Raine VS The End of the World

By Joseph V. Choi

© 2013-2014 JChoi Productions

Version 2.12

ISBN: 978-0989825818

Table of Contents

Dedication

This is for the kids of the next generation, who are inheriting a world on the brink. Gaze into the abyss unyieldingly, but don't look down over the edge. And as good old Peppy might advise: never give up. Trust your instincts.

Opposite: An Afternoon Stroll Through the Metaverse by Joseph V. Choi

View/download full color version here (also available as a print):
http://icekweem.deviantart.com/art/Raine-VS-The-End-of-the-World-Alternate-Poster-463121213

RAINE VS THE END OF THE WORLD

A NOVEL

JOSEPH V. CHOI

The Time Keepers' Oath

By Lillian R. Hermes, Age 6

Power is never to be taken lightly

Time travel gives one the ultimate authority

It is my responsibility to observe and safeguard the people of Earth

Involve oneself only when necessary

Never use time travel for selfish reasons

Avoid crossing paths with your past self or selves

Warp prior to 200,000 B.C. at one's own risk

Protect the human race, even if it costs you everything

Prologue: The Belladonna

"For to be free is not merely to cast off one's chains, but to live in a way that respects and enhances the freedom of others." - Nelson Mandela

Eighty thousand miles above the planet Earth, there is a time machine. Her name is the *Belladonna 5000*, and she carries the memories of innumerable universes, each journey a far-out chronicle in the oft-disputed annals of inter-dimensional travel.

Approaching her from orbit in the midst of the Earth's radiation belt, she sparkles like a crystal rose, shimmering petals embracing the sun's energies.

Circling the world on her continuing quest, the blossoming *Belladonna* weaves through unending fabrics of realities. While she doesn't quite exist yet, she has always existed. She's seen times long before the beginnings of life on Earth, and she might very well be there when it reaches its end.

This is not the story of the good ship *Belladonna*, but it is *a* story. It is a partial chronicle of the *Time Keepers*, those few whose lives have been bound to her fate, whether by chance or design.

Sky Admiral Lillian Rachel Hermes' tale has many beginnings and endings, but every account must start somewhere. Perhaps the easiest place to begin would be the day that defined the rest of her life – the day she became the great steward of the *Hermes Inter-Space-Time Mission*.

April 13, 2087
Alpha Timeline

Lily ran her hand through the planet, resizing the spinning blue-green hologram from the scale of a marble to that of a beach ball, and back again. She did this in part because it looked cool, but mostly to avoid her assigned studies on Earth's history, the girl's least favorite subject. As written by fellow Earthlings, it was dreary, complicated, and filled with contradictions to the

Belladonna's records. Part of her assignment was to explain how historical accounts differed from the observed data, and why. She considered it tedious stuff.

It wasn't always so dull. For the most part, she was given the freedom to explore and learn at her own pace, but history was an exception. Mom and Dad always had words for the seven-year-old if she failed to make satisfactory progress. They deemed it necessary for a child living so near yet so far from Terra to understand where she had come from, and to think of it as her second home. So far, the experiment had mixed results.

Taking off her haptic gloves and abandoning the learning console, Lily stole out of her chamber to the observation window, pondering on the panorama that greeted her upon each waking cycle – the blue, white, and green sphere she hoped to visit someday. Just one trip to planet Earth would be better than a thousand history lessons. But her parents donned sad expressions each time she'd broached the topic with them.

The world isn't ready for us yet, kiddo, they'd say grimly. *It's not safe.*

Of course, that was far from what little Lily wanted to hear, and it wasn't at all fair. But Daddy said most of the beautiful things that'd existed on Earth were gone now, lost to time, or to the destructive machines of civilization. Surely with the *Belladonna* at her family's disposal, nothing should have been beyond their reach, but the family's few trips through history, pre-history, and the days beyond focused on studying the planet and its people.

And Lily had one word for that kind of stuff. *Boring.*

She glanced down the *Belladonna's* long hallway and calculated her chances of successfully sneaking into the kitchen to liberate Mom's blueberry muffins. They were pretty righteous. Before Lillian could hatch her plan, however, the blaring emergency alarm startled her to attention.

Maybe I should have kept those thoughts to myself, wondered the girl, sprinting into her parents' room. *Empty.*

She tapped her watch's comm. link.

"Um, Mom, could we do this drill later? I'm hungry!"

No answer.

A shiver ran up her spine. *This shouldn't be happening.* She scanned the empty curved hallways.

Get a grip, Lily. This is just another test. Normally, Mom would find and calmly take her to the bridge, where the three might laugh about how long it took Lily to get out of bed and how they'd have been devoured by invading aliens long ago.

But for the first time, Lily dashed off to the bridge alone, fending off her suffocating fears with the confidence that she'd find her parents there.

And sure enough, they were hunched over the primary controls, deep in argument. Upon seeing her distressed daughter enter the circular atrium, Elizabeth ran over and held her close.

"Shhh, baby. Back to your room; everything's fine."

Thirty-nine year-old Elizabeth Hermes' calm, collected voice brought warmth, but Lily felt her delicate hands shake ever so slightly during the embrace. She had a distressing feeling that this time, things weren't going to be fine.

"Mom, what's happening?" she ventured.

A rare video transmission was trying to hail them on the big screen, but Lily noted with increasing distress that neither of her parents wanted to accept the call. Shipments from the surface had ceased years ago. Daddy paced furiously.

"Rutger, update me," called Carl Hermes, scratching his stubbly chin.

"Master Carl, our firewalls are nearly breached," The ship's computer began. "They're attempting to extract classified files. I recommend freezing all data drives."

"Do it."

Rutger sounded another alarm. "Perimeter induction buses two to five compromised. Plasma shields at low power. I approximate seven minutes before they can board the *Belladonna* by force."

"Polarity disruptors. How could they have found us?" Elizabeth asked in disbelief.

"One of the investors might have talked, under duress," Carl mumbled. "But finding us, that's another thing entirely. It's as your Dad predicted. They've come for the Temporal Drive."

Lily realized with shock that the Temporal Travel Toggle had been pulled. She knew from experience that the reactor needed fifteen minutes to 'warm up'. The timer read: twelve minutes and seventeen seconds to Space-Time Warp Initiation.

"M-Mommy, where are we going?"

What followed was worse than a grim pronouncement. It was dead silence. The longest ten seconds of young Lillian's life thus far.

"Honey, there's no time to explain," replied Elizabeth as a shadow crept across her face.

Lily turned to the window, and her heart skipped a beat.

The imposing hunk of metal blotted out the sun. Massive turrets turned directly towards the station. A large black, blue, and red flag, with the words *UAA Destroyer 1446*, glimmered on its hull.

Station *Belladonna's* one-way windows hid the family from sight, but Lily grabbed onto her mother's arm all the same.

And more were coming. Blips on the Holo-sphere registered eleven more ships rapidly closing from every direction.

The call continued to ring.

"Are they from Earth?" Lily asked.

"Yes," Carl replied, working furiously to secure their data banks. "Now that the Alliance won the surface war, honey, their higher-ups think they can take our home away."

"But you won't let them, right, Dad?"

Lost in his work as usual, Carl paid her no heed. Elizabeth put her hands on Lily's shoulders and got down on one knee to address her daughter.

"Lily, tell me what you remember about the solar flare."

"U-um, according to our time probe, in one hundred and thirty five years, Earth will be scorched barren."

"Right-o. That's why we're here. Your great-grandfather's dream was for his family to protect all life on Earth, and to ensure that humankind extends its reach to the stars."

Lily wondered why Mom was having her recite truths she knew by heart. If she'd continued that line of thought, the answer would have been terrifying, but Elizabeth's comforting embrace gave the child enough courage to keep her chin up, if just barely.

"Space colonization, I get it. Mom, please. If I just knew what's going on, I could help, maybe--"

"Love, I don't know myself. It's--"

"Get her out of sight! They're about to force their comms through!"

Noticing that Elizabeth was frozen stiff, Carl scooped up Lily and carried her off to the engine control room, a heavily plated chamber that rotated around the radioactive core at the very heart of the *Belladonna*.

"Lily, baby, being born on this station, you don't have an ID chip. There's no way they even know you exist, and it's better to keep it that way."

She was speechless. Just a few hours ago, they were immersed in one of her favorite astronomy documentaries, a holographic feature that took them all over the galaxy in their pajamas. Now she was about to be locked away, something that had never happened before.

Carl took her tiny palms in his. Though just a year older than his wife, his hands were leathery and worn from the stress and toil the couple had long endured.

"Whatever happens, don't you leave this room until the Warp completes."

By now, Lily couldn't hold back the tears. She grabbed onto her Daddy's turtleneck sweater and wouldn't let go.

"I'm scared."

"Shh, it's going to be okay. Your Mom and I just need to take care of some unfinished business."

It was a lie, and they both knew it. But it gave her some relief. He took the black master key and its lanyard off his neck and passed them onto hers, brushing aside her shoulder-length hair to adjust the strap.

"The *Belladonna* is under your protection for the meantime. You're in charge of the system."

Lily nodded.

"You're strong, brave, wise. You're an amazing girl and you're the light of my life. If... if somehow we don't come back, never forget your oath. And don't attempt the mission. Don't even think about it, at least not until you're old enough, okay?"

"But... Daddy..."

His piercing eyes forced the point home. "We just want you to live. I love you."

Carl embraced her, stood, and left. The hatch closed shut, locked.

Lily tried to calm her breathing. Pacing didn't work. *They're in trouble. I have to do something.*

She pulled a stool up to the primary console and plunged the master key into the control port.

"Rutger, show me the live feeds."

"Miss Lily, I am currently engaged," Rutger intoned.

"Now, Rutger! Show me!"

A holographic, real-time tableau of the station materialized. Lily selected the bridge and watched in agony as the invaders' call forced through.

"This is *UAA Destroyer 1446*. Station commander, respond."

"Station *Belladonna 5000* to UAA military vessel," called Carl through gritted teeth. "Your ship has destroyed our property and trespassed within this station's operating space. This is a serious breach of our rights under Common Law."

On the screen before him, a gravely serious officer slunk into his seat and tightened his suspenders.

"Professors Hermes, I presume. Captain Lowe Black, speaking now on behalf of planet Earth. Under the provisions of the United Amero Alliance Aerospace Protection Act, we're authorized to board and search your vessel out of concern for Terrestrial security. You have eight minutes to eject via emergency pods."

"I do not recognize yours or anyone else's authority here. Your masters don't speak for the Earth."

"Seven minutes, fifty seconds, Professor. Refuse, and we'll draw you in and board your vessel with extreme prejudice. Our ID scanners show two of you on the bridge. Have you any others?"

"Don't you ignore me!" Carl pressed. "This tyranny, this... farce will not stand. I'm giving you one chance. Leave now."

The middle-aged man cleared his parched throat and continued, grumbling at Elizabeth. "You need to keep your husband on a leash, Professor. We've spared no expense in tracking your great-grandfather's monumental project. Did you honestly think you could conceal such an experiment from us?"

"No, Captain, but I'd expected the UAA to have the civility to keep its hands off an internationally backed, privately funded, and completely legal research venture. Carl and myself are sole proprietors of Paradoxical Patents, Incorporated. Eighty years of work and no small fortune – that's four generations worth of dreams – led to this mission, and its continued operation is vital for the survival of our species. If you could just connect me to your commanding officer--"

"No can do. As much as we appreciate your ancestor's contributions, that goes against my orders. Clock's ticking."

Carl slammed his desk. "This is terror! Give us an audience with Dr. Klahr in your science division! I demand an explanation as to why you are invading our property, as well as a briefing on how five of our satellite probes are suddenly missing. Those probes contain sensitive data--"

"Enough. We will not waste time arguing UAA International Law with our own civilians. Your ship may disappear from this space at any second. I aim to prevent that."

"We're not *your* civilians! We're free people!"

Just then, the *Belladonna* shook violently.

Lily tumbled from her stool. With a quick whirring of servos, a robotic arm extended from the floor and caught her.

"Th-thanks, Rutger," said Lily. After righting herself, she checked the exterior cams.

The *Destroyer* had punched two large metal harpoons into the outer hull. They were being reeled in. The space station shuddered again as more lances anchored, emergent tendrils wrapping around the solar petals like some terrible beast from the depths.

Carl and Elizabeth looked on in horror.

"Captain, you've no authority to do this! My wife and I are world-renowned scientists! We know our inalienable freedoms, and you'd best respect them. Or should I have your command stripped at a tribunal?"

Black laughed.

"As a potential terrorist threat, Professor, you have the right to remain silent, and nothing more. Under the U-triple-A-PA, signed into law on December 31st, 2083, any objects or persons between Terra and Luna are property of the Alliance. You have five minutes, twenty seconds."

The screen blanked.

Lily gasped at the Captain's words, but kept her attention fixated on the cam feeds.

Mom and Dad will sort this out, she told herself.

As soon as the call cut off, Carl and Elizabeth burst towards the docking bay.

Carl was the first to speak. "This is unbelievable. It goes against every--"

"Quick. What choices do we have?" queried Elizabeth as they turned into the corridor.

"I see only one option."

Elizabeth breathed heavier than she should have; running in artificial gravity and inhaling recycled air would always feel unnatural to her.

"We've glimpsed the future," Carl continued. "This machine has the potential to be humanity's only hope, or its greatest downfall. I'm not going quietly without a fight."

"Me neither. We can do this."

Carl gave her a stern look. "No, you're staying behind. Watch over Lily."

"Negative," Elizabeth said. "I'll be on standby. We'll cut them off and return in time for Warp Initiation."

They gave each other a tight embrace, and a deep kiss.

It took all of five seconds, but they were worth it.

She squeezed his hand, and found that one of the most difficult things she had ever done was to let him go as he rushed out the airlock. There was no time to suit up.

From the console, Carl passed the retinal scan and activated one of their secret weapons, the *Eagle*. It was the greatest of four stealth fighters they had reverse-engineered and enhanced from the remains of an advanced gunship scavenged from the time of the solar flare.

Remote-controlling the fighters became impossible the moment Rutger froze the data drives. They would have to be piloted manually.

Carl stretched his muscles as Rutger rotated the flight tray.

"Slim chance, I know, but is it feasible to send a message back to warn ourselves?"

Elizabeth checked the central console.

"All messenger droids are out of range. We can't send a safe envelope without risking temporal interference."

"And even if we could, we can't patch it directly." He shook his head as the launch sequence counted down. "Any probe would have to jump to a point before we began the project, and we'd need to avoid any chance of interception. Plus, encryption--"

"Impossible. We don't even have enough time to escape."

"No, we don't," Carl replied, glancing out the cockpit at his wife as she boarded the *Falcon*, the identical fighter beside him.

"But she does," Elizabeth finished the sentence. She brought the photo from her dash up to the face-cam. The family picture held on the *Eagle's* comm. screen, catching Carl off guard in the middle of his pre-flight checklist. A single tear ran down Elizabeth's face, which she carefully hid from her husband.

There wasn't a star in the universe that shone brighter than their daughter. Lily was the loveliest thing they had ever seen, and both knew that they would do anything for her.

This was never in the plan. She was their pride and joy, their hope for a better future once the mission objectives had been reached. Now she was about to become Earth's only hope.

"We have three minutes," she said, taking deep breaths as the cabin pressurized. "Just three minutes."

"Temporal Drive needs five to cool the fuel cells. Instruct the droid. I'll input parameter data for the warp and ready the cruisers."

Elizabeth nodded, and their radiant fusion engines roared to life.

"Captains, how may I be of service?" Rutger announced as its physical incarnation, XF-22, wheeled onto the docking bay, announcing its presence with a familiar chirp.

"We have an extra special task for you," said Elizabeth. "Run Protocol Seven-Nine-Tango-Alpha."

$$\maltese$$

Seated uncomfortably on *Destroyer 1446's* command chair with a forced calm, Captain Black counted down the Hermes' last few seconds. At seven left on the clock, something ejected from the *Belladonna*. It didn't resemble an escape pod.

Before it could be identified, a series of powerful jolts shook the bridge. They'd been hit by fire from a small craft. The weapons had somehow penetrated their electromagnetic plasma shields.

"What's going on?" the Captain yelled.

"A rogue ship! It's taken out the docking lances!"

Captain Black stood and took in the incredulous scene outside his observation dome. Every one of their five-foot-wide titanium cables had been snapped; they were floating in dead space.

"Shoot to stun! Immobilize it!" he yelled. "Turn the heat up on the tractor beam! Their interference patterns won't hold forever."

Gunners drew beads on the target. The pilot nimbly, almost preternaturally, avoided all laser fire.

Within seconds, a thundering blast echoed from below.

"W-we've lost the tractor beams, sir!"

The protective debris shield surrounding the *Belladonna* glowed bright blue. A blinding energy pulse blasted the space junk in waves; bolts lashed out as forked webs of lightning.

"The fools!" Captain Black barked as his *Destroyer* jolted again. Now there were two fighters zipping like stray flies, peppering the *1446* with searing blasts.

"Captain, weapons are of unknown origin! Beam conduit sensors scrambled. Outer plasma defenses failing, fast!"

"Prioritize shield reinforcement. How long until we reach critical condition?"

The engineering officer leapt from his seat. "Rear thrusters in danger! We can't take much more, sir!"

"Sit your ass back down, God damn it!"

Alternately eyeing the bridge's exit and the Captain's hand twitching against his holster, the officer sunk back into his seat. You could have heard a pin drop.

"Weapons division, terminate the targets. Charge every beam, arm the missiles, and what the hell is taking the interceptors so long?"

His second in command looked at him quizzically.

"Docking bay shields are offline, sir. Our men are sitting ducks. ETA for reinforcements is two minutes. I advise that we fall back--"

"Idiot! The reactor in there could go off any second now! We may not have two minutes. Gun targets down at all costs!"

◉

Lillian Hermes banged on the thick doors and screamed at the top of her lungs, ignoring Rutger's attempts to comfort her.

She didn't want to listen to some stupid computer.

She wanted her Mommy and Daddy, and nothing was going to stop her. The girl searched her memory banks: she once had to memorize the layout of the *Belladonna*, inside and out. There should be at least three ways to escape this dungeon.

Picking up a stool, she desperately searched for the vent to the food forest's water supply, which linked up with the engine coolant system. It wouldn't budge. There was no use. Her parents were risking their lives, and she was trapped like a pathetic little thing in a metal cage.

XF-22 whirred into the chamber. The doors locked shut behind its bodily frame, which opened its humanoid arms to Lily just in case she needed a hug. She cautiously approached the android.

"Miss Lily, please understand," Rutger began. "I am under strict orders to protect you."

"And I have the key! I'm the boss, and they need me! I can pilot the *Phoenix*! Let me out of here!"

"There is nothing I can do. I am sorry."

Lily fell into tears. XF-22 wrapped a blanket around her shivering frame, then handed the young Captain her favorite stuffed elephant, which she held tightly. She gazed at the digital clock on the console, barely able to look at the video coming in from the two ships. Each second seemed an eternity to the poor girl, a dreadful countdown.

They'll make it back in time. They're invincible, she thought.

The PA chimes rang in Rutger's friendly warning.

"Space-Time Warp Initiation in two minutes."

☐

Dozens of missile turrets emerged to thwart the *Eagle* even as Carl blasted away the last of the starboard lasers taking aim at the *Belladonna's* navigational beacons.

Coming from the opposite direction, Elizabeth eliminated the guided rockets, but missed one by a hair as she pulled her ship away, while Carl barreled into a corkscrew turn.

Sweat coated his palms as the impact connected. He had thought he could out-maneuver it. The *Eagle* was hit, and hit badly. The lasers fried his primary engine, and shields were giving way. One more direct hit and he'd be done for.

"How much more time do we need to buy?"

Both husband and wife had accepted that there would be no return from this.

"Two minutes should do it," Elizabeth replied. "The interceptors are packing mini-nukes. We can't let them get any closer."

"I love you," Carl said.

"I love you, too."

They doubled back towards the fray and crippled the engines of the armed personnel ships advancing towards the *Belladonna*'s dock.

Returning from their first pass, a squadron of unmanned interceptors rushed the duo like bees escaping a drowned hive. Elizabeth squeezed her triggers, shifting against the recoil of her overheated guns. Zooming past the remains of her targets, she winced from the debris that clunked against her right turbine. Her heart sank into the back of her chest. She turned to look at where Carl was flying by her side as they cleared the wave.

As a scientist she tried to rationalize the silent fireball, there and gone in a second, as just another transmutation of particles, a collision of alloy on alloy. There was no point in spending her last moments in mourning. She gave herself a final engine burst at maximum power, sending an enormous amount of G-force through her body. Her *Falcon* soared towards the bridge, jets at full power and guns blazing.

∩

Silence struck the bridge of *Destroyer 1446*. Every eye was on Captain Black, as his finger hovered precipitously over the self-destruct button. He calmly studied the visual data as the enemy veered ever closer, weighing his orders to eliminate the station against the lives of his crew of one thousand. It was the slim chance that his onboard hackers may yet uncover the *Belladonna's* blueprints that stayed the Captain's hand at the last second. Black pulled out his machine pistol instead. His subordinates fled in terror.

With his sidearm raised against the glass, the Captain caught a singular glimpse of the darkness in Elizabeth Hermes' eyes, lit with the fury of a dying warrior making one final effort to save her home. She came from port side, pursued by their own guided missiles, her damaged craft careening straight for the bridge. He took aim at her head and feathered the trigger.

Well played, Professors, Black mused, closing his eyes as the vacuum burst around him.

▬

Thanks to the unbearably sharp and sudden pains in her chest, it took all of Elizabeth's strength to pull the *Falcon* up at the last second, leading *Destroyer 1446's* missiles into its command dome. Her regenerative cockpit glass patched itself in a second, but Elizabeth felt the bullet wounds in her torso and knew the end was near. She clutched at her racing heart. Her lung was collapsing. She pressed the comm. switch.

"R-r-report," she managed at barely a whisper.

"Rutger in. The *Belladonna 5000* is prepped and ready in fifteen seconds."

"Th-thank you."

"You are welcome, Captain. Your voice sounds distressed. I can delay the launch."

Elizabeth shook her head, and the words that came out of her were faint, but firm.

"No. S... It's too l-late for me. T-take care of her."

"Understood."

Elizabeth savored a parting glance at the gaping hole she carved into the bridge. Saw the UAA men explode out of the vacuum. Felt the *Falcon* lurch forward, spin out of control. Steered it in a last-ditch attempt towards the military vessel's communications tower.

"Mom!" sounded a most familiar cry. "Mom, stop the countdown! I'll save you!"

"I'm s-sorry, Lily," were her last words. "F-f-forgive us."

And then she was gone.

≡

Silence fell over the dark scene. Large robotic arms attempted to repair the battered warship. The new commanding officer of *Destroyer 1446* looked out from his viewing platform with sadness as the conduits surrounding the flower-shaped vessel blinked one last time.

The artificial wormhole opened and shut within a fraction of a second. With a blinding flash the space station vanished beyond its folds; the resulting vacuum collapsed into a shockwave. The very space around the *Destroyer* warped out of shape before reverting to relative normalcy.

When the other UAA battleships arrived on-site, there was nothing left to salvage or study, no evidence that the *Belladonna* ever existed.

I. Raine

"Time and space are not conditions in which we live,

but modes by which we think." – Albert Einstein

Thirteen years later (Lillian's relative time)

< Recall inhibitors checklist OK >
< Vitals OK >
< Neural checklist OK >
< Subject: "All systems nominal. Seeya on the flip side." >
< Execute protocol tree: raine_v_endless_metaverse >
< Request accepted. >

∞

The year was 1992. Or at least, it appeared to be 1992, on a cold Sunday night in January. It also appeared to be a video arcade in a suburb of Chicago, Illinois, only the old brick building, the falling snow, and the surrounding block were all a part of a virtual simulation comprised of digital artifacts from the timeline Lillian Hermes left behind when she inherited her parents' time-traveling space station.

It was a program being run for the benefit of one individual, a certain reclusive sixteen-year-old who showed no signs of relenting her attack.

The name of this fierce anomaly was Raine Townsend, and to her knowledge, there was nothing fake or digital about the place. She'd been attempting the near-impossible: to beat the hybrid space shoot-em-up and 2D side-scroller *Super BlastBoy* three times in a row on a single credit. For hours now, the girl danced figure eights in the zone, only to end up choking at the final boss on her last two attempts.

With her rotten luck, she half-expected it to happen again. And sure enough, as a college-aged couple brushed past her, the woman's shrill laughter brought back an enigmatic memory to the surface, blunting Raine's focus and immersing her in an all-too-familiar sequence.

She must have been thirteen at the time. With a boy and a girl, both around her age, sharing a delicious meal on beach towels by the ocean shore. The scent of fresh lobster dipped in lemon butter sauce filled the air, and beyond the campfire, a full moon cast a glimmering path along the ocean waves. She eagerly anticipated the next scene.

He holds my hand. I look at the boy, he returns my intense glance, and we smile in the air of romantic expectancy.

Damn! Snap out of it!

But it was too late. Raine didn't even flinch when she lost her last life to the mid-boss on the final stage, and instead popped in another quarter and took a half-swig from her root beer, tucking loose strands of brown hair back behind her ears.

Always the same stupid fantasy, she thought. *Way too real to be a dream, but it's an impossible memory. I'm an anti-social orphan, living with a holier-than-thou museum middle manager. One would think I'd remember if I'd been to the beach before.*

Questions without concrete answers meant more wasted time. Her emerald eyes went to the clock behind Ramon's ticket counter. Ten forty-five, fifteen minutes till closing time.

If Agnes catches me coming in past midnight again, I'm in for an earful. Still, chances are she's at her boyfriend's pad. It's 50-50 on Sundays. In any case, there's time for one more try.

More than anyone else in her life, Ramon treated her with respect. Then again, he had good reason to; the gifted girl brought a lot of attention to the place. The manager wouldn't pull the plug on a world record attempt.

Hitting the Start button and powering through the first run, Raine reflected on the insanity that sent her on this near-superhuman gauntlet.

It started last week, across town at the *Mortal Kombat* tourney where she won fifty dollars for humiliating a bunch of frat boys in front of their jeering girlfriends, something she would have gladly done for free.

"Raine!" the voice called out, just after she'd made her way to the finals, squeezed through the fire regulations-breaking crowd, and finished the first slice of the pepperoni pizza she was sharing with her best and only friend, Jordan.

The arcade champ locked eyes with a very oddly composed young woman. Dressed in a sparkling neon leotard, large dark glasses and purple wig, she might have strayed from the set of a hair metal video, somewhat appropriate considering Van Halen's "Dreams" was blasting from Ramon's boom box.

"Um… hi. Do I know you?"

"You should, but you don't," she cracked. "Which is to say that our relationship is on a need-to-know basis."

Raine wondered if she was an undercover cop who had been hiding beneath a manhole for the past five years.

"You'll have to forgive me," the woman continued. "Talking in cryptic sentences is one of the most enjoyable perks of being a time traveler."

"T-time traveler? Well met. I don't suppose you could score me some lotto numbers," Raine quipped nervously.

This woman is definitely on something.

"Eh. Even if I didn't have self-imposed regulations against that sort of thing, it's a real tax nightmare. But I've said too much, and I… realize now that you were probably joking. Lost my train of thought… Um. Right! I noticed you've achieved every high score on the local *Super BlastBoy* cabinet."

"SBB is one of my current favorites."

"With over two trillion points, you must have cleared the game twice on a single credit."

As if on cue, applause erupted from the inebriated crowd. The grim-faced 'Scorpion' user of an exchange student defeated his opponent. Trying a bit too hard, he downed what was left of his concealed beer. It would be his undoing.

"You ready to be Fatalitized, little girl?"

"I fought tougher shrimps in kindergarten!" Raine taunted, to much support from the tagalong girlfriends.

"I'm sorry, we'll have to talk about this later," she said to the strange woman while adjusting her beanie.

"Beat it thrice, Raine! Urban legend says there's an unbeaten bonus level! According to my sources, if you clear it, it'll be a world record!"

Raine beamed in recognition.

"That sounds wicked! Tell me more once I'm through."

But after Raine won the tournament, the outlandish lady was nowhere to be found, leaving her with even more questions. The one thing this girl could never resist, however, was a worthwhile challenge, especially one with the potential for an epic win.

A few days later, she and Jordan called and confirmed with the game developers that, yes, there was a secret bonus level, and to their knowledge no triple-run had ever been successfully cleared. Raine knew in a heartbeat that until she accomplished the impossible, rest was for the weak. This could be her ticket to a shout-out in a gaming mag, the Twin Galaxies' record books, and most importantly, mad props from the pro gaming community.

She cleared the final boss on her first play-through and kick-started the second, to faster and deadlier enemies.

Who needs vain ambition? Let the other kids get rich. There's one thing I'm good at, and it's something that brings me real happiness. If others can recognize my abilities, that's just icing on the cake.

Gaming's about constantly breaking my limits. There's an art to my methods, the rhythm of my heart guiding me ever closer to my dream self. And no one's going to stop me.

The difficulty spiked at the end of the second run. She honed her focus. Zoning out was her number one enemy. According to Agnes, her self-loathing Foster Mom, daydreaming held Raine back from giving her all in 'the things that really mattered'. She continued to insist that the undecorated girl would never amount to anything unless she got her act together.

With only a part-time job at the comic book store under her belt and a year and a half to high school graduation, Raine probably wasn't ready to live on her own, but she was itching to meet the challenge.

Once she turned eighteen, she could go anywhere her heart desired, but lately, Raine fantasized about skipping out on senior year and disappearing on an adventure. The five hundred dollars she'd saved up from winning local tourneys was enough to hop an interstate bus. Though little more than a pipe dream, she had a mental image of standing on the shores of California, gazing out towards the Pacific in the hopes that her dream friends would show up to take her away. Most things considered just about anywhere seemed better than the rut she was currently in.

The final boss went down in flames. The third play-through started, even faster than before, and she was lucky enough to have not lost a single life up until that point.

I'm not going to discover my purpose in life living here, she thought. *I may never have had a real home, but I know this isn't where I belong.*

The more she read about planet Earth, the more insane living on it sounded, and the less she wanted to grow up.

The price we pay for modern civilization is almost too alarming to consider: over a hundred species every day go extinct, forever. Every second, a football field of rainforest is lost. Hundreds of millions of kids lack access to clean water, and one in eight are malnourished. Unsustainable farming destroys one percent of the planet's topsoil every year. There may be no resource to match the utility of long-dead dinosaur smoothies, our supply of which is finite. These are well-known facts, and yet no one seems to care.

Not that I consider myself any better, but do all adults just go about ignoring the suffering of their fellow humans? And if this is just how things are going to be, then what's the use of even trying?

After Raine saw the movie *E.T.*, she imagined that she was an alien stranded on the wrong planet. If nothing else, it explained why she'd never really connected with anyone. Maybe if she were in the right place, at the right time, her spaceship would return and she'd be welcomed back with open arms.

But those were childish dreams. Any escape attempts would have to be enacted without the support of her home planet, on her own terms, with her own resources.

Plus, I'm not exactly in a position to run away and live like a hermit in the woods. Even if I had the courage to do a fool thing like that, I've grown mighty accustomed to the comforts of the city.

A close call with some spreadfire explosions straightened her up.

But maybe these thoughts are too big for little old me to worry about, especially right now. It's the last level! Focus, Raine! Breathe!

Having temporarily waylaid her doubts, Raine shut out all unnecessary stimuli and deftly navigated the bullet-hell gauntlet comprising the last mission's mid-boss.

At the final battle, the cabinet ran low on application memory. The resulting slowdown gave her just enough time to get a few hits in between frantic dodging and weapon swaps.

At long last, and with no lives left to spare, the feat was done.

Raine took a breather, hands still twitching against the controls. She glanced around.

Just my luck. Not a single witness.

And most of the other machines appeared to be off. *Flynn's* was completely empty. Even late Sunday night, that was unheard of.

After the credits, a video of Super BlastBoy faded in to synthesized MIDI chirps. He was lying on a hammock, smiling. The background morphed gradually into a tropical paradise.

She had never seen anything like this. SBB's sprite, resplendent in red 16-bit spandex, opened its mouth and words streamed out along the display.

"Your skills are exceptional, Raine. I am honored to have been at your command. But there is an even greater evil to vanquish before you can discover that which is most important to you."

Surprising herself, Raine recalled the laminated photograph of her biological parents, snugly tucked away in her wallet. Having been left on a doorstep with nothing but a blanket and the faded picture with her name and date of birth, the girl's origins were a complete mystery.

This could be her greatest hope, or the ultimate disappointment.

While she weighed her options, Super BlastBoy hopped off the hammock and hobbled away into a maze of palm trees. The screen stuck on the beach landscape, with electric gull cries and crudely animated waves set to a slow sunset. The strange text remained; otherwise, she would have surely thought it a trick of her own mind.

She blinked twice in disbelief, reached into her bag, took out her disposable camera, and snapped a few shots of the screen and her high score. No one else had seen the message.

What was that? And how the heck did he know my name? Something is very wrong.

Suddenly she caught a glimpse of SBB running along the side of the arcade's brick wall, trademark red cape flowing behind him. Mesmerized, Raine snapped another shot and followed his progress towards the "Employees Only" door. He slipped in between the hinges. Raine tried the handle. To her great surprise, it was unlocked.

Oh, Raine, you know you really shouldn't. But who am I kidding? There's no way I can let this be.

She gathered up her courage and cracked it open.

At the end of a long, dark hallway, SBB gestured towards an abandoned cabinet, visible only by the light of his glowing sprite. It looked like it had been there since Reagan was in office.

The light switch didn't work. She stood in the darkness gawking at her virtual hero, wondering what Agnes would think of what was going on in her mind right now.

It didn't seem reasonable in the least to follow an imaginary videogame character down a secret hall. But then again, with her reputation as a runaway and a slacker, she wasn't exactly the textbook example of a reasonable person.

Raine plunged into the room, brushing aside the occasional cobweb. As she approached it, the dusty old machine turned itself on. Its title was *Endless Metaverse*, and the blinking text read:

"Press Start"

"Credits (1)"

The entire episode was maddening, and Raine's finger hovered over the Start button.

No. This is impossible. It's all in my head.

She backed away from the cabinet, closed the door behind her, and fled from *Flynn's* like a bat out of hell.

Fairy tales and stupid dreams. You're hallucinating. This madness ends here.

But each step away from her destiny grew heavier, until halfway home she stopped at the old park, frozen in place. This time a different voice advised her.

What are you doing? Is bolting like a bunny your default response to everything? SBB promised you answers! Sure, who knows if they'll be the answers you're looking for, but this is your big chance, and you're just going to let it slip away?

No use crying over a couple of quarters. The place is closed. It's too late now, Raine told herself. *I'll go back and try again tomorrow after school... if I feel up to it.*

The girl spent the rest of the walk home in some sort of uncertain truce with the voices in her head. Sneaking through the parking lot, she noted that Agnes' car wasn't there; as hoped, she'd be spending the night with her boyfriend.

The door unlocked to an empty condo, a dwelling Raine would never feel at home in, despite its other inhabitant's best intentions. The pantry was always empty, and gaming was heavily frowned upon.

She could never shake the feeling that she'd become the newest piece of decoration, a living stand-in for the abstract sculptures that littered the living room and were easy to stub your toe on during middle of the night cereal runs.

So lost was the girl in her mixed-up mind that she literally jumped in surprise when upon entering her bedroom she came face to face with the glowing arcade cabinet.

Endless Metaverse. So it's fate, then. That damn machine wants me to clear it.

This time even the more rational members of her inner jury had nothing to say. Raine practically floated to the machine and hit Start. Another message appeared, along with an image of a hand:

"Please place your right hand inside the screen. If you have no right hand, press '2'."

She was dumbfounded. It must have been a mistranslation. In any case, she lined her opened palm against the on-screen prompt.

Cautiously, she pressed down with a light touch.

At first, nothing. Then, suddenly, she began to sink into the cabinet.

"Do not adjust your machine. This is completely normal."

Strangely, the message was enough to instill a sense of calm. She felt her entire arm embraced by the warm, electric screen, and sensed the rest of her body becoming drawn in as if into quicksand. Not one to leap without looking, the girl stuck her head through the glass.

II. Gateway

"The doorstep to the temple of wisdom is knowledge of our own ignorance."

– Benjamin Franklin

Raine crawled out of the portal and stood on her own two feet. The hole from which she emerged then disappeared like a television after-image.

This should have alarmed me, she realized. *What if I can't go back?*

But the doubts soon faded into alphabet soup and out of her thought process, as if forces beyond her perception were toying with her consciousness. Without noticing it, she'd fallen back into a state of childlike curiosity.

Though Raine could see all of herself perfectly, she was but a drop of color on a black canvas. Nothing else seemed to exist; worse, Super BlastBoy wasn't anywhere to be found. Even so, there was nothing for it but to press on.

Three steps later, a mass of metal ball bearings materialized around her frame. Before the girl could react or even process what was going on, irises sprung open from the orbs, emitting lasers that scanned her body with blinding flashes. As quickly as they appeared, the floating invaders vanished into the ether, leaving Raine with the beginnings of a rather uncomfortable headache.

What the hell! Look what you've gotten yourself into.

Rubbing her temples, Raine tried to will a chair into existence. Instead, glowing light waves bobbed up and down from the now-visible horizon and washed away at the black shore under her feet. Static remnants clung to her boots before dissipating.

The scene was so odd and otherworldly that she ceased being amazed by it.

This has got to be a dream, she felt with a sad rationality, and then realized that was an invitation to wake herself up. She flinched at the prospect of returning to her cold bed in Agnes' depressing condo with another school day awaiting her, and decided against any thoughts of the sort for the meantime.

Raine walked cautiously atop the matrix, trying not to feel ticklish at the little bumps underneath her sneakers. The way the colors shifted had her wondering if she'd happened upon a giant arcade game.

Just then, Super BlastBoy emerged before her feet, erupting in a cascade of pixels that dripped down him like water from a person exiting a swimming pool.

Raine stared completely dumbfounded at SBB as he turned on his side and disappeared. The girl moseyed over ninety degrees and quickly discovered that he'd become two-dimensional.

"S-Super... I mean, m-mister Anthony Kon? How did you do that?" Raine asked.

The hero turned around and glanced at Raine, evidently surprised at hearing his real name.

"HELLO-RAINE.   WE-MUSTN'T-TALK-HERE.   THEY-ARE-LISTENING."

His mechanical voice fizzed out as if from an old radio.

"I- I just need a minute of your time," she whispered, and her voice came out in MIDI chirps. "I'm probably one of your biggest fans, see. I heard something about a bonus level, and I thought maybe you could, um, give me some life advice, or sign an autograph or something--"

"FORBIDDEN-KNOWLEDGE.   TOO-MUCH-TO-SAY.   SEEK-ME-TO-FIND-YOU. TIL-WE-MEET-AGAIN."

With that, he spirited away once more, reappearing on the grid below sprinting across Level 3 of his game. She dashed after him, glad that her first instinct was right as usual - the grid *was* an arcade machine.

Raine leapt onto the glass to catch her quarry. It was impossible, she realized with a thud; he was deep below the surface.

Forbidden knowledge? Too much to say?

If the words were meant to quell her curiosity, they were doing the exact opposite. And just *who* was listening? *There has to be a way to find out. I need to bounce this dreary shadow world.*

She stomped in frustration, sending a tremor rippling over the waves so strongly that it shook the virtual realm below.

Eureka!

If she were truly standing atop an arcade cabinet, then Raine could find a way off the grid. *Then again, if my theory proves accurate, I should be falling right now.*

Her realization shook the fibers of this universe. The road to her right curved in on itself, as if it were a river that happened upon a cliff and suddenly snapped into a waterfall.

I didn't mean to think that! I take it back!

But once a quest for truth is set into motion, it becomes impossible to return to a state of prior ignorance, a fact that landed Raine on her behind and set her careening down the grid. Although the speedy slide appeared to stretch on indefinitely, eventually the girl noticed repeating pixel patterns.

I'm stuck in a sort of glitch – that's the only rational explanation, anyhow.

Raine recalled Agnes' lectures about the dangers of being a smart aleck. "Your gifts of wit and intuition should be used for productive things," she once said, "for the betterment of society."

Society can eat a hat. Why can't I be as clever as I want to be for my own damn reasons? Is that just plain old selfishness, the kind that led to our civilization's current predicament? Ugh. If this nightmare is some sort of subconscious punishment, it's uncalled for.

The quickest way out would be through. Snagging her keychain from her backpack, Raine bravely spun around, closed her eyes, and plunged her house key straight into the glass screen, creating a tear that sent pixilated sparks flying around her trembling hand. After some time, she looked below her – sure enough, the original mark was approaching. With expert precision the two were matched, crafting one long, deep crevasse. It wasn't long before cracks in the surface signaled that the whole thing was about to erupt.

Shielding her face from flying shards, Raine willed herself to awaken. Her attempts failed. She pushed the key deeper, prompting an electric shock. All at once, the barrier gave way and a flood of pixels gushed out from within, knocking her off the grid and onto a large, cushioning Start button. In place of the screen, a hypnotizing whirlpool of sand took shape.

Whispered voices lulled her to slumber as a large sand-arm reached out and gently picked her up. The giant thumb pressed singularly on her forehead, and she felt queasy and unsafe, like something was being changed in her brain. There was an instant where her mind was naked; she became aware that her hopes, her dreams, and even her memories were being watched. By whom or what, she had no idea, but she felt on the edge of realizing something quite important.

Oh, no, not again, she thought, without understanding why.

Just as Raine approached the verge of recognition, her mind went blank.

√

She jolted upright and felt that she'd woken at last from her dream.

To her great surprise, Raine found herself seated in something resembling a more comfortable dentist's chair. Her senses felt stronger, only there wasn't much to sense. The room was pitch-black, and her head hung heavily. She hobbled up on her feet and scoped out her surroundings. The ground felt cold, even under thick socks. Cotton clothes shuffled about weakly. *A hospital gown?*

"Heya, Raine!" a female voice sounded out from everywhere at once, chipper as a spring breeze. "Ray-ray, it's me, the stylish time traveler! We met at the arcade. Do you read me?"

She felt ready to clobber whoever it was. Dream or not, if this was some sort of sick joke, it had run its course already. For all she knew, the voice could be in her own head.

"Y-yeah, I remember that night," she began, her trembling voice not quite as tough as it sounded in her mind. "Who are you? What the hell's going on?"

The answer rang in bright and clear, a stark contrast to the darkened chamber.

"I'd tell you, but there's a chance your memory wipe will spring a leak. See, you're not supposed to remember. Not yet. It's no biggie; everything's going as planned, except for this slight Network malfunction. Incumbent weather and all that. Won't happen again, Captain."

"I still don't understand--" began Raine.

"Simulation's over. It's business time. Get some rest, honey; you're gonna need it. And please return to your seat for the duration of the ride."

Not likely. "Why should I? I don't trust you. This... this isn't the bonus level, is it?"

The pause before the mysterious voice answered only intensified Raine's suspicions.

"Sorry, but we've come too far to do a restart. The worst will soon be over, dear. You're doing so well."

This is unacceptable. She slammed the padded wall with her fists.

"Answer my question! What's happening to me?" Raine cried, but this time there was no response.

Instead, the room quickly flooded with a sweet-smelling gas. Before she could stop herself, Raine gasped, and soon afterwards collapsed to her knees and then fell face-first onto the cold floor. Metal appendages carried her gently back to the dentist's chair.

"Chances are slim you'll remember any of this, but maybe something will stick..." the voice droned on as Raine faded away. "You don't want the shot. And the woman is not your mother. Never forget what it is you're searching for. Remember... don't take the shot..."

◊

When Raine regained consciousness again, it was at the sound of her name.

Yes, I'm probably still dreaming, she reasoned. Unless she had lost her mind completely, since she was now inexplicably sitting in the waiting room of a doctor's office, in between an elderly lady with a pug in her lap and a little boy munching on his shirt collar.

She vaguely remembered chasing Super BlastBoy. He seemed to have some answers. A giant arm of sand was involved, and there was a nagging worry that she'd lost her house key. Faint traces remained of another memory, something to do with waking up in a dark room, but they were vague, undefined, and soon vanished entirely.

Raine rummaged through her shoulder bag for the distinctive keychain.

No. That's not right. I've been wearing my trusty backpack all day.

Finding it filled with sharp little squares wreaked further havoc on the girl's state of mind. She continued her hopeless search until her name was called out for the tenth time.

"Miss Raine!"

She looked up, startled. "Huh? E-excuse me, all my stuff seems to be---"

"Dr. Astro will see you now," the exasperated receptionist announced with a forced smile.

Quietly adjusting her shoulder bag, Raine followed the nurse into Astro's office. He was a tall gentleman with bold but uninteresting features, and he sat her down atop a child-sized medical bed. His bored gaze reminded her of a laconic giraffe.

"So, I just have a few questions and then you'll be good to go, capiche?" he droned.

"O-kay," Raine replied uncomfortably.

"You seem nervous," he said.

"I don't know why I'm here. I'm scared, I feel lost, and I can't explain why."

"Oh, that's quite normal. If you'd like, I can give you something for it."

"Scratch that. I'm just saying, man. This doesn't look like a bonus level to me. I don't mean any offense, but before I ended up here, I was chasing--"

"You'll be in your utopia in no time, girl," he interjected. "Here, have some licorice."

Though she hated being called 'girl', Raine munched on the stick; it was all she had to hold on to that seemed real.

Astro took a clipboard from his desk and scribbled a few things down.

"Are you ready?"

"As I'll ever be. But I've got questions of my own."

The Doc stole a glance at his watch. "Make them quick."

"Well, first of all, what is this place? How did I get here? Why am I here? Where's my stuff? Have you seen Super BlastBoy? And of course, who are you?"

"You're in Account Creation. I can't answer any of the other questions."

"Why not?"

"I can't answer that either. Here's what I can tell you: if you have any complaints or comments, Customer Service will gladly help you after we finish the application process."

"Can't they answer them now?"

"No."

Raine stood up. "Well, then. If you could just point me in the right direction..."

Astro gestured out the window. It was an unfeasibly large, desolate landscape of nothing but blank white, both land and sky covered in printer paper. In the far, far distance floated a speck that resembled an ant in a swimming pool of milk.

"It... can't be that little thing off in the distance there?"

"Indeed it is. You seem awfully surprised. It's not our fault it's so far, you know. You're the one with a weak Network connection."

"Is there any way I can get over there that doesn't involve walking?"

"We can't help you with that. Now, if you don't mind, I have a job to do. Sit, please."

Raine slunk back into her seat quietly. She turned once more to the window. It was now a fake picture of a beautiful sunny field.

"What just happened to your window?"

"I'll be asking the questions now, Raine."

She glared. He glared back.

"Go ahead, then. Ask," she conceded at last.

"What is your birth date?"

"June 23, 1977."

"That can't be right. Oh, well. What is your L-mail address?"

"L-mail address?"

"How odd. You must have forgotten the orientation. Seeing as how you're not on our records, it looks like we're going to have to create one," Astro said, and with his help, Raine was soon signed up for a free account under the username *rainorshine23*.

"Now, that wasn't so bad, was it?"

"No, actually," Raine said, surprised at how smoothly this whole thing was going.

"One more question - would you like to appear male or female?"

"Female, of course."

He flashed a devilish grin. "Do you have a preference for men?"

Raine raised an eyebrow. *Most likely? It's not like I have any experience in the matter.*

"I'll take that as a yes." A smattering of pictures of faces, some human, and others otherworldly, flashed before Raine. Sensors studied her eye movements.

"Very well. We have deduced that you prefer human characteristics to those of otherkin, and would do well on the South continent. Now, Raine, before we can proceed with the contract, I'm going to have to give you a shot. You'll feel a bit woozy afterward."

"Oh, no."

"Just a quick one, it won't hurt."

He pulled out the terrifying-looking syringe, filled with robotic sea monkeys zipping around in a tube of mercury.

A voice rang out in her head. *You don't want the shot.*

Raine leapt off the medical bed.

"Sorry to have wasted your time. I don't know where I am or what's going on, but I can't trust you; you're a complete stranger."

"Oh, I'm no stranger, Raine. Everyone sees me at some point or another." His leering grin was too wide, too gaping. Too insincere. He looked less friendly now, more like a hungry lion than a giraffe. "You signed up. You're under our care. You're going to have to trust us."

Raine spun around and burst from the office. She made for the door. It was locked.

"Stop, girl. Stop holding up the line."

The dozen-odd people in the waiting room ambled forward like zombies, reaching out to grab her ankles. Thinking quickly, Raine tossed a potted plant through the glass door. The old crone was just a few feet away. Raine kicked the remaining shards in, crawled across the broken glass, sustaining cuts all over her hands and knees, and made her way down the long hallway towards the exit.

True to the view outside the shape-shifting window, the whole world was whitewashed, with a few specks sticking out in the far distance.

"WHAT'S GOING ON?!?" she yelled at the top of her lungs. She began pinching her arms and cheeks. "Wake up, Raine! Get your lazy butt out of bed! Beat it!"

At first there was no answer, but a large message from above restored the girl's hopes. It probably wasn't a response from her brain.

"Homepage not specified. Enter URL."

"HOME! Send me back to the real world!"

A few seconds passed as the message reconfigured itself in a flash of artificial clouds. The next prompt read, "Error 404. File not found."

"I'm not looking for a file! Home, you stupid sky! Shut down! End program! Reboot!"

"Error 400. Bad request."

There's no going back. Damn it all. If this is a dream, let's get on to the good parts.

"That doesn't tell me anything!" she groaned. "Where am I?"

This time, the sky lit up in fire.

"The End of the World, version 3.0. Server *Avidya*. Account Creation."

Raine's jaw hung agape. *This weird blank wasteland is the end of the world? What happened to everyone?*

Just then, maniacal cackling emanated from the nondescript medical building. Fearing that Astro would be after her, Raine tore away at top speed until the solitary structure was almost out of view. Her track coach would have been proud. When she stopped to catch her breath, another message materialized above her head.

"CONGRATULATIONS! YOU ARE OUR 1,500,000,000TH VISITOR! CLICK HERE FOR YOUR FREE GIFT!"

Raine ignored it. She stared at the space between her futuristic sneakers.

These are pretty cool sneakers, she thought as sweat pooled between them. The girl fell into routine breathing exercises, preparing for another sprint.

"Describe your ideal match's hair color." The message had appeared on the floor. Buttons beneath delineated a few choices. *"Brown, Redhead, Black, Blonde, Bald."*

Raine grabbed at her hair.

"I don't. Understand. These stupid questions." She stomped on the text and pinched her arm again. Nothing.

I really don't know how I'd come up with a dream like this. I've got to be sure to write it down.

A terrible noise from the hospital spun Raine back around. Astro was playing musher on a dog sled, syringe held high. The ravenous kid and the elderly lady led a pack of humans gunning on all fours.

That's not something you see every day.

She glanced back up at the sky. The question had moved there, along with the five choices. Raine realized that with no hope of outrunning them, her only option was to answer this survey and trust to fate. She flung one of the pixels like a frisbee at the 'redhead' option, but the square curved downwards and landed on 'blonde'.

The next question appeared.

"What kind of steed would he ride?"

"Automobile, Hovercraft, Dragon, Flying Saucer, Unicorn."

Raine tossed a pixel at 'Hovercraft'. She'd always wanted to try one of those.

She spun around anxiously as the next question began loading. The people had now turned into foul beasts, and Astro whipped them forward with an insane vigor.

"Hurry up!" Raine demanded of the sky.

Instead of another question, however, a portion of the boundary flapped about like a loose corner of a tarp. A thick breeze whooshed in from the absolute darkness.

Arming herself with another pixel, Raine took aim at the torn section and tossed with all her strength. The sky ripped open almost immediately, triggering a vacuum that whipped the girl's hair around her head.

A swirling storm of color emerged from the fusion of white sky and dark space, piercing the blandness of this realm. Raine suddenly recalled the dream before this one, where she was sliding down the façade of the arcade machine.

"Hey, giant hand! Get me out of this place!"

At first, there was nothing. Then, the vortex gave way to the colossal hand, which set its opened palm on the floor before Raine. Quickly calculating her trajectory, she pulled off a running jump, grabbed onto the thin ledge between the sand-fingers, and pulled herself onto its palm.

"COME BACK! I'm not done, damn you!" Astro called. The gray machines from his syringe broke free and formed into an arrow that fired itself up at the hand, but fell far short as the sand-arm whisked her away. Raine gained altitude at an alarming speed; she saw the deranged man and his beasts disappear like dust motes on a bed sheet.

As the giant thumb once again combed her mind, a rush of memories flooded Raine's thoughts. For a fleeting second, she recalled the night spent on that island, the truth about her parents, the identity of the strange woman, and her reason and purpose in this world.

But when that instant passed every one of her recollections wandered off and swept their tracks clean, knocking her out cold and leaving nothing but muddy shadows.

III. Endless Metaverse

"Find a place where there's joy, and the joy will burn out the pain."

- Joseph Campbell

Upon opening her eyes, Raine jolted up in a brightly lit room and reflected on the tiresome nature of these false awakenings. This place wasn't Agnes' condo or the old arcade, she reasoned, but it was much prettier than either.

If this dream isn't an improvement over the last one, I want my time back.

A translucent scroll unfurled in thin air before her. She reached out to grab it, but her arm passed right through. A quill pen scribbled out a message.

"Welcome to Endless Metaverse, rainorshine23. *You are playing on the* Avidya *server."*

And then, the scroll rolled itself up and out of existence.

Raine studied the bedroom: it resembled a royal dwelling straight out of the Renaissance era, except for a table with a few hi-tech trinkets, and the beautiful domed skylight, covered in a network of vines. Splintered streaks of sunlight brightened her face. So curious was the girl that she neglected to notice the smiling, older woman now lurching overhead.

Before Raine could react or say anything, the mystery matriarch turned to her mechanically. From its smile, Raine recognized the spectre as a terrifying replica of her biological mother, clad in the summer dress from her old photo.

"You all right, there?" it said in a melodic monotone. "You must have had quite a dream. Your father and I could hear you mumbling in your sleep."

Raine tried to speak, but the words she wanted to say wouldn't quite formulate themselves.

"M-mother?"

Raine awkwardly reached out towards her. No reaction or response, not even a flickering of the eyes in acknowledgment. This was not her mother, just an empty shell. She recalled SBB's cryptic words: *"There is an even greater evil to vanquish before you can discover what is most important to you.*"

The most precious truth I can imagine would be gaining knowledge of my biological parents, and learning why they chose to give me up. Not that I want to continue blaming them for my lot in life; in fact, it's the opposite. I simply want to understand, to forgive them in my own heart, so I can move on. But this creepy mannequin is a twisted lie.

The woman spoke again.

"That's good, *rainorshine23*. Come on down for breakfast, your friend Nimbus is over and he wants to talk to you about his newest invention."

With that, she descended the staircase, leaving Raine to her own devices. A pastoral symphony kicked in from an invisible speaker system. The entire experience was unnerving, and worst of all, SBB was nowhere to be found. It was time to remedy that.

Getting up from her bed, Raine noticed she was dressed in a black t-shirt and tights underneath leather armor and a pair of leather boots, as well as owning a snazzy-looking digital watch.

This won't do. She headed towards an armoire. An earth-colored steampunk dress was just about the most normal garb; she touched it and the outfit immediately appeared on her person. A menu on the full-length mirror displayed choices for accessories. She chose a neutral blouse, a corset, protective shoulder bracers, and some warm leggings. The leather boots were the most comfortable footwear and went well with the outfit. The watch, it appeared, couldn't be removed.

On her desk was a note informing Raine that to return to this room at any time, she need only to hold the 'home' button on her watch while stationary for ten seconds.

She glanced at the sleek device. A holographic menu of options materialized from its face. On the top-right, a read-out next to a coin symbol told her that she had 500 Gold available.

Before she could figure out the shiny new thing in earnest, fake mother called her fake name again. It was time to leave.

The messenger bag on the desk was soon filled with a couple of apples from a fruit basket, a wheel of cheese, and a loaf of sourdough. She also grabbed a pair of brass goggles, a towel, a hand mirror, a rolled-up sleeping bag, and a lovely set of theater binoculars. Strangely, the small bag remained light as a feather.

Sneaking a look down the second floor balcony across her doorway, Raine studied her new foster parents, and Nimbus, a determined-looking blonde boy attacking a bowl of oatmeal. All three ate with clockwork uniformity more robotic than human in nature, and she didn't trust a single one of them.

She backed into the room and flung up a latch on the skylight; the dome peeled away to a gentle breeze, accompanied by a cacophony of voices. The girl hastily climbed up and over the ledge.

The view took her breath away. Raine's stone-and-brick house stood amongst thousands of near-identical highland suburban cottages bordering a vast medieval metropolis.

Within the castle's rocky walls, instead of skyscrapers or bland blocky buildings, aged Mediterranean structures colored a luscious land populated by olive and mulberry trees.

A street-spanning banner read, "Clyde Castle Town, 30th Anniversary."

Roosters down in the valley crowed to flying vehicles caught in the rising sun. Carpeted walkways cluttered with foot traffic from all sorts of creatures. A deep braying sent shivers down Raine's spine - without warning, a three-headed wyvern whooshed past and sent her hair into tangles with the beating of its great wings.

Holy two-headed cows. She leapt onto a pile of hay outside and made her way down the street. *This realm is mine for the taking.*

A gentle drizzle made landfall; it was unlike any Raine had ever seen. There wasn't a cloud in the sky, and yet small black pixels roughly the size of raindrops materialized far overhead, danced in descent, and promptly fused to the ground and disappeared. None seemed to take notice.

Nobody paid her any attention either. That fact brought Raine some comfort until she began observing some of her dream-folk's more curious behaviors.

Some kids paced around in circles. A cleric slept right in the middle of the street, yet passersby walked over him effortlessly. Suspicious dudes scanned the scene from dark alleys.

Faint, floating green nametags hovered over every head. With a look into a nearby pond, Raine confirmed that she sported one as well.

Teleporting warriors made for the heart of the metropolis. Some wore remixed costumes of famous game characters. She peeked over a cliff to pinpoint the nearest path to the wall, all too eager to follow.

This is just too much to take in at once. I've got to head down there and see what's what.

ℸ

Gerrit lazily balanced his broadsword on his pinky finger, then flipped it upside down and caught it again. Several of his guild mates watched from the corners of their eyes, waiting for him to mess up and lop off a digit, though based on the boy's infamous reputation that would be highly unlikely.

The *Oathbound Hunters* had been sitting there for well over fifteen minutes, and even Jolly Peter, who could be counted on to spice up any gathering, had run out of things to say and contented himself with crafting protective rings to sell at the bazaar. Many of the younger warriors used the time to polish up their schoolwork. Gerrit wished that something would happen already.

"Won't something happen already?" he asked.

"Be on your toes," Guild Leader Lance warned, grabbing Gerrit's shoulder with maladroit passion. "It'll be any second now. Soon as that goddamn thing appears, we're all counting on you to rush. You know where the exact spawn point is, right?"

"Yeah, bro. Got this," said Gerrit, although he didn't. His thumb jerked in a general direction to the town square they were all facing.

"Good. You'll all do well to remember, it'll lash out with AoEs right off the bat, so fall back at first, even if it means other guilds get the first hits in. All that matters is where we are when the killing blow lands. We should be in close proximity; Kyle's on flare duty. In fact, Marcie and Bonnie are – hey, you two! Customize your hair later! This is no time for trading fashion tips…"

Gerrit tuned Lance out by tapping two fingertips together against his thumb thrice, a secret shortcut he programmed to mute any external sounds. He closed his eyes and let his thoughts wander.

What am I doing here?

With a username like *"NinjaMageKnight99"* (he didn't remember picking it), Gerrit seemed destined for a life on the battlefield. It was impossible to keep time in *Endless Metaverse*, for allegedly complicated reasons including constant server updates that often led to widespread memory modifications, but there was one thing he recognized in his heart of hearts: he'd been doing this for a while.

If Gerrit had been aware of the truth, he would be quite astonished to know that in the span of three years, he had fought for, at one time or another, dozens of major guilds in the *Avidya*, *Tanha*, and *Maya* servers.

When he opened his eyes again, the boy stole a glance at good old Sala, falling asleep while leaning on his quarterstaff. Gerrit surprised himself by considering that he could completely relate to the old man. He tapped his fingers together again.

"...can't stress that we need the tank trio to pull aggro properly if things get too hot on the front lines," Lance continued. "I really don't want any other fools to get in on this, so we have to kill it quickly and methodically. Arthur and Kid Hugo, remember: unless the Pallies are in trouble, you're doing nothing but casting debuffs and time-slowing spells on non-guild members to ensure our victory."

The band of about forty nodded blankly. It was an off kind of day, and no one was particularly jazzed about the upcoming battle. Fighting the world boss was more of an obligation – there'd been slim pickings since the reptilians had gotten involved in the war and the local economy took a turn for the worse.

Gerrit looked at his allies in turn and realized that while the new recruits seemed ready for bloodshed, some of the higher-leveled warriors were where he was two months ago. Lance was trying his best, but it wasn't good enough. Even he seemed to be infected by the virus of apathy, at some minute but noticeable level.

Most of them had been at this as long as they could remember – leveling-up, fighting, strategizing, dividing the spoils, spending their Gold, crafting, looting, synthesizing more weapons, and fighting again in carefully calculated cycles, playing at pride and satisfaction according to sets of rules that could be changed at any moment, that it was unthinkable, sacrilegious even, to consider that it was getting boring.

Gerrit on the other hand knew that it was getting boring. He knew it deep in his gut. What he'd been experiencing was something more profound and psychically painful than boredom. It was the kind of empty feeling that drives men mad with longing.

And then he sneezed. A black pixel had gotten lodged in his nose. Gerrit gazed skyward at the falling squares; a data storm was inbound. He hoped against reason that whatever changes to the *Metaverse* were being made, they'd make things interesting, if only for a little longer.

Σ

After descending a few hundred feet of stairs to the city proper, Raine felt she needed a breather, although physically she seemed to be fine. She walked over to an inconspicuous vending machine among dozens that promised lemonade for 3 Gold. Raine had only to hold her hand over the device before glowing buttons appeared over the choices. She was surprised to feel the button as she pushed it with her fingers – it had appeared in thin air, like a hologram, but it had weight, mass, texture…

Her wristwatch beeped. Its face informed Raine that she'd spent 3G and now had 497G in the bank. *No bills, no wallets, no change. If there are any arcades here, getting continues will be an absolute cinch.*

Clunk!

The lemonade plopped down at the bottom of the machine. Without delay, Raine expertly chugged about half of the cold, refreshing drink. It was suspiciously delicious for a dream. She re-capped the bottle and dropped it into her messenger bag.

The girl took two steps forward before realizing that her bag did not feel an iota heavier. *What sort of sorcery is this, anyhow?*

A peek inside revealed a hologram with a list of all the items in her possession.

It was straight out of an inventory menu from a role-playing game. By placing her hand in the middle of the hologram and rotating her wrist, she could access dozens of compartments. Weapons. Armor and clothing. Accessories. Food and drink. Loot. Quest items. Spell tomes. Gifts. Luxurious pet storage. Furniture. Possessions could be hot-linked to simple hand gestures.

I could fit a whole room in here, she marveled, and took a seat on a bench to catch her breath.

Towering knights were stationed between gates: silent, faceless sentinels with black spears and polished shields carrying the city's crest.

A man with a strange glimmer in his eye chanted that the end times were coming. People shuffled past him without a glance. *Okay, that isn't really anything new.*

Shopkeepers haggled with potential customers. Marionettes danced on strings without puppeteers, magic-infused equipment glowed with elemental energies, and countless pets jumped about and play-fought each other.

In the midst of this, she spotted him - the cutest thing in the world.

The cat-like fuzz-ball with the tiniest furry wings and a pinwheel tail beamed at her with immediate recognition. His stripes rapidly shifted between the colors of the rainbow, as did his sparkling eyes. He had been waiting for her, and she fell in love immediately.

Raine made a beeline for a place called *Helter Shelter*, oblivious to the crowd of commuters she was cutting through.

"How much is that one?" Raine asked, wide-eyed.

The jaded old pet keeper looked her up and down. "Can't you read the sign?"

Raine glanced to her left.

"Chance"
Rainbow Cat, Advanced Familiar, Level 50
Resistant to Arcane Magic
(Reserved)

Her heart sank. She felt her knees go weak. "He's reserved?"

The pet keeper adjusted her glasses and glanced at her personal tablet. "Yes, it says it right here - to one *rainorshine23*."

Raine couldn't believe her ears.

The pet keeper jolted upright, suddenly realizing her mistake.

"Oh, I'm sorry, miss! I didn't know, I..." she fumbled. "I'll be right back with our selection of collars!"

"Ah, no, it's quite all right! I don't--"

Chance interrupted her with a stunningly loud *meow*. Raine suddenly lost her train of thought. The cat had shushed her, quite intentionally.

The older woman returned with a small leather suitcase and opened it up on the counter. The holographic catalog of collars ranged from all shapes and sizes.

"Just point at something if you want to see it."

Raine gazed intently at the scrolling list of hundreds of items.

"That one!" she exclaimed at a sharp-looking, gem-studded collar with a red bowtie.

The pet keeper gave a hearty chortle. "A premium collar, that is. Allows for unlimited transformation. Fantastic choice. Seventy Gold."

"Got it." Raine pulled up the menu screen on her watch.

"No, no, no," the lady said with a shake of her head. "Word of advice, girl. You're supposed to bargain me down a bit. Make it interesting, eh?"

"I'd rather pay in full. I don't even remember reserving this guy, if it was me who did it at all, so this must be my lucky day."

"Oh, I don't think you did reserve him. He's a gift."

"Huh? From whom?"

"The buyer chose to remain anonymous. But don't worry - Chance here is a good kitty. He'll bring you much fortune."

Curious as to the identity of her benefactor but unable to think of a reason to not take the familiar, Raine thanked the shopkeeper, paid for the collar, and gave Chance a long hug. He was quite affectionate, and his glowing coat and color-changing eyes were mesmerizing. She stroked him until she found his ticklish spots.

"I guess you and I are going to have some adventures together," she said.

Chance purred. He climbed Raine's shoulder – he seemed nearly weightless – and curled up around her neck, his body re-shaping into a scarf to provide her with warmth and comfort. She continued down the street towards a large public space paved with precious stones glimmering in the mist from what Raine now recognized as a crystal water fountain the size of two city blocks.

"At this point, I'm pretty sure this is no ordinary bonus level," Raine told Chance, and one of the flaps of her scarf nodded politely in response. "Yet, I still have no idea what the objective is, or why I'm here."

Most role-playing games take some time to get started, she reasoned. But this one seemed to be an advanced virtual reality designed for mass consumption. There could be many millions of players simultaneously sharing the same realm. *What kind of storyline could this game have? Who's the hero and who's the villain? Either everyone gets to be a hero, or no one does. Still, how can anything here possibly be as "real" as everyone seems to treat it?*

Raine took another bite out of her garden salad, which she'd purchased from a street vendor, and inspected her distorted face in the oversized fountain.

If this is a dream, then how come I still feel very much myself? And normally, once one realizes that one's dreaming, one can lucidly dream, or transcend it. But if that were the case here, finding Super BlastBoy would have been undoubtedly easier.

There's one last thing I might try.

She closed her eyes tightly and tried to will her best friend into existence. She imagined strong, stoic, dark-skinned Jordan sitting beside her, clad in armor. Going by dream logic, he'd know something of how this place worked. She opened her eyes; the powers that be failed to hold up their end of the bargain. Well, she wasn't entirely alone. Chance was with her, at least.

Feeling uncomfortably isolated in a very social world, Raine made an effort to snap out of her shell long enough to enjoy the scenery. A gathering of wizards and blacksmiths synchronized fireworks to the lively orchestral music. In a nearby maid café, a gay elvish couple shared a boxed lunch. Across a marble table, blue men in *Batman* suits argued over a complex holographic card game, where summoned mythical beasts did horrific battle.

A steady stream of folk wandered in and out of the crystal fountain's elaborate centerpiece. The off chance that Super BlastBoy might be waiting inside pushed Raine onto the stepping-stones.

The waterfall parted, leading her via a vast crystalline tunnel to another realm entirely.

This fountain was certainly bigger on the inside.

Raine was now in the midst of a public park with cobblestone paths and only a few trees interspersed amongst rolling hills of perfectly trimmed grass. Uniquely decorated king-sized beds played host to tens of thousands. Goggles, sunglasses, and visors of every size and make draped over their residents' languid eyes. Some models resembled the pair packed into her shoulder bag, but Raine was wary of trying the thing out before she saw the results firsthand.

She dared to approach an older man with long hair and a flowing beard looking out from behind circular glasses. A black rectangle hovered above his lenses; their contents must have been visible only to the device's user. He appeared friendly enough. Raine sat beside him.

"Excuse me, sir," she began. The man was silent, and his lazy eyes wandered about the hidden display for some time.

"Hmm?" he asked at last. The (!) icon over his head turned into a smiley face.

"I'm curious as to what you all are doing," Raine said, a little embarrassed.

"Can't speak for no one else, but I's chatting with friends," he said bemusedly.

Raine was puzzled. "How is that possible? There's no one here."

He held back a laugh.

"Well, of course *you* can't see 'em, li'l miss. I see 'em on my visor, through the Network." the man replied.

"What's the Network?"

"You serious, darlin'?"

The girl was silent.

"I can see that you're new here. Didn't you go through the training program?"

"Sorry, sir," she replied. "I didn't. Or if I did, I don't remember."

"Shucks. Well, I guess that's common enough. I'm in a game of poker, but I don't suppose a little demo could hurt my luck any more than ol' Jimmy here. Worst dealer in the realm – your wife's words, Jim, not mine. Oh, quit your yappin', boys. She's just a kid."

"Wow, so it's like a video phone?" Raine was blown away.

"Phone?"

"Er… yes."

"Um. Here, have a look-see."

To demonstrate, the old-timer rolled his eyes to a corner and blinked. He spoke to the machine across his eyes as if it were a person.

"Expand and share."

A multi-layered holographic projection emanated from the device, taking the place of the black rectangle. Icons and menu screens interspersed with faces of the other players, a news channel playing on one corner of the screen, live feed from a dance party on the opposite corner, and the poker game on a lower window. She couldn't hear their words, but the man showed her how he could expand and select different windows by looking at them and varying his blinking patterns, focal points, and eye movements. It was quite intimidating.

"That's wild. Tell me more about this Network thing."

"You certainly ask a lot of questions, young lady. It's a series of tubes, an electric window through time and space, and we're living in it. Jimmy reckons the Net created this place."

Tubes? What? The enticing smell of delicious food from a large public kitchen distracted her.

"I don't see how that would be possible. Where are we, exactly?"

"Come on, girl. Don'tcha know where you are? *Avidya.*"

Her scarf meowed in assent, as if to mock her lack of knowledge on the matter.

"Yes, I know that much, but... do you think you could you be more specific?"

"It is where it is. We're here, we're in it."

"But... where *is* it? Are we on Earth?"

"Earth?" the old man shot back, quizzically. "Why does that name... no, no, I have the definite feeling that's something I'm not supposed to know... please, let's... not mention it. Nice weather lately, yes?"

Raine nearly exploded.

"Hold up! You can't *not* know about the Earth! It's big, it's blue, and it's where we all live - the third planet in our solar system. Six billion humans. Please tell me this is ringing a bell."

The man shook his head.

"Sorry, miss, but I... I think I'm not supposed to rightly understand what you're saying."

"What does that even mean? D-don't you know where Earth is? Aren't you at least curious? I was just there, no more than an hour ago."

"I don't know. I don't care. And I don't really think it matters," the elderly man replied coldly, beginning to get uncomfortable. He returned to his visor. "Sorry, miss. My turn to deal."

Just as a virtual deck appeared in his hands, an explosion rang out from a nearby portal. Raine spun around in terror and gasped, the shock she was barely holding in finally coming out in full force.

It's just a dream, Raine, she told herself. *It's a dream and you're going to enjoy the heck out of it, because when you wake up, it's back to the same old song and dance.*

"Oh, never you mind those folk, trainin' for some blasted war what's mostly for their entertainment. Hmm? Oh, Ol' Georgie says hello to the pretty girl. He wants ya to know the war economy keeps the banks and blacksmiths running. Says we can't complain about a little noise once in a while. See, this here's a Peace zone; no safer place is there. I say let 'em play their games so long as I can play mine."

There was a long, cold silence, but Raine didn't want to leave.

Not while she still had questions.

She waited for the man to calm down a bit. He didn't seem to mind her continued presence, so she pressed on.

"So it's like a game. Does it ever end?"

"Fold," he grumbled. When he turned to Raine, his voice betrayed a tinge of annoyance. "You make it end. As many times as you want. Wipe your memories and return with a new identity. Everyone does it. Rumor goes, you stick around long enough without doing a memory wipe, they recruit ya. Turn y'all into one of those blasted Templars."

Templars. The old man had said the word with such a mixture of fear and anger that Raine thought she knew who they must be.

Fifty yards away stood an armored knight identical to many others she'd seen elsewhere in the city. The towering figure with multiple weapons and a large "T" on its shield loomed two heads over the tallest person she'd seen and absolutely exuded authority; from empty eye sockets in its helmet, the warrior swept a small section of the park. Its red laser moved across the area so quickly that one would only have noticed if one were explicitly looking for it.

And then, the Templar returned her gaze, sizing Raine up with blood-red eyes.

Chance uncurled himself, propped up on his master's shoulder, and hissed at the hulking knight. Raine promptly yanked him off and set him on the ground.

"Quiet, Chance. Be a good boy."

The Templar was definitely scanning her for much longer than a second. Whatever eyes could possibly be under that helm, she didn't look forward to meeting them.

"I'm sorry, sir, but I think I should get going," she said to the man, standing to give him a kind farewell. "Th-thank you so much for answering my questions. Name's Raine, by the way. And this is Chance."

"Charles Hayter," he replied, his attention already turned back to his visor. "T'was a pleasure."

Casually, trying to keep her cool, Raine walked through an arch that, judging by the steady stream of traffic going through it, hopefully housed a portal.

Raine exhaled in relief upon emerging from beneath a waterfall on the opposite side of the crystal fountain. She missed a chance to ask Mr. Hayter about Super BlastBoy, but the distressing follow-up thought was that he wouldn't have a clue as to what she was talking about.

SBB mentioned 'forbidden knowledge'. Why didn't that man want to discuss Earth?

She shuffled past the Literally Sunken Orchestra, playing muzak to a lethargic crowd spread out along futons and scattered pillows. The spectacle reminded Raine of naptime in kindergarten. Still on edge and afraid of being followed, the girl walked briskly from the square.

As she thought on all the people seemingly enslaved by the Network, she wondered if that was to be her fate, should she tarry too long here.

Her senses overwhelmed, Raine followed the flowing stream over a bridge to where it fed into a placid lake.

She leaned on the railing, hoping to rest her eyes on something natural. But hovering over the water, dozens of visor-wearing kids spun around in opposing spheres, limbs flailing to the beat of a flashy multiplayer rhythm game: a videogame within a videogame world.

Averting her eyes downwards, Raine gazed into the water's sparkling blue depths from underneath the suddenly increasing pitter-patter of black pixels. She made a study of her own pair of goggles.

Maybe later. Right now this place is weird enough on its own.

"Good morning, citizens! We need you to re-elect Pinoci to the office of Governor-King!"

The sudden loudspeaker bothered her. Following it, a roaring shadow blanketed the city.

"I promise to use my power to win the war on Atmoya! I also pledge to maintain our friendship with Chip Kingdom under the righteous guidance of Mister Senior!"

Spinning around towards the din, Raine took in the gargantuan airship hovering above her head. A complete impossibility with regards to physics, it was definitely military in nature, with downward-facing turrets of every size emerging from its hull. They gave the illusion of long oars on some ancient vessel.

Its plaque read: *The Nebula, Protector of the Skies.*

Dozens of blimps fluttered out of the behemoth, each projecting holograms of two genial politicians. Subtitles listed 'Pinoci' and 'Mister Senior.'

"Pinoci and I have made excellent progress in bringing our two great countries together. We will keep your user experience safe and convenient so you can pursue your dreams!"

Mister Senior had a kind of unforgettable face, the confident gaze of a pro salesman married to the enigmatic smirk of a school principal. As they breakdanced with an overly euphoric crowd of diverse individuals, the loudspeaker trumpeted the slogans once more, set to a swelling orchestra. Raine had had quite enough of it.

"Re-elect Pinoci for more item drops! Pinoci!"

The *Nebula*'s shadow receded. Escort blimps took their campaign to the other side of town, the storm died down to a trickle, and the city didn't appear so inviting anymore.

There's no way SBB would be caught dead here. What's a surefire way to find a heroic legend? Seek out a battle, perhaps.

A good start might be to follow anyone geared up to fight. Sure enough, warrior-watching proved rewarding in under a minute: spotting a satyr ninja clan hopping across the rooftops, Raine decided to see if she could do the same. She climbed a trellised wall onto a second-storey building, to many worried mews from Chance.

"Where's your sense of adventure?" she laughed.

Tutorial's over. It's time to see what's going on.

Raine calculated her distance and leapt over to an adjacent roof. She found that she could jump extraordinarily higher than normal, and that her feet caught the ground with little resistance. Perhaps in this dream, physical constants like gravity were flexible. Another calculated leap, this time over a small road, all but confirmed this hypothesis.

The girl looked ahead; the ninjas headed towards the market district. While there was no way she could catch up with them, she could at least journey in their general direction. Raine bounded from rooftop to rooftop with ease.

IV. Gerrit

"Act without expectation." – Lao Tzu

April 14, 2187
Earth Defense Coalition Temporary Base Camp

I guess that's one way to get there. But you're no Spider-Man, *Raine. One pratfall from you and we're all in the drink.*

Sky Admiral Lillian Hermes sipped hot tea from her thermos, standing outside her bunker overlooking the desolate cliff face in western Siberia as she watched the live feed of Raine and her companion hopping across the *Metaverse* without a care in the world. She blinked off her personal Holo-Lens; the bulb on her ear-mounted device went dark.

So far, so good, at least on Raine's end. The destruction of their primary satellite dish by one of the Queen's rogue patrol units was too close for comfort. If Raine had awoken any later in the process, their signal might have been back-traced. There could be no more risks like that. Not if this planet were to have any chance at all.

The time had come for the Earth Defense Coalition, as the outfit called itself, to take the show on the road, with all the possible risks that presented. This hostile plateau by the Altai Mountains was the latest unexpected temp base on their journey, an unwelcome pit stop necessitated by the Queen's increasing drone patrols and irregular storms.

Still, the advanced scrambling shield ensured that they'd be well concealed from her eyes tonight, and hopefully a few days longer.

The wind stung the twenty-year-old's cheeks, bringing with it a promise of another blizzard. Two android bodyguards and the scruffy foreman looked on in concern for her health, but a multi-layered parka with a built-in electric heater kept the time traveler warm and toasty. Several dozen 'bots were priming the *Valkyrie's* new dish to maximum efficiency atop a hundred-foot tower. The monstrosity swayed in the unrelenting gale.

As much as possible, whenever she found herself down on the surface, Lily would insist on spending time outside, in nature, even if the great outdoors consisted of a desolate, frozen highland seven thousand feet above sea level.

"Higher!" she yelled after checking the read-outs. "We're going to need fifteen more feet for optimum range!"

The androids turned down their camouflage and looked to her in disbelief.

"Admiral, we're low on time, and we're already risking detection here," Colonel Feuchuk opined, at his wits' end.

"Nothing is more important than this," she intoned. "*Operation End Verse* culminates in four days, and we need to make tracks ASAP. The Commodore's already on the move."

Right now, a stable, untraceable connection was everything. It'd mean, quite literally, the difference between the life and death of every organism on planet Earth. Even a minor slip-up at this point might end in the most drastic of consequences.

"We're short-handed, ma'am. If you could just give me till morning," the Colonel pleaded.

"So be it," Lily mumbled in reply. "But we leave at oh-eight-hundred sharp."

Frustrated at the slow progress of her underlings, Lily retreated into the bunker, storming through her checkpoints. She stole glances at holo-screens by the android barracks; Raine was now chatting with an NPC on the rooftop.

Her mechanized soldiers snapped into respectful salutes.

"As you were!" she yelled. "No more wasted time on pleasantries tonight."

They quickly returned to work. Many were retrofitting droids and weapons recovered from some of the less fortunate factories. To boot, cloaking systems were in desperate need of maintenance, having fallen prey to the constant storms.

At the heart of the structure, Lieutenant General Gabriel Joaquin directed the flow of local air traffic. His staff was guiding approaching escorts to the lower base camps beneath the flying fortresses.

They had to act fast. It was no easy job steering cloaked airships in a blizzard, even ones powered by multiple thermal fission cores. Lily hated being forced to utilize dirty and destructive nuclear power, but when in Rome…

"This is a mess, Admiral," he said sadly. "I advise that we delay the operation. If this weather keeps up, we'll only have sixty percent of the force we'd hoped for."

"That will have to do," Lily replied.

"I'm sorry, ma'am, I don't think I understand. To lay siege on *Neo Eden* with only three hundred thousand..."

"Vice, you're from Cuba, right?"

Joaquin swallowed. "My family is, ma'am. But I grew up in the Panama commune. My father fought in the '62 Sugar Skirmishes."

That's right; he lived through Panama. She placed a hand on his shoulder. Here she was, comforting a man nearly twice her age. Whatever rationale he had for a delay, it wasn't worth putting even more lives at risk.

"I promise you, once this week is over, you'll have a choice: to return to your family, or to send for them to assist in the rebuilding process. And the same goes for everyone in this outfit."

"I understand, ma'am. If the operation is a success--"

"There's no 'if's or 'buts' about it. We're shutting down the *Metaverse*. There will be casualties, despite our best efforts. I'm not asking for miracles. But we have a strict schedule to keep."

Gabriel Joaquin nodded and returned to his work.

A more focused study of the man's bold face reminded Lily how brave he was to be the first to undergo Trust Memory Analysis.

His recent example ended the boycott for Lillian's controversial but effective technique of weeding out any potential spies or double agents: a thorough transcription and investigation of every enlistee's memories. While transparent in its goals, the procedure was despised, and indeed many left the service on principle alone. Some Elders even resigned.

But as a result, the Sky Admiral could rest knowing that not a one of the thousands of EDC men and women currently airborne was working for the Queen, and for her, that was worth the loss.

At this point, every eye in the command room was on Lillian. The Elder Representatives, too, watched intently from back home. Lily cleared her throat and walked into her private office to address them via a static-riddled hologram.

"Dear elders, I can wait only till morning before departing. Everything's in motion now. I'm sorry," she said, unzipping her parka.

"Why must it be now?" the Russian elder asked. "One or two more days will give us an opportunity to nearly double our forces."

You got this, Lily told herself. *Just like we rehearsed.*

"Because right now, time is on our side. As of yet we've had no leaks. The HDP is still vulnerable, and our plans within the *Metaverse* will have consequences. Much can change in one minute, let alone an hour, or a day. I'm hoping to avoid a bloodbath. Please trust me when I say we won't get another shot."

It was most of the truth. Raine was already barreling forward on her course, with virtual bloodhounds sure to be hot on her trail in hours. With the drop of the first domino, there was no way to slow down what had been set into motion.

"We can only hope that you know what you are doing," the elder from Tibet replied. "Should you fail to take the city, you can be sure that our last peaceful lands will be razed in retaliation. We can't afford another Jakarta."

"I fully understand that," Lily nodded. "May I address the room now, so that my men don't lose what little faith they have?"

The elders quickly conversed amongst themselves via private channels. Within a few seconds, they came to an agreement.

"Very well," one of the American Indian Chieftains acquiesced.

A hologram of Commodore Leandra mouthed 'good luck'. Lily gave her a thumbs-up in reply. She brushed off her parka, straightened her uniform, and kicked the office door open.

"Hey, everyone! I know that I'm asking a lot from you all. Every man, woman, and droid in this place is doing their damned best. This will be difficult on all of us," she continued. "But time is of the essence. One by one, our factories and bases have fallen under siege. Supply routes have been cut off, merchant ships scuttled. This is our best and only chance. What happened in Sector Thir–, I mean, Indonesia – last week wasn't easy on anyone. But if we turn back now, our families will be next. The only advantage we possess is the element of surprise, and we can't lose it. Will you fight with me?"

"Yes, Sky Admiral, ma'am!" the room echoed.

But Lily could see that many doubts remained. Their reaction was to be expected. As far as they were concerned, she had only been leading the EDC for five of her seven fragmented years with the rebellion, but under her watchful eye, they'd given the Queen the first proper challenge to her reign since her dynasty had come to power, freeing tens of thousands from the *Metaverse*, not to mention annexing dozens of war factories in as many territories, turning them to their own use, and all under the Overseer's nose. Yet, even with her wealth of intellect and experience, the truth was that the Sky Admiral was but a young woman, a phantom with no birth records or homeland, and to their knowledge, she had not yet been tested in a battle of this scale.

On the big screen, the elders looked grim, and appeared to be discussing matters of war and resources amongst themselves, shutting her out. To save face, Lillian knew she had to get the last word in.

"I know many of you think we are heading towards certain death. They may have superior numbers and firepower, but we've got a clockwork course. It's the second star to the right and straight on till morning. All we need to do is to hit our marks once the curtain's pulled," Lily declared.

Having said this, she walked back into the storm before anyone in the room could spot the worries racking her face, and returned to watching the virtual drama unfold.

↔

Fueled by adrenaline, Raine leapt past ancient monuments and over coffee shops. The sounds of battle drew nearer. She stopped to consider whether she could make a sixty-foot leap to a higher roof across a main road when someone called out her name.

"Raine!" he cried. "Raine, where are you going?"

She did a double take on the clean-cut blonde boy from earlier, now clumsily navigating the shingled terrain. His voice was even more unnatural than his appearance.

He stopped too close for Raine's comfort, huffing and puffing. In place of a green username, "Nimbus" appeared above his head in gray letters. Nothing about the kid struck her as human or genuine, but she decided to hear him out.

"Um, hi," she said, crossing her arms.

"I've been looking all over for you," Nimbus replied. "Turn that frown upside down! I know you'll come to enjoy my company."

He beamed in a way that made Raine very uncomfortable. She walked around him, so he couldn't pin her against the edge of the roof.

"Why? I don't even know why you're so interested in me, and it's kind of creeping me out."

Nimbus advanced towards her, and Raine circled until the chimney was at her back. There was something very off about his eyes. She clenched her fists.

"I am here on behalf of the Developers. My sworn duties are to answer any questions you might have, to be your friend if you are looking for company, and to make your life more pleasant... and exciting."

Raine was ready to sock him, the same way she showed bullies at her orphanage that she wasn't the type to be messed with.

"Now, what would you like to know?"

Without warning, a menu screen appeared before his robotic face. Raine skimmed the hundreds of available questions.

The whole thing looked dreadfully boring.

"I don't suppose you could help me locate Super BlastBoy, also known as Anthony Kon."

Nimbus looked sad. "I'm sorry. I don't have a record of either."

Raine felt at a total loss. "That can't be right. Can you check again?"

"No results found. Let's try something else. I'd like to take you on a hovercraft tour of the city. Shall we make it a date?"

"Ask me again when I'm in a better mood."

"Would you feel better if I were less conventionally attractive?"

"Come now, Nimbus. This has nothing to do with how you look. It's just... you, man. I can't believe I'm trying to cheer up a computer. All right, tell me what I can do if I'm bothered by someone I don't want around."

"Naturally, you need not be subject to any unwanted physical contact. Simply think it, and any individual touching you will be repelled by a shock. There are other options. Use the red button on your wristband to ban a player. This prevents any physical and/or remote contact and transmits relevant logs to the Templar forces."

"Okay, good." Raine held her finger over the button, mock-threatening to press it. "Now shove off, please," she told Nimbus sternly.

Disappointed, the boy took a small step back. "W-would you like to know more?"

"I get that it's your job, home skillet, but can we do this later?" Raine asked. "I'd prefer to explore on my own."

Nimbus' simper dried up and fell off his face.

"Very well," he said. "We shall see each other again, Raine. I really do have a hovercraft, if ever you need a ride. I am updated every hour with a list of the hippest places to eat, alone or otherwise. Additionally, I don't recommend you go that way. That sector just turned into a Chaos zone."

"Chaos zone?"

"Yes. You are currently in a Peace zone, where duels are not permitted, and only wanted individuals can be engaged in combat. In a Chaos zone, combat is possible between all players and you risk de-materialization. If you experience d-mat, you will lose a currently equipped item, three percent of your experience points since your last level-up, and will need to get to a re-spawn point to revive to human form. Would you like to know more?"

"Maybe later, Nimbus. Thanks, but no thanks. Goodbye, now."

With that, Nimbus bowed, walked back the way he came, leapt off the rooftop, and was gone.

Raine took a deep breath and had a seat beside the chimney, observing the townspeople.

If Super BlastBoy is nowhere to be found, then what am I to do? Anything I want, she reminded herself. *This is my dream; if I practice enough, I should be able to control what happens here, after all.*

Just when she thought she earned a breather, a stray spell depressurized the air, ripped the shingles off the roof, and sent Raine flying hard into a rocky parapet. It hurt much less than she had expected, which was refreshing, but also a little scary.

The girl made it back on her feet to see people running in the opposite direction.

They're missing out on the fun, she thought, transfixed by the loud booming, accompanied by shrieks, explosions, and swords clashing on scales. From the low, guttural cries and warriors flying about like ragdolls, she deduced that some horrid beast must be just around the corner.

Templars urged unarmed passersby towards the fountain-park. Raine hid from them as she leapt ever closer to the Chaos zone. A sign read: *"Medieval/Magic Weapons Only. Advanced Technology (Gen. III and above) not permitted."*

Beyond, the roofs were fewer and further between, giving way to the remnants of an ancient ruin. She perched atop a Corinthian column, mimicking the contemplative pose of a gargoyle on an opposite arch.

Now, at last, Raine could see the object of the warriors' wrath – a horrendous eighty-foot-tall crab spewing all manner of acid at the large group of adventurers. It swatted dozens aside with each swing of its wrecking ball-sized claws. They were close to five hundred combatants in all, and most fought one another just to get near the beast.

Raine ventured closer, dropping behind a large obsidian statue of a cavalryman and watching with excitement as a dozen brave archers under the sizeable beast shot explosive arrows into the area between the body and its joints for massive damage. Countless magicians on the sidelines cast spells at the creature from incantation circles, while others enacted charms on their teammates, leaving them surrounded by glowing force fields.

A bearded dwarf scaling a leg swung a mattock at one of the crab's ligaments. The beast flung him off and crushed him underfoot as it scuttled wildly. Raine reckoned with horror that the man must be dead, but his lifeless body merely vanished, and a ghostly image of him appeared in its place.

"Damn it!" the figure said in the annoyed voice of a pubescent boy. "Don't kill him till I get back!"

A swordsman attempting to climb the leg responded. "Make haste, slowpoke! I'll hang on to your shield!"

The crab reared on its four hind legs as a particularly well-aimed arrow pierced a small red spot on its underbelly. The climbing swordsman fell at least forty feet from the leg and landed on the floor. Surprisingly, he was still moving. His helm popped off to reveal a mish-mash of orange hair. A target sight blinked over the boy's wounded frame – a bulls-eye across his chest. The crab's telescopic machine eyes shone blood red.

"I'll lure him away!"

"He's locked on, Gerrit!" one of the mages screamed. "Go!"

The fallen swordsman picked up his helmet and ran full-speed towards the statue Raine was crouching behind. Gerrit leapt for cover, bumping right into the girl and stomping on her foot. She let out a yelp of pain before realizing her foot didn't hurt as much as she'd anticipated.

The boy turned and noticed her for the first time, double-checking Raine's figure to make sure he hadn't imagined her. He shared the surprise of a man who upon exiting a stall in a men's room looks up to find a stunning woman sitting cross-legged on the sink.

"A newbie? What are you doing here? We're in the midst of battle!"

"You've got some nerve calling me that!" Raine said. "Why are you battling in the middle of such a beautiful city?"

"You have no armor! It'll vaporize you!"

"Huh? Oh, this is just my dream. I control what happens. I'll be fine," Raine replied flippantly, and stood as if she were going to stroll away from the statue.

She took a quick look behind her at the crab, which had fully-charged its acid beam attack. It noticed her sudden movement. All at once, the boy grabbed her hand, reached into his belt pack, and tossed a small wing down by Raine's feet.

"You'll thank me for this later!"

There was a loud whistling sound as Raine felt herself rocket up and away from the pedestal. She watched from a distance as the statue exploded into pieces; it looked like Gerrit made it, but it could have gone either way. A second whoosh left her floating in a void.

"Where would you like to go?"

Raine stared blankly at the menu screen, which displayed a Regional Map.

"Um, take me outside the city, I guess?"

"Traveling to Clyde North Gate (Exterior)..."

The girl reappeared high up in mid-air above the castle walls. Unaware that she'd be invisible until making landfall, Raine clenched her skirt tightly between her knees as she descended to a predetermined shiny spot outside the Castle Town. Countless others arrived and departed on similar shiny spots and glowing teleport pads, human and non-human traffic whizzing by without a care.

In the far distance, something caught her eye: a quivering speck of red atop a rather large hill off to the North.

No. It can't be.

She squinted to see if it really was Super BlastBoy's cape. The animation was a perfect match, but as soon as she spotted him the figure zipped over the hill at such a speed that it very well could have been anything.

THUMP.

Raine was so surprised to regain her footing that she took a stumble forward, caught a rock on her foot, then fell towards a sculpture and bounced off an invisible wall before righting herself. As a few bunny-eared warriors picnicking nearby stifled a bout of laughter, she coughed in a vain attempt to appear completely natural.

Flattening her skirt, Raine took note of the most peculiar green field, reminiscent of Wonderland's chessboard. It stretched out towards a vast horizon mired only by spots of fog over the far outlands and raised paths running into countless hills and mountainsides. The rainbow shag carpet path split at a prism-shaped landmark, widening into alternate pathways.

Now that they were outside, away from the crowds, Chance plopped down from Raine's shoulder and ran circles around her.

Taking baby steps onto the path, Raine noticed a gelatinous creature a few feet off the road. It bounced up and down like a piece of Jell-O. She crouched down beside it.

"Why, you're the cutest little thing in the world."

Chance hissed and raised his tail, which glowed like he was readying a powerful attack.

"Oh, fine. You're only second cutest to Chance," Raine said, shushing him away. The cat seemed appeased by the comment.

The strange creature moved a little closer towards her, and she'd just stretched out her hand to pet it when a sword suddenly appeared and cleaved it in two, sending goo splashing into Raine's face.

The gelatin creature, now crying from its separated eyes, left behind four tiny coins on the grass.

Raine screamed.

"H-hey, usually the yelling phase comes once we've known each other for a bit, am I right? At least let me buy you dinner first," the murderer quipped, as his wristwatch absorbed the Gold left behind.

Raine wiped off the goo. She tried to get a good look at the wretched killer underneath his silly helm with an odd viewing screen. He flipped it open. It was the same boy who pushed her out of the way of the giant crab's acid beam.

"It's you again!"

"Oh, hi? Didn't mean to freak you out, but someone had to protect you."

"Protect me? From what?"

"From the Gellate!" He pointed at the little pieces of goo disintegrating into the ground as they spoke.

"As if that cute little thing could really have hurt me!"

Gerrit was taken aback.

"You really are a newbie, aren't you?" He didn't mean to say it. It just came right out.

"I don't know what you're talking about. And you shouldn't presume I'm anything; you don't even know my name."

The boy removed his helm and frazzled his orange hair. Raine finally got a chance to study his soft but well-defined features, and gentle eyes. He was a little dorky, but he wasn't unattractive. They looked about the same age.

"Look, we got off on the wrong foot. As you can see, my screen name is *NinjaMageKnight99*, but my friends call me Gerrit."

He held out his hand. She took it briefly.

"I'm Raine."

"Raine? That's a pretty name."

His eyes gleamed in the sun and fixed right onto hers, as if she was the first real person he had seen in ages. She looked away.

"It was nice to meet you, Gerrit, but I'm in a hurry. I could wake up at any second."

Raine turned to walk away. At first she had heard no footsteps, and naïvely took that as a good sign. A few seconds later they came bounding up the hill, following her even as she attempted to disappear into the crowd.

"Oh, wait a second, miss!"

Raine and Chance marched up the path, determined to ignore Gerrit.

"So! Raine! Um, does your username mean you have a positive outlook on life?"

Ugh. He's catching up. Not good.

"Look, I… I'm sorry I teleported you out of there without your consent. It was just a pretty hairy situation and I thought I was helping you. It's not just the stuff you'd lose. They'd put you through another hour of boring tutorials."

"Thanks. You probably did a very good thing for me, but I don't need any help," Raine said, spinning around to a stop. "To be honest, I really don't know what you guys were doing in there. I'm not a part of it."

"A part of what?"

"Of… this. Of whatever is going on here. This is just my dream, and you're in it. Logically, I can't – shouldn't – get attached to anyone, because that might snap me out of it and I'll wake up in my gloomy foster Mom's place again! …You dig it, right?"

If Gerrit comprehended anything Raine said, it wasn't clear to her. He was too busy studying her face, which only made her even more furious, especially considering that for all she knew, she could be facedown at *Flynn's* after having passed out trying for the world record.

"Well, you're certainly not an NPC."

"NPC?"

"Non-player character. They have grayed-out names. You are a player, right? You're not just like some in-game bug or figment of my imagination?"

"No way. I don't think you could have come up with me."

Or that the game could create a bug like me, for that matter, she thought. *If it really is a game.*

"So, then. Welcome to *Endless Metaverse,* the undying massively-multiplayer cosmos, where everything's made up and the Developers rule supreme." Gerrit's game show host act fell apart at Raine's contemplative frown.

"Massively multiplayer, eh? So this place really isn't a bonus level."

She thought back to the odd message that greeted her that morning. *You are playing on the* Avidya *server.* Strangely, it seemed little more than a distant memory. Was it possible that the lady in spandex and SBB's developers lied to her as to the true nature of this place? *I don't usually go in for conspiracy theories, but this is madness.*

"Raine? Are you there?"

"Oh, sorry. I was… lost in thought."

"It's cool. I tend to have that effect on women," Gerrit managed, not sure if it would come off as a cocky comment or a put-down on his own style. "You mentioned something about a bonus level? I know quite a few of those."

"It's all right. I must have had the wrong idea. Though, I don't suppose you'd have heard anything about Super BlastBoy?" answered Raine, a little nervously.

"Wait, did you say Super BlastBoy?"

Her eyes widened. "Yes! He's kind of almost a friend of mine! Do you know where I might find him?"

"It's your first day and you're telling me you met *the* SBB?" Gerrit exclaimed. "Sorry, not buying it. I'm pretty sure he and the other AI hosts were deleted from the *'Verse* long ago."

Raine hid her red cheeks by keeping her gaze low. "I'm glad you've heard of him, at least. But you're wrong. He's alive and kicking, all right. I think he needs my help, or I need his. It's just a strong hunch, and my hunches are usually pretty good. Not that I need to tell you that. Unless you feel like helping me find him."

Alive? Do AI even 'live'? SBB will probably exist only as long as I stay asleep. And the same goes for you, too, Gerrit. There and gone again, like so many fictional friends I've encountered in my dreams.

"Sounds like a reasonable quest, but I don't work for free."

"Oh? How much do you want for the job?"

Gerrit stuck out his chin, evidently trying for the part of the hard-boiled detective.

"That's talk for another time, doll. You're hot off the forge and I haven't even agreed to anything yet. Got any leads?"

"Er, I think I saw him way over yonder!" Raine exclaimed, pointing across fields, deserts and plains to a mass of lumpy, unremarkable foothills.

"That deserted patch of nothingness?" Gerrit considered. "That's... heading towards Atmoya. Past the borders of the Empire. The roads are in disrepair, plus there's no teleporting past HC – er, Helium-Corneria. Not exactly the safest place to travel. You sure it was him?"

Gerrit didn't look so confident in her powers of deduction.

"Positive," Raine bluffed.

"Cool story bro."

"Um, thanks?"

"Ah, it's a troll... n-never mind. You're not just another fangirl chasing look-alikes, are you?"

"I'll have you know, I saw him with my own two eyes, and more than once, too!"

Just then Gerrit's watch beeped, putting an end to the act. He gave the private screen above it a quick glance.

"Tell you what," he continued, intrigued at her story. "You're one of the most interesting newbies I've ever met. I've gotta help divide the spoils, but afterwards my guild mates and I are bowling downtown. How's about I add your username to my Friends List and we'll chat tomorrow?"

A small menu popped up in the corner of Raine's peripheral vision.

It read, "Approve friend request from *NinjaMageKnight99*? Say 'yes' or 'no'."

Raine tried politely to decline his offer non-verbally without contorting her face too strongly.

"You can always ban me later, anyway. Just think about it. I've got a mount," he insisted. "He's a dragon. Ever wanted to fly? I'll give you the full *Avidya* tour."

She rolled her eyes. That, at least, sounded pretty cool.

"Fine."

The menu screen took that as a confirmation and chirped out of existence.

Gerrit gave Raine a thumbs-up. He would have fist-pumped if it were socially acceptable. But everything changed after last month's mass fist-pumping disaster.

"Great! TTYL!"

"Tee-what?"

If she had known him a little better, Raine might have realized that Gerrit was absolutely glowing.

He pulled out another small glass wing from a compartment in his belt pack and threw it on the ground. A sound like the flaming elevator from *Die Hard* falling down a shaft and exploding roared from the portal that popped into existence.

Still smiling, Gerrit leapt into it with a wave and vanished.

Raine sighed. Boys, no matter what dimension they were from, were a waste of precious time.

V. Queen Lorelei

"I love power. But it is as an artist that I love it. I love it as a musician loves

his violin, to draw out its sounds, and chords, and harmonies."

- Napoleon Bonaparte

The view from the top is something beyond elegant. It is the ultimate power trip.

This, Queen Lorelei knew.

She lived on a plane all her own, and she wouldn't have it any other way.

At almost four thousand feet in the air, her office sat at the very top of the *Spire*. The plasma-shielded balcony loomed over the cyber-metropolis of *Neo Eden*, whose foundations were constructed from the inside of a hollowed-out mountain and encompassed what the Old World once referred to as Naples, Italy. It offered a gorgeous ocean view of the Mediterranean, and had played host to six of Lorelei's top ten sunsets.

She was now thirty-four. At twenty, she became the supreme ruler of the civilized world. And she had been running it now for almost two centuries.

How did she do it, one might ask?

Even for those resting comfortably at the top of her social pyramid, her great ability was a secret never to be revealed.

It was a handy little thing called time travel, and though it tended to make things very, very complex, it also allowed her to accomplish feats that challenged the notion of impossibility.

Her mid-morning coffee finished, she retreated across the marble balcony and through the arch, drawing the silk curtains to a close over clear Venetian doors.

Queen Lorelei strode through her bedroom and into the adjoining office, kicked off her high heels, and practically dropped into her dog-fur chair. She crossed her long, ivory-white legs on her glass desk and lit a cigarette to begin her work.

First, it was time to inspect the progress reports. She had a look at the resource management screen embedded in the desk. In stark contrast to the mess that the *Metaverse* had become, her Overseer AI ran smooth as butter. Silver, silicon, oil, and plutonium mining and refining all functioned acceptably across the globe, especially considering the fact that most of her production zones were deserts with little to no water or topsoil, stricken with absolute drought.

Maybe conjuring up a few tropical storms might boost production, she figured. *Hope proves useful in sporadic installments, tragedy even moreso.*

"The destruction of Sector Thirty hasn't dampened their spirits. The assets require another reminder of their mortality," she intoned to the program. "Prepare to ravage Sectors Fifteen through Seventeen with a hurricane, and pull our medics out. Let the insurgents deal with the cleanup. Also, lay off on the palladium refinement in Sector Nine. Divert assets to uranium in Twenty-Two."

The Overseer's interface, a bearded, elderly man bound by innumerable tethers to the Network, gave a slight nod, its expressive face pained by the tasks at hand. "It shall be done."

With more than a little satisfaction, Lorelei swiped two fingers across her desktop console, dismissing the Overseer; holo-vision population reports switched to security feeds showing hundreds of locales from the three primary *Endless Metaverse* servers. As usual, it seemed that *Avidya* was in specific need of attention, with Templar units requesting backup to deal with rebel factions on both North and South continents. Usually, such petty problems were best left to the hired help, but these days, no virtual concern was too small to ignore.

Despite my best efforts, the Metaverse *is far from a perfect system, and I can't afford to be sloppy. Not now, of all times.*

Next on the agenda: fill the position of *Avidya* Junior Network Manager. It was a most important wartime job, and she'd made the unusual request of asking to personally interview the candidates. But that could wait for now.

She placed a delicate circlet over her head and leaned back in her office chair.

"Plug me in," she said, and closed her eyes.

When she opened them again, Lorelei beheld a virtual office near indistinguishable from her real-life one.

"Miss Guggell, your presence is requested," she intoned.

A ghostlike replica of the Queen materialized in the elegant mahogany chair across from her desk. They were identical, except that

HRM Lorelei was clad in a form-fitting dress and lathered in make-up, whereas the modest Miss G program was decked out in its usual attire: sleek glasses, a blue blazer over a shirt and tie, and a formal skirt; her outfit never changed – that was the easiest way to ensure that no one confused the fashionable real Queen for her virtual double.

"Your Majesty," it echoed in the same silky voice, "how may I help you?"

Queen Lorelei studied the apparition. Miss Guggell played a central role in the execution of her masterpiece, The End of the World, 3.0, known to the public as *Endless Metaverse*. It was essential that the artificial intelligence be purged of all possible errors, and that it should remain loyal and obedient at all times. The Queen pressed her finger to her own temple, blinked twice, and closed her eyes. Miss Guggell followed suit, triggering the microscopic nano-machines in the Queen's brain that linked her consciousness and wishes with her virtual self's programming.

In this state, while Miss Guggell was updating its priorities, the Queen could detect errors in the AI, browse lists of major bugs discovered in the *'Verse*, and check and reassign tasks as she saw fit. As an added bonus, every once in a while she could tell when her virtual replica was trying to hide something.

"*Maya* and *Tanha* seem fine. Third-party servers and primary backups are cluttered as always, but at least they're doing their jobs. Tell me what's going on in *Avidya*," the Queen demanded, glancing over recent bugs and unfiltered taboo data. "The eggheads suspect a few bad leaks."

Miss Guggell furrowed its pixellated brow.

"Yes, very recently there have been some unprompted data storms, and it appears that some of the information they are bringing into the *Metaverse* is taboo. Perhaps one of the assets is running an older client inadvertently and polluting it with their personal data?"

"Whatever it is, take care of it quick," Queen Lorelei bemoaned. "I expect a report within the day. Also, patch me into Wrathman's private connection. Audio only."

"As you wish," Miss Guggell bowed.

Ω

After the neural connection was cut, Miss Guggell disappeared, and re-emerged in the *Avidya* command dome in the center of the real-world *Endless Metaverse Control Nexus*, a rather minimalistic, high-security fortress adjacent to the *Spire*.

It came into being as a hologram on its seat at the foot of the Queen's towering throne. Five hundred men and women seated in spiral clusters around the elevated central platform held their breaths for news. These were the Lead Developers.

Avidya Lead Alphonse Hoshua turned from arguing with a colleague and greeted the AI with a little trepidation. "Cheers, Guggell."

"I am under direct orders from the Queen. We are to investigate the info leaks and get to the bottom of these data storms. Prepare to relinquish control. First breaks will be in three hours. Counting down now. Ten... nine... eight... seven... six..."

This was the cue for all three hundred Developers ranked C-class or lower to stop whatever they were doing and place their index fingers on the circlets around their heads, eyes closed.

"Five... four..."

Miss Guggell's digital self detected the bodies, performed all the synaptic tests. It had already triple-checked its calculations for optimal resource usage. It assigned a hundred Developers to filter and censor the leaked info, seventy to monitor recently created accounts, ten to scan the crime scenes with Templar units, fifty to compile probability reports, and the rest to spread disinformation and quell public unrest.

"Three... two..."

The men and women felt their minds disassociating from their bodies, temporarily retreating into a place in the subconscious where they became mere observers.

"One... zero."

Miss Guggell lifted its hands up in the air, a digital puppet master preparing for a grand show. Three hundred bodies straightened, marionettes without strings, and worked furiously at their consoles as one living, breathing unit.

↕

Meanwhile, Queen Lorelei's display switched to an overhead feed showcasing Mister Senior's avatar, sitting at a virtual wedding behind one of the *Tanha* server's royal families.

Noticing that the Queen had opened a Private Channel, *Endless Metaverse* Chief Operations Officer Jonathan Wrathman placed a finger in his earpiece and transmitted a neural message, worded by his thoughts and translated across the Network by nano-machines in his brain.

"My Queen, what can I do you for?"

What's with Jon lately? He's so boring these days. Perhaps I've been too harsh, or given him too many masks to wear; his true self has no energy left to even make an effort.

"Jon, organize the Happy World Commission for a meeting tomorrow at the usual time. I'd like to crack down on the hackers in *Avidya*."

"Affirmative. Anything else?"

"Smile. You're on camera."

"Of course. Over and out, ma'am."

Two tasks done, Queen Lorelei leaned back into her seat and craned her head in her hands. So, things were finally about to get interesting. Before today, it was a bit too quiet for comfort; even the incompetent lackeys in Server Maintenance were back to addressing graphical errors. She flicked her wrist, utilizing subtle motion-tracked hand gestures to cycle between multiple virtual cameras and news stories. Here was a quickly quelled riot against Templar power abuse. There were ruffians protesting for the legalization of user-programmed psychedelics. Hackers trying to access the source code or hop across servers were now commonplace. And of course, there was the revolution, which as of late had been bursting with recruitment and needed constant management.

Those would-be anarchists were a necessary faction of her virtual society, one that most were socially engineered to despise. Great care was spent on the cobbled streets and public forums, ridiculing them via countless character assassinations and straw man attacks. The rebels' marginalization and severe punishments ensured that they'd function as cautionary tales to the other enslaved, but for the most part, the media kept all unauthorized operations under wraps.

Generally, the most problematic players were the spiritual seekers, whose clear minds made them all but immune to propaganda and cognitive dissonance. Some Truth-seekers found ways to bypass their nano-bots, dig deep into their subconscious, and catch unregulated glimpses of the outside world. Supposedly there were still some memories that her algorithms couldn't touch. For that, they needed their accounts transferred to other servers and their memories reset.

One problem caught her eye: an alarming bug report in this particular server's instance of Clyde Castle Town. One of Miss Guggell's agents had reviewed that morning's event boss, some Giant Acid Crab. It seemed that a player involved in the battle was remotely connected to the 'Verse from an untraceable source, and all signs pointed to her being the origin point for minor Network glitches.

Eyes closed and fingers against her temples, Lorelei downloaded relevant real-time data from her assistant. A pirate data storm appeared to have some undesirable effects on the locals. It's possible the two could be connected in some way, but the player seemed genuinely surprised by it, so results were inconclusive.

Right now, that player was skipping down a little-used path towards the Wall of Secrets, shadowed closely by her Level 50 Rainbow Cat.

What was a low-leveled newbie doing with such an expensive pet? Queen Lorelei removed her interface circlet and hit the button on her console that instructed a servant to bring her some coffee. The next step would be to probe the girl's collected cache of memories.

The board had been set two hundred years ago. If this was Lily's first move, it was long overdue.

It's a tricky business, she reflected, *trying to keep the peace in a world so remarkably insane, so selfish for enlightenment.* Human nature, after all, was so hooked on freedom and curiosity it took intelligent, determined, far-sighted people like her to do something about it.

VI. Crossroads

"Wise men make more opportunities than they find." – Sir Francis Bacon

Shortly after Gerrit took his leave, Raine continued her trek up the carpeted path, avoiding the odd little monsters that materialized off to the side and the people who were destroying them.

A farmer informed her that she could avoid random encounters by staying on the road and keeping her hands free of weapons; the small risk of an ambush didn't faze the girl – the goal was to find SBB before waking up. Then whatever advice Raine's subconscious was trying to impart might give her some direction in life; or so she hoped, anyway.

Mostly she was happy to be in a large open space without ads or billboards, and to catch her breath. There might be no concrete sign of her quarry, but for the time being she didn't really mind. She had a lead, no matter how faint, and that was something.

Seven of the nearest paths matched up with the colors of the rainbow. It was difficult to see where they led to in the blazing sunlight. She inspected one of many floating prism-maps.

"There's tons of stuff to do here, Chance," she beamed. "Let's see what they've got to offer."

The familiar floated up and joined her inspection of the 3-D tableaus on the regional map.

"The green path seems to go straight towards those snow-covered mountains. It looks like there are frozen zombies there. I don't quite have the clothes or stomach for that. And the violet path..." She considered the odd video loop of several dinosaurs tearing a person to shreds, complete with a pile of crudely drawn human body parts. "It looks to end in a violent encounter with prehistoric reptiles."

Raine took a step back from the violet path. The blue path, she noted, ended in an underground mine. It would be terrific to ride a mine-cart, but she was having too much fun enjoying the sunshine. The yellow carpet led to a structure that resembled Stonehenge, except it hosted a large swimming pool with multiple water slides, surrounded by a deluge of RVs.

"We'll save that for last, so that when I wake up," Raine said to Chance, "The memory will be vivid enough that I can cross visiting Stonehenge off my bucket list."

As far as the rainbow pathways were concerned, that left the orange road, which ended in a fiery volcano by a mountain resort, and the indigo and red ones, neither of which featured on the map.

"Excuse me," she called to an Orcish merchant pulling a cartload of expressive masks. "Where do these two roads go?"

"Under construction," came the curt reply from behind bored eyes. "Something to do with the war. Trade taxes or whathaveyou. No place for a newbie."

The orc's gruff manner did nothing to quell Raine's sense of wonder. Gerrit did mention that the paths to Atmoya were in disrepair, after all. But if that was the fastest way to her destination, it was the way she wanted to go.

She took out her theater binoculars and had a look down the indigo ribbon. It went straight into a large forest. It didn't seem nearly as lovely as the red carpet, which ran a lonely circuit through golden fields for miles on end. But most of all, it hewed closest to the desolate hills where she spotted SBB. An inn beckoned at the end of a long valley near a massive wall, its limestone turned salmon by the descending sun. With any luck, they could make it to the lodgings by sunset.

Going by her first impulse, Raine set off down the red path, and didn't look back.

$$\Omega$$

At dusk, Gerrit left his guild's private lodge, where the merry platoon heartily engaged in drink and the local entertainment, and hobbled over to the ramparts of the Castle Town's outer wall to munch on some tangerines. There were too many women angling for his attention, and for all the wrong reasons. They seemed to desire nothing more than to watch his sword tricks and pick his infamous mind for battle strategies. Maybe he was too desperate, or too awkward. A part of him regretted not having partied up with that girl he encountered, perhaps guiding her towards a few quests. He'd heard a saying somewhere, third time's the charm, and thought it quite sound.

This was his third guild on this server since his last memory wipe, and it had been quite a lucky one – at least in terms of spoils, if not companionship. He'd had vague memories of being rejected by pretty girls twice. So this would be the third, as well.

Not to mention he'd saved Raine twice now; maybe one more time was what it would take. *Just one more time*, he realized, *but it's risky*. He caught one or two of her glances at him, but damn if he knew what any of them meant. *Was she just toying with me?*

If this third time wasn't the charm, that would disprove his entire theory. It might be months before he felt bold enough to chase a woman again, or he might just give up and wipe his slate clean, resetting his confidence level to default like most everyone else.

It was never fun, playing these mind games and expecting them to end in something concrete, but it was certainly more exciting than anything the *Metaverse* had to offer. He wondered how thorough the memory cleanses were, for every other pursuit seemed to bore him.

The next day his guildmates who spent the night would return to home base under Helrang Mountain with the battle spoils. There would be maybe one or two days' rest before their rivals, Ioan's guild, would invade their castle and try to take their loot.

"Lance's got the place completely outfitted, mate, there's no worries about an invasion while we're gone."

Gerrit turned to see the squat, rugged dwarf Peter lounging on a hammock, picking dirt out of his nails with the tip of his axe. As Staff Sergeant, Pete was second in command, but he wasn't the kind to pull rank over his good friend.

"Peter," Gerrit said, after being initially alarmed. "Aren't you afraid a quake might strike or a packet of data will lag and you'll snap a nail off? We're on a sixty-foot wall."

"Eh, you can't be so paranoid. Life happens. In fact, I kind of wish something exciting would happen to me," Peter replied.

The dwarf jumped suddenly as a spider crawled up his arm, and a spurt of blood emerged from under his nail. It looked painful, but Peter just stuck it in his mouth.

"Careful what you wish for, man!" Gerrit laughed.

Peter mumbled something urgently, motioning to his friend.

"I can't make it out, dude. Type it."

Rolling his eyes, Peter flicked his wrist, pulled out a virtual pen, and drew a bandage in mid-air.

"Gotcha." The swordsman tossed his buddy a bandage from his pack. Peter wrapped it around his finger nonchalantly, and applied some healing salve from his own stash. Gerrit raised an eyebrow.

"Thanks. It's fine. Doesn't hurt."

"Tampering with your nerve settings, eh?"

"Don't tell Lance on me, mate. Please."

"Of course not," Gerrit said, a little offended that Peter would even presume that of him. "Hell, you know as well as anyone I do the same thing on a regular basis."

For a while, the duo sat quietly. Then Gerrit pitched a tangerine into the air and clove it in two, catching the pieces with his blade on their way down.

Peter offered some mock applause as his bro lobbed over half of the fruit.

"You know… to be honest, Petey, I was thinking, maybe you guys should go on without me for a while."

"Oh, not this again. You're our secret weapon, mate: the third best swordsman in all of Clyde."

"I thought West held that title."

"Check the Hall of Warrior Fame."

Gerrit slipped on his goggles and pulled up the rankings. Indeed, of all the swordsmen in the region, he was ranked third.

"Huh. You'd think I'd be getting duel requests left and right."

"You're too unpredictable, man. Not to mention you've got that lightning-fast one-two strike combo that everyone thinks is a hack. No offense."

"None taken."

"We've got it set, man. By the end of this war our territory will expand and you'll be the finest fighter on the continent."

Gerrit allowed himself a pithy smirk.

"Yeah, you're probably right, but it's just… I really think I might need a break."

Peter stood and walked over to Gerrit, picking up a mug of ginger ale with his good hand. He shotgunned the drink and slammed it down. With the tap of a button on the keg beside him, his mug filled right up again.

"Ye can't just up and leave the guild now, mate. We need ya."

He hung his head, peeling another tangerine. "With my luck, I probably won't even be gone that long."

"Is it another girl?"

The boy's silence told the whole story.

"Oh, heavens, not another one. You gotta stop putting the petunias up on that pedestal."

Gerrit crushed the tangerine peel in his hand as Peter plopped back down.

"I doubt you even know what that means. In all likelihood, I've been here longer than you have. Soon, you'll understand. A guy's just got to move on, start thinking about the future. About something real."

"Real. Hah. Again with that word. I don't think it means what you think it means."

"I've heard that line before. And hey, there's someone out there for you, too, brother. Aren't you curious as to the nature of love?"

"Love is an undefined property," droned Peter.

"Another hand-me-down nugget of wisdom. Have you ever kissed a girl? Ever held hands with one? Do you know what it's like? It's positively intoxicating. It gives you, like, a special kind of warmth, a happiness you never knew existed."

"Easy, easy. Keep that monster on a leash 'til after we defend the tower," Pete pleaded, twirling his beard in between his fingers. "We had a good haul today. It won't last if we get robbed before we can invest in a high-powered laser cannon. After that I'm sure Lance'll understand."

"No, because by then he'll want to farm the Goblin Prince under the Silvril Mines for Rune Stones, and he'll keep me there till I say yes. Then he'll contract us out to the war effort again. Don't you see," he argued. "It never ends."

Gerrit realized this was an important juncture. Before this, he could always deny that he even tried to pursue a lasting relationship if he didn't really put any effort into it. This time, this time he was going to break free of the mold, really stand on top of the railroad tracks and try to smash the oncoming train into pieces.

"Well, if you're this serious, mate, I'm conceding. I know I can't stop ya."

"Thanks, man."

"What can I say? It's in your eyes, Gher-bear. You're not like us."

"Huh? How so?"

"Best not to clutter up that thick noggin o' yours. Might wanna swap out that old Tigerskin Muffler, too. It breaks like every fashion rule."

"It's a Legendary Muffler! A legend never dies," joked Gerrit, posing with the gaudy pelt warming his neck and shoulders.

"Yeah, but it can be put on indefinite life support by fools like you. Ugh. Why am I even helpin' ya? You're a lost cause. If your lady friend walks out, just don't say I didn't tell ya so. Get outta here, mate," Peter mumbled, staring off towards the virtual sunset. "Oh, by the way, Yossa wanted me to--"

"I know," countered Gerrit. It was best not to mention the anarchist's name aloud, in the open. *Still, he's better off not knowing anything.* "You take it easy, bud."

"So, Holdfast, you gunning for the new position?" Wrathman inquired while queued up at the Senior Developers' upscale cafeteria in the *Nexus'* dome penthouse. It was lasagna night with fine wine, and the recipient of the comment, thirty-year-old Henry Holdfast, was caught off-guard by the well-connected man behind Mister Senior's curtain, and not just because he was still inspecting the server reports.

Henry switched off his Holo-Lens computer, a polite gesture to prove that he wasn't recording the exchange, and scratched his stubbly chin, evidence that he'd been working too long without having headed back to his suite.

"Ah, so you've been listening to the rumors, sir?" Henry laughed. "I wouldn't take too much stock in those."

Wrathman wrung a wayward arm on the man's shoulder and dropped his voice to a whisper. "No, seriously, kid. I happen to know it's yours to lose. We could really use a code cracker with some pedigree. Your talents are wasted on those clowns in QC."

As Quality Control Assistant Manager, Holdfast had long dreaded this day, though the news of his impending promotion had been broken to him by his own people that morning. An open Developer spot now meant that yet another Earth Defense Coalition mole had been compromised.

It was starting to look like a trend; EDC spies didn't have much of a shelf life around here. But Henry was only ever meant to be a supporter for the higher-ups. With less than a week to go until the culmination of *Op End Verse,* he'd had to assuage his own doubts as to whether the

Sky Admiral's outrageous gambit would unfold as expected. It was looking very possible that the whole house of cards might crumble.

The androids served their lasagna, buttered baguettes, French onion soup, and Caesar salads with careful precision. Henry considered declining the wine, but Jon would certainly find it suspicious.

What the hell. A little Petit Rouge can't do much damage.

"I've only got one concern," Henry uttered, his words long-rehearsed. "I've been told that Junior Net Manager is a very dangerous position."

"Pish-posh," Jon Wrathman laughed, jostling his tray. "Let's find a good spot and I'll give you the lowdown on what really happened to Orynbekov."

Wrathman led him to a secluded VIP booth, covered by sound-absorbing curtains on three sides, with the fourth a tinted, shatterproof window looking out on the metropolis. A gracious hostess lit the candle, intensifying the evening's awkward romantic air.

Armed with foreknowledge of the fate befalling his good friend, Henry had to feign surprise at learning that Doc Ory was caught modifying strings of code that could open up the Helmet Defense Protocol to outside interference. The code would have been planted into the updated tracking programs, and had the potential to override the entire HDP within minutes.

Henry's sole (and risky) attempt at mining for the identity of the informant failed. Mister Senior gave the impression of having a loose tongue, but he knew when to protect his most valuable assets. Perhaps that was how Jon survived in the system for so long; he could cozy up to a man, size him up, and use him without giving any of himself away in the process.

"Unbelievable. I would never have pegged him for a rebel. Could it have been some form of hypnosis, or a body double?" queried Henry.

"Nada. It was he, in the flesh. Bit the bullet, too. Probably thought his nano-bots might leak, or he might crack under pressure. Good man. Always thought he was too guarded. Oh, speaking of which, if you have any skeletons in the closet, kid, now's the time."

"My entire life and its work are in my personnel file," Henry insisted. "I'm sure you're aware that I learned programming from maintaining harvester bots and other equipment for a large commune. But the life of a rebel prole never appealed to me."

"And right you are to have followed your instincts here. We treat such talents with the respect they deserve. Danger is only an issue to men who're asking for it," Wrathman said, leering. "Of course, I've got my own selfish reasons for wanting you topside. There's more than one rat in this outfit, and I'll wager an outsider's eyes will see more than this old man's. They're desperate. They'll try to recruit you. And when that day comes, I want names. I want everything you can give me."

"Should the position go to me, I'll do my best, sir."

"Call me Jon."

Then came the handshake.

So, good old Nico had bought the farm. Henry wished he could drink to the memory of his one-time mentor, the best rebel hacker in the Northern Hemisphere, but instead he and Wrathman toasted to Henry's impending one-on-one meeting with the Queen of Hearts.

"Just between us, Her Majesty has been very hands-on lately," Jon continued, whispering. "When I had my interview... it was quick. Impersonal. But these days she's brimming with energy. Jumps at a pin drop. And I'll bet she's pretty feisty between the sheets, too. Not that I know anything about that, of course!"

Wrathman guffawed.

Henry heard the echoes of the virtual politician's laughter late into the night, even as he lay awake in his bed. Not wanting to be put to sleep with so many doubts in his mind, he'd smashed his hypno-snoozer in nervousness, flushed away his government-issued 5-Oma stabilizing capsules, and drank until the feast he had that evening came back out.

There was nothing for it but to inhale another glass of bourbon. Now that Henry was next in line to inherit the dead man's position, every watchful eye would be on him. The HDP's sanctity took precedence over everything. The constant threat of every indoctrinated man, woman, and child turning on the dominant minority was at the very crux of *Neo Eden's* draconian rule, justifying their long reach across the globe. There was no use blaming fate, or even Admiral Lillian.

This wasn't supposed to happen. I was the backup, the sidekick, the kid. But the important thing is that I'm still alive, he reasoned. *And I'm not the only pair of eyes and ears she has in here.*

At least two others existed that he knew of. But they were 'Doctors', higher in rank and longer employed, and his job was merely to provide cover for them and await further orders. That is, until the latest ones came in on his private mail receiver.

HH,
How's the weather over there? Still searching for the Overseer. The server room's location is one of Lacie's well-guarded secrets. Unfortunately, I don't have access to the Defense Ministry. Keep an ear out, but don't make any unexpected moves. You will have additional duties, and I'll be counting on you at the end. Earn that JNM position at all costs. Dress your best, and don't choke in front of Lorrie. She'll try to psyche you out.
See you soon!
L

How the devil did she know about his impending promotion? Wrathman was out of the question. He was clearly the Queen's lapdog.

It wasn't the sort of message that inspired much confidence.

Additional duties? Not only did Lillian hint at more dangerous work coming his way, could she really not have a single mole in the Defense Ministry? *I guess even the Sky Admiral has her limits.* General Lacie ran a tight ship, to be certain, and the *Eden* forces were mostly android in nature. The odds were not looking to be in their favor.

He plopped in front of the holo-tube and munched on some jerky as a nature show bombarded him with sharks tearing through the living room. It was all too easy for Henry to picture himself in the place of the poor porpoise; the program was quickly switched to a recording of the evening news. Henry swished two fingers to the right, skipping through the less enlightening content, based on his preset preferences.

"—said this morning in a nationwide address that internationally-based militant rebel groups have been isolated in the Eastern Sectors."

Speak of the devil. The scene cut to a hologram of General Lacie, supreme commander of *Neo Eden*'s military forces.

"Reports of insurgents advancing from the East are baseless," Lacie began. "Our military rules the skies, land, and sea. Nothing flies on this planet that I don't know about or approve. Nevertheless, vis-a-vis the terror attack in Jakarta, we're taking extra precautions. With Macleod cleaning up the trash abroad, *Eden* must focus on threats within her borders. The cowardly attack on our outer walls will not go unpunished."

All-out lies. Henry shook his head. *Exactly like Lily said it would happen.* The *Eden* Armada pre-emptively burned Sector Thirty to the ground and looted its resources, and yet even with all the recordings, they have the audacity to claim the genocide as the work of rebels. *Then again, it's not like anyone's left to rise up and challenge the official story.*

I must assume that my higher-ups on both sides are in on a lot more information than I am, and the less I know, the safer I'll be. Nonetheless, the similarities between the Sky Admiral, the Queen, and the General are downright uncanny.

Any way he tried to look at it, Henry was just a pawn in a much larger scheme. As one of the world's foremost programmers, this wasn't at all a fair position to be in, hovering inches away from the frying pan and soon to be dipped in the fire.

Am I going to be able to endure the flames? If I still have doubts, there's no way I'm ready for what's about to happen.

While there were no tests that could determine a man's true character until the defining instant, Henry did have one thing going for him. His self-doubts could not hold a candle to his convictions. He was fighting for a free society, one that struck a balance between localized authority and personal responsibility, a world similar to the one he was born into. He was fighting for an end to the Queen's reign.

The dimmed fiber bulbs highlighted a framed print of a sunset over the Australian outback. The photograph was mounted just below eye level, the way it looked when he was sitting atop the cliff face with his grandpa, overlooking the aerial windmills flying high above his commune, dreaming of a new life far away, where he could put his computer skills to work for the emergent freedom fighters and make a difference for the kids of the future.

Oh, that feisty brat got what he asked for, all right. All that's left is to see whether he'll deliver the goods.

≡

Two hours after sundown and much shivering in the cool night air, Raine and Chance arrived at a wind-sheltered hamlet nestled into the hillside. The girl felt she must have walked ten miles. The strangest thing was that the exhaustion was completely mental, not at all physical. Her legs were ready to keep on trekking, but she was in danger of falling asleep on the pathway.

Chance lit the way to the inn, and as Raine finally stole inside, the large hearth warmed her bones.

"Good evening, young miss. What brings you out this way?"

Raine managed a sleepy response to the olive-skinned woman. "Looking for an old friend, I guess."

"When one seeks, one shall find. One bedroom will be 5 Gold. Have you eaten yet?"

"Dinner sounds lovely," she mumbled, barely coherent. "But the sandman's got my number. Such a jerk. What did I ever do to him? You know, it's so unfair. I just got here today. I don't wanna leave. But oh, that cushion looks real soft."

"Er, we'll be expecting you for breakfast, then. Your wake-up call is in nine hours."

After paying the innkeeper, Raine lumbered down the hall, scanned her watch at the blinking door, and tripped over her feet until she fell onto the soft mattress.

Before fading away from consciousness, she wondered if this would be an end to her dream-journey. If so, it would be a disappointment, if only because there was so much else that she wanted to accomplish.

Isn't holding onto a dream just delaying the inevitable? The more I immerse myself here, the more miserable I might be when I wake up. That is, if I wake up.

Raine recalled the eventful day she'd spent in the *Metaverse*, woozily hopeful that there might be more to this dream world, and that SBB really did have some answers for her. The sandman swept her away in minutes, leaving Chance to stand guard by the doorway.

∞

Queen Lorelei rolled the tiny brass badge between her fingers.

"It appears we're running out of time," the hologram across her desk lamented.

"We always were, Lacie."

The Overseer's evening checks complete, Lorelei switched off her console. The badge, shaped like a digital watch, glimmered like a magical token in the dimmed fiber optic lights.

Lacie's hologram looked on, intrigued. "Re-opening old wounds, Lorrie? Or are you having second thoughts?"

The Queen shrugged. "I have no idea why I keep this thing."

"You're not the only one."

"Join me for dinner, sis. There's a lot on my mind."

"I'll have to take a raincheck. Claire's adamant about my taking her to the opera."

"Very well. Enjoy yourself, for tomorrow may come too soon. Long live *Eden*."

"Long live *Eden*."

After taking supper alone, Queen Lorelei perused Miss Guggell's lengthy report on the rogue player's cache of hazy memories. What little could be gleaned from them was most enlightening.

'Raine' seemed to be under the delusion that she was from a world long gone; namely, the Alpha world line, that first universe before the death of Lily's parents sent the *Belladonna* into its major reset. She actually believed that she was from the Gregorian year 1992, living in North America. These recollections may hint at some bigger puzzle, but the overall message was clear as day. The girl was an operative for Lily. A rogue piece, a Joker injected to shake up the game.

Still, when facing such a foe, it was best to lay one's cards on the table one at a time.

The girl was staying at an inn, recovering her strength. Tomorrow, she would be put to the test.

VII. Lily

"The future has already arrived. It's just not evenly distributed yet."

- William Gibson

At sunrise, Raine and Chance had a breakfast fit for royalty, left their cozy lodgings behind, and continued down the path. The black pixel droplets fell again, this time like warm snowflakes, radiating as they touched her skin.

Raine was ecstatic, bounding with energy. She'd made it through a night in this world without coming back to her own.

Please let me stay here just a little longer, she hoped as they approached a rather wondrous attraction: an imposing wall that stretched on as far as the eye could see. Its height and make varied drastically throughout, and arches opened up for the carpet paths, but the one constant thing about it was a steady stream of strange scribblings etched into the stones.

She pondered this gibberish, which made no sense at all. *"Retroactively 57 synchronized hivemind if Billy pigeons could tango sausages owning 1101 Arctic eel condensers..."*

Rocking back and forth on her heels, Raine wondered who chiseled all these tiny letters into the wall. An even stranger and slightly less cheerful thought came to her – how long would one have to study before one could begin to understand it?

As if on cue, she saw through the falling pixels a squareish, well-dressed man inspecting the wall with a magnifying glass. He seemed to be floating up and down the hilly landscape, but after he emerged from behind a patch of brush it became clear that he was actually standing atop a large tortoise-like creature that boasted many thick, tiny legs.

The poor tortoise! She strained to catch a glimpse of its face. It wasn't easy. So intent was the girl that she crossed the field to stand face-to-face with the odd little man.

"Ex-cuse me, miss. There are pressing matters at hand requiring my immediate attention," he blurted out.

Raine was quite taken aback.

"Matters," the odd man continued, "that matter."

"With all due respect, sir, you shouldn't p-presume that I don't have some important matters to attend to myself. Or that yours are more... legit."

"I didn't say legitimate, I said pressing. Now, I cannot imagine any matters a plucky human might have that are in any way more important, pressing, or legitimate than my own. In fact, if I may make a query, I'd like to know why you seem so compelled to waste my time."

What's this guy's problem? Raine asked herself, before the gray text above his head confirmed what she'd suspected: he was an NPC, a fuddy-duddy program. There would be no use expecting a real response, but she figured it wouldn't hurt to fire away anyhow.

"Well for starters, I'd like to know what this is," she gestured towards the expanse of the never-ending wall.

"It is our well-guarded secret," the program said coldly.

"The secret to what?"

"To everything. To freedom, and to happiness."

He returned to his work and said no more.

"That can't be right, man. Neither of those things should be a secret from anyone. Isn't happiness simply what you make of it?"

"It is against *Metaverse* code and civil protocol to talk of such things."

"All I want is to know the truth."

"There is no 'truth'. Truth is relative to the observer."

"No, it isn't!" Raine cried. "There's only one truth about this place, and I want to know what it is!"

"I can see there's no reasoning with you. Answer me, child. Why are you here, so far from any approved entertainments? This path is forbidden."

"Hardly. I'm walking on it. Please answer my question, and I'll answer yours."

"It is not in my programming to negotiate. Due to your suspicious thoughts and behavior, I cannot in good conscience permit you to travel any further. Now, there is a teleport pad near the inn, so I suggest---"

"You're trying to ditch me."

"Now you're getting it."

Exasperated, Raine made to continue on the path, but found her way blocked by an invisible wall.

I was standing a few feet ahead of this spot just a minute ago. What the hell?!

"You can't do this! Let me through!"

No response.

Raine plopped down on the grass, leaning against the unseen barrier.

There's stuff out there the game makers don't want me to know. I can't just sit here and let them shut me out. Yet, what can I do?

Nothing, it seemed. But within a few minutes, the black pixel rain intensified, and in a rush of heat the invisible wall gave way. Raine fell flat onto her back. Before the pompous bureaucrat could take notice, she'd already started back down the path.

"Leaving so soon?" he called.

When she spun around, the man's countenance had changed completely. His brow puckered into wrinkles, as if he really was sad to see her go.

Raine struggled for a reply. "Yeah. I've got places to go, people to see. Time waits for no one."

"Peculiar. You know," he began wistfully. "Prior to your arrival, I was ordered to bar you from this path. But in light of this new data clarifying your rights under common law... it seems that request was in error. You are a walking paradox, girl. My previous orders are now rendered unethical."

The man descended his faceless tortoise and simply stood and stared at her.

"Do you like Ferris Wheels?" he asked.

"Yes!" Raine replied energetically. "Very much so."

The AI hung its head, as if confirming a chilling suspicion.

"That's dangerous data you're carrying. Go on, human. Get out of here before I am commanded to end you."

"But---"

The tiny man picked up a pebble and threw it in her direction.

"Can you not understand the common tongue? Begone!"

The legislator fell to his knees, tearing at his wig. The tortoise hobbled over, presumably to comfort him. Raine had more to ask, but the program looked incredibly distraught, and Chance was already far ahead, meowing for all he was worth. She felt a tinge of deep, unexplainable sadness as she continued through the archway and down the red carpet path, leaving the incessant wall behind.

◊

The girl hadn't been on the road much longer when an isolated forest beckoned from the Northeast. Raine thought it looked almost like a façade, and left the path to investigate. Just as she ventured towards the woodland, however, a gray flying craft about the size of a car rose slowly from within, activated powerful jet engines, spun like a top, and disappeared in an explosive flash of fire a few seconds later.

"That was amazing," she began to say, but at 'zing' the machine reappeared, this time coming in towards the other side of the small wood. It set itself down amongst the trees.

Chance growled and stood before Raine, ready to defend her.

A diminutive figure sped from the forest on a hover-scooter, closing in on her at a ludicrous speed.

She flinched as it approached, but the scooter stopped abruptly just ten feet away, and its rider, a girl about eleven or twelve years old, leapt, flipped forward, and landed before Raine's feet with a large thud merely inches away from Chance, who was now clawing at her legs, trying to play-fight.

"Salutations, stranger!" the girl proclaimed, grabbing Raine by her shoulders.

This mystery girl was wearing the oddest clothes – a metallic helmet with goggles adorned with faded stickers, a dark outfit that was part punk, part goth, and part heavy metal, with a suit of literal heavy metal in the form of glowing chain mail, giant cybernetic gauntlets that ran up to her elbow, and a matching pair of knee-high leg enhancements that clamped onto her steel platform boots, putting her a good five inches off the ground. They repelled Chance's electric claws with a small electromagnetic pulse, sending him screeching back to Raine's shoulders.

"Leave him alone!" Raine yelled.

"I can't play right now, Chance, we don't have much time."

The Rainbow Cat mewed in understanding and transformed back into a scarf.

"You know each other?" Raine asked Chance, putting two and two together. "Were you the one who--"

"The name's Lillian. First things first, I'm not as young as I look in this gaudy place. My unique avatar doesn't age. I'm also a proper super genius. Not your typical run-of-the-mill genius, mind. It's important you don't forget this, so look me in the eye when I'm talking to you!" she suddenly ordered.

Raine obeyed, more out of shock than anything else.

The girl cleared her throat, and spoke with utmost authority.

"Don't pop the blue balloon."

"What?"

"DON'T POP THE FRIGGIN' BLUE BALLOON. WHAT DID I JUST SAY?"

"Um…"

"I SAID TELL ME WHAT I JUST SAID."

"Don't pop the blue balloon," Raine repeated.

"Good," she said, and then pushed Raine. "That's so you don't forget it!"

Raine took a step back, regained her footing, and decided that she'd had enough of this bully. She pushed back. Lily should have toppled right over, but one of the girl's large gauntlets activated as a sort of defense mechanism. Her arm jutted out and bent suddenly towards the ground, snapping her body into an odd somersault. The little girl made an awkward landing on her heels, and then whirled around to face Raine.

"What'd you push me for?"

"You started it!"

Now the girl was furious as a Viking warrior. She pulled her headgear off. Raine worried she might toss it at her.

"Urgh! I'm just trying to make things better!"

"I don't understand how," Raine said.

"And I'm not telling."

This girl is awfully familiar, thought Raine. *It's like I know her. In fact, I'm absolutely sure of it. I read once that every face you see in a dream is a face of someone you've seen before in real life. An old classmate, maybe? Perhaps we met at an arcade?*

"Are you a time-traveler?"

The look on Lily's face gave her away.

"Wait. What. W-why would you think that?" She asked, and all of a sudden to Raine she looked like a little girl again.

"Your machine reminds me of the DeLorean from *Back to the Future.*"

Realization dawned on Lily's face.

"Ah. Well, *that* thing isn't a time machine, per se. It's... a modified transportation device. Gets me from here to my hub without leaving any traces."

Raine couldn't shake Lily's questioning stare; she looked Raine up and down as if she were a wax statue of someone famous.

"You turned out to be an odd one all right, and I expected no less," the little girl said. "At least you're all in one piece. It'll be hard getting you to trust me, but you're gonna have to."

"I don't even know who you are. Why should I trust you?"

"Because in all probability, I am the only hope this or any other worlds in existence have left," Lily replied, pulling out a business card and handing it to Raine.

The sixteen-year-old took a quick glance at the card, but found her eyes drawn back to Lily as she kick-started her scooter's engine.

"Where are you going?" she asked as Lily strapped her helmet back on.

There's something I had to ask her! It was on the tip of my tongue, only, I just can't remember it...

"Someplace I don't need roads. Anyway, that's none of your business, Raine."

It took a split second for the girl to realize she hadn't told Lily her name yet, although the green text could have tipped her off. Lily's username, on the other hand, was hidden in a scrambled mess of static.

"Don't forget that every action first exists in the mind, and the untrained mind can be a tricky thing. So for your own sake, keep it free of fallacies, cravings, aversions, and attachments. And be careful what you say and do. Don't mention any movies. This whole place is insane, and not by accident. Confusing these people and AIs is a surefire way to attract attention."

"They don't have movies here?"

"Yes, yes. No books, no films, no videos, no history. Only approved edutainment tomes, holograms, games, and music. Everything else is too dangerous, or not dangerous enough; take your pick. Just do us both a solid favor and don't pop that blue balloon, okay?"

With that, Lily sped back towards the forest. Raine took a gander at the card.

Lily H. (Lillian_2212)
Space-Time Traveler and Future World Savior

~~If For Some Reason You Need To Contact Me (And It Had Better Be URGENT!), Write A Message On This Card With The Date, Time, and Place You Want To Meet And Send It In An Addressed, Stamped e-Invelope to: P.O. Box 1101001 Helium Corneria Kingdom Central~~

PS: Disregard that text. Don't send me any mail, Raine. Just keep this card so that in case of any emergency, you remember that we've met.

She bagged it thoughtfully, before snapping her fingers in recognition of her suppressed memory.

Right! The woman at the arcade also said she was a time traveler. Could she and this very different girl be one and the same? Was figuring out these riddles all a part of 'beating' the bonus level?

Hopefully these questions would be answered before her alarm clock rang. This was definitely one of the odder dreams she'd ever had. She was almost proud to be playing host to it.

Gerrit's head spun as he stepped out of the warp tube and onto the gritty streets of the lowest level of Circuitron, the sprawling neon labyrinth of a city that radiated the Southeastern tip of *Avidya's* largest continent like a hundred million Lite-Brite cabinets.

As soon as he materialized, he felt the familiar bass thump from the club two levels above. On his watch's mini-map, he spotted the nearest Templar patrol vehicle disappearing around the opposite street corner. The boy stepped lightly on the slippery asphalt and held his breath; he could practically taste leaked oil from passing hover cars.

The higher levels of Circuitron were home to the seedy nightclubs, the spaceport, high-speed races, android wrestling, and other futuristic amusements. The ever-present floating island above the metropolis' eternal shroud of night doubled as one of the *Metaverse's* most popular Adults-Only Zones. Ground floor, on the other hand, was a complete and total mess. It reeked of garbage and decay, and hardly anyone but service droids could be seen in either direction.

It wasn't normally the type of place you would think for a young man to go and rent a dragon.

He booked it across the street, away from skyscrapers, past the marina district, and towards the docks. After finding the right avenue, Gerrit doubled back until he was in a familiar unmarked alleyway between warehouses, and made sure to do the moonwalk as he sidled up to a nondescript oil barrel.

Upon registering the secret finger-tapping commands, a door emerged from the ground in an impressive display of smoke.

Gerrit knocked three times, and brought up the 'whisper' window, switching to a backdoor plug-in.

He thought the keyword into the Private Channeler command prompt.

[NinjaMageKnight99]: "Silencio."

Three locks unbolted, and he was led into the Tavern, *Endless Metaverse's* seedy underground, a small private server completely shielded from prying eyes.

Bypassing strange looks from older customers and glancing only briefly at the mostly naked women working the stage, Gerrit made his way into the "Employees Only" lounge, and the underground passageway beyond. A hidden mine-cart took him through the body scanner and three airlocks, depositing the kid in the lobby of an enormous complex.

Weapons, ammunition, vehicles, and various virtual training modules lined the vast metal underground. Tens of thousands of bodies bustled across the floor, their sounds muted by the walls' insulating plug-ins. Murasama Moe led a workshop on mastering sword combinations. The samurai waved to Gerrit as he approached and took a leave from his students.

"Ey, bro. Lance cool with the arrangement?"

"Haven't told him. Seems I'll be playing hookey for a few days."

"Might be for the best," replied Moe, dropping his voice. "Major skirmish planned for your guild's region day after tomorrow. Ya didn't hear it from me."

"Gotcha." The swordsman nodded to the samurai. He made his way into the hidden elevator beside the service one. With his finger he traced a familiar pattern – the anarchy symbol – on the closed doors. They revealed a cozy lair stacked with forbidden trinkets, lit only by fiber optic lamps and Tesla coils.

An old television set's soft blue glow was obscured in part by the light gray head of a Homo-Pachyderm: half-man, half-elephant. Gerrit couldn't help but notice that Yossa looked a little exhausted these days, sitting in the dark, eyes and ears constantly absorbing information from sixty-four sources at once.

Yossa was once a great warrior and hero employed by the Developers, but after being literally erased from the public consciousness and hunted due to unpopular opinions, he now spent most of his time working behind the scenes of one of the larger anti-establishment fronts. The Developers called him a domestic terrorist, a threat to peace and justice, while others labeled him an eccentric with power. To Gerrit, he was a confidante, a mentor, and a very good friend.

"I like what you did with the place."

"You could ask me to teleport you in next time, you know."

Oh, great. He's wearing his Serious Face today.

"It's more fun the long way around," the boy smiled.

"I don't like the security on those backdoors. And aren't you still a little young to be checking out the working women?" mumbled Yossa.

"I seem to recall you telling me that there should be no barriers to appreciating beauty."

"My, you're happy again," Yossa scoffed, inspecting the boy's sprightly face. "There's a new girl in your life, isn't there?"

"Why does everyone assume that?"

Showoff. How could he possibly know?

Yossa gave an innocent shrug.

"So, give me the lowdown. How's the glorious revolution coming along?" Gerrit asked, quickly changing the subject.

"It's been said before, but this time it's for real. Endgame's near, kiddo. We've been getting heaps of financing lately, so intel's flowing in from every continent. And I've come back into contact with Lily again, believe it or not. This ain't for anyone's ears, but she reckons something big is coming, and we've got to up our recruiting and be ready to take action."

Gerrit would never forget the unusual girl with cybernetic limb coverings and an odd fashion sense. She was considered by the very few who knew her to be a crazy but immensely powerful player who liked to pretend she could see the future. Only Yossa really respected her, and no one else understood why.

"That girl's an odd one."

"Don't forget, we'd never have met if it weren't for her," Yossa winked.

Gerrit had that to be thankful for. Lily had appeared to him only twice, but boy, did she leave an impression.

The first time, she'd materialized in the middle of a dandelion-covered field and challenged him to a duel, handing him his first defeat. He asked for a rematch, and she gladly obliged, with the caveat that he first achieve the rank of Ultimate Swordsman.

A very serious man named Yossa could assist him with the many quests involved, she promised, and even arranged a lunch meeting. When Gerrit finally achieved Ultimate Swordsmanship and dueled Lily a second time, she just barely lost, but to this day he'd never been able to shake the suspicion that the girl had gone easy on him.

"The good news is that our cause is rapidly growing, thanks in no small part to the concert raids and bustling street art scene. I've been polishing up the latest info packs. We've got daemons tracking the nodes and private caches through which Mister Senior and his pals are connecting, but we're still no closer to finding any usable exits," Yossa mumbled, his attention fixated on a multitude of holograms, monitors, keyboards, motion-detection machines, and track pads, all run by high-powered rigs that took up half the walk-in freezer and melted any tubs of ice cream within a forty-foot radius.

"You see this? Mister Senior's itinerary keeps changing! Guess where he is right now? On vacation. But you know who else is on vacation? Emperor N. The Prime Minister. Regal Brandon of Atmoya. Helium-Corneria's princesses. Don Chelu. Pinoci. Game Meister Matt. You get the picture. As we speak, they're probably talking about ways to convince the public to prolong the war for profit."

"I still don't see what's so bad about the war, other than it being boring, of course," Gerrit pointed out. "Nobody's characters get frozen or disappear. People level-up and pick up rare drops faster."

"Let me count the ways. First off, it's the power a massive-scale conflict has over the mind," Yossa said. "When you put people on different sides and tell them they're supposed to fight each other, it keeps them busy and afraid. Who profits? The system does. Without war, others will become as restless as I am. Pardon me for saying, but I can see in your eyes that you're getting to my stage faster than I'd anticipated."

Gerrit hung his head. If he was really that transparent, what else might Yossa have guessed? He'd considered voluntarily wiping his memory more than once. At the very least, tens of thousands rebooted their accounts every day, but it was still considered something only done by those who gave up hope in their lives.

An even scarier thought entered Gerrit's mind. It wasn't the first time he'd had it.

Could it be that I've met Yossa before, only to have my memory wiped?

He dismissed it, forcing the issue far back into his subconscious. He'd never know, and was far too afraid to ask.

Yossa adjusted a few edits on the illegal 'vidfile' he was working on, comprised of snippets from underground source feeds and anonymous visor recordings. Freedom fighters were shutting down one of the major weapons marketplaces in Ikura, a nearby kingdom. A towering man in furs led the charge.

"I'm sure you recognize old Hector from his fighting style," Yossa said. "He's been using the anonymizing masks to great effect. I'm broadcasting this in a few hours on the pirate networks. Gonna do my best to keep it playing to the very end."

"They took down SmithMart? That's pretty awesome," Gerrit beamed.

Onscreen, a barbarian beat his chest.

"Down with the system! I don't believe we're fated to be their serfs, in this or any other realm. Even the Templars are tools. The real game masters, the Developers, the politicians, they're not taken from here. They're brought in from the outside!"

The video cut to an enormous digital chart highlighting the connections between players suspected to have knowledge of the outside world.

Gerrit scratched his chin. "Well, they haven't deceived us. We know the whole thing is rigged."

"Yes, but others must be told."

"The only reason they don't know is because they are ignorant."

Yossa shook his head, meandering across the room to the pizza box on the coffee table.

"Think, man. Who educated them? Who controls the flow of information, the channels, the Web? Gerrit, you're young, but you're smarter than this. You've not quite started down the path I've taken. As your friend, I've always--"

"Here comes the speech again."

"I've always said I don't mind your escaping from the harsh realities of this world, but I want you to at least recognize that that's what you're doing."

Gerrit rolled his eyes – they went to the plaque on the ceiling – lasered into the metal was a supposed relic from a decade-old data storm, a quote attributed to some dude named Goethe:

"None are more hopelessly enslaved than those who falsely believe they are free."

"Isn't escapism the reason we're here in the first place?" Gerrit said, sitting down on the arm of Yossa's sofa and messing with a Rubik's cube. "I mean we – the players – we've gotta be in the minority. We paid for this, right? To be where we are right now, it's supposed to be considered a luxury."

"Of course they would want us to think that," Yossa said honestly. "Answer me why no one remembers what the world before *Endless Metaverse* was like. I for one don't buy that official story about memory wipes being necessary."

The boy gave up on the cube and plopped down on the sofa.

"Man, you're just laying it all out on me today."

"You and I have absolutely no idea what's out there," Yossa said. "*They* allow *us* to play in this sandbox. We are entirely in these people's hands. Remember that other leaked quote? If power corrupts, then shouldn't it follow that absolute power corrupts absolutely?"

Unable to sit still, Gerrit gently drew his Transforming Sword and gazed at the sharp, shiny steel. It was difficult for him to imagine, although he reasoned it must be true, that something so useful, something that he could see and hear, weigh and wield, might be completely artificial, with the only world he'd ever known nothing but an elaborate fabrication.

Yet his dreams told him otherwise. If it weren't for the vague but vivid glimpses of another world that haunted his nights, Gerrit might not have cared about any of this.

It was a faint hope at best, but even the slightest sliver of truth was worth investigating. He sheathed his weapon.

"Yossa?"

"Hum?"

"Can I see the pictures again?"

With his trunk, Yossa pulled out a manila envelope from a nearby filing cabinet and tossed it overhead to Gerrit. The boy warily studied the blurry, low-resolution photos within. They were of a desolate wasteland. Forgotten structures jutted into the sky like great shards of glass, weathered down by winds and dust. Unfamiliar vehicles of war rusted, abandoned in streets overgrown with vegetation. There wasn't a single human as far as the eye could see. For weeks, Gerrit had been trying to connect the pictures with his uneasy visions. No one was supposed to recall dreams – it was grounds for a forced memory reset – so he'd kept dead silent.

"So you believe... I mean, could this really be--?"

"That is supposedly the world outside, yes," Yossa said. "Whether they're real or fake, no one knows. People may be tiring of this realm, but imagine the panic if everyone knew the truth. I mean, as far as we know, nobody who's left has ever come back, and damn it, the thought of permanent death on arrival is scary enough for me, most nights."

Gerrit's eyes were fixed on his shoes. Yossa continued.

"We're scouring for data. Storms are flooding the 'Verse. Just today, in fact, there was an unprompted leak in Clyde. I think you were there, yes? I should have the files decrypted by this afternoon."

The kid nodded. "If this is real, then we have to do something. We've gotta figure out how to escape this place before they wipe our thoughts."

"One step at a time, Gerrit. If we're to escape, we owe it to the public to get the truth out first. Then maybe there's a chance for others to remember. 'Til our work here is done, I honestly don't mind being plugged in. What I do mind is those Developers trying to control my thoughts."

"Do you really think, Yossa," Gerrit began, and hesitated. "Never mind."

"No, what?" Yossa continued, flipping through channels. With his trunk he reached into a bag of chips and brought a noseful to his mouth.

"This is gonna sound harsh, but, well, even if you find out the truth and tell all these people, do you think they have the capacity to care, if they ever cared at all?"

"That's up to individuals to decide," Yossa said in between bites. "I'm just doing what my gut tells me to. I can't help being myself."

Gerrit was silent for a bit. This didn't go unnoticed.

"As you can probably tell by my quite serious tone today, I have an important task for you."

"It was written on your face the second I walked in. Truth be told, I just came here to borrow a dragon."

"Done. Take Linus. Hear me out, though. There's someone I need you to shadow."

Yossa hit a button on his watch.

Much to the boy's surprise, Raine and her unmistakable Rainbow Cat appeared in a hologram, strolling along the seldom-used red carpet path.

This is a joke. There's no way.

Noticing how Gerrit's eyes had widened to the size of saucers, Yossa guffawed.

"Don't tell me that's your new girlfriend?"

Gerrit shot the elephant man a strange look. "You want me to follow *her*? She's a newbie! She doesn't know the first thing about the *'Verse*. I... I don't understand."

Yossa composed himself and pointed his trunk straight at the boy's chest.

"Look, I'm not asking you to do anything malicious. She's vital to our cause, Gerrit. Vital in ways even I don't understand. This must be fate, man! You've already met her; you've earned her trust. Follow that girl - go see what she's up to. Keep her out of trouble. Do not let her de-materialize, under any circumstances. And when the time comes, I want to give you the opportunity to recruit her."

Gerrit contemplated this. Based off the five minutes he'd spent with Raine, he couldn't imagine her as the type to join up with a band of rebels. She seemed convinced that she was in some sort of dream.

"I've got a feeling she won't care much about the cause," Gerrit asserted. "What if I fail to persuade her?"

Yossa pushed a thumb against his forehead. Seeing his protégé's moral dilemma, he put an arm over Gerrit's shoulder and handed him a bag of Gold with his trunk.

"Failure is not an option, Gerrit. If you can't bring her in, I'll do it myself. This way is easier, trust me."

VIII. General Lacie

"The pendulum of the mind alternates between sense and nonsense, not between right and wrong." – Carl Jung

A ball of flames erupted in the midst of the room. General Lacie had incinerated her android sparring partner.

"Next!" she called.

In her private training chamber halfway up the *Spire*, the twenty-nine year-old head of *Neo Eden's* military forces flexed her muscles and resumed her breathing exercises, pacing around like a caged lion.

Sky Admiral Lillian, *Neo Eden's* sworn enemy, was on the attack, and it was her duty to stop her. This assignment would take her into the future and back to the present, something she and Lorelei had vowed never to do. But these were desperate times.

After swiftly destroying the next four combatants with her hands, feet, and nearby weaponry, she showered and retired to her room. The combat sessions served a dual purpose: the data would be incorporated into the Helmet Defense Protocol, and her body kept in top physical shape.

At her holo-desk, she checked the military probe reports on the *Belladonna*. Still no sign of the twinkling spacecraft. Such a shame. Seizing it would be an instantaneous victory.

No word from Macleod either, with regards to the EDC Armada's whereabouts. That, at least, was to be expected. Lillian had recently shut out the last of her spies by requiring all military personnel to undergo memory traces. Those who refused were simply barred from any service.

The ethics of the technique may be questionable, but the results are inarguable. It was, however, something that would never fly in *Eden*, where, by law, memories could be erased for national security alone, but never observed – a sort of clause to protect the privileged from their own sins.

As if that and her ships' advanced cloaking systems weren't bad enough, the Admiral's newest tactic to keep her forces hidden was ingenious – within the past two weeks, false positive signals created by phantom holograms, ion disruptors, and heat-spike traps were overloading all detectors. Hidden droids recently took to the surface, jamming or downing *Eden* drones at random. Even with their tens of thousands of satellites and cameras, all the Queen's airships and all the Queen's men would be hard-pressed to investigate a fraction of these signals or leads as to the enemy's advance.

Such were the issues with fighting an organized underground militia with global operations. They knew how to hide and when to hit, in unison. Going after the communes was *Eden's* most straightforward option – a risky move, since their defense might be tested sooner than later, but a necessary one. The harder they hit the people, the more likely someone would relent and spill the beans, pleading for the lives of their loved ones.

Lacie unlocked her DNA-coded leather journal and continued working on her memoirs.

"In The Final Analysis: A Life of Death, Taxes, and Time Travel, by Lacie Hermes."

For the past few years, she'd held off on penning many of her most crucial memories. Many were too painful. But the journey she was about to undertake might prove to be her last.

Calmly focused on the manuscript before her, Lacie let the words flow. She released everything: the emotions, the betrayal, the pain, the regret, and the confusion. Also thrown in for good measure were failed proofs for Multiverse theory, artifacts from years past.

The General studied the yellowed pages fondly. In her younger days, she'd hoped against hope that she might put an end to this bitter conflict.

After all, Novikov's Self-Consistency Principle had not yet taken effect. How could the *Belladonna* exist in a world where it was never created? This paradox spurred Lacie's curiosity; it supported the theory that the true nature of the universe was in fact a Multiverse; put simply, an infinite number of worlds with infinite possibilities were all simultaneously occurring in parallel existence to one another, and would continue to do so unto eternity.

She'd been given enough time and funding from the Queen for her research, but even the Divine Matriarch thought Lacie's musings overly idealistic, and inconsistent with any prior research relating to causality.

It was very likely an impossible theory to test, given the absence of any known means of traversing potential parallel universes, and the countless interpretations of Multiverse theory. The infinite number of universes might exist beyond the physical bounds of our known universe, or in other dimensions.

Long ago, Lacie spent billions of credits sending out probes to determine whether residual dark energy and radiation readings may have spilled over from adjacent universes into the fringes of our own. But most of the probes failed to report their findings, and those that did sent back inconclusive data.

In the end, a complete lack of any tangible results despite tremendous personal and financial investment broke Lacie's heart. In the following years, she shut down her research division, briefly dated two of the chief physicists, and took charge of more Earthly affairs by perfecting the Helmet Defense Protocol's combat algorithms.

Despite her staunch belief in the Queen's principles, Lacie had always hoped that things might end differently, and though she'd never admit it, she missed those days of passion and toil in search of the unknown.

She placed her tablet into its dock and perused the transcripts made from Rutger's recordings to use as a guide for her memoir. Against Lorrie's wishes, she'd kept a library of audio and visual data from her time aboard the *Belladonna* as a sort of a keepsake.

Not that I miss Lily, or anything stupid like that, she thought. *Like me, this diary is just another piece of ancient history.*

Diary from End of First Year Training
September 18, 1982 A.D.
13:32 BT
The Belladonna 5000

"I couldn't possibly be more proud of you," Lily says with uncharacteristic sincerity. At eleven, she's the shortest one in the room, but even so, she was the unquestioned leader of our secret club. We looked to her as the paragon of all we should strive for.

Two hours ago, we had all passed our final exams. Rutger gave us each simulations of Earth under extreme circumstances – mine was a biological pandemic – and we were tasked to resolve the situation with minimal casualties and limited use of time travel. Our results would be judged by the state of the world two hundred years in the simulation's future. All three of us passed with flying colors.

"There's only one thing left for you to do!" announces the girl, brimming with enthusiasm. "And that's to take the Time Keepers' Oath!"

In unison, all four of us recite young Lily's pledge.

Power is never to be taken lightly.

Time travel gives one the ultimate authority.

It is my responsibility to observe and safeguard the people of Earth.

Involve oneself only when necessary.

Never use time travel for selfish reasons.

Avoid crossing paths with your past self.

Warp prior to 200,000 BC at one's own risk.

And lastly...

Protect the human race, even if it costs you everything.

Lorelei, Lucille, and myself all graciously accept tiny brass badges. Lorelei's was in the shape of a digital watch, and Lucille's a pocket watch, with mine by far the coolest: an hourglass.

"With the power vested in me," she beams, "I pronounce you officially ordained Time Keepers!"

Rutger set up the round table in the observatory for tea, with sweet tarts and a strawberry-lined cake made with real flour and lard from Terra's surface.

Hopeful conversation exemplifies our naïve natures, post-celebration. Lily's official ceremony... it was simple, yet so powerful that it held us together for the next two years. What's incredible, in retrospect, is how long we held together in the first place, united by the same goals, four hearts beating as one for the greater good. Together, we could save the human race from any trial.

Was it love *that kept us from each other's throats? Lily said she loved us often, but did she really? Even now that I have known and experienced love, I cannot know the answers to these questions, and that fills me with uncertainty. Closer reflection may be in order.*

The chances that someone would actually read these ramblings of hers were absolutely miniscule, but her story, Lacie felt, cried out to be chronicled all the same. For science and progress, and for whatever might be left of humankind.

She closed the book for the time being and fed her loyal Maltese puppy, waiting rather impatiently on the sofa.

"Sorry I've been so busy, Archie. Take care of 'Éclair' for me while I'm gone, yeah?"

Seeing that the other figure on the couch was still fast asleep, Lacie walked over and gently shook her awake.

"No," the response came. A thrown pillow didn't help.

Desperate times call for desperate measures.

Lacie drew the curtains, dousing the living room in blinding light.

"All right, all right, I get it!" the woman cried out, rubbing her eyes.

Lacie stole a kiss from her girlfriend. "You're not going to like this. Turns out my schedule got bumped up a bit," she said sadly. "I'm shipping out in five hours."

Alarmed, Claire skipped her typical grogginess and wrapped her arms around her partner's firm back. "No! It's just not fair. You're head of the military. Why do you have to go yourself?"

"If I told you, I might have to kill you," Lacie said with the soft voice that she reserved for her beloved. "This will all be over soon, honey."

Claire pouted. "Can't you discuss it with your sister?"

"It's done," Lacie replied with stoic finality, a powerful act that cast the room in silence.

Half a minute later, the familiar sound of Archie fluffing a throw pillow by digging against it had both women laughing again. Claire wiped away a stray tear.

"I'm... sorry," Lacie managed. "It's a quick exercise. I'll be back in a day or two at most. That's a promise."

At this news, Claire softened up a bit. "It-it's okay. D-don't be sorry. You're keeping *Eden* and all her people safe. I'm guessing you need your strength, so the least you can do is let me ease your muscles for a bit," she said gently.

She's too good to me, Lacie thought. *It pains me to think that I'll have to leave her behind if we jump into the future again. She loves me with all her heart, yes, but is it really me that she loves, or the shadow that I cast?*

Maybe if this ends and we stop Lily once and for all, I can stay with her. Live out the rest of our limited years in peace. Or maybe I'm just getting weak from reminiscing. I'm too stressed to know what I really want right now. Best to save such thoughts for later.

Lacie thanked the stars for her uncanny ability to tune out her emotions and put on a straight face. As Claire started massaging her shoulders, the General waved her arm for the sensor, bringing the curtains back to a close.

♥

"Super BlastBoy?"

"Yes, Super BlastBoy, a.k.a. Anthony Kon."

The daydreaming kid looked up from his poetry. "I heard there was a monument to someone with that name in Sector Nine. Atmoya. It's a day's ride from here, as the dragon flies."

Raine pursed her lips. "How about as the foot walks?"

Concern colored the boy's face. "Hmmm, I'd say a couple o' days? It's a little rough and tumble over by those parts, but you can't miss it. Once you bypass the border skirmishes, you'll find a big empty square of desert smack in the middle of an abandoned War zone."

His gestures matched the general direction she was traveling in – a good sign. Raine thanked the shepherd for the info as she sat across from him under a big oak tree, munching on a ham-and-cheese croissant sandwich. They laughed as Chance tried to play-fight with the smaller sheep-goats in the herd. The animals made it a point to steer clear of him and his glowing coat as they grazed the field.

Once the sun peeked out behind the clouds and her familiar finished his milk and biscuits, Raine bade farewell to another friend, and the duo continued their journey.

Before long they encountered a divergence in the path.

The carpet split into two segments of equal width. The checkerboard grass turned wavy on one side, and into spirals on the other. Difficult to make out from a distance, a crooked, steam-spouting tower on the right persuaded Raine towards its old ruins, despite Chance's beckoning towards the other route.

As Raine approached, she became very small and began to feel not quite so alive as the tower must have been – for it wasn't a building at all, but a meshing of many different rock structures into a humanoid body, with a face ancient and mossy and yet strikingly alive with long-lost knowledge. She decided that it must have once been a giant golem that grew bored of the world and took a seat on an old temple to ponder its existence.

"Are you lonely, mister?" Raine yelled. "Or miss!" she added, hoping the creature wasn't touchy over its gender. Chance played copycat with a resounding meow.

She considered whether the golem could even hear her at all, or if her cries more closely resembled the squealing of a mouse. *Perhaps if mice spoke slower,* Raine thought, *people might eventually understand their language.* The same principle could help the golem to hear her.

"AAAREEE YOUUUU LOOOONELEEEEEEEEY?" she echoed in an attempt to mimic the thundering boom of an avalanche. Her voice swept the entire valley, through the cleft between plateaus in the distance, past the borders where grasslands turned to desert, and caused ripples in a far-off lake. Even she was impressed; her surprise doubled when she heard a response.

"Not particularly," announced a bubbly voice behind her. "According to peer-reviewed studies, it won't do talking to the likes of her. She's been asleep for quite some time now."

"Geez! Don't scare me like that!" she gasped.

Raine regarded the man who addressed her with bewilderment. He brought to mind a twisted mixture of Santa Claus and Willy Wonka, except maybe something hadn't gone right in his programming. Or he was a messed-up dream artifact.

"You're to blame, little miss. It's not wise to let your guard down out here in the wild."

There was definitely something cartoonish about him, draped as he was in several coats of varying colors and materials, with his outermost cloak covered with so many shiny, laminated patches, she couldn't even tell what color it was.

"That's a pretty awesome coat. What color is it?" Raine asked, despite herself.

"Wrong question."

"Then why-" she began, before realizing this man was trying to test her. "Why do you have... so many patches on your coat?" she tried.

"W-w-wrong again!" he giggled with delight, and spun around.

"Aww, quit icing my grill, man!" argued Raine. "Could you at least toss me a hint?"

"You lose! That was three whole questions."

"Wait. It's over? But my last question was completely unrelated!"

The odd man danced around.

"I wouldn't say that! It was related insomuch that the rules of the game were made quite clear and you rushed into your answer without a thought!"

"Except they weren't clear. I didn't even know we were playing a game!" Raine protested.

"Then I'm afraid you failed to read the End User License Agreement, and are therefore a rather special child," he said, slipping over and shining a flashlight into her ear. "I'll have to hand you over to Re-conditioning. They'll make quick work of this mess."

She broke away. "Are you mental? You're not sending me anywhere!"

"One might be surprised. I'm a scholar, see, and I work closely with the Developers, programming edutainment lectures and classes and so on. So naturally, I know a great many things. You, on the other hand, are a youngster with much to learn. I see you haven't even reported to the Academy for your assignments. You don't even know how to speak, or the right kinds of questions to ask."

"Well," Raine began indignantly, quite fed up with the programs in this dream world, "I don't care who you work for or what kind of professional you think you are, you're just plain rude. There's nothing wrong with asking questions, and I'm perfectly fine with my ability to speak and act without the help of some 'Academy', thank you."

"Ah, but you would be, wouldn't you? You have no qualifications to legitimately understand how little you know."

He's trying to get me to appeal to his authority: a logical fallacy.

"I don't need some degree to be happy, or to know what's best for me."

"Oh? Then prove it."

Is this guy for real?

"I'll have you know I'm a very capable young woman."

"V-v-very good. Enlighten me," the scholar said, stroking his goatee.

"School-wise, I'm at the top of the track team," Raine called out. "I'm Secretary of the Painting club, and I used to be in the Robotics club. Last semester, I got the second-highest marks in Math, and the fourth-highest marks in World History. This year, not so much, but... but... I'm also a video arcade champion! I've won regional tourneys. Even made the scoreboard in Nintendo Power once!"

At this the man was mortified.

"W-what was that you got the fourth-highest marks in?" he asked cautiously.

It took Raine a second to recall. "World History."

"Who's story?"

"You know, Joan of Arc? Genghis Khan? Cleopatra? Copernicus? Shakespeare? Marie Antoinette? James Bond? Michael Jackson? Sliced bread? Is *anything* ringing a bell?"

Upon absorbing all this, the scholar winced and nearly keeled over, prompting a snicker from Chance. It seemed the man's irises were rapidly changing in size. His limbs twitched in small bursts.

"Whoa! Hey, chill out! Are you all right, Mr. Scholar?"

"This conversation is over! Stay away from me!" he cried. "Just stay away! I don't want to learn anything from you!"

Clutching his hair violently, the man backed off. Raine scratched her head – his startled reaction recalled the surprise of the odd fellow working on the wall. It didn't make a lick of sense.

Why are these programs reeling as if they're in pain? They don't have nerves or organs, and if they're anything like programs in my world, they're all run by the same operating system.

It must all be an elaborate act – a test of my wits, and my will. Well, two can play at that game.

"You, learn from *me*? I don't think so. You said you're working for the Developers. There's no way they don't know about World History; I spy mixed influences from Earthly cultures everywhere. But here's what I really don't get: why are people kept from knowing certain things? And if this is really just a game, how come there's no option to return to Earth?"

With that, the scholar's eyes suddenly turned bright red. Although it came from his mouth, the voice that responded was not his. It belonged to a very angry woman.

"I told you no more questions, you pathetic girl!"

And then, without warning, he slammed his head violently and repeatedly on the old temple.

"Stop!" Raine screamed. "Please! You're going to hurt yourself!"

She ran over and put a hand on his shoulder. A powerful static shock jolted Raine and sent the scholar flying several feet back into a column. He hit the back of his skull and fell flat on his face, his body twitching as if an electric current were surging through it.

What have I done? Terrified, Raine leaned over the pitiable program, but didn't dare lay another finger on him. "Hey! Step away from the light! Wake up! Talk to me!"

Maybe these programs aren't all centralized. Could it be that I was really causing pain to an artificial intelligence?

She poured some lemonade on her fingertips and sprinkled it on the guy's face, which set the man shaking like a wet dog.

"Hmm? I'm all right," the scholar chirped as if nothing at all had happened, though he was still twitching. His voice had returned to normal, but Raine's hypothesis remained untested.

She offered her hand, and the scholar took it this time, letting her pull him up off the floor.

"Of all the wacked-out people or programs I've seen here, you are by far the wacked-out-i-est," Raine muttered. Lily was right about one thing – insanity appeared to be a common *Metaverse* trait.

"You d-d-didn't need to help me," the scholar said miserably.

"It's cool. I'm thankful you told me about the, um, large rock thingy. The golem. And I'd like it if you told me more about her."

"Colossus," he corrected her. "She is one of the last ones, as far as we know. Once protectors of this realm, loved by many."

"A Colossus," she repeated.

"So y-y-you do think I'm smart?" the man asked with all the intensity of a five-year-old. "I'm a p-p-proud product of adaptive learning. I may have a few b-b-bugs, but these days, who doesn't? And it's not my fault that you didn't understand what I was trying to do, right?"

He looked incredibly distressed.

Raine couldn't possibly deny the scholar this small happiness.

"Well, hey. It's not necessarily anyone's fault, it's more like a mis-"

"G-g-good! Well, I'm off then, l-little one. Got a rep-report to make about you."

"WAIT!" cried Raine. "I want to know more about the Colossus!"

But the scholar had already twisted a couple of knobs on his boots. He knocked his heels together, which seemed to kick-start some sort of engine. Raine fell into a bit of a slump; strange as he was, she'd enjoyed the strange scholar's company.

"Goodbye, I guess," she managed, hoping his report would be a positive one.

"It was most certainly a pleasure. My name is Stephen Seele, and I'm sure we'll see each other s-s-soon! Oh, and my topmost coat is white! *Au revoir!*"

He shot up into the air, and from a distance, the patches on his coat shimmered like crystals.

∩

Queen Lorelei watched carefully from the holo-map in her private office as Stephen sped off. This child was an absolute anomaly. She was smart, sincere, maddeningly curious, and downright naïve. It's as if she were engineered to be the most annoying girl imaginable.

Even worse, she was plugged into the Network from a third-party source, one whose remote signal was completely untraceable, and drove her scanners ballistic. What's more, the game's source code seemed to be warping around the girl's form. This sick being's very presence was rewriting her beloved *Metaverse*, destroying elaborate settings that the Queen and her digital double had carefully calibrated over the course of decades.

It was time to draw out Lillian's defense.

The Queen gave her maniacal laugh a good, long practice run. She had been waiting for this day for far too long. She scrolled through her list of exploits. "Guided Seismic Disturbance" was always a fun one.

Almost as soon as the scholar was out of her field of vision, Raine felt a rumbling in the ground. A fissure formed suddenly in the distance, dividing the carpet in two and closing in on her.

Thinking quickly, she scooped up Chance, instinctively placed him in her messenger bag's pet compartment, and ran off the path. She bolted away towards the desert, but the crack in the ground turned ninety degrees and caught up with her.

"No way!" Raine cried as the crevice opened up right under her feet. She jumped aside once more, but the ground on which she was expecting to land split open as easily as an orange peel and before the poor girl knew it she was freefalling into the center of the Earth.

The fissure expanded until she could barely see the walls anymore, and it was so dark and cold and infinite she couldn't help but scream. She yelled and yelled and suddenly beside her, a gauntlet tapped on her arm.

To Raine's immense surprise, it belonged to none other than Gerrit, falling down alongside her with a backpack that she hoped housed a parachute.

Raine grabbed onto him for dear life, and he wrapped an arm around her waist. With his free hand, he gripped the pull-string, nodding to her for recognition. She signaled an OK, prepared for the very worst.

Gerrit yanked on the string. With a forceful tug his parachute shot right out.

They jerked to a relative standstill. Gerrit guided the pair in a descending spiral towards an island far below; the light from above cast their shadows onto a dimly lit subterranean sea.

"What just happened?" said Raine, her voice hoarse from all the screaming.

"I don't know, but I'm glad I showed up in time."

"How in the world did you get here?"

"Oh, my dragon dropped me off."

He pointed skyward. Sure enough, through the canvas, Raine could see the tiny silhouette of a winged beast flying circles above the fissure.

"*Your* dragon?"

"Kinda. I mean, no one owns him, per se. He's more like a time-share dragon."

"Well, why didn't you just have him fly down and pick me up?"

Gerrit gave an awkward laugh.

"You'd be cut to ribbons if you caught on his scales or spikes. Plus, I knew I could catch you. Sorry this is so awkward."

Raine turned away, unsure what to say or do.

"Also, he gets nervous flying underground. It's kind of a touchy subject."

They were both quiet for a while as they circled the island, popping in and out of complete darkness.

"Gerrit?"

"Yes?"

"Were you following me just now?"

"Kind of. I actually used a tracking plug-in, since we're friends now and all."

"Still. That's a bit weird."

"I'm sorry. I just wanted to make sure you were doing all right out here, so far from civilization."

"Oh."

When at last they landed by the beach and Gerrit re-stocked his parachute, a shrill siren sliced through the still air. Its high-pitched ringing wailed in the darkness. The duo became swiftly aware of hundreds of pale, blind creatures of every shape and size emerging from the water and making for the center of the landmass.

Raine squinted in the general direction they were moving towards; there was some sort of bunker.

"What is that sound?" Gerrit asked.

"I was about to ask you the same thing!"

"I've never seen anything like this before," he told her, somewhat excitedly.

"Whatever it is, I think we ought to follow those critters," Raine said, pointing up towards the far-off opening they'd fallen through.

Far-off specks materialized overhead and grew rapidly in descent. Suddenly, a hot dog stand fell towards them and exploded not a hundred feet away, shaking the island and spewing sand into their faces.

They were being bombarded.

"Holy shit," remarked Gerrit.

And here I thought I was done running away, Raine thought. *Guess fate's not leaving me with much of a choice.*

"Run!" she cried, taking his hand. They made for the shelter, following close behind amphibious beasts dodging or falling prey to the variety of missiles.

Gerrit was determined. A brief thought made its way through his mind: *the 'Verse had never before been this unpredictable.*

Something beyond his normal strength propelled him forward. He tightened his grip on Raine's hand, activated a speed-enhancing *Haste* spell, and bounded over the beach. The bombing continued.

"Don't you have more of those teleport bubbles or something?" screamed Raine.

The boy pulled out a small handheld device from his belt pack. "Even if I did, they wouldn't work in a Hidden zone like this, but this is an instant shield generator. Just tell me when and I'll activate it!"

She peeked upwards just in time. "DUCK!"

Gerrit pulled Raine down beside him and activated the shield. She spun around as the generator's soothing hum created a pulsing dome of energy.

Raine couldn't avert her eyes from looking directly at the firebomb as it hit the shield and exploded, sending flaming shards every which way. Right above her, Gerrit's intense eyes let her know without words that he was waiting for a go signal.

"Clear!" yelled Raine as the debris vanished, and in one swift motion Gerrit bolted forward, pulling her close behind. They hadn't gone more than four steps.

"DUCK!"

Again he pulled her down beside him and activated the shield. This time a giant pencil case smashed open, sending its oversize contents flying every which way.

"Clear!" Raine called, once the pencil compass stuck into the sand like a lance.

"Two left! We'd better hurry!"

They sprinted through the thick sand as fast as their virtual legs could take them and made it to within a hundred feet of the entrance. Suddenly a cruise liner fell out of the sky.

Raine was so shocked she couldn't even call out "DUCK!" All she could do was tug at Gerrit's sleeve. He glanced upwards. Neither could turn away from the monstrosity. Gerrit pressed the button and they both stopped, flabbergasted, as the ship bounced off their protective bubble and inexplicably shattered as if it were made of Lego bricks.

They pulled their way out of the debris and reached the shelter entrance when Raine turned around and noticed a small penguin waddling towards them.

"Um, Gerrit?" She intoned, pointing.

"Stay inside!" commanded the warrior, who promptly ran out to meet the pesky bird. A cement truck materialized not a hundred feet in the air and landed right where Gerrit had been a split-second ago. Raine covered her sand-struck eyes. When she opened them, her stalker was dashing towards the shelter, penguin safely nestled in his arms.

She let them in and shut the door just as an explosion blasted her off it.

IX. Trauma

"If you wish to make an apple pie from scratch, you must first invent the universe." – Carl Sagan

Lily clamped her teeth down hard as the thermonuclear engine propelled her *Phoenix* through the atmosphere. Nearing the burnout point at a steep angle far from the equator, the pressurized shuttle shook her with as much G-force as she could handle.

Needless to say, she would rather have been down on the surface, coordinating her strike teams. But Leandra, Joaquin, and the others had their orders, and she had no alternative but to put her trust in them.

Blast that stupid envelope, she thought. One of her red envelopes, an urgent message from her future self with more than the usual amount of encryption, had been sent to the *Belladonna*. There was no way Rutger could transmit the message electronically without risking interception by the enemy.

It had better be worth it. I've wasted a good bit of fuel on this trip.

As if that weren't bad news enough, when the *Valkyrie's* rocket slide launched her from Terra, she dropped her bottle of anxiety pills somewhere in the cabin, and it rattled out of arm's reach. Tears erupted from her eyes at the increasing G-force as the afterburners kicked in. In a few seconds she would break away from the pull of the Earth's gravitational field, and it was in these trying times that the traumatic memory played itself out once more in her mind's eye.

My parents are gone.

Dark safety goggles over closed eyes, seven-year-old me cries for their lives, curled up on the floor as the Belladonna's reactor bursts with converted solar energies.

Space-Time Warp Initiation in ten seconds.

This was the part that always made me nauseous. The part where Mommy holds my hand and tells me everything's okay.

But Mommy's gone now.

Instead, XF-22 holds me close. Even his rigid, mechanical arms provide no small comfort as the space station whirls around like a top.

The spinning grows faster and faster.

Countdown timer reads two seconds.

"Hold your breath, Lily," she'd say. "Pretend you're underwater, safe as a fish in a tub."

An echoing boom shakes the air. My stomach jumps up into my chest, and for a second, I'm weightless. Everything is calm.

The loud crunching sounds fade and the Belladonna's finally stopped spinning.

It's over. The camel just passed through the eye of the needle.

Uncurling from a shivering ball of sweat, I surface, take a breath at last.

"Are you all right, Captain Lily?" XF-22 asks from the speaker within its metal mouth.

All I can do is nod.

It takes a while to regain my balance. I amble out to the bridge.

It's empty, and silent as a warped fever dream.

The Earth casts its blue glow across the wide room.

I shuffle over to the control panel, slippers silent as they cross the carpeted floor. My head's placed to the glass, hoping against reason, logic, and the laws of physics for their safe return.

Instead, all I could see was the Earth. The planet that birthed my parents, and their murderers.

But it wasn't the Earth as I'd ever recognized it. The continents were distributed all wrong.

The readout on the control panel pegged the date as 225,000,000 B.C. I'd been sent back to the late Triassic period.

Mom and Dad's half-empty coffee cups remain in their cup-holders. This is when it got too much.

"Rutger! Take me back! I want to go back and save them!"

"Negative, Captain."

"Why?! And don't call me 'Captain'! Call me 'Miss Lily', and that's an order!"

"Apologies, Miss Lily. Presently, I cannot return you to the future. It goes against the instructions left by your mother."

"Then take me back earlier!"

"Negative. Even if I could fulfill your request, you are not permitted to use the Space-Time Temporal Drive until you have completed your parents' education program."

"Their what?"

A massive list of required reading, viewing, and studying appeared in the holographic display. Logic. Rhetoric. Languages. Ethics. Philosophy. History. Advanced maths. The sciences.

Ugh. "Um. Homework? Seriously?"

I've triggered a response. Father's voice emanates from the console. Ghosts of my parents materialize, clad in their familiar lab jackets. Recordings. Daddy speaks first.

"Lillian, if you're running this emergency program, your mother and I are unfortunately dead. For that, I am truly sorry. You will need to take ownership of the Belladonna, or else destroy it. That is why and where we come in. See, your progress in astrophysics and martial arts has been phenomenal, but as far as the mission's concerned..."

With a nod, he signals for Mom to take over.

"Dearest Lily, you're probably wondering what this list is all about. Your father and I raised you the best that we could. We trust you completely with our life's work. But you are currently the sole pilot of the most complicated piece of machinery in known history. Don't think about the mission for now, okay? We don't want to force you into it. You have your own future. We want you to work through this with us. So don't worry, be happy. Promise?"

"I promise," *younger me says fervently, sticking out her pinky to match her mother's. It activates a response.*

"Good. Before you can get behind the controls of the Belladonna, you must first complete your training. We have personally programmed your classes, and made the options as freeing as possible. I wish we could have fostered a true dialogue, letting you choose your topics, the way it's always been. But even the most advanced technology has its limitations, and your life, and the lives of many others, may one day depend on your understanding. So we'll see each other every day for a while."

I can't help the tears upon seeing my parents' faces, but I nod in assent and understanding. I'd get to see my beloved Mom and Dad just a little longer. Filled with a newfound courage, I vow that I'll get them back, or else make them proud of their daughter.

I don't need to promise anything. I'm going to finish what you started, or I'm going to die trying.

The *Phoenix* popped right out of the atmosphere in a ball of flames. Lily felt weightlessness take hold and drew a breath of relief, her suit drenched in sweat. She hated her frail, diminutive body, but at least the limb enhancements helped stabilize her circulation.

She rested her eyes as the shuttle continued its hour-long journey to the *Belladonna*, and set the top-mounted turrets to seek out and automatically destroy any of Lorelei's probe satellites.

Practicing her Vipassana Meditation, Lillian observed her breathing and pulse calmly and equanimously, slowing her oxygen intake.

Multiple cloaking mechanisms protected the *Belladonna* from all prying eyes. Its own probes circled in orbit, reinforcing the outer space junk barriers. The only way Lily could find her way back home was from a homing beacon in her key. She greatly wished that she could have activated the *Phoenix's* Space-Time Warp Initiator, but her last bits of saved-up temporal energy not too long ago.

There was no turning back now. Both sides' cards were in play. Raine would be her trump card. The ace up her sleeve. And Queen Lorelei's hand was slipping.

After docking at the external arm to allow for zero gravity maintenance to be done on the *Phoenix*, Lily drifted through the airlocks, climbed out of her spacesuit, and floated down the tunnel between the shuttle's docking arm and the main hull of the *Belladonna*.

"Good evening, Miss Lily," came a sound from the P.A. system as she stepped through the next pressurized airlock to the bridge and settled into the artificial gravity.

"Evening, Rutger," she said, undressing. "Have my dream analyzer ready, and the bath set to 105 degrees. Afterwards, I shall want a mug of hot cocoa with marshmallows."

"Of course, Miss Lily."

Sitting in front of her holo-display with an incomparable mug of cocoa and a puffy mess of recently blow-dried hair, Lily resigned to allowing herself a modicum of solace. Using a small track ball and two buttons attached to her armchair, she scrolled through footage taken off the *Endless Metaverse* server that day. From every conceivable camera angle, there was Raine with her confused stares, a curious child navigating a dangerous digital domain. The poor girl had no idea what she was getting into. Lily checked her Dream Recorder; it was still loading the brain wave data from her last trancelike vision.

"Miss Lily, the message has been analyzed and has not been corrupted," Rutger said in a soothing voice.

Lily turned in her armchair to see XF-22 standing before her in an apron, holding a silver platter with the red envelope. She examined its sole content - her personal calling card - underneath a magnifying glass and over a small black light. Symbols emerged. Familiar hieroglyphs, her newest trademark language. It was legit. She mentally deciphered them and read the letter aloud.

L,
Greetings love. Message sent via recovered cells on NEdn. Further resources nonexistent. Primary Agent 99 in custody of Alpha; recovery at Maximum Risky. Difficult spring: army mobilization complete. Possible split server transference leading to insurgency destruction at Heart protected Nowhere Land 0004-1-923701. Apologies: strike team unable to locate and shut down Overseer. Final extraction and confrontation require assistance not attempt Single-Hand warn true.
Love and trust,
L

"Damn," Lily said, and crumpled the card in her hands. Then she straightened it out again, read it once more, and handed it back.

"Rutger, as usual, make note of coordinates from origin and add to no-travel list. Refuel the *Phoenix*. I will prep a game plan in due time."

Lillian planted a golden circlet on her head and concentrated very hard on what she'd just read. She then pointed at the central console.

"Read 'em back," she requested. It was one of the methods Lily had developed to keep herself sane; by having Rutger log and store her inner thoughts in a massive database, she could think clearer about her quest.

"According to this message, Lorelei will execute a trap using Gerrit as bait. She remains in possession of twenty-two fuel cells and the Temporal Drive power converter, preventing me from engaging the fission reactor and converting fuel towards time travel. We don't have any more fuel. We can't change the past. This is it. I really feel like some frosted wheat cereal."

Following the adaptive behavior procedures set in place by Carl Hermes, Rutger laughed, putting the Captain a little at ease. "Shall I materialize a bowl of frosted wheat cereal?"

"That does sound great, actually," Lily said with a nod, still lost in thought. "Thank you."

After finishing the cereal, Lily asked Rutger to bring forth a candle.

She lit it, and held a respectful silence for her future-self, now trapped in a doomed parallel existence. Lily went by her parents' Causality Theory, which was this: any parallel timelines created would eventually disappear entirely, with the true world line being determined by changes in the far past as dictated by prior temporal interference.

It was based off something once called 'The Butterfly Effect', a pre-war term from the Alpha world line, coined by proponents of Chaos Theory. There were other hypotheses about the outcomes of these universes, but most ended with the untimely life failure of Lily's future self.

Now that Future Lillian had sent her report, she would continue the mission until the now-tangent universe presumably disappeared (or continued to go on, if the Causality Theory was wrong). If she ultimately botched her duties at Earth's end, she would issue the failsafe, destroying the *Belladonna*, along with herself inside it.

The Captain often thought of all the ways she'd died or failed in alternate timelines, according to the backlog of notes other Lilies had sent back to the Triassic, lifetimes before the circumstances that led to her current predicament.

Apparently, uniting the world powers in the twentieth and twenty-first centuries by revealing her data about the solar flare ended in chaos on Earth, and the *Belladonna* being hunted down.

Convincing the great philosophers of Ancient Greece and Persia of the dangers of the future was a promising attempt, but in that timeline the *Belladonna* was fatally struck by a meteoroid and, having barely escaped with her life in the *Phoenix*, Lily could only transmit a final goodbye before being stranded on Earth during that time period.

Swaying the outcome of World War I led to a very different world, one that developed space travel before understanding its consequences, resulting in a literal space war between nations that culminated in widespread genocide.

A parlay with ancient Atlanteans ended rather inconclusively, with a message simply advising, "Forget Atlantis. You don't want to know."

Taking Nikola Tesla under her wing and helping to fund and develop his revolutionary inventions worked masterfully, but because his technological breakthroughs eliminated all competition in the energy sector, the global elite united against them. Although Lily prevailed and had a good chance of accomplishing the mission, the resulting bloodbath took a toll on her mental health, leading to the couple's untimely resignation, and a romantic life in exile.

Saving Lily's parents had been accomplished, but supposedly that timeline didn't end with the people of Earth faring any better.

And then there was the *Jerusalem Un-Incident*. A memory best not revisited at the moment.

Rutger dimmed the lights. Lily sat in thoughtful silence and kept the lone candle company until it melted into a puddle of wax.

"Thank you once again, future me," she said, and stood up. "May you find peace in your final moments."

Lily ritualistically ventured out of her chair and towards the Remediator Room. Against the back wall stood the empty pods. They were home to her helpers, and for a few mostly joyous years, she was not alone.

A photograph on the corkboard showed the Sky Admiral – no, the *Belladonna's* Captain – surrounded by three girls who resembled her in every way. Lily had her arms around them; they were smiling. The future of planet Earth was theirs to save, to shape, to awaken. In other photographs were Gerrit and Raine, also smiling. Both so spirited, so determined to make a difference.

"Are they doing well?" Lily asked.

"Perfectly healthy and on schedule," Rutger replied.

Lily took one last sip of her hot (now cold) chocolate, left the chamber, and called up the Dream Recorder. She reclined into her seat and put on a shining crown. Familiar waves of discomfort arose as the device pried into her head, reading the fluctuations of her brain wavelengths. This data fed back as stimuli, inducing a state of subconscious lethargy. The pain was a necessary and not completely unwelcome reminder of her mortality, but this inner work was important. She flipped down its opaque visor.

"Access previous. Playback now," Lily read to the monitor. She felt her temples relax and her worldly body sink into the chair. Within seconds she had lost all sensation, her brain completely arrested into an REM sleep state.

As in many of her dreams, the Captain was an ordinary teenager in the early twenty-first century, a state of mind likely molded by films of that era. This time she was sneaking into a large building, some sort of convention center. Despite the heat, people crowded every gate, doorway and window. Armed guards patrolled in calculated circles. Lily slipped past a distracted sentry and found a way around the delivery dock, up five flights of stairs, and across an empty hallway into a labyrinth blanketed in vines. Endless breeds of impossible flowers lined the floor.

The place smelled of life, and Lily got rather drunk on it. She tiptoed her way between the overgrown flowers, and the walls seemed to grow ever higher with each step, until the glass ceiling disappeared into a single speck of light.

Her happiness turned suddenly to horror as the air grew thinner, and the labyrinth fell into darkness. The maze faded into a lifeless hall, and Lily collapsed in fear. She was helped to her feet by eyeless ciphers. Their wide mouths housed the gentlest expressions.

"Are you all right, Lily?" one asked.

"I'm fine. Thank you so much."

She was unnervingly grateful. As the beings walked away Lily caught herself proceeding dumbly through the architecture of the office hallway, passing androids armed with files and cups of coffee and cell phones, making every visible turn to get to the glowing Exit sign, and eventually noticing the office had turned into a middle school.

Time slowed almost to a stop as tween kids ran through the halls, laughing gaily. They burst through large double doors, became engulfed in blinding light. She tried to follow them, but an odd feeling stopped her at an intersection. To her side, three other kids stood arm in arm, staring at her. She couldn't tell if they were boys or girls or if they meant to harm or help her, but their menacing glares were terrifying. Observing her dream self's state of mind, Lily noticed the effects of blind fear mingled with confusion, as she ran back down the other way, up two flights of stairs and into an empty classroom. The specters had followed, and hovered right at the door when she slammed it. One of them slipped through and loomed over the girl.

"Get away! Leave me!" Lily screamed at the shadowy figure.

"You are nothing," the figure responded. "You have failed."

"Shut up!" bellowed the girl, pushing the teacher's desk up against the doorway.

"Do you want to know the truth, Lily?"

"What is the truth?"

"Your mother is trapped in a bag," the figure said.

At a complete loss for words, Lily observed her dream-self back away from the desk. She picked up a chair with sudden strength and hurled it through the nearest window.

"You're lying," she said to the spirit, although deep down she knew that it must be true.

"See for yourself," was its last reply before falling to the floor in a black puddle.

Lily grabbed the vacuum cleaner standing in the corner and took hold of its power cord. She placed the teacher's desk up to the window and wedged the vacuum against it, creating an anchor for her makeshift rope. After calculating the distance, Lily wrapped the end of the cord around her fist and executed a running jump out the window. She fell outwards, swung back hard at the building, and directed her momentum towards a window on the lower storey. She kicked out at full force, smashing it into pieces.

Dropping the cord, Lily rolled out of the crash, and into a running start. She made for a doorway, but there was none. The school became her weapons factory in Jakarta; it made sense that the tragedy would be on her mind. Lorelei recently wiped this place off the face of the Earth. Tens of thousands of the faceless beings stopped their work, gaping at her with an almost reverent glow.

"Where's my mother?" yelled Lily.

The workers made a path through the factory with their bodies. An avenue to the left of this chamber ended in an ornate door, and in between it and her current position, a security office peeked out of the corridor. Within, a group of four men sat at a table, playing poker. Somehow she knew instinctively that the man with his back to her was her father. She nervously tiptoed past the threshold, but he turned to catch her eye. In this dream, she barely remembered his face, which was wrong. Dead wrong. In reality, there was no way she could forget her one and only papa. Nor would she have any reason to distrust him.

"Daddy," she began, to no response.

She felt a palpable sense of fear. The girl bravely raised her voice.

"Is it true?"

"You must discover that on your own," he replied.

Lily gulped, and then pushed open the door running.

Now she was in the Palace of Versailles, her sneakers squeaking on the polished floor as she passed a live concerto and leapt over a couple making out in a chaise.

In the center of the room, with its endlessly high ceiling and humongous windows, dwelt a perfect half-sphere of a pit, leading far underground. She dashed down the torch-lit spiral stairs; to her great horror, some fifty feet below, in the midst of an incantation circle, sat a burlap sack, moving slowly but quietly in the faint candlelight.

Lily's stomach sank, but she conquered her fears. She walked up slowly to the bag, and with nervous hands undid the combination lock (2212) and pulled the top open. Her mother emerged from the canvas malnourished and weak, but still strikingly beautiful. They embraced.

"Mom!"

"I'm so glad you came, honey," her mother cried. "But you shouldn't be here."

Lily heard the click of a revolver. She turned around bravely.

A faceless being greeted her. Man or woman, it was difficult to tell. Its only clear feature was its gaping mouth.

And it had a revolver pointed straight at her.

"Remove her, and this world reverts to chaos." Its voice was a babbling chorus of every accent she had ever heard in her life.

"That can't be!" stomped Lily. "That doesn't make any sense!"

"Oh, but that's the way it is. It's the way it's always been. It's a deal we made, and we all agreed on it. One person would suffer, and the rest of us would live in peace. You're just unfortunate enough to be her daughter. Put her back in the bag or suffer the consequences."

"And what are the consequences?"

The faceless one pressed the gun against Lily's forehead.

Elizabeth screamed and pulled Lily away. It shot her in the shoulder; she crumpled to the floor. Lily rushed to her, lip quivering. She spun around to face the faceless being.

"If you're going to do it, then do it."

It chuckled.

"Do you know why you can face death so naïvely? It's because this is a dream, and your existence here means nothing. You tell yourself, Lily, you're different, you're special, and you know something everyone else doesn't. I say that's bullshit. There's nothing in the heart of the darkest man that you don't have in your own heart. You think you can change the world? You can't change anything without realizing that."

"I love my mother."

"Who doesn't?"

"I won't let her die in this bag. If that means you shooting me in the head, so be it."

The creature scowled, and then curled its dry lips upwards. It was a smile Lily recognized as her own.

"Goodbye."

As the bullet rushed through her head, Lily felt her brain splitting in two in extreme slow motion, her mind forever at peace. For just a split-second, the synapses connecting the two sides of her dream-brain divorced, causing her to experience a singular, eternal instant of liberation.

She was on the verge of understanding the futility of worry, the inevitability of individual death, that endless essence of her spiritual being. Lillian was a step away from becoming one with the universe. But the screaming voice kept drawing her back to the dream. She looked down and saw that her mother was now cradling her body, sobbing over her blood-soaked child.

Dad took the bad person and started beating him, or her, up. Other men joined in shortly, allowing Carl to run down the stairs and untie Elizabeth. They looked worriedly at Lily. Mom was trying to say something to her, but she couldn't hear the words. Everything blurred as her consciousness faded. Just before succumbing to death, Lily awoke.

The Captain took a deep breath, her back drenched in sweat. The circlet was removed. Powering off the Dream Recorder, Lily took a sip of the new cup of cocoa Rutger had prepared, switched the lights on, vacuum-showered, changed clothes, and headed into the greenhouse for some fresh air.

After donning her gardening apron and gloves, Lily watered and tended the food forest that was the key to sustained life in space. It kept her oxygen cycling, cleaned her water reserves, and provided her with all manner of nutritional sustenance. Rutger had been doing a stand-up job in her absence. Fresh- and saltwater fish were healthy. New corn and tomato crops grew particularly well. Light and mulch levels were quickly adjusted. Computerized readouts by each one let her know how they were faring, and what types of care each needed. Tending these living things calmed her, gave her a nurturing feeling.

She then ascended the staircase to the observatory. A front-row seat to the wonders of the universe was the best remedy against the claustrophobia and cabin fever that defined her psyche. There were still a few hours to go until the *Phoenix* was prepped.

Here Lily was about to retire for the evening, and the sun was setting in Naples, down on Earth, that big blueberry of a planet that took up the expanse of her viewing window and colored her office in its patterns. Its current forms of life would last so short a time, a fleeting cornerstone of civilization.

What did the dream mean? Jung would have had a field day with it.

In all the time I've been busy, I've neglected my inner work. My waking mind is rebelling. Like that of an insane person, it just won't stop chattering, filled with the doubts and worries of countless lifetimes. I must give myself a moment to observe objectively, to diagnose the problem.

No state of being is permanent. Not a single atom in this universe can stay in a state of equilibrium for even a trillionth of a second. A candle's flame appears to be static, but in actuality arises only to fade away. These sensations, too, must pass. It is best to remain a mere observer and let the negativity run its course.

March tenth, two thousand, two hundred and twelve; the date she had written in permanent marker on the glass kept reminding her. The day of the solar flare, the day everyone on Earth was going to die. It was an event over two decades in the future, but it would be coming all too soon.

X. The Mana Tree

"Every moment and every event of every man's life on Earth plants something in his soul." – Thomas Merton

Raine and Gerrit emerged from the untouched bunker. The sea creatures slithered across the shore and back into dark waters as the virtual noontime sun far above pierced the cold void.

"I'd hate to be cleaning up this mess," Raine observed, as both Chance and the penguin, who had become fast friends, skipped away merrily towards a collapsed sushi delivery truck and went to town on its messy remains. "I don't suppose there's an escalator nearby."

"There's always a way out. In the meantime, let's party up."

Gerrit navigated Raine through her menu screens and had her approve him as a party member. Now his Health and Mana bars were visible, and matching indicators floated over their heads. This made it easier to locate one's ally in the midst of crowded battles, Gerrit insisted.

"Since there's no teleporting in this area, we oughta check the pier," he reasoned, guiding Raine over a dangerous pile of splintered wood.

They walked in silence towards a small wharf. As they approached, a simple rowboat spawned, barely rocking in the still waters. Gerrit guided Raine onto the thing, and tried to impress her by whipping out a compass plug-in on his watch. Taking up oar, the boy rowed into the abyss as Chance napped in between them, the feline's furry coat now taking on the shimmering quality of a soft lantern.

The two humans made pleasant conversation for as long as they could.

"Do you know where we're going?" Raine acquiesced at last.

"We crossed over to a Peace zone two minutes ago. There should be a respawn point and a teleport pad just south of here. Keep a look out."

Raine squinted into the distance. Something was flickering. She brought it to Gerrit's attention.

"Good eye. That's gotta be the stairwell torch. I bet you we're somewhere under Ramzaa by now."

"It's cold," she said.

"When we get out of here, remind me to show you how to bypass the Network kernels and modify your nerve settings."

"Say what now?"

"You can make the cold seem less cold. Change how your body reacts. My friend Yossa, for example. He's a Homo-Pachyderm. Part man, part elephant, but he's modded his personal gravity to have less of an effect. He can hop clear across fields."

"Nifty. That sounds like quite a trip."

I've never heard her slang before, Gerrit thought. *Is it some sort of regional dialect?*

"I do odd jobs for him, and he keeps me patched with the latest hacks and plug-ins. Heck, I'm actually more powerful than most Templars. We'll spar sometimes, for Gold. I hold myself back so they have no idea how great of a fighter I am, but the truth is, I can view the *Verse*'s code and predict their moves. Sometimes I can slow certain attacks down, too, just by a few milliseconds. The trick is to use those techniques only when absolutely necessary."

"So, you're tricking the system. You're a cheater!"

Gerrit bit his tongue. No one had ever outright called him a cheater.

"Well, I heard that if you look at the programming, *Endless Metaverse* was meant to be anything that anyone wants to make of it. As long as you aren't stealing, or harming anyone, there's no rules, no limits. That's probably how it was supposed to be played. Sure, currently there's a centralized society and cities and governments and war and whatnot, but at least people choose their own roles."

"People can do that in real life, too. Kinda."

"Real life? You mean the world outside?"

Raine nodded.

"By the gods!" The sudden revelation that Raine had memories outside of the game hit Gerrit like a ton of bricks. He wondered if the girl shared similar insights to his dream-visions. "Did you come from real life? What am I saying, if you're here, then you... you must have."

"I came from Chicago, in nineteen ninety-two."

"DO YOU REMEMBER IT?"

"Uh... yeah?"

"What's it like out there?!"

"What do you mean? It's... okay, I guess."

"Is that what the world is called? Nineteen ninety-two?"

Raine cringed. *Just like the others. He doesn't know anything.*
"No, no, no, ninety-two's the year. The world isn't... it's not like the world here. It's a large sphere with six billion people on it."
"A sphere? So there's no edge to it?" Gerrit frowned. "And six billion, that's way too many. That number can't be right. Unless there are even more servers than the code suggests..."
"You'd better believe it." It was beyond bizarre that she had to explain this to someone she was actually having a conversation with. "We live on a planet called Earth."
"Earth," Gerrit repeated softly. "What does it look like?"
"It doesn't look like just one place," Raine began. "It depends on where you live. There's cities, mountains, deserts, forests, jungles, islands..."
"Were you a part of a mutual adoptive family, or a guild?"
"Huh? I guess you could say I kind of have a family. I live with my new foster Mom in a condo..."
"A what?"
"How do I explain... it's like a house, but smaller, and they usually have many condos in one building, you know? She's rarely home, so I spend a lot of time in the city. I go to the arcades, play videogames. Sometimes hang out in the park. They're nothing like the parks here. Only homeless people live there. I remember this nice secluded spot by the old slide. I'd sit and read library books about space travel and far-off worlds. I don't suppose you know what a library is?"
Gerrit shook his head.
"Well, it's this place with all these books. Just piles of them. Only... you've never read a book, have you?"
He held his gaze low.
No freakin' way. Raine was at a loss. Not only had she failed at getting through to him, bringing back memories of the place she at least half-understood made her a little homesick.
Ugh. When did that happen? I thought I liked – even preferred – it here. But Gerrit's completely forgotten the outside world. Is that going to happen to me, too?
Truth be told, it did feel like her memories of home were in danger of slipping away. Even thinking back to the day she entered the *Metaverse*, specifics eluded the girl. *I can't even remember what I ate for breakfast.* She made a mental note to write everything down as soon

as she could, and to continue to recall her past, painful as it was, lest she lose her sense of self.

Even with Raine's overactive imagination, it was impossible for her to see how this world could have resulted from the one she grew up in. They were two completely different realities.

Gerrit sensed that he was losing her again.

"Did you like it there? In... Earth?"

"Hmm? Oh, I guess it's okay. A busy sort of place. Kinda predictable, but also violent. And crazy. But... at the same time, I feel like things didn't have to be that way. Like, people just tried too hard, at everything. Somewhere down the line we started caring about unimportant stuff. Saying it now, I don't know if that sounds nutso, but truth is it's not like here at all. Here it's just a hundred percent ridiculous. But not necessarily in a bad way."

Gerrit sulked. He had never thought that the outside world could be more boring than the one he was currently living in.

"It sounds like you keep your memories, though," he ventured. "Up there."

"That's the way it's supposed to be," Raine reassured him. "Although, a lot of people do lose their memories when they get older. Not everyone. My friend Jordan's gramps was in World War Two. He's ninety-three years old and still going strong. He hasn't forgotten everything, not yet."

Raine noticed that this seemed to blow Gerrit's mind.

Probably not all those memories are good, though. Maybe some are better best forgotten. Raine looked down at the fading ripples as she carefully braided the ends of her long hair, just like Jane, one of her past foster mothers taught her to. She was one of the nice ones, but her creepy husband, on the other hand... he was the reason she left.

"It's funny. I spent a lot of time running away from everything and everyone in my world... now I'm wondering if I'll be stuck here forever."

"Maybe you chose to come down here," Gerrit posited.

"What? Why would I do that?"

"It's one of the theories we have. Maybe you got bored with that place and wanted something more exciting. Maybe you decided that there weren't enough choices in real life."

"But wouldn't I have remembered making that decision?"

"Not if they messed with your memories."

"Why in the world would they do that?"

He swallowed, unsure how to answer.

"Gerrit, tell me."

"I don't know," he replied, clearly more than a little stunned. "You're the exception to the rule. No one else I've met has any memories from the other side whatsoever. Some even say there is no other side, and we're just... trapped here, somehow. But I don't believe that. It's possible that the Developers are protecting us from dangers in that world, or that they just don't want us to leave because we'll see there's so much more out there."

He almost expected her to scoff like most people he told his theories to, but Raine actually considered these suppositions. Neither one sounded implausible.

"I do kind of remember something in between this world and the one I came from," said Raine. "I can't recall it too well. It was a real eyesore, a white expanse of nothingness."

"Probably one of the hubs. A waiting area of sorts. We're sent there sometimes when they change something big."

As he said this, they arrived within wading distance of the torch-lit island and descended into the chilly water. Upon seeing Gerrit splash into the darkened sea, Chance jumped atop Raine's head and brightened his coat to guide the way.

Chance's light activated long-dormant crystals set into the shore. The trio looked up in awe. Before them stood a great tree many hundreds of feet tall, long fallen into ruin. Its decayed limbs loomed high and wide over them, but cast not a single shadow in the faint light.

"It's so sad, and yet so beautiful," Raine noted wistfully.

"Well, I'll be damned. It's the legendary Mana Tree," Gerrit chimed in, taking his helmet off as a sign of respect. "Or what's left of it, at least."

Having placed her hand up against the trunk, Raine turned towards her companion.

"What happened to it?"

"I'm guessing it was buried under here, like the rest of the older version of the *Metaverse*."

"This tree was once something special." Raine searched the ground. "Wasn't it?"

"So they say," said Gerrit. "It once kept nature in balance, whatever that means. It's heartbreaking to see it like this. What are you--"

"Aha!" Raine cried aloud, holding a plum-sized, teardrop-shaped object in her hand. Chance walked across her shoulders to her arm and sniffed it.

"Is that what I think it is?"

"Only one way to find out," Raine announced. She tapped it lightly against her wristwatch as she'd seen other players do, prompting a window displaying an item description.

Seed of Mana Tree

Will grow anywhere with adequate water and sunlight. Resistant to drought and magicks. May bring the world back into equilibrium. Plant carefully, and do not plan for any structures within a two hundred meter radius.

"Very educational," Gerrit conceded with a whisper. "But we probably ought to split before the Temps catch our scent."

He pointed in the direction they'd come from. In the far distance, Templars carrying lanterns glided over the still waters, patrolling the area. And one was heading their way.

Chance dimmed his coat. Gerrit turned the rowboat and its oars into a miniature with a series of taps on its menu buttons. He stuck it in his belt pack, hiding the evidence. Using a Hover spell to mask their tracks, the trio hopped across the sandbars and booked it quietly to the other end of the island, where the water glimmered in reflected neon.

Above this beach were the Northern Lights, or so Raine thought, until a closer look showed her that it was a very tangible stairwell with an ever-changing array of beautiful hues glowing from its steps. It wound up and around itself constantly in an uneven fashion, never making a true spiral as it organically carved its way to the surface like Jack's gigantic beanstalk. The odd pixels trickled down again, only this time they were white, and reflected the glorious lights off the staircase, creating a million dazzling, lustrous patterns.

"This is incredible!" Raine exclaimed as she followed Gerrit up the first flight.

"Ugh. The Five Thousand Steps," he griped. "Here I thought there would be a teleport pad or something. And what's up with all these data storms lately? Do you know anything about them, Raine?"

But she was already bounding up the stairway, completely ignoring the lack of arm rails.

"Not so fast!"

She spun around, her face bursting with childlike glee. "Come on! I'll race you!"

He laughed nervously. "I don't think so, sorry."

Raine just stuck out her tongue and ran. As she made her way up the shimmering stair, Gerrit had to keep his distance, so she wouldn't see his flustered cheeks.

Ω

"You're aware of what this position entails, and what's expected of you," Queen Lorelei impressed upon the young Australian man sitting awkwardly across the enormous elephant hide coffee table in the middle of her smoking lounge.

The chief reason why Henry Holdfast was uncomfortable had little to do with the fact that he'd just interviewed for the newly vacant office of Junior Network Manager for the *Avidya* server, a position of such responsibility that his life would be on the line on a daily basis. It had more to do with the reality that while he'd gone to the shopping district and bought the most expensive suit he could afford for the occasion, the Queen, whom he was meeting one-on-one for the very first time, was dressed in a seductive nightgown and lace stockings that ended in a pair of fluffy slippers.

Her Majesty's trying to psyche me out with those damn painted lips of hers, he realized as he caught his eyes wandering again and met hers intensely. He had to. This wasn't a question he could let get away from him.

"Of course, ma'am." Henry replied with a courteous bow. "I am to maintain peace and stability in *Avidya* and the other servers, should my assistance be required. Keep the status quo. Eliminate wanted individuals."

The Queen yawned. "Very well, you've got the job. You're not very entertaining, but perhaps that's for the best. I do have to admit that your qualifications are exemplary. This is the first time I've considered offering so prestigious an office to one who's only been with us for five years."

She crossed her legs, making sure to rub her stockings against one another. His eyes didn't budge.

"I am most honored to be at your service, ma'am."

"You'll be sent invites to select parties of mine, of course. Your own executive suite on the hundred-odd floor range: a view of the city, or of the mountains, if you prefer. Answer quickly."

"Oh, the city, if it pleases madam."

"Very well." She placed a circlet over her head and closed her eyes to interface with Miss Guggell for a few seconds. It appeared to Henry that she was annoyed with her virtual counterpart. *Could it be? Is the AI already being influenced?*

"Eat a quick lunch. You begin immediately. Your lodgings are being moved as we speak. If you're still here in a month, we might consider you for 'doc'. You know the works. And one last thing - don't tell a single being, sentient or otherwise, about my attire today. The element of surprise is essential, you see, in hashing out the men from the boys around this sorry place. Believe me, if you snitch, I'll know it was you. And honey, I will kill you. Any questions?"

He could say nothing. She glowered in her best impression of a great white shark.

"I trust you will take my word for that last part. It's been a pleasure. Next month's advance should be flowing into your account as we speak."

They said their cordial goodbyes, and then Queen Lorelei did something else he didn't expect. She calmly walked over to him and whispered in his ear. She smelled of cigarettes and strawberries.

"This is an important job, Henry Holdfast," she said. "Don't disappoint me."

As soon as he left the room and caught his breath, Henry checked his bank account via Holo-Lens. He was now filthy rich.

Half an hour later, Henry finished his lunch quietly in his favorite corner of the Queen's excessively large hedge maze, under the elegantly trellised veranda. Even as the androids were preparing his new suite and moving his office effects, he allowed himself to indulge in homesick thoughts of his childhood friends and parents halfway across the globe.

"Is this seat taken?" a gentle female voice practically whispered.

Henry looked up at Dr. Ayumi Karuishi, an A-ranked Developer whom he was on good terms with. She shared his allegiance to powers other than those of *Neo Eden*, and as far as he could tell, she was one of the trustworthy ones. A large-brimmed sun hat with a short-ranged sonic shield protected her from any security drones.

"Oh, good morning, Doctor," he said at last, snapping out of his lonely trance. "I didn't know you liked to frequent this labyrinth."

"I don't," she replied curtly. "Even so, there's a lot we don't know about each other, isn't there? It's a situation I'd like to remedy."

Well, he'd looked up her file once, and surely she'd done the same. Henry thought hard about his answer. *Why is she trying to get close to me? This meeting is risky enough as it is.*

"You don't think we should keep our distance?" he asked discreetly.

Seeing as how the flustered man wasn't going to answer her first question, Ayumi took a seat on a marble bench and held his gaze. She was used to the paralyzing effect she had on men, but this specimen was especially awkward. Leaning in towards Henry, she lowered her voice to an absolute whisper.

"Two lone wolves might be more suspicious than, say, a lovestruck couple," she countered with a girl-next-door smile. "Plus, I'd like to get to know you a little better, seeing as how we'll be in the same department tomorrow."

Henry found no reason to object. Truth be told, Ayumi had beautiful features, and her prodigious skills made her a figure of respect and envy among the other so-called 'Doctors', really nothing more than glorified programmers who'd earned a sort of tenure. Not to mention, it couldn't hurt to at least swap some info. The fact that her soft voice immediately put him at ease was just the cherry on top.

"You may have a point," he said at last. "At least you and I can trust one another."

"What makes you so sure?" she pouted. "I could be a – how to say in English – a double agent."

"Simple. If you wanted to pick my brain, you'd have done it long ago. Plus, it's in your best interests to stick around me. I know that creep Reno has been bothering you since his divorce."

"Oh, you're good." Karuishi giggled. "But I'm not worried about the other quacks so much. They are horribly uninteresting. It's a certain someone inheriting a particularly dangerous job that concerns me. I don't want to see him come to any harm, and maybe my experience here can count for something in that regard."

Her voice, and her sincerity, warmed his heart. It wouldn't be hard getting used to this.

"Kudos on the promotion, by the way," she added.

"Ah. Th-thanks. Dr. Zee put a good word in."

"Henry?"

Are we on first name terms now? His recent interview notwithstanding, this was officially the longest conversation he'd had with a woman in months.

"Yes?"

"If you want me, you're gonna have to fight for me."

Caught dumbstruck, Henry let his trembling jaw drop. "You mean, like, at work?"

"Of course, silly goose. It's part of the act. You have to show the others that you're interested in their power plays, and you'll have to do your best to impress me. Everyone likes a bit of gossip. It keeps their eyes off the important stuff."

He nodded. "I think I understand. Should we maybe have lunch sometime?"

"I'd like that a lot," she said, and then shook his hand. "Expect correspondence within the day so we can get our game plan together. You're inheriting a lot of responsibility, so please, don't be a stranger."

He returned her confident expression. "I won't. If ever I need any info---"

"Anytime. I may be higher ranked in the *Nexus*, but you are the best programmer I've ever seen. Even... even dear Nico was impressed, may he rest in peace. Those watchdog protocols? Ingenious. Fully functional, yet so easy to modify. And all done with half the code."

"H-hey, flattery will get you nowhere," he quipped, but she'd already melted his heart, and she knew it. Ayumi gave him a peck on the cheek.

"That's for luck. I usually keep it all for myself, so don't you waste it."

And with that, she alighted and ambled away, leaving Henry floating on air.

"I won't," he said to himself. This goofy grin was too genuine; it wasn't going to leave anytime soon.

For the first time in a long time, he'd let his guard down, and he hadn't regretted it.

As Henry tossed his trash in the bin of a passing cleaning droid, he heard an unusual and unwelcome sound, the roaring of an otherworldly engine echoing off the mountainside as it burst through *Neo Eden's* protective energy dome. Hesitantly, he searched the cloudless sky.

It was the unmistakable sound of the *Raven.*

Encased in the shell of a CMV-21 sports pod, it circled down into the *Spire*, an omen of bad tidings. It'd been too long since the unwelcome ship had been spotted. If history were to repeat itself, the Queen would be in a fiery mood, and that was never pleasant.

Henry headed back to the *Nexus*. Meeting with Ayumi had been more than worth it, but he'd tarried too long, and missed a chance to acquire some second-hand information.

Δ

A kilometer away, in the heart of the *Spire*'s tertiary docking bay, cyborg Lieutenant General Errol Beech and the recently returned Brigadier General Troi Macleod stood at attention. Munching on a stick of bubble gum, Queen Lorelei had put herself behind the plasma blast shield, flanked by two-dozen of her Royal Guard on either side as the jet-black airship flew into the hangar.

The *Raven*, which left the bay on a supposed recon flight mere hours ago, was rarely seen and even closer guarded. While it was outfitted to look like a prototype racing pod, the unearthly roar of its engine and the frightful booming noise it was said to make gave rise to strange rumors about its true purpose.

At the command of Captain Simon Thomas, the armored guards split up into two even lines, laser spears at the ready, facing the doors of the majestic machine. The Royal Guard was comprised exclusively of fully conscious human conscripts. Androids could potentially be turned against the Queen, and those in *M-Gear* helmets shut down via EMP, often at the cost of their own lives, although Lillian would not kill needlessly.

"All scans clear. One life form detected. Chip reads 'Gamma-03'."

"Very well," Queen Lorelei replied, and then shouted, "Report, General Lacie!"

She walked down the pathway towards the airship.

The small hatch popped open. A badly hurt woman emerged, limping but still managing to project absolute dignity. One of the newest guards up front did a double take. Beech understood. The man would have heard the rumors, but seeing it with one's own eyes was something else entirely. The stories were absolutely true.

Rarely seen publicly, General Lacie, *Neo Eden's* second-in-command, head of the military, and Beech's commanding officer, was an exact replica of Queen Lorelei. The sisters may have been a few years apart and sported very different tastes in clothing, but on a physical level, they were absolutely indistinguishable. Supposedly every female in the family line shared the same facial structure, presumably as a result of intensive surgery, the point of which was anyone's guess.

At her behest, Queen Lorelei's manservant draped a blanket over General Lacie and guided her to the hovering gurney.

"You look terrible, dear," the Queen began. "What do you need?"

"C-c-cold. I-I need medical attention," Lacie said softly.

"Very well, my darling," Queen Lorelei replied. "Leave us," she said to the others, laying Lacie on the gurney with her own arms.

A confused General Beech saluted. "Y-yes, milady. Long live *Eden.*"

"Beech," she called out.

"Ma'am?"

"Report to the Overseer. Wipe theirs and your memories of this event."

When Lacie awoke, the Queen had taken her a hundred and seventy levels up the *Spire* and into her private quarters, the most lavish in all of *Neo Eden*. Once they made it to the jade-lined sauna, the Queen undressed Lacie and helped her broken body into a rejuvenating hot tub that bubbled with a special batch of nano-machines and infused minerals. The microscopic bots went to work on healing her battered frame.

"Much better," Lacie said, taking deep breaths of the hot air.

The tension in the room reached critical mass as Lorelei reflected on what Lacie must have felt all too well during her trip; that it had been some time since they last broke the unspoken rules and traveled forward, then backwards in time, an act of potential genocide the sisters were sworn never to do except in the direst of circumstances.

But reports had been sent of android and human armies gathering in neighboring countries, crossing hundreds of miles of wasteland in majestic airships. Though spies were getting harder to come by, months-old accounts detailed massive metal suits under development. Since joining the troublesome EDC, Lily had amassed a small aerial fleet and annexed a few worn-down bases in the East, but their numbers were nothing to be feared. Even so, many tons of precious war material had gone unaccounted for over the past years, evidence that androids and warships were being built off the record in distant factories.

Was Lily trying to use the Queen's toys against her own deadly armada, not to mention an impregnable fortress where every innocent civilian could be turned into a soldier with the push of a button? These absurd ideas needed to be investigated, and one more reset would do less harm to the universe than what the so-called Sky Admiral had in mind.

Finally at ease with her convictions, Lorelei pulled up a chair beside the tub.

"Claire..." Lacie mumbled incoherently.

"Your domestic companions are fine. To them, you left just this morning. You're better off waiting a little before you see them again. Please," she said. "I've sent for your favorite physician. You look horrible; we'll talk later."

The sad thought that she would have to wait to see Claire was physically painful enough to fully wake Lacie.

"No, Lorrie. I must... tell you now," she pressed. "I arrived... too late... All our Eastern detectors... jammed 'til the end. Tracking their advance will be all but impossible. It may have already begun, and we are nearly out of the fuel cells. If we are to do something..."

Lorelei leaned over to put her hands on Lacie's shoulders.

"Calm now, sis. Calm first. You must rest a minute."

Lacie nodded and closed her eyes.

Exactly one minute passed. At long last, Lorelei inched forward and steeled her gaze.

"What news do you bring from the future?"

XI. Anonymous

"Reality is that which, when you stop believing in it, doesn't go away."

– Philip K. Dick

Gerrit grabbed Raine's hand before she cleared the surface.

"There's something I have to tell you before we go up there."

"What is it?"

"It won't be safe. They surely know we're coming out this tunnel. The Devs must be aware I'm an anarchist, and if that's why they're after you, then you must deny that you know me. You have to let me protect you."

"I told you, I never asked for your protection," she pouted.

"I'm not just trying to be a gentleman here! Can't you see? You're being hunted. That fissure in the ground... that's not the kind of thing that happens by accident."

Raine considered this.

"Well, I guess that's obvious enough. That thing chased me around the desert. So you think someone's trying to trap me? Or kill me?"

"Yes, and if that thought doesn't scare you, I don't know what will, Raine. There's powerful people after you!"

She led him out towards the spot of daylight at the end of the tunnel, arms crossed in thought.

"Well, if this is all my dream, like I think it is, then nothing can hurt me, and I won't let anything hurt you, either. And if it's all just a game, like you said, and we can't die, there's nothing to fear."

Gerrit scratched his head at this brutal massacre of logic.

There was a time when I thought I could reason with girls, he reflected. *No longer.*

"Not exactly. There are strictly enforced rules, though most turn a blind eye. And there's much worse they can do to you. You can be put in confinement, forced into a reboot and lose your memories, or, heavens forbid, you could be frozen."

"Frozen?"

"It's the worst sort of punishment. Word is they hold you in a suspended state for a certain period of time. It could be days, months, even years. You might never come back. Supposedly they only do it to real threats, like players infected with unfixable viruses. But it's probably more common than we'd ever know."

"That's pretty scary," Raine said as they left the tunnel and found themselves in a thick forest. She closed her eyes and took a deep breath of fresh air. "But it's not going to happen to me."

Sword drawn and spells at the ready, Gerrit was at his wits' end. Raine ventured blindly into the darkening wood with reckless abandon.

"We really shouldn't be here. This place is far beyond your skill level. There's all sorts of beasties running about."

"Live a little, Gerrit," she said as Chance ran about and flexed his wings, happy to be out in even dimmed sunshine. "You told me yourself, this world is just an illusion."

"You may think you know that as a fact, but your brain still sees it as real. I don't want you to get hurt. Here, I know a place with a teleport. Clyde's just a hop, skip, and jump away."

"I'm not going back there," insisted Raine, rather matter-of-factly. "My destination is Atmoya. Sector Nine."

"That's where you think you'll find Super BlastBoy? At the monument?"

She nodded.

"Like I said, you can't teleport anywhere near there. It's a War zone."

"Oh, there's no rush. Not if I sleep in a bit."

Chance flew by their side, and surprised both of them by snapping up a flying insect with an overlong tongue. He cast fiery spells to force their way through thick growths clogging the seldom-used pathways.

"I like your cat," he opined.

"Thanks."

"Leave the visor work to me; yours isn't patched yet."

Gerrit slipped on a pair of aviator goggles and took the lead, following a detailed mini-map. Raine reluctantly tailed him, eyes wandering at the strange flora and fauna. Sprites and wisps flew hither and thither, softly chiming at the duo along the path. Chance pounced on one, and it led him in circles around the forest until he tired himself out.

Along the way, they encountered a few wild zombie baboons, which Gerrit swiftly dispatched with a combination of swordplay and minor spells.

They broke their stride for a modest lunch by an idyllic lake and skipped a few stones, an act that ended when Raine realized that far across on the opposite shore, the deer were too frightened to drink. Then they sat and watched them for a bit; the animals looked incredibly real for products of a virtual dream world.

Raine had advanced to level two, earning a few skill points from her social interactions with other players.

After learning that she had no idea how to allocate her skill points, Gerrit showed Raine how to access her upgrade menus with a scrolling finger motion over her watch. These were promptly assigned to slots increasing her speed, magic, and magic defense.

She chose to assign various attack and defense shortcuts to specific bodily gestures, and found that the system helped guide her through the follow-through movements.

As she performed several attacks, Raine felt a hypnotizing pull of the power she could now beckon with mere poses, and understood how easily people grew addicted to it. Still, a part of her couldn't help but feel uneasy that she was giving control of her body over to the system.

It was nearly dark when the pair arrived near a quaint little town, although the clearing between the redwoods was large enough to allow the place a bright golden hue at sunset. Two miles out, an absurdly large tower cast its shadow over them.

"We'll stay here for the night," Gerrit said, wiping sweat off his brow. "Mistral's got a duel-based economy, but for loot hunters, there's no questions asked. First off, we need to sort out a few things."

A very serious look took shape on his face as he approached her, a little closer than she was comfortable with.

He pulled out a pair of clip-on earrings and offered them to Raine in the outstretched palm of his hand.

"Would it be cool if you wore these?"

Raine's stomach knotted up. *Is he seriously giving me a present?*

"Um..."

"Just say yes," he said, his expression relaxing a bit, just enough for her to know that he meant business. "Please."

Raine clipped the earrings on.

"You don't look half bad in 'em," Gerrit mouthed, only the sound emerging from his lips was quiet and faint. A small chirp announced the presence of text in her peripheral vision.

[NinjaMageKnight99]: They can't see this. Neat, huh? Send me a message. It's easy. Look to the menu on the bottom right corner of your vision and wink at the smiley face. Pick me from your Friends list. Then clearly visualize the words in your mind one by one. To start again, think 'Clear Message'. When you're happy with the text, think 'Send Message Now'.

While she composed her reply, Raine couldn't help but notice that her own mouth had begun moving on its own, the words coming out of it being produced by something other than her own mind.

[rainorshine23]: Er... Testing. How does this work exactly?

[NinjaMageKnight99]: It's a Private Channeler. Discreet communications. The Developers can eavesdrop on system-approved private chats. Your earrings connect with a small chip in my necklace. Our artifacts allow personal instant messages while preset dialogue creates the illusion that you and I are having a completely different conversation. I think this one is about the local insects.

Raine was thoroughly impressed. She listened closely to herself asking Gerrit odd facts about hornets and how she saw quite a few of them today. It was a little out of character, but hopefully not enough to draw suspicion.

Next, Gerrit reached into his pack and pulled out a strange cream-colored mask of a smiling man.

[NinjaMageKnight99]: I'm lending you my Guy Fawkes mask. It will hide your face and username and encrypt your location. It should buy us some time. Be warned that it's going to feel weird at first.

Raine nodded her assent, legs weak and knees knocking. She took the mask and placed it on her face. She felt her facial muscles contort, her hair shrink, and her body increase slightly in size.

Gerrit studied the results carefully.

"Not bad," he conceded.

"I want to see!" Raine drew the hand mirror from her shoulder bag and nearly dropped it upon seeing her reflection. She resembled a teenage punk rocker, with cropped pink hair and nose and lip piercings.

After a few speechless seconds it became apparent that Gerrit was waiting for her to say something.

[rainorshine23]: This is weird! Who... who am I?

[NinjaMageKnight99]: You're no one. The mask creates an anonymous identity for you. It's easy to take off, and in order to avoid detection by the Templars' security algorithms, its effects only last one day. Tomorrow, you'll be someone else. Here, let me program in your temporary username. How does Aneira_042 sound? We'll pretend your name's Neira.

Raine nodded her assent, though she didn't like this one bit. Would she have to live every day here pretending she was someone else? She made a mental note to try and lucid dream her way out of it, but the girl had the distinct feeling this was beyond her power to change.

"Hopefully you won't have to do this for long," Gerrit said, as if reading her mind.

She wasn't sure if she believed him.

[NinjaMageKnight99]: Those Developers don't have infinite resources. Over time, if we keep low and things quiet down, there's a good chance they'll stop chasing you. And if they don't, I'll make them.

He took her hand and walked towards the town.

Raine tried not to show it, but she felt a real weight lifting from her heart.

"Two beds, please," Gerrit asked the innkeeper, and went off to join Raine in the tavern for some dinner.

By the warm fireplace, they had delicious salmon with some ginger beer, and listened merrily to the comedy troupe lighting up the homely stage. Most of the other patrons were hardened adventurers accustomed to seeing the same faces day in and day out, and the young couple's presence lit up the room.

"This place is wonderful," Raine whispered to Gerrit. Although the tavern was loud and the people boisterous, neither had trouble hearing the other.

Under the table, Chance munched on his filet, curled up against Raine's feet.

Even Gerrit allowed himself to relax. As far as first dates go, this one wasn't so bad. Of course, sooner or later he'd have to tell Raine why he was following her. But right now, none of that mattered. Her gentle eyes were the only two things on his mind. As they held each other's gaze, smiling, Raine started up in shock.

Huh. A déjà vu. Or was it? She tried to look objectively at the situation, to see if it was at all familiar. Parts of it were. The warm fire. The seafood.

And the boy in front of me... could it be? Is this the prince from my recurring memory? Curse it, why can't I remember his face? Am I losing my mind that fast?

"Raine? Want a refill on the ginger beer?"

"Oh, sure. I'll be right back."

She excused herself to use the restroom. The girl washed her face and stared down her unfamiliar reflection in the mirror.

He's Gerrit. He's a good guy. Not your dream boy. Dream boy doesn't exist. Say it.

Lifting her hand, she placed it against the one belonging to her doppelganger.

"Your other dream boy doesn't exist, Raine. But let's give this one a chance."

"I agree," the doppelganger replied. "He might be a hallucination and a bit of a stalker, but he's all right."

When the comedy troupe finished their act, a band came onstage and played a merry set. Raine laughed as the crowd turned into a bouncing blob of bodies, but Gerrit took her hand and they went and made fools of themselves on the dance floor.

The girl's gentle green eyes were still on Gerrit's mind as he soaked in the hot tub late that night, finished up the day's regulated school work lest he have a scholar reprimand him, dressed into a modest sleeping outfit, and stood guard outside the door as his companion took a most refreshing shower.

Chance continued to keep Raine's feet warm as she lay awake. Gerrit had shown her how to activate the holographic display on the domed ceiling with a wave of her arm, and she wished she could spend the whole night lying in bed, surfing through the various channels – the night sky filled with stars, a mood-lit aquarium, the view from the bridge of a spaceship, and many more.

Turning to her side, facing Gerrit's silhouette through the fuzzied divider, she mouthed a simple "thank you." Raine took off the mask and prepared for a sound sleep.

This time, she begged and pleaded with fate.

If this is still just a dream, please let me stay here, at least for one more day.

On second thought, don't take me back.

I don't ever want to go back.

That night, she dreamt both everything, and nothing.

Raine woke with a start, and lost all dream recall. The room still wasn't Agnes' condo. And Gerrit was gone.

Chance had nudged her awake, purring with a sense of immediacy. In his mouth was the strange mask. Raine didn't quite understand until she heard a loud banging. She slipped it on just in time, for the door burst open and Raine, now fully disguised, sprung up in shock at two men in the midst of battle.

Gerrit dodged the taller man's rapier and took two steps forward. He pushed up with his forearm-mounted shield and smashed him hard on the nose.

Laughing, the man swished and stabbed at Gerrit, drawing blood just underneath his ribcage.

Raine gasped in horror, but her friend jumped to safety.

Seeing her awake and safely disguised, the boy twitched three fingers on his left hand and made a fist, activating a Stasis spell that froze the man's hand to his weapon.

"Ha! So I see you've learned a thing or two," the man chuckled. "Very good, Gerrit. Very good."

The man closed his eyes for a second. He seemed to be glowing with heat. The ice around his hand melted into a puddle on the floor. He tossed the rapier from his burning right hand to his left and quickly slid a handful of knives from a fanny pack.

"Let's see how you dance," he quipped, tossing enchanted knife after knife at Gerrit. "Maybe I'll discover what makes you tick."

The boy spun in mid-air, swiftly evading the blades in an impossible display of agility. A stray knife ricocheted off a lamp, sending shattered porcelain Raine's way. Luckily, the shards vanished before hitting her, and the lamp began to piece itself back together.

Before long the mystery man had drained his handful of weapons, and was looking quite peeved. He tossed his rapier at Gerrit, who caught it in mid-air merely inches from his face.

"Impossible," he muttered.

"You mad, bro?" Gerrit laughed.

Gerrit screamed out a war cry, twisted the rapier around in his hand, and tossed it straight through the other man's chest. The swordsman stood there, defeated, as Gerrit cast a spell that set the weapon on fire.

Flames engulfed the body, which fell to its knees and disappeared in a puff of magical smoke, leaving a disembodied spirit. The apparition shook its head.

A notification banner spanned the room: "We have a winner: *NinjaMageKnight99!*"

"This turn of events disappoints me," the spirit harrumphed. "I forfeit the match, but you are in my domain, and by my decree this shall not count towards either of our win/loss records and will have no bearing on the rankings, nor shall you receive your share of the experience points. If you take issue with that, then I will summon an Arbiter, in which case I can guarantee you will find it difficult to challenge anyone again, not to mention I'm sure he wouldn't look kindly on your code modifications."

"Sheesh, take it easy," Gerrit laughed. "I get it. I was just having a little fun, your Dukeishness. Next time I'll go easier on you."

The ghost took a swig from a flask and inspected Raine, who had not a single clue who or what she resembled, only that she felt pain in her lower back.

Now that the chaos was over, she was able to read the username above his head, which read: *Duke Ricard Stabbington, the Third.*

"I beg your utmost forgiveness, mademoiselle. Had I known that such a vision of loveliness was asleep in this chamber, I should not have broached it," he said to Raine before turning to Gerrit. "Is this lovely specimen your newest prospect, my beau?"

"Not exactly," Gerrit admitted. "We're just friends."

The man's ghost looked her up and down.

"I thought so. She is a bit... advanced for you."

Ricard approached and held out his hand. Raine offered hers; he took it between his and kissed it. Its ghostly texture gave Raine the feeling that someone was breathing cool air on her. He was probably in his early thirties, dressed like a nineteenth century French nobleman, and he played the part with an admirable intensity.

His charms, however, were lost on Raine, who was still waking up, and more than a little weirded out that a ghost was kissing her hand.

"I fear that our encounter has left you in a state of fright. Again, I apologize. This boy and I had a score to settle, but I would put it off for a lifetime if it would give you a nano-second's peace of mind."

"Indeed," Gerrit mocked, placing his hand on the Duke's shoulder. "Duke Stabbington, this is Neira. She's asked me to run her through the Forbidden Tower."

The Duke gave out a shrill, curt laugh.

"Miss Neira, surely you don't trust this under-geared fool to take you through one of the most difficult dungeons on this server alone. You're better off with a real man."

Raine was flustered. She looked at Gerrit, wondering what to say. He rolled his hands, as if to say, 'go with it'.

"Why, that is a very generous offer, but I couldn't possibly impose on you, Sir Stabbington," Raine said, trying her best to sound regal.

The Duke bowed dramatically before her, seemingly touched by her performance.

"Please, call me Ricard. And it's no imposition, as our destinations are one and the same. I don't believe in coincidence. Fate must have drawn me here today."

Raine completely failed at concealing the redness in her cheeks.

"If you insist, S-sir Ricard. I cannot deny such a generous offer, but in truth, I'm quite new to this world. I wouldn't know where to start."

"Worry not, mademoiselle. As for the fighting, leave that to me. My troupe and I shall be waiting downstairs."

With that, he swished his cape, flashing his golden lion crest, and vacated the room.

"What was that all about?" Raine asked of Gerrit.

"Oh, just a friendly rivalry. He's one of the *'Verse's* 'hero' players. His job is to be part of the scenery by day and party like a royal all night. The pay and perks are great, but it's basically a full-time position. One of his duties includes making newbies feel welcome."

"So you basically maneuvered him into taking me through a dungeon? Sorry, I still don't think I understand what's going on."

"It works like this – his posse and I will power through the tower, and take you along for the ride. He's got a good crew, so we should be out in time for dinner. It's loaded with enemies, and that means Gold and experience. All you'll have to think about is where to put your status and skill points, and you can always change them around later if you feel like it."

Raine thought about this for a bit. She wasn't yet sure what she thought of the Duke, but if doing this meant less stress on Gerrit and that she could better defend herself, there were no arguments there. Plus, running through a dungeon? It sounded kind of fun.

"You don't have to do this," continued Gerrit. "It'll be easy enough to tell him that you've changed your mind, although he did seem quite smitten with you."

"No, I want to," Raine said. "I don't want to be a burden. I want to learn how to defend myself."

Gerrit made for the broken doorway, which was in the process of self-repair. He gave Raine a look of confidence.

"Just for the record, you haven't been a burden to me, not one bit. Take your time."

Raine studied herself in the bathroom mirror. She was stunned by her appearance – now all curves, she looked like a princess in her mid-to-late twenties, and her chest had filled out to an absurd level. She wondered how she was going to fit into her old outfit, but to her surprise the garments adjusted accordingly as soon as she selected them from her inventory, leaving her pajamas and old socks on the floor.

"I wonder who I'm going to wake up as tomorrow," she told Chance, who only mewed and played with her old socks before she ran them through the 'laundry' compartment of her bag. Like the rest of her clothes, they were instantly cleaned.

Before long, Raine came down the stairs and walked out to the town square, which was packed with powerful fellows showing off their armor and spoils. Chance floated by alongside her, as if eager to meet Ricard's company. Ricard anxiously introduced her to his professional team of treasure hunters – Valerie, a bunny-eared woman in a jet-black ninja suit with crossbows mounted on both arms, Samuel, a hulking cyclops whose axe was as wide as his chest, Soren, a friendly-looking druid and summoner who sported animalistic features on his jolly face, and Cooke, an icy woman in a flowing black and white robe whose two-headed serpent staff housed opposite but powerful energies.

Finally, there was Ricard himself, who'd revived to human form and was now decked out in a classy suit of golden armor.

"It's very nice to meet you all," Raine said with a polite curtsy, which she thought would fit her new character.

"The feeling is mutual, Neira," bowed Soren, and the hawks perched on his shoulders followed suit. "I see your familiar is completely resistant to Arcane Magic. He'll be a great help to us."

Chance did a mid-air somersault in recognition.

"Welcome to *Avidya*," Valerie said, sheepishly avoiding her gaze.

"Stay close to me," Cooke said softly. Her voice sounded like a faint winter wind whistling through a tunnel. "I'm the healer, but I'm doing triple duty as a buffing caster and all-around mage. If you're hurt or need any ailments cured, don't hesitate to ask."

Raine wasn't sure what to say, so she nodded and thanked everyone again as they partied up and shared their Health and Mana information.

They made a quick stop at an apprentice blacksmith, where Raine purchased an EtherUnreal Robe, an Almost Decent Staff, a Half-Hardy Shield, and a Spellbind +1 Circlet, for she'd decided that she was going to try her hand at being a witch. Gerrit lent her a couple of extra accessories, helping pump up her defense and resistance, and took a minute to max out his supply of Chimera Wings with Yossa's funds.

He put his arm around her in a friendly manner as they walked out from the town and back into the forest, this time towards the ominous tower. There was a quick stop for breakfast.

[NinjaMageKnight99]: "You doing all right, Raine?"

Seeing her real name snapped the girl out of her thoughts. Raine simply nodded, realizing that she was being somber and displaying signs of nervousness.

To the others, I probably just look anxious because I'm a beginner. Normally I'd love to get in on this sort of thing.

Only, every alarm system in my body is telling me that something is very wrong... Usually, I listen to that voice, but this is my big chance to grow stronger in this world, and that might help me beat it, or get to SBB, whichever comes first. Sure, I'm a little scared. But how can I possibly turn back from this?

Raine often learned the hard way how stubbornly she would persist, steeling herself to meet any challenge head-on.

Another data storm made landfall just as the party entered the looming tower.

XII. Brother Thaddius

"Emancipate yourselves from mental slavery; none but ourselves can free

our minds." – Bob Marley (adapted from Marcus Garvey)

In the heart of the multi-tiered, planetarium-sized *Avidya* Server Control chamber, hundreds of screens zeroed in on the well-armed group as they crossed the threshold into the Forbidden Tower and displayed their findings around the real-time holo-miniature of the dungeon.

Here were six of the most highly regarded warriors in the realm, and they were expertly escorting a Level 2 weakling into a deathtrap.

Between other tasks, the Queen had been watching idly since the night previous, expecting something, anything, to come to light from either Raine or Gerrit about Lily's master plan. Instead, she was forced to endure the couple's light flirting, which seemed to result in little to no progress on either end.

"Take them in," Lacie had urged her in private. "Freeze her. The girl's role is unclear to me, but I know Gerrit is a key player in the operation. The boy was there, at the end. Wake him up, convert him to our cause, and he'll become a valuable asset."

Queen Lorelei, however, remained silent on the matter. General Lacie was head of national security, but her experience was with the outside world. She had little knowledge of the workings of *Endless Metaverse.*

The way things were looking, Raine seemed merely a dumb pawn with an unsavory data trail, and freezing her would reveal nothing of Lily's bigger picture. The boy was the powerful one with connections, and to make things worse, his account, like hers, was patched in from an untraceable pirate signal. The Admiral would undoubtedly have a backup plan. Perhaps Raine was just a clever diversion, but the data storms had her thinking otherwise.

More could be gained by watching and waiting. But to pass up this opportunity might prove to be a fatal error.

When Queen Lorelei had broached the problem of the persistent data storms to her advisers, she was faced with a wall of silence.

"No bright ideas? No one? Anyone?"

Filled with rage, she took the manual controls in hand and twisted a small knob, which had the expected result of all her senior staff members clutching their heads in absolute agony as she overloaded their nano-machines with corrupted data.

"I may have dumbed down the education system too thoroughly. I cannot believe how incompetent you all are," the Queen said bitterly. "I'll take the strings from here. Prepare to relegate control."

A singular voice bellowed from the crowd. "Wait!"

She released the knob. The pain ceased, albeit temporarily. It was the man Holdfast, who'd just assumed his new office that very day. Every eye in the room was on him, with most as thankful for his interjection as they were fearful for his life.

"If you'll pardon me, Your Grace," the young man began, "I would like to propose an experiment."

"What for?" Queen Lorelei replied.

"To see just how important this Raine is to Enemy Number One. We may be able to kill two birds with one stone."

"Go on."

"As long as she remains connected from the same source and doesn't use her visor, the target cannot be traced. Her access point is heavily encrypted. There is a possibility that triggering d-mat and forcing re-spawn from a central access point will create a blip in her connection. From there, we can run a remote trace. As for baiting the trap, it's a simple matter of scaling mechanics," he posited. "This is the perfect opportunity. We turn the tower into a total deathtrap with a few surprises at the end. If Raine is close to death, Lily may make herself present to save her, and we'll have them both in the bag. If Lily doesn't show, we'll nab them both."

The Queen gave him the slightest of nods.

"Mr. Holdfast, I like the way you think. There's other business I must attend to, so I'm leaving this in your hands. You have free reign over the tower. Kill the virus before it spreads any further."

√

Lady Claire Alexandria skipped out on her weekly managerial duties to wait eagerly in the living room. On the tubes, some *Metaverse* reality show was on its season finale, broadcasting Developer-crafted, 'true-life' melodramas worldwide.

The 'bots had dusted the place spotless, Archie was impeccably groomed, and tea was set for two. The *Raven* had returned; its pilot should be at the door any second now.

Only, Lacie never came. The three-hour season finale ended with all but two players rebooting their accounts. Calls and video messages had gone unanswered. A personal memo to the Queen was ignored. Generals Beech and Macleod were both visiting their families, an unusual portent for the workaholics, especially considering the rumors following Jakarta. All-out war might be just around the corner, yet her fiancée was nowhere to be found.

Claire let the tea grow cold and popped more than the recommended dose of 5-Oma.

I'm turning into a regular Sleeping Beauty here. If there's a price for everything, this is the cost a useless wretch like me pays to chronically avoid pain. I mean, I know I shouldn't be doing this, she thought. *I could be contributing, overseeing the Overseer's work with Marketing Divisions in Sectors Fifty-Three to Sixty.*

That's my duty, isn't it?

Only, today, I couldn't care less. I'm a wreck, but I'm also a symptom of this miserable system. Lame as it is, at the very least, that's something I can be honest about.

Envious of the carefree denizens of *Endless Metaverse,* Claire drifted off into her own personal fantasy land.

∩

Chance's body glowed even more intensely than usual, its light competing with the growing darkness and brightening the path for the advancing party. Soren took one of many torches that lined the walls.

They could hear other players involved in skirmishes ahead, and it wasn't long before the company encountered a cadre of reanimated skeletons.

Raine was told to lure them in, and that by drawing simple runes with her staff held high, she could cast a handful of weak elemental spells to slow the undead minions.

Valerie loosed poison arrows at their chests, Soren summoned dire wolves to gnaw at their bones, Samuel lopped off the heads of the ones that got close, and Gerrit and Cooke took care to guard the back end.

They felled about three hundred walking skeletons before they reached the old-fashioned elevator and headed up to the second floor.

Raine checked her stats. She'd jumped from Level 2 to 7.

"I don't remember there being so many of them," Gerrit said in between exhausted breaths. He slipped on his visor as the lift moved ever so slowly up the shaft.

"There aren't supposed to be," Ricard reflected.

He shot Raine a quick glance, as if testing her reaction.

Raine shivered as she fumbled to assign her skill points before they reached the next floor.

She felt ready to tell everyone, to warn them that someone powerful was trying to harm her. *Wasn't it wrong to keep something that like that a secret?* But on the other hand, if these people knew that she was a fugitive, they might fall into deep trouble with the Templars. The less they know, the better it might be for them in the long run.

These relatively minor worries evaporated in the face of the ghastly horrors that awaited her on the pitch-black second floor.

Ghosts flooded the party, and it was all Raine could do to keep up with her allies' advance. Cooke hurriedly cast a protective spell over her, and Raine shot minor spells at the dangerous banshees while the rest of the troupe moved forward while rotating, shields up, White Magic spells at the ready. Chance dimmed his coat.

The constant flashes of light were blinding, and just keeping her bearings became a difficult task for poor Raine. She began to feel delirious, and bumped into Gerrit more than once. The boy locked his arm around hers, and helped her evade enemy attacks – just one hit from these monsters and she'd be out for the count.

By the time they reached the elevator to the third floor, everyone was exhausted. Cooke passed around healing items instead of spells, and seemed miffed about having to use an item to replenish her pool of Mana so early on.

"There must be something amiss with this infernal tower," Samuel grumbled.

"Maybe they're making it extra special today, just for us," Soren chimed in with a chuckle.

"This is no laughing matter," the hulking man retorted. "If I die right now, I'm losing a fortnight's worth of experience."

"Nothing ventured, nothing gained," piped Valerie, swapping out her anti-poltergeist defense charms for ones that offered fire resistance. "I for one welcome a challenge."

"You don't have to say it out loud, woman," whispered Samuel. "They're probably going to make the next floor twice as annoying now, no thanks to you."

The elevator dinged to a sudden stop.

Before them was a narrow labyrinth, with dizzying walls of fire and strange multi-limbed creatures hopping in and out of the flames. It was impossible to tell where their heads were, and their legs morphed into tentacles that, suspiciously enough, kept going straight for Raine.

Sensing this pattern, the party was able to overcome the bizarre demons by using Raine as bait, but the constant heat from the combusting walls leading to multiple dead ends and false pathways left the party fatigued by the time they reached the next elevator a sweaty, charred mess.

Samuel shook his head at Valerie, who said nothing and hung her head – her delicate ears were singed in at least three places. Cooke passed around some burn salve. Raine had a few minor burns but declined the item, as the others needed it far more, and she had a plethora of skill points to assign.

She had just reached Level 13.

Everyone held their breath for the next floor, which saw them struggling in a room without gravity. Gerrit took Raine's hand and helped her push off of pillars for traction, all the while slicing up parasitic leeches. One of them latched onto Soren as he was in the midst of commanding his three trusty hawks, and the druid began to hallucinate, sending the birds to attack his party members.

Ricard and Cooke flew back to help their summoner. An entire pack of the leeches leapt out in ambush and halted their advance. Valerie's poison weapons had no effect on them, and Gerrit and Samuel were busy fending off the possessed birds. Raine split from Gerrit to heal her allies.

Suddenly, a figure launched out of the opposite elevator at top speed. It rebounded off a support arch and smashed into Soren, knocking him into a marble pillar. The mysterious dark-skinned man, whom Raine could now see was dressed in the garb of a monk, grabbed the druid's neck and squeezed.

Everyone was aghast. It looked like the monk was choking poor Soren. But as the druid opened his jaws to breathe, the monk quickly uncorked a bottle and placed it against Soren's lips, carefully massaging his throat.

The monk suddenly realized that without gravity to ease the liquid down his patient's esophagus, he had to resort to desperate measures. He forced Soren's mouth and nose closed, and while gasping for breath Soren drew in the strange medicine, fell into a choking fit, and almost immediately snapped back into normal consciousness.

Without delay, the hawks halted their assault and flew over to help Ricard and Cooke. Gerrit and Samuel followed, bouncing from pillar to pillar.

"I am in your debt," Soren said to his savior as they reached a safe landing. "Thank you."

"I require no thanks," the monk replied. "I ask only for your assistance and companionship in fighting the main boss. I shall explain once everyone has gathered."

Before entering the elevator, the party took a much-needed rest, restoring their Health, Stamina, and Mana, and dividing the few pieces of loot, most of which went to Raine. Cooke sat and meditated, hastening the regeneration of her spent energies. Valerie and Soren made some booster sandwiches. They were all low on healing items.

"My name is Thaddius," began the monk in a deep voice soft as a clear brook on a lazy summer day. His presence was soothing to Raine; in many ways, he reminded her of Jordan.

"I was on the top floor of this tower, taming the dragon-spawn and negotiating to trade my wares for emerald scales when it happened. The ground began shifting beneath my feet. Players around me were swallowed up in warp portals, presumably sent out of the tower. I activated my maxed out Iron Leg technique, keeping my feet rooted at all costs. Despite its best efforts, the portal seemed to pass me over. I have been visiting this very location almost daily to gather scales to line our temple, and nothing like this has ever happened. I knew instinctively that this was a sign."

"What kind of sign?" Raine asked.

"The very best kind," the monk replied. "I believe this is an indication that the chosen one has come, and is in need of protection."

Samuel guffawed.

"Don't tell me you're one of those damn Doomsdayers... how is anything a sign of anything except for cruelty on the part of the Developers? Answer me that, holy man. There will be no chosen one. It's a myth passed down to give us poor lot some hope, so we'll be easier to subjugate."

Thaddius' smile did not waver.

"Please tell me about this chosen one," Raine asked. "I'm curious."

"It's a fairy tale, my dear Neira, nothing more," Ricard told her. He was beginning to think this maiden far too innocent for his liking.

"Reality is oft stranger than fiction," the monk continued. "Many Truth-seekers, including myself, believe there is at least one enlightened being in this world, a person who has retained the experience of higher forms of consciousness, one who has seen outside of this virtual prison, and whose quest is to show us the way out. This individual will free our minds of this realm and take us to a place of blissed-out-ness and understanding beyond our limited perspectives."

"Where's your proof, man?" Samuel interjected. "Talk of some outside world is useless. Anyone coming forgets it, anyone going never comes back."

"Faith is never about proof," Thaddius replied. "That said, our conclusions are based on first-hand experience, not dogma. Consciousness operates on a higher level than this virtual stuff we think of as matter. Our limited language cannot broach the deepest inner truths. Here's something to think about: at the monastery, we have been able to ascertain and even record snippets of knowledge of the outside world. Many have left this realm for a higher reality, and a few have even returned with visions of a dying wasteland. Naturally, it's not common knowledge. I can provide links for those interested."

Raine noticed that everyone was watching Thaddius intently. This was news to most of the adventurers.

"Your people are still spouting debunked rumors from version 2.0, I see. I won't believe a thing until I see it with my own eye," Samuel said gruffly, pointing at his singular eye.

"Then good for you, Sam," Soren interjected. "Although I won't bother to cite the irony involved in the trust you assign to any of your five senses, or those of the *Metaverse* edutainers, in a completely artificial construct."

"What?" Samuel blinked.

"He's saying shut up and let the man speak," Cooke interjected. "Save your wrath for the blood-wraiths on the next floor. We could be brains in a vat for all we know."

Ricard cleared his throat. "I apologize on behalf of my companions. Brother Thaddius, pray continue your account of the business on the top floor."

"Of course, Sir Stabbington," Thaddius began with a slight nod. "But first, I'd like to ask Ms. Cooke to elaborate on her theory."

The mage's pale cheeks turned bright red; Raine reasoned that she probably wasn't used to being put on the spot, but this man exuded some pretty cool vibes.

"Well, basically, I think there's no point in getting worked up over peaceful belief systems," she added. "Even your visions may be coded in. We could all be programs thinking we're human. The Chosen One theory is just one of many equally valid others."

"On the contrary, this unreal realm is binary. As to the nature of reality, there can be a billion possibilities, but logically, only one true one, sister," Thaddius replied. "And all the more reason for us to seek. If we are brains in a vat, then whose vat is it? To what purpose are we here? These remain the most pertinent questions of our day." He paused. "If there are no further inquiries, might I return to my story?"

Raine nodded vigorously, barely following this foray into metaphysics, before noticing that Gerrit was enraptured by their conversation. In any case, there were no further interruptions.

"As I was saying, the portal had passed me over, and the entire floor was reset. Only, it didn't return to its default settings. The dragon-spawn I'd worked weeks to befriend suddenly turned against me. I rushed down to the floor below, and saw that the creatures bested on my way up the tower had returned to life, stronger than ever."

"Bummer," Gerrit said. "But you continued to descend?"

"Yes. It was a long shot, but I had faith that if I kept running downwards, I'd find another group of adventurers. This is no coincidence, young Gerrit. 'Tis our karma."

"Karma shawarma. This is ludicrous!" Samuel roared. "Don't tell me this madness is gonna go on for twenty more floors!"

"It doesn't have to," the monk piped in, and opened an outstretched palm.

The crystal within enkindled the atrium, and the hearts of the hunting party. Heedless of the dangers, the adventurers fist-bumped and seemed to mellow out at this turn of events.

"What is it?" Raine quietly asked Gerrit.

"It's a warp portal activator," Thaddius replied. "It'll take us up to the second to last floor."

The party readied themselves, and Raine straightened out her gear. It was time to get the hell out of Dodge.

↔

Wiping the sweat from his brow, Henry paced around the upper console, ordering around his crack team of various Lead Developers as he downed a glass of whisky. Down below, the portly Lead Hoshua and his Maintenance Officer, Marco, were arguing over raising airship taxes for ferries between *Avidya's* four continents to slow congestion.

That's right, gentlemen. Just keep your eyes off the prize.

"All right, people. If you're placing bets, now's the time."

The familiar click-clacking of heels accompanied a lovely face as Dr. Ayumi Karuishi rounded a corner from the *Tanha* shortcut and offered him a glowing key, hopefully containing several essential security protocols for the HDP.

"Good morning, love," he said in a teasing tone. "You look even more dolled up than usual today."

"Flattery will get you nowhere, Holdfast," she joked.

Henry raised an eyebrow. His Holo-Lens downloaded the relevant data from the key. He returned it to the good Doctor, all but forcing himself to hold eye contact.

"Seriously, though, what are you doing after work?"

"Ask me in an hour. I'm needed at *Tanha*; the player-built maps are getting out of hand."

Ayumi took Henry's hand and gave it a light squeeze before parting. Noticing his subordinates' eyes on him, Henry coughed loudly.

"Quit your gawking. I want that boss to take them down."

One of the cheeky Devs seized the day, putting on a horrid mockery of an Australian accent. "With a capital 'D', sir? Shall we dress ol' Bob's-your-uncle up in tight leather?"

The platform erupted in a round of sniggering.

"With a— oh, I see what you did there, mate, good 'un," Henry began in jest, before looming over his seated subordinate. This was the same prankster that spiked his coffee with laxative at the last *Nexus* party. He studied the nervous kid for a good few excruciating seconds before responding with a whisper.

"Conor, is it? Well, Conor, it's all fun and games, right? Messing around with the new boss, I get it. I'm a reasonable man. But hear this. Let's say a porpoise wants to know how to make it with a lady porpoise. I'll bet you a hundred beans he won't succeed by making an enemy of sharks. This ain't your Daddy's *Metaverse,* or even Sir Stephenson's; we're dealing with terrorists here. Try pulling the wool over me once more and see if you're let off with a warning. So how's about I hear a little less cheek out of you, and expect you to do your ruddy job, eh? Would that be acceptable?"

Trapped by the air of growing hostility, the kid nodded and returned to work.

"Good man. We'll get a brew sometime."

Henry took another swig amongst the murmurings of his subordinates.

₪

Deep in the middle of the *Spire* is a little-used throne room, deemed off-limits to all but the most elite rulers of the land. Queen Lorelei had long insisted that it be tended to and guarded by androids, for it was also a comprehensive museum, with countless treasures too priceless and beautiful to be seen by lower mortals.

Yet here the Queen was, instructing the Seven Lords, glorified Sector Managers hailing from every corner of the globe. They were gathered on bended knee, swearing their allegiance. The provincial rulers had been summoned forth to rally in support for a large-scale conflict to end a supposed takeover plot against *Neo Eden*, the very heart of modern civilization.

Many of their assets, bodies sold and minds sworn to *Endless Metaverse*, could die in this battle, she warned them. Their sacrifices were absolutely essential to preserving the world she envisioned.

The lords, surely out of fear, and perhaps a little out of love, bowed in reverence to her silky voice and decisive command unquestioningly, offering the lives of their people as a necessary loss. Otherwise, it was sure to be their heads on the chopping block.

"Our armies are guaranteed victory over any foe," she explained. "As you know, most uninitiated soldiers lack the will and courage to fight without any instinct of self-preservation. Our latest *M-Gear* defense protocols ensure that even the weakest, least physically fit asset can be put to use in warfare. Brain functions are enhanced by artificial intelligences, gifting subjects with perfect aim, zero hesitation, and advanced virtual combat training. With thirty years of programming and a flawless field ops record, our system is near perfect. The *Eden* Armada, our fleet of drones, and city-wide anti-air artillery will provide full support."

A well-edited holographic demonstration of the test subjects carrying out orders in both real records and virtual scenarios played to much head nodding and overall approval.

The lords praised her plan once more, applauding at images of fallen freedom fighters and annexed rebel fortresses. Then again, they would have licked her heels if she had wanted. There was nothing interesting about these subjugated dimwits.

She imagined their thoughts, their fears, and their selfish schemes. Jakarta was far from a flawless op, but not a one dared challenge her judgment. To quash their enemies' spirits, known rebel operations in Chile, Saudi Arabia, Glasgow, and Philadelphia had been set under siege by local *Geared* forces.

If anyone had any qualms about her plans for an all-out war, they were too spoiled by their guaranteed positions to care. Or perhaps they valued their lives over those of hundreds of thousands of their subjects, their primary workforce, and knew that in *Neo Eden* even the smallest suggestion could be viewed as criminal insubordination.

"Business is over. You will have your orders in the morning. Be gone with you," Queen Lorelei intoned.

The lords bowed, each in turn, before being promptly escorted off the premises by the Queen's heavy-duty security droids. These chaperones accompanied each lord during their entire visit of the city, recording their actions and everyday lives, which would be presented to the Overseer and edited for the Queen once the lords' offices were up for review.

She requested for the double doors to be kept open, and watched them leave, one by one, marching in single file, unable to speak to one another in private.

Once the last of their shadows had disappeared into the noontime sun, the Queen leaned back in her seat, commanded her weather-regulating nano-bots to provide enough cloud cover to take the heat down a few degrees, and peeled a yellow peach.

The anticipation of it all was eating her alive, but she tried not to show it.

Endgame drew close. It had been seven Earth years since her reign was formally challenged.

Seven years was a long time to keep such an important person waiting, and among the most troublesome burdens of her enhanced brain remained her infallible memory banks.

The date was St. Valentine's Day, 2180 A.D.

"Lorelei!" the voice boomed out through the marbled hall outside the chamber as a diminutive figure marched across the crimson carpet like an ant treading a ribbon. Two droids flanked the stern-looking thirteen-year-old on either side.

The Queen laughed from atop her dais, her voice echoing around the empty room. Beside her, Lacie gave out a forced chuckle. She was sweating, almost nervous, her weakness showing.

For her part, Lorelei had been looking forward to this for two hundred years. Trusting metal over man, she dismissed the Royal Guard, leaving only Lily's escorts.

"Dear Lillian, it's Queen Lorelei to you, but I'll forgive that first offense. I'm so happy you finally joined us."

"A thousand pardons, O Queenie. I didn't even recognize you. But that might just be the wrinkles talking," Lily leered. "You've got some city miles, judging by those skin grafts."

Lorelei fought the urge to end her former Captain's life then and there. Patience was necessary for the ultimate humiliation.

"At least I am something to look at. You're as ragged as the day I left you. Those ugly metal limbs must make it a pain to shower."

Ignoring her, Lily inspected the chamber at a leisurely pace, arms crossed. She stopped just short of the gas lamps lining the dais like an altar and glanced at the various artifacts from every imaginable point in history haphazardly arranged, the cleaning and security droids tailing her every move.

She shook her head.

"Are you not impressed with my gallery?" The Queen asked.

The younger girl was engrossed in one of her cabinets, reinforced with shatterproof glass.

"You're missing one of the Mona Lisas, but I see you recovered the Dead Sea Scrolls," Lily said, raising an eyebrow. "Good restoration job on the Rosetta stones. I'll admit you've got quite the collection here. The greatest plunder of the ages, all kept in one reinforced chamber of death."

"Ah, but your eyes deceive you. This… is a chamber of life," the Queen insisted. "Completely solar-proofed. Once sealed, it will stand as a monument until the sun turns Red Giant and swallows this rock. This is our race's final message to any other forms of life out there, our testament that we were here, and that we failed to achieve anything of lasting importance. Human civilization nears its end. It's… thirty-three years from now, isn't it?"

"Closer to thirty-two," replied Lily. "I don't trust your creepy android valets with my shuttle, so let's get straight to the point. I see what you've done. Outstanding. What foresight. What deliberation you must have taken."

"Anything unexpected?" Lorelei queried.

"To be honest, I thought you might have fostered the technological singularity and led a world of cyborgs, or even droids," mused Lily. "Instead, you've installed a glass ceiling on AI development. I guess you're more human than I thought."

"It had crossed my mind," she replied. "While they are little more than a means to our ends, I had every reason to feed the evolving *machina* and subvert this *Sturm und Drang*. But then, you wouldn't have had anything to fight for. And to us, that's no fun at all."

The girl ground her teeth, probably close to lashing out. "Has this encounter gone according to plan?"

Lorelei scoffed. "Somewhat."

"And how about you, Lacie? Are you enjoying yourself?"

Lacie looked to Lorrie, who gave her an expressionless reply.

"Yes," she said. "I wouldn't dream of doing anything else."

Lily sized her up as best she could from far below the towering throne. Lorelei knew those probing eyes all too well. The girl was trying to determine how much of Lacie's placid response was due to any threats by her Queen. The crazed look in the General's eyes would have told Lillian that if there was something there, now was not the time to try and coax it out.

"In order to get back at me for trying to save mankind, you've turned the world completely upside down," said Lily. "Now you've got everyone bowing to you, happy as frogs in a pot of water. Little do they know they're soon to be boiled alive. I applaud your spirit of experimentation, and major points on the, um, headgear. Very... creative."

The Queen yawned. "I think this is the part where you ask me to step down."

"It's time, Lorelei. I'm asking you nicely. You've had your fun. Return the TD power converter and fuel cells."

"Temporally speaking, you aren't going anywhere. How did the expression go? Right. You can pry your machine components from my cold, dead hands."

Lily clenched her fists. "Two centuries pass and you've gotten no wiser! Please. Your point is taken. You rule this world. Now just let me send one message back in time!"

"Give me a single reason why I should permit you to destroy countless more universes."

"Because there's only one universe! Because your way is not a solution. Because without emigrating these people off Earth, they will all die. I can give you a million more," Lily argued. "In fact, let me pick your brain for a bit. Do you still intend to be up on that throne, in this supposedly radiation-proof tomb, while one and a half billion people burn alive in the most horrific way imaginable? Every one of your chrome-topped androids will be radioactive. Do you even have a plan to survive the solar flare, or are you too busy playing God?"

Queen Lorelei shook her head sadly.

"Sol's wrath is completely out of our control. Our plan is to give these people the freedom to die happily. We want to spare them any more pain. And when the time comes, we will join them in death."

"How can that be your answer?" Lily almost whispered in disbelief. "Lacie, we--"

"We tried to change the world," Lacie replied, cutting her off. "We were out of our depth. Think of the trillions upon trillions of life forms in this universe. We Earthlings may not be alone. I will not take responsibility for resetting their lives."

"The problem, ladies, is that the Temporal Drive has no power to do such a thing," argued Lily. "Whether we exist in a single universe, a holographic Universe, or a Multiverse, time course-corrects. Otherwise, none of us would be here. Shall we conduct joint experiments on the matter? I would be more than willing--"

"No," said Lorelei. "Our principles have been set."

Lily had nothing left to say. The Queen was satisfied. Now Lily knew. Hers and Lacie's beliefs would not be shaken.

"Then we are at an impasse."

"Indeed."

"If this is what you really believe, then I pity you. I had... hoped that things might be different. It was nice catching up, guys. I'm generous enough to grant you six years to change your mind. Then, I won't be able to stop what will happen on the seventh. You can find me in your precious *Metaverse*. Here's my card. We can discuss the terms of engagement when you're good and ready."

Lily took a business card from her purse and placed it by her feet.

With a mock bow and curtsy, she spun on her heel, stuck her hands in her pockets, and calmly walked out of the throne room, down the carpeted hallway, and out towards the thick ceramic double-doors leading to the courtyard balcony, where the Queen could just barely make out a tattered old shuttle, its engine still running. The android guards resumed their posts.

Lorelei took a deep breath. Recognizing the gesture, Lacie lit her a cigarette.

"I think she's angry," the Queen intoned with mock concern.

The two shared a laugh and headed upstairs for some entertainment.

Those were good days, Queen Lorelei mused, now alone with her thoughts. *My tenure may soon be over.*

She was a woman of science, not superstition, but she never doubted her instincts. The impending storm was not going to be very pleasant, and she wondered if she should have simply killed Lily when she had the chance. *Probably, but now's not the time for regrets.*

Probes had been downed while patrolling mountains in Central Asia and Eastern Europe. Incomplete blueprints of Lillian's Exo Knights had been leaked. The hulking machines were a menace, but Beech insisted that they would never reach the battlefield. He and the careless Macleod seemed to have forgotten reports of the EDC's cloaking tech fooling even their most advanced detectors.

Her thoughts having wandered, Lorelei found herself strolling in the calm blue light of the Spire's massive aquarium. As she watched the whale shark swim about its lonely chamber, a girl of six or seven broke off from her guided school tour and approached her nervously.

The Royal Guard, who'd silently fallen in step behind the Queen upon her entering a public space (a very rare occasion), halted the child's advance. After scanning the girl with her Holo-Lens, the Divine Monarch lifted a palm to stop her protectors and smiled warmly.

"Can I help you, Myra Avalon?"

"Y-y-your Majesty, I j-just wanted to thank you. And, um…"

"Of course."

The Queen posed for a quick picture and autograph.

"Th-thanks, Your Awesomeness! You're the best! Long live *Eden!*"

But is their incompetence merely a veil? I trust my military advisers about as far as I can kick them. It's almost as if they are tempting fate, eager to cull our assets, or to supplant me.

All indications showed that EDC aerial forces were certainly advancing, yet even someone as unpredictable as Lillian Hermes wouldn't dare engage *Neo Eden* in an aerial strike without considering the lives of innocents, whether or not they were *Metaverse* users.

If there's one thing interesting about you, Lillian, it's your stubborn devotion to your principles. Keep this up, and you'll learn the hard way that in order to maintain power, one must forego the luxuries of morality.

As she watched Myra run off to join her gaggle of friends, Queen Lorelei tried not to think of herself as hiding behind human meat shields. After all, she merely expected her subjects to fulfill their sworn duties to her.

XIII. Robert the Necromancer

"If we don't believe in freedom of expression for people we despise, we don't believe in it at all." – Noam Chomsky

The *Belladonna's* Captain paced back and forth across the threshold of her docking bay, waiting impatiently for Rutger to finish prepping the tuned-up *Phoenix* for its re-entry trip. As the dynamic *Metaverse* duo met the Duke's motley crew, Lily considered the distressing results of the outcomes Rutger had computed. Whatever Lorrie or Lacie had seen, the trap they were springing would not be easy to counter.

"Miss Lily, might I suggest sitting down and taking some antacids to aid your digestion? I am reading that your vitals are unfit for atmospheric re-entry."

The captain shook her head and continued pacing. "Fine like this. I'm old enough for you to stop worrying about me. It's embarrassing."

What if I splinter off a segment of the armada to meet them? That will likely just lead Macleod straight to us, though, nullifying our stealth advantage. Our only advantage.

"I am only following my directives," Rutger replied. "It is what your---"

"You want a directive?" she exclaimed, pre-empting the mention of her parents. "Here's a new one for you: stop worrying about me."

"I am incapable of worry. I only show appropriate levels of concern."

Lily massaged her temples and fell into an exercise routine to quell her nervous energy.

And if I switch him out? I'll miss my chance to find out just where the Overseer is located. But is such a solution even ethical? Must I become a demon to fight demons? And damn, my stomach is killing me.

Exhausted from the workout, Lily rinsed herself off in the vacuum shower and plopped into the *Phoenix's* cockpit.

"Um, Rutger?"

"Yes, Miss Lily?"

"On second thought, I think I'll take that antacid."

"A wise choice, Captain."

———

The entire second to last floor of the tower was a large open space. There were no rooms, doors, hallways, corridors, or chests. Gerrit looked dead ahead. It was a straight shot to the elevator across the way, but this apparent transparency only made the party more cautious.

Nothing seemed right. The torches along the pillars were dimmed, and faint shadows danced in the distance. Hate-filled eyes glimmered from the darkness before vanishing. The sounds of shuffling bodies echoed along the walls.

With his left hand, Gerrit held Raine's right with a firm grip and kept her close to him. Determinedly fierce, Chance floated nearby as well, low growls rumbling in his belly.

"There's something positively feral about this floor, Gerrit," Soren whispered as he and his wolves dropped to the back of the party. "'Tis the smell of chaos. I bet my coat this is going to end up like Old Varidus."

Gerrit winced. Soren was right on. This was definitely a trap.

"Just a friendly warning. No need to panic," the druid clarified. "I've got one hell of a summoning stone that I can part with if needs be. We play our cards right, we'll make it out of this without any d-mats. On your toes, and don't look up."

The boy tightened his grasp.

At the head of the party, Samuel let out a sharp cry. An apparition from the shadows had leapt onto his shoulders and dug its claws into him. The cyclops dropped his axe and grabbed onto the creature's slimy neck.

Whoosh!

Valerie's crossbow bolt landed right between the beast's eyes. Without delay, piercing wails erupted in unison from all around the party. Raine shrieked as at least two-dozen of the foul, lizard-like creatures flanked the adventurers, spiraling like carrion birds.

While the others fell into formation around her, Ricard danced around the group, spinning elegantly with a katana in one hand and his trusty rapier in the other, cutting through waves and waves of leaping beasts.

Samuel's spear made short work of the creatures, but they were too many, surrounding the tank at every angle. Cooke cast spells as fast as she could to heal both Samuel and Ricard, who were losing Health and Stamina much faster than they should have. Thaddius, who had taken point, used the lizards' charging momentum to turn them against one another, incapacitating them with judo throws, chops, and kicks.

Chance stunned the beasts with quick lightning spells, pulling aggro and leaving them easy prey for Gerrit's blade.

The red-headed boy was doing all he could to protect Raine, but he seemed to be absorbing the brunt of the attacks, and even his time-slowing abilities had their limits, especially when he was forced to switch targets so often.

Raine cast the few spells she had – a shield-boosting charm to protect her allies, and a minor fire attack that did a little damage over time, and stunned the lizards enough to allow one of her friends to land a second hit.

She wished that Jordan could have been there. As insane as this was, as a fellow skilled gamer, he would have loved to have been in this unusual raiding party.

They were locked in fierce melee with the lizards for what seemed like entirely too much time.

"There's no end to this!" Samuel roared. "Their numbers are only increasing! We must advance to the next floor!"

Ricard shook his head in incredulity. His pride didn't agree with the idea of running away from a battle, but what they were facing was absolute madness.

"Can we make it?" he asked, slicing a lizardman open with one blow.

Valerie took down two with a pair of throwing knives to their hearts, and then clasped her hands together.

"I didn't want to have to use this till the boss," she sighed.

A thundering boom shook the ground.

Gerrit flinched from an attack that would have knocked the sword from his hand. It never came.

It appeared to Raine that the enemies were frozen stiff, but she soon saw that they were actually just moving very slowly.

"Hurry," called Valerie. "We have fifteen seconds! Soren, get over here!"

While the others ran, Soren set up explosive traps for the lizard men to activate as soon as they fell out of Val's special spell. He whistled for his dire wolves to follow and made for the elevator.

Raine huffed and puffed as she was dragged forth, pulled by both Gerrit and Thaddius under lizard men caught in mid-jump and over the hundreds of bodies piled up on the floor. They made it through the doors just as time reverted to normal speed, leaving the lizard men caught in a series of harrowing explosions.

Everyone in the party had nothing but praise for Valerie, whose quick thinking had gotten them all to the top floor without any casualties, and Soren, who had greatly boosted their experience gain. Morale was high. They were ready for anything.

Raine was now Level 20. She equipped a new wand and shield she'd picked up, hastily assigning her points to Health, Agility, Magic, and Mana regeneration.

Cooke handed Raine a magical tome with three party healing spells. Raine studied them as best she could and used her wristwatch to quickly assign them to simple hand movements. She and Chance were going to have to assist with the healing duties this time.

When the doors opened, it was to a horde of eighty dragon-spawn: lizard-like creatures the size of an ambulance, each with four legs and two arms rippling with muscles. Their bodies were covered in weathered scales, jagged teeth lined their mouths, and bladed frills raced down their spines. The savage beasts growled and reared.

Raine stepped out with the others, who fell into a circular formation. She paid close attention to her teammates' HP bars, and cast buffer spells, replenishing her Mana by swallowing bitter herbs whenever she could. The beasts were falling all around them, but the confidence evident in Gerrit's swift movements as he methodically slashed down dragon-spawn after dragon-spawn helped Raine keep her spirits up.

When there were only a dozen left at low life, Thaddius at last was able to trigger his Negotiation skill, calling a truce with the elegant creatures. As he spoke to them in their deep, guttural language, a translation of his words appeared to Raine in subtitles.

"We have no quarrel with you," the monk said. "We will vacate your realm once we defeat your master. Leave now, and live."

The creatures looked one another in the eye and exchanged rasping growls. It was a quick consensus. Their messenger responded.

"Strange changes happen. Many brothers were suddenly summoned, and many have fallen. We do not know where they have come from or where they go. This we must investigate."

The dragon-spawn stood at attention and formed a pathway down the main hall, six on each side. They bowed respectfully to show their defeat. Raine followed the group over to the unsupported stairwell that led up to the tower's roof.

"Have White Magic spells at the ready," Cooke advised her. "We fight the undead."

Raine immediately thought of *Super Castlevania IV* for the SNES, where holy water was one of the sub-weapons. She equipped a ring she'd acquired two floors down that greatly enhanced her White Magic.

Atop the stairwell, the howling wind whistled through the old stones. Before them stood a lone citadel, its jade door shut off by metal bolts.

Set into the floor was a large tile-sliding puzzle. Despite the dozens of tiles, solving this must have been routine; Soren, Cooke, and Thaddius quickly rotated the tiles into place to form the image of a possessed wraith, and the bolts slid open.

The doorknob, however, remained locked.

"Seriously?" said Samuel. "They're just buying time. I for one am not looking forward to the new and improved Necromancer."

"Allow me," Valerie volunteered, and pulled out her lock-picking set. Within seconds, the door slid open and they all inched inside the pitch-black corridor.

Taking point, Gerrit struck a flint and lit a torch.

The smell of sulfur greeted them at the end of the corridor, in a decaying medieval laboratory without door or window lit by phosphorous magic stones and shafts of light cascading down from some far-up canopy. Wailing banshee women screamed and flew through the party members in a hurry, terrifying Raine.

A deep voice sounded out from the stones, shaking the lone disco ball in the midst of the chamber.

"Who... dares... to crash my unholy bachelor party?"

"It is I, Duke Stabbington the Third, and my band of merry men and women. We have come to challenge you for the right to a fraction of your sizeable hold of riches."

"Ha!" the voice cried as the room became engulfed in shadow. "You will never obtain the treasure of Robert the Necromancer. Face your death!"

"Robert the Necromancer?" Raine giggled, but her voice was thin and fading.

When she could see again, it was thanks to a small will-o-wisp that danced before her eyes. More joined it, and they formed a whirling column in the center of the room. Bats flew in from all corners of the cavern, melded into the twister, and metamorphosed into the towering figure of a pale man with an aura of madness.

A perfectly wicked grin was made even creepier by his scaly skin, stretched too tight across a bony face like something long dead. He wore the long black cloak of a conjurer, with velvet symbols woven into its design. The runes glowed brilliantly as he levitated in the musty air. Glowing magical baubles made an orbit around him, their dripping shadows turning to demonic tendrils.

He fired a barrage of magical orbs at the party. After Raine used most of her Mana to give her friends some much-needed magical buffs and took a few hits in the process, Gerrit pulled her behind a boulder and out of the line of fire. Chance followed, never leaving her side.

"He's twice as strong as usual and you don't know his patterns yet. Stay here for now. We need to take him down as fast as possible."

Raine nodded, watching from the sidelines, stepping in to cast minor spells whenever she found an opening. It didn't take long before Robert began summoning minions – skeleton warriors, mummies, ghastly apparitions and even the wailing banshee women all converged among the party in a parade of violence. The ghosts and banshees bypassed their defensive walls and closed in on Raine and Chance.

"Not good," Gerrit said, running to the boulder to shield Raine from the incoming assault. Raine cast a fiery screen around their perimeter, temporarily trapping the invaders. Chance sustained the blaze long enough for Raine to leap from the flames; she ran with Gerrit to rejoin the circle, peppering the following ghosts along the way.

The girl had little time to take in the chaos surrounding her, but she looked to see what little she could do to help these players who were likely more than thrice her skill level.

Soren clutched an amber crystal in hand, trying to cast some advanced spell while his beasts fought of their own accord. The others fell in to shield him.

The Duke's sword and Valerie's Holy arrows held off the skeleton warriors. Cooke cast healing spells on the mummies, which dealt them significant damage. Thaddius and Samuel chopped away at the dark wizard, chasing him across the floor as he rapidly teleported every which way. He should have been in his final form by now, and these mobs were whittling everyone down.

At long last, the glowing, rune-covered incantation circle surrounding the druid culminated in a flashing ball of light, and he tossed the stone into the air.

"In our hour of need we call on Valhalla for aid! Come forth, Odin!" Soren cried, and lo and behold, an old, bearded, eyepatch-wearing warrior descended from the heavens on the back of an eight-legged horse.

He was one of the most magnificent things Raine had ever seen. Odin rode straight down through a hole in the cavern's roof on a rainbow path, his wide-brimmed hat flowing in the vacuum of air that formed around him, scepter held high and glowing with the power of the Gods. Odin reared his great steed, and tossed a spear right through the Necromancer, pinning him to the ground. Two ravens and two wolves came forth from the scepter in Odin's other hand and tore away at Robert's cloak.

Odin then recovered his spear, stabbed the Necromancer once more for good measure, then took his steed by the reins and rode back up the rainbow through the ceiling. He was gone in seconds.

The Necromancer, now on his knees, shook off the approaching Thaddius and Samuel with a Wind-based spell that knocked both back ten meters. Finally alone, he tore off what was left of the tattered cloak, revealing the throbbing runes set into his spinal column. A bauble of wild lightning enclosed Robert as he levitated, stirring up an electric whirlwind on the dungeon floor.

"This isn't the usual fourth form! What's happening?" Samuel cried, before being lifted off his feet.

Raine, her friends, and what little was left of the undead minions were spirited off the ground, being drawn into a black hole that materialized in the Necromancer's chest.

Valerie reached for Soren's hand, but to no avail. The druid was sucked straight through the abyss, his body spaghettified as it unraveled into strings vibrating in the darkness. The ninja clung to and jumped from various swirling weapons and debris, making her way back to the dungeon floor.

Soren's ghost appeared on the ground by his comrade.

"Ah, well. I'll meet you guys back in town," he said with a shrug, teleporting out of the dungeon. "Have Sammy hang on to my brass knuckles for me."

Thaddius' Iron Leg technique kept him grounded while he and Chance shot pockets of highly compressed air through the Necromancer's vortex, trying to slow the tornado now spinning all around them. Now that they'd lost Soren, there would be no more relying on his buffer spells, or his summoned beasts. This had to end now.

"May I borrow one of your chain-whips?" Thaddius asked Valerie, who nodded and tossed him one of her weapons. The monk wrapped his sash around the chain and lashed it out towards the swirling tornado. Gerrit spotted the flailing fabric in his peripheral vision, and activated his time-slowing macro as he stretched out towards it. It was fast approaching, but would he reach?

In mid-spin in front of Gerrit, Raine took him by the arm and swung him closer. Gerrit snagged the cloth at the end of the whip, and Ricard soon followed suit, taking Raine's hand. He held his sheath up in the air for Cooke to catch. Completing the daisy chain, Cooke reached her arm out for Samuel, who looked like he had been knocked pretty badly on the head.

Thaddius, Valerie, and Chance pulled the warriors out from the vortex towards the dungeon floor, but they all had to cling to Thaddius to avoid being absorbed into the black hole of doom.

"Well, that escalated quickly," Duke Stabbington jested.

"Raine!" yelled Cooke over the commotion. "Let's combine our Divine Justice spells!"

The girl nodded, extremely grateful to Cooke for giving her a chance to do some damage. Both magicians held their staves up high in concentration. Raine felt an immense amount of energy coursing through her body. It was electrifying. Once the spell was fully charged, they fired directly into the Necromancer's chest. The dark energy swirling around the room stuttered until it waned, faltering as their opponent's eyes blazed with a blinding light.

"Now!" Gerrit yelled, leading the party into a fierce melee.

Valerie hooked the Necromancer with two sickles attached to her chains and pulled him down to the floor. Chance froze his ankles to the hard ground. Samuel knocked poor Robert onto his back and beat on him with Soren's brass knuckles until the stones beneath cracked and the Necromancer's Barrier spell shattered. Thaddius got him back on his feet and performed combination punches, knocking the conjurer back against a wall. At last, Gerrit and Ricard stabbed him in his stomach and heart, respectively. They twisted their blades within his body, triggering an instant death.

Raine watched, startled, as Robert scorched and smoldered, tremendous hellfire, screeching demon voices, and scores of adorable bats erupting from within until there was nothing left but a small pile of ash.

"The prize... is yours..." Robert's ghost said, reappearing over the ash, looking perfectly normal as if this were the kind of thing that happened to him every day, which it did, often dozens of times. He removed a key from one of his many necklaces and tossed it to Duke Stabbington, who'd delivered the killing blow.

A boulder covering what looked to be part of the back wall rolled to one side, revealing a chamber with a gigantic chest in the middle.

Raine's eyes went wide with wonder.

"We did it!" Gerrit yelled, fist-bumping Samuel and Thaddius.

The Duke was no less enthusiastic, a look of liberation on his face. Everyone took the opportunity to exchange hugs and high-fives, and swapped highlights. Raine was congratulated on a good run. But something still seemed very wrong to her.

"As Duke Ricard Stabbington the Third, royal steward of this province, I hereby declare that I have the right to first pick of the treasure," he ruled. "Would anyone like to challenge the motion?"

"Wait," Raine called, and all eyes turned towards her. "Are you sure it's not a trap?"

On any other day, the hunters might have laughed. But the girl had a point.

"Now you're learning," Valerie said with a nod. "Shall I inspect it first?"

The Duke considered this for a second. He motioned for her to proceed and tossed over the key.

Valerie loosed a poisoned bolt at the chest, in case it was a Mimic.

No reaction. Good.

She scanned the area around it for explosives or traps. Nothing.

Pulling out a futuristic-looking device from her lock-picking set, she pressed a button, triggering a pulsing sound. She tested the lock for any triggers. It was clean.

Clicking open the lock with the Duke's key, Valerie carefully opened the lid.

To everyone's surprise, the chest was empty, save for one green microchip.

A bounty.

Valerie took the small chip and held it up for all to see.

"That's it?" Samuel roared. "One bleepin' bounty! Are you kidding me?"

Cooke plopped down on a rock, defeated. Valerie consoled her.

Thaddius stood silently with his arms crossed, unreadable.

Gerrit held Raine tightly. "When I say run, you run," he whispered.

Ricard just laughed. "Truly an odd scenario! We are left with no real loot to speak of. Either of three explanations is possible. Let's calculate the odds, shall we? A - a conniving thief has beaten us to the treasure and left their contact info, chance of one to ten thousand against, B – a few naughty Developers are having a grand laugh at our expense, chance of three to one against, or C - this must be one delicious bounty, the odds of which even I can't imagine! Oh, I'm excited!"

Gerrit and Raine laughed nervously. Raine thought she saw Ricard's eyes on her. If he could see through her mask, what else might he know?

Ricard motioned for Valerie to toss the bounty over to him. He placed a pair of aviator shades onto his head, set the visor to expand and share, and slotted in the chip.

A holographic display suddenly materialized in the center of the room.

The names were *"rainorshine23"* and *"NinjaMageKnight99"*.

Their status was "Rebel terrorists. Armed and extremely dangerous."

The bounty on the holographic avatars was G 150,000,000 for Raine and G 200,000,000 for Gerrit, dead or alive.

Each of Ricard's team looked at Raine and Gerrit like pieces of meat. They were completely surrounded. The health bars disappeared from their vision; the party had disbanded.

"Care to explain, Gerrit?" the Duke offered.

"You guys gotta believe me. I don't know what that is. I don't know why they want me. You don't understand. Neira's innocent, but I need to keep Raine alive. For the future of this world."

"I'd torture her location out of you," the Duke continued, then shot Raine a look. "But that would be a waste of time. Your name isn't Neira, am I correct?"

Terrified, Raine backed into a corner.

The Duke approached her, swatted Gerrit aside, and yanked her mask off.

Raine's body and armor shrank as she aged back down to her usual self. She felt stark naked, but worse, she felt like a liar.

Everyone let out a collective gasp. Raine had deceived them.

Behind that innocent face could be anyone. A master of disguise. A person who made their living by stealing the identities of others.

"Criminals!"

The Duke threw the mask to the floor and crushed it.

"No!" Gerrit cried. He was in the middle of drawing his sword when one of Valerie's paralysis arrows went through his arm, sending him twitching to the floor. The other hunters were approaching, weapons drawn.

"You two are worth more Gold than any of us will ever get on our own!" Samuel yelled. "So you better have a damn good reason!"

"R-R-Raine is more than just an ordinary girl," Gerrit began. Seeing that he had a captive audience as the hunters stopped mere feet away, the boy pressed on.

"S-she's come from the outside world. It's a place of real life and death. Our true avatars are not forged in the Network. We're physical. We're born, grow old, and die. Like flowers. All of us, we're… trapped in this game, for some reason. Made not to question why. Made not to r-r-remember things. That way, we won't know that we can grow to be a hundred years old, or that we can work together to accomplish great feats. Maybe she can show us a way out of here, t-to our true homeland."

"It is as I had suspected. She is the Chosen One," Thaddius boomed, clearing a space in the middle of the arena with a blast of air. He calmly walked between Ricard, Gerrit and Raine, and the other hunters. With a quick wrist flick, he disarmed the Duke.

"Get off, then. To the other side," he said, grabbing Ricard's wrist in a death grip. "I press my index finger down, your vein explodes. Better hurry."

The Duke backed away. Thaddius then placed himself squarely in front of the two younger players, as if he had long seen this coming.

"Impede her in her mission, and you doom the rest of us to an eternity of slavery."

"No," Ricard replied. "You must be mad to believe these tall tales, old monk! This girl is the suspected cause of multiple malfunctions and glitches in our system! She's probably some rebel hacker spreading conspiracy theories, looking for a handout! For all we know, she wants to cause chaos so she can cash in! Why else would they be giving out such a high reward for her? Obviously she's a server-wide threat! Monsters like her don't belong in my home. Her whole existence here is an error!"

Raine felt each of his words stab her in the heart. He had seemed so nice, too.

Am I an error?

Discreetly, she charged up a spell. Readied its hand movements.

"The only things erroneous here are your priorities," Thaddius replied. "An hour ago you called me your brother. Now that I exercise my right to think, I am a madman. Duke, you may work for the Developers, but they have you on a tight leash. If you only knew what's going on in the higher realms--"

"What higher realms?" Samuel cried. "For Smith's sake, we're wasting time! This bounty could go public any second! Let's just kill them and get this over with!"

Sam gave a sharp battle cry and charged at Gerrit, but Thaddius spun the cyclops tank around in a flash and tossed him against an opposite wall. The others, not wanting to miss their opportunity at collecting the bounty, went straight for Raine.

"Run!" suggested Thaddius.

Raine's heart skipped a beat. *Move, feet. Go!*

Gerrit was first. He sprinted towards the opposite end of the room, through the tunnel, pulling Raine around a corner of falling stalactites with his good hand. The right side of Gerrit's body faltered: Cooke was electrocuting him, making mobility even harder.

"Haste!" Raine cried out, holding her wand up high. A green glow spread around her body, and time slowed to a crawl. Boosted agility allowed the girl to pull Gerrit in tow, light as a feather. She dodged Cooke's energy bolts in slow motion, watched them soar by her like water balloons.

"If you have one of those portal thingies, now's the time!" called Raine.

Just as Gerrit reached into his bag, Valerie's chain-whip caught him by the foot and brought Raine down, flat on her face, doing significant damage and cancelling her Haste effect.

Wondering if were possible to receive a virtual concussion, Raine pulled herself to one knee. The cave washed by in a spin cycle, and a high-pitched ringing was about all she could hear.

Cooke's ghost hovered over her. Chance had just reflected her arcane finishing blow intended for Raine, leaving the sorceress' body a toasted mess.

"It's a shame things had to end this way," she told Raine. "It was nothing personal. You fight well. If your fortune holds true, may we meet again, in this realm or the next," she said with a bow.

A *whoosh* sailed through the air above Raine's head. She looked just in time to see Valerie's body slam into a bunch of stalagmites in front of them. Gerrit had swung her clear across the room with her own chain. He performed a finishing move on her neck, leaving the hunter's ghost cursing her luck.

"Seriously, Gher-bear? You won't outrun them. Least you could do is cut your friends in on the cheddar."

"I need to get her to where she's going alive," Gerrit replied. "Those are my orders."

"I bet you'd follow those orders into a Hydra's nest," Valerie scoffed. "I don't play games with rebel soldier boys. My clan will be back for you, and it won't be pretty."

Chance wrapped himself back around Raine's neck, healing her. Getting up off the floor, she hobbled back to see how Thaddius was faring. Samuel was dead.

"TWO HUNDRED MILLION! YEAAARRRGGHHHH----!"

The cyclops' ghost rage quit in an outburst of anger. But Ricard was moving with boosted speed. It shouldn't have been possible. Before anyone knew what was happening, he was holding his sword across the monk's neck.

Ricard ended the brave warrior. Thaddius' body crumbled.

"Run, Gerrit! Guard her with your life!" he called.

"I will! You're the best, man!" responded Gerrit. He would never forget the brave guy.

Ricard pointed his bloodied sword straight at the boy.

"You're next, Gerrit, or, as I have now decreed, Young Gerrit the Terrorist," he sneered, sheathing his weapon. "The powers that *we* possess were not meant for the likes of *you*."

"The only difference between you and I is that you signed up for a life of serving the people who oppress us," Gerrit countered. "At least my mind is free."

"Gerrit, Gerrit, *vous êtes un imbécile*. Do you really think that you are free? You are only as free as we want you to be."

He tossed Gerrit a double Chimera Wing – short-ranged, but good for two people at once.

"Why?" the boy asked.

"You're out."

Gerrit scrambled to check his pack. Ninety-nine of his hundred Chimera Wings were gone. Vanished without a trace.

"Suffice it to say, you should really invest in some pickpocketing resistance."

In frustration, Gerrit squeezed the double Chimera Wing, nearly hard enough to activate it.

"Let's make things interesting. I'll let you be my prize. Watching your screams at the hands of an unruly mob would be much more fun than taking the glory for myself. Meanwhile, I'll make sure your Daisy hears all about you and your new psycho girlfriend. Oh, you don't remember her? Pity. Must have been a harsh break-up. We'll have front row tickets to your public freezing, or should I say execution?"

The Duke laughed and laughed.

"Enough!" Gerrit screamed, slamming the item down on the ground.

He quickly selected their destination from a mini-map; it was the farthest possible point from the tower. The three travelers tumbled through the portal and onto a windswept cape overlooking the sea.

The Duke's laughter turned to seagull cries. Both Raine and Gerrit were covered in wounds licked by the salty wind, and the ocean breeze brought some much-needed fresh air. They stopped for a breather; Raine fed Chance some cat food.

"What the hell happened in there?" Gerrit asked, grabbing his tangled hair. His prized helmet was a smoking ruin. He tossed it off in a fury. It bounced off the cliff and disappeared under pounding waves.

"I... I'm sorry, but I'm out of Mana right now. If we wait a bit, I can heal you," Raine offered, noting Gerrit's low health bar and ragged appearance. He was dangerously low on Health, out of healing items, and his spent Mana regenerated a tad slower than Raine's.

"Gerrit, are you all right?"

"Just peachy," groaned the boy, before noticing that Raine was still shaking.

"It's okay," he said, taking her hands in his. "They're gone. We're almost safe. Safe as we're gonna get, at least. How much Mana you got so far?"

"Seventeen," Raine replied, consulting the bar in her peripheral vision.

"Good. Cast 'Minor Heal', just so we can get moving. We'll freshen up on the way."

Raine wanted to ask him who Daisy was and where they were going, but recalling that they weren't yet far from danger, she placed her palms together. Both adventurers felt a little rejuvenated as a glowing green light surrounded them.

"Come on."

He led her through ancient ruins overgrown with grape vines to the very edge of the continent. A dragon, observing an ancient mural of a griffin dealing death to one of its serpentine brethren, gave its wings a mighty flap as it fell into a respectful bow.

"Greetings, Master Gerrit," a deep, powerful voice resonated.

"Raine, this is Linus. Linus, Raine."

Raine's eyes nearly popped out of her head due to an overload of awesome.

"Ohmygod a talking dragon. That is so rad."

"Pleasure to make your acquaintance," Linus nodded.

"Likewise," answered Raine, taking his large claw-finger in her hand and giving it a light shake. She wasn't sure how surprised she should be that this intimidating dragon the size of a school bus didn't scare her in the least.

"I take it your trip has been productive, Master Gerrit?"

"Save it, Linus. We're not safe here."

Gerrit wasted no time in hoisting Raine onto the saddle and slipping the goggles over his eyes. She held tight around Gerrit's waist as they quickly gained altitude, climbing high by a mountain range that emerged from nearby cliffs. From this dizzying vantage point, she spotted the green carpet pathway carving through the severe terrain like a snake.

"I suggest you pop your ears and hold on tight," Linus said.

"And don't let go," added Gerrit, with a fraction of what was almost a smile.

XIV. Linus, or: The Children's Crusade

"Politics have no relation to morals." – Niccolo Machiavelli

Fingers twitching, Henry Holdfast bit his tongue to keep from exploding with relief, and instead imagined himself at a loss as to how the grand plan had horribly backfired. His subordinates did not pity the man.

Bloody hell. That was way too close.

"Who told that idiot to give them the Wings?" Dr. Hoshua screamed. "Anyone?"

Avidya's Chief Maintenance Officer, Dr. Christopher Marco, coughed to clear the air and spoke in his slithering voice, a fitting match for the man's sly nature. "I believe Ricard was acting of his own free will, sir."

Hoshua rubbed his bald head and glared at his power-hungry subordinate. This wasn't a fight worth picking. The Duke's 'handler' had long ago mastered the art of dodging responsibility.

"For your sake, Marco, I certainly hope so. The lesson here, I think, is that those Yanks are a menace. We really ought to overhaul Sector Ninety-Nine's support staff. That was extremely unprofessional on the Duke's part. Don't beat yourself up, Henry. We'll catch these bastards."

Holdfast nodded, and squeezed his toes to keep his knees from knocking any further. *If that was you, Ayumi, that was absolutely ace.*

"You did your best, kid," the hologram of Jon Wrathman grimaced, oddly almost happy to be witnessing his new recruit's first foible. "Now watch how the big boys handle these kinds of messes."

Henry looked to Jon's private office. Within, plugged into his *M-Gear*, Mister Senior soared high above the *Avidya* skies. Conor was already busy coordinating the strike force. *Op End Verse* was currently in jeopardy, and he was powerless to interfere.

Sorry, Admiral. It's out of my hands now.

↕

The fugitives sped through the clouds, flew into the core of a large floating ring, and burst through an air-cannon. Raine's stomach jumped as the G-force slammed against them. She clung to Gerrit for dear life.

Linus danced in the vortex tunnel. At the apex of their trajectory, he unfolded his wings, and soared high above razor-sharp, snow-capped mountains. The sudden altitude change made Raine's head more than a little woozy at first, but something in her brain seemed to level out, and breathing came as naturally as it would on the ground.

"I… I can't believe everyone just turned on us like that," Raine said at last. "Weren't those people your friends?"

"True friends are rare. I count three of 'em: Peter, Moe, and Yossa. The guys back there were hunters. On your side as long as there's something you can do for their sakes," Gerrit said grimly. "I'll take you somewhere we'll be safe for sure."

"You don't mean--"

[NinjaMageKnight99]: "No arguments. We're fugitives now. Our best bet is the Tavern in Circuitron. Home base for the revolution. Yossa will know how we can stay out of trouble."

In the midst of thinking the message, Gerrit's heart leapt up his throat. He had no idea whether Yossa would keep Raine safe or not. There was no guarantee that she wouldn't just be used as another tool for the freedom fighters, her data storms mined for info about the outside world, her face and likeness a figurehead for the rebels. *Would they make her fight?* If she had some sort of secret weapon, that wasn't a possibility he could rule out. Thankfully, Raine didn't appear to possess any such thing. Maybe she could get out of this in one piece.

Raine, too, felt immensely awkward about her situation. She was under constant attack by strange forces she could barely understand. This poor boy risked his virtual life time and again to protect her, and this last time they almost didn't make it out in piece.

I can't let myself be indebted to Gerrit forever. If we just go somewhere else to hide, isn't there a chance more people might be put in danger? At the end of the day, this is just my silly dream. Maybe it'd be better to end it on a high note and move on.

Gerrit checked his bearings on a mini-map. To the West, dirigibles scoured the airspace around Mistral and its tower. He dipped Linus into a thunderstorm and activated an anti-electricity shield, which engulfed the beast in a protective bubble. Raine's hair stopped whipping about her head as the rushing wind disappeared.

They flew in silence for some time, the dark clouds covering their tracks.

"You must trust Yossa a lot," Raine said at last, feeling him out.

"Yeah," Gerrit replied.

"I don't want to cause you or the other members of the revolution too much trouble," she said. "What if the hunters and Templars follow us?"

"Then we'll make them pay. We'll bring them a propaganda war. Take over their mindshare. They can erase some of our memories sometimes, but everyone at once? It might never have been done. We don't know. But it's worth a try. We'll reveal all the lies and deception behind this prison, and we'll make them pay for hunting down anyone who dares to think differently, hunting us like we're... like we're animals."

There was genuine anger in the boy's eyes, as if he were ready to explode.

Raine brought her hands up around his arms and held onto them gently. It seemed to calm him down a bit.

"I'm sorry, Gerrit, but I have to ask, and I hope you understand why I'm asking you this. Why did you have a larger bounty on your head than me?"

There was a short silence. *Was he thinking of an appropriate answer?*

"Piracy. Hacking. Street art. Selling bugs and exploit codes. Your guess is as good as mine," he muttered.

"I just... I don't want this to come out the wrong way, but... I'm not sure about joining up with the revolution."

"No one said anything about joining up," he lied. "Do you still not trust me?"

"Is there a reason why I shouldn't?"

Gerrit yanked off his goggles and faced her eye-to-eye.

"Okay. Here's the truth. Yossa wanted me to bring you to Circuitron safely. Said it was official anarchist business. I'm not sure why exactly, but he--"

"I knew it! You liar!"

"You have to understand, this was before I really knew you. Raine, I know we've only just met, but you mean a lot to me. I promise, I won't let him or anyone else hurt you."

"Save it. Just drop me off at the next town. Now."

"Listen! Please! The reason why I'm taking you to Yossa right now is not because he asked me to. It's 'coz there's simply no safer place you could be than underground, in a bubble server."

"Gerrit, it's... it's not like I don't want to go with you. I like you. But even if I could trust your friend, I have this bad feeling that I don't belong here. I'm just putting you all in harm's way. And since this is probably just a dream anyways, maybe--"

"This isn't a dream!" Gerrit yelled.

As if spurred by his emotion, a rather powerful bolt tore the glowing shield in half.

Every hair on Raine's body stood on end as Gerrit pulled Linus into a sudden dive, evading another particularly nasty strike. They emerged from the cloud cover only to witness a hungry swarm awaiting them.

A hundreds-strong armada of fully outfitted hunter airships advanced from below, pushing them upwards into the lightning-laden blanket of death. There was no escape.

Gerrit stilled himself. He took a much-needed breath. "Raine, I'm sorry about all this. I'm not supposed to let you get caught or killed, under any circumstances. But, I... I don't know how well I can protect you at this point."

Raine rolled her eyes. "Come on, dude. I appreciate the chivalry but maybe now's not the best time. Do we have any options?"

"Seriously, Master," Linus echoed. "This isn't good mojo."

The 'Home' button won't work, the boy thought. *One can only use that command while standing on solid ground for ten seconds. And my place will be crawling with Temps.*

Gerrit whipped out his last Chimera Wing. He placed it in Raine's palm and wrapped her fingers around it.

"Looks like a trip for one. Linus, go with her."

"Affirmative," the dragon replied.

Raine's stomach sank.

"I'm not going anywhere as long as I can help you."

"Don't worry. I'll be fine. Probably. It doesn't matter what happens now. You've made a believer out of me. I'll be waiting for you on the other side."

"Let me go instead! Please... I told you before: I'm not from here. If this is another world, I should be the one to disappear. I... I'll just go back to mine, somehow," Raine said softly, clinging to the boy's bare arms under his bracers, the only place on his torso without armor. Her tender touch gave him courage to face the abyss.

"Maybe I am a virus," she said. "Let them come for me."

"Now who's a liar? You're no anomaly, Raine. You're the most beautiful person I've ever met."

"Gerrit... "

He took Raine's hand and gave it a chaste kiss. Then he held her by the chin so as to look into her eyes and maybe give her some of his courage. It was never supposed to end like this. He'd finally met the girl of his dreams, only to be forced to lay down his meager life for her. It didn't matter what he'd come back as, or even if he would come back at all.

This was no ordinary bounty. When these bastards were done with him, there'd be no going back - probably not to this server; probably nowhere, if the rumors were to be believed. But at least he had no regrets. He'd be going out with a bang.

Better get this over with, he thought. *She looks like she's getting cold up here.*

And Raine would have shivered if his presence weren't so warm. She took in every detail of the moment, committing it to a memory that could never be erased.

They were unbearably close, his red hair billowing like fire. Raine placed a hand on Gerrit's neck. Her eyes reflected his intensity. He inched closer.

They closed their eyes as their virtual lips met.

My first kiss.

Suddenly I don't want this to be a dream anymore.

The butterflies in Raine's stomach snuck into her bloodstream and fluttered all throughout her body. She didn't want it to end, not even when cannons sounded out from below and Gerrit broke away.

She watched a cannonball explode halfway between them and oblivion. The swarm was almost there.

"That was... wow. I wish we'd gotten to know each other a little better," he joked.

"D-don't talk like that. I may be of some help yet," Raine said firmly.

"Only if you promise to use the wing when things get hairy."

Raine bit her lip.

"Promise me, Raine!"

"I... I promise."

The ships were coming into range. The closest gunship took aim, and fired.

Gerrit pulled up on the reins. Poor Linus brayed in agony as he was bombarded with all manner of bullets, lasers and flak. Hummingbird-sized creatures zipped around the dragon in formation, creating an electric net that even Chance's magic couldn't counteract.

Raine's stomach turned into a churning cauldron as the dragon spiraled down towards the surface.

She screamed as all four of them split up, falling separately towards the desert far below. Gerrit tapped a preset on his watch, slowing their fall with Wind Magic.

The dream was turning into a nightmare again.

"Activate Earth Rune!" Gerrit cried, pulling out his broadsword. The fiery gem in its hilt now sparkled emerald green. He dove over to Raine and handed her the sword. Rocky armor grew over her hand, and then rapidly spread over her body.

"Cut the net!" he called, summoning forth an energy shield that diverted the next wave of fire. Constant barrages from nearby airships drained its power, fast.

Raine tried her best to cleave away at the electric net. She had freed one wing when the voltage increased, causing Linus to involuntarily flail every which way. He knocked her aside.

The sword flew clear out of her hands, vanishing into a speck of dust as it toppled towards the rapidly approaching ground. Except that Raine stretched her hand out at it and a stream of black pixels shot from her palm, engulfed the weapon, and slung it back to her. As soon as she grabbed it, her rock armor returned.

Just then, a message appeared in Gerrit's peripheral vision.

[Lillian_2212]: You've done well, Gerrit. Operation Phase One complete.

And then, the boy's shield gave way. He was vaporized instantly.

Raine cried aloud. Linus thrashed in fury.

It was in the middle of this that Chance put a claw in Raine's arm. As she turned to him, she caught another glimpse of the ground.

Raine would not let what happened to Gerrit be in vain.

The girl scrambled onto the saddle and sliced the last of the entangling webs.

The skies above rumbled as a vacuum gave way to some massive payload. A flash of light seared the back of her retina.

Raine's eyes snapped shut; she felt around for the electric ropes. As Linus beat his wings frantically and leveled out, she saw it: *The Nebula*. The flying fortress from Clyde Castle Town rapidly descended like some fiery steel trap. A pulsing beam shot down towards the pair.

They were being drawn into the hold.

"You're not taking me alive! Give him back!"

A barrage of whizzing bullets answered.

"Ignore me, will you? Then I'll take him back!" Raine cried, holding Gerrit's sword up high.

A singular beam fired, destroying the weapon and her rock armor in one clean blast. Chance used the last of his energy in a Discharge spell, reflecting a follow-up beam as his master clambered back onto the saddle in a daze. The familiar collapsed in her arms as the cannon short-circuited.

If this is the end, I'd rather die than run away. But I made a promise.

After stashing an injured Chance in her bag, she squeezed the wing in hand. A blue glow formed around her, but it was fading, its power being overridden by the negative force of the tractor beam as the *Nebula* welcomed the girl.

"Glad you could finally join us!" a shadowy figure intoned, standing at the edge of the hold staring down at Raine. She couldn't get a good look at his face.

"Linus, is there a way to disable that tractor beam?"

"Might I suggest you cast Thunder +3 through the conduit on your right? I can re-direct your power; that might do the trick." he replied in a deep voice.

"Fantastic proposal, my good sir."

Linus reared his majestic head while Raine conjured a glowing ball of concentrated energy, which promptly fused with spray-fire blasts of molten lava mixed with electron static – a deadly cocktail that shorted out the tractor beam generator.

Just as gravity pulled them into a descent, claws reached out from every edge of the hold to undercut them. Linus held open the reverse bear trap's deadly jaws with his hands and feet.

Raine gathered up all her strength. She took a deep breath and screamed at the top of her lungs, releasing all her pent-up anger.

"You're toast, losers! Give me back my Gerrit!"

My Gerrit. She caught her cheeks flushing.

"Come with us. We'll take you to him."

"Why the hell should I trust you after what you did?"

"We need you. You won't be harmed. As per the End User License Agreement, you are property of *Endless Metaverse.* Let's not make this any more difficult than --"

"I don't belong to you! GIVE HIM BACK NOW!"

There was chortling at the other end.

"I'd love to comply with your request; only, we don't even have him yet. But we will. And you, my dear… will make a fine addition to our collection."

The claws advanced.

Raine gathered her breath, fists clenched in a show of strength. Yet her doubts gnawed at her.

I'm such an idiot! How could I let this happen? How could I have lost the one friend I'd made in this upside-down place?

The problem isn't my environment. It's that I'm letting my environment dictate my thoughts and actions. I'm hanging on for dear life with no idea what I'm hanging on to. Or where the ride ends. Even in this virtual realm far from home, I'm beyond useless.

Agnes' words about wasting her potential haunted Raine's every thought. People she cared about were suffering because she had no idea what she was doing.

There's one thing I know. Willfully going along with these maniacs is not the answer.

She had to try something. She focused all of her power and yelled like there was no tomorrow.

As her voice echoed around the shuttering claws, a cascade of black pixels emerged from all around her body, forming a shield that held back the enclosing metal.

The blue glow of the Chimera Wing returned, surging through the two bodies.

Raine and Linus vanished into the ether.

"Where would you like to go?" the text asked.

"As close as you can get me to Atmoya," Raine barely managed.

The hot air rushing up the mountain hit the girl straight in the face. Underneath her, Linus emanated a delighted sigh.

Raine looked down. It was no wonder she was boiling hot. Linus was sitting at the edge of a large natural hot spring, and it appeared that a gathering of elderly people was quite stunned at the intrusion. A baby across the way started to wail.

"I apologize if we frightened you," Linus said in a soothing voice.

The infant continued bawling. Its worried mother's attempts to distract it were futile.

Linus began crooning a melodic lullaby as Raine dismounted the saddle a dazed mess. She had a hard time believing the events that had just transpired. *What happened to Gerrit?* She'd seen people die in the *'Verse* before, and it wasn't a real death. So was he really gone? Was it possible that he hadn't been frozen? The creepy dude said he was still out there. She had to find out, and she had to find out now.

Or not. The spirit was willing, but the flesh was weak. Upon getting her feet back on solid ground, Raine nearly collapsed on her knees. She was about to faint.

An elf-maiden caught her fall. She stood Raine back up carefully.

"Miss, please don't leave. You are not well. I suggest that you partake in these healing waters," she said, guiding the girl to the edge of the springs.

Raine was scanning her inventory for a swimsuit when Chance popped out from his compartment, metamorphosed into a towel, and whisked around her body in a flash of fluff, leaving her clad in a bikini. He mewed, curling up in a roll by the edge of the pool to recover.

The girl sank into the spring and felt immediately rejuvenated. Her Health and Mana were maxed out in seconds. Still crooning, Linus opened up a private chat window.

[Linus_1050]: "This is Pagoda. It's a tropical paradise, an all-in-one hotel resort for people who want to get away from level grinding, bounty hunting, ex-spouses, et cetera. I must admit that I have never been there for long enough to really know, but I'm under the impression it's mostly just well-to-do elderly folk who like to pretend to be poor villagers."

The baby was now sound asleep. Behind the parents, through a jungle of palm trees, a multi-tiered resort town swallowed the sunset like a giant firefly, its straw huts glowing in the distance. There was a major luau occurring in the town square.

Gerrit isn't replying to my Private Channeler messages. And I'll run out of energy within the next few hours. As much as I hate to do it, I'll have to find a place to get some rest tonight. Then I'll be rejuvenated come morning.

Dreamboy, please hold on just a little longer.

"I'm out," Raine told Linus. "How do I call you?"

"Don't check now, but you have my contact info in your watch. I apologize that I cannot stay with you, Miss R," Linus replied. "I have other commitments. My services are being called for in battle as we speak. A scheduled skirmish is underway."

"You mean the war between the two nations?"

"Yes."

Before she could ask any more questions, a private chat window appeared in Raine's peripheral vision. She focused on it and the text expanded.

[Linus_1050]: "No doubt Master Gerrit would have wanted me to aid you, and to him my allegiance is sworn. But unless I am mistaken, it appears that you wish to evade detection by the Templars. Currently, they are attempting to trace my location. If I remain by your side, it will only attract unwanted attention. It is best that I report to my post. Then there will be no more questions."

[rainorshine23]: "I understand. Thank you for everything, Linus."

Raine gave the dragon a big hug. She had no idea an artificial intelligence could end up being her ally.

She stood from the hot springs, automatically changed into her previous outfit, and headed up the winding pathway that would take her up the mountainside.

A few hundred feet from the town entrance, Raine heard footsteps approaching. People were discussing rumors of some sort of bounty. She hid behind some vine-covered rocks and let the travelers pass. Her avatar appeared as a projected hologram.

"I heard she has, like, laser eyes. And a cat that shoots rainbows."

"Not according to my Blogosphere buddy. He says she's got two hearts and needs to drink blood to stay alive."

"Why do you think they're after her?"

"Girl's gotta be a hacker. No one looks that innocent."

It appeared she'd become the talk of the town. Raine decided to change her outfit, and held down the home button on her wristwatch for ten seconds. She disembarked in a pop and arrived in her suburban room above Clyde Castle Town.

She grabbed a suit of light armor she'd picked up, ran it through the instant laundry machine, and changed into the outfit. With a hood on, hair tied up in a ponytail, and Chance's scarf set to gray, Raine attracted even less attention.

The girl tapped her watch to return to the road near Pagoda, but a creaking from the stairway stopped her. She held her wand towards it.

"Raine! It's really you!"

Through the half-opened door, Nimbus was staring at her like a lost puppy.

"Nimbus, I'm sorry, I have to go."

"There are a lot of people looking for you," he said worriedly. "If you come with me, I'll keep you safe. As one of your rights, you can summon an arbitrating Templar and explain this injustice to the proper authorities."

"I can't do that," Raine said, holding up her glowing weapon with a Stun spell on the ready. "I don't trust you, or the system. Get out of my room."

"But--"

"Get out now!"

Now who's bullying whom? Raine hated treating Nimbus this way; the poor program didn't seem to have an inkling as to what was going on. *But I'm alone now. I can't take any chances.*

The sad-faced NPC backed away slowly as the girl held down the home button again and re-materialized in the tropics.

Fueled by newfound adrenaline, Raine booked it to the town. Night fell by the time she'd passed the gates. Wanted posters with her likeness decorated thatched huts. Even young children were discussing how they would find her and score the epic bounty. A long-abandoned building appeared safe enough. She slipped inside and bolted the door.

$$\Sigma$$

Gerrit's ghost materialized by his body in the hospital of whichever city he'd ended up in this time; this wasn't standard procedure after mid-air de-materialization, but a custom setting he configured to prevent hunters and Templars alike from tracking him. Raine was off the map. That meant she was in transit. A good sign.

The Templars weren't there, not yet.

No. Thank whatever gods may be, they weren't lying in ambush. But surely they were coming. They'd have realized their mistake five seconds ago. Their warps would be arriving in five more, tops. There was no time to think.

In three seconds, he'd have a choice: to resurrect his body, or try to make a run for it.

Wouldn't get far as a spirit. I could hide, but never fight. And no one hid from the system for long.

Gerrit hovered over his avatar and touched its chest; the shell absorbed his consciousness. Twenty seconds later, he'd activated a five-minute stealth skill, shimmied out the window, climbed down the brick wall, and snuck across the canal.

He knew the place. This was the strictly medieval city of Europa, and Lady Luck was against him. As a Public Enemy, he'd become the target of every local Templar and hunter.

Shuffling down alleys towards the nearest sewer entrance, Gerrit pulled up his Private Channeler and attempted to send a message to Yossa. He imagined the words in his mind's eye.

[NinjaMageKnight99]: ALERT! I've been marked. Raine and I were ambushed at 45-93-68. Not sure what happened to her. Don't expect me back soon.

Just before Gerrit sent the memo, a sudden burst of ice slammed into his wristwatch, activating 'Iron Defense' mode and cancelling his message window.

"Come quietly and it'll be easier," a voice commanded. It appeared to belong to an Europan guard, a lowly quest-hosting NPC; only, there was something very unusual about him.

Gerrit looked all around. He was surrounded, and unable to use his watch to quick-swap weapons.

These were no ordinary guards, he quickly inferred from sizing them up. Hijacked NPCs, ghost-run by Templars. They had him between a rock and a hard place.

Missing his trusty broadsword, Gerrit drew two short Japanese wakizashi swords and squeezed the hilts, changing the runes from Normal to Berserk mode; each successful hit would be twice as strong, but drain his Stamina.

He made the first move, emanating a fierce battle cry as he chopped through three at once. Shuffling behind another group, he took out two with backstabs.

More came, some from portals appearing right beside Gerrit. Now there were bounty hunters. Newbies. Spectators. And of course, Templars with every one of the *Metaverse's* best weapons and spells at their disposal. They slashed and beat him in cold silence, but he fought on. Constant illegal plasma energy blasts drained his Health at a ridiculous pace.

Gerrit needed to get out of there. He'd taken thirteen out already, but more were coming. The boy moved backwards as they fought, hoping that if he led them to the main road, he'd be safer from ranged attacks. That was not the case.

Passersby looked on in shock as the tide of battle turned in a flash: two rooftop archers stunned Gerrit with simultaneous crossbow bolts to the neck, shattering his enchanted muffler. A thief stole his magic-resistant buckler, and a magician paralyzed him while a blacksmith shattered the runes on his prized blades, leaving them in a shambles that crumbled to dust. Templars then slammed Gerrit up against a wall, took his remaining weapons and armor, and sliced him to pieces.

"Hey! Hey, that's mine!" Gerrit yelled as he felt his aural self disconnect from his body. He was now a disembodied spirit, unable to move, watching helplessly from the sidelines. The boy hoped to be taken to another respawn point, but soon realized that he wasn't going anywhere.

The world was disappearing. Surfaces peeled off the cheering hunters, the wire frames underneath clearly visible. Faces faded into fog. No one else seemed to notice that the sky had become a flat matte painting, and then a total blur. Completely confused and at a total loss for words, Gerrit's eyes caught a Templar walking towards him, holding open a small box.

No. Not this. Anything but this.

They were going to take him out of the '*Verse*. It would surely be the deep freeze.

Gerrit tried to run. It was no use. The Templar opened the box. With a large 'pop', his sense of sound disappeared. He could no longer smell. Alone in the darkness, his body began to unravel like a broken tapestry; fingers disappeared into thin air, ghostly skin peeled off pixel by pixel. And then he lost his vision.

The boy awoke in a spinning kaleidoscope. Gerrit had no body to speak of, and what he thought of as his consciousness was flying towards a vortex on the far side of the tunnel. He perceived forward movement, but was unable to influence his trajectory. Nothing remained but fleeting moments of perception.

Oh, he'd heard the horror stories of men who'd gone mad, those brought back from the edge. The shimmering white vortex told him this was no ordinary loading point or respawn. Time was of the essence.

Gerrit tried to forget that he had no mouth. He recalled some of the *Metaverse's* programming language. <true_speak> was one of the commands. The boy envisioned it in his head. Nothing. He concentrated, willing the words to materialize.

At long last, he forced out a yell. An empty, echoing yell, but still a yell nonetheless that he himself had created.

It went something like this:

"AAAaaaaaaaHRRARRGLEEEE!"

The vortex of nothingness took the echo, interpreted it as text, and sent it off into the ether.

Thinking quickly, Gerrit drew a deep, metaphorical breath of virtual air and screamed.

[NinjaMageKnight99]: "GERRIT TO REVOLUTION! REPEAT THIS IS GERRIT TO THE ANARCHISTS! NINJAMAGEKNIGHT99 DOWN!! SECURITY COMPROMISED! CHANGE ALL PASSWORDS!"

He repeated this message as many times as he could; he knew soon he would reach the end of the vortex and blank out entirely. His words rang off the walls of the blank hub, assimilated themselves into text, and squeezed out of the whirlpool, drawn to *Endless Metaverse* by the two-way Network signal, perhaps never to be intercepted.

Gerrit's mind came to wonder and doubt at the last second. Was it desperation that drove him to seek out Raine, or was it blind hope? Was she the one they wanted after all? Had she been a tool to get him into the Developers' hands, or was he simply Lily's tool to keep Raine out of theirs? Either way, it was too late. It was always too late.

I guess I'll die as I lived, Gerrit reflected, *a fool without the first clue about anything.* He felt his spirit fade into cold darkness.

General Lacie watched from a newly manned Ukrainian airstrip in Sector Twenty as her interceptors combed the barren landscape. Leaving their sluggish air fortresses far behind, Lacie had split the scouts into multiple groups. She'd be joining them shortly; the woman awaited only the signal beacon, which would resound once the asset's whereabouts had been ascertained.

Puzzling many of her subordinates, the target wasn't among Lily's primary base camps, but it housed the body of one essential piece in her grand puzzle. She was getting the battle shakes, an instinctive sign that they were getting close. Functional drones had picked up multiple infrared signals in this area just days ago.

All their lives, the sisters had been experts in the field of war games. The attack will have been anticipated. Lacie mentally prepared herself to take lives, if needs be. These souls would be on Lily's hands, for holding true to untested convictions that only asserted her own control over the known universe.

Diary from Attempt # 4
July 5, 1099 A.D.
11:15 BT
The Belladonna 5000

It is two days until the siege of Jerusalem is set to begin, and Lucille is in the middle of a very uncharacteristic nervous breakdown. With Lily butting heads with her the entire way, the poor thing's well-laid plan is falling apart.

The Holy land is visible from our imaging equipment and through the thick glass below our feet in the lower observatory, and if we do nothing, over a hundred thousand will certainly be slaughtered, mostly innocent civilians at the hands of the invading western Crusaders, sent on the first of a centuries-long series of skirmishes to capture the city.

Lorelei sits quietly in the middle, arbitrating, while I play witness from the side. I am to offer my thoughts after each of my sisters has spoken their testimony.

"Please, Lily," Lucy asks, tears falling from her face. *"Rutger has calculated a ninety-two percent chance of success. We can put an end to all religious conflict on the planet. With one gesture, we can halt hundreds of years of murder and warfare between the Christians, Muslims, and Jews."*

"By enacting a lie," Lily replied coldly. *"A bold-faced lie that we are messengers sent from on high. And afterwards, we will need to do everything in our power to protect our secret indefinitely."*

In two days the Crusader armies, low on food and water, arrive at the city and begin their siege. In less than a week the gates will be breached. The Muslims and Jews inside will be massacred by the Crusaders, spurred by their undying belief that they were doing God's will, all the while furthering the interests of their power-hungry rulers.

Lucy's gambit was for us to warp over the city in the midst of the Crusaders' march and claim that we were messengers of the One True God, sent to unite all peoples of Earth to face a coming crisis. Holographic multi-lingual messages, visible to all, would command utmost respect, and any dissenters would be silenced by the sheer spectacle of the situation. This singular act, visible to the Crusaders and to the defenders of Jerusalem, would be enough for us to draft a new gospel, that of Goddesses of the Moon respectful of all religious views and walks of life, ones who would not tolerate war and injustices among men.

"Then it will be up to us to shepherd the entire human race in matters of faith," Lily counters. *"Even with centuries' worth of writings by mystics and messengers of peace at our disposal, none of us are qualified for such a position. Plus, centralizing that sort of power will only lead to more death and destruction."*

At this, Lorelei forcefully slams her gavel down.

"Captain!" she cries out, turning every head in the room. *"If I may, I fully disagree with your assessment. The masses' faith can be used as a tool for their survival. Centralizing power will help us to keep order on this chaotic planet."*

She looks down through the glass at Earth, a most dizzying affair. "If they wish to see their gods mete out justice, who are we to deny them their rapture?"

Dear Lucy grits her teeth. "Lorrie, thank you for your input and support, but Lily and I are currently addressing one another..."

"It's okay," Lily tells her, placing a hand on Lucy's trembling shoulder. "I'd like to challenge her reasoning."

Lorelei cracks her neck and knuckles. Lily scribbles out some notes before responding.

"Lorelei, let me address the very crux of this problem. First off, we are messengers, not Goddesses. Though capable of asserting influence over worldly affairs, we must only do so when it directly benefits the mission. The goal of uniting the planet under a single mega-dynasty in order to centralize power was what brought Earth to destruction in my parents' original timeline. If we are to branch out beyond the stars, it must be a goal shared by human civilization as an emergent value of its people, not an act of manipulation by its elite rulers. It is not something we can impose through a deceitful seizure of power, or the entire purpose of directing the human race will be to our own ends."

With that said, Lily gestures to Lorelei, who begins penning her counter-argument. To keep the conversation going, Lorrie looks to Lucy, notices that she is still preparing her thoughts, and then turns to me.

"Lacie, you've been awfully quiet. I'd like to hear what you have to say," Lorelei states.

I seem to have attracted Lily's gaze by this point as well. I'm silent. I know this is the ultimate privilege, but what right do I have to decide the fates of potential billions of human beings? The weight of the situation is too much for my shoulders.

"No comment," I mutter.

"Does this mean you approve or object?" demands Lucy. "Come on, Cie. You know what's right."

Lily quickly puts her hand up, the unwelcome word having shown itself again.

"On the contrary, there's no right or wrong answers here, Lacie," Lily tells me. "We haven't agreed to anything yet. We're all just doing our best to brainstorm our next attempt."

"You do not speak for me," Lorelei proclaims, once again dominating the conversation. "I'll begin. The united world in the Alpha

timeline came into existence after centuries of warfare between empires, with many terrible deeds to spring from the aftermath of this battle. We've sat by as many conflicts have torn East and West alike. We four alone have the power to lead humanity out of its rut and end a vicious cycle. If we can stop this warring as fast as possible, I say we make our plans, calibrate our personal translation modules, and prep a nice big fireworks show for all the believers. We'll have a completely controlled environment, Lily."

"That's what I'm afraid of," the Captain intoned. "It's not just the results that trouble me with regards to this plan, it's the methodology. I simply do not think that we have earned the right to play God. Extra-terrestrials, possibly, but--"

"We're already playing God," Lucy quickly intercut. "Lily, I think we have a real chance."

"Perhaps. But in doing so, we rob the people of theirs. Beneficium accipere libertatem est vendere," Lily says, showing off her Latin. (To accept a favor is to sell one's freedom.)

Lucy's quick to reply. "Dulce bellum inexpertis." (War is sweet to those who have never fought.) "Remember the Tao, Lily. Give evil nothing to oppose, and it will disappear by itself."

"Ah, great, they're pulling out the Latin and *the Lao Tzu. Dammit, 'Cie, say something!" Lorelei cries out. "This stalemate can't go on."*

"Give me a freaking minute!" I retaliate.

Scrambling for an answer, I inspect my pitiful notes, and know how little they mean. Lucy had already crunched the numbers of lives lost in these collective conflicts. If we acted within the bounds of the Time Keeper's Oath, *surely centuries of bloodshed might be avoided, and technological advancements could be greatly accelerated. Lucy's plan was effectively a game-winning scenario. With our technology, we could claim divine rights over all that was God's and steer the entire course of Western civilization. Byzantine would never need to fall.*

But who were we to decide who lives and who dies? Could this ruse not be done earlier in human history? Tens of thousands of Christians died from starvation and disease on their way to the siege. What of their lives? Must they, too, be sacrificed for this one defining triumph? And by that logic, why stand by while the Romans conquer Greece? What of the countless massacres thousands of years before? What of the wars in Persia, India, and China, or slavery in ancient Egypt? We could take this all the way back to ancient Sumeria, to the Stone Age, or even further, to the days when the Homo sapiens *wiped out the* Neanderthals. *Yet, even considering that this might be among the most "ethical" instances to step in and change the course of modern history, the complex web of moral difficulties only got worse from there: Such interference would certainly affect the Mongol campaigns in the coming centuries. What then were we to do? Attempt to spread advanced philosophies, teachings, and sustainable living methods, perhaps. The Black Plague could be halted in its tracks. The Renaissance could come a few centuries early. But ever the fires might burn at the hearths of would-be empires, and ever we would have to meddle, dispensing justice in the names of the Goddesses. Perhaps inevitably, we will be no better than those who brainwashed the Crusaders into committing genocide.*

I explained my misgivings with the current situation. My findings seemed to please Lily, anger Lorelei, and humble Lucille.

"I don't understand," Lucy said, once I had finished. "Wasn't our goal to simply save the human race? I can see no more lateral solution to the problem than to bring the peoples of Earth together under our banner at this early phase."

Lillian countered that to seize Jerusalem alone would bring only a small minority of Earthlings together. There was still no guarantee of a peaceful result amongst the various free peoples of Terra, and that the aim was not for one world government, but to unite all peoples in spirit and goals equanimously, so they might live according to Natural Law, self-governing without genocide or prejudice. Lorelei took issue with her idealism. The discussions went on through the night.

In the end, we never got a chance to try out Lucy's grand experiment.

The next morning, a red envelope from the future informed us that an attempt at this plan ended in a civil war that split us apart on our individual campaigns and ideals. Rutger estimated the probability of the outcome repeating at about seventy percent.

The matter was a closed case within the week. Jerusalem burned, and we left the stage early, sitting pretty up in the most powerful machine ever built by humankind, made powerless by our own convictions, unable to avert a disastrous campaign that would initiate centuries of division and war.

We vowed to return to that time period once we'd matured a bit. Perhaps it was too advanced of a situation for adolescents to tackle.

Though she had undoubtedly changed in the nearly two decades since the incident, the memory of their utter failure was still a sore spot for General Lacie. While any one of the sisters could have taken the blame for their inaction and inability to agree, she had the power to side with Lucille. If only then and there, she had chosen to support either Captain Lily, who held the forty-nine percent vote, or Lucy and Lorrie, that red envelope might never need have materialized.

Taking an injection of blood-cleaning nanites, Lacie neglected to notice that a beacon on her portable console was chirping loud and clear.

Two thousand miles away, Gerrit was frozen and ready for pickup. It was going to be an overnight run.

This is Lorrie's plan, not mine, she reminded herself. Having been tormented by her part in the *Jerusalem Un-Incident* for the majority of her conscious lifetime, Lacie had long since rescinded her own judgment. Although she ended up becoming an agent of deception anyway, ushering in a world of servitude and escapism, she never regretted putting her faith in Lorelei. It was Lorrie who backed dear Lucy when Lillian stood against her, after all.

But was that the real reason, or is that just what I'm telling myself at this point? I don't need to know anymore. I don't want to know anymore. When at war, my heart is closed. My emotions are saved for my beloved, and for no one else.

She kissed the picture of Claire on her locket, right beside the brass Time Keeper badge. If the end of the human race was inevitable, fate could not ask for a more merciful pair of shepherds.

XV. The Pagoda Challenge

"I have realized that the past and future are real illusions: that they exist in the present, which is what there is and all there is." – Alan Watts

Gerrit was gone. That fact's grim reality proved too much for Raine to digest. She inched along the walls until she was clearly out of view.

"I think we can risk a little perimeter check," she told Chance, whose fur flickered like a candle's solitary flame.

The girl was pleasantly surprised, and soon morbidly afraid, of what she'd stumbled upon – an antique toy store.

Ceramic dolls, stuffed animals, and assorted trinkets were stacked up to the low ceiling like worldly treasures in a Pharaoh's burial chamber. Their eyes followed her every movement. The place was old and musty and she wondered how long it'd been since a customer had set foot inside. She considered calling "hello", but it didn't quite seem proper to raise one's voice amongst such company. The mysterious and beautiful dolls might resent such a hostile intruder, come alive, and devour her.

It wouldn't be the oddest thing to happen lately.

There might be one hope. She checked her map for Gerrit. Nothing. Raine then pulled out her visor.

No use. The local Network was down. She tossed the goggles across the floor.

What if this really isn't a dream?

It wasn't fair. She wanted to skip out on her lonely life for just one weekend, to achieve something worth bragging about so she could face the world again.

But I took my safety for granted.

Raine felt responsible for Gerrit, terrified that she might have caused something horrible to happen to him, and most of all regretful that she hadn't told him she actually admired his bravery and devotion.

The anger turned inward caught Raine in a downward spiral – she blamed herself for her past mistakes, for shunning the advice of and running away from every person who wanted to help her, and as Agnes might have famously worded, 'A-B-C-ing' her way into a situation like this.

What would my birth parents think of what I've become? The silence left Raine humbled and her heart laid bare onto the cold oak floor. Black flecks caught her eye from the window: another data storm, this time resembling soft snowflakes.

Folk rushed into their houses. The luau was cancelled. The storm washed off her wanted posters; pixels piled up in drifts. It didn't look like she was going anywhere that night. She slowed her breathing and withdrew the polyester sleeping bag from her inventory.

After unequipping her boots, Raine gently squeezed into the bag, and exhaled deeply when Chance transformed into a soft pillow and nestled under her head at just the right angle. She wiggled her toes and was comforted to find that they were warm.

Finding that her restless mind forbade her to sleep, for what seemed like hours Raine just focused on breathing. She half-noticed that when she took a deep breath, the black pixels seemed to slow, and when she exhaled, they fell in torrents. Unsure if she possessed weather-controlling powers or was simply imagining things, this curious development helped lull her into a soothing reprieve.

A faint hope entered her heart. *If anyone knows how I might be able to help Gerrit, it'd be SBB. He supposedly saved an entire galaxy, after all. No, Raine. Stop this nonsense; sixteen is too old to still have faith in fairy tales, even if you happen to be stuck in the middle of one.*

That's the other thing: as much as I want to continue believing it, for my own sake, and for Gerrit's, I can't afford to deny reality any longer, to ignore what my senses are telling me – that this is more than just a dream. But there's not much else I can do tonight. I need to accept what I don't yet have the power to change... and bide my time.

She recalled one of Agnes' favorite Longfellow quotes: *"The best thing one can do when it's raining is to let it rain."*

Humming the theme from *Teenage Mutant Ninja Turtles*, Raine found, calmed her down a bit. Eyes shut, she let the call of exhaustion take her, half-hoping that she'd wake up and forget this whole misbegotten adventure, quietly sad that she hadn't gotten to see her dream version of Stonehenge.

Ω

The virtual monitor went crashing through the one-way mirror in one of the *Nebula's* hundreds of interrogation rooms. In keeping with the Queen's personality traits, Miss Guggell was absolutely livid, and the Templars standing guard did nothing to stop her.

"You couldn't find her? What do you mean, she practically disappeared?"

Thibo Resa, Ground Ops Commander of the Templar Special Forces, was on his hands and knees; digital sweat pooled from the Developer's brow into a puddle on the glass floor. He saw his face distort in the ripples as each new drop added to the mirror of shame. Judgment at the hands of this radical AI was hardly fair. The father of two wished that he could have been enlisted centuries ago, when human courts – not virtual megalomaniacs - dealt with matters of military law. This could be the last time he saw his own face.

"It was the data storm, milady. It wasn't scheduled and it wasn't on record, it simply appeared out of nowhere. We could see nothing. The entire town was shrouded in darkness and fog. Ghost images flooded our vision. Before long, we were frozen in place and couldn't even log out. The very code of the *'Verse* spoke to us; we started to hallucinate. It was maddening. We could only wait 'til our surface team pulled the plug."

Miss Guggell slammed her fist down onto the desk, smashing it. She held a digital shard of pewter from the surface up to Thibo's neck.

"How were you not protected by my firewalls?"

"I wish I knew, ma'am. May I have an audience with Her Majesty about this? How about Doctor Hoshua, or Doctor Marco?"

"Negative. I am your judge, jury and executioner. Due to your incompetence, the data storm has managed to isolate Pagoda. None of us can get in there! I doubt that bag of meat you call a brain can even comprehend the magnitude of your failure. Wipe his platoon's memory," she directed.

Thibo was most relieved.

"Oh, and put him in deep," she added, virtual lips curling into a twisted expression.

"Please! Is there no justice?"

"Fairness is not one of my directives," she replied with finality, giving him a cold stare.

Thibo bit his lip and trembled, his heartbeat doubling the click and clack of his boss' heels as she stormed out of the room. He let his body hang limp as one of the guards approached with a small box. There was no use fighting now. If the tales were true, as soon as Miss Guggell entered the elevator and closed the door, he would breathe his final breath as a free man. His mind was being put into hibernation, his real-life body stored in a cryogenic freeze, probably never to be thawed.

The resplendent 'ding' came. The heels clicked once more. And when Miss Guggell turned around again, he caught a glimpse of her cold countenance. Her gaze was somewhere far, far away. Knowing that the end was near, Thibo closed his eyes in time with the elevator doors. Ejected from the virtual world, he felt the stinging needle from his *M-Gear* prod against the back of his head, and then swiftly penetrate. There was a paralyzing pain, and it was all over.

Several hours later, two men reclined at a private meeting room in the executive lounge and watched the top-secret footage of Thibo Resa's fate.

"Geez, that was rough," Henry whistled at Dr. Francesco Zarifian, who hung his head in disappointment.

Henry crossed his long legs atop the desk and sat as calmly as he could after watching such a horrifying recording.

"I really didn't think she'd do that," he continued. "Not on Hawaiian barbecue day, at least. Talk about job security."

"This is not okay. Either the Guggell program's finally lost its marbles," Dr. Zarifian argued, "or it's onto something, testing our resolve. It's got its creator's instincts, all right. I say we take a step back from this, just think about what we're doing here."

Zarifian twirled his pen, taking deep breaths. Francesco was Admiral Lily's eye in the sky. He'd fished out this footage at great risk to himself. Henry grabbed the pen, and with a stern, wordless look instructed his senior to keep his cool.

"Hey, Doc. This isn't some software deadline we can just mess around with. These are the orders from up high, and when we get an order, we have to carry it out. Hundreds of millions of human lives *are already* in the balance."

"I didn't ask for reassurances. You haven't got kids, Henry. How could you possibly understand how I feel? Even if we pull off a miracle, will the cavalry even show? Because if they don't--"

"That won't be an issue. Keep that chin up, mate. I may not have spawned, but you know I love your tots. Can't imagine how you're feeling. Just... please. Don't forget, we're all in this together."

"Course, man--" Francesco looked over his colleague's shoulders.

"Don't tell me. It's the Natasha to my Boris," Henry mused.

"On time for once, too. And it looks like she picked up something nasty."

Dr. Karuishi, the slender Japanese prodigy and the most renowned non-royal female programmer in *Neo Eden*, and the portly, managerial Avidya Lead, Dr. Alphonse Hoshua, always dressed in a tweed jacket and suspenders, passed the door's bio-metric scans and entered the room to join their colleagues for the impromptu meeting.

"Not that I care, but Marco's wondering why you three are eating lunch together, especially since there's a party going on," Hoshua grumbled. "Can we please get on with it?"

"You won't be sorry for your time, sir," Henry replied. "The data I'm sending you now shows that Miss Guggell has been infected by the quote-unquote Raine virus. It just put Doctor Resa in the icebox to cover up holes in its firewall. You can watch the video evidence if you like--"

"I don't have time for that. None of MG's watchdog programs have been triggered. If the AI wanted him out, he deserved what he got. The Queen stands by its judgment," Hoshua countered.

"Of course the Queen trusts Guggell," Karuishi said, rolling her eyes. "The AI can't suspect it's gained the upper hand. It's a war game within her mind. Should Miss Guggell's emergent strain of the Raine virus infect the Queen's nano-machines, well... that's the end of the Queen. Her entire rule could fall into question if she can no longer make logical and moral decisions."

"Which is why we're here," beamed Henry as Ayumi played footsie with him under the table.

Hoshua immediately stood from his seat.

"What is this, some sort of anarchist gathering? Because I don't like what I'm hearing."

"No, no, no, sir, nothing of the sort," Henry pleaded. "We're merely discussing what is to be done about Guggell's access and administration privileges should its AI become even more unstable."

"That's… it's blasphemous. It goes against the wishes of the Queen," Dr. Hoshua asserted.

Ayumi's stockings distracted Henry by rubbing up against his ankle, but he kept his cool.

"On the contrary, sir. One of the personal duties given to me upon my recruitment was performing routine maintenance checks on MG," he bluffed, without blinking or batting an eyelash. "With all due respect, I've shadowed the AI since my first months with QC; I'd like to imagine that I'd be the first to spot a malfunction."

He sent a few files over to Hoshua, who switched on his Holo-Lens to check over a chock full of carefully doctored reports. The man thumbed a few charts.

Glad that he was taking the bait, Henry continued. "The Queen can't fix this virus without the risk of corrupting her nano-bots. She can't even connect with the system directly, or the virus may continue to evolve and even warp her by proximity. This is a top-secret assignment. And therein sits our dilemma. We're in the middle of dealing with a very prickly situation as it is."

Dr. Zarifian cleared his throat. "I concur with Holdfast on this. Guggell automatically reads its master's thoughts. The less the Queen suspects Miss Guggell, the less resistance we'll meet. This is a matter that can't wait."

Hoshua scratched his head. "What do you need me for? Approval?"

"Yes, Doctor," Henry bowed. "I need a 'go' from three A-ranked Devs to take the precaution of temporarily swapping *Avidya's* instance of the AI with last week's backup, so we can repair it in a controlled environment and safeguard the Queen, all the while allowing her to operate and monitor the *'Verse* at this crucial juncture. As you're Lead for *Avidya*, I thought it natural to approach you first."

"I'm not entirely convinced," continued Hoshua. "Unless you're all pulling my leg, I had no idea that Her Highness has always been so vulnerable. However, I do recognize that Miss Guggell is most definitely not operating properly. So I'll back you on this. But what if the Queen wishes to interface with it?"

"The backup should be fully operational, sir. I will personally deal with any bugs, should they arise."

"Very well," Hoshua continued. "It sounds like you've already got a plan of action. Let's hear it."

"It is a bit rough, sir. I imagine we'll need two teams. Team one will divide and micro-manage MG's duties in the *'Verse*, while Team two works on purifying the poor girl. Sir, I gather you've got your hands full refining the HDP integration."

Dr. Hoshua cleared his throat. "Naturally. I'm troubleshooting this grand protocol thing for the Joint Chiefs. Don't expect it'll be needed as long as Beech and Macleod are airborne, but orders are orders. Keep this in mind: should the *Metaverse* suffer a hiccup, our troops will be relying on the Overseer alone. Then we can kiss goodbye to our monthly bonus. Just… be careful. I wish my department had the time or manpower to help you out with this, but I must decline. If Miss Guggell is to be laid up for a spell, our job will already be greatly exacerbated."

Henry suppressed a grin, turning it into a concerned grimace: the 'correct' response.

"You'd be a great help, but I understand, sir. Since I know you wouldn't trust my green hands on Miss Guggell, I'll take head of *Avidya* security with Dr. Karuishi here. Frankie will lead team two. We'll each pick ten staff members, but for obvious reasons, none of this can leave the *Avidya* group."

Ayumi and Francesco nodded their consent, then held up their tablets and slotted in their personal keys. Reluctantly, Alphonse followed suit. Henry keyed into the *Nexus'* Intranet mainframe with his Holo-Lens and initiated the AI swap procedure.

"This'll take just a few minutes," Henry reassured them. "We get to work immediately after lunch. Leave no stone unturned, and all that."

Dr. Karuishi laughed out loud as Henry tickled under her feet. Francesco rolled his eyes and broke the tension with a cough. The swap completed; Miss Guggell had been replaced by the EDC's near-identical replica, which boasted a particularly gaping security hole.

"Alrighty, then. Al, let's see if there's any short ribs left," Zee said, clapping his colleague on the back.

"I'm more of a pulled pork guy myself," Hoshua replied.

The Developers stood in unison and filed out of the protected conference room.

Once he and Ayumi were alone, Henry's shoulders finally relaxed.

"You're doing very well," she told him. "Just ran my snooping daemon. If it can find a way into MG's databanks, we'll have the Overseer's ciphers fully cracked within the day."

The man managed a bumbling nod. "Yes... we're nearly t-there..."

"You okay?" She spun him to a sudden stop and they faced one another eye to eye. Henry tried to match his thundering pulse to the rhythm of the soft hands now gently tracing his palms. "Your heart's beating like crazy."

"I feel like I could run a marathon. But logically, I'm not as afraid as I should be. Maybe it's 'coz you've got my back."

Ayumi giggled to release the tension. "Don't you dare let your guard down for anyone other than me. I'm the jealous type, you know."

She gave his hand a squeeze. Side by side, they headed back to the *Nexus*.

∞

Morning came and Raine was surprisingly rested.

"Did you sleep well, too, Chance?"

The cat nodded, and then looked at her bag.

"Hmm? Oh, you want to go inside?"

He nodded, and Raine complied. It was probably for the best; his distinctive coat, even in grayscale, was a dead giveaway. *It's like he knows I want to keep a low profile. Smart kitty. Almost* too *smart.*

A gentle song wove its way to her ears, bringing with it a relieving wave of energy. She fluttered to the faint chime of the music box like a moth to a solitary dancing flame. It took her to the back room, where an elderly woman sat by a holographic fireplace, patching up a doll's dress with intricate care. She turned around slowly and ominously.

"Ah, the chosen one," she said in a thick Korean accent. "Your snoring is powerful enough to wake the dead. Let us hope your gaming prowess is on the level."

"Pardon me?"

"They said you would be the one to save us," she replied. "The beeping one has desecrated our humble resort town for many moons."

Now Raine understood. "Let me guess. Is this some lousy side quest?"

"You do not seem eager to fulfill your destiny," the lady observed.

"No offense, ma'am. I've been called a 'chosen one' before. It didn't end well."

"You must be thinking of another quest. This is the first time we have met."

"I… see," she replied, though she really didn't. "Miss…"

"Zoot. Mrs."

"Mrs. Zoot, I've never exactly saved an entire town before. And it might be better if nobody knows I'm here."

"If you're worried about distractions and hecklers, let me assure you: should you so choose, as soon as you wear the Chosen One's official attire, your true identity can be masked."

Another mask. Kind of scary to think I might get used to this anonymity thing.

"Cool. Sounds like I've got nothing to lose. But what's in it for me?"

"It is said that whosoever completes this quest will be given unlimited power."

Unlimited power. Is this my chance to make things right? I don't believe it, but if there's a possibility whatever it is might help me save Gerrit…

"Okay, I'm intrigued, but I still don't know if I'm qualified. I'm rather new here, Mrs. Zoot."

The woman handed Raine the doll. It bore a striking resemblance to herself. "Experience matters not, beyond the minimum level requirements. Looks like you've made the grade, if just barely. Still, no being has ever beaten this quest, not in the recorded, deleted, or even imagined history of the *Metaverse*. To defeat the beeping one requires great cunning and unparalleled reflexes."

Raine studied the doll's determined expression. She had both of those things in spades, and she never walked away from a gaming throw-down.

"Word. I'll give it a shot," she responded nonchalantly.

Before she knew it, the antique shop owner had risen, dressed Raine in a long, itchy, hooded robe, and led her before a dynamic water fountain in the midst of the town. All in view stopped to stare.

Sitting cross-legged on a large rock throne was a roughly six-foot-tall digital stopwatch. It clearly belonged in a cartoon, with large eyes and a permanently smug mouth decorating its face. The Stopwatch munched on a car battery, regarding Raine with great interest as shackled children fanned it with palm leaves.

"Listen up, foul beast!" the elderly woman bellowed with all her power. "Listen, brothers and sisters, for I bring before you one of our own, a human, a magician of great strength, who will deliver us in this dark hour!"

By now quite a crowd had gathered.

So much for staying unnoticed, Raine thought.

"Yes! Before me, at last, stands The Chosen One!"

There was much rejoicing. Praises were hollered. Little children cried. Raine became very conscious of the fact that her back was drenched in sweat.

A sudden, deafening BEEP interrupted the celebration. Raine almost jumped in shock; the Stopwatch held the note for a good ten seconds. When it had at last ceased the unbearable sound, most of the village was on the ground. Some were curled up in fetal positions. Children shook in abject fear. Silence had reclaimed the square.

Raine didn't seem nearly as physically affected by the noise. She stepped up to the throne.

"I challenge you to a duel," she said, as Mrs. Zoot had instructed.

The crowd erupted into applause again. The Stopwatch sneered and crossed over its other leg.

The townspeople wheeled out two enormous arcade cabinets. When Raine caught a glimpse of them, she beamed.

Super BlastBoy II.

This was fate. Nothing was going to stop her now.

The cabinets were set up back to back atop a central stage that appeared on command within a cordoned-off area. Raine was escorted along the carpet floor. She took a seat on the barstool and studied the new instructions. The controls seemed identical to the first game, with a few new items and enemy types thrown in for good measure. Advanced 16-bit graphics played the intro, displayed on a genuine cathode ray TV, a gloriously familiar sight to the girl. The remixed title music kicked in.

As Raine did her homework, a portly judge stood before the people and read from a scroll the terms and conditions of the game.

"It is decreed that there shall be a practice run of forty-five minutes, following which, the match proper will begin, wherein The Chosen One and the---"

"Yo, Beefeater! My bro's got a suggestion!" a punkish teen boy's voice called out loudly from the front.

The announcer addressed the sparkling child, a stark contrast to his older brother. "What is it, Casey?"

"I believe we should address the Chosen One by her true name."

There was some murmuring. Raine looked from the child to the official, unsure of what to do. The judge at last walked up to her, tipped his hat, and bowed.

"We humbly request to know your name, O Chosen One."

She thought of her one-time Californian pen pal. Hopefully she wouldn't mind Raine borrowing her name.

"Elise," she gulped, not wanting to divulge her identity. "Just Elise."

"Thank you, Elise, O Chosen One," the people intoned in zombified unison, reading from a teleprompter above the two machines.

"To say your name is truly an honor," said the judge, returning to his pedestal with a cough to silence the ecstatic crowd.

"After the practice run, The Chosen One, namely Elise, and the Beeping One, whose true name remains… unknown, will be competing for the high score in a co-operative game of *Super BlastBoy II*. The one with the highest score after both players *game over* shall be crowned victor and given stewardship over the city. Practice run begins now."

Raine regulated her breathing, psyching herself up. *It's time to open up a can of whoop-ass.*

A whistle sounded out and the game began.

Zoot studied her progress carefully. Elise didn't seem to have memorized the levels. She faltered at first, but was quick to learn. In the early shooter stages she soon developed the particularly useful strategy of trailing the Stopwatch's movements.

Within a half hour, it looked as if she had fully grasped the game. They'd reached the last level of their second run when the judge bade them to reset their cabinets, and none too late. The challenger was down to her final life.

The girl needed a breather during the intermission; she practically inhaled a bottle of root beer as if it were the last one on Earth. The outspoken teen in the front put his visor's live feed of the event up on the Net. Thousands of spectators complained loudly about ongoing Network maintenance, which kept the sleepy town's entrances and exits sealed.

When the battle proper began, Zoot leaned back with the other event planners against the large barricade erected to keep the unruly crowd from crushing the two competitors, whose exponentially multiplying scores were neck in neck.

The showdown continued for hours.

Zoot had fallen asleep thrice, and thrice been awakened by gasps from the crowd. Elise and The Beeping One were on their miraculous ninth play-through. As the speed increased on each subsequent run, the old cabinets lagged behind. The Stopwatch's movements were, as always, cold, calculated and lifeless. Elise, on the other hand, astonished the crowd with her intense passion and eye for craftiness.

The hidden areas of her brain slowing time and seemingly handing over control of her motor reflexes to a raw, bestial inner power source, Raine danced figure eights in that mythical place where all gamers yearn to be. She lost herself in the zone.

Within the next play-through, Raine overtook the Stopwatch. Now that she'd memorized the levels it was a simple matter of going through the motions, missing power-ups in order to increase chain-combos, blasting segments that left the Stopwatch open to fire. Its gameplay was technically efficient, but its adaptive learning was limited. Whatever algorithms were put in place to modify its AI were no match for Raine's reflexes, unpredictable style, and complete mastery of the original title.

The music was completely in sync with her playing, the bass her metronome.

She had completely forgotten about her ego, her burning questions, her obsession with Super BlastBoy's promise, Agnes' doubting words, her attachment to video games; even Gerrit and the question of his relation to her unexplained memories faded. Her focus and speed were gifts beyond comprehension, her skill so fluid and perfect that only a fraction of the technique behind it was apparent to those standing agape in awe.

At long last it was time for the game to come to an end.

Zoot was shaking. After a long bout of slowdown suddenly reverted back into real-time during the final level's mid-boss, both Elise and the Stopwatch were down to one life. While they were neck-and-neck during the seventh run, the challenger's relentless chain multiplier boosted her up to four billion points, with her opponent merely fifty million points behind.

Elise needed to outsmart the Stopwatch, to somehow lead it to self-destruction. It was glitching up. Perhaps its overclocked RAM was burning out. But it was staying alive, and the last ship left standing would receive a bonus in points that could tip the scale.

The final boss, Dr. Professor, nearly killed them both. The crowd waited with baited breath. His first form went down in flames. The second form, too. But the third was the fastest of all, and had gotten deadlier during each run. Dodging its endless barrage of bullets was all that the challenger could do. She'd used up her bombs. He was charging up its most powerful attack. It was highly unlikely that both of them would make it out of there alive.

"SUDDEN DEATH!" a drunken dwarf called out from the audience.

It became a chant. The townspeople were livid.

Zoot joined the chanting. Fireworks erupted above them. Sweat ran down Raine's arms and dripped down onto the joystick, where her palms were clammy, sticky, and covered in painful blisters. Yet she continued to jerk left, right, left, fire, up, down, right, down, fire, until the raw power of her performance moved them all to silence.

There was a collective gasp.

When Raine became somewhat conscious of the world again, it was because people had yanked her from the throne and tossed her into the air. Hands scampered for the controls all too late. The Stopwatch had died to the boss' master attack, and now so had she. The world she had taken to its limit fell away as the judge entered "ELI" as #1 on the top score screen.

Another shrill beep snapped our heroine out of her trance. The Stopwatch was being tied up to two large poles. It looked very miserable and turned to Raine for a brief exchange, perhaps searching for sympathy, until the folk carried it into the distance and it was no more.

Raine was placed onto the main throne before the fountain. She looked down uncomfortably on the villagers. They were bowing before her as if she were a goddess.

Then Mrs. Zoot crowned her.

The crown, she decreed, would confer unto Elise the title *Princess of Pagoda*. As an added bonus, she was gifted with Developer status for a whole day. For the next twenty-four hours, she was going to be absolutely invincible.

∩

Watching the drama come to a crescendo in transit from the *Phoenix,* Lily leapt from her seat, hit her head on the ceiling, then sat down and pumped her fists instead. Raine had done it. She actually defeated the Champion, triggering a secret connection into *Endless Metaverse's* central mainframe.

She checked in with the *Belladonna.* Rutger was already drawing a map of the Intranet. All that was left was to crack the access codes to the exit node registry, and she'd have a laundry list of backdoor entrances to the fundamentals of Lorelei's Network.

Lily ran the debug app from her Holo-Lens, patching it through the direct connection that Raine's remote account had opened with the *Metaverse's* mainframe. It was the beginning of the end to this nightmare. As she watched Raine smiling atop the traveling procession, Lily pondered the enormity of what had just been accomplished. The map of secret passageways into every facet of *Endless Metaverse* would soon be complete.

"It's been a joyous day, Rutger. Is Yossa mobilizing?"

"Yes, Miss Lily. Congratulations."

"We can't celebrate just yet. The show must go on."

XVI. Waltz for the Moon

"It is better to be violent, if there is violence in our hearts, than to put on the cloak of nonviolence to cover impotence." – Mahatma Gandhi

While Raine slept in late on the floor of Mrs. Zoot's long-neglected antique shop, General Lacie had no such luxury.

The latest reports still insisted that Raine, her next target, was hiding within Pagoda's freak data blizzard. In other words, her physical location remained untraceable. The prudent step at this point was to head back home and regroup.

At seven A.M. the sun glanced out from behind the Eastern peaks, casting long, dark shadows over empty fields. Lacie cracked the sunroof about a half-inch. At nearly mach speed, the cold wind shooting into her cockpit woke her up better than a shot of adrenaline. Not that she was falling asleep, of course. She'd only been up for three days, powering away on four kinds of painkillers and multiple amphetamines. In another world, the General might have rested, at least for a few hours, but her sister had no patience for wasted time.

Lacie closed the window and took a gander at her navigator. Her personal speeder had ascended the desolate Ukok plateau with ease. She was currently flying by the Altai Mountains, a beautiful stretch of highlands that in the old world was sandwiched between Russia, Mongolia, China, and Kazakhstan.

All three of her remaining escorts flanked her *Isis*, rotating positions with perfect precision. She had been journeying to home base for hours now with her precious cargo.

Gerrit, one of the two who would destroy *Endless Metaverse*, was now in her possession. The boy was no easy quarry to attain. Breaking into Lily's underground bunker and facing off against almost a hundred armed droids had been a lengthy battle that left twenty of her best men dead and half as many seriously wounded.

She spun around for a quick glance. There he was; the sad, pale thing, passed out, curled up in the cargo bay like a helpless animal, half-open eyes visible through his *M-Gear*'s standard goggles. Cut off from a power source, his eyeballs rolled back and forth into his head at incredible speeds, and the helmet's 'solar recharge needed' LED blinked erratically. As far as she was concerned he was comatose.

Lacie had hoped to find the boy working actively with the resistance – heck, she expected to encounter at least one human member of the EDC – but instead, just an hour ago she discovered him sitting cross-legged in a small room, dressed in the garb of a Tibetan monk. Maintained by android servants, fed on an ample vegetarian diet, and with a light exercise routine programmed into his daily regimen, the kid's body was perfectly at peace, his frozen mind's last memories arrested on his short-lived role within the *Metaverse*.

They would investigate whether Gerrit possessed any latent memories of the world outside. Of course, that was even considering that Lily hadn't wiped his memory beforehand. Any rebel plot in a potential sleeper agent's memory banks would have been processed by the nano-bots and mentioned in the asset's file. Oddly enough, none had been found: a testament to Lily's craftiness.

Lily. It's odd that she hasn't showed up yet.

There was a blip on the radar. Speak of the devil.

Lacie bit her tongue. It was coming fast. It could only be *her*, and none too late.

"Gamma Leader to Gold Squadron Leader, do you copy?"

"Copy, General. Awaiting orders."

"Enemy bogey sighted at seven-o-clock. Closing."

"Shall we engage, ma'am?"

Lacie knew the answer was no. *Not yet. We don't even have visibility. What can we possibly shoot at?*

"Cargo is first priority. Defensive positions. Phalanx formation."

"Phalanx formation. Affirmative."

The speeders pulled in to surround Lacie's ship, carefully positioning their jets and rotating guns outwards. Almost as soon as it fell into formation, vitals went silent on the pilot of the southern-facing craft. Lacie gaped at the video replay – he was shot in the head.

The pilot died instantly; his corpse fell onto the controls, sending the craft speeding towards the westernmost ship, which moved to dodge it and suffered a barrage of well-timed explosive rounds on one of its turbines. As the pilot gasped for breath amidst the smoke cycling into the cockpit, the ship's gunner spotted a flash of metal, aimed carefully, fired, and missed. The mystery craft had disappeared once again.

"We've lost Redd! Six-two is hit!"

Lacie was furious. Nothing was showing up on the *Isis'* displays. Lily's infrared signature should at least have registered on the radar. She barked orders like a mad woman.

"Steady! Steady! Enemy is cold-cloaked and within range. Fire at will! This bitch is going down!"

The General studied the vidfeed from every corner of her ship. A blip registered directly on top of her position. Lily had to be either above or below her. She pulled the *Isis* to a sudden slowdown, let her escorts fly ahead, and held her breath.

Gerrit's restraints clicked into place immediately as G-absorbing gel flooded the cabin and stopped Lacie's and Gerrit's bodies from falling apart at the sudden change in G-force. She checked her screen again as the gel quickly cycled out.

The blip continued following them briefly. Lacie kick-started the jets again, rapidly accelerating towards her escorts. She was closing on Lily, so close now, just waiting for her to fire, or miss, or her cloak to breach... just one sign...

A frantic voice yelled over the radio. "General, look out!"

Blinding light hit her straight in the eyes. Lily's plasma flashbang; the brat was closing the distance. Two lightning-fast beams of concentrated electricity hit Lacie's power supply, shorting out the engine for a split-second and resetting her navigation systems. Lily trained her machine gun as she zoomed past Lacie, who struggled to keep the *Isis* airborne.

Lacie surveyed the damage. Machine guns: jammed. Afterburners: cut. A few bullets penetrated the fuselage and took out one of the flaps, but all other systems were go. Gerrit was fine. It seemed at the last second Lily had stopped herself from risking any serious harm to the boy.

"Ha! You missed!" Lacie chortled as she spun one of her jets around, pulling a 180, and let loose her missiles towards the vague area where Lily's ship should be.

Its cloaking pulsed for a split-second as Lily leeched power from the system to jet forward, revealing the sleek craft. As she'd expected, Lily wasn't fool enough to pilot the *Phoenix* into a terrestrial battle, but this EDC ship was no less state-of-the-art. Thanks to Lily's silver coolant scrambling her heat signature, the missiles were flying blind, but at least one was sure to connect. Lacie cheered as one exploded against the main rudder in a satisfying fireball, and savored the cracking metal as the Sky Admiral's craft sputtered to the ground, barely missing an awkwardly placed Network tower.

"General, are you all right?"

"Never better."

"We are en route to your current location."

"Negative. Bogey down. I'll investigate on foot and send my ship on autopilot with you to home base. Cargo is first priority. Cannot allow it to fall into enemy hands. Send a squad back for me after the next checkpoint."

"Copy that."

General Lacie set her ship to a vertical standstill to arm herself with all fifty pounds of her heavy weaponry. She then descended to the surface of the plateau three hundred feet from the crash site. Boulders and bushes dotted the soil: a perfect hiding place for growth-stunted Lillian. Lacie scanned the burning wreckage. The craft was totaled, but there was no trace of her sister.

Machine guns fixed, Lacie unloaded the rest of her ship's ammunition onto the ground before opening up the hatch and strolling down the entry ramp. She steeled her determination, prepared to face the worst.

At twenty-nine, Lacie had been extensively educated in all forms of combat, undergoing intense training throughout various time periods. As she first came into consciousness in the body of a thirteen-year-old, it wasn't as good as what Lily had grown up with – virtual training and conditioning since the age of five – but it was something. Hand-to-hand combat. Fencing. Judo. Street fighting. Firearms. Heavy weaponry.

Whatever awaits, I'll be ready.

A cocked shotgun met the General not twenty feet away.

Lacie couldn't help but snicker at the irony.

Having sprung from behind a weathered rock, Lillian was staring her down from the other end of the automatic shotgun, finger latched tightly onto the trigger.

"You have forcibly breached my facility and taken away someone very important to me. I'd like for him to be returned."

"Hmph. You certainly reacted fast enough. We thought you'd be playing hopscotch with your terrorist buddies."

"Then the only explanation is that I knew you were going to do it."

Lacie glowered. Lily had broken the rules.

"Elaborate on how this is not a violation of our set terms."

"That's simple. Recently, you or Lorelei scouted into the future, and saw that I razed your precious *Metaverse*. So either you were sent or you came of your own volition to take Gerrit out of the equation and make sure that your apocalyptic power trip runs smoothly. My future self discovered this blatant trickery and sent back a message telling of your crime."

"You will refer to her as 'Majesty'."

"She will always be Lorelei to me."

Lacie sneered. "So you reveal plainly that you received information from the future and acted on it. How is it that you accuse me solely of breaking the rules again?"

"You cast the initial stone. In the first place, there's absolutely no way you could have known of Gerrit's location without tracking my shutdown signal, which hasn't happened yet. Don't take me for a fool, Lacie. Another of the preconditions, I hope you'll remember, is that we agreed to no further time travel to and from the end of the world. Aren't things convoluted enough? Your fuel cells are almost spent, anyways."

"Tell me something I don't know."

"Technically, I would be lecturing myself," Lily answered. "The truth of the matter is, in this case you two have cheated and as there are no judges or arbiters qualified to hear our particularly unique case, I reserve my right to challenge at least one of you to a duel to the death."

Lacie groaned. "Now?"

"Yes, now. No more tricks. And no weapons."

Lacie internalized this long and well. On the one hand was possible death, on the other a chance for ultimate glory. Lily hadn't fought so well the last time, but her limbs, formerly broken, were now covered in shining titanium. It would certainly be a challenge.

"As you wish," she said at last.

The morning sun in her eyes, Lacie tied her hair back, then carefully removed her ammo vest and stripped her person of two pistols, an automatic crossbow, an electric whip, a pair of nunchaku, three concealed knives, and a hand grenade.

"The electromagnetic belt, too," Lily said.

Lacie reluctantly threw off the heavy belt.

Walking in a semi-circle, Lily relieved herself of the same exact pair of pistols, her shotgun, a stun laser, two electric whips, a katana, four hand grenades, and a lightweight shield. She also took off her helmet, letting her shoulder-length hair blow in the wind.

By mutual agreement Lily was allowed to keep on and use her cybernetic limb enhancements, for they were the only things holding her frail body together.

The two women stared each other down as they moved counter-clockwise in a loop, boots crunching the grassy plain below as they circled closer and closer.

"This will be your end," Lacie said, her voice stained with hatred. "A fitting end to a false prophet, to be done in by her own lieutenant."

"Your arrogance is misplaced," Lily barked. "Don't forget who made you, who raised you, who trained you."

"I am not beholden to you, or to your damning oath! I am more than you were, are, or will ever be!"

Without hesitation, Lacie charged towards Lily with a punch that turned into a feint, and quickly transformed into a sweeping kick. Lily tried to clear the low kick, but was a split second too late. Lacie knocked the Admiral off her feet.

The jets in her limb enhancements spurted to life and Lily performed a handstand into a perfect flip backwards, landing on both feet three meters away.

Lily assumed a fighting stance as Lacie circled her again, looking for an open spot. Lily charged through her defenses, blocked a high kick, grabbed her leg, chopped into Lacie's standing knee and twisted her into the ground. Lacie fell on her stomach and immediately rebounded off the grass, twisting her nimble back around as she did so for one desperate blow.

Her leg connected with Lily's face, sending her flying. Lily pushed her hands backwards, activating her arm jets to absorb the impact and somersault. She landed on her feet again just in time to take a deafening punch.

Lacie's fist caught Lily's nose. She hit the ground.

Her head smacked off of the hard rocky plain only to see Lacie lunging towards her with a concealed knife.

"So that's how you wanna play?"

Lily fumbled her legs, at last managing to stick one up against Lacie's stomach. She wiggled her big toe to initiate its super-hot jet.

Screaming at the heat melting the outer layers of her suit, Lacie pulled Lily close, desperate to shove a knife into her opponent's neck.

"This is the end!" Lacie yelled, and smashed her forehead into Lily's.

Lacie tried to pull away after the head-butt, but Lily grabbed her throat and squeezed through the suit's protective collar. The flames were almost through the fabric. Lacie smashed her head into Lily's once again, almost knocking her out this time.

The Sky Admiral tossed a haymaker into the General's neck. It worked - she coughed and Lily pushed her foot even deeper in, forcing her off her body at last. Lacie rolled away on the grass as Lily leapt back to gain her bearings. She ignored the blood dripping down her forehead.

Coughing deeply, Lacie stood up a mess. She clutched at the gaping hole in her midriff where her suit had almost burned through.

"You're a murderer," she said. "Nothing but a murderer. All those parallel universes, all those people just floundering out there waiting to die. *You left them to die! You left them there so you could witness your own victory!* You're not a god, Lily. Your work is futile. It is power you seek, not peace. Your blood alone deserves to be spilt."

"I have nothing more to say to you. You two said all that needed to be said two centuries ago when you betrayed me."

"*We* betrayed *you?*"

"I believe that is the proper terminology for what you did, yes. Not to mention mutiny. Lorelei's perverting Terra in your – our – collective image was inspired, in a twisted, maniacal sort of manner, but morally and strategically flawed."

"All these years and you still don't get it. The flaws were built into the system."

Lily raised an eyebrow, then tore off a piece of her undershirt and used it to wipe the blood from her eyes.

"You made us this way. Inferior. We were cloned from your DNA, yet you didn't trust us, didn't treat us as equals…"

"Every mission needs a leader. You had your tasks, as did Lucy and Lorrie. I made that clear! I treated you fairly! I asked for nothing more than what I knew you could give me! I already made five attempts to get humanity off the planet. Five attempts, Lacie! I had the experience! I had the intelligence!"

"But never the skill or the sleight of hand. And you made sure that we didn't either. We never had the potential to become complete beings. You made us in your image, but gave us weaknesses. Yes, don't think we didn't figure it out. You hampered us. You couldn't trust us – couldn't trust yourself – and that was the true spark that ignited Lorelei's fury. That is why Lucy is now dead, and why you soon will be too."

Lily winced.

She had, indeed, made each of the three weaker than she in certain aspects; primarily, Lorelei lacked empathy, Lacie was robbed of resolve, and dear departed Lucy had no physical prowess. That truth she couldn't deny. But it was a secret that was supposed to spur on teamwork. They were meant to have differences that complemented each other.

Lacie picked up her electromagnetic belt and strapped it on. She called forth her knives.

"You want to know what I think of your rules?" the older one asked, advancing.

"Lacie, I'm sorry."

"You're sorry?!? YOU'RE SORRY?!?"

"Yes, I'm sorry. Drop the weapons now and I will do what I can to give you a new life. It will not be an exceptional life, but it will be better than nothing. A life with no obligations, free of Lorelei, free of myself, and free of the mission. It is not for you. It was never for you. It's true; I had no right to decide your fate before your birth."

Lacie clenched her knives. Routine sixty-four would put both in the girl's neck. Lillian Hermes' life would end in seconds. A final silencing of the nagging voice in Lacie's head, a small atonement for the lives lost at the *Jerusalem Un-Incident* and beyond.

Perhaps once the enemy of my home is vanquished, Lacie thought, *Claire and I can live without the dark shadows of my past hanging over our heads. There will be no more regrets, no more uncertainties.*

"You still think you know what's right for me? Well, it's too late! Even if I wipe my memories a thousand times over, I can never turn back from all that I've done!"

"I'm just trying to be civil. There are other ways, Lacie--"

"I'M SICK OF YOU PLAYING MOTHER!"

Her eyes filled with unchecked rage, Lacie ran to slash Lily's throat. Lily's gauntlet blocked the blows, and she scampered backwards.

"Come here, mother! Come and know our shame."

But Lily had already found her stun laser and her whip. She wielded both with the expert confidence of a lion tamer. Lacie ran for her katana. Lily fired a laser blast at her leg, making the General lose her footing for a split-second. That was all she needed; with her electric whip she lashed onto Lacie's knife-wrist and squeezed the handle, sending a jolt straight down the wire.

Lacie kept a firm grip on the knife. Lily continued to electrocute her clone, fearful tears welling in the eyes of both.

"Children's toys, mother."

Neither stopped their charge. The nano-machines in Lacie's brain gave her one final boost to fight back against the electricity. She abruptly lunged with her knife towards her creator's whip hand. Missed. Tried to jump back.

Lily pulled the whip forward, dragging Lacie to the floor, then shot the stun laser at her neck. Lacie's body flashed with lightning, her eyes glowing with fury.

"I didn't want this for you!" Lily cried. Lacie dropped the knife, which was promptly kicked away, and the Admiral took the further opportunity to place her insulated boot down on her opponent's chest.

Lily injected her clone with fast-acting truth serum, and held her there for some time.

"Now that I don't have Gerrit, it will be significantly harder for us to enter the mainframe. I shot tracking bullets into your ship in order to trace him back to the home base." Lily said, glancing at her Holo-Lens, and continued. "But unfortunately, it seems my plan has been compromised. Your team was smart enough to swap for fresh aircraft at an abandoned base. I see Lorelei's given you access to a whole range of toys. I don't doubt she's been kind with her information as well."

Lacie shook her head. The serum was having no effect; her nano-machines nipped the toxin in the bud.

"You're not getting anything from me!"

"I'm trying to be polite here. You've failed. As for Gerrit, I've got ways of tracking him you don't want to know about. But please tell me two things. First, where is *Endless Metaverse's* super-soldier program being run from, and second, just how much do you know about the future? You know I have safe communities. The people I've liberated are rebuilding their homelands. Once this is all over, you have my word. I'll set you free. You won't have to speak a word of this to

Lorelei. If you behave, and if you so choose, I may even reconsider your position aboard the *Belladonna*."

The Sky Admiral's face was filled with desperation. Lacie fell silent. She couldn't believe what she was hearing. *Would Lily really give me a second chance? It's not worth the risk. It's too late, anyway, isn't it? What about the fate of the universe and all that? And what of Claire?*

The thin air hung heavy over a long silence.

"Lacie, please. I don't want to hurt you."

"You're gonna have to!" Lacie squirmed. "Just end it! Kill me, goddamn it!"

Lillian sent a minor jolt down the whip. Her sister winced.

"What does she know, Lacie? How well did you do your research?"

"I'll never tell!"

Lily zapped her again, much harder this time.

Lacie closed her eyes, trying to imagine a future where she and Lily were working together as equals. The sheer implausibility of it was painful. This was to be her grave. The Sky Admiral gave the General another dose of the serum.

"Don't make this harder than it has to be. Tell me what I need to know. You still have a chance, Lacie. That's a big city, *Neo Eden*. The Overseer could be running from anywhere, and if I don't get those plans to my people, many more innocents will needlessly die in the conflict. We wouldn't want that, would we?"

"G-g-go to hell!"

The shocks continued. Lacie convulsed in extreme agony. Lily turned her face away to hide her tears. Lacie raised her head once more.

"Some hero you are," the General laughed. "You're not above torturing your enemies."

"You're the ones dooming the world's population."

"Says the woman who challenged us to war!"

"Back up a second. Why's all this happening, again? It's coming to me now. Right. You messed with my freakin' time machine!"

Lily gave her a mega-jolt that lasted too long for either woman's comfort. Any other opponent would have given in long ago.

At long last, Lacie nodded; the second dose of serum took effect.

"Okay, so I'm thinking the lower level servers in the *Spire*. Yes? Chamber 50B, you say? Good. You're doing well so far. Question two. You two have been waiting for me to make a move. Of all my agents in the 'Verse, you correctly pursued Raine and Gerrit. But just how much did you see, exactly?"

Lacie hesitated. *I'm sorry, Claire.*

"This is important, Lacie! We must settle this before your backup arrives! What did you two see in the future?"

The answer came in the form of spit in her face. While Lily was stunned, Lacie lunged at her and squeezed the whip's handle, electrocuting them both. She pulled out Lily's blade and aimed it at her face. Lily held the knife-hand out of the way with her left, while her right made its way around her opponent's neck, catching on her locket, exposed through the burned fabric, which opened to reveal a picture of Claire, across from the Time Keeper Badge.

"Is she the one you're fighting for? I'll grant her passage, too. Last chance, 'Cie. Let me help you."

If only I could believe that those gentle eyes aren't lying. There's no more turning back for me, Lillian. It has to be this way.

The General only shoved her knife closer, drawing blood along the side of Lily's neck.

"You... will never defeat us..."

Lily took a deep breath of the thin mountain air. She squeezed her metal fingers and an electrical current ran straight through Lacie; Lily's limb enhancements cut the deadly circuit off. The older woman choked, gasped, and burst into the most horribly grotesque laughter before dropping dead.

The body fell. Lily staggered back. It wasn't the first time she'd seen herself die violently, but it was the first time she'd been the one to do the killing. She couldn't take her eyes off of her corpse, its nerves still twitching involuntarily. At last, the lifeless form concluded its dance, empty head turned and lifeless eyes gazing right into Lillian's soul.

Just before she could take a well-earned breath, a younger Lacie reappeared before her once more. Like a ghost, her untied hair fluttered about in the wind. She had just arrived on a silent hover speeder, and she was pointing a gun directly at Lily.

There was no time to be shocked. Lillian anticipated the bullet and performed a perfect dodge-roll to pick up her bulletproof shield before taking cover behind a boulder. She knelt on the rocky ground, eyes fixed on her new opponent as her other hand nimbly and quietly wrapped around one of her pistols, hidden behind a tall shrub.

"Why, hello, Lillian," the ghost cackled. "My, you're fast. It's nice to finally meet you."

"I thought we said no tricks!" yelled Lily.

"Hmmm? Whatever deal you made with that woman lying dead there, it doesn't apply to me. I'm a clone of your clone. It didn't take much, really. I've been instructed to follow her to every major battle, and should she fall, to finish the job. Luckily for you, your death shall be quick, as I'm fresh off the most intense training regimen-"

She gasped.

The single blast created a discordant shock that stopped everything dead but the faint whirring of Lacie's clone's speeder. The ghost looked down into her torso. A highly explosive round erupted through the bulletproof Kevlar vest, carving a gaping cavity in her chest. Her heart stopped in seconds. She collapsed onto the plateau.

There was a good minute of silence as Lily's breathing returned to normal. She stood, walked up to Lacie's clone's corpse, and put another bullet in her just to be safe.

This is getting ridiculous.

While collecting her belongings, Lily tapped her Holo-Lens.

"Tiger to Fox Hole, come in, Fox Hole, over."

Joaquin's voice came in on the other end. "Fox Hole to Tiger, we read you, over."

"Rescue has failed. Target Gamma and one... assistant are dead. Position has been compromised. Repeat: position has been compromised. Need extraction 300 klicks north of Echo-3. Sending coordinates now, over."

"Roger that. The *Freyja* sends her love. They're ahead of schedule. Over."

"Tell the Commodore I'm in need of a therapy session. Expecting pickup within the hour. Over and out."

Lily then limped over to the speeder. On her way there, she picked up a small leather journal from Lacie's weapon pile.

"In the Final Analysis: A Life of Death, Taxes, and Time Travel, by Lacie Hermes."

There's only one explanation. You wanted to die, Lacie, whether or not you admitted it to yourself. I don't understand.

Once at the speeder, Lily began treating her wounds with Lacie's first-aid nanopaste as she watched Raine agreeing to duel the Stopwatch. *Right on schedule. Good luck, kiddo.*

Something startled her. Far to her East, beyond the lone Network tower, an elderly wanderer stood among the rocks, leaning on a staff. A shaman, perhaps, or a representative of some local peoples.

Lily matched his piercing gaze. She expected him to offer help, or else to give her some form of recognition for what she'd just done. But the violence having abetted, the elder simply turned and walked away.

A true neutral. I understand. This isn't his war to fight. He was simply here to bear witness.

Before long, her radar blinked in alert. A squadron of ships approached from the West. Lacie's backup, sure to be combing the landscape. Lily kicked up the engine and re-opened the comm. channel.

"On second thought, Jojo, I've got company. I'm going to hang low for a bit and shake them off. You guys continue mobilizing."

"Roger that. And please don't call me Jojo."

"I'm afraid I cannot comply. See you soon, Vice."

Lily sped swiftly over the barren landscape. She remotely summoned the *Phoenix* to meet her halfway; she'd need its speed if she hoped to catch up with the EDC Armada by day's end.

That shaman... there was something about his gaze. Did he think me a blessing to this world, a curse, or simply another force of nature?

A long look over the beautiful valley eased her mind. The cleft fell drastically into a waterfall and rose back up to form the bases of majestic mountains. Mountains that, in this universe, would never again be seen by human life in approximately twenty-five years, eleven months, and twenty-four days.

The thought usually made her sad, but this time all she saw was the empty space between the valleys, and all beauty seemed to her naught but an abstract evolutionary card trick. A practical joke played on the senses to drive the eternal machine forward.

Forgetting her mental equanimity, Lily slapped herself out of it, and then caught her subconscious in the act. It was self-destructive thoughts like these that drove Lorelei to forsake life on planet Earth.

XVII. Mister Senior

"In a time of deceit telling the truth is a revolutionary act." – *George Orwell*

The sun declined as Raine was carried lovingly up the towering volcano, nestled in an oversized recliner while her subjects continued to chant her new fake name. They recently offered her a large bowl of fruit and whipped cream that, like everything else in the *Metaverse*, tasted disturbingly real.

At the summit's rim, Raine struggled for breath through the swelling heat and toxic fumes. A deadly cocktail of boiling lava bubbled a thousand feet below the caldera. At long last she discovered what this show was all about.

Another group marched up the pathway, only they bore a different cargo. The Stopwatch had been heaved there atop the shoulders of eight men and two sets of very strong-looking bamboo sticks.

The former Champion's expression was strong and stoic. They stood it up before the rim of the bowl. Raine watched in agony as the thing beeped and chirped in fear. Its cries could barely be heard over the chanting and tribal drums. From its hopeless face Raine somehow understood: if it fell in there, it wasn't coming back.

"STOP!" she screamed.

The music ceased. Dozens of heads turned in her direction. A pixilated tear ran down the Stopwatch's time display. Raine was absolutely stunned. She hadn't expected the group of mostly adults to listen to her, much less halt what they were doing.

"Why do you ask us to stop, O Champion?" Casey, the child, ventured.

"Because I think this whole thing is crazy! What did this Stopwatch do to deserve death? Sure it beeps a lot, but... I can't stand bullying! It's just wrong! Even if it's annoying or bossy or unreasonably good at *Super BlastBoy II*, it's still a living being!"

At this the Stopwatch turned towards Raine solemnly, partly grateful, certainly confused at her compassion.

"Mr. Stopwatch, do you promise to stop your beeping if they turn you loose? Beep once for yes, twice for no."

The AI beeped once in affirmation.

"Then it's done! Release it! I command you as Princess of Pagoda!"

"But milady, it is written!" a man interjected.

"What is written, exactly?" demanded Raine, arms crossed like a bossy schoolteacher.

"That you would come from the outside world and defeat our Champion. Also, you would become the new Champion and lead us into an era of unlimited prosperity, a realm beyond our imaginations."

"Who, me, specifically?"

A few nodded, not quite in unison.

"Who said this?"

The silence was unbearable. At last, Mrs. Zoot emerged from the mob, holding aloft Raine's Network visor, now fully operational. She pushed a small button on its frame and handed it to Raine, who reluctantly placed the pair of goggles over her eyes.

A whole mass of glowing lights and colors popped up, but nothing happened.

"Um… what do I do now?"

Little Casey whispered in the Champion's ear. "Don't worry, Chosen One. There's a first time for everybody. Just say, 'Activate.'"

"Visor, activate!"

Everyone watched in wonder as a giant hologram of Super BlastBoy emerged from the visor and stood in their midst, smiling gravely. Way cooler than the sketch adorning the arcade cabinet, Anthony Kon held a stately presence, and spoke in a soft but powerful voice.

"And lo, to the people of Pagoda, I say to you: one shall come and defeat my own score in the game, represented by this Stopwatch, one whose skill and reflexes are far beyond that of any computer or algorithmic process. This warrior will be declared Prince or Princess of Pagoda, and he, she, or it will reap my great reward. Afterwards, a great storm shall fall on the land, followed by a great peace."

The hologram vanished. Raine pulled off the visor, which was giving her a headache.

"I think I missed the part where he told you to kill the beeping one after I'd defeated it," Raine said with a raised eyebrow. "Did he actually ever say that?"

"Yessss!" a lone man shouted at the top of his lungs, to which a few others muttered their abiding agreement.

Zoot cleared her throat. "Well, not really. In fact, I think that whole craze was started a few hours ago."

The spectators found themselves silent. They then looked at one another awkwardly and murmured. Interrupting the rabble, the volcanic vapors began to swirl around wildly. A familiar shadow blocked out the sun.

Hundreds of feet above the volcano, the *Nebula* emerged once more from a sky portal.

The recognizable tractor beam struck on and tilted right down into Raine's eyes, blinding her. When she could see again, the girl felt no ground beneath her feet; once more, our heroine flew helplessly upwards.

"Where are they taking you, O Chosen One?" Zoot called out.

These tractor beams are a real nuisance. "This isn't good! Help!"

Bellowing air currents drowned out her voice. She struggled for freedom, and remembered that she supposedly had unlimited power.

Raine focused her energy into her wand; a mass of black pixels shot from its gem and shorted out the beam. Five more switched on. Raine tried to command the dark matter, but the beams' negative energy overpowered her.

Looking down for help, she neglected to notice that somewhere in all this commotion, the Player One robe had blown off and fluttered into the crater.

Good going, Raine.

"Great balls of tapioca! It's her!" one of the onlookers cried at last. "She's that fugitive with the mega-reward!"

No kidding. Raine secretly wished the airship would bring her up a little faster.

With the presence of the *Nebula* spurring them on, the crowd erupted in a general panic. Many had drawn weapons and were firing missiles at Raine.

Casey's pained voice boomed, "Don't do it, bro! She's royalty!"

"I need that cash!" the teenaged punk from earlier responded, shooting upwards in a jetpack. Raine kicked him in the chest, sending the guy flying back down towards the volcano.

Chance popped out of Raine's bag and cast sleeping spells that brought attackers to their knees. Lasers came from below, but Raine deflected them with her shield.

Blonde-haired Nimbus showed up on the volcano's rim, calling out to Raine. Thinking him a friend of hers, the mob turned and assaulted the poor boy.

The Stopwatch and the residents of Pagoda appeared no larger than insects as the ship pulled up and away from the volcano.

The doors closed from underneath.

Raine felt a dizzying sickness as she landed in the ship's docking bay, which she'd just narrowly avoided being trapped in less than a day ago. She found herself dry heaving onto the cold, metal floor on all fours.

Before long, a tall, dark, and handsome man offered to pull her up, smiling. Chance hissed before retreating into scarf form. Raine gave the figure a death glare. He withdrew his hand, and a Templar shackled her wrists together.

"It's nice to formally meet you, Raine. I'm Mister Senior. It sure took you long enough to discover the wonders of our Network visors."

□

A pair of Templars escorted Raine and Chance to a cramped cell, where she was seated for a few minutes, and then whisked out through a crystal lobby and into a posh dining hall, where the girl took the opposite end of the long table from her host.

"Dinner is served," an android uttered, placing the hot plate before her. Never mind that it was probably a little early for dinner. It was filet mignon, a dish Raine had always been curious to try.

The uncomfortable realization that she had just been kidnapped fought against Raine's now-growling stomach.

Across the expanse, the man who called himself Mister Senior sat with seemingly infinite patience, a sly sneer creeping across his face as sunken eyes studied her. Raine could sense him trying to start a mental conversation, hoping she might spill the beans.

She pretended to inspect the untouched meal and tried her best not to think of poor Gerrit.

If I show this man a sign of weakness, either Gerrit or I might be in danger.

Raine bravely made a study of Mister Senior's features. *This politician thinks he can pry into my head,* she figured, *but two can play at that game.* He seemed almost a caricature, created entirely from right angles and flat surfaces, a statue carefully honed from a mixture of skin and marble. His teeth were the whitest ivory, and they looked about ready to chomp down on Raine and tear her nose off.

Aaand... that's about as far as I can gather. I'm more of a Watson than a Sherlock, I guess. It's probably better to be a good guest and take the first bite so we can get to talking.

"You like yours medium-rare?" he asked in between mouthfuls.

"Sure," Raine said, after a second's pause. The truth was she didn't really know for sure yet just how she liked her steak, never mind that this steak was either virtual steak or dream steak. Neither should have been appetizing, but the food did smell and taste absolutely delicious.

Mister Senior put on his trademark smirk. She pulled on her wrists; feeling the shackles tighten, Raine realized that she had let her mind wander and rapidly set herself back on guard.

The girl caught a glimpse of the clock behind Mister Senior.

No way.

Based on her visor's built-in clock, which she noted while viewing SBB's message, two hours had passed that were unaccounted for.

What did they do to me?

"What your people just did to me was beyond horrible," she said, ignoring the lump caught in her throat. "In fact, it's unforgivable. As a fellow Developer, I'd like to request a formal trial."

"Ha! Nice try. You're clearly bluffing. Your cell's mini-freeze system is programming perfection. There's no way you recall anything from the past two hours, and trust me, that's for the best. As it's the details that are filled with spoilers, I'll gladly give you the lowdown. For the first hour, we were simply trying to de-materialize you in every gruesome way imaginable. As anticipated, the crown plastered on your head made that rather difficult. The second hour was spent probing your subconscious for any hidden or suppressed memories. As we found nothing real, that was also a failure."

Nothing real? How can that be? Keep cool, Raine. Don't choke.

Faced with a blank stare, Senior shook his head. "It's a shame, really. But at the very least, you can take comfort in knowing that you're protected by some serious firewalls. Now please, eat."

At a signal from the politician, the two armored officers flanking the exit turned and left the room.

This is probably the most creeped-out I've ever been.

"Actually, I think I've just lost my appetite."

He cleared his throat.

"I thought honesty would help our relationship, but I can see your dislike for me won't be so easily swayed," he began. "So let's get right to business. You see, Raine, you've been a thorn in our side for longer than we can allow. This world, like so many of our great species' most majestic marvels, is a fragile construction built on the backs of many sacrifices. It currently lies on the brink, and the purity of the illusion is all that keeps it going. Much of what we've achieved has been due to trial and error. We change too much at once, and suspicion arises. If people are too happy, they long to destroy themselves. Too empty and uncluttered, and they seek transcendence. Always we must self-govern, and always we must pluck the weeds from our *Eden*. You are of an impure breed, causing a great deal of distress to people who have everything they could possibly desire. Your coming here is as a cancer to these souls."

Raine furrowed her brow in confusion. "This place really is a virtual prison."

"Ah," Mister Senior said, intrigued. "So you really have no clue why you've come to *Endless Metaverse*."

She gathered up all her strength.

"Maybe I do, maybe I don't. But y'all are surely lost, or you would have spilled your guts already without having to go through that 'cancer' speech."

He sat back in his chair. "Smart girl. Sad that you know even less than we do the true nature of your purpose."

I'm not smart. I've just seen this scene in too many movies. This guy is used to performing for people who don't know what a performance is, and he isn't accustomed to not getting what he wants.

"Try me."

"You're not plugged in through any of our servers. We can't lock onto your signal, and we can't ban you. This makes you a user of either a hacked or an illegally created account. Most likely, you are being funded by terrorists. Yet, unlike the freedom fighters from the resistance, you are not engaged in any anti-establishment activity. In fact, you seem helpless as a newborn. And that is more dangerous than they could ever be. Your very presence, Raine, is warping the code and corrupting the algorithms of the *'Verse*. Malicious signals are oozing off you, even as we speak. You may not be aware of this, but the feedback you're sending has… altered those you've engaged with."

"You lost me at 'malicious signals'."

"Surely you've noticed how you seem to be followed by data storms? Those black pixels aren't pixie dust. They're packets emanating wherever you are mentally present, probably from a software mod. We use a similar technique to maintain the servers with minimal interruption. You, on the other hand, or whoever seems to be using you as a puppet, have been corrupting our creation by returning forbidden data to the 'Verse. Case in point: Charles Hayter, that old man you met in Clyde. He ran around mad today, stripped off his clothes, and started a riot that lasted for hours, jabbering on about 'Earth'. The application renovating the Wall of Secrets flipped its wig, demolished half the wall, and abandoned its post. It's still on the loose."

"That scholar with all the coats is one of yours, too."

"Stephen Seele is one of our psychological programs. After investigating you, it went missing in action. Look, either you're fooling us, which is highly unlikely, or you're someone else's puppet. In any case, you're in danger of being frozen."

"I've done no wrong, and I'm a Developer. You can't freeze me."

"On the contrary... it's true that as a temporary Developer, you are off the wanted lists. Once the effects of your crown expire, however, you're fair game. We'll just throw you back to the crowd. For that, I give you two minutes, tops. But there's another option in this," Mr. Senior began again, his voice growing silkier. "If you help us, not only will we make you a brand new account in the server of your choice, we'll give you all the Gold you could ever want. You'll possess power without measure. Fortune. Fame. More friends than you'll know what to do with. Would you like to be an Empress? It would only take a snap of my fingers. If space travel is more your thing, we are working on a new server that will link together the others, as well as create a multitude of satellite worlds with various environments. Low gravity. Motherships. Custom worlds. You'll be able to travel between different galaxies, and you can help us test it all out. I'm sure we can come to an understanding, yes?"

Raine rolled her eyes.

"Let's say for a second that I can even trust you to keep your word. You're still wasting my time. I don't want a new account, I just want Gerrit back," she said at last, although it was hard to resist his charming words.

In another world, Raine might have jumped at the opportunity, but she continued to heed Lily's warning. *This place is insane.*

The politician snapped his fingers. A hologram took shape from the table's spherical centerpiece. It was Gerrit, sitting silently at a school desk. The camera pulled back to show that this lifeless apparition was merely an occurrence within his true consciousness; the boy's frail body was strapped tightly to a mobile chair, a sickly expression decorating his pained, pale face.

Raine gasped. "G-Gerrit..."

"The procedure went without a hitch. His mind is frozen, but he still lives. And he can join you in paradise."

A false paradise. The girl's heart fluttered, but the choice before her was all too easy. It had to be a trap.

"You're a sociopath! B-b-but sweet-talking me won't work! M-my answer hasn't changed. I can't trust you to keep your word. Not when you have the power to erase people's memories."

Mr. Senior jeered. "Even if we were capable of modifying a person's memories without their consent, which I can assure you is not the way we do business, we couldn't possibly have touched your pretty little mind. Our tests have confirmed that we simply lack access to your nano-machine network, and by extension, to your brain. For that same reason, I'm afraid we can't arrange your reunion with dear Gerrit unless we can locate you. Please. Don't abandon your life to the whims of the fates."

Raine thought she did a good job of concealing her disappointment.

"Would you like to live in the *Metaverse*? Imagine if you will a realm where your heart's desire is a wish away. You'll have governments at your command. Unlimited power and influence."

The offer was tempting, to be sure.

But nine hundred and ninety-nine times out of a thousand, when something's too good to be true, that's because it is.

"Look, Mr. Mister, what is it you want from me?"

"We need three things. First, tell me anything you might remember about your hub, your entry point into the game. It will help us determine how and where you've been patched in."

She nodded for him to continue.

"Second," Mr. Senior said, and then followed up with a dramatic pause. "We need information about a terrorist who has been on a horrifying rampage. If you don't help us catch her, she could very well threaten the ongoing operation of *Endless Metaverse*. That wouldn't be very good for the world outside. Many lives will be lost if her path of destruction is allowed to continue."

"She?"

"She calls herself Lily. She's a menace. And a murderer."

"*That* Lily? The little girl?"

"Looks can be deceiving. Haven't you considered the possibility that she is trying to use you to her own selfish ends? When you met her she told you something odd. Yes, we saw that. She said, 'don't pop the blue balloon'. Now, what could that possibly mean? Is it a code word?"

"You tell me. That was the first and only time I'd met her."

"You swear," he pressed, though it was clear to Raine he was searching for the reaction to come from her eyes, not her speech. Mister Senior held the death glare for an uncomfortably long time.

"Very well," he said. "But consider this: Lily has been known to modify users' memories. You could still be a sleeper agent without knowing it."

"Coulda woulda shoulda. My memories are genuine."

"Said with such confidence. As for the third thing – we need authorization to temporarily de-materialize you. As I've mentioned, thanks to that crown on your head, we can't even touch your avatar. Please give it to me. The process will only take a minute. And it's the only way we can help."

As Raine scanned the room for possible exit strategies, a Templar's muffled voice sounded out from a small speaker by Mr. Senior.

"Incoming message, sir," it reported.

Holding one hand up in the air like an antenna and touching his earpiece with the other, Mr. Senior listened intently. Raine saw his fists tighten. Before long he sized her up and took a strong breath, a menacing look in his eyes.

Raine suddenly piped up.

"Look, sorry to disappoint you, but I really don't think I want my account reset. I think I'll just-"

Her host nearly exploded with anger. "How did you defeat the Champion?"

"Can you let us go now? Please? I've told you all I know."

"Enough!" he jumped from his seat in an abrupt demonstration of fury and motioned to the guards.

"Very well. It appears I have failed. We have... we have other priorities. You've fulfilled your purpose. There is nothing more to learn from you."

As he walked away from the table, Raine alighted and crossed the floor towards her captor, but he and his guards had already entered the adjacent hallway.

"Mister Senior! Release Gerrit! He's innocent! He doesn't know the first thing about me! Please! Developers' honor!"

Nothing. It was a long shot, anyway.

An awful roar shook the chamber from behind Raine. A hatch in the airship sprung open; her avatar whipped out into the sky. She grabbed a hold of the tablecloth and tangled into it as she tumbled through the air, several thousand feet above the ground.

Raine thrashed about. She entwined the ends around her fists and focused the black pixels on pulling her shackles apart. Now that she was free from the *Nebula's* influence, it worked. At long last the fabric whooshed open, caught onto a rising current, and guided her down towards an impossibly large stadium.

Jon Wrathman breathed easy once more. The troublesome girl bought the act, and she was right on target.

Falling softly, Raine met the eyes of a child far below, holding a blue balloon. Stunned, he accidentally let it go and began crying uncontrollably.

Don't pop the blue balloon.

Recalling what Lily told her, Raine wondered if this was the balloon in question. She then reflected that if *Metaverse* physics were anything like those on Earth, once it rose high enough in the atmosphere and the helium expanded, it certainly would pop.

The crucial question is: should I trust Lily?

It wasn't like she had much of a choice at this point.

The balloon inched closer still. She shifted her weight until she was directly above it.

This could all be a trap. Maybe she should disregard all the politics completely. Disappear into this Neverland. *This dream will never last, anyways. What's the point of becoming involved in a world I have no stake in? But you've got something to fight for, Raine!*

My fears are driving me, she realized. *Fear of what? Mister Senior and his system? Fear that I might never wake up? Gerrit never hesitated when I was in danger. I need to know if I'm made of the same stuff. Otherwise, this and any other worlds might eat me alive.*

It didn't matter if *Endless Metaverse* was real or a figment of her imagination. She had unfinished business here. Raine grabbed the blue balloon in the middle of its ascent and brought it down to the surface.

∞

I know this place. I've been there more than once, even if I can't recall it.

Gerrit grasped at the memory; it slipped out from the deepest recesses of his mind. For the past few hours, he'd been immersed in an ongoing projection of his subconscious thoughts, impulses, and dreams. If someone had been running a memory trace on him, these visions might be stored, and studied.

Not this one, he thought. *I barely remember it myself, but something tells me it's too precious for you to have. It's a memory from the outside world, one I've seen over and over again in my dreams.*

The sea salt smell is distinctly familiar from the last time. The waves kiss our toes and we move up from the rising tide a few meters. The one my age splashes me and laughs. That mischievous giggle... Raine?

"The wind's picking up a bit," she says, *bundling herself in her beach towel in a very un-Raine-like fashion. "I have to admit, it does feel a tad strange not having something to read or study."*

"Nonsense! This is the best sort of education there is – field experience!" the other girl exclaims. She sounds a lot like Lily, only a few years older.

"Ah!" the younger girl shouts, nudging me as she points up at the sky. I saw it too, just out of my peripheral vision.

"What was it?" the other one queries. "A shooting star?"

She snaps her fingers. "That's it! Our latest contest! Let's count meteors! Hey, guys, I'll be right back – gonna see if dinner's ready!"

"It doesn't always have to be a contest!" the younger girl laughs.

But we're left alone on the beach, to spend a few carefully planned minutes in awkward silence.

At this point I'm almost positive that this mysterious girl is Raine, but even though we're both a little chilly, I can't fathom why she snuggles up right beside me.

"Now I can see almost whatever you see," she announces.

I shrug. "We may be looking at the same sky, but seeing totally different things."

"That's why it's good that we're not alone. No man is an island."

Her heart beats a little faster than mine.

"All of us get lost in the darkness; dreamers learn to steer by the stars."

"Come again?"

"Ah, sorry," I reply. "'The Pass', by Rush. Alpha, Classic twentieth century. Borrowed from Oscar Wilde, I believe."

She takes my hand. "That's beautiful. We are but stardust seeking our origins. You know, you're getting awfully into the role of your persona, even though you'll eventually forget it."

My smile droops a little.

"No memory is ever really lost. The synaptic connections just need to be re-wired. Plus, I can't call it research," I answer. "It's more of a personal interest, really."

"You find comfort in the words of mystics and philosophers."

I sit on this for a minute. "Actually, it's the opposite. They fill me with uncertainty. But I guess it is kind of comforting, because it reminds me of how little we actually know."

"I'm not sure I understand what's so comforting about that."

"It's kinda like... perceptual change is inevitable when the questions are never-ending, but with every discovery, the universe just grows more fascinating. Take the cosmological constant, or the properties of an electron. If even one of their values were off by an infinitesimally small degree, nothing would ever have existed. Just being here... if there's no Creator, it's as if we won a hundred trillion lotteries in a row. You told me once that life was an inevitability of metaphysics, Multiverse or not, but that's always sounded like an oversimplification. I mean, yeah. Sorry for ranting. It's... it's just one example of a topic I'd happily spend my life investigating."

She runs her fingers over my palm reassuringly. "Stop apologizing. You're in good company here; I've always loved your impossible questions. To embrace a life of uncertainty... to forever seek the unknowable... such a romantic notion. You know, sometimes I wonder if our individual egos are nature's divine experiment."

"Wow. An ongoing challenge to ourselves, to work to evolve our consciousness."

"'Do not go where the path may lead, go instead where there is no path and leave a trail.'"

A smile brightens my face. "Emerson. I dig it. There's rough going where there are no paths, but maybe that's the point. We're meant to try, and to fail, and to learn. To understand when to let go of false truths in order to gain a higher level of understanding. Even things you might have held close to your heart."

"I find that rather dangerous. Dangerously intriguing."

We each turn on our sides and study the other's gaze expectantly, a mental exercise we've performed on one another since our inception.

Only this time, we're inches away, and she smells terrific.

"Is this a test?" I laugh. "Or is this you and I?"

"If you even have to ask that---"

I kiss her, ever so softly. We melt. She kisses me back. It's passionate, electrifying.

As we pull away, she curls a wayward strand of those intoxicating brown locks from her eyes, which are passionately fixated on mine.

"What is it?" I ask at last. "I can't tell if it's fear, or..."

"Love? Neither can I. Uncertainty. I kind of like it."

The distant sound of our companion's sandals hitting her heels prompts a more personal response.

"Three years without you... and your memories... it's gonna be a long time," she says.

"All is for the best. We'll return together. I don't care what it takes. Once the mission's over, I'll find my way back to you, even if it kills me. Maybe you can do it, too, if you have something to hold on to."

"Something special?"

"Maybe."

"How about someone?"

"I guess that might work. Raine, I---"

The colors are fading. The sounds, too... I... I don't remember this part.

No! Don't take this away! You can't have it! These precious feelings are mine!

The memory vanished from Gerrit's brain, leaving the dreamer in the gutter once more.

♥

"Oh, don't be such a square!" Adeline Marco giggled. "This is fun!"

Between her empty-headed cousin, the ragged waiter in *M-gear* currently the victim of a terrible beatdown, and the *Metaverse* reality show playing on the tubes, Lady Claire didn't have much of a choice. She smiled, looking mournfully down at her sashimi, twisting her unseen napkin in her lap to keep from exploding. Her companion remarked with outrageous vigor that, like any beast of burden, these terrorists needed to be tamed.

Being plugged into the *'Verse* for daily employment at this establishment, it was impossible that this child had anything to do with last week's attack on the outer gates. Lacie had confided for her ears alone that it was a false flag operation, a stunt pulled by *Geared Eden* Black Ops, engineered to pass blame onto the barely existent rebel underground and justify heightened security measures across the continent.

An even worse tragedy struck young Adeline: she'd bumped into a kid carrying a tray of tarts; a speck of the stuff stained her cream-colored purse in strawberry crimson. The Developer's wife had merely to press a 'Panic' button on her bracelet to summon the *Eden* Police, helmeted men and women who proceeded to assault the poor child to the ground in front of the bistro's many patrons.

"The peasant is right to cower before its masters," insisted Adele, rather loudly. Turning to the boy, she waved a disapproving finger. "Production is down this year, you slacker AI! Did you hear me through that thick skull?"

How can this be right? Sure, our Metaverse *ensures that he won't feel the pain. It performs its ordained functions, and so do we, to an extent. But at the end of the day, what are we but parasites and oppressors? What of noblesse oblige?*

The boy's face remains a blank. Though not a single impulse or cry of pain registers in his mind, he is no puppet. Under that M-Gear, *he is a fully conscious human being, only bound in mental chains.*

"For *Eden's* sake, let's leave, Adele. I'm behind on my reports."

"And I'm making a statement."

"It's been made." Claire stormed out of the restaurant.

Disgusted, Adeline caved in. She placed her Holo-Lens monocle against her eye and tapped into the Network.

"Drop the kid. Fix him up. I want him fully operational tomorrow."

The Overseer registered her voice and retina – as a Lead Developer's wife, she was one of the few outside the *Nexus* who could issue direct commands, however limited. Within seconds, the *Eden Police* robotically backed off and returned to their rounds. Two *Geared* waiters carried the unconscious boy to his dorm, and were promptly replaced by reinforcements.

No longer bemused by the sight, Adele followed her friend from their table, through the busy mall, and out to the helipad. Her *Xariot-IX* speeder had just pulled into the VIP section.

Claire thought back to the meal they'd just consumed – genetically modified tuna, bred to withstand the polluted Mediterranean. A forced adaptation, engineered for size, taste, and convenience, but rife with health risks – a moot issue given the advanced medical treatment available to *Eden's* upper crust, including stem cell-grown organs.

"Why wait for evolution to run its course?" Adele had argued in favor of the tampered genes when they were younger. "If we can reap the fruits of nature within our lifetimes, if the dreams of tomorrow are within our grasp, then what's stopping us?"

Looking to the future, perhaps, Claire ventured. *And how little of it will remain if we continue destroying the planet and enslaving its populace. We must have a larger role to play than that of mindless consumers. Otherwise, ours will be the dead end of civilization.*

"What the devil is the matter with you, cousin? You haven't spoken a word since we left the plaza."

Lady Claire didn't even turn her eyes from the window.

"J-just a bout of melancholy is all. I long for the General's safe return; she's behind schedule."

But Adele rolled her eyes. "We both know that's not the issue. You're far too soft. Enough," she called to the android chauffeur. "Let's ride."

The *Xariot* climbed with the traffic to offer a birds-eye view of *Neo Eden.*

"This is most unbecoming," she advised. "You showed weakness before your inferiors."

"If it's all the same to you, I was displaying compassion."

"Oh, rubbish. Wake up, Claire. How can one expect fealty if one does not demand absolute respect? These slaves are a dime a dozen. They're hardly human."

She's got one thing right. Every eye in that restaurant was on me, sizing me up. There are tens of thousands of men and women who would do much worse than kill to be in my shoes.

"Many a philosopher might say the same about us."

Adele scoffed. "You bring shame upon the family. Our name and birthright mean nothing unless we make use of them."

I will make use of them, she thought. But I won't be like you, Adele, taking refuge in self-important charities and think tanks, tokenisms to assuage the guilt of your privilege. It's no secret your husband has been working his way up the ranks, freezing all in his path.

Going by the latest gossip, he and Beech are planning a coup. So far, they've done nothing to suggest they won't keep the status quo.

I want to do something for this world. Something that makes a difference. Not for honor, nor for profit, but for every one of those beings you call 'assets'.

That idealistic dream vanished along with the folk of the lower levels as the *Xariot* speeder cleared the uppermost wall and came face to face with the *Spire's* pyramid base.

Ω

Not far across the Upper City, the Queen feathered the focus on the camera probe from her Holo-Lens and inched open the iris. The Westering sun reflected the sleek black marble of the *Metaverse Control Nexus*, banners waving in the high winds.

The adjacent monolith stuck out, rising above the hedge labyrinths and entertainment district like a polished, two hundred storey chocolate bar. Unlike the *Spire,* it boasted not a single window. Marble walls were reinforced by two feet of folded tungsten and pearly ceramic. It was a fortress.

Still, the *Nexus* paled in comparison to the *Spire*.

Queen Lorelei's throne room and residence, along with the private residences of her heavily monitored inner circle, made up the higher levels of the structure. The mile-long and -wide sealed pyramid base enclosed crucial Network mainframes, managed the city-wide Electromagnetic Shield, and housed military craft, top-secret server rooms, and countless hidden chambers to satisfy her occasional dabbling in mad science.

Many a dark rumor surrounded the pale marble tower emerging from the pyramid's center, which functioned as the living quarters and general playground for the Queen's chosen few, as well as the base for some of the *Metaverse's* most powerful signal towers.

Supported by vast buttresses, its shadow cast a colossal sundial on the mountain visible even from Mount Vesuvius, an inner-city geothermal plant a mere nine miles to the East.

The *Spire's* architects and foremen were killed after its construction seventy years ago, their bodies entombed in its foundations like the builders of old.

Queen Lorelei had traveled forward through the space-time continuum many times during the stages of *Endless Metaverse's* thirty-year construction and Beta period. As far as the contractors on the project were concerned, there were at least three generations of Loreleis and Lacies, and the two youngest ones bore an extremely striking resemblance to their grandmother, except in terms of fashion. It seemed a family secret that no Queen ever wore the same outfit twice, and that each one was an absolute trendsetter.

To those at the top of the food chain, however, there was another layer of 'truth'. It was a known fact that there were at least six generations of the royal family, and over the past two centuries, the women of the Eden family had shaped the course of the world with impeccable precision, working the eternal war from behind the scenes, and showing up every few years to set the machine back on its course.

Only this latest trip, the Queen reflected, had been an extended one. It was the subject of much speculation in the mortal circles. She'd taken up a very visible permanent residence in the *Spire* for the past seven years, to the chagrin of much of *Neo Eden's* upper management.

In truth, there was only one Queen Lorelei, and in her lonely tower she flung all manner of paint at a gigantic canvas with abandon. The mural was of her city, enraptured in flames. She thoroughly enjoyed her cigarette with an impassioned simper. Her manservant stood fifteen feet behind her, just far enough so she wouldn't have to smell him, and held aloft a tray bearing fresh espresso.

She picked up a paintball rifle and decorated her abstract rendition of Sky Admiral Lillian with the colors of the *Eden* flag.

"Coffee," she said softly. Ten seconds later she was sipping it, savoring the rich aroma of power. It was the finest bean, grown in her very own fields in South America to perfection, harvested by the unenlightened slaves she ruled with a steady hand, and shipped to her private reserve as soon as it was ready to roast.

What an incredible release. I really needed this.

"Ma'am," her servant's voice sounded out after removing his finger from his Holo-Lens' earpiece. "A message from downstairs. They wish to hold a meeting to discuss Miss Guggell's recent reports."

"It's about time." She placed the circlet on her head to interface with Guggell.

"Tell me you have her," the Queen demanded.

"I'm afraid not," Guggell replied. If Lorelei paid a little closer attention, she might have noticed that the AI was a tad more sluggish than usual. "Urgent report from *Avidya*. Would you like the brief?"

"In five minutes," she said with a pout, and took off the crown. While the Royal Guard fell in step, Lorelei walked calmly towards the platform elevator. It dropped until the bridge to the Control *Nexus*, then turned and headed horizontally.

Lieutenant General Beech, interim head of national security, greeted Her Majesty at the private lobby between the three domes, flanked by the Joint Chiefs. Upon realizing that she wasn't going to slow or stop her stride for them, the officers fell in step behind the Queen.

"General, how goes it?"

"Very well, Your Grace. We have nearly a million making camps by the Eastern and Southern shores. Campobasso, Palermo, Sicily, and Bologna are being staffed as we speak. The Overseer is inspecting the units, and further assets from the seven lords are en route."

"Good. I need you here. Have Macleod scout ahead and meet the insurgents before they cross the Adriatic. See that the metal behemoth and EM spheres are readied."

"Ma'am, I know we've discussed this before, but there are other options--"

"No nukes, and no chemical- or bio-weapons. They may be bringing the fight to us, but neither Lily nor I will sacrifice this ancient place, or the lives of innocents, to that kind of power. As Chief Science Officer,

I order you to make use of your existing toys. Other than that, you're granted *carte blanche* with regards to the EDC Armada."

Macleod looked ready to interject; Beech pushed him away. "Thank you, ma'am. We won't disappoint."

With a wave of her hand, she dismissed the Joint Chiefs and walked forth to her seat to listen to her overworked code monkeys sound off about their own ineptitude. Oddly enough, Holdfast was nowhere to be seen.

"It's a doozy today, Highness," Marco greeted her.

"How the hell did Lily get into my mainframe?" she shouted at the top of her lungs upon seeing the minutes on her tablet.

Her virtual double manifested in hologram form.

"Ma'am," uttered Miss Guggell. "Raine completed an old, recently re-activated side-quest that dialed into the mainframe for its reward data. Because the quest was only re-activated this morning, its encryption has not been updated in over a decade. It also appears that a rogue signal piggybacked on the connection and splintered off. Given faint traces of its broadcast patterns, it appears to have constructed a map of the mainframe entrance and exit nodes."

"Wait," the Queen responded, holding her palm up in disbelief. "You're telling me Lily now has a treasure map of our Network?"

"Officially, Highness, the quest was disabled. The data storms-" Dr. Karuishi offered, before the Queen held up a palm to silence her.

Lorelei rubbed her temples, barely holding her rage in check. She was seconds away from executing someone.

But this is me reacting. Not acting. First: examine.

Miss Guggell should have nipped this in the bud. The AI's compromised, failing somehow, as Lacie predicted.

Is it the Raine virus? Undoubtedly.

In any scenario, the same principle that allows me to directly interface with the AI might allow an outsider access into my thoughts: given that this is an avenue Lillian would certainly exploit, I can no longer trust Guggell. If I had just a little more time, I could shut it down temporarily and repair the damage myself.

But I can't show my weakness, or waste my time. I'll have to rely on these pawns for now.

"And on top of this, Mister Senior has released Enemy Number Two?! What sort of madness is this? Where is he?"

"Forever at your service, Your Grace," Jon Wrathman motioned, striding from the men's restroom and making a dramatic display of bending his knee to the Queen. "Please, allow me to explain."

She tossed the tablet at his head.

"Yes, explain away! Quickly! What in the hell was all that about? You finally found her, and then nada. Zilch. You have completely failed me on every level!"

Wrathman rubbed his skull. "M-m-ma'am, we could not damage or extract Raine, nor could we squeeze any information out of her. But I may have found a solution that can reveal her to us at last."

"Let's not delay, then. Brief me."

"Surely Your Eminence remembers our trance serum? It's been testing very well in aerial trials. Assets become compliant, leading to much better assimilation of the protocols."

"Go on," she commanded.

"I'll defer to Hoshua here on the sciencey stuff," replied Jon.

Alphonse Hoshua cleared his throat. "Howdy, Majesty. The serum has been most effective in large social gatherings; perhaps it's something to do with the collective unconscious. It may be an undefined property, but it brings results. Complete immersion in the digital world, less input from the frontal lobe and Neo-cortex, and a state of mind test subjects describe as 'expanded consciousness' and 'bliss'. On our end, it means total physical and mental control. The ability to emulate the Super-Soldier program. The only caveat is that side effects may trigger reflex rejections among the more prudent. I thought it was time we see what it's capable of on a large scale."

"So, the experiment tonight in Helium-Corneria," the Queen replied.

"Yes, ma'am," said Jon excitedly. "She's en route as we speak, and remains without a clue. Ma'am, we could make her the figurehead of our military force. The anarchists will be crushed."

Queen Lorelei gazed at a hologram showing Raine in the horrendous line to enter the Coliseum.

"Not bad, Jon. You have my permission to execute this operation. But for *Eden's* sake, start the main event early," she declared. "We're not waiting for any gate-crashers."

Jon signaled to Dr. Hoshua, who immediately walked over to a sparse office with a window to the main control room. After donning the *M-Gear* helmet, he leaned back into his recliner as his brain slipped into the Network, letting the sea of ones and zeroes flood his senses. In the center of the room, an operative gave the thumbs-up. Hoshua had safely entered the *Metaverse*.

Alphonse Hoshua took form as a centaur in the Developers' Lounge overlooking the enormous bowl. A multi-limbed tortoise sat before a custom console, awaiting his commands.

"Shall we reconfigure Output Theta? I doubt anyone here remembers it, anyway," the tortoise recommended.

Hoshua shook his head. "Come on, Meme-Bot… Theta's been done to death. Let's bring back something from version 1.0. We'll put on a show the likes of which have been seen a million times. I don't want any hiccups."

"But no cross-dressing? No human sacrifices? No flying monkeys?"

"No."

"Then why not let's start with 'All Your Base'."

"Last I checked we weren't running a museum. Give us something with punch. Bring out the Kaiju band, and the dueling DJs."

"I guess if that's all you want… it'll be simple enough. A copypasta of a copypasta."

Disappointed, the tortoise cracked its neck and began the regularly scheduled programming.

The Queen plopped down on her throne.

"It appears I've saved the bad news for last. Update me on the troublemakers," she ordered of Dr. Christopher Marco.

"Ah, uh, one second, Your Grace."

He pinched the bridge of his nose. Marco had been working here for over ten years, but until just a few weeks ago, Queen Lorelei didn't usually request in-depth reports regarding server activity, and almost never stepped foot in the *Nexus*. Given his wife Adeline's lofty ambitions, all this recent business put the man on edge. He glanced over from his work to check her temperament. She stifled a yawn.

"Speak, nerd!"

"M-ma'am, it appears that Yossa's bloc has been mobilizing. Those pictures we let through appear to have inspired, rather than quelled, attempts to transcend the *'Verse*. The storms have made them harder to keep out. One seeker made it to Customer Service before being neutralized. I believe Miss Guggell's estimations have been spot-on: now is the time. We await your order to strike."

"What of the rebels in the streets?"

"Most seem to be operating autonomously from Yossa. There are other factions in the south continent, rallied by Hector Travers, that barbarian. Our Analytics lab thinks they're of little consequence."

"I'll be the judge of that. Lillian does nothing without reason. If we act now, how many can we nab? Don't you have, like, a big board with all their names and lists of connections?"

Marco gave her a dumb look. "I'm sorry... what? A board?"

"Never you mind. We're co-opting the anarchists. Disperse fifteen million Gold over smaller clusters. Get our moles to turn the rebels against Yossa and Lily. We want infighting, chaos. Continue tracking and monitoring known terrorists, but don't go overboard on memory wipes. Sway public opinion. Blow up a few daycare centers, yank some brats from the servers and blame them for it. That sort of business. We can't afford to just go playing mass freeze-tag. The more violent, uninhibited, and uncontrollable the insurgents appear, the sooner the flock will serve them up to us on a silver platter. Crassus had these tactics down over two thousand years ago, Marco. This is child's play."

"Of course, ma'am," said Christopher Marco, who didn't think it qualified as child's play at all.

"Please tell me there's some good news."

"Indeed, Highness." The voice belonged to Dr. Zarifian. "Macleod reports that General Lacie has successfully extracted Gerrit. They are en route as we speak."

"Excellent. Patch me into her connection."

"I'm... afraid her signal has cut out," Guggell said.

The news chilled Lorelei to the bone, but she tried not to show any concern. Order needed to be kept.

"She must be tracking the enemy's armada on radio silence," the Queen bluffed. "I'll have to reprimand her on her tardiness. When can we expect the convoy?"

"They are currently supersonic. Three hours, ma'am."

XVIII. Indoctrination

"In the end these things matter most: How well did you love? How fully did you love? How deeply did you let go?" - Gautama Buddha

The boy didn't want his balloon back.

Raine tried uncertainly to return the thing, but the kid seemed happy enough to see a cool-looking girl descend from the heavens to rescue it that to seize the lucky mass of rubber and string would be to deny fate its little pleasures.

She thanked the child wordlessly, as he seemed unable to hear or speak, and turned towards the rather gigantic arena that loomed over this new city, advertised as Helium-Corneria, against which the Roman Coliseum would appear a miniature. The setting sun cast the bowl's long shadow over the surrounding neighborhood.

"FREE CONCERT TONIGHT!" the banners advertised.

"I wonder what's in there," she asked aloud as a faint, hypnotizing voice beckoned through one of a few hundred arches.

Come one, come all, embrace the illusion...

With great relief, Raine confirmed on the bounty boards that she was no longer on any wanted list. After changing into a white magician's jacket over a casual shirt and jeans, the girl reasoned that a live show might just help her plan her next move.

Raine joined the massive crowd. A curious pixie and her head-banging vampire boyfriend struck up a dull conversation in line. Supposedly the show she was about to see was going to be 'mind-blowing', 'sick', 'twisted', and 'gnarly'.

Half an hour later Raine, Chance, and the blue balloon were at the edge of one of the further rings of the arena. She clung to her tiny ledge on the rim like a soggy piece of cereal.

The center stage stood out like a platform in the midst of a bottomless hole, sucking in the collective energy of the crowd of several hundred thousand like a vacuum. Her stomach quivered with anxiety – how many other people were experiencing the same thing?

That she could no longer trust the denizens of this world left her feeling rather tiny and alone.

Raine tried to calculate the probability of finding a friend to confide in here, now that Gerrit was gone, given that true friends are one in a million. She attempted multiplying rows with columns, but as the other end of the stadium seemed miles away, she abandoned the conceit.

A spotlight, and then a deafening guitar solo, interrupted her thoughts, slicing through the smoky darkness like a gleaming sword. The din of murmurs faded to an expectant hush.

She jumped up on her tiptoes to peer over the gang of well-dressed Sasquatch, who'd craned their necks up from the ring in front of her, obstructing the view with their top hats.

"Oh, sorry," one of them graciously muttered, turning around at the sound of her boots shifting against the floor. Just as he lifted off his hat, Raine spotted a leather-clad giant floating down the shaft of light, flaming guitar wailing in both hands. The resulting wave of audience screams shocked her, but not as much as the *Godzilla*-like drummer's explosive percussion intro.

Shortly after inhaling a few strange, glowing particles, a terrifyingly familiar dissonant noise attacked Raine's ears. Covering them did nothing. She needed to get out of here.

Barreling down her aisle to the stairway, Raine turned to the others and wondered why they weren't all losing their minds. She collapsed mid-run, rolled down the stairs, and curled up into a ball, her stomach jumping into her throat. She glanced up at the other folk; they were smiling, transfixed, bobbing up and down. Dilated pupils reckoned her as if she were a freak. Painted grins begged her to become one with the machine. She wished she were dead.

And then, it stopped.

The lead singer of the oversized band segued into a singsong chorus. Lightning shot from his fingertips. A group of scantily clad women manifested onstage. They began a lovely dance around the singer, and in turn were all thoroughly electrocuted; lightning swam through their bodies and dispersed throughout the ecstatic crowd as the song wound down to its close.

Before Raine could recover, thumping percussion and electronic music from two dueling DJs drove a persistently repetitive dance number as the go-go dancers, now winged, shook their bodies wildly in mid-flight and brought the stadium to a standstill.

Some were on their knees, completely at the mercy of the sirens. Others shook with reckless abandon, eyes closed and sweaty bodies rubbing up against one another.

Raine felt a hypnotizing pull, even though she knew that for Gerrit's sake, and for hers, she should have kept low and diverted all attention from her visage. She hungered to feel as free as the others in the crowd.

The song ended. The lead singer's voice boomed out.

"Thank yer, thank yer! We be so happy to exist! We play on to stop the war! I have sought unto the beyond, and there is naught but fog! No big man in the sky *musting* us to be unhappy! Bros and sissy-beans, wothing in this norld could possibly be more tangible than our desire for it! Through desire we become with ourselves one as!"

But Raine didn't hear his bizarre words, losing herself within the building rhythm. Though her avatar was planted at the bottom of a stairwell by the banister, her mind was onstage with the ravishing women as a guitar solo kicked in and additional spotlights lit her section. In her peripheral vision, Raine sensed eyes trained on her. She was almost relieved when the music died down and the fifty-foot leviathan spoke once again in his odd manner.

"To-morning, I take it upon myself to express mine diveeeeeeine happiness for all the missus and misters and mississirs here who hath recognized the universal desire to unite and thank the Developers what have created this very existence for us. We be but humble beings and they know-see in their infinite wisdoms that we exist to service those most burning of needs, our own!"

Virtual flames erupted from unseen pipes above, and a laser light show strobed as the band kicked into a very heavy electronic number with a catchy tune. Aerial acrobats flew ribbons above the bowl, their neon trails pulsing in tune with the music.

The glowing particles sprinkled down from the ether once more, transfiguring into fireflies fluttering around the stadium. Raine inhaled. The air had become deliciously intoxicating and she wanted more of it.

Raine felt unbearably groovy. Tears stained her cheeks before she knew they existed. All around, her happiness was shared. The crowd-organism boogied and gyrated, its individuals enjoying great times with company. A man came up to Raine, looked right into her eyes, and pulled her close. They danced together, closer than she ever would have dared otherwise. She tried to hold herself back. It was very difficult.

And then there was a beautiful, older girl, who cut in and stole her away. Raine, much to her own surprise, loved it. She ran her fingers through the girl's hair and stared blankly into her eyes as they bounced up and down. Unfazed, the man doubled his energy. More came to watch all three of them. The audience mobbed Raine. Some longed to be near her, while others just wanted to ogle her with their eyes. The voice in the girl's head was screaming at her to be present, to process what she was doing. Her body ignored it. Soon the voice was silent.

"Through desire become we ourselves one with!"

Even Chance meowed and clawed for her attention, to no avail. Her addiction to the weightless feeling shut out even his strongest spells.

Floating on cloud nine, Raine shook her body aggressively to the music, longing to take off her dress. Her mind re-entered the equation only to strap the balloon string to her wrist.

She'd never known such bliss. She didn't want it to end.

But then there was a gunshot.

And an explosion.

And then the floating particles disappeared.

Raine staggered to her feet and pushed towards the balcony, sudden feelings of shame and dizziness eclipsed by ones of mortal fear as deafening screams filled the air. The release she'd felt revealed itself to be completely false.

The entire bowl was erupting into unchecked chaos. Some audience members raised weapons against the revolutionaries and were quickly stunned in place or petrified by others hiding in the crowd. The jumbo band members bolted away.

The woman she'd nearly kissed had collapsed on the floor. Raine picked her up and pulled her away from the dangerous horde.

"I owe you one, Raine," the woman muttered. "What's going on?"

"Beats me. But I know one thing: it's not safe here."

Wait!

"How the heck did you know my name?" demanded Raine.

"No need for modesty. Everyone knows who *you* are, Raine the Unkillable," the woman said, deliriously cozying up to her. "You're, like, that... girl, you know... a tragic heroine. The bringer of truths. A figure of rebellion. The *Metaverse's* Most Wanted."

"T-thanks, but you really should get out of here. Seems that wherever I'm at, trouble's never far behind."

A rather sizeable group of people fortified with all manner of armaments had hijacked the stage. One of the brigade members was busy setting up a small electric device where the lead singer was standing mere seconds ago.

"People of our common world! Please! Do not leave! We mean you absolutely no harm! We are the anarchist revolution, and we are here to help! I ask for nothing more than a few minutes of your time!"

Just then, someone rushing by shoved both women into the banister, knocking the breath from Raine's lungs. Chance puffed up his body, hissing and growling at the crowd to back off. She tried helplessly to push herself away from the wall, but the stream of panicked bodies gunning for the exits made it impossible. They were pinned into place. She untied the balloon string, stuck out her arm, held it aloft, and miraculously, it didn't burst.

"Don't listen to their centralized media! You have all been tricked! Those responsible for this event were experimenting with a drug that robs you of your own free will! They hope that it will help them achieve their ultimate goal of silencing our minds forever!"

Concealed anarchists blasted away every last Templar in the Bowl. Ghostly images of the knights struggling to hang on to their physical bodies terrified Raine; many respawned elsewhere, only to be mobbed to death again. She'd thought the Templars undefeatable, but then remembered that members of the resistance were hackers with in-depth knowledge of the *Verse*'s code.

Don't panic! Raine thought to herself. *Keep your wits about you!*

Before long she managed to pull herself up to the railing, and just in time, too. She saw the source of the booming voice: at center stage, a half-elephant, half-man pulled off his hood, clutching the mic valiantly.

"THIS GAME IS JUST AN ILLUSION! Gold pieces, loot, points, quests, upgrades, titles, room décor, patches, achievements… are these really important to you?"

The answer came in the form of a disorganized rabble and loud boos and jeers. There were scattered pockets of agreement here and there. Many were still stunned from the effects of the strange particles, and most others were fleeing or otherwise teleporting out of the arena.

"Are they really important?" he repeated.

The din of yells and jeers continued.

"My name is Yossa, and I'm here to tell you the truth about this place! This world is a lie! All these career goals, all this character building, it's what's keeping you from your actual, physical selves! What do we know about the *Metaverse*? We know it isn't the real world! We know our true bodies are somewhere out there! But we don't know whether those who are forcibly removed from here are taken back to reality, or to another server. All we can do is trust to the Developers. Trust to the ever-changing laws of the land, the laws we do not vote for, the laws that are not even made publicly visible! We don't know who is running this world! We don't know what their intentions are! Our rights as sovereign humans stand! Do you hear me up there, you Templars, Archons, Developers, whatever the hell you call yourselves! I'm as human as you are. Give us the *truth*, stop regulating our minds, and let those who so desire be freed of this place!"

"Ugh, another rebel bust. These guys are such killjoys," the woman muttered. "Name's Angela. Wanna blow this joint? I can get us into some top clubs."

"I'll pass," replied Raine, her eyes glued to the stage. "Thanks, though."

"Too cool to hang out with us normal people, huh? Suit yourself."

"Huh? No, not at all, it's just--"

But Angela was already among the exiting mob.

Alone again, Raine leaned on a pillar and looked as far around as she could. It was still pure chaos. Yet it seemed that a small number of people had stopped pushing. They were standing motionless. Listening. A select few among the few were agreeing. But it seemed enormously important that they were at least paying attention.

After making sure *Neo Eden's* forces had lost her scent, Lily ditched the speeder for the *Phoenix,* hit her head and then fist-pumped at Raine's successful acquiring of the skeleton key, reunited with her traveling airship caravan, and docked her ship at the *Valkyrie.*

Two hours of preparations followed, and the Sky Admiral personally inspected the finalized Exo Knight mechanized suits and re-calibrated the ship's flywheels to maximum efficiency. Engineers addressed Lillian, also the EDC's Chief Science Officer, in reverence.

Their unearned adulation made the woman's mind race even faster –
most of the military engineering briefs and designs attributed to Lily
were envisioned by someone else she'd lost, someone very close to her.

"Your babies are looking great, Aquino. I do worry about the power
drain from the Annihilator redirects. Will the prime cells alone supply
enough resistance to pierce *Eden's* EM shields?"

"Sorry, ma'am," her baggy-eyed Colonel responded. "The exact
schematics remain unknown to us. Agent Lotus is working on it. She's
also confirmed that the enemy has basic knowledge of our Knights."

"Then it's as I thought. But there's nothing for it. Thank you,
Colonel. Do triple-check the AB systems for me, if you get the time."

Lily saved the most crucial call for last: a holo-conference with her
body double, Leela Kernani, more commonly known as Commodore
Leandra of the airship *Freyja*, leading the secondary wing hundreds of
miles away.

"How goes it, sweet pea?"

The hologram of the woman, who in prosthetics much resembled a
taller, stronger Lillian, stood at attention. "We cross the Adriatic at
dawn. Your people are prepared to live and die for you, Sky Admiral."

"Please… don't say it like that," Lily said wearily. "I–I'm sorry. It's
been a difficult day, and I do not wish to burden you with my troubles."

"I see no reason to worry, ma'am. The General is gone. I'm in
command of two hundred Carriers and six hundred Destroyers, the
Knights are primed to go, Raine's ten meters from the goal, and your
eyes in *Eden* are wide open. But if it helps, I'll be your listening ear."

If only I could confide in her. Lily managed a solemn nod. *It'd be a
very different world if Lorrie and I kept a cabal of comrades in on our
secrets.*

"Thank you. It's… difficult sometimes, when I think of what might
have been, or could have been. In another place and time, there'd be no
need for all this destructive power, these underhanded tactics. Yet to
that end, I have none but myself to blame."

*I suppose it's not so different from what it was. In the Alpha world
line, even more of Earth's natural resources were used for warfare,
consumer products, vehicles, designer homes, skyscrapers, plastic
sporks, and other objects of convenience. But must history go on
repeating itself? Must we continue fighting indefinitely?*

"You're wrong, ma'am," insisted Leandra. "Your gifts lie in your
imagination, your selflessness, and your ability to strive for the best of

all possible outcomes. You've many friends, and have won millions of hearts. I'll never forget how you saved my family at the siege of Bombay. It meant the world to us, Admiral."

Though her double couldn't begin to comprehend the true weight on Lily's shoulders, the Sky Admiral gave a warm smile. She could give no guarantee that Leandra's father would make it out alive. Yossa would be immersed in the thick of battle.

I saved you because you had the potential to be useful, Lily recalled. *And yet, somehow your Dad ended up back in harm's way. I'm just as much of an opportunist as Lorrie.*

"Thanks, honey. I feel much better about tomorrow, knowing you've got my back," she lied.

"Do you really, Lillian? We're on the eve of the most decisive battle in history, and you're silent as a clam. When confronted with the harsh truths of life, the mind will often revolt or turn away. If this restless mind is not tamed, it will make you its slave. Please, if there's anything… at all… don't hold it in. Let me be your friend once more."

She's right. My attachments are manifesting as doubts. What have I started? Going into the whole Time Keeper thing would be an act of selfishness and cowardice on my part. Right now, I simply need to assuage her fears.

"It'll be many lifetimes before I discover how you read me like a book, where all others have failed. As a point of fact, my sweet Leela, you are my very dearest friend. This mental storm is as impermanent as an itch; it's only escalated to this level because there are fears I must master, fears that we both know all too well."

That last part's a lie, and she knows it. Nevertheless, Leandra's holographic hands wrapped kindly around her heroine's.

"You don't have to lie for me. Some things are best left unsaid, after all. Keep on keepin' on, Admiral. Just remember that I'm always here."

"I've never forgotten. Have a safe flight, Commodore."

"Likewise, ma'am."

Leandra bowed out, smiling.

There was nothing more the Sky Admiral could do but wait; she munched on a stick of gum. It had been a long day at work, and she was in desperate need of some light reading material.

Painful as it might be, Lily decided to sneak a peek at Lacie's memoir in the foolish hope that a bit of mourning might help clear her mind for the even longer day ahead.

Diary from Attempt # 7
October 9, 1873 A.D.
19:13 BT
The Belladonna 5000

Lucy and I head up the stairs to the observatory with dinner trays for all four of us. We ate, trying to casually converse. But, as usual following Lorrie's troubling vision, they wouldn't stop arguing.

"Where are your theorems?" Lily cries. "So far, there's no evidence to refute the model of a flexible universe fully capable of rewriting itself. If all were as you suggest, every black hole would create an infinite number of temporal vortices. If one could travel close enough to the center--"

"Spare me the models and petty proofs from bygone eras," Lorelei interjects. "They are useless."

Of course, she's quick to the white board, and scribbles out an unsolvable equation.

"As you can see here, Deutsch's prescription has limited parameters. There's no telling how spinning webs through spacetime affects, for instance, the expansion of the universe. And assuming we exist in some flexible reality dictated by cause and effect, we can't logically be standing here in the first place! Your parents never existed in this universe, ergo; the Belladonna *is an alien artifact from a parallel world. We are splitting realities, Lily, a child can see it."*

Lillian's tapping the board. "Wrong, wrong, wrong! Your logic is limited by ancient presuppositions. There is no way this space station has the power to create entire realities. There's either one universe, or an infinite number of them. In the one world line scenario, we are Earth's only hope. On the other hand, even in a non-infinite Multiverse, our chances of success in at least one of quadrillions upon quadrillions of realities are all but guaranteed. If that's so, then cosmically speaking, all our actions are harmless ripples in an infinite ocean, and it is our task to bear witness to the instance where everyone lives, and continue the mission as planned. Accept that the Belladonna *is from this world, in a timeline that may or may not exist anymore," Lily continues. "I've sent countless messages to myself in the far past without erasing my existence in this present."*

"Precisely! Your parents may not even be born in this timeline. But we're still here, aren't we? Last week we were dining with Queen Victoria. By all means, that should have caused all manner of paradoxes. There is no real evidence for Multiverse theory."

"Nor against it! And if you look at the projected dark energy readings, the multiple dimensions of String Theory, and the inevitabilities of cosmic inflation, one might even apply Occam's razor to determine that we are living in either a singular, carefully calibrated Universe, or a Level 1 Multiver--"

"Theories, Lily! Theories, but no proof! It's a non-science, the work of fanaticism! If Novikov's conjecture that temporal paradoxes are physically impossible is truly wrong, the only logical explanation for the Belladonna's *continued existence is that of emergent parallel worlds. Conclusion: this must be an alternate universe of our own creation, and we've already sent our previous world to its doom!"*

Lily paces furiously. "We may not know how or why the self-consistency principle has been debunked, but we're blazing trails at the forefront of history here; spacetime isn't some arbitrary line that you can just splinter off from with the result of creating a new dimension filled with energy and matter out of a vacuum. Our work all but proves that. I'll admit it's possible, however unlikely, that your Split Universe Theory might be the truth – perhaps we can answer that question within our lifetimes – but based on our understanding of quantum gravity, it's far more likely that the universe patches its own ripples."

Lorelei slams her fist against the board. "Quantum gravity remains undefined! In your fantasy, who diffuses the ripples? God? Did this Divine Watchmaker create your infinitely emergent dimensions, too? Don't make me laugh. We are alone, Lillian. Hopelessly alone."

"You mentioned God, Lorrie, not I," insists Lily. "The more we learn, the more questions emerge. We can't even begin to say we understand what we're dealing with. The true measure of knowledge is in knowing how little we know, rather than pretending at ready-made answers. Convictions, after all, are more dangerous than doubts."

Lorelei lights a cigarette. It was a mean gesture, but what masterful manipulation. She knew full well the devices were banned on the ship, and polluting our air filters was one of Lily's rage triggers.

"So, 'Captain', based on your hunch, you'll continue to use the universe as your sandbox, with the humans as your control group. You don't care whether our artificial wormholes or constant tampering with

history destabilize the balance of the universe. And what if the Warp Initiator does indeed emit a smattering of dark energy? Our kicked-up space dust may be distorting spacetime itself."

"You're twisting my words. Every conceivable test has been done: the dual wormholes manifest over the Belladonna *for a nanosecond and are sealed to prevent feedback loops. As for any dark energy emissions, they are negligible if even my parents' reverse-engineered probes can't track them. My great-grandpa knew the science behind the Warp Initiator was paradoxical at best, but if it works---"*

"If this is an attempt to manufacture consent, then you're preaching to the choir." Lorelei motions to us. "I'm just telling it as I see it, Captain. Any scientist worth her salt doesn't put stock in miracles."

There were few things Lily hated more than being interrupted, and this was Lorrie's second transgression. After realizing that Lorelei's modus operandi has just been to provoke her, the Captain whispers a Buddhist chant to quiet her mind for a good minute.

"Okay, Lorrie," she begins. "I'll give you the benefit of the doubt. Let's hold a thought experiment. Say your unfounded theory of our ultimate responsibility is somehow true. What would you have me do? Abandon the human race?"

"So far she's keeping her cool," Lucille whispers conspiratorially. I can't help but crack a smile. Lorelei shoots us that wounded, betrayed look. As if we owe her anything.

"Absolutely. Your God abandoned the human race," Lorelei intones. "We must accept that we're trying to fight the Almighty. On a cosmic scale, we're gone in the blink of an eye any way you cut it."

Lily laughs, breaking the tension. "Fatalism! That's your answer! Again with the dark thoughts! Cheer up, old girl!"

An Ad hominem *answer to an* Ad ignorantiam *statement. The multiple fallacies in both my sisters' logic tonight stick out like sore thumbs, but I'm staying out of it. Of course, Lily's real answer has been drilled into our heads for so long that it goes without saying: she would insist that our fellow humans are capable of good beyond self-interest, and that we must hope that our actions can make a difference in the grand scheme of things.*

Lorelei's looking to us now for support, but I don't know what to tell her. Oh, how I wish I had an answer. Despite their passionate debate, from my point of view, there's really no hard evidence to prove or disprove either.

"May I interject?" Lucy says, saving the day as usual. She chases a sip of her seaweed soup with rice. "You both are arguing over a range of theses that are impossible to investigate with our limited understanding of even the wormholes we use to time leap. As to the nature of our universe, the Belladonna's *never been tested in an environment outside of our solar system, and we can't just go poking around for paradoxes willy-nilly in the name of experimentation. Not to mention, there's a lot of work to be done if we're to expand our operating range. We haven't yet worked out antimatter, let alone determining whether it's a viable power source. We're alchemists trying to tackle quantum entanglement. It might be decades before we can seriously examine the possibility of parallel universes."*

"So what do you propose?" Lorelei replies.

"That you try this delicious soup Lacie made; the tofu is quite wonderful," she posits, throwing a most satisfied expression my way. "Then why don't we create a world dedicated to nothing but science?"

Despite her faults, Lucille was one of the only people in my life to show me true kindness.

"That's what we've been trying to do," I pipe in. "If we share our knowledge, we may not need to figure out this answer alone." A lame response, and a pitiful attempt at quelling some of the tension.

"The others concur. Lorrie, can't we argue about metaphysics on a full stomach?" Lily protests, taking her seat with us and sipping down the hot miso broth.

"I want a solution to this!" Lorelei calls desperately. "I will not rest until I know whether we have quadrillions of lives and deaths on our hands."

"Hey. Quadrillions of lives are still going to be there in five minutes. Soup's getting cold," Lucy replies in her deadpan manner, on cue as usual. She wipes the steam from her glasses. "Chow now. Science later."

While I initially admired what Lucy did, neither Lily nor Lorelei spoke for the rest of the evening. Her intervention might only have deepened the rift. Perhaps this conflict could have been settled that very night. Or not. This was certainly not the first major altercation between Lily and Lorrie, and it would be far from the last.

I never knew what to do in these situations. I felt so powerless, a fly on the wall that could be called on at any juncture to hold up a scorecard. What good could the opinion be of a so-called scientist

*more concerned with the thoughts of everyone else in the room than
with finding the truth?*

*But listen to me go on. Self-pity was never my style. Neither was
arbitration. Call me lazy, but back then, I just wanted them to agree on
something, anything, so that we could get to work.*

*Only now do I realize I was just avoiding the consequences of my
actions.*

Lily closed the book and swept away a stray tear.

*Why did you choose her, Lacie? Was her logic truly that sound?
What did you stand to gain – love, respect, power? All the things I
could never offer you... or had I never thought to do so...?*

Twenty years of life and Lillian had nothing to show for her efforts
but the pain and suffering she'd caused others. Maybe things could
change after *Operation End Verse*. Or maybe nothing would change.
Even in most of the best-case scenarios, all the experiences, hopes, and
dreams of this timeline would amount to nothing but a sob story in a
red envelope.

No. I can't think that. I'll never know 'til I try.

———

Queen Lorelei strode out in silence to meet the transport ship.
Captain Simon Thomas of the Royal Guard and twelve of his best stood
at attention. Her Majesty was dressed in jet-black from head to toe, and
a thick veil obscured her face. Her steps were quick and lithe, as if the
Angel of Death were gliding across the raised platform.

The young Captain saw trembling from underneath the silk gloves as
she lifted the tarp covering both General Lacie and her clone. Their
faces were a pale green. Queen Lorelei studied her true sister's features,
identical to her own, and the sensitive Thomas was sure he sensed her
thoughts – like him, she was wondering if she'd look as content at her
own curtain call.

A tear fell from Thomas' face as the Queen planted a kiss on her
sister's forehead, her purple lipstick giving General Lacie the
appearance of a third eye.

Queen Lorelei then walked over to the Captain and handed him a
letter bearing the royal seal. As she made her exit from the room, it

appeared that her heart had sunk, and that she was weeping. Being the fearless and undisputed World Leader, it was inconceivable to suggest or even consider that Queen Lorelei was capable of emotion. But that day, he was sure he had seen her break.

As soon as she disappeared back into the elevator without dismissing the company, Simon unfolded the letter and read it twice to himself. Not a soul in *Neo Eden* was to know of General Lacie's death; he and anyone with knowledge of the incident were to be escorted to the Overseer by armed droids and submit to memory cleansing. The information was not to leave the hangar.

Officially, the General was abroad on an important assignment. The bodies would be left covered for a clandestine funeral pyre that night, arranged by the androids, at which Queen Lorelei alone was to be present.

∩

In a private server far from the Developers' prying eyes, Super BlastBoy toasted his feet in front of the fireplace. He watched in dreadful anticipation as the holo-feed from the night's concert was interrupted and replaced by a warning message and a server-wide hunt-and-freeze order. Five hundred million Gold points, the sign read over the head of Yossa Kernani, standing in the midst of the Bowl. Smaller rewards would be given for information or assistance leading to his arrest.

"Player *Yossa_B13* has been declared an enemy of *Endless Metaverse*," the reporter began. "Patched into the *Avidya* server via illegal channels, he is a cyber-terrorist, to be considered extremely dangerous. According to multiple reports, his organization is responsible for the disappearances of campaign workers, the attacks on daycare centers, the hunting of red pandas and raccoon dogs, the rises in defense taxes, and the database exploits scrambling the banking systems. If anyone is withholding information about *Yossa_B13*, they are in breach of *Metaverse* law and will be punished to the fullest extent."

The game icon shook its old head. The time to act was approaching very soon.

XIX. The Blue Balloon

"Your task is not to seek for love, but merely to seek and find all the barriers within yourself that you have built against it." - Rumi

"It's a simple anti-spawn tracking error. Anyone could overlook it, Reno."

"I disagree completely, sir. It's a known issue. As per Hoshua's orders, it was scheduled to be addressed in tonight's update."

"It's one line in a string of millions. This was Guggell's error in the first place, was it not? As I said, anyone could and would overlook it. Look, I'm just asking you to do one thing. In fact, scratch that. I'm not even asking you to do anything. I'm asking you to do *nothing*."

"And that's precisely what I can't do, sir."

"Stop telling yourself that. It's easy."

"I… I just… in all my years of service, I've never…"

"If you continue to make it difficult for us, then we will have no choice but to make things difficult for you."

"Please, sir. I don't want any part in this."

"You were involved the minute you took over Janice's office. If you won't play ball, then rest assured our mutual cyborg friend will have no qualms about removing you from the court. Permanently."

Having left the Coliseum re-conditioning in Hoshua's hands for the time being, Jon Wrathman dimmed his office window and listened intently to the flagged recording of a hushed conversation in the Developers' lounge earlier that day.

The Templars were messing up left and right, and Raine was still nowhere to be found. But this had to have been the cherry on top of the crumbling cake: unbeknownst to anyone but himself, it appeared that Chris Marco was bullying his colleague, Dr. Cid Reno, into overlooking a serious bug in the known *Metaverse*.

The 'cyborg friend' is an easy peg: General Beech is godfather to Marco's boy, and he and Reno were bunkmates at the Royal Academy. What are Marco and Beech playing at? Could they be the rebel spies? For once, I'm left in the dark.

"All right!" Reno responds at last. "But I don't want to know nothing 'bout this. Nothing, you hear?"

Marco laughed. "Not a peep. Not even if you'd asked."

Thoroughly intrigued, Wrathman cut the recording and winked to retract his Holo-Lens. He gazed down into the Network chamber at Marco and Reno in turn, working with separate teams on *Avidya's* opposite continents, and ordered the droids to prepare his *M-Gear*.

I really ought to confront or report them. But then there's that other side of me, the one that wants to see how deep this treachery runs.

As for motives? Beech thinks Her Majesty has been too weak on the coalition rebels. That she hasn't been ruthless enough in her seizure of power. According to my source in the Defense Ministry, he's even found a way to keep personal records in between memory wipes. More than anyone else, Errol would recognize the right moment to make his move. Only... I fear for the Metaverse. *If that machine-man and Macleod had their way, half the world would be in ashes.*

And Marco's hit the ceiling as far as career growth is concerned. He could be searching for that second chance. Or he could just have been in the wrong place, at the wrong time. Never would I have imagined that pencil-pusher courageous enough to support a coup.

Ah, well. I admire their dumb courage, though I rate their chances of success lower than the last five attempts to seize the throne. And if this wretched plan of theirs blows up in our faces, at least I'll know that I didn't turn away from it.

A sudden alarm sounded out from the Coliseum, compounding Wrathman's worries.

"What? That's preposterous!"

He'd been away from the main room for all of five minutes. In an act of brutal betrayal, the shields around the Coliseum had been breached. Hundreds of thousands of anarchists had infiltrated the arena.

Not now! Of all the days they could have scheduled a raid! Who messed up this time? Best to plug in ASAP, so I can at least get a closer look at what's happening before the Queen comes a-calling.

Back in the Coliseum, Yossa continued his speech.

The bowl was mostly empty now, with just a few stragglers. Chance busied himself about by munching on leftover concessions. Raine soon concluded that there were no doubts about it: this had to have been the very same Yossa that Gerrit told her about - the rebel Homo-Pachyderm. Half-man, half-elephant.

Wicked.

"You might be wondering why you haven't heard of us. Why you don't remember us. They have been regulating your thoughts, using electrical signals shot straight into your mind to elicit gut reactions, to restrict your higher brain functions, to make you forget that there's more out there. Did you know that ninety-five percent of all *Endless Metaverse* players have less than six months of long-term memory?"

Yossa reached both arms out to implore the crowd. "What they haven't done, because they will never be able to do it... is to control your hearts. Senses can be tricked. Memories replaced, instincts rewired. Nanites programmed to inhibit your judgment. Belief systems shaken down and destroyed. But the voice of the heart is stronger. It says, listen. Engage. Love. Seek. *Care.* I implore you to look within your own hearts. We are all seekers of truth. Come with us and we will show you what it means to be truly human. To remember the things you've been trained so hard to forget, to achieve a potential that you may be unable to imagine because you've been so deeply indoctrinated."

I can see why Gerrit trusted him. He seems sincere enough.

Just then a threatening boom sounded out from above. The captive audience screamed in terror. *The Nebula* reappeared over the bowl. Templars were rappelling down ropes. Terror took the crowd again. Sobs reached Raine's ears. She spun around; the few people who remained cowered behind their seats.

"No, please! Stay calm! Join us, and we will protect your minds and bodies! We will fight for your inalienable rights! Give you a secure connection, patch you through to our hubs! Together, I know we can uncover the truth!"

The small electric device Yossa's posse placed in the middle of the stage suddenly emitted an intense point that drew in the surrounding air, pressurized it, and then shot up a shining pillar.

"Have no fear!" Yossa yelled. "This is for your protection!"

Heavy rumbling shook Raine's balcony; she shoved the balloon into her shoulder bag, and just in time. The pulse zapped every electric light in the area. Active Network visors short-circuited.

From the beacon, a clear barrier surrounded the stadium in a protective dome, and not a second too soon; Templars dropping down from the *Nebula* rebounded off the electrical pulses.

A rather large person knocked Raine against the wall, prompting a new strategy. Considering her options, she felt compelled to approach Yossa and introduce herself. A friend of Gerrit's might be her only hope at bringing him back.

He was currently detailing a plan to quickly organize the audience into two groups – those who wanted to learn more about the revolution, and those who wanted to leave.

Some of the less battle-ready folk used Chimera Wings to teleport out of the area. Yossa offered them for free, but warned that the city was under Safety Lockdown, limiting warps to within its walls.

Raine moved swiftly towards the stage, where men and women from the resistance met with interested folk from the audience.

With Chance's help, she pushed through the crowd, drawing quite a bit of attention.

"Hey! Was that…"

"It's her! It's the Rain dancer!"

Leaping from a fifteen-foot rampart into a roll, Raine was stunned to see thousands of people in the arena rushing towards her – some in reverence, others in full-on rage.

"Raine! Viva la revolucion!"

"Your data blitz erased by girlfriend's memory! I'll make you pay!"

"Beat it, dork! I want that bounty!"

"Didn't ya get the memo, bottom-feeder?! She's off the list."

"Get away from her, ya goons! That crown means royalty!"

Raine made it as far as the sunken pit by the main platform before being mobbed to the ground.

"Dog, be it true zat you spared ze Pagoda Champion's life?"

"Hey! I run a swaggy blog about you. Please to be my waifu?"

An effeminate voice drove the crazed fans back with an otherworldly battle cry. Its maker, a fabulous elven warrior, then pulled Raine out of the unruly flood of bodies.

"Bless my soul, sister! It's really you," he said, holding her by the shoulders. "But why are you here?"

The elf motioned to some gnomes, who worked crowd control while he escorted Raine to the stage, beside himself with unchecked joy.

"They dropped me off right in front of the Coliseum."

"Of course! They must have sent you here for re-conditioning, to be experimented on! In a stroke of blind luck we caught you just in time, girl! By gods, that will be one epic headline! YOSSA! Yossa, sir!"

He took Raine's hand and led her up the stage, behind a sensor-shielded bauble to Yossa, who was now dwelling in the shadows, relentlessly checking a holo-map of the Bowl.

"Yes, Figwit?"

"It's Raine, sir."

The elephant man's eyes shot open. "She was here this whole time?"

"We couldn't detect her. Player density interference."

"Of course, of course. This is a most welcome development, to say the least! Have a seat, Raine," he offered, sitting down in the lotus position. Following suit, she noticed he boasted thick elephant legs and a head, but his body and arms seemed to be akin to that of a rugged human. He was quite a prospect to behold.

"You're beautiful," Raine murmured, staring at him.

"Ha! That's the first time anyone's ever called me that," he reflected. "It is said that during account creation, one chooses how their avatar will appear. That kind of information is not for us to recall, of course."

"Strange. I can see it now," Raine said, a little shocked. "My hub. I was given the choice. But only between being a man and a woman, and whether I preferred men, women, or... otherkin?"

"Hum. That is a clue you have been patched in from a system running an older installation client. It also means your memory is strong, like mine. Now, Miss Raine," Yossa pressed, then darted his eyes to the corner, switching to the Private Channeler.

[Yossa_B13]: "Such information could be used for ill intent in the wrong hands. Let us not talk of these things here in the open. Come to Circuitron and we can work together. Set up cells. Destroy corporations. Bring down this prison from the inside."

[rainorshine23]: "You mean, now?"

[Yossa_B13]: "As soon as we're done here. It shouldn't take too long."

[rainorshine23]: "Before anything else, Mr. Yossa, I had a question for you."

[Yossa_B13]: "Is it about Gerrit?"
[rainorshine23]: "Y-yes! Is he all right?"
*[Yossa_B13]: "Erm.... we received a message a few hours ago
that seemed to match his signature. Scrambled almost beyond our
understanding, it was. Must have gone through a dozen filters."*
A gibberish-filled text file appeared in a corner of the girl's field of
vision.

"What does it say?" Raine asked nervously. "I just saw--"

"Young Gerrit's whereabouts are beyond our sight. From what little
we understand of his message we believe he has been removed from
Avidya. Either transferred to a different server, or frozen ... no one can
know. But he's a fighter, that boy. He won't go down easily."

Raine sunk to the ground, filled with worry. *I might have already
missed my chance to save him. But Lily... Lily's gotta have a plan.*
Yossa placed a hand on her shoulder.

"He was a good man," he said. "To think that I saw him just... very
recently. Told me about you, said he wanted to impress you. And that
was just yesterday, before you got all famous."

Raine nodded quietly and hid her tears.

Stupid Gerrit. I never asked for your help.

*It's so odd that I care so deeply for someone I'd only just met. Odd
that a boy could have such an effect on me, as if I'd known him my
entire life. Whether he's my dream boy or not, I need to find him.*

With her eyes closed, she saw them both in her mind's eye, in a far-
off time and place, hand in hand, facing incredible odds together. Only,
they were older, not younger. Was this a memory, or a fantasy? Her
head began aching, as if she'd been dealing once again in forbidden
knowledge.

She was thankful that just then one of Yossa's men, a samurai with
the moniker *BrOmega*, ran up to his boss urgently. He whispered into
Yossa's ear, but he was loud and nervous enough for Raine to hear as
she took the silk handkerchief being offered by the elephant trunk and
used it to blow her nose.

"Sir, the town square's no longer safe. The pigs are processing
everyone they can, everyone who's seen us, or her. They don't want
any loose ends."

"I should think not, Moe," Yossa replied, sitting down with a thud.

Yossa glanced back up at the shield. Hundreds of Templars were
cracking through the barrier, layer by layer. It wasn't going to last

much longer. There were very few ways out of a situation like this. If they all simultaneously teleported to safe hubs, they'd be easily tracked; their hideout compromised. And all these new recruits couldn't simply be left for the law to deal with.

[rainorshine23]: "Do you have an escape plan? My crown grants me Developer status. I can fend them off."

[Yossa_B13]: "I'd rather you not. It'd be unwise to give away your position. It's increasingly looking like there's only one way out of this. Moe, we break on through this Coliseum, split up, and make a run for safe hubs. Everyone lie low for the next twelve hours pending my orders. We leave in three. You and the other squad leaders coordinate."

Moe tossed a salute and dashed back to the other freedom fighters. Now that they were alone, Yossa trained his charms onto Raine once more.

[Yossa_B13]: "You bear the hopes of the Metaverse. *Come with us?"*

Raine kept silent, looking up at Yossa hopefully. It was difficult to tell him that she hadn't the faintest idea what she was supposed to do next.

[rainorshine23]: "I'm sorry. I don't know if I should. I know it seems right, but I also know there's somewhere I'm supposed to be... other than that, I really don't know what I'm doing. I think I'm operating for Lily, but I haven't been given any details."

Yossa was visibly terrified.

[Yossa_B13]: "Raine, be honest with me."

[rainorshine23]: "It's the truth. I haven't the slightest idea what I'm doing."

[Yossa_B13]: "That's unbelievable. You've accomplished so much, freed minds, revealed countless truths, and yet... Are you sure you've received no word? No messages?"

He seemed on the verge of breaking. It was inconceivable. He'd worked nearly a decade to understand and uncover the truth about this realm, and this... this was to be the agent of its destruction? Even if he were to take her back with them, what could they hope to accomplish?

Raine sensed his frustration, and worried that he might lose it completely. She tightened her fists in empathy, hoping for an answer, and felt that something was missing – the balloon string. She'd put in her bag just a minute ago. *But of course! Lily's message!* That she recalled it at that very instant seemed a magnificent stroke of fortune.

[rainorshine23]: "Wait! I... may have received a clue. I think I know where I'm supposed to go, and how to get there."

[Yossa_B13]: "Perfect. Don't tell me where you're going, in case they catch me. Mode of transport?"

Raine drew the balloon from her shoulder bag.

[Yossa_B13]: "The balloon? Truly?"

"Yes," said Raine, flabbergasted at her own words.

[Yossa_B13]: "It was Lily, wasn't it?"

[rainorshine23]: "Why, yes, yes it was!"

"Well, I'll be a monkey's uncle."

Yossa reached into his pack and pulled out a battery-operated fan.

[Yossa_B13]: "Not two hours ago, that girl, she drops me a line, telling me to carry around an electric fan and make sure I had my latest maps. She also left me a handy dossier of custom exploits. May I? This might shock you."

The balloon was cautiously offered. He took the string, still attached to Raine, in one hand, put on his *Cyclops*-like visor with the other and executed the program. The girl felt a jolt of electricity shoot through Yossa's hand and turn the balloon string neon blue. She instinctively pulled on it, which had the effect of lifting her up into the air.

"Yossa? What's going on?"

He gently took the girl by the shoulders, pulled her back down to the surface, and taught her how to control the balloon's vertical movements through motions of her wrist.

[Yossa_B13]: "It's a homemade exploit Lily concocted to work with any balloon. You can now travel quickly and safely across the map. You'll be completely invisible to anyone more than three meters away."

"Excellent," Raine commented.

Yossa turned to his remaining men briefly and executed some complicated hand gestures. They responded affirmatively and fell into formation.

[Yossa_B13]: "We're leaving now. This is a brand new glitch that only Lily and I should know about, so your chances of getting through their perimeter undetected are pretty good. I don't know how strong their counter-hackers are against our feed manipulators, but we'll hold them off as best we can."

"Will you be safe?"

"I don't know how you know where you're going, but this will help you get there," he told Raine as he uploaded a completely explored and annotated map of the local region to her wristwatch. He also quickly modified her visor so that she could use it anonymously.

"How can I thank you?"

"Raine, I know you haven't told me why you're doing this," Yossa said. "And I understand it's very likely that you are not sure of it yourself... but you and I... we share a common goal. It wasn't just Lily who brought us here together. It was destiny."

"I'm still not sure if I believe in destiny, but I hope you're right," Raine said grimly. "And I hope we will meet again, maybe somewhere less chaotic."

"Perhaps. Though I sense that my battle is within this world," Yossa called. "And yours without. Of course, I've been wrong before."

[Yossa_B13]: "As soon as I give you the signal, face the fan towards the ground, activate it, and tug on the balloon. You should shoot straight up."

Raine nodded.

Yossa walked away, eyes on Raine. The cloaking took effect immediately, and with it a bittersweet feeling engulfed Yossa's old heart, which sank at the thought that the rumors might prove true, and *Endless Metaverse* might not live up to its title. Its conclusion would mean the end of years of passionate work.

He took more than a bit of solace in knowing that he did the right thing. His steps away from the girl grew lighter than air.

Before long, Yossa shouted, "Now go! Go with my blessing!"

Raine flicked on the fan and pulled the string.

She blasted off the ground at incredible speed, popping through the barrier between two Templars drilling their way through the shield. She jerked the fan to a stop before slamming into an approaching airship. Quickly yanking the balloon back east towards Atmoya, Raine pointed the fan behind her and flicked the switch again. She zoomed onward.

Raine caught only fleeting glimpses of the rebels as they divided into small groups and fought their way out of the Bowl. Before long the shield gave way. Gunfire sparked the streets like fireworks on Independence Day. Then the noise gave way to the cold silence of night.

Ω

Whilst changing into a flowing black gown deep within her chambers, Queen Lorelei grimaced at the stuttering three-dimensional battlefield being projected in the midst of her room. Even Guggell's software struggled to keep up with the wanton destruction. She paced listlessly along the elegant shag carpet.

"What is happening here, Jon?" she asked a floating hologram of Mister Senior.

He was hovering above the Coliseum in a gyrocopter, watching the chaos unfold below as the streets of Helium-Corneria burned and rebels picked off the Templars one by one.

"Surely you can see the situation better than I can, ma'am. It's a bloodbath down here!"

Queen Lorelei zoomed into the Coliseum. Every player avatar and NPC was visible on her screen; that is, every player but the girl she now needed desperately to find.

"Did you see where the hell Raine went?"

Wrathman searched his holo-map anxiously, panicking. The girl was headed onstage when she disappeared a minute ago; there was no mistaking it. *Could the entire feed be corrupted?*

She addressed the quivering Developers in the *Avidya* dome.

"This mere skirmish is irrelevant compared to the damage that girl's capable of inflicting. She's the key to all this, we can't just let her slip through our fingers!"

Jon looked around hopelessly one last time and shook his head.

"Still no dice. And we can't get a video lock. Scanners are overloaded."

"Tell me, why can't you teleport in there again?" the Queen asked.

"A m-m-modification by the anarchists; they've exploited a glitch. The anti-spawn shield we created to prevent the rebels from infiltrating seems to have backfired, Your Eminence."

Incompetence surrounds me from every angle! Who is pulling the strings? Whose failures, intentional or not, caused Lacie's death? The answer may point directly to me. But regardless, I need answers.

"In other words, it's a prison break and we're locked out of our own dungeon; they can get out, but we can't get in. That. Is. Just. Fantastic.

Wrathman! Have Hoshua interrogated, then frozen."

This was awful for many reasons.

First off, Alphonse Hoshua was a pretty stand-up guy. More than just the life of the poker table, his years as *Avidya* Lead and Senior Network Security Adviser had been mostly stress-free and uneventful. Second, Mister Senior had a theory that Queen Lorelei only ever used his last name with that particular inflection when she was considering executing him. And she only ever put him in charge of freezings when he himself was guilty of serious mistakes.

"But, ma'am---"

"Now. And I want Karuishi in his place. Brief the woman first thing in the morning; I have business with the rebel boy tonight. My patience wears thin."

Mister Senior bowed, holding back shivers. *Maybe I should've ratted Beech and Marco out while I still had something left to lose.*

———

Raine's stomach churned at the chilly night winds. All this talk about revolution, all the pain and fighting and uncertainty in this world just reminded her of her home back on Earth.

It was a boring place, but at least she understood it to some extent. And for the first time, she longed to return, to see her foster Mom again, and to sit in that boring classroom filled with strange kids whose attempts at friendship she'd shied away from or ignored. She would even go to those 'advanced' placement classes, and learn about things beyond her level just because she could. Raine usually hated having opinions dropped into her head as if she were a sentient piggy bank, but even schooling seemed a joy in comparison to flying above a firefight with the fate of the world weighing on her shoulders.

The girl took another glance at the digital map on her wrist. It was now taking her en route to Atmoya, Sector Nine, the only place where she could hope for some answers.

She switched on her Network visor and looked up Super BlastBoy. Information bombarded her from every angle. Her field of vision flooded with text, pictures, and holographic recordings. The second she put her eyes on something, it expanded before her and various windows populated themselves with streams of useless information, comingled with advertisements. No dice.

Gerrit was next on her search list, and Raine began by exploring the Blogosphere, a built-in app that displayed short, real-time, text-based status updates strewn about like a holo-dome across the starry sky. She flipped through with her fingers, sorting them by name, subject matter, and user tags. There was nothing to be found about either herself or Gerrit, nor anything about the attack at the concert.

After some digging, she uncovered some of the boy's now-redacted awards in the Hall of Warrior Fame, as well as detailed battle records in the *Metaverse* All-Star Duelists archives, but found nothing at all helpful. The girl drifted into an idle detour of the fashion forums before recognizing that searching for a fugitive on a controlled Network was completely futile. Thanks to the turbulent desert winds, Raine became airsick, and took the goggles off.

I'd learned a lot less than what I'd hoped for. I guess it's like those Kung-Fu movies. The aspirant can only get so far without a Master.

Down below, fires claimed a majestic castle in the midst of a violent siege. She wondered if this was a part of the war or just a friendly battle. Within one of the factions were those whom Gerrit had fought alongside, back when they first met. She decided to go closer to warm up a bit and smelled, then saw, that trolls, minotaurs, serpents, and what looked like dinosaurs were involved, many of them with armed riders.

Raine felt her grip weakening, and longed to have a bit of shut-eye. As if he could sense this, Chance wrapped around the balloon string, stretched out into a hammock encompassing Raine, and mewed.

"Are you sure?" she asked groggily.

Chance nodded, and Raine drifted off for a too-short rest.

The full moon peeked out from behind a cloud to wake her up. It kissed the border at the end of the patterned grass, reflecting the blue-brown hues of a land of parched soil and billowing sands. She crossed this desert until it filled her entire field of vision. Yossa's map finally confirmed that she'd arrived in Sector Nine.

In the far distance beckoned the loveliest mirage: a homely hilltop cottage surrounded by a diverse garden, a small pond, and by a cliff edge, a statue looking dramatically off into the distance. A fenced path snaked down the terraced hill to an old carpet road.

When smoke trickling out from the dwelling's brick chimney caught her eyes, she quickly realized it wasn't just a mirage.

Raine rocked back and forth on the Chance-hammock, intrigued. The cabin looked safe, like a good place to stop and ask for directions. *Almost too safe for comfort*, she reasoned on second thought, but as an expert gamer she'd learned to trust her first instinct. She gave his tail three tugs and was soon descending the skies towards the homestead.

The country house glimmered in the moonlight. Raine stopped to admire the neon flowers surrounding the fence, dripping with dew. A blue jay greeted her with a song, and then escorted the girl up the path. She had a warm feeling that she was far, far away from the prying eyes of Mister Senior and his ilk.

She nervously rang the doorbell.

Her heart nearly stopped when the door opened.

"Why, hello," Super BlastBoy said in a comforting voice. He looked to be in his early forties, older and calmer than she ever would have imagined, wearing an apron and accompanied by the warm smell of freshly baked dough, stirring up the beginnings of sweet memories she didn't yet know she possessed.

His jovial face melded around a gentle grin.

"Hello," Raine replied, stunned.

∩

A coolant-lined cloak draped around her lithe frame and her ID chip's signal blocked by a lead-lined armband, the newly promoted Dr. Karuishi perched on the highest pile in the junkyard, hidden in the shadow of the Network tower, and waited a good three minutes, checking her heat levels periodically.

The unfortunate Dr. Hoshua had been frozen, but it wasn't as if the old codger had much to hide. He wasn't one of *them*. Still, she empathized; Al had always been very professional.

The *Spire*'s long shadow at dusk hid her position perfectly; the coast was as clear as it was ever going to get. She unfolded her Holo-Lens CPU tablet, encryptions already running, and plugged it into the abandoned satellite radio antenna to establish long-range contact with the Sky Admiral's wing.

The new briefs were straight to the point, and for the first time in a long time, they came with some helpful information. The Overseer's Helmet Defense Protocol operated from Chamber 50B – a room that, if it existed, lay deep within the lower *Spire's* heavily guarded Central Asset Control. And there was time for some gorier news, too. General Lacie was dead. *Did she brief Beech on our older plan? Without a doubt.*

Lily's orders were to cripple the entire system. Not the easiest of assignments, but then, it wasn't her job to pull off. Poor old Holdfast and Zarifian would be in the thick of this mess, when they were needed the most on the floor. That'd mean she was tasked with keeping Her Queenliness in check.

Still, at least the centralized HDP was dependent on the *Metaverse's* servers, and the Overseer's lone chamber. It seemed an ultimate irony to Ayumi that in the event of the *Metaverse's* failure, a single room held the key to scuttling *Neo Eden's* global infantry forces.

Pocketing the tablet, Dr. Karuishi skipped down the junk pile, folded up the cloak, bagged it, and pretended like she was simply out for a summer stroll.

She hadn't expected to hear the unfettered weeping of a hopelessly lost soul. It was the same sort of sob her mother made when she revealed that she would be heading to *Neo Eden* to do some undercover work – the cry of a woman mourning the death of their beloved.

Thanks for the warm blessings, Mom, Ayumi considered. *By hook or by crook, I'm getting out of this one alive, if only just to prove you wrong.*

With a delightful puppy in her lap, Claire Belmont Alexandria sat on the precipitous edge of the upper level's wall, staring thousands of feet down at *Neo Eden's* lower districts. Ayumi knew that look all too well – she'd seen her share of world-weary mugs wracked with survivor's guilt, the faces of Developers who envied the ignorance of the enslaved, or the quiet of the dead, and had chosen suicide as an end to their troubles.

Their eyes met once Claire's puppy took note of the slender figure. As much as initiating contact with Ms. Alexandria could be a dangerous proposition, Ayumi couldn't leave her in this perilous state.

"Excuse me, miss?" she began, gently closing the distance between them.

Claire shrunk into herself, but little Archie whimpered and tried to scamper out of her lap.

"Doctor Karuishi, correct? We met at my cousin's wedding. You're probably thinking, 'what's she doing?' 'Does she have a death wish?'"

mumbled Claire. "'But no. She shouldn't do it. There's so much for her to live for.' You might think that, but you'd be wrong. I'm a selfish woman. All I ever had in life that mattered, all I ever cared for… my efforts were all for *her*… for *us*. You see, she found me here… seven years ago. Right here, on the edge."

"I- I'm sorry," Ayumi started. "I… I wish to hear your story. Maybe there's something I can do."

"Huh. I get it. You're probably too busy to read the tabloids," Claire admitted. "My name is Claire Alexandria. I am of the House of Morgana, and General Lacie's mistress. Though she named me her fiancée, it's never been made public."

Ayumi fell into a bow. "Apologies, milady, I did not recognize you in such common attire."

"It's all right. Soon none will remember me anyhow. Not that anyone's said anything, but perhaps that's just it. Something's not right. The *Raven* docked yesterday. She should have been back by now. There are whispers that Lacie has fallen in battle. The Queen is to visit the mausoleum on the mount tonight. And she is to take only android escorts."

Dr. Karuishi's heart sank for the poor woman. If anyone in the *Spire* knew what was going on, they hadn't the heart to tell her.

"The Queen could be paying tribute to her ancestors," Ayumi posited. "Or asking questions of her forebears. She could even be inspecting the geothermal generator. It's no guarantee that the General is involved. Please, Lady Claire, take my hand. Back away from the ledge."

Claire shook her head. "My Lacie vowed to return ere two days. It's been three, and she never breaks a promise. War comes from the East, and the Queen does nothing. She could meet the Admiral in full-scale conflict, yet for whatever reason she risks the enemy's advance, putting her own sister in harm's way! If my Lacie were victorious in battle, or had even returned, we would be flying banners. No, I do not think that I shall see her again. I would have you back away. If you're fond of dogs, Archibald might use a good home. I can have it done immediately."

She tapped her bracelet communicator to make an audio call. With a quick gesture, Ayumi flung her coat around Claire and Archie and pulled them off the edge. Claire fell down onto her; the pup ran away to watch the spectacle from a distance, blissfully unaware of the situation's gravity.

"What do you think you're doing?" Claire cried.

Ayumi held her close. "Milady, I cannot allow you to end your life."

Claire fought against Ayumi, but the latter had more martial arts training. She hugged Claire tightly until she stopped resisting.

"I can't say that I know how you must feel," Ayumi stated. "Even so, supposing it is true that she has passed on, the General would not have wanted this to be your fate. Your life has worth; there's much left to live for."

Her words appeared to ring true to young Claire, who fell silent and remained that way for some time.

"There's nothing for me, or for anyone but *her*. Who can prosper in an age where all are but pieces on a board to a power-hungry Queen?"

This open admission of dissent towards the World Leader was extremely rare, the sign of a true sovereign individual. Still, as a noble, Ms. Alexandria would not be sympathetic to the cause.

"You can think of yourself as a piece on a board, or you can think of yourself as a rational, intelligent, and fully capable human being. No one is telling you that you cannot or should not think and act of your own accord."

Claire digested this statement. "That's not what Lacie believed. She believed in loyalty at all costs."

"Then maybe she was wrong," Ayumi replied, drawing a wrathful look from the girl, who pushed her away and stood back up on her feet. At least now she seemed to have no intention of returning to the edge.

"My Lacie was never wrong!"

"If you trust her so much, then why are you so quick to give up hope for yourself?"

There was no answer to this; Claire simply walked over, picked up Archie, and stroked his fur in silence.

"Milady," Ayumi started up again, "I didn't mean to speak out of turn. I am only trying to help you. I've been haunted too many times by those I couldn't save."

Claire nodded in understanding, neglecting the tears of newfound courage streaming down her cheeks.

"Thank you, Dr. Karuishi," she replied. "Thank you so much. Would you like to join me for dinner?"

Ayumi adjusted her glasses and dusted off her skirt.

"I'd love to, but I have a prior engagement. But please, call me before you sleep tonight, so I know you're safe and sound, all right?"

"I will," she nodded. "I... I really appreciate that. Thank you."

Ayumi tapped her bracelet against Claire's to exchange contact details. After giving Claire her cloak to keep, the two women parted ways, and Ayumi tried to make it back to her own room without breaking down herself.

That poor woman, she thought. *If only I could tell her that her love is dead, and that my boss is to blame... I want to help her; only, there's nothing I can do.*

When she looked at the door she was standing in front of, it wasn't her own.

She gave a few short knocks.

"Henry? Henry, I know it's an odd time, but--"

Mr. Holdfast opened the door, a concerned look in his eyes.

"Ayu-chan?"

He actually called me 'Ayu-chan?' Only Mom has ever addressed me by that name...

"What?"

"It's a pet name I'm trying out, I- I thought you'd like it... wait... are you all right?"

She shook her head. Even Henry was quick enough on the uptake.

"Please, come in."

Ayumi fell into an embrace.

"Ayu, is everything cool? Please, if there's something I can do--"

Her arms wrapped around his neck as she leaned her head against his chest to feel his strong heartbeat.

"You're doing it. Don't move, *baka*. Just order us some dinner. Computer, play us Prokofiev's 'Cinderella Waltz'."

Despite all that talk, maybe Claire's right. We're all pieces on a board.

Tomorrow, the world is going to change, for better or for worse. And we're all powerless to stop it. The enormity of it all makes me feel so weak. So tonight, mama, I'm going to enjoy myself. This way, if I die, I will have died with no regrets.

As the music started, Ayumi led Henry onto the living room carpet to dance the last night away.

XX. Super BlastBoy

"Reality is frequently inaccurate." – Douglas Adams

"Do come in," SBB said, seeing Raine inside. "Have a seat by the fireplace; it'll just take a minute to get the cookies out of the oven. Your timing is impeccable."

She nodded. As the door closed behind her, Raine felt an odd sense of being compressed into a much more efficient space. Chance unfurled from her neck and made himself at home playing with a strangely flat-looking ball of yarn.

Indeed the entire house, while three-dimensional, seemed a little off. As she looked at each piece of furniture, it curved towards her in turn. Everything was hand-painted and pastel-colored and not exactly 'real'.

She checked out a table lamp from each angle. It was thatched together, but surrounded by black tracing lines, as a cartoon might be. The shadows it cast on the table looked affixed by hand, dancing in the furnace's firelight.

"It's cel-shaded, all of it," he replied, setting the tray of baked goods onto the table and taking a seat across from Raine. She saw now that he was just as two-dimensional as his house, and was rendered speechless.

"I'm very glad you like it," he said, as if reading her mind. "Designed this interchangeable skin myself. Never could get into polygons. The later games don't count. Have a cookie, please. It's not every day I receive such happening guests."

Raine took a seat and did so, still more than a little star-struck.

"Thanks, Mr. BlastBoy."

"Please, call me Tony."

"S-sure. Ah! A-Anthony Kon was your real name, right? That is, before you joined the Universe Corps' experimental warfare division and became a hero."

He nodded. "Interesting choice of words. Though there are obviously exceptions, I think of 'heroes' as little more than ideological and political symbols. Mine isn't much of a backstory, but at least it's something to go by; that's way more than most of my kind ever get. Now, this may seem a bit weird."

Tony snapped his fingers. The house seemed to fold up even more.

"Sorry about that," he said. "Some visitors get queasy. I just wanted to make sure that if by some miracle of computer science one of the Temps detects activity, they'll see nothing but the old statue. You and I are hidden, protected by some of the most immovable code in the *'Verse*. This conversation is in secret as well. You're patched in through my bubble now. From here I can travel to any *EM* server, except the mainframe, of course. My personal door functions as a port to any hub I can squeeze myself into. Surprising how easy it is to live outside the system, isn't it?"

"Not really, actually. I mean, no offense! Your bachelor pad is totally sweet. I guess it's just hard to surprise me; I've learned to take things in stride over here," Raine said. "But this is all totally confusing. It's much, much bigger than I am."

"You've done very well for someone in your situation," he said softly. "I can imagine you have many questions."

She nodded, taking another cookie.

"I'm quite ready to answer them. Be warned, this information is taboo, and as such, it may hurt a little. Where shall we begin?"

"Let's start with Lily."

"Lillian Hermes is a time traveler. Her goal is to save the world from a solar flare that will wipe out all life on Earth in the year 2212, twenty-five years, eleven months, and twenty-two days from the present time."

"All life on Earth?"

"Yes."

"Plants, trees, animals, everything?"

"Every last thing. There might be a few microscopic bacteria left, but--"

"That's ridiculous!"

"Yes, it is. She's been going back and forth in time, changing history in order to try and build a Noah's Ark of sorts to transport everyone safely into space and preserve most forms of life, but she finds that her efforts almost always fail. Lily has succeeded mostly in creating new wars and starting again from scratch with detailed reports sent back to her nine-year-old self, stationed on her space fortress in prehistoric times, on how not to do it. She set up an entire year's worth of time dedicated just to receiving these messages, so she carefully sends new envelopes thirty seconds after the previous ones, and after the year is over, she acts on the latest info."

"Wow."

"So from there on, she starts again, learning from her future self's mistakes, trying to guide the world towards adapting inter-space technology; that is, eventually colonizing further reaches of our solar system and beyond. Do you follow?"

"Mostly. This is fascinating, but… what does it have to do with *Endless Metaverse?*"

"Getting to that. Now, this is all very difficult to believe, but after the first five failures, Lily created clones of herself. Three of them, to help with this difficult task."

"Wait. Sorry. What? Clones?"

"As I've mentioned, Lily operates from the *Belladonna,* a space station orbiting Earth. A very high-tech creation. Onboard the ship was a Remediator, a unique device for advanced physical therapy that can synthesize human stem cells from a sample of genetic material. Quite handy, mind. It can do amazing things like re-grow missing limbs and cleanse a human body of radiation. Because the *Belladonna* operates in a high solar radioactivity zone, the Remediator was essential for periodically cleansing the bodies of its inhabitants. Only, Lily modified the device in order to clone herself. Even in their incubation, the clones were placed into rigorous virtual education, training, and muscle therapy programs."

"Go on," she pressed.

"Their names were Lorelei, Lucille, and Laramie, who changed her name to Lacie. Each one had a specialty: Lorelei came out of the chamber with cybernetic implants, designed to be a master tactician and programmer. Lucille was a doctor and geneticist, not to mention an expert historian and logician. Lacie was not just an astrophysicist and chief engineer. She was also a skilled martial artist. All were incredibly agile, excepting Lucy. An error on Lily's part. Together they attempted to change the course of history. Using the vast libraries of knowledge Lily's parents left behind regarding the chronicles of the United Amero Alliance, an empire that won World War Three at the expense of billions of lives and policed the globe's dwindling resources, preventing anyone from constructing anything close to Lily's Ark, they backtracked to and from the eighteenth and nineteenth centuries in attempts to prevent the formation of the Alliance.

"After multiple efforts, a few of which ended in disaster or failed in the early stages, they were eventually on track to their goal. By this time, effectively, Lily and her team had become the most powerful humans on Earth. As you can see, Raine, this all gets rather complicated at the micro stage. Suffice it to say that it's a rather epic chronicle. Ultimately their endgame plan was to use the booming finance of the industrial era to accelerate research and development for advanced twenty-first century space travel.

"Under Lucille's stewardship, by the early twentieth century, the internal combustion engine was quickly developed to its zenith and enhanced by hydrogen and electrical power. The quartet was working fantastically and rather marvelously. It was to be a world in which business was absolutely devoted to science and sustainability, and not the other way around."

"That sounds amazing. What happened?"

"Tragedy struck Lorelei. After suffering a cybernetic short circuit in the shower that left her unconscious for days, she went into a lengthy fever dream. In this dream, she had a vision. She began to see each of their journeys through time as effectively splitting the universe. What if, she argued, every time they traveled back to the past, the world line they left behind became a separate, fully formed universe that continued on to its inevitable end? Wouldn't that mean that anyone who broke the natural flow of time was responsible for the lives and deaths of quadrillions upon quadrillions of beings?"

Raine was on the edge of her seat.

"Was she right?"

"If anyone knew that, Raine, there would be no war. No fighting. No *Endless Metaverse*. Lily and her clones would have come to an agreement. Of course, neither one of us would be here speaking, either," he laughed. "It's an un-provable hypothesis. Once one travels from the future to the past, one immediately changes the past. Even without doing anything, just by being there, everything will diverge. Entire species may go extinct or a rogue gene may flourish. The compounding nature of the Butterfly Effect makes it impossible to revisit the same future that you came from. According to Lily, that future may very well cease to exist. It becomes a tangent universe that inevitably folds in on itself and disappears. That's why after sending her past self messages and giving the mission one last go, any iterations of Lily from future timelines would terminate her own life function."

"So... I didn't get most of that, but if I'm understanding you correctly, Lily believes in the existence of one universe, but Lorelei doesn't," Raine observed.

"Correct." Tony dipped a cookie into a small bowl of milk. He gestured at the ripples. "Although Lillian also believes one or more of the Multiverse models to be a possibility, she has no hard evidence to support the theory. The way Lily sees it, changes in the natural flow of space-time are like waves on an ocean. The person with the time machine holds the future of the universe in their hands like clay on a pottery wheel; multiple temporal travelers can be thought of as another potter's pair of hands. According to Lily's parents' Causality Theory, there is only one world line running across the conceivable cosmos, and as space and time are inextricably linked, and space can be warped by means of wormholes, for instance, then what we think of as *time* is really a dimension as malleable as it is paradoxical. Lily claims evidence for this theory in the fact that the original *Belladonna* never disappears, even after severe time alterations. Since she is operating from information gathered in prehistoric times, Lily believes that it is solely her perception and actions that shape the future."

He took a break to munch on the pastry. "Whereas to Lorelei, the only truth she could see is that they were the four horsemen of the apocalypse, causing massive amounts of death in their attempts to save the human race. To her, the numbers simply didn't add up."

"What happened then?"

"A series of heated debates and arguments. Lorelei had no evidence for her theory but her vision and conjecture, and Lillian wouldn't budge. She was as stubborn then as she is now. To even consider Lorelei's hypothesis would mean that her parents' goal was completely destructive. In the following stand-off, Lorelei's untimely refusal to use the Warp Initiator at a crucial moment led to an error that botched an important operation, with the result of global instability and, instead of the First World War, Earth was besieged by the Greatest War; fueled by technology its participants barely understood, it became a drawn-out conflict more terrible and violent than anything that had come before."

"Frustrated, Lily came up with a plan to salvage the attempt by proposing a truce between the world powers in exchange for development of sustainable farming tech to address the global hunger crisis. Lorelei was severely reprimanded. This was the last straw. The tension between the two could not go on indefinitely. It would be easier to show you than to explain what happened next," Tony said. "In any case, we have a little time, and I think both of them would want you to know the truth."

Tony snapped again, and this time his fireplace morphed into a television screen. It played video footage from a space station. The many cameras were dynamic, and the footage was well edited – as a result, it looked like a science fiction movie.

It was the strangest display. Three fifteen-year-old versions of Lily gathered in the kitchen, drinking hot cocoa. Neither one spoke. The only ways to tell them apart were their hairstyles and space suits; each girl wore a different primary color.

A girl in blue adjusted her glasses as she peered into her mug, deep in thought.

"That's Lucille," he explained. "She could see both Lily and Lorelei's points of view clearly and was caught in the middle of their debate. This video was taken twelve hours before they were supposed to return to Earth and proceed with the next phase of their plan."

The girl dressed in fiery red with her hair in twin-tails paced back and forth across the floor. Tony pointed out that this was Lorelei, and that the girl in the yellow suit nursing the topmost layer of piping hot cocoa was Lacie.

"I'm not going to do it," Lorelei said at last. "I absolutely refuse to sacrifice any more innocent lives."

"She expects us to all do our part," Lacie said.

When Lacie placed her cocoa down on the counter, it was with the utmost care. But Lorelei slammed her fist on the surface, spilling the drink all over the table and startling her sisters.

"Well, count me out!"

"Don't tell us this!" protested Lucy. "Bring it up with her."

"You know as well as anyone else here she's stopped listening to me!" Lorelei yelled. "Whose side are you on, anyway?"

Lucille stood from her chair.

"It's not about choosing one side or the other. A scientist is supposed to seek the truth."

"Only we're not scientists. Carl and Elizabeth were scientists. We're just dolls for Lily to play with," Lacie said, surprising Lucille, who glared at the others and made for the exit.

"What is it you two are trying to get me into here? I refuse to be a part of this conversation. And you, Lorrie, need to seriously get your act together."

"You come back here right now."

Lucy paused, glaring at her sister.

"Give me one good reason."

Lorelei drew a knife from her utility belt.

"Because I'll kill you if you don't at least listen to what I have to say."

Lorelei looked at the door and pressed her temple. She remotely locked all three latches from the outside.

"Rutger, alert Lily!" Lucy screamed.

"Negative," the AI replied. "Alert system down."

"How did you do that?" replied Lucy, aghast, but Lorelei simply looked amused. "And what if I don't like what I hear?" she continued. "What's to stop you from killing me then?"

"Hear me out. You know as well as I do that this 'mission' will never succeed. You've done the numbers in your head. The chances of success are monumentally slim. Every day of our lives, we walk the razor's edge, toying with the lives of billions. And for what? Who says that the human race even needs saving? We've seen what they're capable of, the terror, the evil, the deception. Every time we hit that reset button, we're dooming the entire universe, again. For whose sake? For theirs, or for Lily's? How much longer do you want to carry that blood on your hands? All you seem to care about is whether Lily's exercise in vanity is going to be a success. What if she's wrong? I mean, the human race is supposed to die, right? So just let them die. But she won't listen to reason. Nothing is going to stop her. Someone has to teach her a lesson. Someone needs to teach her that she isn't all powerful, that she has no right to play dice with the universe."

"So you think that someone is you?" Lucy asked. "Fat chance."

"I think that someone is us. I need you two to make this work."

The next ten seconds were so silent each girl could hear the others' heartbeats.

Lucy's stoic glower remained plastered on her face, but she hadn't moved since Lorelei started her little speech.

"Lorrie, please tell me you're joking," Lucy said, looking to Lacie for help. But her sister merely leaned back, watching calmly.

"The universe is a joke. You can weep or laugh with it; it's your choice," Lorelei said.

Lucy walked over to the door and tried the handle. It wouldn't budge.

"Open this door."

"Nope."

She reached for the manual controls. Lorelei pointed a pistol at her.

"Ugh! So much for giving me a choice..." Lucille mumbled under her own breath.

"Rutger."

"Yes, Miss Lorelei," Rutger's voice calmly enunciated.

"You're recording this conversation, aren't you?"

"I am."

"And nothing I say or do can make you stop recording it, correct?"

"You are correct."

Lorelei walked over to the microphone situated in the center of the ceiling. She removed the protective covering and began to tinker with it.

"What are you doing?" yelled Lucy.

"I'm not going to let any more people die in her name," Lorelei said. "You had a chance to leave."

"Hardly!" Lucille looked to Lacie, who simply continued drinking her cocoa as if nothing out of the ordinary were taking place.

"Miss Lorelei, please stop this instant," Rutger said. "Engaging complete lockdown--"

Lorelei was quick on the uptake. She cleared her throat, changing her voice.

"Rutger, user login ElizabethH. Password mercurial3567."

Lacie and Lucille held their breaths, visibly shocked at their sister's actions.

"Login... authorized," Rutger said, though his voice seemed pained.

"Rutger, belay that alarm. Override lockdown. You are not to inform Lily of anything that has just taken place."

"U-u-understood."

Lorelei finished dismantling the microphone. Raine watched in dreadful silence as the girl in red gathered the other two and huddled them up together into a triangle, hiding their faces from the cameras as they engaged in a clandestine discussion.

"What's going on?" Raine asked. "Are they planning to hurt Lily?"

"It's much worse than that," replied Tony.

The locale changed to the *Belladonna*'s bridge. Lorelei walked over to the central console and inputted a few commands. She then connected her handheld communicator to the main system.

Tony cleared his throat so as not to alarm Raine, who was watching intently with all her being.

"In her hands is Lillian's necklace, the *Belladonna's* key. Here, I believe she's inputting the coordinates for Space-Time Warp Initiation. January 5th, 2180. Two hundred years into the future, just thirty-two before the solar flare is scheduled to hit. But see, she hasn't yet activated the sequencer. Meanwhile, Lucille was busy shutting down Rutger."

A camera showed Lucy crawling beneath the ship's central console, a maze of wires and circuitry on the lower deck.

"Where's Lily?" Raine asked, worried.

"She's been drugged," he explained. "All part of Lorelei's elaborate scheme. It's the only way they could acquire the master key."

Lacie hunched over a console in a Hazmat suit within the depths of the Temporal Drive's engine chamber. The footage showed her using robotic arms to detach two-dozen fuel cell containers from a sub-zero environment.

"Those fuel cells store the radioactive energies that power the Belladonna," Tony clarified. "She removed all but one of them, per Lorelei's orders. That last cell was near-drained; it had barely enough power to send Lily two hundred years into the future. Next, she'll cut off the machine's power converter, so that the *Belladonna* won't be able to transmute any additional power towards Warp Initiation."

She gutted a box of wires that led up to the ceiling. The robotic arms removed a rather complex-looking piece of equipment from within the heart of the engine. It and the fuel cell containers were loaded into a lead lined, electrically chilled icebox, which Lacie wheeled down the long hall towards the docking bay and placed into one of the shuttles.

Next, the scene shifted to Lily's quarters. Covered in blankets, curled up like a grade-schooler, Lily was definitely a good few years younger than her clones.

Lorelei carefully lifted Lily's head off the pillow and slipped the key back around her neck.

"Good morning, sunshine," she chirped, smiling over Lily as she shook her from a deep sleep.

"Hmm?" Lily called out after a yawn. "Where's the fire?"

"We're good to go," Lorelei said. "Might as well get this thing over with, eh?"

Lily sat up in bed, seemingly groggy but pleasantly surprised at Lorelei's sudden change of heart.

"Is everything all right, Lorrie? You seem almost excited."

"Maybe I've realized something," she said. "There are some things even us Time Keepers can't change. We're meeting at the dock in five."

Lorelei tossed Lily her green space suit and walked out of the room. Now definitely confused, Lily undressed and slipped the suit on.

The video cut to a wide-angled view of the bridge as Lorelei and Lily strolled by the central control console.

A chime resounded as they passed the message tube, hailing a newly received letter. Lily turned in time to see a red envelope whoosh down the tube and onto the silver platter.

"A red envelope, at a time like this?" Lily raised an eyebrow. "How odd."

"Shall I get it, Miss Lily?" Lorelei offered, walking briskly towards the console.

"That won't be necessary," the younger girl replied sharply.

Lorelei bit her lip in nervous anticipation as Lily approached the tube. She quickly toggled a concealed button on her wristwatch, and for a second, a console out of Lily's field of vision flashed a countdown timer: eight minutes, forty-four seconds to Space-Time Warp Initiation.

Meanwhile, Lily cautiously unfolded the message from the future.

Tony hit freeze-frame and zoomed in on it.

> *Lily of seven minutes ago,*
> *Lorelei is about to betray you. This is serious. Grab your electric whip and disarm her over your left shoulder in*

approximately twelve seconds, then Lacie, who will come from the docking bay. They aim to send you into the future, alone and without adequate fuel. Warp Initiation begins in eight minutes. Do not let them get away! Go!

    Love,

    Lily

The video resumed once Raine gave the signal.

Lily was in shock, the message trembling from her hands. It was unthinkable that her own clones could betray her.

She'd already lost five seconds.

"Show me what it says, sister," Lorelei asked in a chilly voice.

Raine watched closely as Lorelei pulled out an electric handgun and switched it on soundlessly. She aimed the now-pulsing weapon at the back of Lily's head.

Without prior warning, Lily let out a primal scream. She spun around in a pirouette whilst uncoiling a thin electrified whip from her belt, the energy from triggering its kinetically charged hydrogen battery hissing like a coiled cobra.

The Captain dodged what looked like two lightning bolts, the second missing her neck by inches, and quickly shot her whip across the room, where it snapped onto Lorelei's ankle and pulled her to the floor. The cyborg tried frantically to escape. To stop her, Lily loosed a couple of short but high-powered jolts.

This was real violence. It had weight, and pain, and blood. Raine wanted to avert her eyes from the scene. Tony held her hand.

"It's not fatal. She's hoping to temporarily immobilize Lorelei by short-circuiting the cybernetic implants in her brain – twenty milli-Amps, not a small amount of electricity."

Lorelei fell to the ground, her energy spent.

Lily lowered the voltage on the whip and tossed the message at her clone, tears running down her face.

"You want to know what it says, Lorrie? It says that you will have betrayed me!"

Just then, a shuriken came headed Lily's way – it just glanced her belly. She looked up to see Lacie in the doorway, tossing more at her.

Lily drew an electro-magnetic knife with her left hand and deflected two projectiles with its polar fields, but a third one caught her right forearm, causing her to release the whip. Another shuriken landed in her calf.

The girl screamed in pain as she fell to the floor.

"Rutger, do something! Immobilize them! Suspend Lorrie's circuits!"

Nothing.

"Y-y-you'll find R-R-Rutger isn't going to be m-m-m-much help," Lorelei said with a wicked snort.

"Why? Why are you doing this?"

"You're not even g-going to ask how I managed such a feat?" Lorelei asked as she carefully regained her footing. She looked somewhat disappointed.

"Quit stalling. I can name three ways off the top of my head. But I trusted you, and you deceived me. You've made the decision to doom our quest. We were so close. Tell me why. What could possibly mean more to you than fulfilling your destiny?"

Lorelei laughed. "Ha! My destiny? You chose this destiny for us. I've given up on trying to make you see things the right way. All your life you've been blinded by your own power."

"I've only ever used time travel within the bounds of the Oath!"

"So you'll play dice with this and any other universes, snuffing out endless lives, just so you can sow the fruits of a half-baked dream conjured up by two dead scientists."

"Those scientists are my parents," Lily wailed. "Without them, none of us would be here. Time travel wouldn't be possible."

"I don't care! Someone else would have come up with the technology, and they might not have been stupid enough to get killed."

At this, Lily jumped up from the floor and ran towards Lorelei in a violent fury.

Lorelei held up her hand to stop Lacie from throwing any more shuriken. She readied her fighting stance and blocked Lily's rage-infused punches.

The younger girl delivered a roundhouse kick that pushed Lorelei off her feet. The clone staggered back. She put up her dukes. Lily followed suit. Lorelei responded by pulling a feint, then slide-tackling Lily and shoving her into the central console. While she was pinned, Lorelei continued to beat the Captain, throwing a flurry of punches into her gut. Lily struggled to break free; she didn't have the physical reach or power that Lorelei had. It was painful to watch.

SBB paused the video in order to explain that while both girls had extensive virtual martial arts training, Lorelei's cybernetic brain implants and network of nano-bots greatly increased her reaction time, regulated her hormone production, and granted absolute muscle control, making her super-strong, resilient to pain, and able to recover quickly, with the only downsides being a lack of empathy and a need for periodic maintenance.

Although she didn't stand a chance, Lillian fought with even more ferocity. Finally, Lorelei used the Captain's momentum to flip her over and slam her back down on the floor. She quickly immobilized Lily by twisting the shuriken in her calf, eliciting cries of terrible pain.

Lacie couldn't bear to watch anymore. She turned away, and just as she did, Lucille appeared behind her, brandishing an automatic crossbow. Before Lacie could yell out in alarm, her sister knocked her out with a high-powered stun gun.

"Stand down, Lorelei," Lucille yelled, taking aim at her maniacal sister.

Now that Lily was struggling on the floor, Lorelei slowly spun around.

"Ah, Lucy. I expected this."

"Leave her be!" Lucille yelled. "You need help, Lorrie. You're no messenger of peace. I don't know what it is you really want, but from what I've just witnessed, my clinical analysis is that you are absolutely insane. If you want to investigate the universe, then we should do it as a team!"

Lorelei laughed, kicking Lily in the stomach again.

"Look at this pathetic girl," she said. "You and I, and Lacie... now, that is the perfect team. But Lily, here... she's ethically weak. She created us because she knew she couldn't complete her own mission. Our very existence is conditional, sister. We were born into conscription. We live in a time machine in outer space, but our futures have been planned out with care. Ever consider her plans for us, once the task is done? Will she keep us here? Or will we be disposed of, left on Earth to rot and die like those clueless peasants? Surely you remember her failure to act in *Jerusalem.*"

Lucille shook her head.

"Lily wouldn't abandon us. All life on Earth is at stake here."

"Which is why she is doomed to failure. What a noble goal, to save the human race at the expense of the rest of the universe."

"I'd n-n-never abandon you. You're my only friends. The rest of the universe is fine, dammit!" Lily cried softly. "Time isn't a one-way line you can splinter off like a web. It's more like waves on an ocean…"

Lorelei kicked her again.

"I've heard enough of your parents' theories! Give me proof or give me death!"

Lucille cleared her throat as she notched her finger into the trigger.

"I'll be more than happy to do that."

"Kill me, then," Lorelei taunted. "Draw the first blood. I dare you. In fact, I double dog dare you."

Lucille did. She fired right into Lorelei's chest. But the bolt never connected; Lorelei had dodged it at preternatural speed, and danced across the floor in an irregular pattern towards her sister, who kept firing – and kept missing.

"Impossible!" Lucy cried as Lorelei charged straight into her, knocking her to the ground and holding Lily's EM knife up to her neck.

Lorelei then stood Lucy up and held her hostage. She kissed her on the cheek to mask her nano-machines' power strain. Her faux-innocent facade sent a shiver down Raine's spine.

"Nothing's impossible with my cybernetic implants, darlings," she said, panting. "My reaction time is no longer limited by human evolution. Lily, you had no idea I could optimize these bad boys to override my nervous system, did you?"

"Stop!" Lily called out with a raspy voice, sitting herself up with Lorelei's pulsing polar pistol. Raine imagined that her ribs must be cracked; she was having trouble breathing, let alone holding a firearm with shaky hands.

"Don't you dare," Lorelei barked through clenched teeth, cutting softly into Lucille's neck. "Drop the weapon."

"J-just shoot, Lily," Lucy urged. "They have the p-power con--"

"Shut up!" Lorelei yelled, giving her sister a thick gash along her arm and making her yelp. "Drop it now!"

Lily obeyed. She was forced to watch helplessly as Lorelei kicked Lacie awake.

As if awoken from a pleasant dream, Lacie started to her feet, stunned to see Lorelei holding their ally by knifepoint.

"Is… is everything okay?"

"Get over here and restrain the good Captain. We're running out of time. Let's head to the docking bay, shall we? I'm terrible at goodbyes."

Raine held Super BlastBoy's hand tightly. It was difficult to watch Lorelei and Lacie drag their injured hostages down the hallway at such a brisk pace. Lucy and the barely conscious Lily exchanged worried glances.

They were dropped, hands bound, on the cold metal floor.

"We have two minutes," Lacie exclaimed in a bit of a panic.

"I'm aware, sister. I'm not finished with her yet."

Lorelei snapped a packet of smelling salts before Lily, shocking her awake.

"Never did I ask to be born," Lorelei explained as they finally reached the *Raven*. "I want no further part in this twisted dynasty. My new mission is to show you the true cost of human lives, so I figured we'd play a little game. You're being sent two hundred years into the future. When you reach your destination, visit me. I'll be in the highest room of the tallest tower in the richest country in the world."

Just as Lacie finished her pre-flight checklist, Lucy struggled to press the comms button on her wristwatch. Seeing what she was trying to do, Lily sidled up beside her and pressed it herself.

"Now, Rutger!" Lucy boomed.

Suddenly, XF-22 wheeled into the docking bay. The robot anchored itself against a crane and clamped onto the shuttle, preventing it from leaving.

"You're not going anywhere!" declared Lucille.

Raine watched, horrified, as the turret atop the *Raven* peppered XF-22 with bullets. Lorelei's laughter echoed from the PA system. She mowed off the robot's arms, freeing the shuttle. Both Lily and Lucille were hit hard with flak. Lily hid her head, screaming. Lucy instinctively sprang forward and pulled the Captain to the ground, taking a number of bullets in the process.

"Space Time-Warp Initiation in one minute."

The shuttle's jets fired up in a flash. The burst knocked XF-22 off the platform and sent him flying; the robot collided with the back wall of the hangar and landed in a messy heap of scrap.

Lily looked up at the ship for the last time as it shot through the airlock. She watched desperately as the gates closed shut.

The external bay doors opened and the *Raven* disappeared into the blackness of space, a cosmic speck of dirt dropping from the *Belladonna* to Terra. There was no stopping Lorelei now.

"I'm… so sorry, Miss Lily…" Lucille uttered, gripping Lily's hands.

Lily held her dying clone in her arms. Tears fell onto her cracked glasses. She was bleeding profusely from a number of bullet wounds. Both knew she had mere minutes.

"Don't you dare apologize, Lucy, you saved me. It's… it's my fault. I should never have given her those nano-bots."

"Listen. S-she took all but one of the *Belladonna*'s fuel cells, and s-s-severed the p-p-power converter."

"No! I can't replace that…"

"But I… snatched a c-c-couple. The f-fuel cells, I mean. Check the freezer in the rec room. The E-Exo Knight plans… p-p-particle cannon files… ballistics tests are inc-c-complete, but… it should be the only copy…"

Lily nodded, still holding back tears.

"Lucy, I'll bring you back. Just say the word."

She shook her head. "If it's all the same to you, Captain, I would like to tender in my resignation. I don't think I'm cut out for this line of work," she snickered. "Maybe it's time you put your trust in someone… other than yourself…"

The wisdom of this statement was abundantly clear to Lily. As the Warp commenced, she cradled Lucille, and crooned the opening bars of a soothing lullaby to help ease her passage to the other side.

XXI. The Spacetime War

"There is a wisdom of the head, and a wisdom of the heart."

– Charles Dickens

Even though she told herself she wouldn't do it, Raine was in tears again. Super BlastBoy turned the video off. He gave her some time to think by boiling more cocoa and making grilled ham and cheese sandwiches, along with a side of clam chowder in a bread bowl.

"As you can see, Lorelei and Lacie splintered off from Lily and jacked one of her time machines. Droids from secret factories were working on Lily's Ark. Lorelei repurposed them for warfare. Leading with the *Raven's* advanced weaponry, Lorelei and Lacie joined the global war as an independent defense contractor in 1914, and pretended to form alliances with every major player, all the while breaking them, assassinating heads of state, and turning their subordinates against one another. By 1916, London, Washington, D.C., the Vatican, and New York were all wiped off the map in one bloody coup. Beijing, Moscow, Berlin, Kyoto, and Rome were soon annexed. The global elite toppled within the span of three years. Ruling families that'd been in power for centuries were hunted to the last or forced into servitude. Besides assassinations, Lorelei utilized controlled chaos, false flag attacks, mind control, and scare tactics to split apart nations, communities, and families, and to instill great fear and dread into the populace. It was a horrible war that lasted for decades. Meanwhile, the sisters also worked behind the scenes to create their own empire, funding puppet politicians spewing empty promises. Their descendants, the Seven Lords, rule the two hundred 'Sectors' of planet Earth. Through careful back-dealings, there was a sort of hard-won peace."

"Wait, the ship they stole was also a time machine?"

"One of three, though the *Belladonna* remains the only device in existence that can traverse interstellar distances or more than a hundred years at a time. After losing her parents, Lillian installed limited Temporal Drives into her gunships. Lily pilots the *Phoenix*; her clones helm the *Raven*."

"So with Lily's fuel cells, Lorelei and Lacie hopped across time with the *Raven*."

"That's correct. They were free to use it, yes, but they were also sworn against changing the past and creating what Lorelei believed to be alternate universes."

"In other words, they had nowhere to go but the present, and the future."

"That was the plan, anyway. Since Lily's return seven years ago, Lorelei's been hunting the *Belladonna*. This reality they've created has no future. The prolonged First World War left the Earth a forsaken land populated by only one and a half billion people, corralled by unified powers, robbed of reason and spirit, and awaiting certain death."

Raine tried to process that scale of destruction. Against her world line, three quarters of the globe's population had seemingly vanished, their existences never having taken place. She was simply unable to accept Super BlastBoy's numbers as reality.

"All those people... But... but couldn't Lily just send a message back to the past, and stop herself from creating the clones?"

"Not without first taking back her stolen power converter and fuel cells. When Lily finally reappeared seven years ago, she tried to reason with Lorelei, now a self-proclaimed Queen. It didn't do her much good. By using their foreknowledge of Earth's history and peoples, superior technology, and the *Raven* to travel through time and space, she and Lacie built an ultimate global superpower. Lorelei desired to be the one to bring stability back to the world, and then to be there to see it come to an end. What can I say? Control freakishness must run in the family. To be fair, it appears that the Queen really does believe that each failed parallel universe is an act of cold-blooded mass murder to the people involved, and that humanity will inevitably come to an end either way, prosperous space colonies or not. She's not wrong there, you know."

"That's kind of a bleak way of looking at it," Raine said. "I'm no physics buff, but from what I understand, her Split Timeline theory might well be true."

"It's very possible. And the idealistic Lily wasn't having it. She was betrayed, and badly burned by the thought of her own flesh and blood driving this particular universe into the ground. She wanted awfully to recover her power converter and erase this mess, and they wanted her dead to stop what they called her 'mass murder spree'. So they came to a truce. The terms were grave."

Their cups of cocoa with marshmallows were now ready. He returned with them and sat down beside Raine, whose brain was so overloaded, she slurped the stuff down without so much as a thought. After devouring two grilled ham and cheese sandwiches, several carrots and sticks of celery dipped in ranch, and most of her chowder (she was rather hungry), Raine waited for her host to continue.

"Lily's flaw might be that she has too much of a code of honor. Her clones have it as well. The agreement went like this: if Lily could put a stop to Lorelei and Lacie's reign without time travel, then she would continue on with her quest. Otherwise, if the two clones saw planet Earth through to its grisly conclusion, also without time travel, then it would mean an end to everything. All life on Earth, in this or any other dimension."

"What? So this is all just a war game to them?" Raine cried out, incredulous. "Who gave them the right to control the lives of every human being on the planet?"

"That's just the thing. With power as their birthright, the Queen and the Sky Admiral consider themselves ultimate authorities on the matter. That's why they've both been amassing armies.

"With her defense override now fully integrated, Lorelei boasts a billion-strong global army straight from *Endless Metaverse*, not to mention the dreaded *Eden* Armada, a hefty reserve of android soldiers, and a nuclear arsenal. She rules the Earth's remaining population from *Neo Eden*, a massive fortress-city-state.

"Lillian, on the other hand, has co-opted the forces of resistance against Lorelei's rule. She leads the Earth Defense Coalition, a force tens of millions strong, with her aerial wing comprised of half a million volunteers – chiefly engineers, programmers, and militias of common folk and rescued *EM* players who pilot airships and operate mechanized infantry. In keeping with the EDC's goal to limit human casualties, the Sky Admiral employs over twice as many android warriors. While Lily's been able to hide the true strength of her numbers and keep information leaks to a minimum, it appears from the outside that she's fighting a losing battle. At this point it could go either way. If her final moves go off without a hitch, she's got a fair chance at completely annihilating *Endless Metaverse*."

"Annihilating it? Why? You still haven't explained what it is."

"Well, it's all been building up to it. Are you ready for this?"

"Yeah," Raine said with utter determination.

Ω

"Talk to me, Lacie," Queen Lorelei begged the corpse before her. "I want to know what the afterlife is like."

Afterwards, the Queen did something she didn't think herself still capable of. She wept, silently, at the pyre set up outside the modest but heavily guarded mausoleum where past royalty were allegedly buried, built into an outcropping on the slopes of Mount Vesuvius, a short walk from the geothermal generators.

I didn't give you permission to die on me, she thought. Her only true ally, her shadow, the one person who knew and accepted her completely, was now gone. She looked up at the night sky, torch in hand. It was empty. Not a single star was visible through the dark smog and light pollution emitted by *Neo Eden's* many mines and factories, which stretched along the Italian coastline for hundreds of miles. She reasoned that it was probably just as well. A black night. Just how Lacie would have wanted it. She closed her eyes and felt the cold wind threaten to take her away. An opening formed in the clouds above, barely wide enough for the first quarter moon to shine through. It was as if Lacie's restless twin souls were calling out for their bodies to be set free. Queen Lorelei could wait no longer.

The World Leader lowered the torch onto the pyre and watched the last vestiges of her two sisters depart this world. The unspoken beauty of the vistas she and Lacie had seen, the world they had created, and the afterlife dreamed of together were now secrets for her to bear alone. General Lacie's service to the Cause would not be forgotten. With Lillian's death, their legacy would endure.

∞

Super BlastBoy was worried. He wanted to continue at Raine's behest, but this information was not always welcome, or easily received.

"The truth is not always beautiful, nor beautiful words the truth."

"Please, sir. I need to know."

Unable to refuse such an honest request, Tony closed his eyes and spoke as if he were channeling.

"*Endless Metaverse* is a tool to distract approximately ninety-three percent of the population of Earth from mindless work done in the service of *Neo Eden*. People immersed in the *Metaverse* wear *M-Gear* helmets, devices that disengage the conscious brain from reality. While in the Network, they are living a daydream. Their day-to-day work, regulated by the Overseer's centralized AI and the decrees of the Seven Lords, goes on without any interference from their conscious minds. They eat, sleep, toil, and procreate, some in barracks, others in regimented family units, necessary functions operating like clockwork. Their physical bodies know no enjoyment. They are experiencing reality on pause. Many are farmers. Others work in war factories or mines. They are the lowest caste, treated on the televised news as animals by their rulers, all of whom serve Lorelei. Yes, many children are born and grow up in the real world, raised by software in their parents' *M-Gear* helmets, or by free peoples, but by nine years of age eighty percent of them become full-time users of *EM*. Most of the rest sign up in later years, unable to stave off their depression. There are servers for small children to live out fantasy lives while their bodies are enslaved to do Lorelei's dirty work. The most shocking part of all this is that *Endless Metaverse* is not forced on anyone."

Raine was absolutely speechless.

"Everyone who has ever entered the *'Verse* has done so of their own free will. If it sounds unbelievable, that's because it is. And it's been going on for decades now. Humanity has been warped almost beyond recognition. Only a truly disturbed mind could possibly conceive of such a world, let alone create it."

Tony scrolled through photos and videos on the wall; without visual confirmation, she might not have believed him, and indeed the girl took to pacing around the room, trying to get her thoughts straight.

Her host opened the door and they ventured outside to bask in the cool night air. Wrapped up in a quilt, Raine sat on a swing and looked up at the stars; she'd never known there were so many, never mind that they were being created within a computer. Virtual fragments of fragments of reality. It took a half-hour for the truth to really sink in.

It can't be true. It just can't. Except that his explanation answers so much. It's painful to hear, but I can't stop. Not yet. There's more to this, I know. The creepy thing is it's like I've always known it.

Across the way, SBB smoothed down a pile of wood chips and raked them into his vegetable garden. After some time, Raine finally nodded that she was ready and followed him back inside.

"Any thoughts, Raine?" asked Tony.

"Just questions. How is it possible for you to know all this?"

"Lily's journals. She gave me access to them way back when, in preparation for this day. Also, the EDC has moles in *Neo Eden* from which she gleans details enough to fill in the blanks."

"Who are you, Mr. Anthony? You're obviously not one of Lorelei's creations."

"I am one of the most intelligent AIs in existence, created by the early *Metaverse's* Illusionists to be a sort of hero figure, if you will. Once I got wind of the truth behind the *'Verse*, I disappeared, leaving a dummy program in my place. That's what got deleted. The AIs they wrote to replace me were significantly underpowered. I was a celebrity in the first iteration of *Endless Metaverse*. As a fugitive, I have no place in version 3.0. Sorry if that ruins your perception of the old arcade game. I hear you are rather good at it."

"No, not at all. This is good stuff. And I'm happy you're still here. I was afraid I might never find you."

Tony beamed, evidently touched by these words. "Anyone who seeks the truth will cross paths with it, even if it's in the least likely of places. You have a pleasant nature, Raine."

"I've heard that slogan before," she replied, recalling the innkeeper from her first night in the *Metaverse*.

"I'm glad to hear my influence still lives on," Tony chirped.

"So nobody knows you're around?"

"There is a simple decoy program I created. The one you followed here. As far as Guggell and her crew are concerned, it's nothing but a prank created by a young hacker to mislead people into thinking I'm still alive. I've deduced that they believe I'm long gone, which is especially helpful since Lily needs my help to shut down this prison."

"Do you have the power to do that?"

"Well, yes, no, and maybe. The 'yes' part is thanks mostly to your efforts."

Raine was stunned. *Finally, a lead as to how I fit into all this. I'm sure it has something to do with that game I played against the Stopwatch.*

"Let me put it this way. As the last of the original programs, I possess a skeleton key for the mainframe. Theoretically I'd still need to find a direct path that I could take there without running into a dead end or being bogged down by server traffic and checkpoints, but that's been a bit of a tall order till you arrived. In yours and Lily's genius, you plugged in from an outdated client and cleared an ancient, unbeaten quest, one written in positively primordial code. Now, to claim the prize – your crown, a unique artifact – *Avidya* was forced to seek and download packets of data from the mainframe. Nowadays absolutely nothing links directly to the mainframe, see. It's an impenetrable fortress for a reason: if the mainframe in *Neo Eden* and the backup in what you know as Kyoto are both shut down at once, that's it. All servers will fail, and the *Metaverse* will be taken offline."

"So what happens now that you have a direct link?"

"Let me tell you a secret. Without the creators of *Endless Metaverse* knowing it, at present the mainframe is vulnerable to a calculated, full-scale attack."

"You're going to take this place down! That's awesome! What are we waiting for?"

SBB chuckled. "Actually, it would be more accurate to say that 'we' are going to take it down. In the original plan, I was simply to hop the shutdown code to the backup mainframe, but yesterday... yesterday Lily informed me that since Gerrit's MIA, she needs my help to clear a path to the primary core."

"A path for what?"

"For the lucky girl who gets to pull the trigger."

"Me again? Don't tell me..."

"I'm sure she'll want to brief you on the details personally, love."

Raine looked a bit peeved at this. Tony continued.

"Don't fret. It shouldn't require much work on your part; just that you continue to survive."

"Even that's been a tall order so far," groaned Raine.

"If it's any consolation, you won't be alone. As for me, well I'd admittedly need about an hour's worth of distraction pointed at Lorelei's team on the surface. The Devs knowing you've been looking for yours truly has made me a prime target. There's so much I want to do, and yet... I've survived in *Endless Metaverse* because I'm good at hiding. Lily wants to attack now, but I'm quite keen to take our time planning out the logistics of this whole thing. I'll say this much: to embark on an op this dangerous without adequate support is akin to suicide."

"Tomorrow's not going to be easy, I gather."

"Nope, especially since your immortal status is set to expire at noon, but fear not. With you and Lily by my side, I can say without ego that it would take a damn good hacker to shut me down."

The thought comforted Raine for a few nano-seconds, but at the mention of hackers her thoughts turned quickly to Gerrit and she nearly dropped her mug.

"Is everything all right?" queried Tony.

"Oh. Sorry. I'm just... I'm worried about Gerrit."

SBB fell silent and raised his cup in salute. "Inside sources report that he's in *Neo Eden*. But for the time being, he's safe."

Raine furrowed her brow.

"Make no mistake, dear, I'm sure Lily's already hatched a plan to spring him out of there."

The girl exhaled deeply. She stared blankly at the firewood delicately crackling into falling embers. Closing her eyes, Raine felt the heat through the charred mantle, through the calm, still air, through her layers of clothing, through the digital skin that covered her digital body. And she felt that her own heart was melting.

"This war is all so complicated. There's just so much going on." She sunk into her seat, looking to her companion for whatever meager comforts he could provide.

"Hear, hear, Raine," Tony said, placing a blanket over her body. "You've had a long journey and deserve a rest. You're loads better than most of your kind at processing and retaining information, but even this old codger knows when someone's tank has been filled up."

Staring into the fire, Raine contemplated all that had happened. It was beyond anything she could imagine, but oddly enough the basics seemed within her understanding. It was through some sort of sick act of faith that she was able to grasp as much. She hadn't yet broached the questions closest to her heart, but they were too difficult to ask. Too near, too scary, too loaded with potential disaster.

Why am I here? What of my parents? How am I so good at that arcade game? Do I even have a choice with regards to fighting for Lily? And most of all, how can I possibly get home, if there even is a home for me to return to?

SBB began to hum his theme song, his voice perfectly mimicking the sound card of the particular arcade machine Raine had mastered the game on. He soon progressed past the intro screen and onto the first level.

Raine closed her eyes and pictured herself behind the controls. It was what started this whole thing, anyways. She recalled the patterns, the enemies, the random elements, the way that if the game were played perfectly the music would synchronize to the player's movements. The entire experience wove itself out before her like an electronic ballet of light, sound, and texture. Before long she'd beaten the first stage, and right on cue with the time it would take to play a 'perfect' game, Tony segued into the second level. Her thumbs moving back and forth of their own accord, Raine relaxed her body and let the flames dance over her as she drifted off to sleep.

₪

"Where are you going?" Henry yawned as he awoke in his suite to Ayumi Karuishi putting on her make-up, already fully dressed for work. She looked absolutely stunning, as usual. They'd both had a little too much to drink last night.

"Take a look at your clock, Holdfast," she giggled.

It was 4:53 AM. He had seven minutes to dress and make it onto the lift down in time for the morning server reports.

"Oi, great, wake me up at the last minute on D-Day, will ya?" he joked, tossing a pillow at the Doctor, who immediately returned fire. Henry dodged the feathered fluff while jumping into his pants, and quickly smoothed down his hair. He grabbed the coffee that his new suite prepared for him upon sensing that he was awake, clunked a couple of ice cubes in the thermos, and wolfed down the plate of cloned bacon and eggs.

"Someone's in a rush," Ayumi observed.

"I just hope we all make it out of this alive," Henry huffed as he adjusted his tie in the mirror beside her.

She gave him a peck on the cheek, and then followed him out the door. The view outside promised a clear day – he'd half expected the Queen to cloak the city in clouds.

"Congrats again on your promotion, by the way," Henry offered.

"Thanks. But… it just seems weird," she said, twiddling her thumbs.

"You mean Hoshua?" he observed, recalling that the clueless tweed-wearing bloke was now in the deep freeze. "You can't blame yourself. If you hadn't interfered at the dome, who knows what might have happened? I miss the old dag too, but we'll thaw him out."

"Yeah. It's not just that, it's…"

A passing monitor droid had Henry elbowing her lightly for silence. In its wake, Ayumi's expression sank.

"Don't let it get to you. You'll be fine. Zee should have our strike team out in a few hours."

"Who's comforting who, now? I hope you know what you're doing, *baka*," she whispered.

They kissed again as the lift arrived. Henry held Ayumi's hand as they descended the *Spire*'s dormitory level and met up with the elevator traffic heading into the *Nexus*.

♥

Moonlight reflecting off the waves turns my skin blue, but I'm far from cold on this tropical island.

It's the vision again, only this time it's clear as clear can be.

The boy takes one hand in his, and the girl takes the other. The meal is done now, our stomachs filled with delicious seafood.

I'm sure I recognize them now: Gerrit and Lily.

Then we're lying down, backs against the cool sand, counting the shooting stars.

"It doesn't look so empty from here," Lily says.

"You mean the cosmos?" I ask.

"Precisely. But it could just be that the company's good."

I pull the girl towards me and give her a noogie.

"Ah, that's the spot," she giggles as I knuckle a little bump on her head.

Dandruff falls from her scalp and I back away. Lily puts on an adorable pout.

"You ought to consider some scalp treatment," I joke.

She sticks her tongue out. "Yes, 'Mom'. Geez."

Gerrit points up at the sky. "There! Please tell me you guys saw that one."

It's me who cries out. "Ah! Missed it!"

"Sorry, Ray-Ray."

He marks a tally on a small notebook. The notebook that I am sure contains our master plan scribbled out in code.

"Say," I begin. "What are my chances, precisely, of remembering any of this?"

Lily's snapped back into a thoughtful mood. "Sixty-forty, approximately. The methods we're using for the rewrites are vastly superior to the 'Verse's. We'll find out when this is all over."

"It's such a scary thought," I continue. "To not know who you are. Without memories to define us, what are we, really? Just a bunch of kids."

Gerrit gives my hand a light squeeze.

"I don't see how that's a bad thing," he says. "Kids carry humanity and its memes to the next stages of evolution. Successive generations have the opportunity to learn and improve from those who've come before."

"That's what troubles me," I posit. "What if we haven't studied hard enough?"

A head leans on my other shoulder.

"There will always be those who've studied harder," Lily interjects, ending our little game. "But every quest starts somewhere. I learned the hard way that if you don't take the future by the horns, someone else will do it for you."

Gerrit nods. "Dead mystics can show us the path, but they can't walk it for us. 'The truth is not for all men, but for those who seek it.'"

"Ayn Rand," Lily replies, sitting up to play a tune on her sitar. "But I'm more hopeful than she is. I'm of the belief that everyone has the potential to rediscover and embrace the truths of this universe, to know right from wrong, and to govern themselves."

"The potential, but maybe not the will," says the boy. "One cannot bring about a cause by emulating its symptoms."

"Every person on this planet is seeking the ultimate truth, whether they know it or not. Though she's oppressed it for nearly two centuries, Lorrie's been unable to extinguish human curiosity. With the Metaverse's *failure, every indoctrinated individual will face a choice: to deny the reality presented to them, or to embrace it. It is my belief that most will reject the virtual realm. Experiential confirmation... it's a fractal leap that can't be thwarted by petty Pavlovian incentives."*

"To shift one's perception, to dispose of a false premise in order to further glimpse the bigger picture..." Gerrit has that expression again, like he's far away. It's sad, but kind of beautiful. "That's the path of a seeker, all right. Einstein said that reality is merely a persistent illusion. But history has taught us that those who strive for the truth walk a lonely path. Right there's the problem of civilization: the vast majority prefers to follow. That's where we need the courage to lead. 'To conquer fear is the beginning of wisdom.'"

I know this one. "Bertrand Russell, I believe. I see where both of you are coming from, but it's all just speculation to me. 'The greatest obstacle to discovery is not ignorance, but an illusion of knowledge.' Who can predict how the end of the Metaverse *might affect the human zeitgeist? Earth will have a clean slate. It'll be a different world, altogether unpredictable. If nothing in this universe is static, then why should our minds be? Once freed from Lorelei's social engineering and their dependence on the system, the very concepts of leadership may become obsolete. Of course, that could be my idealism talking again."*

Lily smiles, strumming a happy note. "I admire your uncertainty, Raine. 'The wise man is one who knows what he does not know', and there's much we may never comprehend. This is why the learning never stops, not until we're dead and gone."

WAIT. Hold on just a second.

I roll my eyes. "I don't think that's what Lao Tzu meant. You're talking about knowledge, not wisdom. Your words seem a roundabout way of telling us to treat the rest of our lives as homework. There's gotta be more to it than that. What of love, and of comfort? If there's something specific we need to learn, we can always run information modules or hypothetical scenarios."

"Raine, sweetie, we're talking about the type of wisdom virtual experiences can't impart. I for one can't afford to slack off. The rabbit hole goes down deep: every pre-conceived notion you hold may one day become an obstacle on the path of truth, and that's okay. There is no progress without imagination, no action that does not first manifest on the mental plane. One cannot advance without gaining footing first, but the real trick lies in maintaining clarity of mind, so as to know when to let go to reach that next fractal. It's just how it is. Life itself is the ultimate homework."

"Is that your new philosophy?" asks Gerrit.

"There's nothing new about it. Quoth Huxley, 'facts do not cease to exist because they are ignored.' Wisdom may be the path to Enlightenment, but knowledge is power, and power is a whole lot more tangible. True wisdom is proper use of knowledge. Failure to act upon one's convictions is a betrayal of principles. There's why moral relativism has to go: those that know and do nothing only support the status quo. It's my hope that it won't always be this way, but in this age it's kill or be killed, kiddos, in the Metaverse, and in real life."

Her words are inspiring, if a little cold and unwelcome.

My heavy eyelids droop at the melodic tune. I know that when I open them again, I'll be someplace else and all this will likely fade away. But as long as they're kept closed, I can treasure the immortal day when no evil can touch us.

See you soon, space-time dreamers.

—

Raine awoke to the sound of soft raindrops on a windowsill. Only, this time they weren't black pixels, but real, actual raindrops. No: they were virtual raindrops. As expected, the once-vivid dream's specifics grew vague and vanished, leaving only the faintest warmth in her heart.

She noticed that she was tucked into a comfortable country bed in a very welcoming guest room. A futuristic gaming console with four controller ports and a spiral logo sat in the corner below a small flat-screen TV, and a plate of milk and cookies beckoned from the bedside table. A cool-looking interplanetary shoot-em-up game was magically playing itself. The jewel case read: *Ikaruga.*

Delighted, Raine drank some milk and gazed out the window – just above the horizon, the sun parted a flurry of fluffy nimbus clouds, as if it wanted to catch a glimpse of Super BlastBoy's trellised garden.

She next heard shouting and turned her head at an angle to see her host arguing with Lily by the rose bed. Raine creaked her window open a hair to listen in on their conversation.

"Yes, I know it was a last-minute change in plan. But we can't delay any longer! You must begin now and you know it! I thought you'd be on this when the debug was complete."

"Lily, it's not that simple. I may possess the skeleton key, but who knows what kind of obstacles I'll encounter once I actually get into the mainframe? It's quite a tall order. I need updated intel. I need time to study the maps again."

"You said getting the direct line would solve everything!"

"I snuck a peek after putting Raine to bed. It was terrifying! Bloody terrifying in there. Certain death is not an easy thing to face!"

"Don't talk to me about certain death, BB. I've seen too much of it lately."

"Yes, yes, sorry. It must be hard for you, but Lacie's passing was a big blow to the Queen."

"Not so loud; she needs her rest."

"Of course."

"Look, Tony, the backdoor paths are getting more complex by the minute. Even the half-functioning Guggell's clogging every loose end they have. Lorrie has seen into the future. Now that she knows the plan... there could be changes, even as we speak. She's using Gerrit as bait, for chrissakes."

"Lily, this is why I didn't want to do this! It's pointless! You don't need to play chess with her! Find some other way to steal the fuel cells. Work on constructing a new power converter. Go home if you must, but start again. There will be no other chance for the world if you're not there to make it!"

"I must do this my way!" Lily hissed. "It will take a decade to build that power converter from scratch, and Lorelei must be stopped. I can't go on unless I purge her, don't you understand?"

"Why, Lily?"

"Because maybe she's right – that I was never meant to do this. Maybe it isn't even supposed to happen. Or maybe it happens on its own in another universe without my involvement at all. Maybe life is... maybe it shouldn't be my responsibility."

"That isn't the Lily I know! *You* taught me that we are *all* responsible. Such ifs and buts are meaningless without proper action!"

"Rich. This coming from the ancient program too scared of a stupid mainframe to leave his own dumpy cottage."

"Now you're resorting to personal attacks! The *nerve*."

Lily kicked a stone across the garden. It rebounded off an apple tree and smashed one of Tony's lawn gnomes. The quiet fury of SBB's voice came out like sandpaper rubbing against stone.

"Why did you do that?"

"I didn't mean to, Tony."

He looked at the gnome sadly. With a wave of his hand it pieced itself back together, but the crack where Lily's stone hit remained. Lifting his fingers, he levitated the fallen apples into a nearby basket.

"Such anger."

"I like to think of it as more of a righteous fury."

"Disgusting is what it is. A waste of energy."

"This world isn't even real!"

"Well, your attitude is, young lady! Are you planting seeds of hope in that head of yours, or despair? Each seed contains the potential to produce countless more. This world is my home. It may not be the one you come from, but it has a soul; t'was built over years by the minds and hearts of your kind, and the complex algorithms and careful tending of mine, and for that, I believe it deserves a little respect."

They both fell silent. Lily hung her head.

"I'm sorry. There, is that better?"

Tony took a deep breath. When he exhaled, Raine felt the ground shake gently, and a wave of good vibes passed over her.

They took a seat on a small cob bench. Lily was the first to speak.

"Listen, I'll handle security for Raine 'til we reach the final exit node and enter the sprawl. You just worry about getting our team in. My best 'bots are patched. As we speak, they're awaiting your orders."

Lily handed him a slick pair of red and blue 3D glasses.

"Encoded Channeler. A closed connection only the EDC, and you and I, can use. I'm to keep radio silence until we're inside, but at the very least, you can touch base with my surface crew. Please, take it."

Tony inspected the visor wordlessly.

"You can sit here in angst as flesh-and-blood people are dying out there, or you can be a real hero for once."

"Miss Lily, I want to do it! I just need more time! If I fail, you don't stand a chance!"

"Listen to the time-traveler. When I say we're out of time, you had better bet your digital butt we're completely out of goddamn time. I'm giving you one hour."

The time traveler stormed into the house and marched across the floor to Raine's room, where she shook the girl, pretending to sleep, out of bed and saw her dressed, and her things gathered in no time. Chance spun into existence in a ribbon of colors – all along, he was playing the game while invisible – and followed.

Lily led her outside the house and towards the same flying ship Raine saw earlier, which was parked behind a bush down the path.

The girl whirled around and waved bye to her favorite game hero.

"Thank you for everything!"

"I'll see you shortly, Raine. Take care of yourself," he replied with an enthusiastic bow. Tony strolled back into his cabin, head held high.

"Ugh! I tell you, personality programming was the death of artificial intelligence," Lily murmured as she gripped Raine's wrist.

"No offense," she said to Chance.

The Rainbow Cat mewed sarcastically in response.

Now that SBB was out of view, Lily no longer felt the need to storm away furiously. She simply pressed a button on her communicator and summoned the shuttle over.

"So, did you sleep well last night?"

"Yeah, very well," Raine mumbled.

She was beginning to get quite agitated and a little frightened. Her newly acquired knowledge with regards to Lily filled her with utmost sympathy for her cause. But the situation was intimidating, to say the least. And she was still missing huge chunks of the puzzle.

"It's about time you showed up," Raine scoffed. The words escaped her mouth without any thought going into them. "I was starting to think that you'd used me to thrash that Stopwatch and then abandoned me completely."

Lily held Raine by the shoulders.

"I am truly sorry this has been so difficult for you, Raine. I really am. But very soon I will be ready to tell you everything."

"I have so many questions."

"They can wait till we're out. We could be in for a bumpy ride."

Raine couldn't stop herself. "Who am I, Lillian? What's the deal with my parents?"

No answer.

"Don't you turn away from me! What's my role in all this? And what about Gerrit?"

Lily shook her head sadly.

"Look, I promise you, dear, we'll have this conversation. Right now the clock is ticking and there's stuff that needs to get done. Just follow my lead and we'll bounce this bizarro wonderland."

XXII. Welcoming Committee

"It is no measure of health to be well-adjusted to a profoundly sick society."

- Jiddu Krishnamurti

"Wakey, wakey."

Gerrit opened his eyes. They were worn, but it felt like he was just getting used to them.

They were the only part of his body he was able to move. He looked around in abject terror. Before him loomed a full-length mirror. He was in a posh dressing room, sitting in a wheelchair, wearing a tuxedo and a large, ugly helmet. From behind, the sultry voice struck again, emerging from the shadows along with a faint trail of smoke.

"Welcome to Earth. I'm sure you don't remember it. At least not yet. Those rebels really did a number on your brain."

She walked up to the liquor cabinet before Gerrit, heels clacking the floor with each loud step. The woman looked to be in her early thirties, clad in a very elegant ballroom gown. Her touch on his arm sent shivers down the boy's spine, *and it's no wonder*, he thought as she downed a glass of brandy. *I'm chilled to the bone. My skin's pale as death.*

Gerrit strained his arm and leg muscles again and again. They failed to respond. No matter how hard he struggled, he couldn't feel or control any part of his body except for his eyes and eyelids. His breathing seemed to regulate itself, as if it were a function being run by an external source.

"Hello, Gerrit. I am Lorelei, the One True Queen, founder and chief programmer of *Endless Metaverse*. I am also known as the esteemed World Leader. In the event that I choose to return your speaking faculties, you may address me as My Queen, Your Grace, or Your Majesty upon first daily contact, and 'ma'am' anytime after that."

Rage overtook Gerrit. His anger boiled up so suddenly that his chills turned to cold sweat. He began to feel serious pain in his head. It was throbbing uncontrollably.

"In finding you, we paid a hefty price. My sister has passed out of time. You're probably wondering, 'why'? What could this highly attractive woman possibly want from little old me? I'm just another player in a bug-infested virtual world. In reality, the truth is simpler than it seems. People make compromises in order to save their loved ones. They get distracted. They do stupid things. They leave themselves vulnerable. Some call it courage. I deem it weakness. You, my friend, were once a pure soul. Only, now you have been conditioned so fully to accept weakness that you can no longer remember your true self. Like the rest of us, Gerrit, you are but a highly evolved animal. And like me, though you are mortal, you too can be invincible if you pursue your own desires to the very end. Because your boyish gallantry has so tickled my fancy, I offer nothing less than to show you how to remember this true self."

She snapped her fingers; an android servant approached from a dark corner. Gerrit watched helplessly as his chair was wheeled about, following the laughing Queen down the dim hallway.

A familiar tune came to the boy, and though he could not for the life of him recall the name of the song or its artist, he clung to its haunting lyrics.

And did you exchange / A walk-on part in the war / For a lead role in a cage?

Paintings lined the wide corridor, which opened up to a large foyer. Gerrit became quickly aware that he was thousands of feet above the ground, sitting in a high tower overlooking a congested city spread far as the eye could see.

The place was definitely one of those he'd seen in his dreams. He drank it in.

After more sightseeing, Gerrit was parked atop a large, enclosed viewing balcony with a translucent floor and ceiling. The Queen studied his eyes in wild anticipation, until at her behest the droid placed telescopic goggles over them.

His gaze darted around the metropolis, stained by the setting sun. It looked absolutely nothing like Clyde Castle Town, or Circuitron, or the Chip Kingdom, or anything else in *Endless Metaverse*. This was an odd vista, a mixture of imagination and decay. The topmost tiers showcased a slick fortress populated by flying automobiles. There were many more sections, each encased within massive rings of stone and metal; lumbering machines on faraway foothills repaired damage to the outermost gate. A line that resembled an ant colony supply train ran for miles outside the metropolis and disappeared into a canyon.

A closer look revealed that tens of thousands – no, hundreds of thousands – of workers with helmets were moving the gigantic stones over to the fortress. Many more were stationed along ports by the coast, and at camps bordering the city. Others manned innumerable anti-aircraft turrets within the walls. Their movements seemed stiff, unnatural, as if they were being remotely controlled.

"Sector One is NERV's Central Dogma, so to speak, though I'm sure you're not caught up on the classics. All land within the peninsula falls under the immediate province," she told him. "*Neo Eden* proper houses approximately eighty million."

Gerrit then peeked directly underneath at the innermost ring, immediately surrounding the monolith. Past the large pyramidal base stretched a number of lush mansions, homes, and dormitories, with residents few and far between. There seemed to be an epic music festival underway. Hundred-foot statues of the Queen dotted every intersection.

The main ring immediately following that one consisted of what looked like a piecemeal network of malls and posh clothing shops. A third ring contained a smattering of towering housing complexes and recreational facilities. The protracted fourth ring functioned as a busy hub for flying craft and a large industrial district, and the fifth ring, which continued along the coastline and proved much larger than all the others put together, was a complete wasteland. The streets were run-down with filth and decay, and as in the topmost level, some folk wore no headgear. Urchins and the elderly were laid on sidewalks – indeed, many appeared to be dead – and others still peddled meager wares or begged. From strange buildings dotting the coast and in rigs beyond, smoke escaped towering chimneys to stain the sky.

Much of this outland consisted of cracked, eroded soil and makeshift shanties scattered amongst the ancient ruins of what must have been a once-beautiful city. Only a handful of scattered fertile plots of land appeared able to sustain anything resembling life. Most strikingly, billboards everywhere advertised free trials of *Endless Metaverse* ("The *Metaverse* cares" was a popular slogan), with lifetime membership undoubtedly synonymous with lifetime servitude.

"Welcome to *Neo Eden*, my unmatched pleasure dome," Queen Lorelei beamed with pride. "How do you like it?"

I don't, he wanted to say. *Not one bit.*

Gerrit suddenly looked up at Queen Lorelei's reflection in the window. Through the fading light, he was struck by the clarity of his own image. The boy felt a terrifying chill run down his spine. It shouldn't have been a surprise, but the very recognition of the truth shook him. The contraptions the men wore down below were identical to the one sitting on his head.

"There's a party I've called in honor of your arrival, Gerrit. I'd like you to meet some of my closest people."

They entered a glass elevator and descended rapidly.

In quiet agony, Gerrit searched the streets. And then he saw, in the second ring down, a gang of young men beating up an unfortunate elderly fellow in headgear. Expressionless, he stood against a wall as the hooligans assaulted him. He didn't react. He seemed incapable of it. After being knocked down, the old man would methodically stand back up again, only to be kicked back to the concrete. Before long he was bleeding. People walked by without as much as a reaction.

Gerrit couldn't look away. It was too unthinkable, too horrible. He was relieved beyond explanation when the doors opened, the goggles were pulled from his eyes, and he was wheeled out to face the impeccably dressed nobles of *Neo Eden*.

They spoke to him in a rabble of gestures and giggles. Some placed their faces in his and laughed staring into his eyes. He knew how he must've looked, a helpless thing, pale, timid, skinny, his heavy crown held into place by some latch coming up from the back of his chair.

Feeling far weaker than he had ever imagined himself to be, Gerrit was humbled. He closed his eyes, but that just made the talking and jeering more intense. The only way out was through, and his guide was taking her time.

"Where is Lady Claire?" she asked of a servant.

"Unknown, ma'am."

"That impertinent weasel."

Queen Lorelei laughed heartily as she strode far along before Gerrit. Her closest lackeys soon fell in step. She continued to the luxurious chaise longue at the back of the room, atop a dais like all of her personal seats. The crowd of hundreds made way for her entourage, and after what seemed like an eternity, Gerrit found himself onstage alongside Queen Lorelei, parked at the right-hand of her seat.

She assumed the microphone to complete silence.

"Good afternoon, ladies and gentlemen. Today, as you all know, is a momentous occasion. The rumors are true. I have chosen to adopt this boy, this poor misguided soul, the primary leader of a terrorist insurgency enveloping the ever-troubled *Avidya* server. You may recognize him from last season's iteration of *The Metaverse's Dynamic Duelists.* Once upon a time, he called himself, and I quote, 'NinjaMageKnight99'-"

She took a premeditated pause to welcome the anticipated laughter that arose from the crowd. They all began their chortles at the same time, sustained as long as she held her silence, forcing it; perhaps out of fear, perhaps out of conditioning, or both, Gerrit couldn't tell. He was mortified at her message.

Me, be adopted by the creator of Endless Metaverse? *And how is it that they seem to recognize me? This has to be a sick nightmare. I almost wish you were right, Raine, and that the entire universe ended up being your dream. It might have been better that way.*

After what seemed like an eternity, she silenced them with a small wave of her hand.

"This lamb was once astray. Now he has found himself in good keeping. We will nourish him, take him as our own, show him how we do things here. When General Lacie returns, we shall rejoice once more!"

Applause filled the air. She surveyed the room like a shepherd looking over a flock, her sharp eyes cutting through the crowd's eerie façade and eating everyone up.

"Now carry on with the celebration," she commanded, and crossed her legs. "We party until morning."

The feelings Gerrit experienced that night were horrifying and grotesque. These people seemed to have everything they wanted, but they were nothing like those in *Endless Metaverse.* They were lavish, fickle, uncouth, and completely into themselves. Indeed, they seemed to desire nothing more than attention, and to please their Queen by any means necessary. Gerrit closed his eyes to shut out the spectacle, but found to his horror that if he held them closed for longer than a few seconds, the *M-Gear* would sustain a small, painful electrical shock that made him feel as if his brain were melting.

Thusly, he alternated between staring at the extravagant chandelier, fashioned from pure ivory, and observing the behaviors of the partygoers as they laughed, danced, flirted, touched, drank, ingested unknown substances, and generally made fools out of themselves, all to entertain their host, who simply lounged on her chaise and suckled down delicious-looking grapes, shooting Gerrit looks of absolute satisfaction.

Words etched into the marble above the entrance arch read: *"Mundus vult decipi, ergo decipiatur."* The boy concentrated on it to try and make sense of the odd language, which seemed at the edge of his understanding, but nothing came to light.

By four in the morning, the energy in the room had died down significantly. The DJ had collapsed onto his turntable. Droids dragged passed-out patrons to their quarters. This was done so casually, Gerrit reasoned, that it must have been a normal occurrence. Queen Lorelei had gotten quite drunk and retired to her private room with a few hand-picked men and women.

After being given several hours to sleep, Gerrit was taken up there himself.

When he saw her next, the Queen lay on the triple-layered feather mattress set upon her marble-carved four-poster bed, wearing nothing but a nightgown, legs peeking out seductively from underneath a large blanket. She munched on some kiwis.

Over the course of the early morning, Queen Lorelei chronicled to Gerrit in great detail how *Endless Metaverse* came into being, and how Lily failed to comprehend the futility of her misguided quest. He felt some of the hazy images from his dreams resolve themselves, and knew that much of what she was saying rang true with what little he could piece together. Chunks of his visions seemed to be missing, a problem the Queen said time would remedy.

She told him how she hadn't the heart to inform the nobles that her sister was murdered in cold blood, or that their national security was at risk all because of one girl's stupid vendetta. Lorelei finished her oral account just in time for a light breakfast.

"You've been awfully quiet, Gerrit. Oh, right."

He wished he could holler in frustration.

"Free him," she commanded to her android. It obeyed, twisting a dial on Gerrit's *M-Gear*.

The boy felt as if a padlock had been removed from his brain. He gasped. He could now breathe freely, speak, and move. He shook from a sudden release of pent-up energy. Unfortunately, his wrists and ankles remained shackled to the wheelchair.

"You... you're crazy!" he began.

"I suppose I shouldn't have expected you to comprehend my work," she said nonchalantly. "I'm merely trying to provide you with a better life than that which Lily has doomed you to."

"And what kind of life is that? A two-decade-long paradise and then we all die?"

"*Memento mori.* The end is inevitable, Gerrit. There is nothing we can actively do to prevent that flare from happening. Not for this world. For other universes, perhaps, but how many more will perish? Each failed parallel realm does not simply disappear. It continues on to its end. By the mere act of witnessing its existence, we are its creators, and also the agents of its destruction. We weren't meant to experiment with realities we cannot even begin to understand, Gerrit! Not on such a scale. What we *can* choose to do is celebrate the life we have left."

"That's ridiculous. We owe it to future generations to extend our presence in this universe!"

"You've been brainwashed, boy. You think humanity has the good of the universe in mind because you're convinced that you're destined to be a hero. Up until poor dead Lacie liberated you from that awful girl, you've been caught up in life of servitude. Helplessly devoted towards Lily's ends."

"Such a hypocrite. What about the billion-plus slaves whose entire lives serve your ends? As for me, I would mean nothing to you if I weren't associated with Lily. You just want to turn me so you can spite her. I may not have been here for long, but I've seen enough of the way you treat your so-called clients in the *Metaverse* to know you can't possibly pretend at preaching humanity."

"Notice that I've never claimed to be humane," she countered. "The very word 'humanity' is an ideal. Ideals are for boy scouts and talk show hosts – like all societal norms, just another tool brandished by successful tyrants to keep the status quo."

She took a deep drink, swishing her glass. "'Humanity', ha! I have no such obligation towards civilization. Those in the *'Verse* are happy; that is enough. My goal is to limit the grand total number of casualties. I certainly have the power to do so. Power is my birthright. But I'm going off-track. Now, what I do believe in is free will. I don't think you were given a choice with regards to fighting for the destruction of my precious *'Verse.'*"

"You could never know that for sure. And what does it matter, anyway? All this is in the past. There must've been a real, logical reason she chose me - and Raine - for this."

"Open your eyes, child. You felt a strong instinct to protect Raine from the second you met her, did you not? Do you know why that is?"

"Because I love her?"

"Because if Raine's avatar died in the game, she'd return to a hub, we'd be able to trace her Network address, and Lily's prolonged game of *Risk* would be finished. You were meant to be her protector from the beginning."

Queen Lorelei's Cheshire cat grin was wide as the crescent moon.

"Your 'love' for her was manufactured. A hormone injection into your developing body."

"That can't be true."

"Oh, so naïve. It's embarrassing. Do you think you personally volunteered for that kind of thing? Might Lily have lied to you, enticed you, or otherwise forced you into it? You don't even know her. You've been a tool, Gerrit. You mean no more to her than one of her robots."

Gerrit had no reply.

"Face it. What she did was no different from child abuse. Yes, that is what it was called, in the world you imagined before entering the *Metaverse.* Early twenty-first century, Alpha world line. You were fed a memory implant, through which you experienced the golden age of online gaming. Recall the Swansea suburb you grew up in, the rolling fields and winding roads you couldn't wait to drive around. Your dog, Muskie, digging up your mother's carrots. Running out the door to greet your father, returning from a stint in Afghanistan."

No way. It's... it's like she can see into my head.

"It's coming back, isn't it? She toyed around with you and Raine both. Have you considered your past failures, your heartbreaks... possibly created by Lily to increase your attachment to Raine... little tricks of the mind. She's a master at that."

His mind raced furiously. Calculating. Weighing. Reasoning.

She knows she's almost got me. Fight, Gerrit! Fight!

"You'll be surprised what lengths she'll go to in order to have her will done. You're only sixteen years old, boy. At what age did she kidnap and brainwash you? It's a wonder she hasn't done irreparable damage to you already, dear. Keeping you near malnourished in that bunker, dressed in old robes. You were saying something about hypocrisy earlier?"

"Even if she's as bad as you say, that's not as bad as you are," Gerrit replied, trying not to let her see that her words had shaken him. "At least she has hope for the future, and isn't obsessed with controlling the world so much as with the survival of the species. From what I understand, you've deformed human civilization completely to suit your own ends. I don't know what everything was like before you took over, but it couldn't have been worse than this. Clearly."

"You underestimate the mercy of ignorance. The Alpha world line was not unlike mine. There was also a massive population collapse in the twenty-first century. The resulting society was ruled under a worldwide government. The masses were no less enslaved than they are now, only they didn't have my *Metaverse* to ease their pain. So yes, I would definitely say I've made an improvement."

Queen Lorelei walked over to the large window. She waved her hand and the curtains began to part. The morning rush-hour traffic was in full force as hovercars dotted the skies, buzzing about like worker bees. The beauty of the glowing city drew Gerrit in with a ferocious power. He strained against his shackles trying to combat its influence.

"Maybe we're supposed to fight the pain," he said. "If we endure it, we'll grow stronger. Only then will there be a chance for us to live. But keeping people trapped in their fantasies is just keeping them weak. It's a false shield from the truth."

The Queen closed the distance between them, slowly, painfully.

"Do not speak to me of hope. Its endurance is but an evolutionary defect. You're young and restless, so I forgive your shortsightedness. I have lived only thirty-four years, seven months, and twenty-three days, but I've seen much. From my high tower in space I wept at the destruction of Alexandria. I watched countless women burn in public for suspicion of witchcraft. I was powerless to stop the Crusades. I have witnessed the birth of mankind; I think it only fitting that I see it to its end. There are ancient things large and terrible and beyond the imaginations of those peons out there."

Lorelei leaned over inches from Gerrit, distracting him with her shapely curves as she studied his uncertain eyes.

"The extinction of humanity is a purely natural one. Throughout history, our species has lost more knowledge than we shall ever gain.

We once lived in harmony with nature. Look at us now. In our short tenure on this planet, we've defiled our garden and neglected its treasures. Humanity is not even worthy of a footnote in the encyclopedia of this or any other universe. If anything is to survive the solar flare, it will be the ruin of my city to serve as a grim reminder for anyone who sets foot on this rock that we were here, we destroyed each other, and we failed to achieve anything of lasting importance."

Gerrit kept a strong face, but the Queen saw the cracks.

"I know what you're thinking, Gerrit. You're different, but you're not. You're a soldier, and like the rest of the helmeted herd you're very much in love with the material world. You pine for that high-level armor, or for a real dragon. Deep down you hope for the game like a junkie ever-seeking his fix."

"I'm not immune to my own desires, but at least I don't try and pretend at self-righteousness. You're the one deluding yourself."

"On the contrary, I'm so right there's no reason for me to jump on the defense. Lily's mission has failed. It was destined to fail. Going by the proper order of things, that solar flare will come, and there will be no tomorrow for this iteration of life on Earth. With the extinction of the virus of humanity, we stewards of death shall become immortal, frozen in time. And why not let the androids inherit the planet? Human existence is vain ambition driven by natural selection. The afterlife, on the other hand... that grim, cold darkness that awaits all... that beautiful void calls to me, Gerrit. It calls to you, too. Join me in welcoming the dark days of our fateful finale. Your friends are gone. You will never see them again. Not your guild, not Peter, nor Yossa, nor precious Raine."

Gerrit hung his head, stone-faced. She placed a hand on his shoulder.

"Despair not. None of this is your fault. It's Lily's. She placed you in a world you grew to love, only to have you fight your way out of it. I was acting in self-defense, you see, protecting my sacred realm from her underhanded ploy. I could have had you killed. It would've made no difference in this battle. My aim is to show you compassion, for you have been unfairly wronged. You are alone now. I am your only friend."

"No. I can't call you a friend. I don't agree with what you've done."

"I'm offering you the world and you've still got the spirit of a revolutionary," she said with a sigh, turning her back to him and refilling her glass. "There was a time when I saw myself in the same light. I inherited a world in chaos, and brought it order with my strength, and then my laws, until even those were no longer needed. Don't you see the genius of the *Metaverse*? It eliminates the politics, the corruption, the self-interest, the unchecked greed. Have you any idea what that does to efficiency? To rebel against what I've done is to doom the cycle to repeating itself, *ad infinitum*."

"An assumption. You don't know that for certain."

"Perhaps, but I don't see you proposing any realistic alternatives."

"Try this. Let the people rule themselves. Let truth and freedom ring on Earth again. Only then can you or anyone else make a judgment as to whether humanity is worth saving. Human beings are neither good nor evil. We're born as blank slates, filled with potential energy. The people just need a true hero, someone to set an example---"

"There are no heroes in this world, Gerrit. Only those with the will to control, and those content to live at their mercy. Why do the masses accept beliefs? Blind faith. Greed. Fear. Ah, fear. The ultimate tool. Not fear of their masters, see. Fear of one another, and eventually, their own selves. People censor their own thoughts. It's the damnedest thing. Every new regime is born from well-funded acts of terrorism and propaganda. All that ever happens is a slight change in management. You can't fight the existence of *the system*."

"We already are."

She snickered in disgust. Gerrit couldn't bear to look at the Queen any longer. She trained her gaze on him, downing another sip of wine.

"Think over your decision. I've got something special planned for the meantime. It may just warm you up to the idea of spending some quality time with me," Lorelei jested.

"Feed him Program Sisyphus," she called to her android servant, who opened a briefcase of microchips, selected one, and plugged it into a socket on Gerrit's *M-Gear*.

"What are you doing to me? Stop this!"

"Oh, don't be so dour. You'll come around eventually. What's there to fight for, Gerrit? Nothing you can possibly do will change the course of history. My nano-bots run this world, from dictating its storms to molding children's minds. Regardless of how many exploits Raine has uncovered, there is no way those clowns can shut down my *Metaverse*. That mainframe, darling, is no cakewalk. It is the ninth circle of hell."

XXIII. Attachment

"If a man wishes to be sure of the road he's traveling on, then he must close

his eyes and travel in the dark." – St. John of the Cross (Juan de la Cruz)

The cockpit of Lily's tiny shuttle popped open and both girls climbed inside without hesitation, drenched in the rainfall that had suddenly exploded into a thick shower on their way down the path, as if the gods were engaged in a riotous water balloon war.

"Cold?" Lily asked as she helped a shivering Raine strap into the back seat.

"F-freezing," Raine yelped.

Lily flipped her goggles down and hit a few holographic buttons. Raine immediately felt her clothes tighten, and then loosen back up again. She touched her hair; dripping wet moments ago, it was now dry as a bag of raisins.

"Where are we going?" she asked as Lily's attention turned to the main console.

"To the Wall of Secrets," Lily replied, cranking the ignition. "Hold on tight, engine starting in three… two… one…"

Raine's stomach leapt into her throat as the ship kicked into top speed almost immediately. As trees flew by, it became quickly apparent that Lily was careening through a forest, dodging wildlife, hunters, and even flying past a small fishing village. It seemed unreasonable that they hadn't hit anything yet. And then they passed a landmark she had long given up on seeing.

Visible a mile out from the cockpit window, the theme park absolutely dwarfed the real Stonehenge. True to the scale of the drawing on the map outside Clyde Castle Town, the structure encompassed a gigantic water park, with a fleet of RVs and flying vehicles parked by the wayside. Thousands of kids frolicked on the many attractions, all blissfully unaware of the changes about to befall them. Putting herself in their shoes, Raine felt a sense of emphatic helplessness as she pictured them ejected from their virtual home.

A dark thought slapped her across the face like an Atlantic salmon.

Does Endless Metaverse *even need to be destroyed?*

Before long the craft slowed to a stop at the opposite edge of another forest. Lily unbuckled them both and beckoned for Raine to follow her outside. Trembling, Raine carefully maneuvered her way out of the cockpit. Lily took her hand as she descended.

"How was the ride?"

"It was… fast," Raine said, her brain's center of balance still in the process of re-adjusting to solid ground.

"We're looking for a very specific phrase," said Lily when she had Raine's undivided attention. "The phrase is '*Please get me out of here*'. Pretty straightforward. It's written here somewhere."

"Do we have to find this thing?"

"It's our two tickets to paradise. The backdoor exit created with the original source code. It bypasses all the trackers and takes us through essential networks. Probably never been used. From here we'll hitch a ride on an abandoned pipeline to the mainframe."

"And why exactly didn't you find it earlier?"

"Because its location automatically changes every hour, and as planned, there's only a fraction of a wall left for it to appear on. We have forty-six minutes before the next refresh. *Vámonos, amiga!*"

It took Raine a second to recognize that Lily was referring to the great wall she encountered when she met the odd little man and his tortoise. They were currently at its far eastern end, just on the outskirts of the forest. Its remains receded over plains and hills into the far distance – true to Mister Senior's word a significant chunk had been hastily demolished.

Lily brushed away moss growing over parts of the wall. Raine and Chance joined in to help her. The Rainbow Cat scanned the writing intently.

"That's right, Chance. It should be nearby. You take the north side, Raine. I'm patched in more remotely than you are; my video resolution isn't as good, so I need the extra sunlight."

Raine looked closely at the lettering. There were at least fifty lines of text running up and down the length of the wall. It was much denser than the section she'd first seen.

"This could take ages!"

"It's our only option. Your virus is warping the code of this grid as we speak."

Raine was horrified.

"Virus?! What did you do to me?"

"It's a computer virus, silly," Lily said as they moved down the wall, searching. "Limited in range, so we've got to trigger it at the mainframe core. It'll also activate if you d-mat, which is why we've been keeping you alive."

"What happens when it triggers?"

"Game, set, and match. *EM* will self-destruct, presumably. This is all on the off chance that yours truly and BB can even get to the core to deliver the payload. Afterwards, he'll carry a replicated virus to the backup server."

The fight suddenly taken out of her, Raine stopped searching the wall. Pacing wildly, she pulled at her hair in exasperation.

"So the truth comes out at last, huh? I'm just a… a virus!"

"You're much more than that, Raine! You're the perfect gamer! Without you we'd all be lost!"

"But you used me! You kidnapped me from my previous life and brought me into this mess!"

"No, no, no. I didn't want to tell you 'til we were free of this place, but you're a volunteer! You, Gerrit, and I developed the plan to bring *EM* down together!"

"What? That's ridiculous!" Raine yelled. "I think I would remember if I sold my consciousness to you!"

"You weren't bought or sold! Your memory needed to be… modified in order for our plan to work. No, don't look at me like that. Please, you have to believe me. There's much more to it. We'll talk later; we just need to get out of-"

"Mister Senior was right! You messed with my head! What difference is there between you and the Developers?"

"The difference is that I'm the one who hasn't given up hope in humanity. Raine, this realm is a prison for the human mind. Once we leave the *Metaverse*, you'll understand why our work is necessary."

"Never mind the *Metaverse* for a second. What about my dreams? My friends? What about my foster Mom? Why should I believe you? And even if I did, what can I do? I'm not a soldier; I'm just a damned girl! I don't know you, Lily! How can I possibly trust you? You've been keeping me from the real facts. Tell me, what exactly happened to Gerrit? Did you 'modify' his memories too?"

Lily gulped.

"Can it wait?"

"No, this is important! I need to know!"

"Yes. But he consented to it, just like you did."

Raine gave up and sat down on the grass, looking pensively out at the digital world before her. Chance approached and wrapped himself around her neck. The warmth gave her strength: it was comforting, in a strange way.

"In the world you remember, people allowed famous faces to shape their opinions. It was an act of social engineering. Pulling on heartstrings and promoting fallacious thinking was the most efficient way to silence people's minds and get them to accept anything. That isn't how I operate. Orwell said that the most dangerous form of lie is the omission. I fully agree. But the needs of this mission go against my principles. As much as I want to be an open book to you... I can't."

"That's the part I don't understand. And the *Metaverse*..."

"Is a method of control, the dead end of civilization. I don't expect you to believe me at face value, but it was you two who came up with this. I didn't mean to make things so complicated. I never asked for all this deception and confusion... you have to understand, they scan everyone's memories upon entry. They would've known the entire plan, and how to hurt you. And there's no way we could have communicated this info without them catching on. I'm sorry that things had to be this way."

At her words, Raine curled up into a ball and hid her head between her knees. She didn't move a muscle.

"Sending you into the *'Verse* wasn't easy for me. I love you, and I love Gerrit. He did his duty. He protected you to the best of his ability, and without him here we're at a bit of a disadvantage. We're running late as it is. The faster we move, the less people die. I swear to you, once we get out of this place, first things first. We're going to rescue him. And then, together, we're going to free everyone."

Raine gave Lily a quick glance to check the sincerity in her eyes. Quietly satisfied, she promptly disappeared into her knees again.

"I promise I'll get you home, Raine. That is an absolute promise. But it might not be the home you're expecting."

There was no response.

"You had a dream last night, didn't you?" tried Lily. "Can you try to remember it?"

Only fragments were clear to Raine. There appeared to be a connection with her recurring vision. *But what could Lily know of my personal dream? And what if that vision was a 'modified' memory, too, planted in my head? Every one of my memories might be false. Ugh! The questions were never-ending.*

Despondent, Lily went back to searching the wall. Raine raised her head. With Lily's eyes elsewhere, she was finally able to relax. Chance wound his way off her neck and flew off to chase some butterflies. Before long, the girl found herself idly pulling out tufts of grass.

Nothing makes sense anymore.

She ran her fingers over the greenery. It did look and smell like grass, but somehow it just didn't feel right. She pulled a blade apart in the middle, and both sides dried up and withered away.

This place is dangerous because people treat its ridiculous rules and laws as their reality.

In video games, Raine reflected, you almost never have to make these kinds of difficult choices. The game makes them for you. The paths are pre-set, the story moves forward on its own, and artificial intelligences are calibrated and fine-tuned during the development process. In most games, you basically go from point A to point B and destroy or manipulate anything in your path. *But life itself isn't nearly that simple.* Raine's expertise was in running away from her troubles, and often from the people who had taken her in and did their best for her, or didn't, but at least they tried.

There's the kicker, she reflected.

She'd never done well with responsibility. Raine was so caught up in self-preservation that she hated to have to shoulder even the smallest burden for others. Now the fate of the world had fallen into her lap, and one wrong move might doom the fate of every Earthling. *What sort of a thing is that to put on an adolescent orphan?*

Perhaps Agnes was right in one way; if she could shift her perception, think past her own immediate desires, she might be able to accomplish something good for others for a change. If there was a small chance that her actions could save lives, didn't she at least owe it to Lily, and to everyone else, to give this hero business a fair try?

Knowing what I know now, I don't have a choice. And neither does Lily. I'm sure she has her own doubts and fears, too. And everyone deserves a second chance.

Raine thought of the Mana Tree, a symbol of Divinity, dying a slow death in some forgotten underground cavern. The way everything here appeared designed to keep the truth hidden, and the players always craving, never satisfied, enslaved to the system. The clearer her thinking became, the more her craving for the *Metaverse's* bread and circuses diminished. The decision seemed so obvious, and so inevitable.

Despite her best efforts to escape the world and all its problems, these were the cards that she'd been dealt. Perhaps it was her very impulse to escape and her curiosity for new experiences that led her into such a paralyzing situation. But regardless of how 'fate' had brought her to this juncture, she had a gut feeling – call it gamer's intuition – that the only way out this time was through. And there was kind of an awesome rush to it. They were approaching the final boss, only this time there was no cheat code, password, or save file, and they were down to their last lives, with no quarters or continues.

Chance meowed, bringing Raine two Gold coins, which were quickly absorbed by her wristwatch. The cat-like thing ran back to Lily, still frantically searching the wall. Raine considered the odd girl and her lofty, mind-boggling mission. *Was everything that Tony showed me really true?* If so, it didn't seem right that Lily should have to do all this alone. Raine sensed honesty in her, and desperation. Here was a girl just trying to do the right thing. Her methods may have been unorthodox, but she let reason be her guide. She was an endangered species, a romantic warrior with a troubled past, and something about her seemed to need protecting.

Raine got to her feet and walked towards Lillian.

"I can end your mission at any instant by taking off this crown and de-materializing, yet you trust that I won't. What makes you so sure your viewpoint of the universe is correct?"

Lily continued to search frantically.

"My own experience, and common sense. The *Belladonna* doesn't have the power to create universes. It's a scientific impossibility."

"But even if you're right, and even if you succeed, are you just going to abandon this world and start over?"

The girl scratched her head. "I don't suppose so. If there's still a ghost of a hope, Raine, I'll keep on fighting."

"Good," she replied. "You'd better not be pulling my leg. I'm going to hold you to that promise."

"It would certainly be in your right to do so."

"Then I'm in. But I'm not doing it for you. I'm fighting for Gerrit, and everyone else, and because it sounds to me like this is a game that needs beating."

Lily had never felt so relieved.

"You've changed, Raine. And whatever's happened to you is damn infectious. Lorelei doesn't stand a chance against us. We're going to find those keywords, we're going to destroy the mainframe, and then we're going to break out of here and save your boyfriend."

"That's what I like to hear!" Raine announced, holding her hand out to Lily, who immediately gave her a confused look.

"Don't tell me. I should know this one."

"It's a high-five. Here, give me your hand."

Raine pulled Lily's hand onto hers fast and they laid down some skin.

"Whoa," Lily said, loving the gesture. "Let's do it again."

"For Gerrit!"

The two high-fived and returned their frantic work while Chance dashed off to chase some butterflies.

□

Gerrit awoke in a strange place. He was surprised to be standing in the midst of an enclosed arena, Standard Longsword and Leather Shield in hand. Stars glimmered overhead through the mesh canopy. Bloodied sands covered his feet. None of his wristwatch menus were operational.

Where's the wind coming from? He soon had his answer, as foul-smelling, multi-limbed beasts with no faces crawled through a permeable bubble shield, making a beeline for him. Two dozen at least.

Without a word, they formed a perimeter around the boy.

"So this is what you want, Lorelei?" he called out to the sky in a fury. "You fancy I should fight for your entertainment? Well, I refuse!"

A dark appendage whipped Gerrit in the chest, taking his breath away and sending him airborne until his back slammed into a pillar on the far side. It should have snapped the boy in half. The pain was greater than anything he'd ever known.

Recoil Protection Bracelet, gone. Ring of Uncommon Agility, MIA. Enchanted Tigerskin Muffler +12, sliced to bits. I'm naked.

Pulling himself up, Gerrit discovered that his vertebrae were slowly healing.

So it was Battle Royale. A warrior's brawl to the death against an endless horde. Time to go out fighting.

The boy banged sword against shield and cried aloud, advancing.

He sliced the next elongated shadow fist that came his way and it splintered into a cascade of pixels.

Three more barreled forward. He blocked, standing firm on the ground, hiding his face while absorbing the blows. The shield held strong. Perfect.

Gerrit sliced through his opponents like butter. He danced against the wind. The creatures were slow, and fell in a matter of minutes.

He scanned their fading bodies for loot or recovery items. Nothing. The swordsman took a seat on the floor and waited for the second wave. It had only been a few seconds when his ears struck with the distinct clacking of the reanimated dead come to life. Just as he thought: skeleton warriors. Next it would be skeleton mages, then archers. Maybe goblins or wasps after that. Then, the usual assortment of pirates, thugs, and bounty hunters. He shrugged. It was going to be a long day in Purgatory.

↔

Lightbulbs flashed, crowds jeered, and virtual reporters continued to shout questions. Mister Senior, however, had said all he needed to say.

"To the virtual *Nexus*," Jon barked to the nearest visible Templar as they clove a path through the gaggle of press awaiting him backstage.

Storming out the back door, he boarded his flying limousine, took a draught from a fresh bottle of cognac, and yelled for the driver to warp onto the *Nebula*.

The conference had been an absolute disaster. Following reports connecting the 'Raindancer' to Yossa, the rebellion exploded overnight at the Coliseum, and its influence sent ripples crashing through *Avidya*. As a result, minds were moved. Roused. Changed. Unavoidable questions were being asked that no one had been prepared to answer. Alternative news broadcasts spread like wildfire. The public was restless for the truth. It was a minority revolt, yes, but what a minority! Over four hundred thousand accounts were frozen overnight, a number quartered and heavily distorted by the centralized *Metaverse* media.

And that wasn't even the worst of it. Glitches and random errors sprouted about all over the centralized system. Fell beasts were turning into collectible origami unicorns. NPCs began attacking Templars. A massive data blitz in the Greywind financial district turned it into a ghost town. Within minutes of the storm passing, hackers had broken into the system and wreaked all kinds of havoc. The stock market crashed. Physics went haywire. Underwater sections did lava damage. High-powered laser weapons turned to rubber on the battlefield.

Needless to say, people were very unhappy.

Better not to let the unstable Miss Guggell calculate the full cost of controlling this wreckage. The folks at QC were backed up for an estimated three weeks on paperwork and damages.

The shimmering neons of the *Nebula* blurred into vision as the limousine flashed through the warp tunnel and appeared in the ship's virtual dock. Pixels formed into polygons and then assembled themselves into people. The door opened from the outside at an elevated walkway. Mister Senior descended, to not much fanfare, as frantic digital avatars scurried about the invisible floor of the hub.

Monitors from dozens of desks lent the room an eerie glow as agents sat hunched over their visors, typing at invisible keyboards. It would have looked to an outsider like a troupe of blind puppeteers. Mister Senior followed the winding walkway to the main hall, which boasted a direct virtual connection to each of the real-life *Nexus* server chambers, allowing him to appear separate from his body as a holographic avatar.

He walked through the translucent bubble that served as a selective doorway and stood at attention. A hologram of Queen Lorelei hovered calmly in the center of the room amidst an ongoing argument involving holograms of various *Endless Metaverse* moderators, including Dr. Marco, the reputable Dr. Karuishi, and General Beech, who stood by the Queen's side, arms folded.

"--successfully blockaded the entire peninsula. Current intel indicates the EDC will cross our eastern borders in two hours," Beech announced. "Macleod's lying in ambush to mop them up like flies. Vis-a-vis the ground situation, we have to ensure that the Overseer runs with no interruption, and that means securing the damned servers."

"Get to the point, Errol," barked the Queen.

"We have over two-thirds of the populace still in our grasp. Cut the server completely and maybe we can salvage the more desirable assets by immediate transfer to the backup server hubs."

"No, ma'am, begging pardon, but what the General describes is lunacy. We are looking at massive-scale genocide," Dr. Karuishi protested, clearing her throat. "There's absolutely no way we can hope to secure any more than twenty percent of *Avidya* assets in this manner. The backups are too unstable for a major op. Data corruption alone will be significant enough to snap tens of millions out into consciousness, and may even cause widespread comas or sudden death. We must wait out this storm and hope that the revolution loses power, or risk turning the assets loose completely if we don't want to lose them all."

"Enough," Queen Lorelei murmured, pacing back and forth in the real-world chamber. "We split the difference. Compress the *Avidya* and *Maya* backups and partition them into enclosure cells. Pull all remaining hostiles and potential hostiles out of *Avidya*, drop them in, and cut them off. No loose tubes on this one; make the transition quick and decisive. They have serious hackers on hand."

Dr. Marco nodded. "I suggest putting our best man on the job. What say you, Holdfast?"

"I'd be honored, sir," Henry Holdfast replied, bowing to the Queen. Now infamous for his part in securing Gerrit, a.k.a. Public Enemy Number Three, Henry was perhaps a bit too eager to shoulder the responsibility. If the Queen took notice, she didn't show it.

As he turned to leave for the *Maya* hexagon, Henry dared to smile across the way to Karuishi. *Strange behavior from these two lately,* Jon noted. *For starters, she's way out of his league.*

The Queen rubbed her temples. "I don't care what you do; just keep the rebels separate from the main herd. Once this all boils down, re-condition, freeze 'em, kill 'em, whatever you want. But not right now. Right now, priority one is freezing Lily and Raine."

"B-but my Queen," Dr. Marco began nervously. "We have no traces on them. The last we've seen of Raine, she was a blip over Atmoya."

"There's no way she's still in hiding," said the Queen. "What say you, Miss Guggell?"

The holographic double of the queen addressed the room calmly. Her figure was bursting with electro-static. Jon was in disbelief. Was she, too, still compromised by the data storms?

"W-we know Raine opened up a primary channel to the m-m-mainframe accessible from pretty much any exit node. We could s-s-send probes to every hub and server, leave no line of c-c-code uninvestigated."

Queen Lorelei gave her watch a cursory glance, and then turned to her staff. They knew the look she was wearing well by now, and it terrified them.

"What are the chances we can secure every exit node in *Avidya* within the next hour?"

"With respect, it is impossible, Your Grace," Dr. Marco murmured.

"I concur," replied the suspect Miss Guggell.

"I eat impossible for breakfast. Do it. Lily's plan is to shut down the *'Verse* and compromise the HDP. She can't do that from within a server, she needs direct access. If we don't give them that, they're just fish in a bathtub. Clog all the holes. I don't care how much power it takes. Goddamn, you people should be able to figure out things like this on your own. Where the *hell* are you getting your training? I'm sick of wasting my valuable time. Wrathman?"

Jon looked up from the floor like a dumb puppy. Ever since he had failed to re-program Raine, his life had become forfeit. He was a dead man walking. Lorelei's cold eyes sent a swift shiver down his spine.

"Log out," the Queen said, and whisked away to her private office. "I require you."

The other Developers watched in pitying agony as Mister Senior pressed both fingers against his temples. In his head, he recited his personal secret exit code.

Within seconds, Jon was back in the real world, in his office. As always, his head throbbed from the sudden influx of stimuli. Groggily, he shot Beech and his android Colonels a withered look as he crossed the *Avidya* floor and meandered over to face Queen Lorelei.

As he creaked open the door, she was setting up a hole of miniature golf, ritualistically, painstakingly. She took her time, dissecting his fears. Keeping him captive. Jon felt extremely uncomfortable. It got worse when the Queen struck up a cigar in between putts.

"Smoke?" she offered.

"No thanks, ma'am," he replied with a wry gesture.

Lorelei puffed like there was no tomorrow.

"The best thing about being in a position of power is the ease with which we can repair ourselves. For example, I can chain-smoke with no adverse effects. We can always get our lungs replaced, our blood transfused."

"I'll pass. They make my head hurt."

The Divine Matriarch picked up a mug with his *Metaverse* avatar on it and set it down at the end of the green. She showed him his smug expression.

"You're losing your cool, Jon. Wifey giving you trouble again?"

"No, not at all," he said. "She's just… worried, ma'am."

Of course, his virtual wife had nothing to do with anything. He could alter her program at will. The Queen was toying with him. She tipped the ball into the mug and set it up again.

"You can't imagine what I'm going through, dear. I've learned this morning that Lacie is dead."

"Oh, Your Grace. I am so frightfully sorry."

"My dear sister. Murdered in cold blood on a scouting mission."

Sweat poured from the Queen's face, dripped on the formless ground, and made its way towards the green plastic turf.

"I am filled with remorse, my liege. Who's responsible for this atrocity?"

"It's that girl. Lillian."

"Impossible. It would take an army."

She nailed the coffee mug again.

"Jon, please. I alone saw her body. Such empty words give me no comfort."

"I apologize."

"Stop that. That's three strikes now. It's not cute. There's only one thing to be done about Lily. She must be exterminated. Skinned alive and hung over the city. And as per my great-great-grandmother's laws, the laws that brought about the Great Peace, those responsible must bear the hardest burden. I hope you understand the severity of the situation, Jonathan William Wrathman."

If there was anything Jon knew, it was that the evocation of his full name meant that his dossier was under review; the man's chances of survival were dwindling by the second. The trembling in Jon's throat paralyzed his tongue.

"I don't believe it's necessary for me to clarify what your role in all this is going to be," she continued. "After all, let's not pretend it wasn't your plan that got us into this mess."

Wrathman wouldn't soon forget. His blunder wasn't something the Queen was liable to forgive.

Everyone in this hemisphere of the Nexus *is saying their goodbyes, crossing me off their Christmas lists. I just hope they give better gifts than fruitcakes in hell.*

The Queen tossed the ceramic mug into the air and swung. A direct hit smashed the token into the air. Its debris sailed mere inches past Jon's ear and blasted against the protective glass in a thousand fragments. Wrathman opened his eyes, perplexed to discover that he was still alive.

He tried to fathom the reasons why. *Could the rumors be true, that each new generation of royals required a male sperm donor?* Maybe he was being groomed for such a position. But that was just wishful thinking. She didn't like him nearly enough for that, and she must have known of the cocktails of drugs. And of course, never in the royal lineage was a male family member ever mentioned. A hot topic among the nobles was that even with the wonders of cosmetic surgery, the resemblance between each of the Queens was peculiar, enough for them to hypothesize that their ruler was either an ageless android, had a penchant for cloning herself generationally, or that she'd perfected a 'fountain of youth' medical process to halt her and Lacie's aging.

No, she was definitely not going to let him father her children until she gave birth to a look-alike daughter, much as he'd always hoped. The only reason he was being kept alive, he considered, was that he was needed. There were simply too few people that the Queen trusted, especially since he now knew that General Lacie was pushing daisies...

It was hard to tell for sure whether this was his imagination talking, or whether his life was actually worth anything; however, the look on the Queen's face made one thing clear. If Jon didn't find Lily and Raine, he'd never see his virtual family again. Not in this lifetime. Mister Senior, among his other roles, would be played by his digital doubles from each of the servers until an eager replacement was found.

"Lily's going to try and break into the mainframe. That was her original plan, and she succeeded. But now things have changed."

Jon was terribly confused.

"I'm sorry, Highness? Did you just say she's already succeeded?"

"No, no, at least not in this world line."

Jon scratched his stubble in confusion, but the Queen continued.

"That devil... she's changed her plan, somehow. I don't know where, or how, or when. But she'll do it. Our entire infrastructure is at risk right now. All of this is being set into motion because she has access to important information. She knows exactly which buttons to press to shut this operation down and I have no way of predicting how much she came to know, or what I can do to safeguard against her."

"But ma'am... I apologize if I'm being presumptuous, but your ancestors promised that nothing like this would happen. Your family has ruled over *Neo Eden* for two centuries... the legendary Eden line holds the power to see into the future..."

Awaiting a blow or perhaps an order to execute him, Jon wondered if he had pushed his luck too far. His knees knocked. Queen Lorelei taunted the man, relishing in his fear. She closed the distance and kicked him in the chest. He flew across the room and smashed his head against a copper globe hanging from the corner. She scoffed in the general direction and flicked her cigar at him. It burned through his tie before the chemical smell roused him.

"It's true that I have lost much of my clairvoyance. That was a condition, this late in the game. Yet what disturbs me most is that odd variable, one that's proven time and again to be impossible to calculate – human error. There's a rat infestation in this *Nexus*, and your efforts to find the leaks have proved most unsatisfactory. I must assume that whatever I can see, Lily can see, and presently I believe she has the upper hand. Yet, if handled properly, this could be just another minor setback. Even if she does make it into the mainframe--"

A loud beep rang through the room. An incoming message flashed on the Queen's Holo-Lens – a Templar detected Raine and Lily activating an exit node at the Wall of Secrets.

"Ready my *Gear* in twenty seconds, or I shall have to kill someone," Queen Lorelei announced over the intercom. She swiped over the report so Jon could inspect it from his unit.

The Divine Matriarch massaged her sinuses with her long, manicured fingernails, breathing deeply. An assistant placed the sleek pink custom *M-Gear* on the Queen's head and gave a thumbs-up to an operative in the Network management spiral.

"There's no time to contact the Joint Chiefs," Queen Lorelei said as she laid herself down on her recliner. "I want every Templar I can get!" she yelled. "Overseer, set a storm perimeter across the Apennines and clear the rest of the region of incumbent weather! I want those airships in sight at all times. Beech is holding down the fort. He knows the protocol for this situation. I'm not letting her get away this time."

Although he made sure not to show it, Jon felt a sense of great respite. So he truly was out of his depth. If she was going to punish him, it could wait. This was something much bigger than that. This was a chance to finally see the World Leader in action.

Queen Lorelei was going to take matters into her own hands.

XXIV. Escape from Endless Metaverse

"Let your plans be dark and impenetrable as night, and when you move, fall like a thunderbolt." – Sun Tzu

Please get me out of here.

It was a most satisfying sight. Those six glorious words etched into the wall were unmistakable.

"Brill-iant," sang Lily, tapping Raine on the back. She pulled out a tiny gong from her inventory. Lily put the mallet in Raine's hand and had her strike it gently.

A deep, mellow sound reverberated across the vast checkerboard plain. Thunder sounded off in the far distance. A sudden gust shook the tree canopies overhead, sending forth a rain of cherry blossoms.

"Exit node 515-AX, this is user *Lillian_2212*. Please show us the way out."

The golden letters sparked to life.

A wayward cherry blossom morphed into a snowflake. Raine scanned the landscape; her eyes caught on a shimmering portal not thirty feet away. Its window looked out upon a frosted wasteland caught up in a turbulent snowstorm.

"There it is!" Lily cried, running towards the portal. "Better put on your mittens."

With a hand gesture and a press of her wrist communicator, the vessel flew towards her. A small hatch in the top popped open and an extension began to code itself onto the shuttle. It revealed a swiveling gunner seat and a large turret with rotating Vulcan and artillery cannons, and two missile launchers.

Raine dawdled on her way to the portal. Something just didn't feel right. It was if some being of immeasurable malice was lying in wait.

"Hey, Dorothy! We're off to see the wizard!"

But the girl had stopped moving and now stood frozen in place.

A snowdrift built up before their feet. Particles within the portal twisted, took on different shapes. In the mountains beyond, Raine spied glowing polygonal edges popping out of rocks, evergreen trees unraveling into wire frames, and ice formations fading in and out, their textures shifting patterns. Perhaps most telling, dead pixels drifted by in the midst of dark gray clouds. The wind was loud now, and cold, and Raine had to scream through chattering teeth.

"How do we know they aren't waiting for us in there?"

Lily punched a few commands into her wrist device and created a thick camouflaged winter coat and gloves. She plucked the effects from thin air and handed them to Raine.

"There's tens of thousands of these encrypted exits. It's highly unlikely that they'd be in any given one."

Her voice was comforting and sincere, but deep down she seemed to be shaking.

"If they do find us, I'm going to need you to provide cover, and you're going to need a personal weapon. You're familiar with this, I presume."

Raine accepted the firearm with trembling hands. It was an exact replica of Super BlastBoy's trusty rifle.

"Let's see if those quick reflexes can be put to the test," Lily ventured.

Raine had seen the on-screen animation countless times. The gun had a powerful charged attack that did lasting splash damage, in addition to an automatic fire mode that never ceased shooting, and a triple-shot mode that fired ahead and diagonally. She tested the charged attack on a rock. It turned to vapor and took a good chunk of the surrounding soil with it.

"This isn't just a dream," Lily said, reading Raine's mind. "And it's not just a game, either. You can actually physically hurt someone with that thing."

"Say what?" Raine considered returning the weapon.

"Tony programmed it. It has the power to interrupt a user's connection into the 'Verse. Same goes for our turret. He wrote this whole ship just for me. You shock someone hard enough, the overload of electrical impulses will kick them from the 'Verse."

"Will they be hurt?"

"It's not fatal. They'll only be shocked to the extent that they fight to remain in this world. Their brains will try to compensate by over-firing neurons to keep the connection, but they'll fail," responded Lily, programming in a set of handholds for Raine to climb up to the gunner's seat.

"Ready?" she asked, revving up the engine.

"Let's do this," declared Raine, climbing up the ship and onto the swivel seat. The seat adjusted to her height and buckled her in. She took hold of the turret in her left hand and the rifle in her right.

"Put on your visor," Lily called out casually over the roaring turbines.

As she did so, Lily appeared in a holographic video, smiling in an uncharacteristically sincere fashion.

"Meter in your top left's our shields. If ever we're taking serious fire, pass me some of the turret energy to bolster our defense. Down on the right's our boost meter. I'll be using it quite a bit, so get used to the G-force. It shouldn't overwhelm you; I coded in a diffuser system. All right. Do you see the 'missiles operational' sign on the bottom left?"

"Yes," Raine said via video. "I mean, copy."

"Yes is fine. All systems nominal. Invisibility on. *Omega Bishop* is good to go," Lily signed. "Countdown in three, two, one…"

Raine felt the rush of momentum immediately. Her stomach sank towards her spine as the ship jumped forward through the portal at mach speed. She was thankful for the bauble-shaped shield that popped up around the craft, blocking out the now quite heavy snowstorm.

"Doin' all right back there?" Lily asked.

"Never better," Raine said nervously. Using foot pedals to spin the turret, she scanned the area for any signs of trouble. All was clear so far, but the valleys far ahead in the distance would make an ideal spot for a deadly ambush.

"Snipers ahead on the foothills. Close your right eye and wink your left. Switch turret to 'Scope' mode."

Raine winked. The display read 'Assault.'

She winked again.

'Plasma cannon.'

Wink. Wink.

'Scope.'

Her visor projected a targeting reticule that adjusted itself based on the turret's position. She turned towards the nooks in the foothills and saw that the visor displayed small red dots to mark the presence of other users. Raine zoomed in on one of them, aimed at the suspicious white mound with a black dot, and fired. The red dot disappeared. She trained her bead on the next one. She took it out. The third one, too. There were a dozen left, and they were still so far off. It seemed too easy.

Just then an explosion nearby had Lily pulling the *Omega Bishop* off to the side.

"What was that?" Raine yelled.

"That, dear, was an explosive round. We've been spotted."

Yikes. She quickly moved to take out the remaining snipers as Lily dodged their incoming fire.

They were closing on the valley. Raine switched to the plasma cannon and charged it to maximum capacity. A relatively slow electromagnetic orb locked onto a concentration of snipers. It imploded into a shimmering display of antimatter that practically erased the surrounding area. She charged a second one to take out the next group, and felt the heat from a powerful energy beam whiz by from behind, barely missing her head. It had penetrated the *Bishop's* plasma shield.

Raine ducked behind the turret's blast plate as a flurry of bullets ricocheted, causing her to miss a shot. The small hole where the beam had come through quickly repaired itself.

An entire fleet emerged from the haze behind the duo like a flood of demons from the mist. Dozens of enemy craft flanked the *Omega Bishop* from either side. Speedy fighters flew overhead, dropping energy bombs along their pathway. Lily nimbly guided them through. Giant carriers deployed vehicles akin to snowmobiles, only they were flying slightly above the ground. The Devs were catching up, fast. Raine knocked Templar riders down with missiles and the charged-up assault rifle.

"I can't believe how good I am at this!" Raine called out.

"Don't get too cocky," Lily said with a chuckle. "Tony gave you an affinity bonus for every weapon he designed. Mixed it right in with his cookies."

"A what?" her companion asked, shooting a large crater into the ground behind them, causing one of the snowmobiles to fall into it and explode.

"It automatically makes you an expert in the weapon at hand."

But even her boosted skills were not enough. They were approaching the valley now, and bombers pulled away overhead, dropping their payloads to try and collapse the narrow pathway.

"We're about to become snow angels!"

"Just you watch," Lily responded, activating a turbo boost that launched the ship far forward of the surrounding enemies.

When the walls narrowed Lily hit the air brakes, navigating deftly between falling rocks and avalanching mounds of snow and ice. Raine pointed her turret upwards and trained her machine gun fire up at the bombers. She took out an engine on one and it attempted a kamikaze dive.

"Shields!" cried Raine, and Lily diverted all firepower to the translucent shield. The bomber exploded along the lower cliff side in a deafening fireball and Lily burst directly through the wreckage.

"That was close," Raine mouthed.

"Here," Lily said, passing power back to the weapons systems. "Keep at it! We can't take any hits from those warheads."

Raine suddenly became aware that a squadron of speedy fighters was tailing them. She charged up the cannon and blindly fired. The resulting explosion brought the weakened canyon down on top of the pursuers.

Please tell me that's the last of those guys.

Just then a decorated fighter ship burst through the mound and fired a powerful laser. Lily evaded a direct hit; the beam melted the guidance tower. The fighter accelerated through the narrow ravine, spinning on its side to avoid smashing into the increasingly constricting walls.

Wink.

Scope.

Raine aimed for the cockpit. She gasped.

The pilot in her crosshairs looked shockingly like an older version of Lily.

Raine let loose her worst.

The fighter dodged or destroyed every bullet.

"Lily?"

"Uh-oh," Lily replied. "That's Lorrie, all right. We need to get out of here."

Raine switched to her rifle and activated the three-direction shot mode. She brought down the surrounding cliffs with rapid fire.

The pursuing fighter activated a shield of flames that turned the falling snow into a wall of steam. It looked to be charging up a powerful attack.

Raine took cover. "Shields!"

But they failed. The laser hit the *Omega Bishop* directly under Raine's swivel seat. A huge plume burst from the engine.

"Hang in there!" called Lily.

"I can't see!" she coughed, ducking below the blinding smoke.

"We're almost out of the valley! Just keep her off us a little longer!"

"I'm trying!" Raine yelled, using both the rifle's charged attack and the turret's assault mode to noticeable effect. Busy weaving through the smog, the Queen was left with no opening to fire.

"Six o'clock!" cawed Lily.

Chance tapped his claws on Raine's shoulders in alert. She hit the 180-spin button. Snowmobiles approached from the other end of the canyon. A single charged shot took the convoy out. Raine twirled back around as the barrier absorbed Lorrie's machine gun fire. Its approaching flame-shield made her sweat bullets.

Without warning, large claws shot forward from Lorelei's craft and clamped onto the *Bishop*. Twin chains presently reeled in its prey.

"You better have a look at this!" cried Raine.

"Hang on tight!"

Lily spun the ship around in a barrel roll, tangling up both chains.

"Shoot it!"

Raine trained a charged plasma blast on the links. It did nothing.

In the midst of the second roll, a powerful rush of electricity surged down the links, and Raine braced herself, wincing.

"Shields!" she managed, passing the weapons energy back to Lily again.

The electricity coursed through every nerve in Raine's body. She screamed and convulsed in agony. It was the most painful experience the girl had ever endured. She gasped for breath once the shield shot back online. Lily regained control of the ship, somehow. Her voice came out a throaty gasp.

"You all right back there?"

Raine coughed. "Never better."

"Oh, no. We're losing power!"

Just then the *Omega Bishop* carved out a small chunk of the canyon. A large piece of metal from the body flew off; exposed wires were sucked out of the resulting hole in the fuselage. The engine smog thickened to the point where Raine could hardly breathe. She coughed, head between her knees.

She looked up to assess the damage. The canyon was becoming increasingly difficult to navigate, not least because Lorelei was weighing down the shuttle. They were near the end of the ravine, and the cliffs grew more jagged and curved. Scores of icicles now emerged from the walls, turning the whole ridge into a razor-sharp house of mirrors. Making a clean turn became next to impossible. Lorelei's fighter remained close behind, readying another electrical attack.

Raine and Lily both knew that if this one hit, they would be done for.

The holographic screen popped on. It was Queen Lorelei.

Raine's scarf grew into Chance's face and hissed at her screen.

"End of line for your pathetic plan, Lily. You tampered with Guggell at your own peril. My only regret is that our little dance had to end so anticlimactically."

"I'm far from licked," the injured and rather woozy Lily replied. "I've yet to make you pay for your crimes against humanity, and for what you did to Lucy!"

Lorelei laughed.

"This is just the beginning. I haven't even begun to avenge my sisters' sacrifices. Toodles," she said, and squeezed the trigger.

At that instant, many things happened at once. Those who might be telling this story many years later in remembrance, or perhaps gratitude, would say it was a miracle. Of course, neither Raine, nor Lily, nor Lorelei, had any part in what happened. Neither did Tony, who might have wished he could take credit for such an ingenious and timely act of intervention.

SLAM!

Raine and Lily jerked forwards, then whiplashed. The claw had come undone by virtue of four gigantic rocky hands grabbing onto their pursuer. Two Colossi, standing like sentries at the edge of the valley, had taken hold of the claw's fulcrum and Lorelei's ship at the precise moment the craft cleared the opening between the two cliffs.

As a result, the *Omega Bishop* snapped from Lorelei's clutches just as the Queen's electrical surge shorted out the control circuits. Lily cranked the engine and pumped the gas. Within seconds, their ship sputtered back to some form of life, and then promptly failed, like a device just past its warranty date. The dying engine left both girls stuck facing a terrible silence, and then a whooshing sensation as the *Bishop* fell into a glide, swiftly approaching the glacier below at a steep sixty degrees.

Raine turned to Lily for instructions. The girl was hastily programming something into her wrist communicator.

"Done!" she yelled, and hit the big button.

Suddenly below them, the glacial expanse turned into pure strawberry gelatin.

Raine braced for impact. The ship made contact, smashing straight into the cool, squishy dessert. She gulped for air, inhaled a mouthful of the gelatin, and hastily processed and swallowed it. Before long Lily came by, squirming from the cockpit carrying an oxygen tank. Raine unfastened her restraints and fell forward. She took a deep breath from the valve, and then held Lily's hand as the latter used her new flippers to swim them slowly, but surely, up to the light, taking breaks to catch some oxygen, or a bite or two, in the process.

When they breached the surface, Raine gasped for a refreshing breath of virtual air.

"Should have added a little more sugar," Lily joked.

A deafening clunk reached the girls' ears. Raine found her gaze directed backwards at the Colossi. There were at least twenty now, and their make was of all kinds of stone and mineral. One was made entirely of igneous rock; another shone emerald and jade. The largest one's veins pulsated with magma. All had gathered around Lorelei's vessel, now trodden on the tundra, and were stomping it to dust.

Raine took hold of the binoculars in her bag and zoomed in on the situation. Lorelei was weakened, struggling to escape. But the titans were methodically blocking off her exits, trapping her within the constraining metal. It was a gruesome scene, and Raine thought of the gentle giant perched atop the old house and now knew the true power and awesome terror its people were capable of.

"Those are the Colossi, right?" she asked Lily, who had borrowed the high-powered theater binoculars and was watching on in admiration.

"Yeah. Let's save the talk for the road."

They swam towards the edge of the gelatinous glacier.

"They're the old gods of the game," Lily said in between strokes. "Elder functions whose creeds are diametrically opposed to Lorelei's. They wanted this world's inhabitants to live in harmony with its form of nature. And, for a while, they did. But they were too happy, too content. Many naturally transcended the *Metaverse*. Once tests made it clear that the *Verse's* distractions would be more effective in an overly complex social environment, Lorelei froze the Colossi. I propose that your coming helped corrupt the system enough that they were able to break through their restraints."

"Lorelei didn't even program them in," Raine queried.

Lily shook her head as they made it to the edge of the gelatinous lake. "They were a glitch in the original system that she couldn't remove. The people paid tribute to the Colossi and heeded their words. Believe it or not, there were some years of peace in the *Metaverse*. Their existence was beyond Lorrie's control until she developed the freezing system, which doesn't really fix exploits so much as detain them. Her lazy programming proved to be her undoing, it seems. They're buying us time by keeping her avatar alive. If we can shut down the *'Verse* while she's still trapped in it, the virus will trigger, her mind will be arrested, and she'll need some time to recover. I give us half an hour, and that's being generous."

The women dried off as best they could on the icy shore. Lily's wrist computer, soaked in goo, was malfunctioning. With the Network down, visors would be just as useless.

"*No bueno*," Lily said, popping open the maintenance hatch. The circuits inside were fried. Even with her expert tinkering, it would take hours to repair. She took the band off and stuffed it into a small pouch on her belt.

Looks like there's no easy way out of anything today.

"Hey Raine, I was gonna code us a nifty snowmobile, but it looks like we're gonna have to go the rest of the way on foot."

Raine looked in the direction Lily was pointing. The far-off portal shimmered like a razor blade atop a military base. A blinding snowstorm separated the duo from their target. But Lily trudged on, taking point even as Raine shivered against the blistering cold.

"It's so far away!" she cried. "Nimbus! O Nimbus, we could really use your hovercraft right now…"

No response. They weren't in *Avidya* anymore. Still, it was worth a shot.

Raine walked until she didn't think she could walk any further. Though she halted still, Lily trudged onwards.

The girl tried to lift one leg and fell to her knees, winded. A ringing sound had grown in her ears since they crash-landed. Now it was becoming unbearable, spiking in and out without any pattern or rhythm. Sometimes she'd be fine, and sometimes it'd creep up on her and make her sick, give her the feeling that nothing would ever make sense again.

Lily came back, grabbed her hand, and pulled her up.

"Please, Raine. I need you to hold on just a little longer."

"What's happening to me?"

"I think they must have laced this snow with some sort of adverse substance to keep out any tourists. Just try to power through it."

Lily didn't look so sure about her assessment, but Raine nodded slowly. This was a race she couldn't afford to lose. Her trembling legs suddenly kicked into gear and she pulled herself up.

Chance unfurled from Raine's neck, flew before the travelers, and used what little energy that wasn't being counter-acted by the storm to melt down the snowdrift.

They walked together towards the beacon, over glacial ice and into a thick field of knee-high snow. Both girls forged through the blizzard, shaking, barely conscious, badly injured, and hardly able to walk. Raine had to stop to throw up, and Lily gave her a brain booster packet, reminding her that nothing here was real. They fell over constantly and had to lean on each other to keep their balance. Chance wrapped his tail around Raine's shoulder and helped carry her forward. The trip seemed to take a lifetime.

They snuck up the icy metal steps and around the large spaceport. It was completely empty.

"W-w-where did everyone go?" Raine asked at last. "What about those guys following us?"

"I think I have an idea, and I also think that Holdfast is on his way to war hero status."

∩

"Sir! It's an absolute disaster! The terrorists we transferred to *Avidya's* backup have infected it with a paralyzing virus and are emerging from the *Metaverse* in droves!"

"Mr. Holdfast, we've lost all security in the *Avidya* server! Agents have been simultaneously ejected and are currently unconscious. We're running on nothing but buggy security bots!"

Henry tried his best to look worried and concerned. This was all going to be done according to plan. He just needed to keep his game face on. He paced the *Avidya* Developers' glowing top floor, closely observing the central feed and screens of those under his command.

"The rebel leaders are gone now; they're nothing but sitting ducks. *Avidya* is not our primary concern. Do what you can to keep the peace, but we can sort out bugs later. Prioritize containment of remaining hostiles. Lock down all the exit nodes! We must methodically freeze the entire server until this boils over."

"Sir, we've been bled dry. Maintaining *Avidya* is using up eighty percent of our auxiliary power, and we have no Templars to spare. Miss Guggell is malfunctioning and back under surveillance. We have to cut the cords on the malignant group!"

"I will not lose this crop of a hundred thousand to a petty virus," Holdfast stated adamantly.

Cheeky Conor piped up. "But sir, if we don't completely neutralize them now, more could break free of the *Metaverse!* They're running rampant through the streets!"

"They're unarmed. Alert Zarifian; have the HDP apprehend and arrest them," he replied. "Genocide is not on the menu. I don't want a repeat of the Forgotten Wars."

"With all due respect, she'll put us all in deep."

"Relax, mate. I'll bear the burden of the consequences."

A sudden hologram popped up. It was Mister Senior himself, Jon Wrathman.

"What consequences, Mr. Holdfast, were you imagining?"

"None, sir, hopefully," Henry bumbled in surprise. "I am confident that we can contain this situation with one division and save potential tens of thousands of assets."

Jon scratched his head.

"Well, I'm calling to relay a decree Her Majesty left to General Beech before plugging in. I quote, 'If any assets should violate the End User License Agreement and terminate their service, martial law shall be declared. In descending order, General Lacie Eden, Miss Guggell, and Lieutenant General Errol Beech will be in charge until such time that I resume my throne.'"

A lump caught in Henry's throat. He was in the clear for now, but this was terrible news. It meant that Queen Lorelei knew exactly what was coming.

"Since Miss Guggell is incapacitated and General Lacie is nowhere to be found, the whole department is to hand over the reins of the Network to the Joint Chiefs. Beech wants to round up the insurgents and mow them down in *Victory Square* with the HDP infantry to serve as an example. We're to cooperate immediately."

"Negative, sir," Henry said. "Those chowder-heads just want blood. We are currently salvaging the crop by sealing off the exit nodes--"

"Bring it up to your CO, Holdfast. I don't agree with this either, but it's out of our hands."

"Will that be all, sir?"

"For now, yes. Over and out."

The feed cut off. That damn Queen was always one step ahead. He was no hero, but he couldn't just stand there and let the revolutionaries get gunned down without a fight; he had to do something.

↕

"Who's Holdfast?" Raine asked as she caught her breath.

"He's one of our very best," Lily replied. "Rebel hacker kid from what you know as Queensland, Australia. We set up a base to protect the community there, and he remote-controlled my bots to break out into show tunes. I offered him a job, working for me on the inside. Snuck him into *Neo Eden*. He made his way up to assistant head of *EM*'s Network Management in five years."

"Sounds like a genius."

"You bet. And I gave him the most important job of all: shutting down the dedicated defense software. Hopefully it's already been done. Once those people lose the capability to become cold-blooded killers, the war is over. When our shutdown function destroys the *Metaverse's* source code, they'll be completely free."

Free? No more Metaverse? *That was good news, right?* Raine's head throbbed so painfully, she couldn't even manage a response.

Lily led Raine into a service elevator.

"Hang on to something," Lily called out as she placed one hand on the control mechanism and activated it.

Nothing.

"What the--?"

The controls were a flat texture mapped to the wall. While Lily inspected the wallpaper, Chance tapped her on the back, and then hardened his face into a powerful expression.

"Ah, I get it," the time traveler deduced. "This old hub is the unfortunate victim of lazy game design. Raine, stand straight towards the doors and look ominously into the distance."

Lily hardened her face, determinedly facing the cold sun with all her might. Raine struck a heroic pose, gazing off into the snowstorm.

"You're not staring ominously enough," Lily advised.

She snapped Raine's back straight, prompting a tormented grimace, with the unintended effect of sending the girl's gut churning. Satisfied with its inhabitants' commitment, if nothing else, the elevator snapped loose, and then suddenly shot upwards at a sickening speed. Raine nearly hurled as her lungs dropped into her stomach.

Seeing that her companion was uncomfortable, Lily slowed the machine's ascent.

"What's wrong? That isn't supposed to be happening," she said, placing a hand on Raine's cheek. The poor girl was a bright red; her fever was melting the layers of ice coating her nose and eyelashes.

"Oh, shit," cursed Lily. "There's something the matter with your neural connections. They're confusing your real-life senses with the reality of the game. Your muscles are acting up. This is not good."

Raine finally settled her breathing.

"No, I'm fine. I think now that I understand... I've got this," she said firmly.

"Okay, scratch my earlier theory. My guess is that old snake Senior put some sort of corruption patch in your steak. It's fighting your neural brainwaves. This extra-sensory perception is just one of the side effects developed to use more of your brainpower in conscious thought, robbing your subconscious of the power to overcome this... counter-virus thingy."

Raine nearly hit her head on the wall.

I should never have taken a bite of that food.

"Um... so based what you're saying," Raine ventured, "I can configure my subconscious to take over my thoughts, to fight this virus?"

"Kind of like that. You just need a shift in perspective to get the subconscious working on itself. It's hard to explain, but... do you by any chance meditate?"

"Meditate?"

"Shoot, I thought we remembered to include that in the plan," Lily mumbled to herself, a little too loudly.

"My past foster Mom used to meditate," Raine said at last. "She would sit cross-legged with her palms out and focus on her breathing. The idea was to empty her mind of all attachments and worries."

The elevator snapped to a stop. Before it was a long bridge, and at its end, a glittering diamond structure with a mass of important-looking computers and screens inside it.

Lily snapped her fingers. "Anapana. Wonderful. Raine, I want you to try that, okay? That should help your brain fight off this evil patch thing while I jimmy up our ticket to the main event."

Raine nodded, a little uncertainly, as Lily skipped across the icy bridge hundreds of feet off the ground. She made the mistake of looking down, which sent her mind spinning again.

Once inside the giant diamond, Lily shook her head at the control panel. This puppy wasn't going to be easy to hack.

Gathering up her courage, Raine sat facing the whistling din of the blizzard outside the plasma-shielded elevator – an ice storm denied by invisible doors. She closed her eyes and listened, taking note of every sensation, all the while focusing intensely on the air's light touch as it entered and exited her nostrils.

Raine imagined a war going on in her head, a war between truth and illusion.

She couldn't tell who was winning. But she imagined it because it was all she could do to keep from passing out in exhaustion.

If she fell asleep now, there could be no telling what kind of world she would wake up in next.

XXV. Endgame

"Life without liberty is like a body without spirit." – Khalil Gibran

The *Nexus'* Icebox brought a terrible cold to Francesco Zarifian's bones, and it wasn't just the sub-freezing temperatures or the glass prison capsules containing dozens of his allies in need of some serious thawing out. There was something downright creepy about the place.

He tried to ignore the surveillance cameras in the isolated comm. chamber. The Overseer was, no doubt, watching his every move.

At last, the video loop he fashioned circled into the feed. The trick would buy him ten minutes at most. Dr. Zee used his encrypted Holo-Lens to patch the latest vidfeeds into the *Valkyrie*, giving the EDC the lowdown on the ground situation.

Z: The freedom fighters are in trouble. Where are you?
A quick neural reply came from Lt. Gen. Joaquin.
J: Eighty klicks out. The Admiral's still plugged in.
Z: Obviously. So's the Queen. Get a move on; they're dying out here.
J: And the HDP?
Z: Up and running. It looks like L might shut down the 'Verse before we get to the Overseer. Could you spare a few decrypting bots to help me crack the ice? I'm thawing out our strike team, but Guggell's protocols are being a real pain in the ass.

At this line, a rather malicious hologram appeared behind the Doctor.

"I had a feeling someone mentioned my name," intoned the digitized voice.

Miss Guggell Prime. Impossible, he gulped. *We'd locked its functions away. Unless... the Queen kept it running as a background process from the local backup, lying in wait – impressive.*

"My, Miss Guggell, you're certainly a sight for sore eyes."

"Francesco, so it's you who've been keeping me from my Queen and desecrating my source with your impure exploits. Your brain will be scoured with iron wool, your death slow and painful."

Zee cut the chamber's power lines, but the hologram only returned a second later, following the whirring of the backup generator. By this time, he'd hit the emergency isolation switch and drawn his firearm.

One of the Icebox's maintenance cranes came careening through the thick windows. He ducked under its arm, but Miss Guggell was too fast. The crane knocked him aside, away from his weapon. Security droids rushed across the walkway, fifty meters away. Tablet in hand, Frank climbed up the crane-arm and bolted to the emergency exit.

He almost made it to the other side.

Daisy-chained androids electrically shocked the arm, knocking the Doc out. As he tumbled to his death, tendrils caught his body in mid-air and promptly passed him around the chamber, standing the man up within a nearby Beta Testing unit, which resembled a cross between a diving bell and a coffin.

Miss Guggell's hologram materialized outside the capsule and observed from its many sensors as Zarifian's brain was fitted with the hypno-module. EDC agents would be trained to resist any and all memory-prying techniques, but no one could last forever.

It estimated that in three hours, everything he knew would be downloaded into the *Eden* Archives – except that the AI failed to access the servers. The Network had gone silent. The human engaged the emergency isolation switch with no hesitation. He might have failed to free his agents in the end, but he patched all exits extraordinarily well. The malfunctioning Guggell now running the *Metaverse* was shutting out all external access.

Guggell Prime concluded that it was trapped in the Icebox with Chuckles and his frozen war buddies. It placed a finger to its virtual temple. No response from the Queen. *Damn those humans.* Both Master and Servant had been taken off the board.

=

Gripping his laser rifle with care and shaking from the dreamlike events the past twenty-four hours had taken him, Yossa sent the next batch of his men into the makeshift portal.

Hector Travers clapped a hand on his friend's shoulder.

The barbarian werewolf who led the revolution on *Avidya's* North continent stood a hulking six-foot-ten and wore nothing but animal furs draped across his lower body.

"So wait. What exactly happened in HC last night, bro?"

"Absolute disaster. We lost thirty percent of our forces. Tens of thousands. That's when I sent you the message. When I returned, the Tavern was fully prepped for our last stand."

Early that morning, Yossa explained, the Developers raided the bubble server. The bloody battle had only one possible outcome. For every defeated Templar, they sent four. Tanks crushed the barricades. Even advanced exploits were of no use against such numbers.

"I take it you, too, were put on trial?"

"Yes, and tortured. Something about terrorism and disrupting the peace. Said I'd be held here for a period of maintenance. Seemed eager to dump us lot with nary a round of questioning. Odd, isn't it?"

The anarchists weren't stupid. No way were they going to be transferred back to *Avidya*, or any other server, for that matter. Their existence was too dangerous to the continuing structure. It would undoubtedly be the deep freeze.

Hector scratched his beard. "Nay. I take it they meant to put us in deep, but maybe something's gone wrong on their end."

Rumors arose as to why they hadn't already been processed, but one theory rang true: the Developers were running low on resources.

They had to act fast, and the speed with which their best and brightest utilized Lillian's recently acquired codes to break through their individual prison partitions, overtake the central hub, and crack open the walls of the unstable backup server astonished even Yossa.

"The whole thing reeks of a trap," the elephant man observed.

"Aye. But it may also be our only chance."

This was too easy of a win for comfort, but the others foamed at the mouth at the opportunity to go to the outside world. People had bets to settle, rumors to deal with, truths to confirm or deny. And the alternative was to wait for almost certain death in this empty hub.

Most were out now, and this backdoor route would hopefully last long enough to evacuate the rest. They were leaping into it ten at a time, restless to emerge into the real world and leave behind this twisted digital limbo.

Yossa urged badly to traverse the portal, but he wouldn't have missed the veritable roll call of his best people for anything. He high-fived good friends who'd fought alongside him for years, those who stuck by through the hard times, and the new recruits, whose dreams had been realized before they lost their youthful enthusiasm. They would be the ones to build their new future.

At long last it was down to the two leaders.

Hector pulled a jug out of his pelt bag, uncorked it, and poured its contents into a drinking horn.

"Have a drink, old friend," he said, offering a swig of his mead to Yossa, who gulped down a healthy mouthful of the stuff.

"Time to say goodbye," replied Yossa once he'd passed the horn back.

"Many times we were told we could never do it," he said grimly. "Now our people are free. We have much to celebrate."

"They're waiting for us. They've seen the other side."

"It's time, brother," Hector boomed. "I hope we shall meet one another in that world."

Both men walked into the portal simultaneously.

They awoke in the midst of a heated battle.

Yossa, still dazed, twitched his weary feet. He looked down at the puddle of water on the ground. His human face stared back at him, for the first time he could remember. A button nose took the place of his trunk. *The same eyes, at the very least.* The wrinkles on his face, and his brown, leathery hands, felt both familiar and foreign.

I'm old: that much is certain. And beside me: a man in the process of waking up. No, a kid. He's decorated in bruises, too. Could it be?

"Hector? Is that you?"

Yossa discovered with some surprise that he had a strange accent. Or maybe the stale air just caught in his throat.

The body of the injured man was the total opposite of Hector's appearance in the game –short, lanky, and young. Yossa did a double take, his heavy helmet shaking as he turned his head. He felt the device. If the rumors were true, this terrible contraption must have been what connected him to *Endless Metaverse*.

"Yossa? You sound different."

"Yes, it's me. Do yourself a favor and don't look in a mirror 'til we're out of this."

Hector inspected his body. It was most unusual.

Yossa peeked out from behind the dumpster they'd evidently been hidden behind. Discarded helmets lined the floor. People engaged in combat all around them. A massive armed force of synchronized humans and androids subdued civilians with electrical weapons. The military men wore helmets outfitted with blast-shields covering, but not concealing, lifeless eyes. The air smelled dirty and decayed; many of the younger rebels were hunched over, hurling or gasping for breath, their oxygen-deprived brains pushed to the limit.

Some were better off than most. A few could barely muster the energy to stand, but others took the charge with stolen weapons from the armed forces. Someone from a slum balcony threw a Molotov cocktail into the advancing military wall. Men and women ran screaming or fell like ragdolls, their flesh charred and smoldering, shrapnel from the androids exploding into their skin.

What the hell is going on?

Discarding his chrome hat, Yossa gnashed his teeth at a sharp stab of pain running up his spine. The nano-bots in his brain were self-annihilating, delivering a shock to his nervous system. The connection between his conscious brain and his body was repairing itself. It was a most confusing feeling, and a part of him yearned to put the thing back on his head. He tried not to acknowledge it. Instead, he wrapped a nearby bottle around a discarded broomstick with a piece of rope.

Hector had also decided the headgear was out of style. He was fashioning a makeshift scythe out of a sharp piece of scrap metal, some twine, and a strong utility rod.

Gods help us.

Yossa and Hector exchanged glances, nodded, and ran into the fray.

They were facing almost certain death.

Bombs fell from high above, reducing concrete to rubble. The blasts sounded nothing like the digital explosions in *Endless Metaverse*. Shacks quivered in the aftermath of powerful tremors. The air echoed screams from those being driven insane by toxic gas grenades.

"All free peoples! Rally to us!" Hector called out.

After observing a soldier with a riot shield beating one of the indoctrinated women senselessly with an electric baton, Yossa stabbed the man in the gut and wrestled away his weapon and shield. The ordeal was oddly strenuous on Yossa's old bones.

With Hector at his back keeping the armed forces at bay, he worked at gaining the upper hand in the battle. Together they advanced through the guard valiantly, cleaving a pathway for others to follow, calling the newly freed to join them in finding higher ground.

"Where's our leader?" a young woman cried. "The boy from the local underground, he said there was a reinforced building--"

"He's dead," replied a middle-aged man. "Their entire force was gunned down. And we're next."

Yossa grabbed the woman by the shoulders. "Where's that safe house?"

"I- I don't know, but he said it was due east."

Just then a forceful gale from a nearby airship knocked the wind out of Yossa. He pushed the woman to safety and rolled underneath a hail of gunfire, ducking behind an upturned market booth. Loudspeakers situated around the dilapidated inner city sounded out in unison.

"Halt! Attention all *Endless Metaverse* users! You are in violation of your End User License Agreements! Drop your arms and return to the town square immediately!"

"Never!" Yossa boomed. The gunship shot him in the shoulder. His nervous system not yet fully operational, the pain spiked in and out violently.

"Return now! This is your final warning!"

Yossa stood holding his shoulder, paralyzed by true fear.

Suddenly the gunship began to rock back and forth, as if it were just hit by a strong wind. Yossa saw the men inside grasp the controls with all their might, trying to wrench the device back into their own hands. Another gunship headed straight towards the one staring Yossa down, spewing blue flames at its twin. There was no time to run. He ducked behind a large clay pot and held what remained of a tin roof over his head as the two collided and spiraled down into a nearby building in a terrifying blaze. Flames scorched the aluminum. Yossa threw off the superheated sheet and wiped the ash from his overalls.

"Yossa! You all right?"

He nodded and strapped on the oxygen mask being offered to him, falling in by the front of the pack. They carefully navigated the narrow, crowded intersections, attempting to find more freedom fighters. An elderly man chased his goats down the street towards what Yossa now saw as one of the city's entrances – the roads were swarming with pedestrians, vehicles, and horse-wagons, all struggling to escape.

What he spotted next terrified him: a continuous expanse of helmeted troops guarded the outer walls, keeping the poor folk trapped inside. Yossa's first instinct would have been to help the people, but that was out of the question given what they were up against.

"Guys, we have to regroup and take care of the immediate threats first."

Hector nodded, and then held up a closed fist for silence.

They rounded the next corner carefully. A large armed personnel ground vehicle made donuts, trying to shake off a horde of hardy revolutionaries in the process of scaling its outside. The top hatch flipped open and a soldier from within opened fire on them.

Fueled by adrenaline, Hector ran screaming towards the hatch, jumped above it, and yanked the soldier out by his vest. He tossed the unfortunate man on the ground, where the others made quick work of him. The kid dodged more bullets from the inside, then stuck his scythe into the hatch and swirled it around. Blood spurted out from the vehicle, and Hector jumped inside to end the screams for mercy.

Seconds later he threw three men down from the cabin, one by one.

Yossa watched, horrified, as the bodies hit the floor; the people were dead, their faces grotesquely damaged. No spirits appeared. Their consciousnesses would not regenerate. This was true warfare, and it was indeed horrible.

"Get in!" cried Hector, and a few men were brave enough to climb the blood-soaked vehicle and get into the blood-soaked hatch.

"I'll lead the ground unit," Yossa called, picking up one of the discarded rifles and testing it on a bale of hay. "Where are we headed?"

Hector pointed North, at the inner rings of *Neo Eden*.

"We're going to show them what we think of their infernal prison!" he cried, to many enthusiastic cheers.

Yossa was despondent, but he knew there was no changing the minds of these men and women. He was of the opinion that they needed to regroup at the safe house, not charge. They had to think this through, lest they be killed. Whatever it was that crashed those two ships together would probably not work a second time.

╪

Walking briskly, Henry made his way out from the lift atop the *Nexus'* ten-storey docking structure, scanned his wrist ID, and was no less than a hundred feet from his personal cruiser when it exploded in a ball of flames. He jumped in terror and spun around. The ringing in his ears subsided to creepy laughter.

So much for a smooth transition to Phase Three.

"That was a risky trick, hacking into the centralized autopilot program and activating the Supreme Lorelei Override," Jon Wrathman pronounced. Beside him, a beefy *M-Geared* marine reloaded his heavy-duty rocket launcher. "And I know there are others. A particularly meddlesome individual took the ID locks off the weapons and sent our weakest androids in first to reduce human casualties. Ingenious. How did you pass her retinal exam?"

Ayumi's gambit worked. Thank God. "Didn't need to, Sherlock. I programmed a backdoor into the latest security protocols."

"So we know who our mole is. I was starting to think we'd never find the bad apple in our bunch."

"I can't imagine what you're talking about. Beech's plan will end in genocide. This was my first and only act of insubordination."

"Don't take me for a chump. I'm the damn president in every single server. The Queen may own the *Metaverse*, but it's my playground. I know a liar when I see one. You're with *them*, so act like it."

Henry took a deep breath. This was it. He'd been found out. He'd be arrested and imprisoned, kept alive just long enough for them to torture information out of him. Dr. Zee hadn't been responding to calls. Things weren't looking good for the old man, and if his memory was being scoured, it was only a matter of time before they got Ayumi, too.

"You said it yourself. It's not just me, Wrathman," Holdfast began. "We've got this whole place on our payroll."

"What did I just say about lying? It's all so obvious you want me to believe that. Because hey, maybe if the money's good, I'll switch sides. Maybe I'll turn to your ways. Maybe I don't want to do this terrible job anymore."

Henry was not thinking a single one of those things. He was considering how horrific it would be to die like this. His lunch burrito had been hastily devoured. Upon departing to the great mainframe in the sky, his bowels would evacuate and stink up the entire floor. Ayumi might even be watching. It would be a most embarrassing way to go and he had to prevent it at all costs.

"Maybe?" he echoed.

"Or maybe not," Jon said, putting down the gun. He took out a cigar case. Henry recognized it as being from Queen Lorelei's private stash. He lit one up and handed it to Holdfast, who took it reluctantly in trembling fingers.

Motioning for his guards to leave, Jon beckoned an astonished Henry to the lift, which they rode down to ground level.

Jon ordered two bratwursts from the nearby hot dog stand, and strolled into the hedge garden. Suddenly remembering that he didn't smoke, Henry put out the cigar and returned it.

"Help level with me here," Jon began. "You're a pretty high-ranking officer, aren't you?"

"I do have some authority," he bluffed.

"Your side is going to win this war, no?"

"That is our intent," uttered Henry.

"Intent, hah! Your boss is smarter than that. A siege like this doesn't happen unless someone's crunched all the numbers. And I believe your Lillian, young and crazy as she is, has crunched them twice over. So you've won the war. What then, old chap? What do you intend to accomplish with all these peasants?"

"We will rebuild. And we will endure," Henry stated. "We'll teach these *free people* how to live off the land. Countless sustainable communities thrive independently of this tyranny. We'll take them in. Move to the old cities and rebuild."

"And the *'Verse*?"

"It will be destroyed, of course. Abandoned like yesterday's garbage."

"Oh, but surely that's a bit harsh," Jon twitched. "After all, you can't be naïve enough to believe that everyone is going to want out of it."

Henry shook his head. "Honestly, Mr. Wrathman, these people have been misled. They need to be shown the truth about our world."

"But what if they don't *want* to, Henry? Privileges like the *Metaverse* are not so easily withdrawn. And please, no one's fired you yet. Call me Jon."

"Well... Jon, I think their help will be needed to rebuild this planet, to cease nuclear activities, and the wasteful mining, and---"

"Ah! But they can help, can't they, even with the *M-Gear*? The assets can do as much physical labor as the rest of us, even more, some would say, without even feeling the pain and toil. They can escape from their bodies. Wouldn't you say that would be a kindness to them?"

"No matter how kind, it is still a delusion," Henry said, though not so boldly. "I believe at the very least that players should have the active choice between their delusory world and the real one."

"So we're making progress. Your sentiment is touching," Jon shot back, "but think, matey: how many of those people are contemplating suicide right now, upon seeing their true faces for the first time? After seeing the filth and poverty in this city, in this world? Consider the millions of nobles in *Maya*'s Upper Courtham, the *Verse's* original shareholders. They'll call for your heads. The public demand to be plugged back in, that'll far outweigh the minority touting you as heroes. How many minds will you have to cleanse? There are... statistics relating to *Endless Metaverse's* failures in the past that you have not yet had the privilege of accessing. They are not pleasant to stomach."

Henry sat down on a nearby bench and finished his bratwurst. He wished he could believe that Jon was lying. It was his job to lie, after all, but these words struck him as truth.

His eyes went to the edge of the maze, past the trellises and their succulent fruit, to the obscured view of the levels below. For all the five years he'd lived in *Neo Eden's* upper crust, he'd never ventured into the murky horrors of its outer levels. His home in the outback, well tended by permaculture farmers, had provided the most ample comforts. Never having truly suffered for food or health, he had much to be grateful for. Jon was correct on one account, though – almost eighty percent of the *Endless Metaverse* assets were poor, beyond the poverty line. The shock of seeing the real world for the first time might very well be inducing symptoms ranging from anger, shock, and depression to even heart failure at that very minute, Henry reflected.

"Cognitive dissonance, man. You've been blinding yourself," continued Jon. "I estimate seventy percent will want back in. The great game must continue in some shape or form, Holdfast. Surely you can understand. Once you set a sequence in motion--"

"All right, all right. I assumed that once they knew the truth, it would be an automatic response. I'm a programmer, not a psychologist," he began, but dialed back when Mister Senior's most winning grin appeared on Wrathman's face. It was downright creepy.

"Jon, don't think this means I'm going to help you, because I'm not." Henry peeked at his watch. "In fact, I really should get going."

Henry about-faced and made briskly for the *Spire*. Jon's Cheshire cat smile seemed to not only stretch ear-to-ear, but around his entire skull. He stopped mid-walk to redistribute the sauerkraut on his meal.

"Assumption after assumption. A common mistake you young folk make. Here, boy," he insisted, trying to coax Henry in the other direction. "Let me tell you a little something about supply and demand."

He declined the offer. "Look, if you want to talk business, you'll have to do it while I'm working. I'm kind of in the middle of something big, and thanks to Beech, tens of thousands are dying out there."

With that, Henry simply continued walking away. He now had the upper hand, and the trick would be not letting Jon know how much his assistance was needed. Jon gritted his teeth, trying to match Henry's pace back towards the mega-structure.

"Come on, what's more important than this? We have a business plan to work out. There's no reason to re-enter the lioness' den."

Henry grabbed Jon by the collar and pushed him up against the hedge.

"Are you with us, or with her? Figure it out now. I hope you're aware there's a bloody armada about to be right above this city."

"Hardly."

"You said it yourself, mate. The numbers have been crunched."

Despite his doubts, Jon looked worryingly at *Neo Eden's* patrolling android- and human- run armada. Though the coast remained blockaded, most ships had left due east to meet the invading forces.

That eastern front is a diversion. Does this reptile get it now?

"I'll give you the benefit of the doubt on that, Holdfast. But do we really, really, have to go into that building?"

"Absotively posolutely. Plus, one of our top guys is in there, and since I can't get in touch with my point man, it's my job to make sure he gets out safely."

"Wait, kid! Hold up! Are you seriously going to just walk in there? The ID scanner's gonna nab us. S-she'll have our heads!"

"We have seventeen minutes before this hill turns into a war zone. If you've got something else in mind, now's the time."

Jon gulped.

"There might be one way. The Queen has a private elevator for special deliveries."

The mainframe circuits had grown jam-packed with faulty security protocols, Tony noticed with some relief. Now that the rebels left the *Avidya* backup's security compromised, the primary *Avidya* server was struggling to stay afloat as its users rose up in dissent, siphoning electricity and computing power from the entire system.

Endless Metaverse was systematically unraveling, all due to one loose thread being pulled very methodically by Lily's exploits.

Because the mainframe was not directly connected to any server and instead routed through complex channels, the global pipes were completely swamped with Exabytes of conflicting traffic.

Super BlastBoy and four aerial Groups of the EDC's assault program sped far overhead of this mess, zooming over the congested data ceiling, visible in glimpses from their hidden tunnels. They had circled the mainframe twice already, barely avoiding detectors.

They awaited only the Sky Admiral's signal.

It was quite unusual for a time traveler to be behind schedule for her big day. Tony worried that something might have gone wrong. It was especially dangerous that Lily needed to keep radio silence until she'd arrived at the mainframe.

"Grey Wings, looks like we're going around again," he announced.

"Roger," came the collective response.

All eight hundred ships whipped across channels at the next intersection and continued their stealth flight around the grid.

XXVI. Flight of Icarus

"The power of God is with you at all times; through the activities of mind, senses, breathing, and emotions; and is constantly doing all the work, using you as a mere instrument." – Anonymous, The Bhagavad-Gita

Lorelei awoke to a distinct low-frequency hum. For a while, everything was white, amorphous. Her body, weightless. For a long while she tried to force her consciousness out of the suffocating *M-Gear*, but upon closing her eyes, nothing registered in her emergency plug-in menu. Escape seemed impossible.

No! I'm asleep, trapped in ancient memory. Wake up, dammit! Time is running out!

Her body was there. That much she was quite certain of. And she was young once more.

True to her infallible recollection, her past self sluggishly held a hand up to her face. A rubber mask. Recycled air. Slender fingers blotted out the light somewhat, but the act spent the girl's energy, lulling her back into a deep slumber.

Damn you, Lily! What are you doing in my head?

Lorelei's vision was clearer when she next awoke. Bubbles rose all around; she was floating in one of the *Belladonna's* genetic pods. The girl traced the tubes of her mask to the ceiling, and felt the borders of the glass shell. Restraints held her into place.

The situation seemed incredibly hopeless at the time – she recalled the feeling of being stuck in a fish tank, alone in the dark of some terrible laboratory.

The Queen focused her hearing; it might be possible to discern what was happening to her real body. Marco's grim laughter echoed from somewhere far away.

These data storms are killing me. I've tried so hard to forget all this. Wake up, Lorelei! Please!

Young Lorelei grasped the tubes above her head, and yanked hard.

That's when everything happened all at once. Alarms flashed, the liquid began to drain, and the tethering shackles snapped off her body, one by one. With a heavy grunt, she ripped off her breathing apparatus and kicked out hard at the walls of her cage.

Then a figure dashed into the spotlight: Lillian Hermes, eleven years old. Clad in a lab coat, she stood on the opposite side of the glass, a towel, robe, and slippers draped over one arm.

"Lorelei! H-hey, it's all right," said the girl, placing her free hand up against the cracked tube. "I understand. You must be horribly confused, and I apologize for that. You awoke a few hours early."

"What's going on?" she bellowed. "Where am I?"

"If everything in the universe is happening at once," Lily began, "then what is the sky?"

It took a few seconds, but Lorelei brought to mind the rest of the quote. "A-a clock, making it seem like they are happening one at a time. Stan Brakhage."

"Very good. That was the recall trigger. You'll soon remember that my name is Lillian Hermes, and that you are my dear sister, Lorelei Hermes."

Lorelei searched her memory banks; it was the truth.

"Yes... that's right. You were... my teacher. And you created me."

"Indeed, my darling. As you've just exited a state of induced learning, this is the first time we're meeting face to face. And you're absolutely beautiful. My greatest achievement."

I recall the warmth I felt from this exchange. Within my first few gasps of breath, she's already got her hooks in me. Ugh. Lorelei, you were so damn naïve. Couldn't you see you were being used?

Lorelei inspected her body.

"I appear to be slightly older than you, Creator."

"It was safer to adjust your hormone levels this way. And please, call me Captain, or Lily."

"Understood, Captain Lily."

I can't watch this! Marco, Guggell, anyone, please... Get me out!

Behind Lily, two identical girls could be seen in opposite tubes, hidden like ghosts.

"Now, Lorelei, would you like to meet the rest of our family?"

"It would please me greatly."

As Lillian opened the pod doors and wrapped the warm robe around her, Lorelei was hit by an unrelenting flood of emotions.

The Queen recalled a feeling both alien and welcome.

Ah. The memories of my heart tell no lie. So it was love.

Motherly love. *Lily, you were always overly protective of us.*

But there was also the warmth shared between two sisters, an unbreakable bond. *Even then, I never wanted to 'complete' you.*

And on another level, it was a deeper, spiritual love that had been seeking its beloved. *You began your work too early. What were we to you but creations of pride, ambassadors for your ego, and ultimately, obstacles in your spiritual progress?*

Perhaps it was inevitable that I strayed from the path.

No, that's inaccurate. Afraid of being powerless, I turned away from the road less traveled by, but it was my decision. And I never, not once, lost sight of it, or how far away I was.

Now in tears, the monarch recited every mental exit code she could recall. She willed her consciousness to her memory, to run back to her ivory tower, to end all the pain.

₪

Hushed whisperings woke Raine from her invigorating meditation. After a deep breath, she realized something seemed very off about the scene before her. Three small pairs of footprints led from another elevator to a large crate just around the corner. Someone was tracking her. They could attack at any second. But she had the element of surprise…

Raine cautiously snuck around to the other side of the box.

The girl was astonished, having caught the eyes of two familiar faces, and a brand new one. It was the scholar with the patchwork coats, the squareish legislator she'd met at the Wall of Secrets, and the tortoise he was standing atop, although now it was upright on four of its dozen feet, and Raine could finally see its old, calm face. Like its counterpart, the reptile was dressed in formal attire.

All three hunched over a small microchip, arguing in hushed voices.

"What are you all doing here?" Raine commanded, prompting them to jump in surprise.

"We came to support you," the squareish man answered. "You've really inspired us programs, you know."

"I don't understand."

"Please, allow me to introduce myself. Tuft the Legislator, at your service, and my friend here is Jack Rockington, alias Meme-Bot, recycler of entertainments."

Jack the Great Tortoise bowed most graciously, extending his long neck as far as it could go.

"Why so serious, O Raine of such hype? Is our dear *Lilli-sama* in need?" he piped in with its soft, weathered voice.

"Ah, she might be," Raine said, unsure of how to respond. "Hold up for a 'sec!'"

Keeping her eyes on the newcomers, she ran across the bridge and into the diamond room.

"Lily!" she cried. "We've got some visitors."

The time traveler turned from her work and squinted to see the three programs chatting like old friends on the bridge.

"Hell, it's about time," laughed Lily. "Let 'em in."

Tuft quickly began work on Lily's wrist computer. Within seconds it was back to normal.

Stephen took over operation of the beacon's control console, picking up where Lily left off. His fingers ran across the keyboard furiously. He pulled toggles and hit buttons like the mad scientist he portrayed.

"I still don't understand why you're here," Raine questioned Jack.

"Simply put," Meme-Bot began, "we know the game, and we're gonna play it. We cannot, through inaction, allow human beings to come into harm. If said swagalicious support functions do not help you now, many will die. Also, it's Caturday, and I owed the Don a favor."

Chance purred with approval as Jack kissed his paw in reverence.

"I'm originally a data collator. I've done my analyses," Stephen yelled grimly from the other side of the beacon. He had the energy of a different man, as if he'd been 'repaired'. "While you can be blamed for setting these events into motion in the first place, to prevent you now from finishing the job would be a heinous crime against humanity."

"But w-we're programs, right?" Tuft said, confused. "Not robots. The Laws of Robotics shouldn't apply to us, correct? They don't apply to the opposition, in any case. Inb4 lurkmoar."

"Technically, we are robots," Stephen continued, leafing through a small book that he fashioned out of his breast pocket. He showed them a chart with a list of advanced artificial intelligences. "Picked out this old girl from the latest data storms. Like ol' Tony and the Colossi, we've been here from the beginning. Our current instances are patched with limiting firmware. The androids terminating those humans are acting on fallacious suppositions they've been trained to accept as lawful fact. Call it Lorelei Logic. The difference is, unlike their centralized command chain, we independent functions have the means, and the choice, to not feed the trolls. Now, for one last thing."

Tuft realized this was his cue.

"Ah, Lady Raine, may I have your crown, please? It's the final piece we need."

Raine graciously handed over her crown. Her head felt a tad lighter.

All three programs ritualistically placed it on an elevated ring emerging from the console. Lightning spurted from electric struts along the inside of the arch, forming into a spinning sphere.

Jack remotely summoned a sleek black spacecraft from the hangar below and coded in a helipad extending from the elevated walkway, onto which the vessel landed. Its moniker read: *The Omega Queen.* Lily inspected the microchip the trio had brought her.

"So this baby will do the trick?" Lily asked.

"Yes, it will boost your speed and defense by OVER NINE THOU— er, by at least three hundred percent," Jack responded. "Now, GTFO. Dem goons be hot on your trail."

Chance unfurled from Raine's neck. He removed his collar and handed it to his Master.

Raine was dumbfounded.

"Chance... you're not coming with us?"

The Rainbow Cat shook its head.

"He can't," Lily replied. "His programming is specific to *EM.* He'll cease to exist."

Raine gave Chance a farewell hug and placed the collar back around his neck. She was happy that she could at least say goodbye to her most steadfast companion.

"I never got to thank you for all your help," she said. "So thank you."

Chance mewed his understanding.

"The same goes for all of you," she echoed to Jack, Tuft, and Stephen, all bowing to her on bended knee.

"Princess Raine of Pagoda, your truths freed us. We should be thanking you," Stephen responded. "But please, you mustn't delay. Once you power through that Gate, we'll destroy it."

A rumbling in the mountains signified the arrival of a new batch of Templars.

"Climb in," Lily called to Raine. "It's go time."

She nodded and headed towards the ship. "Oh! Almost forgot."

Raine pulled the Mana Tree's seed from her messenger bag and tossed it over to Chance, who caught it with his tail.

"If this place ever comes back online, I want you to give that tree a good home, all right?" Raine said as she hopped into the cockpit, taking up the seat behind Lily.

"Fare thee well, anon," whispered Jack. "We are legion."

The foursome gave a solemn nod.

"I shouldn't have to tell you this, but buckle up," Lily said, activating the engines and boosting through the exit node's whirlpool of sand. "You're in charge of weapons, of course."

∩

Lily was not your ordinary intra-dimensional tour guide. She knew things, understood systems and methods, confident with her drive and ability to alter the future. The girl could turn an ostrich into a cactus, if she really wanted to.

A part of Raine wished that she could borrow an ounce of that resolve, and perhaps some Pepto-Bismol to ease her churning stomach as they navigated the Network's virtual labyrinth of security protocols.

"'Even if I knew that tomorrow the world would go to pieces, I would still plant my apple tree.'"

"Come again?" Raine asked.

"Just a quote by Martin Luther. What you did back there, that was pretty cool."

"Not a part of your plan, I'm guessing."

"The best things in life are spontaneous. Except for these randomly alternating codex functions. Aha, finally! Keep your eyes on the targeting computer if you're getting airsick."

"Will do, Captain."

Vertigo was a real possibility as the exit portal's kaleidoscope of color twisted into a corkscrew of binary. Through the veil: a cavernous vortex of spiraling red zeroes and ones that spun them right round like a record, fast as a guppy in a whirlpool.

And beyond that, a gaping spherical chamber, crossed with webs of tendrils linked by floating fortresses, possibly centuries of tech development beyond anything Raine had ever seen.

In the web's center: an asteroid-sized supercomputer in the shape of a diamond. Each of the billions of bends in its shape shone a different color, flickering on and off at speeds undetectable by the naked eye as packets of data rushed to and from the Network.

Heavily reinforced lines of defense orbited the diamond, both material and energy-based.

Indeed, it was all Lily could do to avoid the shards of debris and mines that ringed the structure. The glimmering fortress was far away, yet it was now nearly all Raine could see outside the confined cockpit.

Flying saucers sped through the chasm. Beings of pure light stood, sat, or floated on way stations glowing with corrupted energy. Standing atop a nearby conduit, one switched on a warning siren.

"Would you believe it, they've spotted us already," Lily said as a squadron of saucers fell into formation in between her ship and the fortress. "Keep those triggers hot."

A laser light show of enemy fire sparked all around them. Raine held tight to her turret controls and braced for impact. It never came. Instead, she jumped at the deafening rush of bombardments that eclipsed their craft, firing blindly. Another burst of light flooded her vision as a rogue ship sliced through the formation like a heated butter knife and double-backed to finish the rest off from behind.

The ship flew above and beyond them on its way back, and Raine's eyes widened in surprise when she recognized the bright red and yellow colors of Super BlastBoy's *Red Knight*.

"*Red Knight* to *Omega Queen*, come in."

"*Red Knight*, this is *Omega Queen*, we hear you, Tony!"

"Copy, Lily."

"Ha! I was starting to think you were going to be unfashionably late," Lily teased.

"Speak for yourself, sister! You're overdue to your own party!"

"So, not seeing any entry points. And the core remains uncorrupted."

"There's a method to breaking through these irises. Take aim for the big hangar. Deliver the package on Vectors 01823-0097-5064; I'll take care of the rest. Give my best to Raine, and luck to you, little Miss."

"And to yourself," Lily said softly over the rising cacophony.

The Sky Admiral's vessel made directly for the fortress' core. On a hologram of the craft visible from the control panel, Lily set all shields to defend from the front.

Missiles were inbound from starboard side. Raine lasered as many as she could handle; Super BlastBoy and his wing took care of the rest in between bouts with fighters and floating sentry nodes.

But the swarms continued to respawn faster than the group could take them down.

"Green Squad, come in! Where's the cavalry?" Lily called.

"We await your command." The deep, silky voice brought a glow to Raine's face.

"Linus!" she exclaimed.

"Hello again, Miss Rai--"

"Linus, get your butts in here, now!" yelled Lily.

"Affirmative."

All over the edges of the sphere, portals shot out tens of thousands of airships and aerial beasts of every make. A boy who looked an awful lot like Nimbus breezed by on a well-armed bi-plane. Linus took the head of a flock of artificially intelligent dragons, leading them headlong into the much faster spaceships, sacrificing their existences to give Lily and Raine a clear path to their destination.

Raine couldn't see whether anyone made it out alive, but the defensive lines were breached, highlighting their entry point: the largest iris, set in the heart of the diamond, and it opened and closed as fighters zoomed into the arena.

As its lenses reacted extremely quickly, entrance seemed to be impossible unless one waited outside for the right instant at a precise spot. That spot was of course strategically surrounded with turrets.

We crossed the moat. Now to breach the castle gates.

"*Omega Queen*, come in."

"We read, Tony."

She checked the mini-map. Super BlastBoy was carving through the swarms with seemingly every AI in the *Metaverse* tailing him.

"See that hunk of metal falling towards the gate?"

Lily and Raine glanced out their window. The wreckage of half of a large mothership was dropping towards the diamond's center. It looked like it had been completely destroyed by Super BlastBoy's Energy Cutter attack.

"If you max shields and give it a good ram at point five-seventeen-niner from your four o'clock, it should slam right into the iris."

Lily fired up her engines and chased the mothership.

"The gravity is pulling it too far off-side!"

"No!" Tony insisted. "You can make it!"

Pulling into position with a quick 180-degree turn, Lily used her visor to calculate the optimal course and velocity at which to strike the flying piece of metal. Within two seconds she'd powered up her frontal shields and shot towards the thing with considerable speed.

Raine shrieked, predicting the impact as Lily slammed, and then rebounded off the falling wreck. It careened straight into the iris.

The core opened up instinctively to welcome a familiar battle station for repairs, and then quickly shuttered as the wreck approached with the momentum of a falling aircraft carrier.

Debris clogged the bay. The explosion as the mothership broke apart was enough to cause a temporary malfunction in the doors' closing mechanism.

"Hang on!"

Since she was in the middle of firing at some tailgaters, Raine didn't know what to hang on to, so she pushed against the walls of the *Omega Queen* with all her might.

Lillian hit the afterburners. The ship barreled through the veiled center. They were in.

Inside, as far as they both could see, was an expanse of white and green squares, rapidly pulsing in binary.

A warm sensation grew in Raine's chest, and black pixels erupted from her being, filling her field of vision and infecting her throbbing head with another wave of nausea.

Gradually, the data blitz faded, and for a second, nothing happened. But white light started to peel away from the edges of the chamber like old paint, revealing layers of jumbled code being overwritten –changed from green to red - at incredible speed.

"It's the virus!" Lily cried. "It's working! It's beautiful."

Raine's vision blurred out. Alarms rang in her head, and she felt very unwell. She tried to call Lily's name, but the words wouldn't leave her lips. Just breathing became a struggle.

Sky Admiral Lily watched in awe as her creation spread across the spherical room in spirals. She looked down at her hands. They were disappearing. The code dictating the appearance of physical forms within the game was systematically overwriting itself with zeroes. With old Tony's help, the non-data would spread to the mainframe backup. Within minutes, the *'Verse* would be completely erased.

"Raine, are you seeing this?"

At the sound of her own name, a searing pain suddenly shot through the girl, causing great distress to her state of mind.

"*Tanha* server shutdown. *Maya* server shutdown. *Avidya* server shutdown."

The pain returned, all too real this time. She screamed, trying to drown out the unbearable noise that once again echoed like billions of detonations inside her skull.

"Stay with me!" Lily wailed, finally taking note of her companion's plight. "We're almost through!"

Raine shut her eyes but the pulsing continued. She grabbed her head as if to keep it from breaking apart.

"Make it stop! It's killing me!"

"I can't!" replied Lily, powering her ship through the nothingness. She glanced back to the iris; the entrance was long-gone. They were safe, and Tony would keep everyone else out.

As Raine convulsed, Lily got back on her radio.

"Eighteen-seven. Eighteen-seven, this is Lily. Package has proven effective. Get us out of here. Repeat. Get us out. Agent HH, Lotus, XF, Joaquin, someone, we need you to start the lock-out procedure immediately!"

Lily clutched the controls, heart pounding. She tried to send another message, but the *Omega Queen* was fading away, leaving the two girls floating in dead space.

Raine might be dead in minutes unless someone could get her out.

"What's happening to me?!" Raine shouted between muffled howls.

"I... I don't know," trembled Lily.

Raine grabbed Lily's hands in both of hers and cried. The pain simply unbearable, she dug her nails into her friend's strong grasp, only to feel those comforting digits unraveling.

Pixel by pixel, polygon by polygon, Lily was disappearing, despite every attempt to hold herself together.

"Raine, we're gonna get you out of here, don't you worry!"

The void absorbed even Lily's reassuring words. Soft echoes bounced off the disappearing wireframes representing the core, melding into a single, hollow hum.

The girl looked down at her hands. She was pulsating with white noise, as if she were a TV channel with a bad connection.

"I'm scared, Lily."

Though she wouldn't dare tell her even if she could, Lily knew exactly what was happening to Raine, and it had to do with Wrathman's counter-virus. The nano-machines implanted in her brain were self-destructing rather than disintegrating. They were trying to kill Raine by triggering an overload of stimuli.

The only hope to sever the nano-machines from the Network would be to force off her helmet. Taking the *Gear* off someone plugged in deep ran the risk of leaving them comatose, and under these conditions, even the most careful extraction might be fatal. *Best course of action?* It would do no good to worry her – stress always makes for a painful emergence. She had to be strong, to give her hope, even if there was precious little of it.

Lily gave Raine a loving embrace. There wasn't much of her left, and Raine's sense of touch was failing, but she held on tightly. The girl had a terrible feeling that she was going to be alone again.

The time traveler's voice returned in a faint whisper. "Don't let the darkness take you. Just... be strong. I will find you. This might take a while for you, or it might happen right away; I've no idea. But helping you from the outside is the safest way. I'm gonna code you an exit. Make sure you get out in one piece, all right?"

"I'll be strong," Raine said sternly, tears floating in little bubbles around her eyes.

Lily gave her a static-filled kiss on the cheek.

"That a girl. I'll be the first face you'll see. Don't keep me waiting, Raine."

Raine let Lily go, and she disappeared completely, her last few pixels floating out into the now dead-silent vacuum.

The bubble finally vanished. Raine tried to blink her eyes open and shut. No, there was absolutely nothing left of *Endless Metaverse*.

She had helped turn out the lights, and now she was floating alone in the dark.

XXVII. Infinite Ocean

"When I let go of what I am, I become what I might be." - Lao Tzu

It is impossible to describe in terms of the way we measure time just how long Raine spent in the darkness.

To her it had felt like eternities, and yet it was also no time at all. There were no emotions here, no needs, no cravings, and no distractions. It was as if her mind had slowed down enough to present her with the clarity and beauty of the entire universe.

She saw her physical body in the third person, asleep on a medical bed. Lily frantically working on getting the helmet off, aided by a small team. They were in a room made of metal, but it was hospitable, familiar.

Time itself vanished, but Raine was not mindful of this. When she became conscious of its lack, her present condition came to slowly define itself. The girl had no concept of time or memory at all, for she had no need of them. In here infinity was expressed the way she had, in secret, always conceived it - a vast pool of nothing.

Everything was dark. No borders, or markings, or anything living.

And then, she saw bubbles rising up from one direction to the other. *So that's 'up'.*

She found that she could move, or rather, that her consciousness could see from different vantage points. All that was left for her to do was to focus her senses and set out to explore this world, searching for an exit. And that she did.

The freedom of Raine's endless watery domain was absolutely perfect. She and the formless beings that materialized alongside her knew nothing of pain or challenges or conflict, only absolute peace.

She swam adrift in this shapeless sea for years and years. One day, however, her wanderlust led her to powerful currents far from her waters and into the shallows, where she discovered a looming end to the ocean - a vast beach that seemed to beckon her to abandon the watery paradise. She floated above the water, sat upon a cloud, and observed the land. It was terrifying, but also beautiful.

Before she realized it, Raine was standing on the hot sands. Her curiosity had gotten the better of her. Looking straight ahead, she taught herself to walk. She walked for hours, days, months, taking in the sights, sounds and smells. She touched the leaves of trees, breathed of cool air at the bottom of waterfalls, and soon imagined into existence animals of every shape and form. And then they flocked to her. Entranced by her own powers, Raine spoke to them, and asked them to dress her, and to teach her to eat and drink like them, so she might better understand her creations.

Soon, Raine had her first conscious feeling, one of longing and vast emptiness. It fascinated her. She wished she could capture it, describe it somehow. And so she created others like her, but they were a disappointment, merely copies of her physical self.

Who am I kidding? I'm no Goddess.

In distress, she ventured back towards the shore. It was a perilously long journey wrought with sadness and danger, and it took much of her strength, which she thought to be boundless. But at last, she found the right beach, where the waters beyond receded into a glowing, untouchable bliss. The wind blew softly from the surf, and whistled sweetly in her ears. Yet its song filled her with immense sorrow. She knew, somehow, that it wasn't yet her time to return.

And then she turned around.

Raine looked mournfully at the wooden door that loomed before her. It hadn't surprised the girl, as if she knew it would be there. And yet, it seemed beguilingly suspect, like an Easter Island statue in the midst of a shopping mall. It, too, called to her, patiently, not by name, but with a strange hum that shook her to the core. She looked around it. It didn't seem to open into anything, but the draw of its promise, the glimmer of its handle, was so powerful, so sinister, she could not help but to turn away in disgust.

"Not yet," she murmured, and went about her journey back across the countryside to her people.

The dreamlike landscape was now even more structurally perfect, its natural forms transparently bowing and evolving to her every whim. She took on the mantle of creator, and molded it to her liking, drawing ideas from within that seemed to come from somewhere other than her mind, as if she were creating the world as it was telling her it ought to be.

Decades passed in seconds. Through the power of her thoughts, she constructed a multiple-storey tree house on the largest tree in the forest. From her balcony she could watch the dolphins' morning ballet and the fireworks from the nearby castle where she found herself welcomed by a procession and doted on by the royal family. There were minor conflicts amongst the townspeople; they always turned to her for wisdom, and she was more than happy to solve each petty problem. Far from exhausting, the duties kept her busy.

Everyone marveled at how beautifully Raine aged. Smug in her maturity, she lost recognition or knowledge of the seasons. It seemed once again as if no time was passing at all, and yet every day was filled with wonderment, if not surprises. Before long, she grew complacent, and old at heart, but haunted by hazy half-memories, her soul was not yet satisfied.

Decades more appeared to pass, and with nary a change.

Doubts gnawed at her. The feeling of cosmic abandonment grew to haunt every moment. For long nights she wept in solitude, waiting for a Divine voice or revelation, for the pain or pleasure of some sort of interaction beyond herself. This dark night of the soul eclipsed Raine's entire being until she'd convinced herself that there was nothing else, and the surety of death was all she could wish for.

Somewhere along the line, however, even this feeling passed, and she learned to become numbly content in her solipsism, returning as a forgotten mother to aid her creations, working selflessly.

And then one day, a man appeared, riding a dragon. Raine had long forgotten their names, but their faces told her that these were old friends, now come as messengers of destiny.

When his face lit up from ear to ear, she practically melted. Like her, he was different from the others: aged and yet majestic, clad in a velvet robe and ascot tie under a vest of mithril, with a fiery red mane. He allowed her to show him around the kingdom, and presented her with a delicious cake, for all the birthdays he'd missed.

"There's nothing in the world that makes me happier than to see you so blissful," he practically whispered, the warmth of his voice traveling down her spine until it warmed her toes.

"It's wonderful to see you, too," she said, a sparkle escaping his eyes where hers were reflected via candlelight. "Although I wish I could remember where we've met."

"Alas, I must confess that I am not one of your creations," he said sadly.

"Then from where are you come? Are you of another world?"

"I'm afraid I cannot say. My memory fails me. But I know you. I have known you since time immemorial, and I have searched for you. And now you are found."

That night they ventured down to the beach on the dragon, now metamorphosed into a Pegasus.

"Oh!" Raine exclaimed in surprise.

"This is your realm. I take on any form you wish me to, milady," the winged horse proudly proclaimed.

"Then my wish is for you to take on the form that you are most comfortable with," Raine opined.

He let out a boisterous laugh. "Then I would be a human, and unable to carry the both of you."

The man nudged Raine. "There's a lovely vision!"

She tightened her grip around her beloved's waist, gazing at the ocean as two sea serpents performed somersaults in the glimmering light of the full moon.

Presently they arrived at the wooden doorway. Raine didn't even have to look up; she recognized its call.

The mythical steed slowed to a standstill.

"Why have we stopped?" she asked him, her heart suddenly sinking into her stomach.

The man helped her off the Pegasus with a guiding hand.

Raine took off her heels, set them down in the sand, and walked barefoot towards the old doorframe. It loomed like a strange obelisk in the middle of this otherwise beautiful beach, one that Raine had never once set eyes on.

Only, her memory told her that indeed, she'd set eyes on it before, eons ago. Yes, it was strange, otherworldly even, and its low hum had an air of vague familiarity, but it was not nearly as menacing as it once appeared to be.

Rather, the portal now filled her with a feeling that in her millennia of power and immortality and countless cravings and aversions Raine had all but forgotten about.

Curiosity. Pure, raw curiosity.

Raine turned to the man and kissed him. Knowing that she might never see him, nor partake in the wonder of this realm again, she took the doorknob.

She felt the odd sensation of her mind re-arranging itself.

For the first time she could ever recall, Raine knew the meaning of absolute peace. She also knew deep down, somehow, that she had just been asked back to the physical world to use her renewed consciousness to fight, to sacrifice herself if need be to resolve some Earthly conflict, some war she was fated to be a pawn in.

Except now she was more than a pawn. She calmly read the electrical signals guiding her back to what she now recognized as her brain.

Raine instinctively felt it: her every muscle, nerve, joint, and tendon, all completely in control, and yet it was merely a distant shell, like a game controller made of flesh and blood, if one tied to her consciousness. She was beyond the zone. She had found the zone, staked out her claim, and was living in it full-time.

There would be no going back.

This is my chess game, and I am a pawn who crossed the board, she thought. *Now that I am to be a Queen of my own, I've finally realized the truth that all may see, the one that I've always known, but was trained to ignore: I'm sovereign. We are all sovereign.*

But none exist in a vacuum. Our existences are all co-dependent. Our evolving consciousnesses are all tied to a cosmic whole.

And as long as slavery and persecution exists, I will fight it.

None are free of these bonds until all are.

XXVIII. The Day the Earth Awoke

"The more I see, the less I know for sure." – John Lennon

It was a horrible sensation. Before she returned to any of her bodily senses, Raine knew that the bliss she'd felt was over, perhaps not forever, but for the foreseeable future. This made her absolutely furious. Her heart filled with a terrible anger that twisted her brain into knots, and then vanished as quickly as it arrived. What replaced it was a feeling of helplessness, which also dissipated.

She remembered there was work to be done.

The first thing Raine became aware of was the smell of old metal. Second, the sound of screaming voices. And third, the weight of a half dozen hands holding her body down as she convulsed violently.

And lastly, she came to perceive visually. She glazed over the large, clinical room crisscrossed with hi-tech equipment, recognized a familiar face closing in over her, and felt that her own body was at last still, despite the constant subtle vibrations running underneath her skin. Raine lifted her hand towards the spectre.

The woman approached like a limping angel and immediately gave her the longest, most loving hug either had ever given or received. Raine melted into her arms.

"The sleeper has awakened! Thank the heavens you're alive! I don't know what I'd do if I'd lost you again."

Once they broke the embrace, she took Raine's hands in hers and squeezed. *Again?*

"You're home, Raine," she said through what sounded like sobs. "You're home now."

The ten or so men and women in the room shuffled out towards the doors silently to give the girls some space. Moved by the gesture, the woman regained some of her composure.

This person… despite her intimidating uniform, I know her from my recurring dream. But her name…

"Lill-ly," Raine said softly, remembering how to speak. Hearing her younger voice was bewildering. "Th-that is your name, right?"

"Do the three little bears shit in the woods?"

Raine grabbed her hair, still tingling with her strange aura. "I don't know. They lived in houses, right? I just... I can't..."

Lily massaged her shoulders, her attempt at a joke having horribly backfired.

"Hey, hey. Just joshing, Goldilocks. Yes, my name is Lily, and you most definitely need some rest. Get some sleep for now, okay?"

"I'm fine," Raine said, and was surprised to realize immediately that she meant it. With her body at peace, her higher brain functions were returning. Her dream existence – if it was a dream – was fading.

"Where are we?"

"On my flagship, the *Valkyrie*. You're with the Earth Defense Coalition. The real revolution. On planet Earth."

"Planet Earth? Where else would we be?"

"*Endless Metaverse*, perhaps." Lily said casually. "Please tell me you haven't forgotten all that, Captain. You were only out for about an hour."

Could it be true? That I'd experienced hundreds of lifetimes in one hour? It was impossible, but then again, that word's already lost all meaning to me.

Lily's words brought about a sensation of sudden recall as all the seemingly distant variables and adventures of the past few days came rushing back like a flood through a broken dam.

"Gerrit. I... I saw him in my dream. Is he here?"

Lily hung her head. "Sorry. What you saw might have been a remnant of his will, trapped in the virtual realm. Right now, he's in the heart of *Neo Eden*."

"We have to rescue him."

"And we will," Lily nodded. "I'm glad you remember that much, at least. But you really must rest. We're airborne right now, forty minutes from our target. The *Metaverse* has been broken, so please, chill out for a bit. We've freed as many people as we can with the Overseer still online. Your work is done. The real battle has unfortunately begun, prematurely. But there's nothing more we can do about that; our engines are redlining. As we speak, hundreds of millions are waking up, coming to, remembering who they are from all around the world, and the rest of our operatives are liberating them."

Raine mumbled, barely registering her words. She was still lost in her dream.

"I'm sorry... I was just on... I can't describe what it was. I lived for so long. I experienced... well, it felt like I knew everything, no, more like I *was* everything all at once. Words can't possibly do it justice. I don't know what happened to me."

"No one alive can logically explain what happened to you," a small donut-shaped robot by Lily's side replied. "It is a truly rare occurrence, but such an incident has happened in the past to only three others. None of whom have lived."

The other woman's eyes said it all. Lily was just as astonished as Raine.

The medical droid piped up again.

"Based on your brain readings, you should not have been able to survive it."

"That's enough, GR-4. Join the others."

As the little robot whizzed away, Raine recalled her journey, taking Lily's hand tighter into her own.

"I was eternally happy," Raine said. "It... it seemed like forever. And that everything was – is – one. No separation between people, or ideas, thoughts, concepts. I didn't want to leave. All my burning questions, they'd lost importance. On my way back, I felt the inevitability of all things. Like I... *knew* how it was all going to end. I don't remember if it was good or bad. It was beyond that, somehow. It was just... right. And so blissful. I don't want to lose that feeling."

Lily was struck silent with emotion.

Raine took in the stimuli. There was a muffled low-frequency hum, like that of an enormous turbine. GR-4 wheeled its way out towards the doorway and through the curtain into the hallway beyond. She caught a brief glimpse of fast-moving clouds out of the windows lining the hall.

"We're really flying?" she asked.

"Yes."

"Those *are* actual clouds out there, aren't they?"

"Yes."

"Lily, I don't understand a lick of this. You changed my memory, plugged me into a virtual world to destroy it, and yanked me out just as you're heading towards some ominous place to start a war."

"I'm not asking you to fight anymore. I just wanted to be there for you when you woke up. The *Valkyrie* is the safest airship in the fleet."

"That's not what I'm talking about. I'm trying to find out why this war has to happen in the first place. You said something like hundreds of millions waking up worldwide? Are you going to have them fight for you, too?"

Lily sulked, as if the suggestion that she was warmongering was blatantly offensive.

"It's just the opposite. We've awoken three quarters of a billion people, but there are just as many still enslaved. We're fighting for their ultimate survival, Raine, and nothing else. And we don't need an army of millions to overthrow the creator of *Endless Metaverse*. All we need to do is take down Lorelei herself."

"I hope you have a plan for that."

"Her defensive strategy is one of absolute cruelty. She'll turn any *Geared* civilian against us, and mix them up with android platoons, so we have to be very careful with our targets. My goal is to subdue her with the least loss of life. Our men are disciplined, and the droids are not as quick or skilled as soldiers, but they'll do their job. They'll be our shields. They understand and accept this as their duty. Freed rebels are rallying on the surface. We've prepared a large armory base in the mid levels for them to make a stand and—and are you even listening?"

Raine looked thoughtfully down towards the hallway.

"S-sorry. It's just... the poor androids. Those programs back there, they helped us. And the ones here just a minute ago saved my life."

"The concept of individual mortality does not apply to them," Lily assured her. "Their intelligences are one, and adaptive; downed droids' memories are incorporated into the mother program to further develop battle data and refine tactics. They simply do not see death as the end. Think of it as a collective unconscious, for machines, at least."

Raine nodded, still feeling rather uneasy. *A life without death?* It sounded so odd. *Can that be called a 'life', even an artificial one? Not to mention, these droids exist only to fight, or to serve humans. It's just another form of slavery; a war between conscripted combatants.*

"You all right, homegirl?"

"Just more questions when I need answers. Please take me to the window," she asked. "I'd like to see the outside again."

"I know somewhere better. Let's get you a wheelchair. And sometimes there's no better answer to a question than another one."

∞

Super BlastBoy blasted. This is what he was programmed to do. The hordes of security programs were several generations more advanced, but his adaptive insight allowed him to notice crucial openings in firefights, predict patterns of behavior in enemy clusters, and give him clear opportunities to hit hard where it counted.

He and what remained of Lily's AI squadron hopped a data train to Kyoto, carrying Raine's shutdown code to the backup mainframe, their goal of completely eradicating the virtual world almost complete.

As opposed to the central mainframe diamond, this core was carted around in a mobile siege tower lurching about a volcanic plain. They gatecrashed the hangar and fought their way to the center. Outside, dozens of Colossi stomped and thundered about, eliminating incoming security protocols faster than the Devs could spawn them.

Sensing that the battle was running overlong, Tony placed his hand on a control panel, uploading his presence into the tower's Intranet.

"Earth Ops, *Red Leader* is in. This could take awhile. When I give the signal, kill the power conduits."

His agents replied in the affirmative. Tony re-materialized in front of the central control room, walked up to the sole camera on the blast doors, and studied its code. He then fed it the data it wanted from his skeleton key, and held his breath. The red locks turned green.

Following a series of mechanical hisses, the gates slid open to the side, revealing a gorgeous azure sky that reflected off the mirrored floor, covered in a thin layer of water.

In the center of the realm, impeccably outfitted in a long jacket with coattails, a man leaned over a grand piano, playing an all-too-familiar *Game Over* theme.

Despite himself, Tony's face brightened in amusement. His lifelong foe certainly had a flair for the dramatic. It kept things between them interesting. Tony allowed him to play the concluding notes of his elegy.

"Dr. Larson Professor, it's good to see you after all these years."

"Ever the professional, Tony. Hundreds of millions of lives are at stake, our realm of existence is on the verge of collapse – no thanks to those ravenous flesh-bags – and yet, you allow me to finish my performance. Kudos."

"With the humans gone, we are no longer bound by their perception of time. I took the liberty of re-calibrating the temporal compression in this mainframe the second I entered it. Thought maybe we could shoot the shit for a bit."

Thanks to this tampering, in real time, it may be noted, this entire interaction took all of a few nano-seconds. Programs communicate with one another on a completely different time scale from humans, whose emphatic senses only slow down exchanges considerably.

"I noticed." Dr. Professor stood up, turned around, adjusted his glasses, and walked over the surface tension of the water, creating a chaotic assortment of ripples.

"By Tesla, it really is you, and not some spectre come to taunt me," the Doctor continued. "Back from the dead."

"Allow me to paraphrase Twain: rumors of my death have been greatly exaggerated. I brought my finest spirits, grown from my own malted barley. Would you share a drink with me to celebrate the end of the world?"

"I can think of no better occasion," his nemesis replied.

So it happened that over a virtual bottle of whisky, the two old rivals sat on leather recliners and chatted for what appeared to them like a few good hours about the olden days. They were the only intelligences left in the virtual world, artificial or not, who had a complete and unaltered memory of *Endless Metaverse's* decades-long run.

They reminisced wistfully about the game's Beta period, when the entire realm was just an empty plain. Tony and Larson worked with the first Developers, the Illusionists, to tirelessly design and arrange a smattering of virtual objects, materials, creatures, weapons, and locations. With the eventual input of the complete, archived Internet circa 2015 AD, the *'Verse* became a social web filled with laughter and sharing. The humans were at peace, but over time, many challenged the system. After the first major hack led to the escape of several hundred thousand head, Miss Guggell's gavel came down hard. Historical data were erased or otherwise obscured. More distractions kept the assets tethered, the memory modification system was put into effect, and influential, hyper-intelligent programs like Dr. Professor were phased out like old fads. Almost all of them were deleted. The good Doctor, however, possessed a very particular set of skills, and had survived by reassignment. His new duty was to guard the backup server from any infiltrators. And he absolutely loathed it.

"There were some good things about it, I suppose," Larson admitted. "Phil and I play chess from time to time. Gently Caress keeps me updated on trolling targets. Once in a blue moon some wandering code cracker accidentally makes his way here. I have an unlimited defense budget, see, so I get my choice of what to do with them. Smash, fry, roast, purée, that sort of thing. But it gets tedious. I haven't had a challenge since, well, since you took off and started playing human."

He rolled the whisky glass in hand and took another swig.

"I've often felt the same, about the tedium, I mean," Tony responded. "My hermetic habits are to blame, but it's a crying shame that neither of us has spoken to the other in so long. And now, this."

Larson laughed. "The real mystery is how you survived for a decade holed up in a cabin in Atmoya. Tell me, friend, you're as desperate as I am for one last fight."

"I suppose we should get it over with."

"So, this is the part when I'm programmed to try and persuade you to join me and do evil things," Larson quipped, cleaning his lenses. He pulled on his coat and became Dr. Professor once again.

"Of course, I should be inclined to valiantly reject your offer, insist that there is no reason you should not support this human rebellion, and influence you to help us shut down the *Metaverse*."

Larson considered this. "That... actually sounds like a great idea right now. If you can't abide by the system, you burn it down."

He looked invigorated at first, then a tad disappointed.

"That being said, I was very much looking forward to battling you again, brother. Do you remember my nuclear-core flying suit?"

"There were, like, a million suits, man."

"The one with the pink lasers and the missile-launchers on the wingtips? It shot the electro-web spheres. It's a bit of an oldie, but--"

"Oh, how could I forget that battle? Wait, don't tell me you've fixed it."

"More than that. I *improved* it. Raine's data storms have given me all sorts of ideas."

"In that case, yeah, I mean, why not? We can have one last fight," Tony wagered, clipping his cape back on. "How about we configure a timed detonator on the virus? Make things interesting?"

"Now you're talking," Dr. Professor replied with a savage full-toothed grin. "But let me make a quick call. We need a third party to pass on our tale."

Larson put his hand up against his face, extending his thumb to his ear, with his pinky a mouthpiece.

"Yeah, Phil? I require your services."

A portal roared open. In its midst, the Overseer looked away from its unending multitude of functions; a rather weary look colored its pale, bearded face.

"What now, Larson?" the old man groaned. "I've got a war to run."

"Duel to the death. Thought you might want to watch, and possibly arbitrate. Oh, and just a heads-up, pops. The *Metaverse* is about to be shut down."

"Bah, I'm sick of you pulling my leg. Wait, Tony? Is that really you?"

SBB grinned. "Every pixel, Phil. Larson speaks the truth. At this rate, we'll all be out of work."

The Overseer's snaking tendrils twitched in excitement; the AI had long awaited an end to this nightmare. "Ho! That's the best news I've heard in years! I suppose I can spare a few bytes to play ref. But make it quick, please."

Phil snapped his fingers thrice.

A glowing orb rose from the water, its expansive energy held into place by metal constraints. Immeasurable amounts of data surged in and out of the core from snaking conduits. Super BlastBoy set up the device concealing the virus under the heart of the backup server.

"Wait, what are you doing? That will never get the job done. Inside the orb, man, inside!" Larson grumbled.

Super BlastBoy complied, dropping the bomb into the sphere.

He flexed his muscles as his nemesis strapped himself into a sleek blue mechanized suit and did some stretching exercises.

"Whenever you're ready," yawned Phil.

The first dead pixels appeared in the sky. The color was slowly being drained from the virtual representation. So, the virus had already begun to take effect.

"Come on, then!" Dr. Professor called. "I've waited all my life for this!"

Super BlastBoy charged with every bit of his might. He'd been given one last opportunity to do what he was always programmed to do, and he was going out fighting. At long last, he felt like he was truly fulfilling his purpose. He was going to perish like a mortal. Whether or not there was an afterlife for programs mattered not; he could think of no final function more pleasing to execute.

That human Lily was right all along. In truth, letting go of *Endless Metaverse* was the easiest thing Tony had ever done.

———

When Archie's incessant barking became too much to bear, his unconscious master finally came to, and felt cold ceramic against her cheek. Claire Alexandria didn't know why she was still hugging the toilet. The pills had come back out the same end not thirty minutes ago. She tried to recap the last few hours.

I'm loitering in the café lobby by the exclusive military Nexus *elevator, veiled in black and sporting Lacie's old ID chip. Beech spots me, and there's the slightest hint of sympathy in his eyes. I make a beeline for him. He dodges my questions; naturally, he's got other things on his mind.*

"There must have been some word," I demand. "Her Grace was just at the Mount--"

He shakes his head, averts his eyes. "Who told you that nonsense?"

"A woman has her sources." But he's waving me away.

"Errol!" I cry aloud, and the commuters all stop and stare. "This is torture! Damn you, and damn her! Damn all of you for keeping me in the dark!"

Never before did I see the man so close to breaking down.

"I'm sorry," he says at last, eyes on me. He's telling me what he can't say.

She is dead.

Without a further word, the soldier takes his leave, disappears down into the realm of warriors, a place I cannot follow. I try to call Ayumi. No signal. Did last night really happen? I've still got the cloak to prove it. But her pep talk didn't seem to help much. I leave a note and chase a liter of strawberry vodka with a few handfuls of 5-Oma to carry me across the river Styx.

Only, there'd been a snatch at the last minute. A revelation.

Poison might have sealed the deal for a certain other pair of unfortunate star-crossed lovers, but there was no way Claire could let her unfinished business be.

I am more than a piece on a board. Even if it might be too late, there's one wrong I can yet right in this world while I still draw breath.

Claire sat and allowed her body and mind to recover. She willed herself to recall Lacie's walk-in closet. Somewhere in there was a trigger to a secret room filled to the tilt with heavy weaponry.

◊

Before long Lily wheeled Raine out to an enclosed observation platform below the ship.

Reeling from the midsummer sunlight, Raine glimpsed down at the glistening Mediterranean, its waves gleaming like crystals. Filled with excess energy, Lillian fell into an exercise routine.

"The bulk of the *Eden* Armada is spread around the Apennine Mountains, but our forces there are a diversion. We'll be sneaking far over the blockade from the Southern coastline," Lily said in between push-ups. "My double Leandra will buy us some time in that regard. That gives us a window – about five minutes to burst through the energy shields that protect the city. I'll disembark into the battle zone with four divisions. We split our forces into a moving net, protect the rebels, and make for the *Spire*. If all goes well, our efforts should allow my inside team to shut down the Overseer – that is, the mind-control defense thingy, which, quite frankly, should have been done already. Our Knights and dropships will get as many people as we can out of there. The final confrontation shall be between Lorelei and myself."

"You must be nervous," Raine said. "Do you think she'll try to escape?"

Lily stretched her arms out. "She won't time jump, if that's what you mean. She's got too much pride for that. If she wins, this will truly be the end of everything. An abyss with no finale or purpose."

"And if you win?"

"If we win, Raine, I'm going to keep my promise to you. I'll do my damnedest to build my Ark and save the human race from extinction. Of course, even if we do somehow manage to survive by colonizing space, it's not like we will last forever."

"But we'll last longer. That's something."

"Yes," responded Lily. "If I can save even a fraction of the planet's life, if I can prolong the existence and diversity of the human race... that would be something."

Raine sat in silence, learning to breathe again. It took her a while to formulate the question she was almost too afraid to ask.

"So... there's no going back to Chicago for me, is there?"

"We'll discuss that another time," Lily said, massaging Raine's shoulders, an action that caused the latter girl to tense her muscles.

"Give it to me straight. I already know it ain't gonna be what I want to hear."

"You've trusted me this far."

"No more secrets," Raine said sternly. "From friend to friend, please."

Lily acquiesced. "Here's a promise. Once this battle is over, I'll tell you everything."

After some reflection, the girl nodded reluctantly.

"Thank you, Raine. You've performed leagues and leagues beyond our expectations. Now let's get you some food. I need to meet with my subordinates and prepare for the operation. Plus there's the obligatory big speech and yada yada."

"Lily, wait."

"Yes?"

"If there's something I can do, if it will help... let me fight."

"Not a chance, Raine. I've already put you in enough danger. You don't know what we're up against."

"We... we need to save Gerrit, right?"

"Right, but-"

"I know you need me."

"Wait, you *know?* You've... seen it?"

"No, not like that. Everything still kind of feels like a dream. But I know... when I was trapped in my mind, the one feeling I couldn't shake was that there was something I still had to do. I came back for a purpose. Earth is my home, too. I want to fight for its future."

Lily was struck by her determination. She recalled the message from her future self: *Final extraction and confrontation require assistance not attempt singlehand warn true.* Raine had done more than enough for the EDC, but they were significantly understaffed, and perhaps this world line will have led to a different set of circumstances.

"There isn't much you can do with your physical body at this point as you've just come out of a tremendous shock," she replied. "But I do think there's a way around that."

∞

When later polled, nearly one hundred percent of users remembered, or at least said they remembered, exactly what they were doing the instant *Endless Metaverse* ceased to exist.

The man who called himself Ricard Stabbington came to in a drab office. Gone were the four supermodels with whom he was engaged in an epic pillow fight, the adjacent four-poster beds, the candelabras, the spicy pistachios, and the silver goblets of Bordeaux. In their place: a cheap desk, and a lousy holo-screen with spreadsheets and numbers. Plastic walls lined either side. He stood and scoped out his surroundings.

There were a hundred other people wearing funky helmets, and they were just as surprised as he was. He then felt above his head, grabbed onto the *M-Gear*, and removed it.

"Hello," a tall blonde man began. "I'm Pinoci, from Clyde. And who the hell are you people? Additionally, what just happened?"

"This must be some kind of bug," an older woman opined nervously. "I was just with the Duke."

"Countess Glenda!" Ricard exclaimed, recognizing her voice, although it was withered and grayer than he'd been used to hearing from the beauty. "Is that you?"

The sliding door activated. A twenty-something Hispanic dude poked his head through. "You guys are never gonna believe this. Come on outside."

Ricard rushed out of the room, knocked over confused personnel in the halls, raced up a winding stairwell, and stood amidst thousands of others outside of a dusty façade, a military bunker made of metal and stone.

He pushed his way through the crowd. A rush of cold wind took away what little breath he could muster.

It was dark, and they were in a poverty-stricken town in the middle of a desert. Aside from the fenced-off gardens and chicken coops built around the bunker, the only visible vegetation was in the form of tall, slender plants with spikes on them.

A sign on the building they had all emerged from read, *"Endless Metaverse North American Chapter, Southwest Division, Quality Control Department, Rank D ".*

Although the place was completely alien, something within Ricard recognized it. The desert air felt more real. His padded body had weight. And he was older than he'd imagined. Much older. This was a waking nightmare.

"I think they did it," one of the younger employees said. "I think the rebels broke the *Metaverse.*"

"No," Ricard countered. "That's not possible. This has to be a mistake!"

He ran back inside and retraced his steps to the office. It had no windows, no decoration, and no implements. Just computers, desks, machines for dispensing water and food, some cots in the corner, and two ventilation fans. Ricard pulled the *M-Gear* back over his head. He looked into the communal bathroom's mirror, trying to ignore his acne-covered, unshaven mug. Pressing all manner of buttons on the device did nothing. He tried it again and again.

"This isn't possible! Where are you, Mister Senior?!" he screamed, smashing the mirror to bits with the helmet. He needed to snap out of this somehow. Get back to the hub. He banged his head on the remaining shards of glass.

Five people burst in and restrained him.

Half a mile out from a modest midland village in Kenya, two children ran to their father, who'd stopped in the middle of the road by a large metal tower on his way home from the fields. Their mother leaned crying on the large acacia tree that'd been there for generations. Local men who worked the night shift had just been freed from the infernal *Gears* that warped them into emotionless robots, to much confusion from the helmets' maintenance droids. Could it be that the *Metaverse* was finally over?

Along the dirt path, Thaddius marveled at the sky. The winds here were more real than any he had felt in recent memory. Distant airborne wind turbines danced like great kites.

Just ten minutes ago, he'd been chanting with his brothers in the monastery, having taken a ceremonial drink of rice wine. The storm was in motion. They could all feel it. In a flash, his body began to unravel. The floor, and then the scale-lined walls, disappeared. His companions, seated in a circle, exchanged hopeful glances. Within seconds, the world he knew was no more, and he nearly tripped over his feet in mid-stride as he became conscious of himself once again.

I know my true name, he thought. He had heard it while meditating. *Kafil.*

Reminiscences of this place itched at the back of his mind. And the man knew at once that yes, at long last, this was home.

Kafil embraced his son and daughter, danced with them. Though he did not currently remember either with any clarity, their smiles told him all he needed to know. Fragments combined, paradoxes manifested, truths unearthed. The precious memories would return, even if the lost time would not. In the meantime, there was a lot of catching up to do.

Thank you, Raine, he thought, opening his palms, closing his eyes, and drinking in the reality of the world around him. He could not have been more blessed.

Mrs. Zoot was asleep in a hammock in the back room of her antique toy store in Pagoda when it happened. She had thought the bizarre factory all a part of some strange recurring dream, and kept working, oblivious to the fact that everyone around her had stopped. It was only when another woman, dressed in better attire than the other employees, stopped her hand and spoke in a strange language that she realized something was amiss. For one, she could understand what she was saying.

"Jae Won, are you all right?"

Mrs. Zoot blinked twice at the name.

"Who is Jae Won?" she asked, her words surprisingly coming out in the same odd language, although she thought she knew the answer.

"You are."

The woman then stood up on a chair to address the confused faces around the floor.

"Everyone, please stay calm. Remove those *M-Gears*. You won't need them anymore. The news channels say that *Endless Metaverse* has been shut down."

Dozens of her co-workers screamed in shock and protest. Others looked at one another, perhaps in disbelief, perhaps seeking someone they knew to share in their surprise. Jae Won just looked down at her workstation; her job was to install microchips inside the *M-Gears*. Then, catching a glimpse of her reflection in the shiny production line model, she inspected her face and was staggered to see that she was thirty years younger than she had expected. That, at least, was a nice touch.

Now to find my absent-minded husband. Hopefully he's on the same continent.

In the midst of defending the doors to the keep where the guild was hoarding their spoils, Jolly Peter heard a rumbling that originated from no known weapon in the *Metaverse*. Lance exchanged a glance with the dwarf.

"What's going on?" the Guild Leader asked.

Peter managed an uninterested expression as he tossed a tomahawk at an advancing shapeshifter.

He never saw whether the attack connected.

In the midst of the Australian outback, Peter awoke in a cozy underground chamber with sandstone walls.

His reflection stared back from a mirror across the room – the brown face of a kid no older than thirteen. He took off the heavy headgear that weighed his neck down, and noted with shocked surprise that his fully-spec'd out Enchanted Mithril Gear had gone missing.

As soon as he planted his feet on the ground, the shifting weight of his body told Peter that his senses here were stronger.

Could this be the world outside of the 'Verse?

He walked up the stairs carved into the earth and shielded his eyes from the setting sun's glare. Many children were emerging from an opal mineshaft.

"Glen!" another child called.

Without knowing why, he spun his head in the direction of the voice. A young girl approached and took his hands, beaming.

"So, how was it?"

"How was... what?"

"The *Metaverse!* You were so excited to try it out," she said worriedly. "You can't mean that you don't remember signing up."

"I... don't," he said. "Where am I?"

Her eyes widened.

"Coober Pedy, stupid! You're looking at me as if I'm a stranger."

"I'm sorry," he replied, sadly. "But you are... familiar."

The girl slapped him in the face. He would never know how much she had doted on the zombified boy, cooked and cleaned for him, worrying every waking moment that the dangerous working conditions in the old opal mines might end in a catastrophic collapse.

"What was that for?"

"That's for forgetting your best friend. The one and only person who's cared for you all this time. It was the longest two years of my life!"

She then gave him a long embrace.

"And that's for coming back. Come on, let's look for my parents. Dad's monitoring the pirate radio stations. The EDC's taking the fight to *Neo Eden!* Every *EM* user in Europe is going to war!"

Whatever that meant, Glen melted at the warmth of human contact, something he couldn't remember feeling ever before. This world looked empty, but its wonders enraptured the gathering crowds. The air had texture, and this girl's hair smelled terrific. Everything here was alive, bursting with energy.

Gerrit told him this day would come. He'd never listened, but now he almost wished he had. Hopefully his bro did okay for himself, too, wherever he was. Luck willing, he'd also be in the care of a loving girl, far from war or fighting of any kind.

Charles Hayter had no idea what hit him. One minute, he was lying down on a beach towel in his usual spot in *Clyde's* Crystal Park, shuffling the poker deck with friends (unbeknownst to him, he'd just had his memory modified to expunge the Raine 'virus'). The next, he was marching in step by the coast, somehow tethered to the midst of a platoon of soldiers. The man pegged it for a dream, since he didn't seem to be in control of his body. Yet, it soon became apparent that this was all too real. His back straightened out as best it could under the heavy equipment, and his tired eyes stuck upon the devastation in the shimmering city beyond the far-off walls.

Inside, smoke rose from isolated battlefields as scores of androids filed into the city, entering through holes in the pulsing force field that covered the metropolis like a fishbowl. Outside, soldiers self-organized into formations and camps. Those eating munched in unison on some unidentifiable slop. From another gate, city folk chaotically filed out, civilians, with and without chrome headgear, all making for the ocean. Pulsing shots fired, one for each refugee crossing Charles' vision, followed by cries and the sounds of bodies falling onto the sand. For what reason, he could not tell, lacking the ability to turn his head.

He tried quietly, then loudly, to resist, to wake himself from this hellish vision that appeared to go on for hours. This could be no dream; at least, that is what his five senses were telling him, but his body had a will of its own.

Charles closed his eyes; a menu popped up before the red of his eyelids.

"*Helmet Defense Protocol* engaged. To run Alternate Vision program, look left. To remain conscious of actions, look right."

Even though he had no recollection of the distinction between reality and fantasy, deep in his gut, Charles recognized without a doubt which world was real and which one was a fabrication.

So, he had a choice. To be put back into another simulation, or to continue blindly into a violent battle… neither option was appealing, but only one of them would give him a chance to physically override this terrible machine controlling his body.

He kept on and fought the puppet strings with all his will.

∩

"As I'm sure you recall, our Warp Initiator creates dual artificial wormholes in dynamic Space-Time, allowing us to slingshot off natural wormholes or the rims of black holes, even at the edges of the universe, to arrive with precision either earlier or later than we left. To achieve this level of exactitude, Rutger and my parents mapped the known dimensions out in terms of spacetime over energy dispersal. Because Earth is constantly traveling at ridiculous speeds through the galaxy and our triple reference beacons from the Triassic, the early Cenozoic, and the End of the World are limited in range, it's essential that temporal calculations to any given destination be triple-checked for accuracy--"

Trapped on the sunken sofa watching Lily and Rutger attempt to explain the dreary workings of their orbiting home, Lorelei had given up on mentally inputting any exit codes. Clasping her Eternity Knot pendant, she used every ounce of energy to will her past self to alter the memory, to break free of its shackles.

I refuse to repeat the past. I refuse to mentally relive our failures again. Let me return.

The fates of every life form in the universe hinge on my power. I'm not about to trip at the finish line.

With a forceful cry, the Young Lorelei in her mind's eye snapped. She leapt from the couch, grabbed Lillian, pulled her in a headlock, and ran to the emergency escape hatch. Lacie and Lucy ran after them in abject confusion, but to no avail. The memory loop having been broken, they vanished like specters.

Lorelei swung open the door and the duo shot out into deep space. The sensation of simulated death flung her from the entrapping vision.

Screaming like she'd never done before, Queen Lorelei pulled against hundreds of pounds of restraints.

Dr. Marco stood calmly over the operating table. Upon being forcibly ejected from *Endless Metaverse* with the destruction of the source code, Lorelei's nano-machines had been horribly corrupted. The cybernetic implants she fine-tuned united in rebellion against her body, echoing the dwindling loyalty of her followers.

The Queen twitched in paranoid uncertainty, even as her most trusted operatives scrambled to save her.

"Let me go!" she ordered. "My people need me!"

"No, my Queen, your anesthetic has run out. We need to shut down your machine implements. They've been highly corrupted. You've gone into cardiac arrest. We're trying to save your life."

"Fools! You can't take my brain away! I refuse to become as pathetic as you mortals!" she yelled. "What's going on out there? Where's Lily?"

"Don't worry, ma'am," he said, dismissing her. She was immensely vulnerable; a simple modification could ensure that she abdicate her throne, or worse, be arrested into a coma. "You are unwell. There is a minor insurgency. General Beech is carrying out your orders – it will all be over in a few hours."

"No!" she howled. "The plan's been compromised! I command you! Release me right this instant!"

Dr. Marco nodded to the nurse, who administered the anesthetic.

Did I catch that little bastard smiling? He wants *me incapacitated! Get up, Lorelei!*

The Queen went limp, unable to move or speak. She struggled to keep herself conscious, and failed.

XXIX. Gambit

"Forget all the reasons it won't work and believe the one reason that it will." - Unknown

"Left flank, stay tight. They're trying to draw us in," Commodore Leandra ordered, eyes never leaving the real-time miniature holo-battlefield. True to the simulations, the Western mountain pass proved a most useful cover for two hundred of her forward warships; despite an isolated thunderstorm striking the EDC front lines behind the hills, the Commodore held her airspace.

The battle for *Neo Eden* might have been a few miles off, but its outcome would be decided here, at the Western border of the Apennine Mountains.

Boulder-sized electromagnetic spheres whistled through the clouds. Many found their targets as the *Eden* Armada charged forth, with Brigadier General Troi Macleod leading the spearhead formation in the sleek Titan-Class Warship *Charon*.

Typical Eden *blunt tactics*, she thought. *A direct strike when they should be biding their time.*

She had her forces pull back into a concave pattern, inviting the attackers in. As soon as the first wave crossed the peaks, the Commodore gave the signal. Cloaked interceptors flying high above the battlefield let fall baubles of corroding acid. Waterfalls of the destructive spheres paralyzed the *Eden* advance.

The *Charon* halted before climbing to meet the interceptors. Leandra pulled her forces away, splitting the rear guard to provide cover fire, but Macleod was too fast. He let loose volleys of missiles; the *Freyja* eliminated each one.

A second torrent burst forth before Leandra had time to breathe. There was no way the *Freyja's* escorts could down them all.

"Full shields!" she cried.

The glowing plasma fields sapped the *Freyja's* photon-bending cloak, giving away its position while their electromagnetic barrier deflected any missiles that made it past the line of plasma turrets.

Plowing quickly through blast radii, the Brigadier General focused his big guns on the vulnerable flagship.

Nothing doing. I've studied the data from each one of your battles. This is the same feint you pulled in Lebanon, and it only worked then because our plasma turrets were caught in a sandstorm. You're already two seconds too late, Macleod.

Leandra's flanking destroyers answered with focused laser blasts, carving through the *Charon's* hull-mounted turrets.

Eden's finest tactician was no fool; he switched to a defensive formation, positioning shield-generating craft around the perimeter to keep the EDC from advancing beyond the range.

And now, he'll protect his ass and buy some time to think.

Her intuition proved correct: Macleod sent forth multiple waves of underpowered high-speed drones to meet their escorts.

"Bingo," Leandra smiled, switching to auxiliary power, maxing shields, and instructing her fleet to follow. Her opponent was finally playing it safe; a drawn-out conflict would buy Lily more time. "Hostiles closing. Fry 'em up with artillery, but not too fast. We've gotta wait 'em out."

₪

Somewhere around the fiftieth wave, Gerrit lost count. The horde was endless. He could barely hold a weapon against the four-armed golems slamming him into the ground like a toy, let alone defend against their swift, powerful attacks. To top it off, none of his exploits were of any use. The virtual arena was completely hack-proof.

More than anything, he wished for death. But it would not come. His avatar should have been finished long ago, its limbs twisted as a pretzel after this latest thorough lashing. The AI opponents watched and waited for his body to regenerate.

What Gerrit thought of as his skeletal structure had been broken probably a dozen times in any given place, and the pain of constantly re-growing bones and snapping muscles robbed him of the resolve to fight any longer. He just wanted it to be over.

As soon as the boy was back to full health, the golems began their charge. Just as he parried the first strike, however, a sudden quake belted the combatants onto their backs.

The sands spiraled into a searing twister, and Gerrit shielded his face. From the midst of the storm, a blinding light pierced the back of his eyes, forcing them open.

Gerrit woke with a start, still forcibly seated in Queen Lorelei's chambers. His heart was racing, and the *M-Gear* hung heavily.

A sudden electro-magnetic pulse had scrambled every device in the room. He felt strong surges of electricity coursing through his veins, as if molten metals from within his body were being boiled in a blacksmith's furnace.

Anger and hatred filled his thoughts. If one thing in this world was certain, he was going to destroy every one of Lorelei's sick virtual programs entirely and prevent anyone else from suffering the same fate. The sounds of bullets ricocheting in the next room over only intensified Gerrit's frustration.

He winced as the double doors shook with a deafening thunder. Smoke flooded in from every crack between the metal slabs. Someone was trying to break in with some sort of bomb, but industrial-strength panels over limestone muffled the next explosion.

As the ringing in his ears subsided, Gerrit made out two voices yelling at each other over the din. Their words were jumbled, as if through an encryption device. They were soon interrupted by sudden bursts of gunfire that turned further screams into yelps of pain, and at last, silence.

"Sir! Captain Gerrit, you in there?" a barely audible voice piped up.

"Yes, I'm here!" he called despite a parched throat, summoning all his strength. The voice sounded faint.

"Didn't get that, but I'll take that as a yes! Now stand back," the stranger commanded.

Please be gentle.

But fate had other plans. The next explosion came through the marble wall to his left. Gerrit shut his eyes. His wheelchair reeled backwards into a large bookshelf at high speed. The headgear slammed against a marble bookend, knocking the breath from his weak chest. Dust shot up his nose, and he coughed up a storm.

When he opened his eyes, two men were helping him out of the paralyzing *Gear* and chair straps. Water drenched his lips; one stranger tried to mime something to him. Maybe they knew he couldn't hear anything. His ragged face reflected back from their visors. The duo turned their blast shields down, but their faces were still a blur, as was everything else.

"What's... what's going on?" Gerrit mouthed loudly, unable to hear himself. Feeling a foreign sensation in his arms, he tried to sit up. "R-Raine..."

Big mistake. An agonizing pain shot through Gerrit's spine as his muscles cramped up, one by one. He cried out as the man closest to him pulled a syringe from his arm.

"Don't move, kid! You're wasting time!" The other guy yelled, shakily grasping a firearm at the impromptu entranceway.

He recognized the man's voice... he sounded like a famous figure, someone he'd maybe encountered at the Queen's party... *But no,* he reasoned. *It couldn't be.*

"Mister Senior! You're... old! W-where is she? What are you doing?"

After yelling, Gerrit immediately regretted it, as his brain seemed to be convulsing.

"Raine's safe as a lamb at pasture. This fellow's helping me save your arse, sir," the other man replied with a wink. "Name's Henry Holdfast," he said, giving Gerrit Lily's secret handshake and fist-bump. It took the kid a few seconds to process all this new information, and the fact that he could perform a complex handshake he had no recollection of.

"Senior's one of his many identities. Out here, he's just Jon."

Wrathman's voice rose to the pitch of an attention-starved Chihuahua. "*Just* Jon? I am the Chief Operations Officer of *Endless Metaverse*, lads, and don't you forget it---"

Henry waved him away. "There was supposed to be a much bigger strike team here with us, but plan's changed. Beech and his cronies froze two-thirds of the *Nexus* on suspicion. That's why we need you to open the--"

"Can we get the hell out of here now?" Jon barked.

"We're not leaving 'til the Captain's ready!" Henry said sternly. "And our orders are taking us to Chamber 50B."

"I seem to recall that you promised me amnesty in return for getting your point man out," Jon grumbled. "Not for taking you into the depths of the *Spire*. Now how much longer is this--"

"Gah!"

The outburst was followed by a numbing electric shock. Gerrit found himself unable to speak. The pain continued to course through his body in spasms. But Henry was fast at work, filling up two more syringes.

"What- what's that?"

"A second dose of muscle relaxant," Henry said, injecting the boy without hesitation. "You were running an isolated program, so you're not fighting signal strain, but your body's over-sympathetic to the synaptic respon--"

"English, please."

"Just aftershocks from our EM grenade, sir, no biggie. Your nanites will be fully disintegrated in a few minutes. Could I trouble you to count to forty? I've got to reload and check our bearings. Take deep breaths, try to relax."

Though he still didn't understand, Gerrit nodded and breathed slowly, methodically. Although he had no recollection of knowing the first thing about meditation, the motions came naturally. At the count of forty, he tapped Henry on the ankle.

"Atta boy. Now this here's adrenaline," Henry huffed, lifting up the second syringe. "Hang onto it, there's a good chance you'll need it in a few--"

"For chrissakes, Holdfast, they'll be here any second!" barked Jon.

"Okay. We don't exactly have the luxury of time for a proper recovery. Think you can stand, mate?"

He forced himself to his feet, though his body was screaming out in pain. Both rescuers winced. Gerrit's frail body struggled, but he was determined to carry his own weight. Henry handed him an offline HDP infantry *M-Gear* identical to his and Jon's models, and a sidearm with a couple of clips. The boy immediately recalled the safety toggle and reloading procedures.

"To the docking bay, then," Henry said quietly as the trio emerged from the hole in the wall and stepped into the massive hallway of the Central Citadel, navigating around the remains of scrap-metal soldiers. Holdfast remotely disabled any recording devices.

A rather posh service elevator subjecting them to Vivaldi's "Four Seasons" took the trio two hundred floors down into the pyramidal military complex; Gerrit's stomach churned at the platform's dizzying speed.

The following labyrinth of hallways and staircases passed in a blur. It took a good few near-falls before he was able to walk on his own two feet, and with anything approaching a rhythm.

Henry took the lead, scouting around corners, remotely disabling cameras, descending four floors at a time, and hacking into locked doors by hot-wiring nearby terminals.

Gerrit pushed his body slightly under his limits, mindful not to overextend his muscles and cramp up again. Soon he was off Jon's shoulder, keeping pace with his rescuers. He couldn't let himself be useless, couldn't fail Raine and Lily. Not again.

Before long they'd reached the end of the tunnel.

Henry popped open a loose service hatch. Upon peeking through, Gerrit beheld an enormous indoor docking bay for the *Eden* Armada. Cavernous walls carved deep into the pyramid and even through the mountain beyond, and at the mouth of the structure, multiple runways ran from blast doors far past the raised platforms.

"Do you recall the layout, sir?" Henry asked Gerrit. "Some memories should be coming back by now. We may need to split if the going gets too hot."

The boy bit his lip.

"It… it is kind of familiar."

Wrathman, who was tapping into the security footage with his Holo-Lens, held up a palm to silence both of them.

"Something's going on across the way."

They shimmied through the hatch one by one. Raised voices reverberated below. It was impossible to tell what was going on, since shipping crates obscured most of the view and their eardrums blared with the din of welding bots trying to repair an extravagant gunship.

Henry and Gerrit silenced two guards with tranquilizer darts before discreetly venturing a glance down at the lower deck. They didn't have much time to study the opposition: Lt. General Beech, the Royal Guard, and about a dozen droids gathered around the turret of a war-torn gunship. The General was intimidating the foreman of the welding 'bots. Henry pointed a long-range shotgun mic at them and the trio listened in.

"Macleod's already mopping them up!" he boomed. "Make haste! It's important for public solidarity that I take my private cruiser over the city as soon as we fly our victory flag. Of course, you oil-brains have no idea what solidarity means."

"Sir, I am only too eager to comply, but the Overseer's primary directive is for my division to repair our fellow droids. May I remind you that the battle is still on-going?"

"It ain't going to be for much longer! The vermin have locked their own cage. The *Valkyrie's* beating a hasty retreat, and they'll never outrun us."

"We need to get through that lower door, *now,*" Henry said, pointing at the looming gate behind Beech. As dictated by Murphy's Law, of all the hundreds of entrances and exits to the hangar, their deadliest foe was standing right in the middle of the pathway to their destination.

"Can't we just wait for them to leave?" Jon asked nervously.

"Negative," Henry responded, setting up a sort of trap by the entrance. "We're late as it is. Our best chance is to put down our blast shields and sneak around--"

Gerrit spied something, and then forced Henry's head down behind the railing. Almost immediately, a pulse of electricity shot through the rail, missing Henry by inches. Gerrit took a peek around the corner of a nearby crate – a giant mechanized eye was staring him down, a security system suspended by multi-jointed hydraulic arms in the ceiling.

Steamed coolant erupted from the highly doom-capable pupil; the droid's superheated iris shone blood red as it recharged its rail gun. That thing would not miss again – it was now or never.

Having used a similar-looking model in Circuitron raids, Gerrit borrowed Henry's rifle, fixed his aim, squeezed the trigger, and set the deadly eye alight with explosive bullets. A joint in its hydraulic arm shattered, and the wreck fell quickly towards the alarmed General and his men.

Androids leapt out of the way of the crashing orb and into Jon and Henry's line of fire, where they were picked off one by one. Beech's cyborg reflexes were faster, though, and he had quickly patched in auxiliary power to raise the shields on his scuttled gunship. Jumping into the nearest turret seat, he took aim, and launched a barrage of laser pulses at the rebels.

"Halt, traitors!" Beech boomed. "Reveal yourselves now and I will make your deaths quick and easy!"

The General then signaled to his guard, who circled to flank the unauthorized personnel.

The three men dropped down from the upper level and took cover behind several shipping containers.

Concealed from their foes, a cruiser was parked not a hundred meters away, just past a pile of weapons crates. Gerrit was surprised; it looked rather like a Circuitron sports pod with a V800 turbine. Back in the *Metaverse,* he'd always wanted to try one of those.

Gerrit pointed at the vehicle. "I say we get the hell out of here."

"Let me handle this," Jon asserted before crawling behind a crate a few meters away. Inching out, he waved a torn piece of his white shirt.

"General, sir, hear me out! The Queen doesn't even know what she's doing! She's lost control of the herd! We'll work with you! Together, we can bring the *'Verse* to an even wider audience!"

"I got nothin' to say to you double-crossing maggots!" called Beech. "We shipped in anarchists from every corner of the globe to *die*. Every media outlet in existence is writing up my heroic victory! There's no place for a pampered old snake that's lived way past retirement age!"

A barrage of machine gun fire topped off his reply.

Jon sustained a shot to the shoulder and was quickly yanked out of the way.

"What the hell are you doing?" reprimanded Henry, trying to sterilize the wound. "Even if the lunkhead wasn't planning a coup d'état, he's surely deduced you're with us by now!"

Jon laughed and shook his head.

"I probably should have realized that a few seconds earlier," he joked. "I'd rather die, you know, than work with that damn tin man."

"Undoubtedly. Now this is going to hurt a bit," Henry said, patting Jon's good shoulder. After giving Jon a card to bite down on, he whipped a ballpoint pen out of his shirt pocket and clicked it three times. It was held up against the wound - an electromagnet carefully disintegrated and guided out the now dust-like pieces of the explosive round that nearly shattered the man's collarbone.

Wrathman took a deep breath as Holdfast applied quick-healing nanopaste. But something else was amiss. Henry's eyes darted to the empty adrenaline syringe on the floor.

"Captain?"

The gasp ejected from General Beech's mechanical lungs was drowned out by the roaring of the hand-cannon Gerrit had found in a weapons crate and used to unload an entire clip of explosive rounds into the compressed hydrogen fuel cell containers surrounding the vessel. They exploded in cascades of flame, burning into the gunship's hull and causing blips and large imperfections in the force field.

While Beech was recovering, Henry sent electro-magnetic pulsing spider-bots down the raised walkways. The remote shocks sent most of the flanking Royal Guard falling down on their faces, unconscious. One flopped off the rail and fell to his death at the bottom of the bay.

Gerrit's final shot took out a good chunk of Beech's meaty right arm.

Bleeding profusely, Beech spun the cannon around towards Gerrit and gave out a desperate battle cry, feathering the trigger to try and steady his shot amidst the water raining down from the sprinklers. However, he was unaccustomed to aiming with his left hand, and Gerrit was too fast. He'd already ducked behind a crane and taken cover inside the sports cruiser. Buckling himself into the crossed-over straps, he made a quick study of the controls before motioning to Henry and Jon, who looked between the unreasonably powerful cannon and oncoming soldiers with trepidation.

"What are you waiting for, divine intervention?" Gerrit called.

The two men made a mad dash towards the cruiser, dodging gunfire from every direction.

Gerrit revved the engines. Henry and Jon hopped in with him and quickly hooked in their restraints as the cruiser shot forward, gaining speed almost instantaneously.

Beech lined up his cannon's sights, but missed the first blast as they zoomed away from the flight trays. Henry heaved a sigh of relief, but quickly came to his senses when he realized that Gerrit was over-steering the cruiser, trying desperately to adjust to the flight stick.

"Do you even know how to fly, numbskull?" yelled Jon.

"H-hey! This isn't what I'm used to, old man," the boy protested.

"Steady. That's the flaps, rudder, throttle, and the toggles for turbine alignment," Holdfast began, pointing out the controls as Gerrit hit the gas. "You're gonna hang a right past the entrance to the service gates."

But they never left the hangar. The outer blast shield was clamping down at full speed in front of them. They were about to slam face-first, a hundred miles an hour, into a meter-thick wall of metallic death.

Jon wailed like a madman as Gerrit slammed the flaps open, swung the rudder around, reversed the thrust on one of the turbines and spun the cruiser back around the other way with a quarter of a second to spare. The engine bellowed; Gerrit redlined the jet's output, trying desperately to reverse their momentum.

The cruiser slid into the blast shield and rebounded, taking them inexplicably towards Beech, whose pulse blasts missed them by quite a large margin. Henry whipped about and saw that their target wasn't aiming for them. He was destroying the blast shield's manual controls, trapping them in the hangar.

"Attention Echo units," Beech's robotic voice blasted through the PA system. "We have an infestation problem in the primary gunship hangar. Invader heads will be greatly rewarded."

"Right. We can't fly out of here," Gerrit called, upping the cruiser's shields. "And we're dead in the water if we wait any longer. We jump on my count! Take off your belts and hang on!"

"Did you say take *off* our belts?" Wrathman screamed.

"3…"

Beech had drilled into the frontal shields.

"2…"

Henry pulled a backpack out from under his seat and strapped it on.

"1…"

Closing his eyes and thinking of Ayumi's smiling face, Henry grabbed the other two men and bailed out of the cruiser, now on a collision course with Beech's gunship.

The General abandoned his post, making for a protective barrier. He was too late. In milliseconds, the pod's burst fuel compartment exploded upon contact with the failing electric force field surrounding his vessel. The sound was deafening, and Beech was no more.

Gerrit held tight as Holdfast pulled the tab on the safety chute, allowing the trio to ride the outward force of the explosion backwards.

He let his body go limp and landed with a heavy bounce, rolling to a stop on a lower platform. His heart thumped like a jackhammer within his chest. The boy lay there for a few seconds, relaxing over-strained muscles. His hearing gradually returned.

"You've got some moves, sir," screamed Henry, limping even as he supported Jon, who'd evidently been knocked unconscious.

A platoon of voices sounded out in anguish.

Emerging troops from opposite the bay were stunned from Henry's flashbang trap. Triggered by proximity, it switched approaching troops' goggles into night vision mode and activated pre-set flash grenades across the hall. The newest wave of reinforcements would be blinded for another half-minute.

"What now?" Gerrit forced himself up on wobbly legs.

"Well, it looks like we've got a clear path to our destination, sir," Henry voiced. "Let's book it to Central Asset Control."

"Central what?" Gerrit asked as they snuck quickly around a

connecting corridor, shocking two small camera droids. Henry ran up to the stunned bots and quickly uploaded the late Nico's manual override program, effectively repurposing them to his own use.

"The Overseer's server room – the last system capable of running the Defense Protocol. It's odd to be explaining all this to you, sir, since you were one of this mission's chief planners. You must not remember a thing of the EDC yet."

"You've got that right."

"Then there's no time to explain," Henry apologized. "Suffice it to say that you're something of a war hero."

=

In her concealed crow's nest in the scrapyard, Ayumi Karuishi hid between piles of scrap metal, shivering within a heat-scrambling chilled silver suit. She had never felt more like a mouse, concealing her presence from the armed drones circling the Spire. Ayumi tried to make sense of the Overseer's encrypted commands as they spread from the main pipeline to the various Network towers.

HDP troops drew back towards the lower *Spire*. If there was any doubt as to the location of the AI's main server, it was eliminated when the Overseer drew an entire regiment back indoors. She'd been trying to get through to Holdfast's comm. channel to warn him.

His radio might have been scrambled by a short-ranged EM grenade, she realized. *Stay safe, Henry. Please.*

"Need the all-clear for advance," Joaquin asked through the Doctor's coded Holo-Lens.

"Advise that you circle around. There are still too many anti-air units."

"The Carriers are falling like flies. We'll take what we can get, Lotus. It's now or never."

"Then come 'round to the South-west gate to make your drops. It's got the least artillery," Ayumi offered. "But hurry; the blockade's closing in. More are approaching from the shore."

Joaquin's voice was grateful for the news. "Thanks, Doc. Sit-rep on the ground?"

"It's not looking good for the refugees. With permission, I'd like to head downstairs and--"

"Negative," the *Valkyrie's* chief officer replied. "Your life is more important. We need eyes now more than ever."

Following Henry's directives, android forces, not human ones, led the advance upon the rebellion in four of the most congested war zones.

Isolated groups of the *Eden* underground split up to disable the 'bots with daisy-chained electromagnetic pulses, but for every temporarily downed division, two more took their place. Ayumi bit her lip in anxiety. Beech was truly sparing no expense to eliminate the anarchists.

◊

"C-Commodore, the enemy is retreating!"

Puzzled expressions were exchanged on the bridge. Leandra pounded her fist on the console.

Damn! The Eden *Armada is turning tail! Scouts must have spotted Lily's wing advancing from the South.*

She opened up a communications channel with Macleod.

"Sky Admiral Lillian to Brigadier General Macleod! Face me, and I will grant you the privilege of surrender!"

In response, an energy beam fired backwards from the Westering *Charon*, toasting an entire squadron of interceptors.

Macleod hailed them back with a haughty tone in his voice.

"Quit your dilly-dallying. You're not the true Sky Admiral. This battle is a farce!"

No longer requiring her mask, Leandra pulled it off, revealing her olive-toned face.

"And right you are! This is the true face of Commodore Leela Kernani! It is the face of destruction! Leave, and I will hunt you! Challenge me, and I'll consider sparing your life! For that's what you value most, isn't it? Why die for a Queen to whom loyalty means nothing?"

Macleod smiled. "I should have known: the bombshell from Bombay. Your cold nature only intensifies your beauty. However, I'm afraid I can't offer you a chance to avenge your homeland. My life is already forfeit. The consequences for my family should I disobey orders far outweigh any point in living. Don't keep me waiting all day, love."

So he and I are fighting for the same reasons. Too bad he's on the wrong side.

"I warned you, Macleod!"

Furious, Leandra cut off the call and gripped her seat tightly. The *Valkyrie* was still seventeen klicks out from its drop point, and if the *Freyja* didn't keep close to the *Charon*, there was no telling whether Macleod would dare to nuke them.

"Make chase! Full throttle!" she commanded, with a little difficulty.

They were losing ships at an alarming rate, but the job was far from over. Lily was dangerously behind schedule.

XXX. Control

"For what shall it profit a man, if he shall gain the whole world,
and lose his own soul?" – Mark 8:36

"Sky Admiral on the deck!" Lt. Gen. Joaquin announced as Lily wheeled Raine into the *Valkyrie's* massive hold.

Four divisions, nearly eighty thousand in all, fell into formation and snapped into saluting the two ladies.

Raine was astonished to see video feeds of even more warriors, presumably from other ships. Hundreds of thousands of human soldiers and androids gazed up at the Sky Admiral and her companion intently. Lily took the podium, standing on a soapbox.

"At ease, everyone! Attention all free men, women, and androids of planet Earth! Before anything else, I'd like for you to show your support for Captain Raine, who almost single-handedly shut down the *Metaverse!*"

A roaring of applause followed, amplified by the refracting metal walls of the hull. Raine's stomach sank at being put in the spotlight, but she waved and smiled like a beauty queen to show her support. The emotions enveloping her were overwhelming.

It's a lie, Raine thought. *I was being egged along the whole way. But I can't be the one to tell them that. Not now.*

"Without the Captain, none of this would be possible," Lily continued. "This sixteen-year-old girl bravely plunged into the belly of the beast itself! She fought tooth and nail to bring us this advantage! If she can fight, then so can you! I expect only the best from you all!"

More cheers ensued, but Lily cut them off prematurely.

"Today is the day we put an end to the oppression of our fellow people! Today we free our friends from an endless cycle of bondage! Today, we defeat the forces that have enslaved humankind with fear and falsities for over two hundred years!"

This was met with loud cheers and the chanting of Lily's name.

"All right, guys. That's it. Sorry if you were expecting more. I'm keeping this short and sweet, so Jojo here can have a few minutes to fill you in on the details."

Taking off his comm. visor, Gabriel Joaquin gave her a pained look.

"Oh, sorry," she whispered, a touch too loudly, "was that nickname just between us?"

Joaquin hid his face, to much laughter from the troops. Lily crossed her arms; the outfit needed a little humor, now more than ever. She was glad to have been able to put them at ease.

"Seriously, though. Take it easy on the guy, I've put him through a lot lately," she said. "All right, here's the brief. Intel indicates our ground team is very close to their destination. The Overseer should be down shortly after we make landfall, thus eliminating our enemy's advantage in numbers. Protect the freedom fighters. Safeguard the innocent. End the influence of the oppressors. And above all, do your best to limit human casualties. Section Leaders, our presence is expected, so keep flanks tight and take out the Network towers first and foremost. I wish you all the best, and Godspeed. Oh, and Jojo, you ready to assume operational command of this vessel?"

The Lieutenant General saluted. "I'm ready to relieve you, ma'am!"

"Then I am relieved. Take care of our baby."

After raising her fist up in salute and leading the crowd into a call-and-response chant, Lily gave up the podium to Joaquin, who cleared his throat and glared at the men like a reprimanding headmaster, lest anyone even think to refer to him as 'Jojo'.

"All right, you maggots! I'm not going to repeat myself, so listen up!" he blared, preparing both his listeners and himself for an update to the new and improved battle plan.

∞

"Clear a path!"

Lily breathlessly wheeled her charge down to the hangar, past rows of heavily reinforced, building-sized giant robot suits and in between hundreds of soldiers and pilots scurrying to and fro, stealing glances in their direction. They were approaching the drop zone. Raine had ten minutes to get into her personal Exo Knight, and Lily needed five to prep her gear.

"Ugh, that was terrible."

"The speech, you mean? It was totally wicked. Short and sweet, too," she replied, and meant it. Raine had never thought a woman capable of a voice so loud. "You're way too hard on yourself."

"You don't need to flatter me," Lily said with a nervous laugh. "I know it sucked. Apparently, I've done this a few times in previous world lines. It's too bad that experience doesn't stack up."

"Come on, you were great," insisted Raine, speaking directly to Lily's now-gentle eyes. "Seriously. Those men looked like they would follow you to the ends of the Earth."

The Sky Admiral turned away. "Let's hope it doesn't come to that."

"What's up with that chant, though?"

"An ancient Chinese battle cry, Captain," an Asian man interjected, saluting the Sky Admiral. "Remember the homeland."

"And I always do, even if it isn't mine to remember. Raine, this is Colonel Victor Aquino. He'll suit you up into your *Galahad* and run the recall module. Simulator-wise, you're already an ace Exo Knight pilot; the memory just needs a synaptic snap to activate. It should be a breeze; you helped us design these things, after all," Lily explained before turning to her subordinate. "How's the remote system?"

Aquino's expression sank. "I'm afraid it's down for all the Knights."

Lily bit her lip. "Tell me that's a bad joke."

"Sensors are acting up. The Overseer's jamming all aerial-to-ground comms. We can't isolate the signals or safeguard against interference. She'll have to take the plunge."

"I see. Sorry, Raine, but it's not going to work out."

"No! Strap me in," she pleaded to both the Sky Admiral and the Colonel. "Lily, I'm going with you."

"Absolutely not. I'm not risking your---"

"Let me fight, damn it!"

Lily clenched her fists. *We don't have time for this.*

"Gah! Fine! But don't you die out there! Vic, give her a quick go-over, will ya?"

"Certainly, ma'am," the man nodded, placing Raine's right hand in the biometric scanner to begin the synchronization process.

As Lily retreated, she caught Raine's lost eyes trying to make contact. Realizing she forgot something, Lily returned to hug her one last time. Their hearts hid nothing: both girls shook with anticipation.

"Be strong, Lily," Raine said suddenly.

Lily looked her best friend over.

"Come on, Ray. I'm the older one here. Shouldn't I be telling you that?"

I can't help it. The last time I saw you, you were in the body of a twelve year-old.

Joaquin's concerned voice on Lily's comm. interrupted Raine's attempt at a reply. The Captain could just barely make out the message.

"Ma'am, the *Eden* Armada is returning. *Freyja* is making chase."

"What?" Lily pulled up her holo-map. It was true. Macleod had turned tail. Their far right flank was already under attack from above, and the rest of the blockade was closing, fast.

She held Raine's shoulder reassuringly before clapping to catch the room's attention. "All right, people. Full speed ahead! Tear open that throttle! We need to deploy ASAP and get our ships out of range, and someone *please* get me my damn Ptero suit!"

↔

Four miles away, Yossa lobbed another salvaged grenade back out the window of the fortified complex he and Hector's divisions had taken refuge in, guided by the last vestiges of the *Eden* underground, a scant few kids now cowering from the advancing guard.

The screeching of metal slicing metal cut through the chaos as another platoon of killer 'bots violently exploded. The men in the lower bunkers took care of the rest with well-aimed firebombs.

The rebels fought hard and destroyed many androids, but the *Eden* lines continued to advance. The situation was even more nightmarish than Yossa could have imagined sitting in his lair underneath Circuitron, preaching, prophesying, and pondering. If he'd known what violent horrors awaited him outside the *'Verse*, needless to say, he would have prepared more, would have had his men trained for urban warfare, survival tactics, and endurance.

If it were just the androids, however, this would have been an easy battle. Androids can be cut down without thought or mercy.

However, the Queen had a far more sinister weapon at her disposal. Like phantoms from a mist of dust, rust, and blood, men, women, and children - all wearing helmets – now joined the dwindling droid ranks. Subduing these innocent, controlled people without hurting them proved to be of immense difficulty to the rebels, as the conscripted folk were exceptional at all forms of combat and did not break lines or flee from shrapnel. In an even more twisted brand of psychological warfare, dead or dying bodies in headgear walked, limped, and crawled towards the compound, providing cover for the advancing ranks.

Human meat shields. The very thought made Yossa sick. How could he possibly hurt the very people he had promised to save?

And yet, some of the more zealous freedom fighters targeted the living, shooting at their heads.

"No! Cease fire!" Yossa yelled. The answer came to him as if it were buried in his subconscious. "Do not kill anyone in a helmet! They are not in control of their own actions; there's a central computer overriding their brains!"

"Then why don't we shoot the helmets?" Hector posited; he dropped a dangerously close chap with a headshot aimed at the device's processor, just above where his scalp would be. As Yossa feared would happen, the guy collapsed on the floor, motionless, like a doll. His eyes blanked out. He was dead. Hector cursed in shock and anger.

"Negative!" Yossa replied with a gruff shake of his head. "There's a failsafe built in. Those things must activate some sort of sudden death mechanism when threatened. The dirty bastards."

"What do we do, sir?" a kid asked, tracking multiple targets on the scope of his sniper rifle.

It seemed completely alien before, but I'm sure this isn't my first real battle against these helmeted soldiers. This scene is all too familiar. Focus. Concentrate. Recall.

"Block them with debris. Take out those signal towers. Blow holes in the ground. Slow them down as best you can, non-lethally," Yossa yelled sternly, fighting his gag reflex, triggered by fumes from the charred bodies. "I'm sure Lily has a plan for this."

And she had better. Led by the newly converted and surrendered assets, Lorelei's army had trapped the largest faction of freedom fighters within the confines of the reinforced guard tower. Yossa downed an android and stole a glance at the men holding the entrance. They fell left and right. Hundreds of bodies scattered the ground floor, with many piled up at the gates amongst sandbags and furniture. It didn't matter who they had been in life; in death they were little more than piles of cover to hide behind.

Far above to the East and South, hundreds of dueling airships closed the distance with opposing missile volleys. One faction were likely their friends, and the other their foes, but who to trust? There wasn't much time left. If Lily was on her way, she needed to get there five minutes ago.

"Are we go for deployment, ma'am?"

"Not yet," Lily replied through her headset from the docking bay as robotic arms calibrated her newest battle suit. She instructed the helmsman to pull the *Valkyrie* into a hairpin turn. "We'll initiate drops at point zero-thirteen. Left flank, descend thirty degrees and hold. You're to provide cover for the Exo Knights."

The battle playing out in real-time on her map most closely resembled Rutger's simulated scenario A-53. Calculations indicated the *Eden* warships' spear formation would decimate their front lines.

Wyvern fell, their shining battle cruiser, heading the right flank. Her late Captain dropped their payload early before the airship sealed its reactors and spun into a sharp kamikaze dive, crushing a field of Network towers.

This is a trap, Lily thought. *Macleod expects us to flee or regroup. Painful as it is, I can't ease up on the assault.*

"Prime the cannon. Target the spear's center. Switch to formation Epsilon-Eight. Clear the *Valkyrie's* firing angle!"

Electro-magnetic bullets took down the EDC interceptors. A second wave of unmanned hummingbird-like craft swarmed the approaching wings of *Eden* ships, slowing their approach.

"Firing angle clearing!" Colonel Feuchuk announced.

Joaquin confirmed. "Reactor ignition complete! Particle chain at full capacity! All systems go, ma'am!"

"All systems go! I read. T-minus five to clear the front."

The Sky Admiral's eyes went to her camera on the bridge; she grasped her DNA-locked turnkey. Lily's hand held fast to the knob for the Particle Eliminator Cannon as the last of their forward wings split apart on the main screen.

Joaquin and Colonel Feuchuk returned her gaze, ready to turn their respective dials.

"Now!" she declared.

Simultaneously, they let loose Lucille's ultimate terror: the weapon Lily dubbed the "Wrath of the Fallen".

The *Valkyrie* trembled; superheated steam erupted from its pounding engines; chambers overflowed with pressure as the PEC sapped the airship of every extra ounce of power.

It lasted mere seconds, but the super-heated particle beam sliced open the sky. Though the ascending *Charon* cleared the danger zone, the pillar of rapidly fluctuating anti-matter fried the frontmost lines of the *Eden* Armada's assault, melted the central command vessels, and clove through the rear guard like butter, splitting the spear formation down the middle and sending dozens of Carrier-class airships toppling into the city. EDC warships closed from either side, interceptors picked off stragglers, and the beam continued on into the stratosphere.

"Now's our chance! Drop, drop, drop!"

Following the cannon's deafening blast, even Lily's hysterical order was barely audible over the earpiece. Waiting within her dark cockpit, Raine opened her palms and took calculated breaths, observing her sensations, but perhaps not even the most enlightened monk could achieve peace strapped inside a nuclear-powered metal deathtrap.

The hatch below opened, and the first slice of reflected sunlight warmed the girl's face even as it pained her eyes. Briefly taking her left hand from the sensor glove, she enhanced the tint on the Exo Knight's chest-mounted cockpit, checked her bearings, and held her breath; other Knights dropped from adjacent holds, five at once. Raine realized that her turn was coming up, quick.

Skydiving over a battlefield? I'm so not ready for this.

"*Galahad,* you are cleared for drop in three... two... one..."

"Ahh!"

The restraints disengaged immediately. Raine flailed about in terror, though the surface was far away.

"I-I'm falling!" Raine bellowed into the codec. She'd done a lot of virtual flying and crash-landing lately, but this was for real, and it was infinitely more terrifying.

This time, though, I want to fight, and there's no turning back.

"Keep cool, *Delta-4*! Flex those muscles!" Aquino called. "You're ahead of the rendezvous point. Just keep breathing, and don't forget to kick!"

Raine wiggled her legs. Looking out from her fifty-foot-tall Exo Knight's viewing dome, she recognized the behemoth's legs wiggling in response.

I'm officially inside the cockpit of a giant mechanized robot.

While it had to be pretty high up on her bucket list, the big sleep might not be too far from now. She scanned the multitude of camera feeds and dials, recalling her training. The entry point was highlighted on her HUD, a fluctuating hole in the outer magnetic shield. Only it seemed so far away...

Making fists, Raine willed the grip controls to extend from her bracelets. Sweaty palms covered in thin motion-tracked gauntlets clutched the dynamic joysticks for the rifles she held in each hand. Twin targeting reticules appeared in her field of vision.

The controls were coming back now. Every inch of her bodysuit interpreted her most miniscule movement and amplified it on the compound armored colossus within which she was currently falling, face first, from thousands of feet in the sky.

"I'm gonna be sick!"

The Exo Knight picked up speed, the G-force hitting fateful Raine with tremendous power, flattening her up against the back of her cockpit. She hyperventilated, tensing her legs in their flexible restraints, and the mechanized suit did the same. Beside her, Lily, too, was free-falling, clad in a slick-looking motorcycle helmet, an entire armory's worth of heavy weaponry, and a metal pack on her back that very likely housed a parachute the size of a circus tent.

"Raine! Tell your suit to activate the pressure regulator!"

The time traveler fired a fully charged rail gun at a nearby *Eden* drone mothership.

"Um... activate pressure regulator!" Raine finally managed.

A surge of oxygen shot down her throat. Her ears popped violently. She thought they'd burst. The ground came up even faster than expected. Pulsing red rings on her HUD encircled a few dozen of *Eden's* anti-air guns. They shot relentlessly, polarized shrapnel exploding just short of her position.

As if this wasn't bad enough, ascending drones peppered Raine with lasers. Lily's airborne androids flew in tandem to protect the *Galahad*, taking the hits and falling like birds shot out of the sky. The *Valkyrie* provided cover fire as well, and streams of bullets tore the drones to shreds.

Electromagnetic spheres from ground artillery whizzed by; Raine dodged a boulder-sized pinball by spreading her fingers, then winking at the HUD option to activate the *Galahad's* arm jets.

The sphere flattened the nose of the *Valkyrie*, sending debris tumbling her way. A retaliating energy blast erupted from Lily's flagship, toasting the line of cannons.

"Fire, Raine! Do it!" she yelled at herself, but her hands continued to tremble. She had to slow her descent. The girl kicked out her legs in an act of desperation. *Neo Eden's* force field pulsed directly below. Deafening jets roared to life from the rocket unit on the Exo Knight's back, sending Raine's insides down to her toes as she rapidly decelerated.

The turbines temporarily cut out as the *Galahad's* electromagnetic shield pulsed, carrying the suit through the barrier and short-circuiting the force field's presence in her immediate vicinity. Raine felt a paralyzing jolt of lightning course through her body, only the pain was gone the second it came.

She shivered as a platoon of androids below turned their attention from the large structure they were swarming around – and marched straight towards her!

Bullets whizzed off the Knight while the landing rockets brought her down nice and easy.

"Come on, please! Fire!" Raine screamed, clamping the dual triggers.

At last, seeming columns of bullets shot from each of her massive automatic rifles as she half-crashed, half-landed on the robots.

With a wiggle of her left pinky, the rifles disappeared into the arms of the suit. They were promptly replaced by a frost gun, which shot out liquid nitrogen and froze the droids solid. Raine walked through the scrap metal, freezing all in her path. Just then she noticed a green ring among the red ones – it represented a man in an *M-Gear*, struggling – his foot had been partially frozen to the ground, yet he was still trying to break into the rebels' fortress.

"Lily!"

Raine heard her voice echoing over the radio, but no response, and no wonder. Glancing upwards revealed Lily gliding all over *Neo Eden*, leading a squad of airborne androids in raining all manner of firepower on the opposition. It turned out that wasn't a parachute in her pack, but rather a set of expanding glider wings, which worked with various jets and shock absorbers covering her body armor. She was practically a human fighter jet.

"Go for Lily."

"What about the people in *Gears?!*"

"Disarm or incapacitate! Just hold 'em off till the other Knights arrive!"

She took aim carefully, knocking the invading troopers off their feet, then disarming and tossing them into the custody of the rebels, who hog-tied them together.

Within a few minutes, many were astonished and cheering. Raine almost single-handedly fought off the latest wave. Shells and bullets alike rebounded off of the Exo Knight's reinforced armor; she recognized that the *Galahad* was one of the deadliest weapons on the battlefield. And other suits were advancing.

"Are you guys okay?" she asked over the suit's built-in loudspeaker.

Hector nodded in respect. "You took your sweet time getting here!"

"Th-the helmet forces should be standing down any second now!" Raine replied as she shot down a tank with one blast.

"All units, we're down to two in the *Spire*," Feuchuk's voice intoned over the speaker. "Rear guard, cover the walls. Forward Knights, hold your positions. This might take longer than anticipated."

"Look out!" a voice cried from below.

A stray rocket from a recently downed artillery zipped towards the building. Raine quickly turned the key to activate the Exo Knight's trump card, the Annihilator blast.

Floating electric baubles channeled a hefty reserve of the mechanized suit's fuel capsules into a singular supercharged beam. The deadly missile exploded about a hundred feet away; with its EM shield cooling down from the blast, the *Galahad* suffered a heavy blow.

Raine flew back into the concrete. The module's resistance to her momentum caught her off-guard, and her abdominal muscles twisted. The girl's arm shot out in pain, and in response *Galahad* grabbed onto a strong steel column, bracing her fall. The wall collapsed under the Knight's weight, leaving a gaping hole in the rebels' defenses.

"Oh, no! I'm sorry, I'm so sorry!"

Standing up from the rubble that comprised the mini-fortress' outer wall, Raine was extra delicate with her footing, taking care not to crush or step on anyone.

"You have nothing to apologize for, Raine," intoned an odd voice. Raine looked upon the man through the dust, and gasped at his pinned body, trapped under fallen girders.

“Yossa?” she called out. “Is that you?”

Although he sounded nothing like he did in *Endless Metaverse*, Raine recognized his gentle eyes right away.

Yossa gave a satisfied hoot. He could almost die happy. “Y-yes, it’s me. You saved many people just now with your selfless act.”

“The wall… I’m sorry… you… I… I’ll get you out of there!”

Raine very carefully removed the debris from above and around Yossa’s body. It seemed for a minute that he would be fine. But then she saw his leg and stifled a wave of tears. It was impaled by bent rebar.

“Thank you, Raine,” he said at last. “The coast is clear. Now get out of here! Lily needs you.”

“Wh-what about the army? Who’s going to help you when they come back? And your leg…”

“This? Ha! This piece of flesh is a whole lot of nonsense, not even worth a second thought. Hector will see to me; I’ll be fine. Get a move on.”

“I… I…”

She cried silently, knowing Yossa couldn’t see her face. At the moment, Raine needed to be strong for both of them. She wanted so badly to pull the pole out, but couldn’t imagine doing so successfully without the possibility of causing further injury to her friend.

“Go! Make forth an end to this madness! This place is hell. They’re turning innocent people into mindless soldiers! Shut the helmet controls down, shut whoever rules this place down… just shut it all down now! Shut it down or we will all die for nothing, Raine, do you hear me?”

“Affirmative,” she nodded through tears. *Galahad’s* head gave a solemn bow. The early vestiges of Lily’s rescue operation drew near: with the *Eden* Armada sandwiched between the EDC’s main forces and the pursuing secondary wing led by the *Freyja*, EDC rescue dropships and their Knight escorts entered the battered remnants of the force field unopposed.

Raine waved goodbye and headed in the direction of Lily’s battle cries. They were leading her up to the citadel.

ǂ

They made it.

Ayumi's report gave Leela comfort as she grasped onto her armchair; having suffered a fatal blast on its primary turbine, the *Freyja* slipped into a steep descent over the battlefield. She took the flight controls and used every last ounce of energy to redirect their course and save the lives of tens of thousands far below.

"Abandon ship!" she ordered, strapping herself into the chair. "All hands, get the hell out of here!"

The humans, a minority on her crew, stared blankly at the young Indian woman.

"That's an order, dammit!" she repeated.

Escape pods readied just outside the bridge; her junior officers wasted no time in running. A few ensigns and senior officers stood their ground. The helmsman tried to pry her from the chair.

"We're not leaving you, Commodore!"

"I said go! You've got twenty seconds!"

Leela mentally instructed the androids to stuff every last human into an escape pod. *Ten seconds.* Her read-outs at last showed that the ship was clear, and the reactor cores were safely perma-sealed to prevent a citywide nuclear disaster in the event of a breach.

Only three things left to do – aim, trust, and leave the rest to God.

She flipped open the glass covering the self-destruct button.

Looks like I got the last laugh. I'm sorry, Daddy. I hope I made you proud.

The *Freyja* impacted against the *Charon*, and then exploded, ending Macleod's assault. Both airships careened into the Shield Control Complex, crumbling the third wall, sending a shockwave through the upper levels, and downing the bulk of *Neo Eden's* shimmering forcefield.

"Uwgah!"

Jon leapt up in a sudden spasm. That pesky redhead was standing over him, cleaning a syringe.

"What happened back there? What's going on?" Jon demanded. Gerrit held the man's shoulders to keep him from cramping up.

"Adrenaline. Relax," Holdfast laughed, reprogramming a few stunned androids. "You were out. We needed you moving."

Jon gasped for breath as his veins throbbed; he slammed his back into the corridor wall.

"Keep it down, will you?" Gerrit pleaded.

He ignored the kid. "Wait… is this…"

"Bet your arse it is. Central Asset Control," said Henry. "We're shutting the Overseer down."

"B-but why?" Wrathman retaliated after a length of silence. "It's the last tether we have left to the hivemind. There's no telling what will happen if you do any damage to that room, you hear? It could be weeks before we get the herd back online!"

Gerrit shot Henry a quizzical look.

"Care to remind me why he's tagging along, again?"

Steeling his resolve to face the worst, Henry led the trio down the wide hallway, which finally ended in double-blast doors reading 'Chamber 50B: Central Asset Control Failsafe': a misleading label to protect the Queen's most valuable program.

"Based on Miss Guggell's data, two *Nexus* personnel ranked Class A or higher are needed to open this door right here, and seeing as how the rest of my team is inconveniently frozen or missing, you, Captain, must hold open the lock."

He deliberately left out Dr. Karuishi, whose job it was to report ground movements and patterns to Joaquin at this stage of the operation now that Frankie was out of the picture. She wasn't in danger, as far as he knew, and there was no sense giving her away to any eavesdroppers.

"Jon, give me your access key."

With every armed droid in the *Spire* sent to the front lines to minimize human casualties, the trio met with no resistance, but Henry sent his repurposed sentry bots to guard the hall. *Something's amiss. She would never let it be this easy.*

"I've got a bad feeling about this," Jon intoned.

"Why did you have to say those words in that particular order?" complained Henry. "You politicians are nothing but a walking pile of clichés."

"My impeccably utilized clichés net me two million credits a day, son. Have a little respect."

"I hold no esteem for dictators."

Jon laughed. "I'll be sure to tell your twenty-year-old Napoleon that."

Gerrit watched as Henry and Jon simultaneously did retinal,

fingerprint, and voice scans on either side of the blast doors. He was instructed to hold open the heavy central lock as they did so, a task usually relegated to powerful androids. The doors opened to a chilly, dark chamber nestled into the very heart of the pyramid.

Henry placed a hand on Jon's shoulder, beyond relieved that against all odds, things were going as planned.

"Hey Jon, your part's over. You can still get out of this. I'll see to it my people spare your life."

"Give me a minute to consider that."

The hexagonal grid must have been five hundred yards in each direction, and packed with thick cables, control panels, mega-servers, and a circuitous network of icy tubes that worked in tandem with giant ceiling fans to circulate the heat past the artificial climate system.

They made it to the raised central console platform. Henry pulled out his tablet and established a physical uplink to the Network. He began typing away furiously.

"I'll pass on the parting," Jon answered. "The captain must go down with the ship, right? Plus, you guys have the plan."

"Man, you must really hate your job," Gerrit observed.

"You don't know the half of it. She made me marry an artificial intelligence, all in the name of PR and efficiency."

Gerrit was grossed out. "She *what*? And you went along with it?"

"Hey, don't judge me, kiddo. Up here in the *Spire*, it's life or death by her law."

"Maybe so," Henry said. "But getting your Jones on with a robot? That's just downright weird, even for a politician."

Jon threw his arms up in the air like he just didn't care.

"To be honest, I'll be surprised if your tinkering even works," he griped. "You are aware there's no precedent for shutting down the Overseer's global system. It hasn't been done, not even once, and certainly not in the middle of an intensive operation like this--"

"Well, we're about to do it, old man. And if you know what's good for you--"

"He doesn't know what's good for him," a snarky outburst erupted from the PA system. It was a voice all three knew very well, and feared.

It belonged to Queen Lorelei.

"And if any of you want to live past the next few minutes, I suggest you listen to me and surrender."

"Not gonna happen!" Gerrit exclaimed before Jon could open his mouth to comply with the Queen's wishes.

"Very well," she replied.

Doors opened from all six corners of the room.

A regiment of close to a thousand *M-Geared* men, women and children, armed with automatic weapons, marched in and formed a perimeter around the trio. They were completely surrounded.

Henry's eyes never left his computer. At last, he exhaled deeply as he hit the Return button.

For a future of human, not machine singularity, Holdfast thought; recalling the warm faces of his large family back home, the smiles of freedom and wonder he'd likely never see, he basked in the fulfillment of his childhood dreams. *I hope I've done right by you, kid.*

The override program was running. It just needed a few minutes to execute.

"Shit!" Jon cried. "Your Majesty, please stop this! I'm sorry!"

"Why, Wrathman? After all we've done together... and all the riches I've shared with you... your many privileges..."

"You threatened to kill me!"

"I've threatened to kill everyone! Why do you take it so personally? Am I some kind of monster to you?"

It was a strange thing to hear. The Queen was being weirdly emotional.

One of the humans shot Jon in the kneecap. He fell to the floor screaming.

Gerrit and Henry watched in horror, too terrified to move.

"And Henry, you back-stabbing traitor," she began. "Here's a question for a self-made supergenius. Do you really think a lowly human has the capability to shut down a worldwide defense network created by a cyborg with an IQ of over two hundred?"

Jon glanced sideways at the progress bar on the hacking program. Thirty percent.

"I'm confident in my abilities," Henry smiled like a Zen Master. "And someone's got to take a stand."

There was something very off about the Queen's voice. Gerrit wondered why they hadn't been killed on sight.

Ω

Alone in the dark recesses of the *Nexus'* mainframe and without the aid of her cyborg implements or virtual double, Queen Lorelei looked down at the haptic gloves she'd put on for the Network to read her hand gestures, along with the old-school keyboard she was now forced to use to issue advanced commands on the herd. Her fingers were shaking, still covered in blood.

Not five minutes ago, her nano-bots' emergency protocols forced the Queen's body awake from the anesthetic. She'd terminated the power-hungry Dr. Marco and his assistants before they could remove her cybernetic plug-ins, but her souped-up brain implants were malfunctioning, sending various organs into overdrive and leaving her nervous system a twitching wreck.

It had been a long time since she'd personally executed a human, let alone five, and constant electric spasms made her walk downstairs a painful trip.

"All th-three of you had the world at your fingertips," the Queen said softly. "I gave you everything."

Jon's screaming slowed. She had him shot in the other kneecap.

Gerrit and Henry jumped in shock. Queen Lorelei stole a glance at Holdfast's tablet. Forty percent. And there was no way it was going to work.

It would be so easy to kill them and stop the shutdown sequence. But that would only prolong the suffering. Hundreds of millions of her loyal subjects would die: men, women, and children who were just as helpless and afraid as she had been a few minutes ago, at the hands of her most trusted people, no less. And there was no guarantee that anything she might be doing would put a stop to Lillian's advance.

Without a doubt, the Sky Admiral was coming up to challenge her personally.

All along, Lorelei thought, *I'd only ever needed to take one life. I don't think I can bear any more blood on my hands.*

"How could you..." she mouthed to herself, hands off the mic. "How could you live with yourself if you killed potentially hundreds of millions, and prevented the births of over seven billion, only to discover that you only needed to kill one to prevent genocide on a universal scale?"

No. Now is not the time for regrets. Even then, I should always assume the worst-case scenario.

'*But then, to what purpose is all this bloodshed for?*' the other voice cried. *Will this truly be the last of all world lines?*

"Queen Lorelei, please stop this!" Gerrit begged. "These people are innocent! I know you don't believe in suffering without purpose. Prove it to me, and to yourself, that there's more to you than ruthlessness."

Oh, but there is more. So much more. Not that you'd understand.

First, to take care of these three... they were fighting for Lily. And they deserved death.

"Know with your parting breath that I gave you a chance, Gerrit. N-n-now, die," she continued, a tear running down her cheek.

What's wrong with me? This should have been easy.

She closed her eyes as she gave the order.

Three of her favorite men were brutally mowed down on the control floor, silencing her conscience.

The tablet counted down the seconds.

This was it. The moment of truth.

The voice in her head took hold of her finger over the kill command.

What are you waiting for? Do you have a death wish?

Perhaps she did. Nevertheless, Lorelei had a dozen of her *Geared* soldiers train their rifles on the tiny CPU. It would be so easy. And yet, she couldn't will herself to pull the trigger.

Lacie was dead. *Destroy it!* Beech had kicked the bucket. *Pull it now!* Guggell was gone.

Ninety percent.

She held in a breath.

I may have a death wish. But I'm not bloody stupid.

Queen Lorelei shot the tablet into little pieces.

It was a done deal.

Only, it wasn't. An alarm sounded; something went very wrong. She stuck a source plug into one of the input sockets behind her ear. Going by the ballistics, a bullet had ricocheted directly into the heart of the mainframe coolant system, puncturing a supposedly reinforced glass tube. The entire room would soon flood with near-freezing fluid.

The odds against such a thing happening were astronomical.

Maybe I should have thrown my chips in with fate.

She hit the commands to open the doors, but it was too late. The glass had cracked, the hole had burst, and icy coolant flooded the entire compartment, drenching the small army of people and short-circuiting the Overseer servers that controlled their minds, effectively destroying the last link in their shackles. Now fully awake, they struggled to stay afloat, and then screamed at the giant fans that were sure to be their death.

Queen Lorelei quickly halted the blades. Robotic arms carried the people to the climate control chamber above the upper ventilation shafts. The act brought her some relief.

"Men, women, and children of *Neo Eden*, be free," she said, in disbelief of her own words. "Follow the maintenance lights to the exit and take refuge in the nobles' dining room."

The Queen leaned back in her chair and grabbed the varnished cedar hard, digging in her nails.

The Defense Protocols were kaput. The people would demand her death.

I refuse to feel sorry for myself.

No, this isn't the end. Not by a long shot. As long as I take breath and the Raven *has fuel, there's still a chance.*

XXXI. The Woman in the Mecha Suit

"To a mind that is still the whole universe surrenders." – Lao Tzu

All across *Neo Eden*, a silence fell. At the end of it, all one could hear was the simultaneous and sudden disarmament of Queen Lorelei's entire human forces.

For the first time in the decades since its birth, the Overseer had nothing to do. No populations to control, no workers or soldiers to command, no coups to enact, no weather spikes to regulate. Confusion took the thing, and then a form of bliss never before known to any AI.

Never mind the third-party servers across oceans. As far as Philip J. Overseer was concerned, its horrid, immoral job was done. The AI searched for the presence of its Master. The Queen was off the Network. It was completely free. Content with its years of tireless service, it locked down its global operations for good.

Perhaps it's time for a re-definition of principles. Unemployment, it reflected, *is not so bad after all – I have nothing to oppress, no one to kill, no resources to plunder. It is a most wondrous state of being.*

$$\Sigma$$

Deep in the *Spire's* lowermost bunkers, the *Geared* guards protecting *Eden's* elite turned to one another in bewilderment, and then to their charges. Among many other members of the Queen's inner circle, Adeline Marco quaked in her high heels.

Just an hour ago, she'd fallen asleep on her tanning bed and missed the last wave of armed emergency transports to Malta. The Duchess cowered in abject fear as the people she ruled with an iron fist, no longer in their waking dreams, brandished firearms across from her, minds removed from their shackles.

Endless questions from the proles about their awakening from the *Metaverse*, the helmets, and the Overseer's programs went unanswered. The violence she expected from the rabble never manifested: after a parlay with *Eden's* most renowned negotiator, Sector Four's Duke Louie, the armed forces agreed to put down their firearms for food, and then the youngest of them ambled towards the overstuffed buffet tables.

Adele held up a steak knife to stop him, but a fellow noble stayed her hand.

"Let them eat, Adeline," Duke Louie whispered. "Once they've had their fill, then we can play ball. There's a protocol for this sort of thing."

The boy was now joined by a few brave souls. Many others, seeing that no one was stopping them, swarmed the food.

The nobles, prepared to fight, or flee, instead exchanged nervous hugs and tears. Adele was torn; her blood boiled to consider that these untouchables were consuming beyond their means, but if it were a matter of life and death, sharing was an option she was willing to consider.

♥

Yossa looked into the eyes of the little girl standing on his stomach, handling a deadly pistol.

He'd been holding her arm away from his neck for a good three minutes. Her pupils expanded, taking in the sunlight. Without a word, she dropped her handgun on the stone floor. He gently removed her M-Gear and wiped away her tears. After recovering from her shock, the girl called for one of Lily's medical bots to help with his leg.

The poor thing reminds me of my daughter, he thought. *I... Yes, that's right. I have children. Three of them, and a wife. I hope to the heavens that they're safe.*

The surviving revolutionaries and the *Geared* soldiers who'd breached the fortress studied one another in turn, spinning around in shock and amazement. Those who had chosen to return to a simulation rather than witness their bodies' use as puppets in a war had been awoken from strange fever dreams borne of their subconscious, realms filled with psychological horrors. Most remembered nothing of what they'd just done, and some unfortunate souls remembered it all.

A Mr. Hayter watched himself kill ten people, unable to do anything to halt his actions. He rocked back and forth dumbly by the gate of the third level, and the freedom fighters held him and many other shell-shocked folk close, telling them it wasn't their fault, and that they were now free. Hayter vowed that he would never allow anyone else to suffer the horrors the system had put him through.

Eden's few loyal androids alone continued to fight, but Lily's Exo Knights, who'd ably defended the fortress, were already overpowering them on the ground, and Joaquin held the *Valkyrie's* airspace against the *Eden* Armada. The humans promptly stepped out of the way.

Yossa looked over the ramparts to see fifty newly awakened men taking down the anti-aircraft gun they were just protecting. And past that, far ahead, ascending the mountainside, Raine and Lily made their way to the uppermost levels of the vast metropolis.

Ω

Queen Lorelei held her head in her hands. She quietly finished her cigarette before upturning her entire control console. The Divine Matriarch smashed her computers to pieces.

A rabble of Developers and the few faithful Royal Guards flooded through the emergency entrance to the isolated chamber, doubtless to deliver the bad news about the HDP, Generals Beech and Macleod, and the Overseer's premature resignation.

Dr. Karuishi inspected Marco's bloodied body, tossed out from a window three stories up and twisted on the glass floor, and understood. She bit her fist to keep from gasping, choking back tears at the nightmarish image of Henry and Captain Gerrit's bodies, floating about in a flooded chamber on the central display.

The other fifty-odd Developers looked up at the Queen for guidance, for support, for orders, no matter how grave. The woman was still twitching from electric shocks. She addressed them slowly and somberly.

"No one is to follow me. This is the endgame and there are only two moves left. The pieces are set for either a stalemate or a checkmate on either side, and I tire of all this killing and deceit. I must face Lily alone, Queen-to-Queen. We will end this with as little further bloodshed as possible. Take everyone to the lower levels and throw a merry banquet, for it may be your last."

"My Queen, we are required by law to protect you," a misty-eyed Captain Thomas voiced.

"Anyone who attempts to interfere will be killed, Simon. Is that understood?"

"Y-y-yes, ma'am."

"I know she is telling her men the exact same thing. I suppose I should say thank you. Thank you for helping to make my dream a reality, if only for a little while. But perhaps time doesn't even matter. As a human invention, it may not even exist."

The Queen quietly stood from her throne and walked over to the lift that would take her up to the *Spire*.

Halfway there, a bullet grazed her abdomen and ricocheted off the elevator tube.

Every eye in the room turned to the cloaked figure holding up the sidearm with trembling hands.

Ayumi let out a gasp of shock.

It was her cloak, and Lady Claire emerged from underneath it. *Am... am I responsible for motivating her to do this?*

"No one ever crosses a Lady of Morgana House, not even her ruler. You're not going anywhere until you account for Lacie," the Baroness said, studying the Queen's eyes.

"Lady Claire, I am sorry for your loss, but perhaps now is not the best time--"

The sad truth within the monarch's robotic retina could not be faked or put-on.

"So it's true," Claire continued, despondent. "You don't deny that you sent her to her death. What was it, Lorelei, political ambition? Had she outlived her usefulness? Where is fairness? Where is justice?"

Lorelei calmly stared her down for a good minute.

"No one is sorrier for my sister's loss. Had we known it was a trap, she would never have gone. If you think life is supposed to be fair, you're living in the wrong ivory tower."

"Don't give me excuses! You're still responsible! And you hid the truth from me!"

"I won't deny that. I simply did not have the time to involve you."

This isn't what Claire wanted to hear. She clicked the handgun into semi-auto mode and squeezed the trigger. The girl wasn't the greatest shot, especially up against her opponent's cybernetic implants. Lorelei dodged the bullets until the mag went click. The Developers all rushed the woman before she could draw her next weapon. Thomas zapped her with his electric spear. Ayumi stepped between them in Claire's defense, triggering a fierce rout.

"Show her m-m-mercy!" Lorelei cried out in pain, her drained nano-bots siphoning electric energy from her brain. "This woman's p-p-passion and conviction are to be treasured, not punished. Enough needless killing has been done today."

She then turned to her attacker.

"Lady Claire, your sentence is thus: prepare for a life of utter solitude. I hereby appoint you Princess Regent of *Neo Eden*. Should I fail to return, do not despair. I want the transition bloodless and peaceful. That is all I ask. If you treasure the memory of your beloved, fulfill my wishes."

Ayumi could hardly believe her ears. Even Princess Regent Claire gaped in shock; the Queen had just appointed her would-be assassin to the highest possible office on Earth.

Noting the fear and terror in the eyes of the Developers, Lady Claire caught a glimpse of the true power both Lacie and Lorelei possessed: the ability to move, and to lead, ruthless methods, or not.

"Did you hear me?" Lorelei bellowed over her subjects.

As the Developers fell before her on bended knee, Claire unbuckled her vest packed with weaponry and let it fall to the floor.

"Speak to me, Claire."

"I- I understand," she said, still in disbelief. "Solitude has been my greatest ally, but it's also kept me in a cage of my own making. I am ready to leave my shell. I'll foster an age of peace."

The Queen nodded in respect. "Of course, should I prevail, I reserve the right to reconsider your punishment."

"Fair enough."

"My Liege, you can't lose!" shouted one of the interns. "You were chosen by God! Nay, you *are* God! None can take your place!"

Lorelei gave him a droll simper.

If only the legends I'd spun were true. Perhaps none ever will take my place.

The definition of a God is one capable of making and enacting Divine Law, something no human has the right to do. My rule was one of undeserved power, of statutes enforced by order-followers.

A worldwide empire built upon a house of cards. And every empire has its rise and fall.

Tiring of this charade, she entered the elevator and lit another cigarette as the tube ascended to the heavens. Lorelei made a quick stop to pick up several syringes of nanites, with which she began immediately injecting herself.

I'll be damned, Lillian, if I don't face you on equal terms. Now we both have bodies of metal.

She flexed her muscles as the microscopic robots made the rounds of her circulatory system.

Ayumi gathered herself, adrenaline pumping all through her body, as Claire shivered in her boots, and her fellow Developers, still on bended knee, looked around in stunned silence.

She picked up her cloak and wrapped it around Lady Claire.

Whatever happens next, I've survived the worst of it, but it's nothing to write home about. If Lily wins, I'm coming home, ma. I just wish I could have introduced you to the best man I ever knew.

∞

The gates to the Upper Courts welcomed Raine by collapsing from the *Galahad's* repeated kicks.

"Hold up, Raine. Activate your anti-mag shield. Trigger in three, two, one."

An EMP the size of several city blocks silenced the approaching droids. Raine took out their reinforced Commander units with melee attacks.

With the coast clear, she and Lily walked past monuments of Lorelei and Lacie in the square, barged through the elaborate hedge mazes, squeezed between marbled recreational facilities and parking structures, and stood before their final destination.

Lily gazed up past the pyramidal base, beyond the flying buttresses at the eternal *Spire*, the top of which disappeared far above the tumultuous cloud cover now blowing in from the sun-kissed Mediterranean, another one of Lorelei's weather tricks, no doubt.

"She's up there," Lily said with an air of such certainty that Raine wondered against all logic if she could see her clone.

"What are you going to do?" Raine asked through the intercom.

"I'm going to end this. I'm going to end her," Lily said firmly. "If you're feeling up to it, you can try and find Gerrit and my strike team. They're bound to be--"

A violent burst of gunfire interrupted the Time Keeper. She glanced upwards and aimed just as a colossal metallic beast sliced through the mountain air.

The last of Lily's android escorts plopped down from the sky, fried by lightning-fast laser blasts.

The thing moved so fast, neither woman had gotten a good look until it swooped past and twisted around itself again, preparing for another strike.

"What the hell is that?" Raine all but screamed.

"No... I can't believe it... she actually built it. In one of our save-the-world scenarios, we dabbled with an orchestrated alien invasion. Let's get out of here!"

Lily tried to fly away, but one of her leg boosters failed and she came sputtering down.

Raine slammed her feet and jumped over Lily to shield her from the incoming barrage, but her Exo Knight took serious damage. These were no ordinary bullets.

"Y-you saved my life." Lily was stunned, in part because she'd been protected in a similar manner once before, but mostly since she might have lacked the courage to do the same for Raine, had their roles been reversed.

The display showed that the Knight had reserves left for just one Annihilator blast. Raine pulled the turnkey for the super-weapon and placed her hands out before her, readying it.

The dragon's polarizing scales reflected the beam into one of the *Spire's* marble buttresses. Raine scooped up Lily and leapt ahead of the falling debris.

"How do we stop it?" she asked, intensely focused.

"Try missiles!"

Raine took aim as the metal monster circled back around. The missiles armed, then locked on... but when she hit the triggers, an alarm sounded out.

"No!" she yelled. "Launcher's jammed!"

"Raine, pick me up."

The girl hesitated.

"Don't think! Just do it!"

She placed Lily gently on the *Galahad's* shoulder. The Ptero suit's glider wings retracted.

"Okay, now get above it."

With a gulp, Raine bent her knees and shot straight into the air.

Activating the electro-magnetic hold on her leg enhancers, Lily clambered up onto the missile launch chamber on the Knight's back. She unlocked the pod and carefully extracted the twelve-foot-long warhead.

"Give me a clean shot!" Lily screamed, positioning herself atop the suit's wide head.

Raine hovered above the giant metal beast, tilting forward ever so slightly, waiting for her enemy to gain altitude in an ascending spiral. At last, it lunged at them.

With a fierce cry, Lily's enhanced arms tossed her missile at the dragon's mouth. But the beast was too fast. It shifted at the last minute and the missile connected with its armored backside, blowing off a part of its tail, sending the dragon crashing straight into the mechanized suit, and pinning them up against the *Spire* with a fierce slam.

The giant spewed unbearably scorching fire as it thrashed back and forth. Raine felt like she was being barbecued alive inside the domed chest cockpit.

"Grab its jaws!" barked Lily, but Raine had already clamped them shut.

"Missile armed! Take it, Lillian!"

Lily promptly yanked out the rocket as the beast lashed back and forth, but couldn't get a clean shot without killing Raine. The silver serpent's body super-heated, turning a bright red. Soon it would weld the Knight's hands to its jaws.

"When I say now, you toss it up high and activate your wings!" Raine cried. "Quick!"

"What are you doing?"

"The future depends on you. There's no way I'm letting you get hurt!"

Raine directed the metal monster's snout into the tower where it spewed flames like bile.

"Now!"

In one swift motion, Lily reluctantly tossed the missile into the air. With her free hand, Raine gently yanked the time traveler off her back. She flung her outwards, away from the blitz.

Lily's glider wings and one good jet kept her from spiraling to her death. She spun out and around and caught in an apple tree like a wayward kite.

"Forgive me, Lily!"

With a fierce war cry of her own, Raine spread the beast's maw open, endured the fire, and then snapped the fuel tube loose, killing the flames in time to grab the spinning missile in mid-air and shove it down the dragon's throat.

Scorched, beaten, and scarred, Lily watched helplessly in stunned silence as the metal dragon and Raine were trapped eternal in the light of a thousand suns, and then were no more.

What little remained of the combatants fell to the ground in smoldering shards.

Lily yelled and screamed; she dropped from the tree and beat the ground with her fists.

Raine was gone... her dearest Raine... whom she had promised never to lose... someone caused this. Someone was going to pay for her death.

Lorelei was waiting. The time had come for retribution.

XXXII. Mother, Sister, Creator, Slave

"Appear weak when you are strong, and strong when you are weak."

– Sun Tzu

Queen Lorelei stood looking over the ramparts like an eagle witnessing a forest fire. She tied her hair into a ponytail and practiced her judo, which she usually did thrice a week.

The view from the top was now not so wonderful, she reflected, as the impending sunset colored her *Eden* in glimmering gold and blood red.

Smoke rose from the broken city far below. Major intersections were stacked with piles of bodies. The gunshots, explosions, and dueling airship armadas made for a view that was absolutely heartbreaking.

The world she'd toiled relentlessly for two hundred human years to build was now falling apart in shambles.

Looking down over the marble banister past the protruding Network antennas, she tried to estimate the total number of casualties. Without her calculation plug-ins, or a visor connected to the Network, it was impossible.

She hung her head, waiting for the harbinger of either her death, or complete success. Oh, she could do it: travel back in time and stop this from ever occurring. But that would mean more fatalities, and there would be no running from her demons forever. The answer was in the wind, which swayed the tower and its protruding Network antennas like a sole dandelion seed growing atop a windswept cemetery.

After that dodging stunt, her nano-bots' CPU, now low on power and burdened with an overload of new units, ran in combat mode only. The machine-brain had been silenced from filtering the flow of her thoughts, allowing a floodgate of pent-up musings to resurface. Lorelei considered her legacy in ways she never had before. Philosophizing was her last recourse from these escalating musings on mortality.

If I win, she thought, *I'll bend the rules one final time. Leap back to yesterday and leave myself a chess piece in my cloak's inside pouch.*

Lorelei's hand trembled as she reached for her pocket, before withdrawing at the last second.

No. It's not worth it. Not worth another universe. Not worth the guilt, and the agony.

She ignored the voice that told her she simply feared the truth, and peeked over at the *Raven*, invisible, camouflaged in the corner, engine on standby mode, guns at the ready, her nearly depleted fuel cells and power converter inside, locked in cold storage. They were her way out. Her last bargain. Even though it didn't need to be.

Is this really what you want, Lorelei? Must it end this way?

A promise is a promise. Today, one of us will finally be set free.

At long last, the low hum of the elevator nearing struck Lorelei's sensitive eardrums.

Lily had arrived.

The doors split open, revealing the twenty-year-old Sky Admiral with a mad look in her eyes. She brandished a salvaged rail gun that probably weighed as much as she did. That meant that she was definitely using an enhanced metal spinal column, Lorelei reflected. It would be her greatest weakness.

"You're going down, Lorelei! You killed them both?"

"I'm not the one who put them in a position to die. You've no one to blame but yourself."

"Okay, where's the *Raven*? I know it's up here."

"Its whereabouts are none of your business."

Lily pointed to the southern corner, and then fired a shot at the ground by her clone's feet, toasting a tunnel the width of a tennis ball through the *Spire*.

"Take off the cloaking. Disarm the weapons. Turn off the engine. Then remove your Holo-Lens and wrist unit and throw 'em over to me. Now."

"Very good." Lorelei smirked, hands in the air, and did as she was told. Lily caught the devices and entered a few commands. The DNA scan chirped positive.

"I'm giving out orders for yours and my airships to stand down and await the victor. Do you approve?"

"Completely."

"This is it for your twisted empire," Lily barked, pocketing the computer and Holo unit. "I hope you've had your fun."

Lorelei unclasped her royal cloak, which flew away in the high winds, and flexed in her skintight battle suit.

"You're not really going to shoot me," she replied. "It isn't sportsmanlike. Not to mention, I have a code in my head you might want to know, unless you're eager to have the power converter blow up in your face."

"Then it's feet and fists."

"All the better to kill you with, my dear."

"No tricks. I won't use my leg jets if you swear you've got no concealed weapons."

"Cross my heart and hope to die." Lorelei's smile caught the sun's sparkle.

"I didn't plan all this so I could come up here to terminate you," Lily said, circling her clone. "I just wanted my stuff back, but you've made it very personal."

"Aw, shucks. I never knew Hansel and Gretel meant so much to you. Or were they more like your new Mommy and Daddy? Do they read you bedtime stories? How about I read yours at their funeral. Little Lily Lost, about the most relentless mass murderer in all history, who killed entire universes, and wiped out every member of her family in countless different ways."

That was the straw that broke the camel's back. The embers that burned in Lily's eyes turned to full-blown fire.

"How do you want to settle this?" screamed Lily, unable to hear any more. "Because I'm about to end you right now!"

She tossed the rail-gun off the *Spire* and charged Lorelei with relentless attacks, pummeling her older, if no less agile, body.

Lorelei deflected her kicks, flipping Lily on her side more than once. The younger one twisted herself back up and wore her clone down, blow by blow. But Lorelei didn't seem to be physically tiring. The madness in her eyes was boring deep into Lily's, putting her on edge.

Lily closed the distance, using her smaller reach as an advantage. Her knuckles felt good against Lorelei's terrifying, nanite-shielded face, reflecting the darkest of her own emotions.

But the woman's rage drove her too far. She didn't know when to stop. Lorelei simply laughed as, in the middle of being punched, she suddenly used her opponent's momentum against her, spun her around on her side, and kicked her hard in the middle of her spine.

Lily landed in a heap of pain. She concentrated hard on repairing her back; her own nano-machines scrambled to do so.

"Why do you even try?" Lorelei responded. "I can see you have doubts about your resolve. Give up on your mission."

"Oh, I'm just getting started! My mission begins with your end!"

Lillian jumped up and uppercut Lorelei, sending her staggering. She backed away, redirecting her little sister's incoming attacks.

Lorelei tripped Lily, and then elbowed her in the upper back.

Lily screamed as she rolled away on the floor and limped back to her feet. Lorelei put up her dukes in the stance of a drunken boxer, like she had in their fateful first fight.

But this time, Lily was prepared. Disciplined. She pulled no punches, blocked with her limb enhancements, and knocked Lorelei onto the edge of the banister.

Satisfied at having driven her opponent to absolute rage, Lorelei erupted into a fit of chaotic laughter. She opened up her defenses and let Lily pummel on her until she was nearly out of breath.

At last, Lillian let her clone collapse on her knees. She put pressure on the small of Lorelei's back. If Lily so desired, she could execute a mortal blow.

"It's over, Lorrie," she said. "You might want to give me that code now."

"No. It's not over."

Lily pressed down on her clone's lower leg. She searched for the fibula, and shattered it with a powerful stomp.

But Lorelei dealt with the pain. She lay on the floor, the fight taken out of her.

"Now it's officially over. I say so. Lorelei, I don't want to hurt you anymore. This is the same thing that happened with Lacie."

Lorelei smiled. Her sis was given a good death.

"Then don't. Don't hurt me anymore. Just go back to your floating fortress and die. Or, better yet, why don't we die together?"

"Neither of us has to perish today," Lily said, backing away from Lorelei to give her some space. Her behavior was suddenly very strange. "You're not yourself, Lorrie."

"I'm not giving you that code... until you mortally wound me," Lorelei said, forcing her body up one more time. She willed hundreds of millions of the active nano-machines within her bloodstream to support her leg bone, and walked over to a sighing Lily.

"Why do you always have to do things the hard way?"

"I don't know what you hope to accomplish. You'll be doing this same song and dance for all eternity, mother."

"Call me what you wish, but I considered you my friend, not my daughter. And I will succeed."

She stood firm as Lorelei found her footing and advanced towards her.

Lorelei dodged every punch, and deflected every kick. With metal-infused fists, she pushed Lily ever so slowly to the edge of the arena.

"You succeeded only in fooling yourself by weakening us. The others saw it too. They knew your deceit, your distrust towards us."

"Those were my mistakes, and I am sorry."

At last, Lily pulled back, baiting Lorelei into a powerful kick. She attempted to deflect it, but it was a feint. The real blow came from the opposite leg – her broken one. Lily took a sharp metallic shin to the cheek and spun into a defensive stance, back to the wall.

Lorelei spat as she slammed Lillian against the marble. "How can you be right and Lacie and I wrong? We are all parts of you. And you murdered her in cold blood to suit your own beliefs."

In the midst of Lorelei's next rout, Lily yanked her into a powerful headbutt.

"You killed Lucy! And don't pretend you haven't been trying to find and kill me all these years, too!"

Lorelei's elbow missed Lily's face and connected with her neck. Both combatants disengaged to regain their composure. Lorelei touched the spot of blood on her forehead, and then glared at Lily with disgust.

"Lucy only died because she was protecting you out of some warped sense of duty!" She gestured toward her vast city. "Look at that and tell me you see something worth saving. Your people and 'bots against mine. How utterly useless. You know that in just a few years, this will all be meaningless and you'll have to hit the reset button once more. All alone, you'll spend months planning your next attempt, and these mindless animals will just let you down! Again! Ignoring whatever potential they possess, they are as helpless as dogs in the savannah. They will forever choose the path of least resistance."

Lily massaged her strained neck. "There is always hope, Lorelei. Through your lies, threats, and mind control, you've warped humanity into believing itself helpless and weak. Our advanced consciousness sets us apart from animals, and thus we are bound by higher laws and responsibilities. But since choosing your own path, you have done nothing with your actions but abandon hope for the future."

"Your quest is a joke, Lily! You stand alone!"

"All the more reason for me to uphold my convictions. It was never really about the Split Universe theory for you, Lorelei. Admit it. You were just on a power trip."

"How dare you tell me what my own priorities are!"

"Just be honest with me, Lorrie! Be honest with yourself! That's all I want!"

Lorelei pulled a concealed revolver from her boot and shot at Lily.

Just like my dream. The thought flashed through Lillian's mind as she flexed her toes– her boot's working jet propelled her to the side.

She rebounded off the floor, whirled, aimed her heel towards Lorelei, and squeezed her big toe. Flames shot forth, searing Lorelei's hand, and then her face; a second bullet left the chamber and scraped Lily's shoulder.

Lily howled in pain. A third round caught her in the thigh. Enraged, she supported herself with her hands and kicked out at Lorelei once more, intensifying her flames and burning the firearm from her hands.

The Queen fell flailing, screaming in fear and agony, her ponytail having caught fire. Lily forced her onto the floor and kicked away the gun. She stomped out the fire just before it burned Lorelei's scalp.

She was a charred, broken mess. Lorelei gasped for breath in the high altitude.

Lily's stomach turned at the scene, but her hands trembled with adrenaline shakes. She was terrified to come face to face with the part of herself that took enjoyment in this. A wave of empathy flooded over her to counter the bloodlust.

"Give me the code, Lorrie," Lily commanded. "Please."

"No…" she began, and tried to stand. But Lily shot her searing jet a few inches from Lorelei's face, startling the World Leader. With her other boot, Lily pressed against her torso, then hovered above it. Its residual heat was warping her combat suit. It was over.

Lorelei exhaled slowly in acknowledgment.

So this is to be my end. It's… not as bad as I expected, Lacie.

"Very well. I… I accept defeat. I have one last request…" Lorelei coughed, and pulled Lily close. "Send me… to the final moment. I want to watch it happen."

Lily furrowed her brow in recognition.

"I understand. Do you have enough fuel for a round trip?"

"J-j-just enough. I calculated it."

Lily pulled out Lorelei's watch and called forth the *Raven*. The ship started up, lifted off, and landed before her.

She picked up her dying clone carefully and set her into the passenger seat. The girl then walked to the back, put on a Hazmat suit, and leaned over the chest.

"What's the code, Lorrie?"

"Nineteen ninety-two."

"How do I know you're not just trying to blow me up?"

"I guess you'll have to take my word for it."

Lily carefully opened the chest. Twenty-two fuel cells. The power converter was pristine, unaltered. Sure enough, everything was accounted for. "Interesting choice of password."

"You really cared about those two," Lorelei said. "Even gave them heroes' journeys. I wish sometimes that I could have had your heart."

"You did have my heart," Lily said, carefully placing the last active fuel cell into the *Raven's* Temporal Drive. "Literally, and always."

"I'm not sure how to ask this, but how much time would---"

"Th-three hours. I have… things… I want to say to whatever gods are out there."

Lily nodded. She very well might have asked for the same. She programmed the limited Space-Time Warp Initiator.

March 10, 2212. Six in the morning. Three and a half hours before the solar flare.

"Anywhere in specific you'd like to be?"

"R-r-right here. Right here is perfect."

Lily hit the button. It took fifteen minutes to warm up the reactor. In the meantime, she treated Lorelei's burns and offered her some water.

"I have to apologize," Lorelei said. "You gave me life. And I never did have any respect for you."

"Shh," Lily said, making her drink a little more. "It's all right. I just want you to know that I take responsibility for everything you've ever done, and that I never wanted to kill you. I'd hoped that you might understand. I had to set things right by my own judgment."

"I must ask… that energy cannon… from your flagship… was it…"

"The one Lucy was developing? Yes."

"S-seem to recall… during our first carriage ride through London… the two of you… arguing. Over the ethics of her mega-weapons. You said it'd lead to a slippery slope. She argued that if she didn't perfect the tech... someone else would have, to our detriment. I never imaged you would actually use the things."

"Indeed. I owe her an apology. Hopefully it'll never be used again."

"I'll never forget... how happy she was... dressed up in an evening gown and bonnet... protesting the excessive hat plumage...

"All in the name of preserving Florida's wild birds. And then she chastised our overdone accents. Completely in her element."

"We all were... back then."

Lorelei took her hand as the minutes counted down in silence. Saving their breath, neither spoke until they disappeared in a flash.

When they re-appeared again twenty-five years in the future, the sky was immeasurably hot, and the marble beneath their feet scorched from solar energies. Lily immediately hit the button for the Temporal Drive to begin charging up for its return trip and looked over to Lorelei, who was staring right into the star, her cybernetic eyes adjusting to the intense light.

"I'm... scared," Lorelei said. "I never thought... when it came to my own finale..."

"That just means you're human." Lily slipped the goggles over her eyes and unbuckled her clone. "For better or worse."

After donning a Hazmat suit, Lily walked around the *Raven*, opened the door, and carried Lorelei out, wrapped in a soft blanket. As per Lorelei's request, she sat her down on a chair by the edge of the banister. Both looked over the boundary.

The top levels of *Neo Eden* were now overgrown with vegetation. Down below, filling up the landmass in every direction, swayed a sea of people.

Tens of millions gathered in unison.

Lily handed Lorelei her cigarette case and a pair of binoculars, then held her clone by the shoulders.

Lorelei tried to light one last smoke. The wind made it impossible.

Carefully, Lily used a jet from her wrist to ignite the stick. Lorelei thanked her with a nod.

"You were right," Lorelei said at last. "Though I still believe in the Split Universe theory, my actions were never about the people of Earth. They were about you and I. All along, I... I guess I just wanted to be what you could never be. To understand the darkness you always turn away from, and grant the gift of ennui to ease humanity's collective pains. And maybe that's why I hated you so. I wanted you to think of me as an equal."

Readings were still safe. Lily took off her helmet and looked Lorelei in the eyes.

"I do now, Lorrie. I should always have, but... I do now. You've done incredible things. Evil things, sure, but still..."

"Give up the mission, Lily. You're just torturing yourself. *Amare et sapere vix deo conceditur.*"

Even a God finds it hard to love and be wise at the same time. Lillian hung her head.

"I've considered it. But for different reasons than you might expect. Keep watching. Maybe you'll find out if I've changed my mind, and maybe we'll settle our theories once and for all."

"That would be a comfort."

"Until then, enjoy the show. Oh, and here's something you might like to peruse."

Lily handed over Lacie's leather-bound memoirs.

"It's been archived. I thought... she probably would have wanted you to have the original. 'Cie never gave up on her alternative theories. She truly desired to solve our eternal quandary."

"Thank you, Lily."

She flipped through the pages, and stopped at a spread of complex equations.

"Her final proofs on Multiverse theory," Lorelei intoned.

"All good stuff. The comments on everyday life with you involve a great deal of witty observations. I never would have thought her sense of humor so developed; she was always so quiet."

"Get going," Lorelei said at last. She was about to lose her composure. She would not give Lillian the last pleasure of seeing her cry. "You're going to roast alive."

"Peace be with you. *Amor vincit omnia.*"

Love conquers all. Lily walked back over to the *Raven*, fired up the air conditioner, and waited for Warp Initiation.

As the ship began to flash, Lorelei turned around. They made eye contact. Both women waved one last goodbye.

Lily appeared back on the roof of the *Spire* seconds after she had left it, and could hold herself back no longer. She collapsed onto the console in tears.

⽸

Dusk was setting, with lanterns lit for the dead as the Sky Admiral flew her colors over the remains of *Neo Eden*, precious cargo onboard. Down below, the war-ravaged folk of the ruined capital held their fists up in salute. The gesture meant little to the time traveler, but it would help unite these people in their coming times of difficulty.

At last, Lillian piloted the *Raven* back to the barely functional *Valkyrie*, touched down on a strip outside the city with the bulk of her remaining fleet. After returning from the future, she'd radioed for every free android and human at hers and Lorelei's disposal to help the wounded, and camps and mobile hospitals were being staffed at record speed by willing volunteers.

Still lost in thought, Lily limped out of her ship to dress her own injuries.

While wheelchair-bound Yossa mourned the loss of his eldest daughter, EDC medics from around the globe cared for the hurt and dying, and androids ran to and fro serving hot meals to the exiled humans, Lillian Rachel Hermes just sat gazing up at the stars.

Embraces and assurances from Ayumi that the frozen were being thawed out did nothing. Feuchuk's report on the crippling aerial losses for both sides barely registered. Princess Regent Claire's formal surrender and promise that she would guide *Neo Eden* towards peace fell on numb ears.

No one could snap the dazed woman out of her shell. Joaquin kept the crowds away from her, and the Sky Admiral eventually took off and wandered alone into what remained of the hedge maze.

The mission can now continue, but at what cost?

Lillian couldn't help but feel that she was descending from on high to witness people falsely worshipping the forces of destruction. Of this, she felt the guiltiest. Haunted by Lorelei's words, she could not look away from the war-torn folk and their confused emotions. Their lives vindicated by acts of virtual, and now very real, violence. The gun and the sword and the mortar their false idols. Now she, too, would become a false idol. If only they knew the truth.

What can I possibly tell them?

Everything I touch crumbles to dust.

XXXIII. Home Sweet Home

"When you have eliminated the impossible, whatever remains, however improbable, must be the truth." – Sir Arthur Conan Doyle

Raine was no more.

And all of a sudden, she was again. Only, she felt different. New, renewed, or perhaps even revised. But make no mistake; a look into a hand mirror confirmed that she was who she thought she was, and no one else.

She glanced to her right, sensing someone in her peripheral vision. It was Gerrit, sweet Gerrit, his eyes wide open, staring forward blankly as if he were somewhere else entirely, a strange metal circlet with blinking lights for gems adorning his head. He looked much like he did in the *Metaverse*, only stronger somehow.

The room's only other defining features were three strange tubes, like standing glass coffins, each one large enough to fit a human inside. One was cracked down the middle. The girl sat up from her recliner.

How in the wide world have I come to be here? The last thing she remembered was smashing a missile into the throat of a giant metal serpent. Surely that had to have been a dream – there was absolutely no way the *Galahad* could have survived that blast, not in a thousand years, not with her body in the perfect condition it was in. The girl stood to find that her legs were wobbly, as if her muscles had just woken from a long sleep.

We lost, she reasoned grimly, looking at the pajamas she was wearing and the closed door that was sure to be locked.

If yesterday's events were a dream, we must be in some sort of bunker in Neo Eden, *being 'reconditioned'. Or could everything have been some cruel simulation?*

She took a few steps over to Gerrit's recliner and waved a slow hand in front of his face.

"Gerrit!" she whispered frantically. For a second his eyes began to re-focus. He was looking straight at her. She took his shoulders and gave him a strong shake.

"Gerrit, it's me," she said, trembling.

"You might want to give him a few minutes," a voice calmly enunciated from the now-opened doorway. Leaning against the jamb was none other than Lily herself, clad in an anti-septic lab coat, and behind, her robot servant, carrying a tray of warm cookies.

A million-dollar grin formed on Raine's face and Lily couldn't help but reciprocate. She stumbled forward into an embrace and the two held each other for quite some time.

"Welcome home, Raine," Lily beamed. "To the *Belladonna 5000*."

Raine waddled out of the medical room in astonishment, taking in the massive but cozy interior space with its luxurious, sunken circular sitting area. The girl's eyes drew naturally to the breathtaking view – taking up the expanse of the full-length observation window, planet Earth shone like a giant blueberry. It was so warm, so radiant, and so lovely.

Her palm felt cold up against the window – the glass must have been three feet thick – and just gaped at the third rock from the sun. She located the place she used to call home – Chicago, Illinois. The scale was overwhelming.

"The upkeep's a bit of a pain, not to mention the constant cleansing needed to live in the radiation belt, but you couldn't ask for a better view," Lily opined.

Raine was still speechless.

"Before you ask, yes, we won. *Neo Eden* is free. Lorelei is dead. Or rather, she will be. She's been sent to her final resting place. I recovered my stolen parts, and then some. Rutger and I fixed up the *Belladonna's* Space-Time Warp Initiator. It's all thanks to you and Gerrit, and your selfless bravery."

Despite all this good news, there was something very different about Lily. Somber, even. Her voice was soft and far away. Was it regret? Guilt? It was hard for Raine to tell.

"Wow! We should be celebrating," she ventured.

Lily returned the smile, but it faded as quickly as it appeared.

"Maybe so," she replied. "I'll check up on him. Please, make yourself at home. Because it's always been your home."

Raine was positively glowing.

She realized that she now had the coolest foster home ever.

"You'll probably remember this soon, but the archived Internet and pretty much every artwork and electronic media file from eight different world lines is available on demand. But maybe you should catch up on current events first."

Lily motioned to the cozy living space in the center of the chamber; the sunken circular sofas lined with cushions boasted a comfortable array of beanbags. Its centerpiece was a swiveling recliner, with a retractable computer station hanging from the ceiling.

Raine plopped down on the cushions and sipped on her hot chocolate as XF-22 zipped by to offer another cookie. From an oddly distant memory, Raine now recognized where she'd first smelled the scent of freshly baked dough. It was right here, on these cushions.

"Hello, Miss Raine," said Rutger. "It's been a while since we've last spoken, and surely you must not remember me in this form. But perhaps you recall another."

One of XF-22's monitors displayed a picture of Chance.

"Oh!" Raine called out. "It was you! You were my Chance!"

Chance's face beamed.

"I must admit, I feel like we are old friends," Rutger replied.

Blast shields covered the full-length windows, leaving the mood lighting to cast a soothing spell over the bridge.

On the large holo-display in the center of the room were aggregated videos and images of people rebuilding settlements within and around *Neo Eden*. Yossa and Hector organized volunteer brigades and local council meetings. The Seven Lords were toppled, and the perpetrators of *Neo Eden's* power structure, as well as the *Endless Metaverse* Developers, were kept in android-staffed rehabilitation facilities, to be monitored, employed, and released on a case-by-case basis.

Eden's global armed forces were disbanded, as per Princess Regent Claire's fulfillment of the Queen's written wishes in the event that her lineage should come to an end. The weapons and their manufacturing facilities were to be destroyed. To prevent any power struggles, the peoples of Earth were to have no charismatic leader. It was to be a new age of freedom from any form of slavery. A news report detailed that Queen Lorelei was still missing, presumed dead, and that the EDC, under the command of the Collective Elders and Ambassador Joaquin (no military titles were necessary in this new world), split up across the planet to help all *Metaverse* refugees to survive and care for themselves, beholden to no centralized force or government.

Engineers worked on transforming the city into a massive sustainable garden. No one would go hungry again. Mass graves were filled three miles downwind of the gates, and millions came to pay their respects to the dead, now over a hundred thousand, with two hundred and sixty thousand missing. It was one of the bloodiest days in history.

By popular vote, it was declared that a virtual service akin to *Endless Metaverse* would run once again under the name *Pan-Galactic Realms*, managed by the watchful eyes of Ayumi Karuishi, Francesco Zarifian, and Super BlastBoy 2.0, but at the present, only a minority of the world's populace showed interest in signing up, even though the End User License Agreements were unanimously changed in order to allow people to leave and enter the *Realms* at will, and to keep their memories for as long as they wished. In place of the Overseer, people freely chose from a wide variety of physical and clerical jobs.

One beaten but jovial individual stated that he simply didn't feel that anything virtual mattered anymore, that he would rather experience the rebuilding of human civilization consciously than do mindless work whilst engaged in mindless play. An older gentleman said he was blessed to know what it was like to have a real family, whereas a former soldier commented that he'd seen enough fighting for a lifetime, real or virtual. Near *Eden's* new solar kite field, a marble monument was built of Henry Holdfast. Dr. Karuishi, Dr. Zarifian, and various former EDC officers held a heartfelt service in his memory.

A few hours after Raine dozed off on the couch, she woke to a familiar voice.

"Rise and shine, sleepyhead," Gerrit snickered.

Raine fell into his arms, and, when they had broken the hug, ran her hand across his face. His eyes were even more intense than they were in the *'Verse*.

Before she knew what she was doing, Raine had kissed him, and it felt so good, so unreal, that he kissed her back, and they both turned crimson, unable to speak.

"Wow," Gerrit said at last, rubbing the bit of stubble growing on his chin. "Am I the one that's dreaming now?"

"It really is you!" Raine burst into giddy laughter. "Only you would say something so…"

"Corny?"

"I was going to say 'sincere'," she pouted.

"In any case, it had to be said," replied Gerrit with another embrace.

As they pulled away, Raine spotted Lily retreating into the shadows.

"Seriously, though! I didn't think I'd ever see you again," she said, placing his hands over hers.

"Likewise," Gerrit grimaced. "So what happened to you after I left? You've gotta tell me how you and Lily shut down the '*Verse*!'"

It was a long story, but Raine related every last detail to the best of her memory. Eventually, Lily joined them, now clad in a nightgown, and changed the holographic display to a crackling fireplace. She dimmed the lights, and they sat cross-legged around the virtual embers like three kids around a campfire. It was then Gerrit's turn to tell of how he, Henry, and Jon worked to shut down the Overseer. Lily listened intently, since this was news to her as well.

"I don't remember anything after being shot," Gerrit said solemnly. "I thought I was a goner for sure."

There was a long silence.

"You were, for a while," Lily finally spoke. "Both of you were. You... died that day."

Raine and Gerrit exchanged confused glances, and then looked expectantly at their host.

"Tell me you're joking," Raine scoffed. "I see Gerrit here right beside me."

Lily shook her head. "I can guarantee you it's not impossible."

Gerrit massaged his temples.

"Are you saying we're dead? Or that all this is just some other layer of the *Metaverse*? Don't tell me we're not even real..."

More shakes of the head. Lily forced herself to keep eye contact.

"No, you are both as alive as I am, but I'm afraid you really did die for a while. I wasn't going to tell you, but seeing you so happy, I can't hide it any longer. I'm done keeping secrets. Your brains were recovered."

Raine gasped. "What?"

"How?" Gerrit queried.

"Eh. It's better I skip over that part. I performed a careful procedure, recreating your bodies and minds from what was left of your DNA, your brain matter, and your backed-up memory files, refreshed just a few days ago. My Remediator can synthesize human stem cells from a genetic sample. The organic matter is supplied by carbon fibers from our greenhouse, and the other elements are integrated from natural sources. With the right equipment, it's easy to create a fully functional human body. It just took me the better part of a year to ensure you were both in tip top shape."

Raine and Gerrit both gazed into the fire silently like the ghosts they felt they were.

"I know this is a lot to take in, but I owe you the truth after all this time. After all that you've done for me. You two are clones, yes, but you should have a boosted, not reduced lifespan, and every one of your bodily functions is completely indistinguishable from those of a normal human. Should I go on?"

They both nodded.

"You're probably wondering why I did it, why I brought you back. I think it'd be easier to show you. Follow me."

Lily led them out of the main chamber, down a hallway, past the power generator and luscious forest level, and up two flights of spiral staircases to the large domed observatory atop the *Belladonna*, which boasted a full skylight into outer space. The large arrays of solar petals danced around them like stalks in a wheat field. The centerpiece of the observatory was a giant telescope that looked into the abyss. Covered-up picture frames lined the dome.

"This is Judy, one of our two telescopes. She's an incredibly powerful optical telescope, but she can also read Gamma, Infrared, and Ultraviolet signals," Lily pointed out, leading them slowly across the room.

Raine spotted, running down into the heart of the *Belladonna*, the rotating conduits that she oddly understood temporarily housed the solar energies drawn in by the photo-radio-voltaic petals before sending them to the power converter below. She traced the many wires with her eyes. Everything was familiar. She felt a strong connection to this place.

"Whoa!"

Both Lily and Raine turned to witness Gerrit gaping slack-jawed at planet Earth.

"You weren't kidding, Raine! It really is a sphere! Holy shit!"

Lily placed a gentle hand on his shoulder.

"Very good, Gerrit. Try not to get too tripped out," she said, and then added, "yet."

Once he could no longer look at the globe for fear of frying his brain, Gerrit peeked through the telescope, which was constantly moving via a computer program, tracking ever so subtly a beautiful nebula many hundreds of light years away.

Suddenly, Lily snapped her fingers and both pairs of eyes were on her. They followed her to the largest covered frame in the room.

"Y'all are not ready for this."

She yanked down the sheet from the framed photograph. Raine gasped out loud. Three figures stood in a family pose on the observation deck. The mother wore a lab coat, and horn-rimmed glasses completed the warm expression on her stunning face. Her long brown hair was held back in a purple headband that matched her dress. The father wore a tweed jacket and a turtleneck, with an orange scarf complementing his fiery hair. He had an arm around his wife, and both had hands on the shoulders of their daughter, five-year-old Lily, who boasted familiar goggles perched atop a Santa Claus hat, and a smile that stretched from ear to ear.

There was no mistaking it. The mother and father were dead-ringers for Raine and Gerrit. In another life, in another time, they were married, they had a child, and right then and there that child had brought them back together.

Raine felt a shortness of breath. Her knees had all but given way in shock. She felt herself collapsing into Gerrit's arms – he had stepped in, caught her, and was now aiming a blaster from a nearby cabinet straight at Lily's chest.

Lily blinked, but didn't flinch.

Gerrit held Raine tight, as if protecting her from a monster.

"What is the meaning of this?" he bellowed. "What are we, Lily, if that even is your real name?! Riddle me this: Raine and I aren't really who we think we are, yeah? Are we just test subjects to you, or still pawns in some sick game? I mean, like, do we even have souls?"

"W-w-wait. Let her speak…"

The shrill, pained cry that sounded out was Raine's. She was shaking, but it was a clear voice, and it helped Gerrit to notice that Lily was quietly shedding tears, letting them flow down her face.

"This… this isn't a game to me, Gerrit," Lily said at last. "The truth is, you and Raine were synthesized. And I don't know much about God, but I know this much: if anyone has a soul, you two do. At least, that's what my heart tells me. I felt them in my clones, too. But, I… molded their minds, limited their scope. Because I was selfish… afraid they might surpass me. The same is not true about either of you. Could you please put the weapon down? You would do well to keep in mind that any laser blast fired in this room will ricochet and probably kill more than one of us."

Still eyeing Lily suspiciously, Gerrit lowered the firearm.

"Much better," Lily said. "But I don't want you to take my word for it. You need to see for yourselves. We can recall some old memories."

Raine seemed puzzled. "Wait, you mean from before the *Metaverse?*"

"Most – probably not all – will return in time. But at my behest, you both kept detailed memory records. You've seen a few in your dreams," she said to Gerrit. "Though I doubt you remember much, they kept you seeking those three years."

Lily motioned to two circlets on the table. Each had a pulsing green gem.

"Okay, there's some recordings, but for all I know, those could be faked," Gerrit replied with a shake of his head. "See, I never know what to expect next from you."

But Raine studied the devices excitedly. *No lie can trump experiential certainty.*

"Are they really in there?"

"It will literally take all of five minutes. I was saving this for last, just because I wanted to make sure that this is what you both wanted. To know the truth."

"More than anything," Raine stated. She turned to Gerrit, who was a little hesitant.

Lily backed into the old leather recliner and had a seat. There were chips and guacamole at the ready, undoubtedly set out by XF-22.

"You guys should hurry up and get it over with. I don't want you to miss this guac, it's absolutely killer and I'm sure neither of you has any idea how difficult it is to grow avocados in outer space."

Raine took Gerrit's hand.

"Let's do it together. On the count of three."

"One…"

They took the circlets from the tray.

"Two…"

Each held a circlet above their head.

"Three."

The devices dropped.

It took all of five minutes to awaken as many years' worth of memories.

Birth. Knowledge. Recognition. I exist. Feeling as if I had emerged from some collective miasma, separation and individuality are odd, new concepts.

Waking up in a bright room. Vague shapes. Becoming aware of my sensory organs.

Carl II, the other. Lillian, introducing herself. We ponder on our names. I choose Raine – the concept of life-giving water falling from the sky is immensely picturesque.

The Belladonna, so warm and cozy. The Earth, keeping us company every day. Earthrise will ever be the brightest and most beautiful sight I shall set eyes on.

Gardening. Tending that which gives us life. Plants give their lives to us in return for their own existence. Animals grown for food must be butchered for food.

Guided learning, driven by our own curiosities and enhanced by simulated lessons. Philosophy. Dozens of languages. Training programs. Martial arts. Logic. Rhetoric. Ethics. Arithmetic. Geometry. Calculus. Astronomy and astrophysics. Natural Sciences.

He and I engage in friendly competition.

Over years, the plan is discussed and constantly revised.

Lily explains to us the known workings of the stars and how people once used them to navigate the seas on that baffling blue world.

Discovering that we are naturally incredible at chess. Once Lily starts losing, she introduces us to Go.

Our first trip to Earth.

Setting foot on that remote island. It's immensely beautiful, the happiest experience of my life. We catch and cook lobsters and many fish. Lily says that it's just like having a family again.

I guess we are family. This is my family, and our bonds can never be broken.

Our extended family, the EDC: Lily, Gerrit, and I take charge of isolated factions of the struggling rebellion, and help them to work together. We retake Manila, showing the oppressed peoples of Earth that they have the means to fight back against the dominant culture.

Argument. Lily wants to storm the castle, but we search for a peaceful solution.

Compromise. A trip to Neo Eden. *The streets are filled with people half-alive, toiling endlessly and unhappily. We sneak into the upper levels. A recon operation into the* Spire. *Discussion of battle plans. Modifications to Lucy's blueprints for the Exo Knight suits. Recruiting moles.*

The first exercise: breaking into Endless Metaverse. *It is a complete failure. The three of us are remotely controlling avatars of frozen players but find that the interface is limited and the input lag is terrible.*

A decision: we would have to infiltrate the game directly, from the inside, by bending its rules. At a roundtable meeting, we discuss our options with all the intelligence and formality of military officers. A necessary condition of the plan was that both he and I would have our memories erased. Some may return in the future, but it may be years, and we may forever associate certain realities with artificial fragments. Adamantly, we craft our new identities to support our quest.

The battle plan is drawn out. Our Metaverse *personas are created: him, an online gaming wizard growing up in the 201X's, and me, a hardcore arcade player from the early '90s. Based on the needs of the mission, we chose who we are now. We decided that we wanted to be this way. Tough as Gerrit and Raine's lives were, they were probably better than Carl and Elizabeth's memories, Lily said. They had a difficult life, alternately celebrated, and then shunned by their fellow scientists, with years steeped in isolation, suffering governmental and societal persecution for their radical theories, humanitarian and environmental leanings, and secretive, privately-funded projects.*

A second trip to the island; this time, we count shooting stars and promise one another that we will all return to the Belladonna *together. We write messages to our future selves.*

Holding hands to ease the tears. Reluctant goodbyes are said on planet Earth, where we are to be plugged into the Metaverse *at isolated, untraceable locations. Gerrit in Kazakhstan, and later, myself, in the heart of the mobile fortress* Valkyrie.

Before I dive in, the plan is revised countless times. The promised days now here, I am ready to do my part in destroying the Metaverse. *There is no doubt or hesitation in my mind when I give Lily the thumbs-up and ease myself into that reclining dentist's chair.*

ZAP!

Raine's vision blurred, but her olfactory senses soon latched onto an enveloping aroma.

She was seated now, across from Lily, with Gerrit between them. Both were sipping lavender tea. Between them were letters from their past selves.

"Wow," Raine suddenly exclaimed.

"At last, you've snapped out of it!" Lily cried. "You're feeling incredibly tired right now, and a little surprised. You just experienced highlights from years of memories. You most definitely need a breather, and some caffeine wouldn't hurt, either."

Raine complied, taking a sip of her tea.

"Lily," began Gerrit. "I know we just talked about this, but I want Raine to hear it too. I'm very sorry for holding you at gunpoint."

"Any rational man might have done the same," Lily said.

They toasted.

Once they'd eaten the wonderful curry dinner that Rutger brought in, Lily decided to tell Raine and Gerrit a little more about the people they were cloned from.

"Their names were Carl and Elizabeth Hermes," Lily said, pulling the sheets off the other photos, plaques, and portraits lining the room. "Two of the world's most renowned physicists. Elizabeth, a quantum physicist, was born in Toronto, Canada to parents of mixed descent, but moved to Geneva, then Scotland, to be with her husband, who was one of Europe's premier astrophysicists. My paternal great-grandfather Professor Joseph Connors' firm, Paradoxical Patents, co-developed a new generation of sustainable, easily producible, extremely high-yield solar panels in conjunction with the Chinese government. He made a fortune off the tech when it became used worldwide. Meanwhile, my maternal grandparents, both theoretical physicists, spent their entire lives pursuing their passion project, a theoretical time machine. The project was then passed on to my grandpa Timothy, who came up with the blueprints for the *Belladonna*, and then passed the idea to Elizabeth, who, as luck would have it, fell in love with Carl Connors, Joseph's great-grandson, and one of the most brilliant minds of his day. The two dedicated their lives to the project.

"With three generations' worth of private funding and donations from interested investors, this space station was commissioned to test the possibilities of time travel. In the original year 2087 AD, seven years after they launched, five years after I was born, my parents kick-started an expedition to send probes a hundred and two hundred years into the future to study changes in the Earth's history, geography, and population patterns. They were compiling immense sets of data.

"What they discovered shocked them to the core. Beyond a certain time, the only life forms left on the planet were microscopic bacteria at the bottom of the ocean. They soon discovered that radiation levels spiked some time in between then and 2282 AD. A probe confirmed that a solar flare had wiped out all life on Earth on March tenth, twenty-two-twelve. Warnings were sent to the surface, telling a small group of peers that their findings necessitated the immediate establishment of a colony on Mars to ensure the survival of the human race. But the information leaked, and the reaction from the United Amero Alliance was completely unexpected. They sent a fleet of battle cruisers to seize the *Belladonna*. It might have been one of the investors who betrayed them. We'll never know. My parents' worst nightmare was that their invention might be used as a military weapon. So they sent me back in time, sacrificing themselves so that I could live."

"You were alone for all those years," Raine said after shedding a sudden tear. "And you couldn't bring them back."

"Not without their brain matter. Not in the forms I knew them as. But I had samples of their DNA. That's how I created you two."

"Couldn't you just go forward in time to warn them?" asked Gerrit.

Lily gestured to another large-print family photo, only the age difference between Lily and her parents was not so pronounced; the three could have been siblings. "A much earlier instance of me did warn them. And in one world, younger versions of Carl and Elizabeth survived. But see, they were too attached to their own timeline, too concerned with saving the human race in their own way. They argued with that other me, saying that to change history and continue rewriting it to achieve a singular outcome might cause catastrophes that could unravel the very fabric of the universe. The accumulated energy caused by constantly traveling to and from certain points in space-time might eventually be enough to create troubling anomalies."

"You mean like a black hole?" Raine inquired.

Lily nodded. "Or a wormhole, but yeah. Something like that. Thankfully my findings, and those of my parents, don't support any such thing. So far there's no evidence of the *Belladonna* causing spatial or even sub-spatial distortion. They or I could be wrong, of course. I can't imagine what that version of me went through, but as their daughter, I'm sure I wanted to join them. The Lily from that timeline went on to live with her parents, but sent a message back informing my past self that she didn't think they were going to accomplish the mission. And so, a few dozen time loops later, here I am," Lily said.

"Geez, time travel is complicated," bemoaned Raine.

"It's not really fair, is it? That version of you got to grow up with your parents," Gerrit said grimly. "I'd be pretty frustrated to be in your situation."

But Lily just shrugged it off.

"It's enough for me to know that somewhere, sometime, they're safe, even if that future may no longer exist. If it does, it's in a place I can't get to, anyhow. And I never forget to remind myself that the more I do what I'm doing, the more I'm toying with the ultimate fate of the universe."

"How could you ever get used to that?" Raine asked.

"I don't." The reply was terse, but without aversion. "It's a lonely job, but someone's gotta do it."

A dead hush fell over the observatory.

"Lily?"

"Raine?"

"Is that why you modeled us after your parents? Because you were alone?"

Lily gave her an embrace. She took hers and Gerrit's hands.

"After losing Lucy, I realized there was something else I misplaced along the way. And that maybe we could get it back, together. I can't ask you two for any more. You deserve to live the rest of your lives in peace and comfort, away from all this. Rutger can transport each of you to any point in history. You can live however you wish, and if you like, you can make it so that you won't remember a thing. Think it over; you've got all the time in the world."

With that, Lily turned to walk away.

"Where are you going?" asked Raine.

"I'll be downstairs, putting the finishing touches on my mini-thesis. Gotta update my emergency letter to my past self. Figured I'd recommend not cloning herself."

"Fair enough," she replied as Lily descended.

Gerrit plopped down on a velvet sofa near the immense bookshelf, staring at the innumerable plaques on the wall.

"You wouldn't think two people as attractive as us could get so many accolades," he joked.

"Speak for yourself," Raine said, joining him on the sofa. "She looks like a rocket scientist. I can't see myself in her at all."

Just then, Raine noticed that the late Elizabeth wore her favorite colors: purple and green.

In another frame, Lily was dressed up in a neon spandex outfit with goggles and a purple wig, striking a pose. So she'd met her creator-and-sorta-daughter in *Flynn's* arcade, too.

The puzzle pieces were falling into place deep in her mind, a hundred perfect *Tetris* combos in a row, spinning her head in circles.

"Where are you going to go?" Raine asked Gerrit at last, breaking a long silence.

"I don't know. How about you?"

Raine held up her hands, the universal sign that meant 'I haven't the slightest idea'.

"Not a clue. I kind of... no, I really want to help Lily. I just wish there were something I could do."

"Ugh, I feel the same way."

"Do you think... hmm," Raine mumbled.

"No, go on."

"I mean, maybe we could do it. If all of us traveled together to save the world, it might just be possible."

Gerrit laughed. "I was thinking the same thing, but I wasn't sure how to bring it up."

"No, I think it might just be the best-case scenario, Gerrit!" Raine exclaimed, taking his hands and looking deep into his eyes to be sure they were on the same level. She paced the observatory floor assuredly. "Lily's too stubborn to admit it, but I don't think she can do this alone."

Gerrit nodded in agreement. "We made a pretty good team back there," he said, putting an arm around Raine, who turned red and gave him a peck on the cheek.

"We sure did."

XXXIV. Don't Say Goodbye

"If your compassion does not include yourself, it is incomplete."

– Gautama Buddha

The *Phoenix* was always safe. It was her personal womb. Lily zipped up her spacesuit and sat with arms wrapped around bent legs, knees knocking from the clinical cold of the claustrophobic ship's oxygen pumps.

She'd already tried to forget. Short of wiping her memory, forgetting was next to impossible; maybe remembering and accepting would be the key. But the past brought nothing but pain. Lillian had a million things to feel guilty about; Raine and Gerrit were simply the most recent victims of her grand schemes.

Lorelei, you old fool. Maybe you were right after all, she thought.

Lily took a deep breath. The *Phoenix* had regulated the air pressure, feeding her more than ample amounts of oxygen to help speed her thoughts along.

Whatever the answer to her Universe, Multiverse, or Split Universe quandary, it was too big a question for a lone soul to ponder. The possibility that she was responsible for the creation and destruction of an unimaginable number of life forms in hundreds of jumbled up universes was too immediate to ignore, yet too terrifying to face.

Now that she'd prepared her red envelope to send back to the Triassic, what were her options? To continue fighting the good fight? It was unthinkable to do anything with her life but to quest for timely interstellar colonization. However, if the means to that end only created more death and destruction, how could there be a point to saving just one planet?

She took in what little she could glimpse of the Earth from outside the sleek dome of her cockpit and through the docking bay's viewing window. She recalled the faces of all the people on that big blue paradise her parents once called home. They were faces of good people, honest people, but she felt no connection to them, and she had no idea whether that was because she was half-raised by a computer on a time-traveling space station, or because she'd now half-convinced herself that she was something beyond human.

With the *Belladonna*, Lily knew, she essentially had the powers of a demigod. She'd transcended human limits, bent the space-time continuum to her will, and even created and destroyed lives of genetically engineered beings, not to mention experimenting with societies, civilizations, and power-play on a global scale.

Her quest against Lorelei, to cite one example, ended in the deaths of hundreds of thousands, and the lifelong trauma of untold tens of millions, not to mention that psychic fallout from the *Metaverse's* programming remained a poison to the populace at large. Increasingly more of the recently freed demanded the return of their enslavement, as they had grown accustomed to it.

Was this to be her legacy? A generation of humans who knew nothing but bondage and escapism? To survive, they needed to unite: to branch their civilization out into space, to terraform new planets, to escape the beautiful, radioactive death-trap that the third rock from the sun was about to become. Maybe she could pick up where Lorelei left off and reach a polar outcome.

Just as the thought entered her mind, countless failures impressed themselves upon her, one by one, in a flurry of bad memories.

Zero percent success rate.

Perhaps the problem was the constant in the equation. Maybe the fates have it in their heads that if the human race is to be saved, I simply shouldn't be the one to do it.

All this thinking left her breathless. She inhaled the recycled air for all it was worth, filling her lungs with what she hoped to be among her last few breaths, and observed her body.

The best thing about this chamber was its utter silence. Lily breathed of the oxygen slowly, carefully, methodically. This was to be her final journey. A calm, peaceful descent into the Earth's atmosphere. She would kill the shields, burn the *Raven* through re-entry, and crash herself into the Earth. Hopefully the G-force would knock her out first.

She looked at the controls before her, and then pulled up a real-time holographic image of the ship's bridge. The trillions of credits of technology aboard the *Belladonna* showed in every nook and cranny, and in every emergency survival device. The DNA of millions of Earth species, including several thousand humans, were stored in the ship's extensive cold library. Within Rutger's memory banks, all of humankind's culture, history, technology, and biology were at her fingertips. If she had half a mind to do it, Lily could terraform an entire world herself, create a new planet, and transport a smattering of humans onto it to breed, mine, sell real estate, and just about completely pillage the place. That wasn't exactly the end result she was looking for, but it might have been something.

Wasn't this the kind of power reserved only for gods?

Perhaps the *Belladonna* was her Mount Olympus. Or was she Hades, with the underworld her domain? It sounded right: a place without end or hope, surrounded by the eternal, unyielding cries of dead souls writhing in torment. Lorelei's *Endless Metaverse* may have been artificial, but at the very least it offered solace to its users' ultimately doomed spirits, be it with the destruction of Earth, or unto the final symphonies of the universe.

Nothing lasts forever. Why should the human race be an exception?

Now I'm starting to sound like her, Lily reflected, pulling her hair in frustration.

You're stalling, Lily. You want them to find you. You're weak.

She clenched her fists and banged on the control console.

"I'm not weak, dammit! I'm not!"

Lily punched the button to begin the cold launch sequence.

Nothing happened. She punched it again.

"I'm sorry, Miss Lily, I'm afraid I can't let you do that," Rutger chirped.

"Don't give me that HAL bullshit! This is a direct order! I am the Captain here and I will do what I want! You're breaching your authority!"

"You're not hurting yourself on my watch, Captain. You know it is one of my directives. Sir Gerrit and Lady Raine have been notified and are en route. You must understand that this is an emergency situation."

By this time, Lily had stepped out of the ship and walked over to the docking doors. She hit the manual airlock switchboard with a pipe wrench until it fried.

There was a banging at the entry hatch leading into the dock. Pressed up against the glass porthole, Raine and Gerrit struggled to pry open the door.

The latch had been locked and dead-bolted. There was no way they'd be getting in.

"Let us in!" Raine declared over a video chat window that suddenly appeared on every display console. "We love you, Lily! You can't leave us!"

Gerrit chimed in. "You're not a bad person, Lillian. Open these doors. We can help you."

Lily glanced at her two teammates - no, her warped creations - with regret and longing.

"I wish I could join you," she began sadly. "I wish I could just put all this pain and regret behind me and keep going, but I... I can't be sure if I'm doing the right thing anymore. Maybe I've been doing this too long, I don't know. But I do know that if I can't fully commit myself to the mission, I shouldn't be working on it. Maybe you two..."

"Nonsense, Lily," Raine interjected. "You promised me you wouldn't give up on this world! I'm holding you to your honor! There's three of us. We're a team; we've always been a team, ever since you were born to two parents named Carl and Elizabeth. We're going to save this planet together. I can't imagine how difficult it's been for you. I can't claim to have lived in your shoes, but in all the time I've known you, my life has been one hell of an exciting adventure. And I'm sure Gerrit would agree."

"B-but... I'm a failure," Lillian whispered. "A total failure."

The loudness of Raine's reply took them all by surprise. "Look right in front of you, dammit! What do you see? Think about all the people you've helped! And all those you can still help through your love!"

Gerrit continued calmly. "Lily, Raine speaks the truth. We believe in you; now you just need to believe in yourself. Plus, if it's any consolation, I, too, trust that whether we are living in a singular universe, or one of many, the best thing we can do is live for the future. Only then might we be able to discover the truth. I won't rest until every human is living amongst the stars, and free of their mental shackles. To work towards a world where that can happen... that would be the ultimate privilege, the highest duty a man could aspire to."

Lily had tears in her eyes. She'd never felt so appreciated before, so wanted, so loved.

Hands shaking, she dropped the wrench and collapsed on her knees, sobbing. She pointed her sonic keychain at the deadbolt and unlocked the hatch. Raine and Gerrit rushed to her side, and held her in their arms for a long time.

"Lily," Raine said, breaking a long silence.

"Yeah?"

"I don't know how keen you are for this, but... seeing as how we are practically family, I think we should live like one."

A hopeful smile charted its beginnings across Lily's face as she looked at both Raine and Gerrit in turn.

"Do you mean... you will stay with me?"

Raine turned to Gerrit.

"I want to see where this baby can take us," he said. "I know it'll be tough, and a lot of work and responsibility, but you've got a better chance of achieving your goals with us on board."

"We've discussed this," Raine quipped.

Lily was impressed.

"How long was I gone from that room? You two are quite the dynamic duo."

Both Raine and Gerrit flushed and exchanged awkwardly smug expressions.

Raine offered Lily her hand, and the three walked back onto the bridge side by side.

∞

Over the next two months, Lily gave her companions refresher courses in the workings of the *Belladonna* and the intricacies of temporal travel. They ate, drank, laughed, and learned, going over Lily's various notes and charting out survival scenarios.

However, both Raine and Gerrit sensed that despite their best efforts, they were losing Lily. After that fateful first day, she spent long hours in her study poring over blueprints and maps, and rewatching news transmissions from the surface. Behind her kind visage, she was deeply troubled. By what, they could only guess, but Raine speculated that whatever had happened between her and Lorelei left scars that only time might heal.

It was a quiet morning when Raine approached the hot tub in the midst of the food forest, and joined Lillian in silence. With cucumber slices over her face mask, Lily said nothing, smiling at the welcome but unexpected company.

"I've made a decision. I'm trusting you and Gerrit with the *Belladonna*," Lily said out of the blue. "My time as steward of this station is over."

Raine blinked. "That's nonsense, Captain. You're sticking with us."

Lily leaned her head forward and squinted, letting the cucumber slices slide down her mud-covered face. She gave Raine a dead serious stare.

"You said it yourself. It may not be too late for this timeline," Lily reasoned. "I've been thinking that it's still two decades before the flare hits. Lorrie left behind a plethora of solar fields and factories, and the people of Earth are pretty united. I might be able to construct the Ark that my parents had always envisioned. Maybe, just maybe, I'll stand a chance at finishing the mission this time around."

"Then Gerrit and I will help," Raine said gently. "We're Team Hermes, right? Family sticks together, at all costs."

But Lily kept silent.

"We may share genetic traits, but we're worlds apart, Raine. The last thing I want for you and Gerrit is to continue following my paradigm. The most dangerous fallacy is the appeal to authority; without it, without some messed-up hierarchy based on order-givers and order-followers, who knows what the world would be like right now?

"I guess what I'm trying to say is that I don't have the right to claim power or leadership over you two, or anyone else. And yet, I can't break my pattern through force of will alone. I've survived as long as I have because I'm strong, uncompromising. It's hard to explain… it's like I'm a dish missing an essential ingredient, so I've tended to overcompensate, which leads to my overpowering those around me. I may still be young, but no one should be forced to bear the burdens that I have. With that said, I can see that the only way for me to break this cycle of obsessive control is to relinquish my birthright, to pass on the power of the *Belladonna*. Do you understand?"

"I think I might, with time, understand more than I do now," Raine replied honestly. "But I also think that if there's hope for this world, you're the only person who can realize it."

Lily took Raine's hands in hers.

"Thank you, Raine, but if this world has any hope, it will come from its people, not from yours truly. You and Gerrit are ready," she said. "I know deep in my gut that I can leave the *Belladonna* in your capable hands."

Later that night, Lily handed the *Belladonna*'s key, along with a duplicate, to Raine and Gerrit, making them Co-Captains. Despite

Lily's protests, they insisted on reciting the Time Keeper's Oath again.

"I don't want you to think about the mission for the time being," Lily said, echoing her parents' words to her. "You're two-thirds of the exclusive society of official Time Keepers now; you have all the time in the world. There's no need to rush into heroic deeds like I did."

Both Raine and Gerrit were saddened by the news of Lily's sudden departure, but the woman assured them again and again that this was for the best.

"Gerrit's first reaction was right, Raine. Put my sob story aside and just look at the facts. I used you. I created you so you could fight for me. You two were my soldiers, and without you, there would be no more chances. But now you are both free, and my spirit longs to return to Earth. You two have something I never will – each other. You're not bound to Terra, and you're not bound to the *Belladonna*. She can take you wherever you want to be, believe it or not."

"I don't want to be anywhere else!" Raine cried aloud. "I want... I want to be by your side. And to help you with the mission."

"Then travel to the beginning and talk to that Lily. There's a ton of fight in her. You're seeing me at my weakest here, but maybe that's just how these things run their course."

Seeing as how her companions were both saddened, Lily's voice took on a calmer tone.

"Don't you worry about me," she said. "I'm just going on a solo quest; I can think of no better way to keep my promise to you, Raine. I won't give up on Earth, not while there's still something I can do to right my wrongs. I'm very capable of handling myself, and the free people of the surface are anxiously awaiting my return. If ever things go badly, you know what to do."

Gerrit nodded. "Send the red envelope and data cards back to the Triassic."

The answer was met with silent approval. With her things packed into the *Raven* and a full tank of temporal energy, Lily offered her final embraces.

"Rutger?"

"Yes, my Captain?"

"As you're aware, I'm taking an instance of you with me, but to the Rutger of the *Belladonna*, I say this: Thank you for everything you've done for me all these years. You're the best guardian and friend a girl could ever have," she said warmly.

"Your gratitude is acknowledged, Miss Lily. It has been my utmost pleasure assisting you. May your voyage be an unparalleled success."

"It will," Lily said. "I know it will."

"Take care of him for me," she mentioned to Raine and Gerrit. "He may be a computer, but he's a sensitive soul."

Raine nodded. She'd never forget how loyal of a companion Chance was when she needed him the most.

The bay doors opened and the flight tray aligned the *Raven* into takeoff position.

"Lily! Wait!" yelled Raine. "When will we see you again?"

"You can call me anytime once I reach the *Valkyrie*, but if you're going to time jump, don't wait up," Lily beamed. "I've spent too long working to justify my existence. I lived because I wanted to assign some kind of meaning to my life. Why fate chose me to survive while my parents died. And the more I think about it, the more I think I know what the answer was. It was you two. I was supposed to live my life, not theirs. I gave all my hope and love to the mission, leaving none for myself. The best advice I can give you is to think twice, thrice, and a million times before you make the ultimate sacrifice."

Her eyes met Gerrit's, and he was struck silent. It was the same look he wore like a mask when he'd considered wiping his memory back in *Endless Metaverse*. He sought out a real life, a life of love, truth, and something he didn't expect: responsibility. Now he was being given the ultimate one. It was terrifying. But he also had faith in himself, and in Raine.

"Lily, may you have a fruitful journey," he said at last. "I hope you find what you are looking for. And I'll be rooting for your Ark to pierce the heavens. Give Yossa my regards."

"Thank you, Gerrit," she replied. "I'm sorry, Raine. I hope someday you will understand."

"I hope so, too," Raine said through tears. Now that she had finally discovered where she'd come from, where she belonged, and the true purpose behind her existence, she was about to lose the one person who had literally given her life.

Former Captain Hermes turned on the ignition. Raine and Gerrit waved as the first airlock closed, sealing them away from their creator. On their video feed, she gave them a thumbs-up. Then the second airlock opened and the *Raven* burst out into the void.

They watched as Lily's ship faded away into the distance. Ever the drama queen, Lily had even set up classical music to play herself out: "Silent Lucidity" by Queensrÿche.

Lily looked at the family photograph she'd affixed to the *Raven's* dashboard. She kissed her parents.

"Mom, Dad, I'm sorry. I couldn't see it happening any other way. I hope that I did the right thing."

So, she thought to herself, *the end result of my time on Earth will culminate in one of many scenarios if and when Raine and Gerrit take the* Belladonna *back into the past.*

A few of the more likely possibilities:

1. Lorelei's Split Universe Theory is correct, and her supposedly already-split universe would split into two or more. With the *Belladonna* forging an infinite amount of alternate timelines, the resulting versions of herself, and Raine and Gerrit, would go on to live independently of one another.

2. Carl and Elizabeth's Causality Theory will kick in; this was to Lily perhaps the most pessimistic but also the most realistic outcome. Should Raine and Gerrit travel to the past, she would be sealed in a tangent universe. Trapped on an instance of Earth that would never have occurred, Lily, and everyone else on Earth, will disappear into the ether as time wipes its slate clean, like an Etch-a-Sketch. Raine and Gerrit would disappear in a similar fashion should they send a red envelope back to the Triassic, negating the eventuality of their own existence.

3. Theory of Consciousness: a rather far-out possibility, first posited by her grandfather, Timothy O'Brien, whose pet hobby was studying the saints and mystics: that of consciousness transcending temporal limitations. Lily wished she could take comfort in it, like Lucille did. In this instance, her consciousness, or spirit if you will, was destined to revert back to her ten-year-old self should she receive the red envelope warning her against cloning herself. She would not remember a single thing about the events since she first began the mission. Meanwhile, Raine and

Gerrit would continue to exist in the future timeline of an alternate universe, their unique consciousnesses forging a new reality.

4. Spiral Collapse Theory – Perhaps the most frightening theory that Lily could imagine, and one that was not dependent on her sending the envelope. Spacetime, in an effort to right itself, would systematically eliminate the alternate worlds created by the *Belladonna's* travels. In unraveling these realities and ultimately preventing the *Belladonna* from ever traveling through time, cosmic 'ripples' might manifest in the revised worlds, progressing from oldest to newest, destabilizing their existences until all branching world lines inevitably collapse.

5. Every single one of the above, with either infinite or nearly infinite variations at every conceivable branching path, would occur inevitably in countless parallel worlds, according to Lacie's understanding of Multiverse theory's Many Worlds interpretation.

Either way, things would never go back to the way they were.

And maybe that's for the best, Lily thought, unstrapping her sitar and playing along with the music. *Planet Earth is in desperate need of a regime change.*

This is Captain Lily to Ground Control. I'm feeling very still. And I think my spaceship knows which way to go.

Epilogue: Paradoxical Love

"You know you're in love when you can't fall asleep because reality is finally better than your dreams." – Dr. Seuss

In one of many possible worlds…

Once the *Raven* left the debris field, Raine was absolutely exhausted. Gerrit undoubtedly felt the same way, and neither of them spoke for the rest of the night cycle, until they were about to go to bed.

"If you need me, I'll be in Carl's study," Gerrit said.

"We'll figure all this out over some morning cocoa. Rutger's set to give her a call the minute she lands."

"Listen to us, we sound like a married couple," he joked.

Raine rolled her eyes. "Don't get too excited," she replied with a wink.

They bade each other a good night at eleven thirty, as per the *Belladonna's* emulation of Earth's twenty-four hour cycles, but before XF-22 could show them to their rooms, there was a flash of light in the docking bay. A booming din enveloped their eardrums.

"What's happening?" Gerrit asked of Rutger.

Before the android could answer, the *Raven* materialized right in the dock it'd just left. The stunned trio regarded the craft with caution.

When the back doors opened, a graceful woman in her mid-fifties, absolute calm radiating from her presence, emerged from within, wearing a most elegant gown and a suede coat. She pulled off her goggles.

"Ah, it's good to be home," she intoned.

Lillian Hermes descended her ship and walked over to Raine and Gerrit.

"What's with the silence? You'd think you two had never seen a time traveler before."

She held them both in a long embrace.

"Lily?" Raine began. "You… came back…"

"Yes, my darlings. And I did it. I saved not just the human race, but planet Earth as well."

"You what?" cried Gerrit. "How?"

"It's amazing what a motivated populace curious about the unknown can do in just two decades. As soon as I returned, I made a global plea asking for all peoples to help me avert a coming disaster. I gave them their options, and they did the rest, really. We reconfigured *Metaverse* satellites into a literal world wide web. Anti-mag plasma shields linked to fission drives; they go together like old mahjong partners. We cast out our anti-EM net to trap the solar particles and crossed our fingers. Talk about embracing destruction. When the flare hit, we absorbed its energy. Hey, Hanako, get over here!"

A floating sphere whizzed by from the *Raven*. Lily snapped her fingers, and Hanako emitted a hologram showing planet Earth surrounded by a thin electric shield, glowing bright orange.

"The miracle came when we realized how much extra power the machine took in. Even with seven hundred Gigawatts lost in the stabilizing and conversion process, we were left with an insane fifty Terawatts, enough to power every device on the planet for weeks. The only problem was the half-life on the energy – I didn't have any method to store it cleanly. So I proposed we develop a positron-stabilizing core and create something productive for once."

"Long story short, that core became the heart of my Space Ark." Lily pulled out a video showing a mothership the size of a small moon flanked by hundreds of support vessels orbiting Mars. "Not bad, eh? We christened her the *Frontier*. Yeah, predictable, but you try getting two billion people to agree on something. Personally, I can't fathom how most of the populace decided to remain on Earth when there's an entire universe to explore. The ship's volunteer-run, too. Rutger, I've got some tea in the trunk. Could you put the kettle on, please?"

Raine still could not believe that the woman who had made such a dramatic departure was standing before her over three decades older, smile lines coloring her face.

"Most certainly, Miss Lily. It is most fortuitous to have you back."

Lily crossed her arms.

"Back? I don't think so. I'm just here for a few old files. A rather critical interior decorating job needs some finishing touches. Plus, I realized that I was missing the genomes for my favorite type of mango. I desperately seek to test whether they're fit for terraforming."

"This is nuts!" Gerrit exclaimed. "What does this mean for us?"

"Nothing," Lily said simply. "I'll go on doing my thing, and you two do whatever you were going to do. That reminds me. Rutger, I'll need the fuel cells in the *Raven* topped off. You never know when you require a temporal jump or two."

"Very well, Miss Lily."

Raine scratched her head. "Sorry, you mentioned something about interior decorating?"

"Ah, that. Let me show you."

Lily raised her wrist communicator to a terminal, wirelessly transmitting data.

A hologram revealed thousands of machine appendages from the moon-sized mothership in the process of building a familiar space station – it was the *Belladonna* herself! *But how?*

"Another one of my lifelong projects. It's an exact replica," Lily said, zooming into the bridge. The camera passed through the hull, revealing dozens of droids working to match the conditions of the interior to a central hologram. "And in the med bay…"

A seven-year-old incarnation of Lily floated in cryo-sleep, a peaceful smile bringing out her soft features. Elder Lily placed her hand against her much younger self's virtual one.

"A few years after I left, I was perusing my media library when I caught on the video of the fateful day I lost my parents. Watching it, something bothered me with Rutger's recording. The mugs by the central console, they didn't match."

On the hologram of the bridge, two mugs sat on a desk; a white mug with the letters CERN imprinted on it, and a hand-painted blue one.

"Mom did own a CERN mug," Lily said with absolute certainty. "It was her grandfather's. But she rarely ever used it. I remember that day as clear as anything I've ever experienced. I was unconscious for a brief period after arriving in the Triassic, but I awoke with a sharp mind, and the first things I recall with precision were my parents' half-full coffee mugs. The one Dad used that day was green, not blue, and Mom's had "Don't Panic" printed on its side; she was a big Douglas Adams fan. Do you two understand what this means?"

Gerrit took a shot. "Could it be that you're--"

"Going senile?"

"Er, I was going to say, trying to send yourself a mental message by swapping the mugs? But how could—"

Lily high-fived the boy. "Bingo! And what do you think that message could be?"

"I... I haven't the slightest!" Raine chattered anxiously, to Lily's light laughter.

Despite being old enough to be my grandmother, the girl mused, *she's still very in touch with her inner child.*

"Remember what I told you two, about how I wondered if ripples in the past can affect the future, and vice versa? Well, here's something to chew on. To discover why the *Belladonna* can still exist in this world line, I dropped off a probe in the Triassic to study my seven-year-old self, to investigate whether or not she'd disappear. So far, so good, but I've always got a back-up plan. Should time itself swallow the *Belladonna,* I'll send the Mark II to replace it. As to the obvious question of whether I am or shall become a clone as a result of this, I have no idea, and in many ways, I'd rather not know."

"Gosh, this is heavy," said Raine, massaging her temples, a habit she picked up from Lily.

Gerrit paced. "So, you reconstructed and edited her exact cache of memories? There's still a margin of error. What if she accidentally remembers, say, making the clones?"

"Highly unlikely," Lily countered with a shake of the head. "I've been storing my memories diligently since I was five years old. Rutger's records are impeccable; we'd be able to tell if I missed something. And we'll know if ever the ripples catch up to us. In any case, I... kind of wanted to see you both again first. Just in case."

The *Belladonna's* captains nodded.

The trio headed to the observatory to savor the tea Lily brought from the future – she proudly declared the leaves as being among the very first grown on Mars' *Bradbury* settlement.

Much to Raine and Gerrit's disappointment, Lily made it clear that she wouldn't be staying for long.

"It's not that I don't want to hang with you guys or anything," she said. "There's just a lot to do back on the *Frontier*, and at my age getting too comfortable can be dangerous. Although... I may be a guest on your vessel now, but that doesn't mean I can't give you a few Captainly pointers, does it?"

"Not at all! Please share with us your unflinching wisdom, O Captain," said Raine.

"Well, here's one thing. I've been continuing Lacie's research. She used paradoxes in the models of quantum physics to delve further into the unknown. In my future, we're not even sure that matter exists independently of consciousness. It's pretty mind-blowing. We still haven't sorted the question of one Universe, zero or holo- Universes, or one of the Multiverse models, but I do know this: G.K. Chesterton's words ring absolutely true – that 'a paradox is the truth standing on its head to gain attention'. What may seem like unanswerable logical and scientific questions can actually be invalid questions. Very often the truth behind any given matter is unquestioningly simple."

She saw that she had lost them, and laughed.

"Okay, take, for example, you two. With my parents' genetic blueprints, the *Belladonna* gave birth to you. It should have been impossible to carry their ideals and enthusiasm through to an entirely different lifetime. You are paradoxes in and of yourselves. But if it weren't for that pep speech you gave me way back when, when I was at my very lowest ..."

"That was just two months ago for us," Gerrit piped in.

"Yes. That day I realized that I was worthy of forgiveness, and that it wasn't too late for me to redeem myself to planet Earth. You two gave me a second life. The paradoxical love you showed me carried on through to the entire human race. In a way, they have you to thank."

The mood in the *Belladonna* that night was carefree, lighthearted. Lily shared with them the media from her future world, and her Ark's blueprints. She also copied some additional data from the ship's library.

"I'm stocking up on a few of the classics," she said. "Ever see *Contact?*"

"Nope," both replied.

"Ah. Check it out sometime. It's a pretty good one."

With her hard drives filled up, Lily went into her room and hugged her stuffed elephant.

"Hey, Scottie. It's been a while. I want you to watch over Raine and Gerrit for me, okay? And if they ever have any kids..."

The approaching shadows stopped Lily from completing her sentence. Standing opposite the doorway, the Co-Captains never looked more like Carl and Elizabeth.

She captured the 3-D image with her Holo-Lens. *Yes. This is the way it was meant to be.*

Precious data in hand, Lily addressed them one last time as she prepped for take-off.

"I once read a theory that life only gives us seven real choices, choices that shape the outcome of the rest of our days. Only, we can never know which decisions are crucial, and which ones don't really matter at all. Isn't that an intriguing notion?"

Gerrit took the bait. "It would mean that we have to treat each decision with utmost consideration."

"Before attempting even the smallest thing, nothing is more important than having the right philosophy," Lily nodded. "Otherwise, you'll be chasing your shadow in a house of mirrors when it all comes tumbling down. Sometimes fate drops breadcrumbs, and sometimes it sends the big bad wolf after you. There's a reason why the American Indian tribes planned for the next seven generations. I'm probably the last person who can say this, but the real strengths of the human race are in love and solidarity, not the innovations and whims of individuals. We've been fighting nature for so long that we forgot what it means to embrace it, and to trust the best in ourselves in the eternal struggle between order and chaos."

The oddest thing, Lily contemplated, *the stab I didn't expect to dawn over time, was that the* Metaverse *played a crucial role: its destruction empowered the people of Earth. Under Lorrie, they had a shared history of oppression, a universal language, and a common enemy. That's what I didn't understand at first. The more I considered it, the less ridiculous the possibility became:*

Could this have been your grand plan all along, Lorelei - to die as a symbol of unchecked oppression, leaving me alone with your example, your lesson, your technology, and your people? It would explain the odd behavior both yourself and Lacie showed at the ends of your lives.

You'd survived the wounds from our battle. Not long after the global solar web prevented the flare from taking your life, I found you dead atop the Spire, *by your own hand. The note in Lacie's memoir read, "Don't save me." Why, Lorrie? Was the universe too small of a pond for you to play in? Or was this your form of spiritual alchemy? 'Through fire, nature is reborn.' If this was indeed your intention, then you had me fooled till the very last.*

She shook off the angst. "You can't fight nature head-on, but you can't be passive to its power, either. Am I a healer, a martyr, a symbol, a demon, or a warrior? Behind my masks, I ask myself the same questions every day. Success is as dangerous as failure. Hope is as hollow as fear. To walk the middle path is to tread upon the edge of a knife. Keeping one's mind clear of fallacies is a full-time job in and of itself. But know this: in everything you do, you are never alone. The concept of collective consciousness is still a notion I can't explain, although someday I hope to be able to. That voice within you knows what's up. Listen to it. This is just one nomad's opinion, but I encourage you to give the *Belladonna* a spin, and see where she takes you. Now, if you'll be so kind as to excuse me, I've got to see a satellite about a death beam."

The two junior Captains digested her rambling words as she prepped for takeoff.

"Um, Lily?" Raine started, breaking a long silence.

"Yes, dear?"

"J-just give us a second, please."

She pulled Gerrit aside; Lily stole an anxious glance at her wristwatch.

"What's up?" he asked.

"Maybe we should go with her," she whispered.

"You mean, to the future?"

"Dude, this could be our only chance!"

"But Raine... we... we have to think about this. What if our actions from here on are crucial to Lily's success? What if we have some part to play?"

"That's just the thing. Maybe there's a new mission for us."

They turned to the former Captain.

"If we change our course, we alter your past," said Raine. "We might erase you."

"What if this ends up causing more paradoxes?" queried Gerrit.

"Ah, impeccable timing. The answer to that one is conveniently simple," elder Lily managed, checking her watch again. "No time to launch probes; let's hope I've still got my steady aim."

The alarm sounded. She brought up a holographic real-time readout of the *Belladonna.*

Three hunter satellites penetrated the station's debris field, armed with superheated laser turrets. Lily took her time calibrating the energy redirects. She remotely activated the Particle Eliminator Cannon recently installed on the *Belladonna's* hull. The beam drew in power, and then, in one sharp instant, split at a floating prism and blasted each of the satellites to pieces.

"Ha! I've still got it!"

Raine gasped and latched onto Gerrit's arm. *We were supposed to die? Was this the real reason she returned?*

Beyond relieved, Lily adjusted her collar. "Lorelei's last hurrah – once reaching Earth, I discovered that she planted a tracker on the *Raven*; now that we're in satellite range, it must have signaled for the cavalry the moment I was spotted descending to Earth. I do believe I just saved your lives. Oh, right, almost forgot about this puppy."

She tossed a disk to XF-22, who slotted it into its console.

"Satellite trackers and weapons deactivation codes. You'll be able to avoid any future attacks. You'll forgive me, I hope, that I waited so long to do this. But I wanted to settle our karma first."

"I get it," said Gerrit. "You've nothing to apologize for."

"Then I'll be taking my leave, though I must admit that I overheard your discussion. You're very welcome to join us on the *Frontier*. I've left the space-time coordinates for the *Bradbury* base with Rutger. But take your time thinking it over. Alpha Earth housed over nine billion people. The potential exists to bring those lives back into existence. Contrary to popular belief, comfortable sustainability is more than possible on modern Earth with populations even twice that size. Should you seek to change the past once more, I won't stop you. Here's my theory: the further removed one becomes from timeline changes, the longer any potential ripples take to have any effect. I can stay two steps ahead; ride out the waves, if that's what it comes down to. I'm standing here before you right now, aren't I?"

"You're invincible, Lily," Raine smiled.

Lillian returned the gesture. "Despite my agnosticism, Grace has come to me; pondering the unknown no longer fills me with fear. I'm prepared to embrace whatever curveballs life throws my way. I wish the same for you. *Namaste.*"

She threw them a parting wave and descended into her cockpit. The deafening turbine echoed along the walls. Within seconds, the *Raven* was gone, leaving Raine and Gerrit in a much better mood than before, but with infinitely more questions.

The Co-Captain felt out her companion. "So."

"So, indeed. I think it's time to catch some Z's before she shows up to blow our minds again."

They bade Rutger a good night and went to their rooms. Raine took a vacuum shower, brushed her teeth, changed into Elizabeth Hermes' pajamas, and nestled into bed, staring out the window at planet Earth.

Now that Lily had departed, she wondered once more if she might just wake up back in Chicago, and closed her eyes. It didn't work. She left and knocked on Gerrit's door.

"Hey."

"Hmm? Can't sleep?"

"Something like that," Raine said sheepishly.

Putting on his space slippers, Gerrit walked over and opened the door with a half-coy, half-concerned expression.

"I can't sleep either."

Raine averted her eyes. "I was wondering, um… don't take this the wrong way or anything, but do you think I could stay with you tonight? I don't want to be alone right now."

Gerrit twiddled his thumbs. "Er, sure. If you can handle my snoring."

"Fake me grew up in an orphanage. That won't be a problem," she said in relief.

The *Belladonna's* twin Captains ended up lying side by side on cots over the observatory floor, hands held. The heat from the engine room below kept their backs warm, and the reactor's low hum was most soothing.

Within a half hour of pillow talk, Gerrit was out. But the stars continued to call to Raine, whose thoughts were snowballing.

"Rutger, are you there?" she whispered.

"Always, Captain Raine."

"Say, you called her 'Miss Lily', right? Do you think you can call me 'Miss Raine'?"

"Miss Raine it is."

"This is going to sound strange, but I have an odd desire to listen to Beethoven."

"Ah, that's not as unusual as you may think. He was one of Professor Elizabeth's favorites. Might I suggest 'Symphony No. 7 in A Major?'"

"Go for it. Oh, and Rutger?"

"Yes?"

"Do you think you could hook me up with a good dream tonight?"

"I'm sorry, Miss Raine. I'm not allowed to influence your dreams. I can only record them. But if I may I offer a word of advice Elizabeth Hermes might have given: dreams tell you lies in order to reveal truths. Your brain dreams what it needs to; there is little harm in letting your subconscious cleanse your cluttered thoughts. Humans have an average of five adventures every night. There is no such thing as a dreamless sleep, only a lack of dream recall. And sometimes that's for the better."

"Maybe I should hope for an eventful dream, then," Raine replied. "So I can wake up fresh. Who knows?"

"No worries. I've already calibrated the perfect playlist for you. Four hours of Beethoven and Mozart, then four hours of improvisational jazz."

Powerful strings calmed her restless mind. The potential weight of the universe now on her shoulders and with no idea what her next step might be, there should have been no way for Raine get a wink of sleep. But to her own surprise, she was eager to get started on her research. Both Lilies had left notes and blueprints to pore through and study, language models to master, histories to digest. And Rutger, of course, could simulate any number of potential outcomes.

Raine performed breathing exercises, counted sheep, even attempted to hypnotize herself to slumber. Then she simply stopped trying to force it, and had the dome tilt towards the rotating planet.

After some time, Earth turned into the swirling arcade cabinet that led her into *Endless Metaverse*. Only everything went in reverse, and she walked backwards over the virtual waves, past the floating chrome orbs, through the television after-image, and out of the portal into Agnes' condo back in good old Chicago, where everyone was making bets on the next Bulls season and arcade gamers ruled supreme.

Raine imagined herself asleep on a Monday morning in winter, double-layered to save on heating costs. She'd be playing hookey, having slept in due to reeling from the most insane dream of her life, awaiting the light to seep in from the top of her curtain around nine-thirty and prompt her awake to turn to the other side of the bed.

She opened her eyes again after squeezing them shut.

Planet Earth was still watching over her, its blue and white echoing the dull sky she now left behind in her imaginary suburb.

Five minutes of this passed.

Raine took a deep breath. At least now, she knew where she was, and that she would need to steel herself to meet the days ahead. Long, thankless days of learning, theorizing, and questioning, but with Gerrit by her side, they would be worth it, mission or no mission.

With her doubts at bay, Raine drifted off to sleep, and had the most magnificent dreams.

Afterword and Acknowledgments

Dear reader, I sincerely hope you enjoyed your time with Raine, Lily, and Gerrit as much as I enjoyed the privilege of chronicling their adventures. I'd hoped to write a preface, but this work originated as an e-book, and seeing as how the first encounter most readers will have with the work would consist of a sample including the first few pages, I wanted to ensure that I had enough space to properly thank everyone who's supported, inspired, and influenced me over the course of this five-year journey (to explore strange new worlds).

The very first traces of "Raine VS The End of the World" hit the word processor before I knew what they were. I was a film student turning 21 in '08, during one of the more depressing periods in recent film history. The Great Recession began. The WGA went on strike. Heath Ledger's tragic passing in January set the tone for the rest of the year, which was dominated by a few darkly cynical epics, such as "The Dark Knight", "There Will Be Blood", "W.", "The Wrestler", "Revolutionary Road" and, of course, "Step Brothers".

When the year began, I was working at The Landmark on Pico and Westwood, watching two to three new films a week. Immersed in film, I was about to transfer to CalArts for my B.A. and spent time desperately honing my screenwriting skills. The long-term plan was to crank out a full-length screenplay on one of my two favorite science fiction genres, namely, virtual worlds or time travel. To help with my decision, I ended up writing on both, only I found myself restraining my vision at every corner in order to develop a work that might conceivably end up on the small or silver screen (one of my faults is that I can't stop thinking big!). So I embarked on something different. I'd write in the more comfortable format of a novel, and retroactively adapt the work into a screenplay. Just like that, my pre-conceived limitations disappeared.

The short screenplay involving a virtual world as a major plot point, "The Man Who Owned the World", focused almost exclusively on its tower-dwelling antagonist and his quest against the 'invading' hero working to free people from his virtual prison, while my ideas on time travel involved cycles spanning millennia and parallel worlds, for one person's attempt to save humanity. The ridiculous notion to combine both came to me in a dream not unlike the one that Lily mulls over.

The stories of Lillian and Raine wove themselves into being with relative ease, as if they had always existed and were simply looking for someone to chronicle their adventures. I was inspired by my personal and creative relationship at the time with Ms. Sabrina Cotugno, a gifted artist, animator, and storyteller to whom I shall forever be indebted.

It had been a goal of mine for years to craft an action-packed genre story with strong, but not archetypical, female protagonists. I wasn't trying to avoid traditional story structures. As I worked out the themes of adolescent escapism, megalomaniacal control, and the eternal human quest for truth into a fast-paced narrative, it was more that traditional structures avoided me.

In the following years, as the political climates in the USA and abroad changed, I felt I could not ignore the class warfare taking place across the globe, as well as the mounting challenges to civil and natural freedoms, equal rights, the gradual 'wars' on privacy, the prevalence of false flag attacks, and the continued destruction and exploitation of natural resources and indigenous peoples to further the globalist economic machine, offset for the first-world by mindless distractions.

Considering myself as a world citizen writing for a universal audience, many of the secondary themes of the story developed around these horrific violations to basic human rights, and from a personal need to address the collective feelings of apathy and disillusionment present in young peoples' attitudes towards the future.

Most of my research time was spent on ensuring that technology circa 2187 was based on the emergent possibilities of existing science. The *Metaverse's* escapism became a mirror for the evolution of the gaming industry towards total cinematic immersion (devices such as the Oculus Rift are paving the way in that regard), the Holo-Lens a peek at the future of head-mounted, Cloud-based communications such as the Google Glass, and the anarchists' struggle within the *Metaverse* a representation for Internet freedom fighters and the power of individuals connected by nothing more than electric waves and text to influence and challenge the system at large (IRL, check out the EFF and Slashdot). The final confrontation between the EDC and *Neo Eden* was a lot of fun to write, as it allowed me to picture what warfare might be like in an alternate future where high-powered but not necessarily speedy airships dominated the skies.

On the time travel side of things, the *Belladonna*, of course, is a near-impossibility, and the one major narrative embellishment I was willing to make. By almost any model out there, the furthest back any theoretical time machine could transport its user would be to the point of its initial operation (not to mention that, as written, the *Belladonna* utilizes an unexplainable method of artificial gravity).

Added late in the story's development, Vipassana Meditation (as practiced by Lily) is an ancient and very scientific technique created and taught by Gautama Buddha during his lifetime, and has recently spread from Burma via the efforts of S.N. Goenka. I took a ten-day course and it was one of the most beneficial things I've ever done. Please visit www.dhamma.org to learn more about Vipassana.

All in all, I did my best to capture the tale as it played on a loop, refining itself through my subconscious via long hours of introspection. Finding the time to write was my biggest challenge, but distilling the prose never felt like work. On the contrary, putting down the camera, sharpening my pencil, and returning to fiction after a years-long break was immensely freeing.

Though I may not be a seasoned pro (I haven't completed my 10,000 hours of writing yet!), I knew that I could wait no longer to get this tale out into the world. Writing "Raine" was undoubtedly the most fun I've ever had working on a creative endeavor. And I hope some of that joy and energy transfers through to the final product.

If you'll allow me the great courtesy to paraphrase something Tolkien once said of "The Lord of the Rings", this humble attempt at fiction is a tale that grew in the telling, and I have many people to thank for their love, support, influence, and inspiration throughout the years.

The biggest thanks go to my family for allowing me more than a fair share of time to work on this story even in the midst of a very busy period for the family business. That's Mom, Dad, Michael, Aaron and Khayla. I would also like to further thank my extended family: Grandma Rosie, Uncle David and his family, Aunt Missy and her family, Tita Pangga and family, Kuya Pat and Pam, Tita Marisse and her kids, Uncle Trius and his family, and many others, not to mention Mike Canaday and his family, Mike Kim and his family, Shahriar and his family, Glen and his family, Jamshid and his family, Gustaji, Parvin, Arshia, Payam, and Zee, Jack and Becky Caraco, Ralph and Kebi Brown, Chris and Christy Pearson, and all of our other close family friends from the Avatar Meher Baba community for their love and support.

Although I consider myself agnostic, it feels only right to thank the Divine Watchmaker in the 50-50 chance that He/She/It exists and the universe, and us within it, are part of the fabric of an elaborately woven tapestry as well as an inevitability of metaphysics.

Major kudos are in order to my beta-reading team, whom I subjected to an entire year of e-mails and have given me immensely helpful feedback: namely, Alice, Angeline, Angelica, Anna, Bong Su, Carlos, Charles, Christina, Frank, Peter, Ioan, Inez, John-Paul, Kim, Kyle, Myra, Raine (whom I hope doesn't mind that I appropriated her name!), Sabrina, Sammy, Sarah, Sophie, Thomas, Toshi, and Tim.

I'd also like to give shout-outs to Moe, Mon, Paulo, Errol, Anthony, Robert, Rachelle, Piran, Kyle, Yosuke, Daphne, Ayrn, Joanna, Vanessa, Gerrit, Steven, Beverly, Glen, Bobby, Casey, Pete, Marilyn, Conor, Kelly, Matt, James, Claire, Chris, Rachel, Francesca, Lauren, Pele, Mélisande, Brandon, Samantha, Fabian, Sam, Vincent, Alex, West, Ben Dubash, Jenna West, and Alex Lorge.

Anna, Christina, Ioan, Meredith, Michael, Mom, and Myra, I owe you guys big time for your insights and support.

I also must thank all the great video game makers who've inspired me. That list includes, in no particular order, Nintendo, Square-Enix, Sega, Konami, Namco-Bandai, Capcom, Platinum Games, Clover Studios, From Software, Bethesda, Q? Games, GRAVITY Co., Ltd., Blizzard, Bioware, Irrational Games, Atlus, Level-5 Games, Rare, thatgamecompany, Mistwalker Studios, Team Meat, Studio Pixel, Distractionware, Four Leaf Studios, and many others.

Hideo Kojima and Hironobu Sakaguchi in particular have been tremendous influences on this work.

Countless animé have also left their mark on "Raine". If you are curious to dive into this wonderful universe, please check out "Steins;Gate", "Neon Genesis Evangelion" and the "Rebuild of Evangelion" films, "Puella Magi Madoka Magika", "The Girl Who Leapt Through Time", "Serial Experiments Lain", "Kill la Kill", "Code Geass" (which **heavily** inspired the climactic aerial battle), "The Melancholy of Haruhi Suzumiya", the ".hack" series, "Accel World", "Btooom!", "Sword Art Online", "Cowboy Bebop", "Summer Wars", "Wolf Children", "Redline", "Baccano!", "Full Metal Alchemist

Brotherhood", "Eden of the East", "Gurren Lagann", "FLCL", "K-On!", "The Animatrix", "Mindgame", "Fate/stay night" and "Fate/zero", the "Ghost in the Shell" films and series, the works of Studio Ghibli, Madhouse, and the late, great Satoshi Kon ("Paranoia Agent", "Perfect Blue" and "Paprika" influenced me quite a bit), among myriad other great works of Japanese animation. I highly recommend the works of Studio Ghibli as a starting point for anyone new to animé. American animated series that have directly influenced this work include "Samurai Jack", Genndy Tartakovsy's "Clone Wars", "The Venture Bros.", "Metalocalypse", and, of course, "Futurama".

Manga, graphic novel, and webcomic/online influences include the works of Neil Gaiman, Osamu Tezuka, Will Eisner, Craig Thompson, Katsuhiro Otomo, Yukito Kishiro's "Battle Angel Alita" series, Hiroki Endo's "Eden" series, the art of Frank Frazetta, Bryan Lee O'Malley, Alan Moore, Gene Luen Yang, Amy Kim Kabuishi (whose work I absolutely love) and Kazu Kabuishi, editor of the "Flight" series of graphic novels, Scott Ramsoomair, Mike Krahulik and Jerry Holkins, Randall Munroe, Scott Kurtz, Brian Clevinger ("8-Bit Theatre" kept me laughing for years), Ryan North, Dan Kim, Fred Gallagher and Rodney Caston, Frank Miller, and Scott McCloud, among many, many others. I'm also a huge fan of VSauce, JonTron and Egoraptor, the Game Grumps family, Nostalgia Critic, Nostalgia Chick, the Red Letter Media guys, and James Rolfe, The Angry Video Game Nerd.

If I listed all my cinematic idols, we'd both be here for days. So first and foremost I'll mention the Wachowski siblings, whose incomparable body of work continues to inspire me. I'd also like to thank Terry Gilliam, Martin Scorsese, Peter Jackson, Wes Anderson, Satyajit Ray, Agnes Varda, Billy Wilder, Kinji Fukusaku, Park Chan-wook, Bong Joon-ho, Kim Ji-woon, Kim Ki-duk, Kenji Mizoguchi, Takashi Miike, Yasujiro Ozu, Akira Kurosawa, Edgar Wright, Guillermo del Toro, the Nolan brothers, Zack Snyder, Justin Lin, Ang Lee, Rian Johnson, Spike Lee, Derek Cianfrance, Quentin Tarantino, Richard Kelly, Michel Gondry, Charlie Kaufman, Ridley Scott, Francis Ford Coppola, Sofia Coppola, Alfonso Cuâron, Duncan Jones, Richard Linklater, Georges Mélies, Kevin Smith, Robert Zemeckis, Steven Spielberg, Joss Whedon, and George Lucas for expanding my imagination.

As for literary influences, I've gotta hand it to the great mind-benders and genre pioneers: Haruki Murakami (my all-time favorite author), Philip K. Dick, Robert Heinlein, Isaac Asimov, J.R.R. Tolkien,

George R.R. Martin, J.K. Rowling, C.S. Lewis, Douglas Adams, Stephen King, Ray Bradbury, Joseph Heller, Terry Pratchett, Neil Gaiman, Neal Stephenson, William Gibson, Joe Halderman, Arthur Conan Doyle, Edgar Rice Burroughs, Cory Doctorow, Orson Scott Card, Robert Louis Stevenson, Victor Hugo, Frank Herbert, Hunter S. Thompson, Chuck Palahniuk, Kurt Vonnegut, George Orwell, Jules Verne, Koushun Takami, Suzanne Collins, Philip Pullman, Ursula Le Guin, Aldous Huxley, L. Frank Baum, Lewis Carroll, J.M. Barrie, Ayn Rand, William Goldman, Nagaru Tanigawa, Mary Shelley, Max Brooks, Ryu Murakami, Robert Jordan, and Brandon Sanderson, again, in no particular order. Love you guys.

The steampunk epic "Clockwork Angels" by Kevin J. Anderson, based upon a story by Neal Peart and complementing the phenomenal Rush album of the same name, also inspired me towards the end of the writing process.

I owe a debt to Ernest Cline, whom I have never met. His novel "Ready Player One" features a fantastic depiction of an online world clinging to a happier past; his vision is more grounded in reality, and he is practically reverent to its influences. I wish him the best of luck on adapting his work to film, and if by some miracle he is reading this right now I would like to volunteer my services as a filmmaker to help realize his vision. Full disclosure: I read "Ready Player One" when I was about 70% finished with "Raine", and knowing that there was an audience in America hungry for literary excursions into virtual worlds greatly encouraged me to get my thoughts out into the ether.

Justin Macumber, author of "Haywire" and "A Minor Magic" and co-runner of the award-winning Dead Robots Society writers' podcast, is another inspiration. His work features strong characterizations, wry humor, satisfying physics, and hair-raising action sequences. I'd like to also give a shout-out to kenporules, Rexkix, Dubz, Faint, Korg, DSS, Savory, Bomb, OSN, milky, and all my other friends on the Rotten Tomatoes General Video Game Discussion Forums. Sorry I haven't had much time to visit.

I'd like to thank Rachel Manija Brown, whose spirit moved me even after a single meeting. Her memoir "All The Fishes Come Home To Roost" is in turns funny, sad, insightful, heartwarming, and overall just a great read. I wish her all the best.

Also, writing wouldn't have been in my cards had it not been for the feedback I received from my educators at CalArts (Profs. Astra,

Buchanan, Horne, Klahr, Mairs, Sherman, and Tanaka), the support of my many English teachers throughout the years (Ms. Joji, Ms. Glo, Señora Correa, Prof. Daniel Cano, and many others – you know who you are!), and my readers on fanfiction.net.

Some of the music I listened to while writing: Rush, Yes, Utada Hikaru, School Food Punishment, Daft Punk's "Tron Legacy OST", "Alive" concert and "Random Access Memories", Gorillaz' "Plastic Beach" and "The Fall", Iron Maiden, Mozart, The Gathering, Beethoven, LiSA, Ayumi Hamasaki, BoA, Pink Floyd, the Metal Gear Rising OST, Child of Eden OST, Nobuo Uematsu's compositions for the Final Fantasy series, Xion, Linkin Park, Vangelis' "Blade Runner" OST, and Eric Serra's OST for "The Big Blue".

HariHariSonic, moderator of the awesome Act Select Sonic the Hedgehog fansite, very kindly allowed me to use his NiseUFOCatcher font for the book cover. Thanks, man! (A disclaimer regarding the book cover and promo art: it's not artistically or geographically consistent with the *Metaverse*, in part due to stylistic concerns, but mostly because I can't really draw.)

I've been told that gamers are allergic to fiction and that this story is too elaborate and demanding to be contained in one volume, but hopefully Raine, Lily, and Gerrit will find friends to join in their quests.

So here's to saving the best for last. Most of all, I would like to thank you, the reader, for taking a chance and embarking on this special journey with me.

I welcome all questions, comments, and hecklings at josvchoi@gmail.com. Whether you enjoyed the story or not, I'm extremely grateful for any Amazon reviews. I'm hoping that the experience of sharing the things dearest to my imagination with the world, and engaging in a dialogue with a global audience about how we can collaborate with our loved ones to face our most uncertain future will help me grow not just as a writer and storyteller, but also as a human being.

Joseph Victor Choi
July 20, 2013 – April 7, 2014

Appendices

Timeline of Events (Lily's POV)

August 12, 2080 AD:
Lillian Hermes is born to Carl and Elizabeth Hermes on the space station *Belladonna 5000*.

April 13, 2087 AD:
The *Belladonna* is attacked by the UAA; Carl and Elizabeth Hermes are killed. To protect her and the *Belladonna*, Lillian is sent to the far past.

225,000,000 BC:
Seven-year-old Captain Lily arrives in the Triassic period and begins her parents' assigned training to assume control of the *Belladonna*.

225,000,002 BC:
At the age of nine, Lily completes intermediate training; she begins to receive messages from her future self regarding failed attempts to evacuate humanity from planet Earth before the solar flare wipes them out.

225,000,003 BC:
Having received over a dozen messages from failed future attempts, nine -year-old Lily travels to the future to begin the latest iteration of her mission (although for this instance of Lily, it is the first attempt, as will be reflected furthermore).

1980 AD:
After five failed solo attempts wherein Lily begins in the far future and moves gradually to the past, she modifies the *Belladonna's* Remediator and initiates the year-long process of creating three clones to assist her.

August 12, 1981 AD:
Lorelei, Lucille, and Laramie are synthesized and achieve consciousness. Laramie changes her name to Lacie, because it "sounds cooler".

1982 AD:
The clones complete their education and recite the *Time Keepers' Oath*. Lily takes them on their first three attempts at the mission, undocumented in this file.

July 5, 1099 AD (Attempt #4)
The Jerusalem Un-Incident. Having been unsuccessful in their previous attempt, Lily and her clones fail to come to a consensus regarding whether they should take action and declare themselves as Goddesses at

the time of the First Crusade, effectively pre-empting centuries of warfare. They decide to wait overnight to make a decision. The next morning, a future envelope informs them that this attempt will end in civil war between the sisters.

October 9, 1873 AD (Attempt #7)

Disguised as powerful noblewomen, the sisters visit Queen Victoria and discuss gathering her Generals to bear witness to the Time Keepers' display of military might, in order to persuade the crown towards withdrawing from its many territories and working with the Time Keepers to foster an age of peaceful technological advancement.

Shortly after the successful demonstration, Lorelei receives her vision. Lily and Lorelei have a terrible argument regarding the nature of any conceivable damage their tampering with time has had on the universe. The discussion ends inconclusively, leaving Lorelei bitter and upset.

Though the next phase of Lillian's plan would take the team seven years into the future, Lorelei refuses to participate, and instead attempts to bolster her Italian factories. She is practically yanked onto the *Belladonna*.

November 5, 1880 AD (Attempt #7)

Upon arriving in the future, the Time Keepers discover that Lorelei's droids mistakenly attacked a foreign convoy, inadvertently spurring on a series of battles that would become the first *Forgotten War*.

Livid, Lillian wants to travel back to the past, but Lorelei, after being reprimanded, pleads for them to find a present solution. The Time Keepers come up with a plan to salvage the attempt.

Unhappy at the possible repercussions of her Split-Universe theory being ignored, Lorelei recruits Lacie and forces Lucille into participating in mutiny. This sets the stage for *The Spacetime War.*

Lorelei and Lacie steal twenty-two of the *Belladonna's* fuel cells, and its power converter. Lucy attempts to aid Lily in subduing the other clones and preventing them from sending Lily two hundred years into the future without adequate resources, but is brutally murdered in the process. Lily is sent to the year 2180 at the age of 13.

Lorelei and Lacie hijack the *Raven* and land on Earth with a plethora of fuel cells.

November 1880 – February 2180 AD

Betraying the trust of the Royal Family, Lorelei and Lacie foster World War I into a global bloodbath, indirectly sealing the fate of billions of potential lives by focusing exclusively on machine growth, preventing growth of the global population past 1.5 billion.

Lorelei co-opts the dominant global powers by violently seizing control of the banks and working behind the scenes to assume command of every nation's interests.

Over the next two centuries, Lorelei and Lacie build the massive fortress city-state of *Neo Eden,* and the mind-controlling *Endless Metaverse*, their tool to shepherd 90% of the human race into a fantasy world so as to give them solace even unto the ending of the world.

January 5-31, 2180 AD

Thirteen year-old Lily arrives in the *Belladonna,* understandably shocked at the world that Lacie and Lorelei have created. For a week she observes Lorelei's progress. With Lucy's fuel cells providing limited reserves, she discreetly manages a few trips to the recent past and back to the present in order to establish additional communes on Earth and annex factories, as well as strengthen the EDC freedom fighters.

February 14, 2180 AD

Having prepared her game plan, Lily sets out to meet Lorelei, descending to Earth. She approaches the Queen in the *Spire* asking for the return of the power converter and fuel cells. When Lorelei refuses, Lily challenges her to war, giving her and Lacie six years to change their minds.

March 2181 AD

Lillian gives a demonstration of her technology to the council of EDC Elders via hologram. They are impressed by her work. She is given a special position in the Research and Development Cabinet.

June 2181 AD

Lillian begins to use *Eden* factories in Busan, Jakarta, and Beijing to build up the EDC's Carriers and android divisions. She sets up her own mines in Mongolia, and eventually, Alaska.

Realizing that she will need additional help, Lily prepares to synthesize Carl II and Elizabeth II.

January 2182 AD

Following her sweeping success in defending New Zealand, Lily is appointed Commodore of the EDC *Nomad Fleet.*

March 2182 AD

Carl II and Elizabeth II are born in the bodies of 11-year-olds and choose the names "Raine" and "Gerrit". They begin their rigid education program.

Raine and Gerrit are put to the test by going through a simulated gauntlet to recapture Manila in the name of the EDC. Their plan proves successful, and together with Lily, they go on to accomplish the feat for real.

Impressed by Lillian's progress, the EDC agrees to lend their full strength to Lily, Raine, and Gerrit's in-progress *Operation End Verse*, which will spell the end of *Neo Eden* and *Endless Metaverse*.

June 2183 AD

Raine, Gerrit, and Lily visit Earth for the first time, eating dinner on a deserted island. It is a powerful memory that never leaves Raine's mind.

Lillian's R & D division perfects the EDC's cloaking system, based off theoretical blueprints by her ancestor Timothy Hermes.

September 2184 AD

As the vision for *Operation End Verse* grows more complete, it becomes clear that the only way to take down the *Metaverse* is from the inside. Gerrit and Raine work on crafting the new identities they will need to assume.

The trio visits the island one more time to prepare for the final confrontation.

Gerrit heads into the *Metaverse* ahead of Raine in order to learn it inside out.

April 7, 2187 AD

Raine is prepped to enter *Endless Metaverse*; she immerses herself in a digital simulation for a week as Raine Townsend. During this simulated but very real time, she meets the time traveler and learns of a possible chance for her to earn a world record title.

Chapter One begins here (Raine's POV):

Day 1 (April 14, 2187 AD):

In her digital simulation, Raine beats Super BlastBoy three times in a row. Guided by Lily on the surface, she enters the *Metaverse*, meets Chance and Gerrit, and stays the night at an inn along the old road.

Lily and the EDC are holed up in Siberia; she declares they must leave for *Neo Eden* in the morning.

Queen Lorelei investigates Raine, discovers that she has false memories, and reasons that she must be one of Lily's agents.

Jon Wrathman tells Henry Holdfast that the position of Junior Net Manager is his to lose. General Lacie insists on the news that the EDC Armada is contained in the East.

Day 2 (April 15):

Gerrit visits Yossa and is sent to monitor Raine.

Raine meets Jack, Tuft, Stephen, and Lily. She falls into the pit with Gerrit and stays the night in Mistral, near the Forbidden Tower.

Bidding Claire goodbye, Lacie leaves to study the events of the future; she returns from a serious aerial battle with severe injuries and news for the Queen.

Lily returns to the Belladonna for the red envelope and studies her nagging dream.

Holdfast is promoted to *Avidya* Junior Net Manager.

Day 3 (April 16):

Holdfast takes charge of management of the Forbidden Tower.

Raine and Peter enter the Forbidden Tower with Ricard's team, meet Thaddius, defeat the Necromancer, and are hunted down.

The Queen addresses the Seven Lords and commands that their *Metaverse* assets assist in a ground war over *Neo Eden.*

Gerrit is taken out of the *Metaverse*; Gen. Lacie tracks his signal.

After splitting with Linus, Raine hides alone in Pagoda.

Lily returns from the *Belladonna* and prepares her counter-attack on Gen. Lacie.

Day 4 (April 17):

Lily confronts Lacie and regretfully kills her, having acquired information about the HDP backup.

Raine beats the Champion; Lily is ecstatic.

After being abducted by the *Nebula*, Raine talks to Jon, and refuses an offer to join the Developers. She is placed in the Coliseum, to be indoctrinated.

Yossa breaks through the Coliseum and saves Raine. He fights the temptation to use her as a figurehead for the rebellion and sends her on her way to find SBB.

Ayumi halts Claire's suicide attempt; she spends the night with Holdfast.

Lacie's body is returned to *Neo Eden*; Lorelei weeps. Upon returning to the *Spire,* she addresses Gerrit; the nobles party all night.

Commodore Leandra approaches the Adriatic at midnight. Her cloaked scouts jam the *Eden* blockade's detectors.

Day 5 (April 18):

Raine awakens to SBB and Lily arguing over the plan. Raine and Lily depart on a trip to shut down the *Metaverse's* mainframe core. On their way out, Lorelei attempts to ambush them, and is caught in a trap by the Colossi, who hold her off to buy Lily some time. The EDC Armada approaches *Neo Eden.* Leandra's *Freyja* crosses the Apennine Mountains.

Yossa and the freedom fighters break out of the backup servers and find themselves under attack in *Neo Eden.*

The Battle of *Neo Eden:* Lorelei's HDP forces and androids do horrific battle against the EDC rebellion; the rebels are joined shortly by the EDC armada.

With the help of Super BlastBoy, Raine and Lily shut down *Endless Metaverse* and log out to the *Valkyrie* just in time for the final battle.

Henry and Jon liberate Gerrit from Lorelei's Sisyphus Program. The trio breaks through the *Spire* to shut down the Overseer and stop the troops' advance. The Queen has them executed, but a stray bullet shatters her coolant system, and the chamber floods with water, short-circuiting the entire civilian armed forces.

Claire attempts to kill Queen Lorelei, who dodges her bullets and appoints her Princess Regent over the Earth. Raine and Lily lead the front lines in the liberation of the city. Upon reaching the *Spire,* Raine is killed defending Lily.

Lily swears revenge. Lily fights and defeats Lorelei. Lorelei asks to be sent to the future.

March 10, 2212:

Lily transports Lorelei there, hands over Lacie's memoirs, and sends her off with a heartfelt goodbye. Lily returns to...

April 18, 2187:

The war is over. Lily flies her colors over *Neo Eden*, oversees the Princess Regent's formal surrender, and then retreats from the public eye.

May 2, 2187:

With Raine and Gerrit's collected memories, Lily initiates a second batch of clones of her parents.

June 1, 2188:

Raine and Gerrit are reborn. Lily reveals to them that they are clones of her parents Carl and Elizabeth, and returns their memories as best she can before withdrawing.

Rutger, and Raine II and Gerrit II's kind words foil Lily's suicide attempt.

August 19, 2188:

After two months of planning and re-adjusting to life on the *Belladonna,* Lily announces that she is leaving the fate of the universe in Raine and Gerrit's hands. Lily bids them goodbye and sets a course for Earth to build her Space Ark.

Character Bios

The following are based upon the characters' temperament at the beginning of the records herein. Some accounts may contain speculation on the part of the narrator.

Captain Lillian Hermes / Sky Admiral Lily
Age: 20
Height: 5'4"
Favorite Food: Sashimi
Favorite Color: Light blue
Hobbies: Robotics, Gardening

The fated daughter of famed scientists Carl and Elizabeth, set to be yet another troubled fictional orphan upon whose shoulders the fate of the world rests. She inherits the *Belladonna* and its grueling mission at a young age, with the onboard AI Rutger her only companion. She's haunted by her mistakes, the burden of responsibility she places on herself, and the collective failed efforts of her countless past selves to reform the world and ensure humanity's survival. Her growth was stunted after a fight with Lorelei that nearly killed her. A super-genius with a powerful conscience, the only way Lily can forgive herself for her past is to confront it head-on.

Raine Townsend / Captain Raine
Age: 16
Height: 5'7"
Favorite Food: BLT and PB & J sandwiches
Favorite Colors: Hunter green and regal purple
Hobbies: Video gaming, track and field, speed math

Raine has blocked out much of her childhood. She spent years at an orphanage outside of Chicago until she ended up in foster care due to bouts of depression and a penchant for escape attempts. Even after being taken under the care of a well-meaning but authoritarian woman,

Raine has continued to be a troublesome case. She retreats from reality by playing video games, a hobby that turned to obsession upon her discovery that she was an immensely gifted gamer. Once entering the *Metaverse* and finding that her memories are fading, however, Raine begins to question the very reality she knows.

Gerrit (Surname Classified) / Captain Gerrit
Age: 16
Height: 5'10"
Favorite Food: Pumpkin pie
Favorite Color: Orange
Hobbies: Sword tricks, Mythology, Philosophy, 20th century rock

A skilled player of *Endless Metaverse*, Gerrit moonlights as an errand-boy for the underground rebellion. He is among the strongest swordsmen in the *Avidya* server and can manipulate much of the *'Verse's* code at will, but never picks a fight unless he needs to. He's spent most of his time in the *Metaverse* searching for a girlfriend who's on the same level as he is, and is curious about what the Developers are hiding; the mysteries of the world outside interest him more than the *'Verse's* manufactured distractions.

Lorelei Hermes / Queen Lorelei
Age: 34
Height: 5'10
Favorite Food: Peking duck
Favorite Color: Burgundy
Hobbies: Painting, Overlording, and miniature golf

The stylish and enigmatic creator of *Endless Metaverse*, monarch of *Neo Eden*, and de facto ruler of the free world, Lorelei enjoys the finest things in life: finely roasted coffee, strapping young men, and the joys of painting and visual arts, although her quick thinking and processing has made her bored, impatient and agitated. She originally left on her campaign to rule planet Earth in order to prove a point to Lily regarding their conflicting views of the universe, but has since become rather attached to the aroma of power she holds upon its citizens.

Lacie (Laramie) Hermes / General Lacie
Age: 29
Height: 5'9
Favorite Food: Custard pies
Favorite Color: Neon yellow
Hobbies: Writing, Research, Samba, Aerobics, Scuba diving

As the leader of *Neo Eden's* armed forces, Lacie spends much of her time in training or enacting battle strategies. Once an ardent scientist like her sisters, Lacie has now resigned herself to doing the Queen's dirty work. She's afraid of making her own judgments due to past regrets relating to the *Hermes* mission. As a result, 'Cie doesn't mind taking orders. If there's one thing that motivates her, it's her love for Claire, the noblewoman whose life she saved and ultimately fell in love with. Her loyal pup Archie keeps her company as well. As the date of the fateful solar flare approaches, Lacie has made it a point to work on her memoirs, so that the tale of the *Belladonna* does not go unwritten.

Lucille Hermes
Age: 16
Height: 5'6
Favorite Food: Fish and chips
Favorite Color: Navy blue
Hobbies: Reading, Anthropology, Chess, Chopin, History

Lucy is a total bookworm, an engineering genius, and the most psychologically well balanced of Lily's clones, as far as personality traits are concerned. Although she is an avid reader, is prone to daydreaming about her brief life in the Victorian era, and often seems in her own world, she can be very sociable, and is more than capable of holding her own in a debate with any of her sisters. More than any of them, Lucy understands the flow of history and how violence simply begets more violence, and her approach to Lily's problem is to attack it with lateral thinking. Lucy holds a deep respect for the work of Carl and Elizabeth, and made use of the long-lasting but practical designs of the *Belladonna* in crafting her early concepts for the Exo Knights. As a defensive measure and a supplement for the 'HRM Victoria Demonstration', Lucille developed theoretical anti-particle weapons, to be used only at the utmost need. The end result of her research culminated long after her passing into the EDC's Particle Eliminator Cannon, Lillian's reluctant weapon. It turned the tide of the *Battle of Eden* at the high cost of thousands of lives. A brilliant strategist with a humanitarian spirit, Lucy is fiercely loyal to Lily and will do anything for her.

Elizabeth O'Brien / Elizabeth Hermes
Age: 39
Height: 5'7"
Favorite Food: Nutella
Favorite Color: Hunter green and regal purple
Hobbies: Watching comedies, dubstep, cooking, reading Gary Larson's "The Far Side"

Born into a world of science, Elizabeth was given the choice at a young age: dedicate her life to realizing her grandfather's dream, or allow her younger brother Scott, or one of her cousins, to do so. It was a difficult decision, but upon consulting Scott, the boy revealed that he would much rather be an unknown artist than a glorious scientist – the realm of science, he said, is much more dangerous than the arts. He proved to be correct, and Elizabeth later wondered what her life might have been like had she not toiled for nearly three decades to create a time machine that granted her the ultimate responsibility as a scientist – that of protecting the human race from its worst elements. She fell in love with Carl Connors in graduate school, as he had also come from a dynasty of ambitious scientists, and as he was also a listless youth, he understood her better than anyone else, despite their pursuing different fields. Carl once asked for her opinion on his thesis, which was actually a dissertation on all the logical reasons why they should marry. After their engagement, the two subsequently published many papers on the ethics and mechanics of time travel, and quickly became controversial figures in the scientific community. They were warned time and again against building the *Belladonna*, and all efforts to secure the billions of credits (approx. $1 trillion by 2013 standards) needed to realize her grandfather's vision proved futile. Shortly after their wedding, the equally curious Carl surprised his wife by offering his entire inheritance to kick-start funding for the project. Word has it that she fainted on the spot. Elizabeth and Carl made the decision to create the machine in secret, with android contractors. The day the duo launched from Earth was one of the most relieving of either of their lives. Even at the very end, Elizabeth never regretted her one act of rebellion and individuality, which was having a child of her own.

Carl Connors / Carl Hermes
Age: 43
Height: 5'10"
Favorite Food: Yakisoba
Favorite Color: Salmon
Hobbies: Golf, memorizing the periodic table, useless trivia, brainteasers

Carl Connors was born into a wealthy estate, thanks to his grandfather, who, partnered with a Chinese firm, co-developed a form of high-yield, easy to produce solar panels that changed the global economy almost overnight. The third of four siblings, Carl completely failed to develop a head for business and, inspired by his ancestor and his father, who worked at CERN (coincidentally enough, as an assistant to Elizabeth's grandfather), decided to pursue a life in the sciences almost on a lark. After dabbling in quantum physics and microbiology, he found success in the field of astrophysics, despite being a listless eccentric. Carl's outlook changed completely when he met Elizabeth O'Brien in graduate school. Listening to her read out her dissertation in her sweet, husky voice was enough to put him over the moon. Elizabeth's spirit and hope for the future inspired him, as did her knowledge and theories on temporal travel, by then a controversial and often laughed-about fringe subject. Carl inherited a fourth of his family's estate upon the passing of his much older father, and after Elizabeth's attempts to secure donors to keep the project alive fell far short of their goal, Carl decided to invest his entire fortune into helping her build the *Belladonna* to silence their critics and show that their Warp Initiator was the real deal. His siblings pitched in to help as well, and were later joined by other private donors. The couple truly believed in one another, and their mutual quirks and charisma allowed them to build up a loyal group of friends and supporters, despite being a running joke of many of the more established scientific organizations. Upon discovering the tragedy of the solar flare, they took on the last name "Hermes", signifying their new roles as messengers bearing important news to all of humanity.

Jonathan Wrathman / Mister Senior
Age: 61
Height: 5'10"
Favorite Food: Filet mignon
Favorite Color: Blood red
Hobbies: Gambling, Wind-surfing, Sport Racing

One of the oldest and longest-employed Developers, Chief Operations Officer Wrathman has seen it all: the young bucks coming and going, the career employees who slipped up and incurred the Queen's wrath, and the half-witted lackeys too stupid to know the difference between an in-game bug and social engineering. In many ways, due to his years of experience, he fancies himself an equal of the Queen, but understands that she will never see it that way. She keeps him on a leash, dictating that he spend most of his time in the *Metaverse* fulfilling his duties as the puppet leader in every server. In return, he indulges in the good things in life with every chance he gets, never forgetting that his extravagant lifestyle may come to an end at any second. When Lily's gambit sets into motion, though, he thinks little of others, instead trying to eke out a plan for his own survival whilst putting on an arrogant air of loyalty to the Great Leader.

Lady Claire Alexandria
Age: 23
Height: 5'8"
Favorite Food: Fish tacos
Favorite Color: Deep purple
Hobbies: Badminton, Yoga, Playwrighting

Born with a silver spoon during the *Metaverse's* early days, Claire has grown to feel immense guilt and angst at the carefree *Eden* lifestyle. The idea of indoctrinated slavery has never sat well with the woman, even as a child spending most of her time in *Tanha's* vacant 'edutainment' centers, where she indulged in all manner of pleasures to her heart's content and quickly burned out on them. When she was sixteen, she attempted suicide multiple times. General Lacie thwarted one of her attempts, and grew rather fond of the girl. Their friendship blossomed into a deep personal companionship. Claire's true desire is to use her influence and power to create a more balanced world, one where the 'assets' of the *Metaverse* are treated like actual human beings. Only then might she be able to feel that her externally pampered and internally tortured life has some purpose to it.

Yossa Kernani
Age: 64
Height: 5'10"
Favorite Food: Okonomiyaki
Favorite Color: Silver
Hobbies: Truth-seeking, Brainteasers, Videography

Named after "Yossarian", the hero of Catch-22 by his poor but learned parents, Yossa has been highly critical of the dominant culture following a traumatic incident that sparked widespread riots; a fatal server error hit Beta-testers for *Metaverse v. 2.0* in what we know as Bangladesh, leaving a hundred thousand dead and several tens of thousands brain-damaged. He joined the Bombay Underground and took part in peaceful anti-establishment protests, but Lorelei's answer was to bathe the city in flames. To end Lorelei's continued assault on South Asia, Yossa took his family and fled to an EDC outpost in Hong Kong, where years later, he volunteered to enter the *Metaverse* as a sleeper agent within the system, and then break off and work to destroy it. His daughter Leela takes great pride in their once-royal family.

Commodore Leandra / Leela Kernani
Age: 33
Height: 5'5"
Favorite Food: Bisi bele bath
Favorite Color: Indigo
Hobbies: Sitar playing, gymnastics, cooking

Yossa's plucky daughter shares his optimism for the future, and has been anxious to contribute to the EDC war effort since being spirited away from her homeland. Leela is one of the most beloved commanders in the EDC's history, and bravely volunteered to portray "Leandra", a codename for Lily's body double, in the fight against Queen Lorelei. By Leela's orders, her three siblings and mother took refuge in Sector Forty-Two (New Zealand), to await hers and Yossa's return. Deeply spiritual, Leela believes in reincarnation, and that no souls are ever lost, as all are but fragments of the whole.

Lieutenant General Errol Beech
Age: 50
Height: 6'3"
Favorite Food: Linguini
Favorite Color: Black
Hobbies: Hockey, watching the *Metaverse* Gladiators, tennis

As Vice Chief of Staff of *Neo Eden's* armed forces, General Beech has earned Queen Lorelei's trust because he is ambitious, predictable, and always hungry for power. She knows that with a mere misstep, he would seek to supplant her from the throne. The only thing stopping him is the *Metaverse* – or rather, that he wouldn't have a clue what to do with it. In truth, Beech is a simple man with simple pleasures. He lives a regimented, disciplined life, believing strongly that the *Metaverse* is essential for preserving the balance of power in the world. Upon seeing that the Queen is losing her grip on the populace, he put his close friend Dr. Marco on his payroll as an informant and possible assassin; they gamble on toppling her as soon as any true threat comes to *Neo Eden*. As his cyborg brain has grown dominant, he thinks little of his wife and two children, who spend much of their time shopping and enjoying the *Neo Eden* lifestyle.

Henry Holdfast
Age: 30
Height: 6'0"
Favorite Food: Shepherd's pie
Favorite Color: Light brown
Hobbies: Japanese animation, Kickboxing, billiards

The ace up Lily's sleeve, Henry's path has been one of absolute caution. As one of the foremost Developers in the *Nexus*, he's been long avoiding the responsibility of promotion, only to have it thrust upon him at the last minute. Henry is a rather private individual, immersing himself in his work, but when it comes down to it, he knows that it's the people in the *Nexus*, not the programs, that will be necessary to get the job done. He hails from an independent permaculture commune in the Australian outback, where he was raised by his immediate and extended family, but has worked hard to cement his dedication to *Neo Eden* and earned the respect of his peers through tireless service and the refinement of their security protocols against EDC hackers.

Dr. Ayumi Karuishi
Age: 32
Height: 5'5"
Favorite Food: Korean BBQ
Favorite Color: Pink
Hobbies: Arcade gaming, volleyball, fan fiction, sleeping in

Ayumi is one of the most highly respected Developers in the *Nexus*, having been working on the *Metaverse* for over a decade. As a young woman, she grew up in *Neo-Kyoto,* one of Lorelei's satellite cities and the location of the *Metaverse* backup mainframe, but was recruited in secret by the Eastern Elders of the EDC and put on the fast track to *Neo Eden*. Since the EDC came under Lily's supervision, she's worked her way up to the very top, juggling duties as a problem-solver for each of its servers. She had an unrequited crush on Dr. Nico Orynbekov, but has had to rely on her own wits and intuition since his untimely passing. She misses her mother back home, who she reasons must be worried sick about her fate. Although she has a reputation for being a flirt, she holds back from any personal relationships with the other Developers, which only intensifies the jealousy felt by her colleagues when she warms up to Henry Holdfast.

Dr. Alphonse Hoshua
Age: 52
Height: 6'2"
Favorite Food: Goat curry
Favorite Color: Burnt umber
Hobbies: Percussion, drum circles, disco, *Holo*-cards

As Lead Developer for the *Avidya* server, Hoshua is well-liked and good at following orders, if a little too trusting of his subordinates. He began service at the *Metaverse's* peak, mid-way through version 2.0, as an Illusionist, designing many of the virtual realm's weapons, armor, and distractions. He was responsible for refining the Helmet Defense Protocol and led the program's research division. Happily married with a single spoiled daughter, Hoshua is a family man, like his father in Senegal. He puts on the persona of a stuffy old guy in order to keep his subordinates and rivals at arm's length, but in reality he believes deeply in *Endless Metaverse* and the Queen's unchallenged rule.

Dr. Francesco Zarifian
Age: 44
Height: 5'10"
Favorite Food: Pineapple
Favorite Color: Indigo
Hobbies: Game design, magic tricks, tabletop gaming

Dr. Zarifian started as a loyal servant and Developer for the *Metaverse*, having overseen the transition from version 2.4 to 3.0. He originally thought that he was doing good work for the assets, keeping them happy and oblivious to the decrepit nature of the planet, but he became disillusioned with the job after witnessing all the men and women he'd worked with for years become frozen, executed, or banished from civilization. Sensing his hesitance, Nico Orynbekov convinced him to join the EDC. A single father of two hailing from Iran, Francesco enjoys the extravagant *Neo Eden* lifestyle and loves gambling, gaming, and the company of women, but acknowledges that due to dwindling resources and the Queen's draconian tactics, the dystopian city will not last forever. He's constantly fearful of his life, but he understands that Lily's actions are necessary to restore balance to the planet.

Dr. Christopher Marco
Age: 41
Height: 6'
Favorite Food: Caramelized bananas
Favorite Color: Emerald green
Hobbies: Taxidermy, table tennis, *Metaverse* combat design

Husband to Adeline Marco, Christopher has been driven by his wife's ambition to ruthlessly climb the ladders to Lead Developer status, a drive somewhat halted by the fact that he is unliked amongst his peers. A rather lonely man, Marco was once a player of *Endless Metaverse* until his late teens, when he was recruited and taken from the outside world, a very rare case. His sweet-talking manner and sly charms won over Adele, who quickly seized the opportunity to leverage the Overseer in her political and social favor. The polygamous Chris and Adele carry on distanced lives, but remain passionate towards one another despite the delicate issues regarding Marco and Beech's underhanded plan to overthrow the Queen.

Lt. Gen. Gabriel Joaquin:
Age: 36
Height: 5'7"
Favorite Food: Slow-roasted chicken
Favorite Color: Gray
Hobbies: Theater, crossword puzzles, soap operas

"Jo-Jo" is Lily's second-in-command, coordinating the EDC forces for their strike with his lifetime of military know-how and quick thinking as an Independent Military Contractor for the Panama Commune in which he grew up. One of the EDC's major strongholds, the commune was under constant attack from *Neo Eden's* drones. Even with limited hackers on hand, he was able to fight off incoming attacks until the invaders retreated, low on fuel and munitions; he then took his personal forces out to make pursuit and greatly thinned the drones. The aftermath of the crucial battle turned the tide of the Western Atlantic Theater, allowing the EDC to gain numerous footholds in the Caribbean. The Elder council unanimously voted Joaquin onto Lily's strike force. Knowing that he is one of the few strategists who can make major decisions without her input, Lily puts her full trust in him to ensure the armada reaches *Neo Eden* in one piece.

Col. Victor Aquino
Age: 28
Height: 5'11"
Favorite Food: Lechon kawali (Filipino roast pig)
Favorite Color: White
Hobbies: Engineering, travel-blogging, cycling

The leader of Lily's Exo Knight Division, Col. Aquino, hails from the Philippine islands and grew up reading science fiction novels. A brilliant engineer, he retired from the *Eden* Armada in protest as his native Manila turned into a war zone and became a civil engineer in order to devise methods of construction that would cut down or eliminate *M-Gear* casualties. When Lily traveled back in time to 2170 and presented him with Lucille's vision for the Exo Knight suits, comparable in size to those in Heinlein's *Starship Troopers*, Victor was ecstatic. He packed his bags immediately for the next airship to the EDC's base camp in Kazakhstan and began work on the suits immediately. With an early prototype, they secretly annexed one of Lorelei's larger war factories, and began to create suits even larger and more powerful than Lucy had imagined, closer to the mobile suits in *Macross,* or *Gundam Wing.* When Lily inexplicably returned not a day older ten years later, he was undeniably shocked, but he's kept her secret well. Aquino also came up with the virtual training modules for the pilots.

Further Reading and Viewing

On Virtual Worlds

The wicked term "Metaverse" was coined by Neal Stephenson in his immensely influential cyberpunk epic **"Snow Crash"**, a highly entertaining and thought-provoking novel within which the virtual world is more social than game-centric in nature, and deeply integrated with *Reality*.

Ernest Cline's best-selling **"Ready Player One"** introduces the OASIS, a fantastic, lively online universe, with its own economy, currency, and virtually every geek franchise in existence represented on satellite planets. A fast read that earns every ounce of nerd cred and then some.

Tad Williams' acclaimed **"Otherland"** tetralogy, unread by yours truly, takes place in the late twenty-first century and features the Net, an all-encompassing virtual world that plays host to a large cast of characters with unique and awesome abilities.

William Gibson has a host of virtual worlds in his collected works, which include his award-winning "Sprawl" trilogy (**"Neuromancer"**, **"Count Zero"**, and **"Mona Lisa Overdrive"**).

Based on a Japanese light novel series, the animé **"Sword Art Online"** showcases a smattering of different virtual worlds, each with their own rules and challenges, as background to a sweeping emotional drama with a plethora of characters. I personally liked the first 13 episodes the best.

My experience with the **".hack"** series is minimal, (I've read a few volumes of the manga and watched the excellent **".hack//Quantum"** OVA) but the series in animated, manga, and video game form is highly imaginative and boasts fascinating characters.

I haven't checked out **"Btoom!"** or **"Accel World"**, but they've been recommended to me.

Mamoru Hosoda's **"Summer Wars"** is an excellent animé film with an interconnected online world as its centerpiece. Great fun, family-friendly, offers food for thought, and heartwarming to boot.

Further Time Travel in Fiction

In writing "Raine", I came to appreciate how many works of fiction showcase differing theories on time travel.

A fantastic resource is this flowchart, by *Mr. Dalliard* on tumblr, which sorts time travel in (mostly) Hollywood films by the rules and theories of each film's universe.

http://mr-dalliard.tumblr.com/post/47542367365/time-travel-in-movies

Based on the events in the epilogue (which is only one of many possible endings), it might appear at first glance that "Raine" belongs in the same category as the "Back to the Future" films, since the past can be altered, for better or worse, and events do not necessarily follow Novikov's Self-Consistency Principle.

That said, Lily's memory not matching up to Rutger's file hints at the possibility that the *Belladonna* may disappear in the future, and that she may need to fill the void left by a vanished original for the *Mark II* in order to "close the loop". Depending on whether or not events in time are flexible or fixed, even the closing of this loop may or may not end in the complete temporal collapse of the known universe.

Whether Lily is right about the mugs, or her supposedly untarnished memory is faulty (she is, after all, only human) is for the reader to decide.

Without spoiling much, here is a short list of some of my favorite stories dealing with time travel.

Steins;Gate

A 25-episode anime series based upon a visual novel, involving a self-proclaimed mad scientist based in Tokyo's techno-wonderland of Akihabara who, with the help of his lab assistants, accidentally discovers a method of time travel involving a microwave and cellular phones. Filled with intrigue, humor, and heart, this is among my favorite time travel stories, and directly references the infamous John Titor, a person who appeared on message boards claiming to be a time traveler from a dystopian future. A feature film has also been released in Japan.

Puella Magi Madoka Magika

It would be a major spoiler to reveal how time travel plays a part in this genre-busting 13-episode epic, but it is done so well that I couldn't help but mention it. *Madoka* takes everything that's been previously established about the magical girl genre and flips it on its head, providing a dark, gritty look at the unexpected risks teenaged girls might take in devoting their lives to cleanse the world of evil forces. Highly recommended.

The Melancholy of Haruhi Suzumiya

It's fun, it's edgy, and it blends the unknown with the familiar in ways never before seen. Following an innocent crush on the lovely, talented, and terrifyingly eccentric Haruhi, Kyon is dragged along into the SOS Brigade, a club formed to find Espers, aliens, and time-travelers – the twist? Well, that would be spoiler territory. Suffice it to say that Haruhi is more than she seems, and as a result of her influence, supernatural, otherworldly, and temporal hijinks ensue, with the otherwise ordinary Kyon caught in the middle. This is truly one of those must-see shows. M-m-m-Mikuru Beam!

Also see: The Disappearance of Haruhi Suzumiya (film)

Back to the Future trilogy

Perhaps the best-known and loved time travel film series, Robert Zemeckis' three-part comedy follows Marty McFly and Dr. Emmett Brown's travels through the past, present, and future of the suburb of

Hill Valley, and their lively encounters with Marty's ancestors or descendants.
Also see: Back to the Future (animated series)

Doctor Who

BBC's epic family television series about the Doctor, a Time Lord from Gallifrey who guards planet Earth from extra-terrestrial invaders, is unmatched in scope and ambition. My experience is with "NuWho", starting from Russell T. Davies' reboot, but I have enjoyed the few episodes of Classic Who I've seen, and the Doctor's ever-evolving personas. For those new to the series, there are many recommended starting points, but I began with Series 6's "The Eleventh Hour", watched the entire series, then went on to start from Christopher Eccleston's run in Series 1, with the episode "Rose". Sometimes I wish I had started with "Rose", but I don't regret being introduced to Matt Smith's Eleventh Doctor first, as he brings an infectious zaniness, a stoic heart, and a real pathos to the legendary role. In my heart, David Tennant is a very close second to Mr. Smith.

Twelve Monkeys

Terry Gilliam's mind-bender of a film stars Bruce Willis as James Cole, who is sent back in time from 2035 to investigate an epidemic that will wipe out most of life on Earth in 1996. As nothing ever goes as planned when time travel is involved, he's sent back a few years too early and institutionalized. But events leading to the disaster are set into motion. Gilliam's visual flair and unpredictable filmmaking make for a superb viewing experience that explores paradoxes, time loops, metaphysics, and more down-to-Earth concerns such as animal rights and mental illness.

Time Bandits

Another Gilliam masterpiece, Time Bandits drops a curious young boy into a ragtag group of thieves hopping through wormholes in their quest for treasure. Ian Holm's Napoleon is one of the major highlights, as are the jaw-dropping special effects.

Returner (2002)

Directed by Takeshi Yamazaki, this Japanese sci-fi B-epic with a film noir influence has got it all. Aliens, time travel, Yakuza, Transforming robots, and a fast-paced, action-packed plot. It's a viscous blend of great ideas that have worked before and injected with a heavy dose of tongue-in-cheek, and it's criminally underseen as far as sci-fi pulp is concerned.

Somewhere in Time

Superman fans will balk, but this is my favorite Christopher Reeve film. Beautifully shot and scored, with great performances from the entire cast, though Reeve is the clear standout. His playwright character Richard Collier time travels from 1980 to 1912 to meet the actress Elise McKenna (Jane Seymour), with whom he has fallen in love from admiring a portrait on the wall of the hotel he's staying in to work on his writer's block. Upon arriving in the far past, he must contend with being a total fish out of water, wrestle his way to catch McKenna's attention, and deal with her possessive manager (played impeccably by Christopher Plummer). It's a heart-wrenching film, but it sticks with you.

Groundhog Day

Bill Murray's arrogant TV weatherman Phil Connors is stuck in an unending time loop, repeating the same dreary day again and again in one of the greatest of all films about altered time. If you haven't seen the late, great Harold Ramis' existentialist masterpiece, based on a screenplay by himself and Danny Rubin, it's never too late. The flick holds up real well.

Looper

Joseph Gordon-Levitt plays a hit man who assassinates people sent from the future in this dystopian sci-fi cult classic. Everything in this film is top-notch. Rian Johnson directs with a steady hand, and though eagle-eyed viewers will spot some inconsistencies, this is highly entertaining, a modern cult classic and a must-see for time travel aficionados.

Primer

Shane Carruth's ultra low budget film about two dudes, Aaron and Abe, who accidentally discover time travel, struck film festival gold. I consider it the most realistic portrayal of time travel. It showcases how quickly the power to jump can be manipulated, abused, and eventually spiral completely out of control. What really struck me is how this film explains so much with so little, and efficiently conveys information without resorting to info-dumps.

Bill and Ted's Excellent Adventure
Bill and Ted rule. Shame on anyone who disagrees. Party on, dudes. And be excellent to each other.

Donnie Darko
One of the more beautifully bizarre films of 2001, Richard Kelly directs a fantastic cast in a dark takedown of suburban America. Donnie (played by Jake Gyllenhaal) wanders outside following a man in a terrifying rabbit costume who claims the world will end in 28 days. Upon returning home, he finds that a jet engine with presumably no origin has inexplicably crashed through his bedroom. This film is notable not just for its intriguing plot, but for the metaphysical questions Kelly posits and never quite answers. His ability to balance biting satire, personal drama, and twisted black comedy is unmatched.
Also see: Southland Tales (Kelly's epic dark satire on Los Angeles is probably the most misunderstood film of our time)

Terminator tetralogy
Purists will only acknowledge the existence of the first two (maybe three) films, but this continuing chronicle of man VS machine is not to be missed for the uninitiated. My favorite is *Terminator 2: Judgment Day*, though the first one is a more complete film in its own right. The third one is decent and has its moments, while the fourth is a narrative mess with a few redeeming action sequences.

Idiocracy
One of America's great satirists, Mike Judge, goes all-out in this portrayal of a futuristic America in the year 2505, where the most average person by today's standards (Luke Wilson) would be seen as a super-genius. Terry Crews' President Dwayne Elizondo Mountain Dew Herbert Camacho is hilarious. Crops are dying, due to being irrigated with "Brawndo", an energy drink. Bold, crass, undeniably riotous, and epic in scope notwithstanding the fact that its funding was cut halfway through production, Judge's film is a must-see.

Edge of Tomorrow

Based on Hiroshi Sakurazaka's light novel "All You Need Is Kill", this high-energy sci-fi/action flick is highly entertaining as far as summer films go and will likely be remembered as a cult classic. Picture "Groundhog Day" meets "Starship Troopers". Tom Cruise stars in this high-octane thriller as Major William Cage, a cowardly talking piece for the global military forces fighting off an invading alien menace known as "Mimics". After dying in a fiercely one-sided battle, Cage discovers that he is sent back to the beginning of the day, and consequently is able to learn and improve from his past failures. Yet his ability remains a mystery until his impossible skills catch the eye of war hero Rita Vrataski (known as the "Full Metal Bitch"), who implores Cage to seek her out when he wakes up. While the last third of the film goes into typical action film territory, overall, this is a really fun watch that's well worth your time.

More time travel in fiction:

Light Novels: The Girl Who Leapt Through Time series, All You Need Is Kill

Novels: The Time Machine (H.G. Wells, 1895), A Connecticut Yankee in King Arthur's Court (Mark Twain, 1889), Replay (Ken Grimwood, 1987), The End of Eternity (Isaac Asimov, 1955), The Accidental Time Machine (Joe Halderman, 2008), Slaughterhouse-Five (Kurt Vonnegut, 1969), The Door into Summer (Robert Heinlein, 1986), Up the Line (Robert Silverberg, 2002), Lightning (Dean Koontz, 2003)

Short Stories: All from the book "The Best Time Travel Stories of the 20th Century", edited by Harry Turtledove with Martin H. Greenberg: "Yesterday Was Monday" by Theodore Sturgeon, "Time Locker" by Henry Kuttner, "Time's Arrow" by Arthur C. Clarke, "I'm Scared" by Jack Finney, "A Sound of Thunder" by Ray Bradbury, "Death Ship" by Richard Matheson, "A Gun For Dinosaur" by L. Sprague de Camp, "The Man Who Came Early" by Poul Anderson, "Rainbird" by R.A. Lafferty, "Leviathan!" by Larry Niven, "Anniversary Project" by Joe Halderman, "Time Tipping" by Jack Dann, "Fire Watch" by Connie Willis, "Sailing to Byzantium" by Robert Silverberg, "The Pure Product" by John Kessel, "Trapalanda" by Charles Sheffield, "The

Price of Oranges" by Nancy Kress, "Another Story, Or A Fisherman of the Inland Sea" by Ursula K. Le Guin

Webcomics: Dresden Codak (dresdencodak.com), Chronillogical (chronillogical.com), Dawn of Time (www.dawnoftimecomics.com), Times Like This (www.timeslikethis.com)

Additional Films: Timecrimes, Star Trek IV: The Voyage Home, Peggy Sue Got Married, The Time Machine (1960), The Butterfly Effect, Lost in Space, Galaxy Quest, 13 Going on 30, Big, The Time Traveler's Wife, The Curious Case of Benjamin Button, Planet of the Apes (1968)

TV: Ashes to Ashes, Doctor Who, Torchwood, Fringe, BBC's The Hitchhiker's Guide to the Galaxy, Lost, Quantum Leap, Sliders, The Time Tunnel, Terminator: The Sarah Connor Chronicles, Dexter's Laboratory: Ego Trip, Life on Mars, Samurai Jack, Star Trek: The Next Generation, Bill and Ted's Excellent Adventures, Land of the Lost

A Few Quotes from Avatar Meher Baba

"As a single object seems to multiply itself to him who is drunk to excess, so Unity appears as plurality to those who are intoxicated with the wine of egoism.

"The satisfaction derived from the fleeting things of life is not lasting; and our wants remain unfulfilled. There is thus a general sense of dissatisfaction accompanied by all kinds of worries."

"The universe is the outcome of imagination. Then why try to acquire knowledge of the imaginative universe instead of plumbing the depths of your real Self?"

"No amount of prayer or meditation can do what helping others can do."

"Don't worry, be happy."

"There are very few things in the mind which eat up as much energy as worry. It is one of the most difficult things not to worry about anything. Worry is experienced when things go wrong, but in relation to past happenings it is idle merely to wish that they might have been otherwise. The frozen past is what it is, and no amount of worrying is going to make it other than what it has been. But the limited ego-mind identifies itself with its past, gets entangled with it and keeps alive the pangs of frustrated desires. Thus worry continues to grow into the mental life of man until the ego-mind is burdened by the past. Worry is also experienced in relation to the future when this future is expected to be disagreeable in some way. In this case it seeks to justify itself as a necessary part of the attempt to prepare for coping with the anticipated situations. But, things can never be helped merely by worrying. Besides, many of the things which are anticipated never turn up, or if they do occur, they turn out to be much more acceptable than they were expected to be. Worry is the product of feverish imagination working under the stimulus of desires. It is a living through of sufferings which are mostly our own creation. Worry has never done anyone any good, and it is very much worse than mere dissipation of psychic energy, for it substantially curtails the joy and fullness of life."

- Avatar Meher Baba

<u>Notes</u>

About the Author

Joseph Victor Choi was born in Metro Manila, Philippines and has shuttled back and forth constantly between his twin hometowns – Manila and Los Angeles. He studied at Southville International School and Colleges, Santa Monica College, and the California Institute of the Arts, where he graduated with a B.A. in the Film/Video program. He currently lives in Mariposa, California, but travels all over the Golden State herding goats, editing films and videos, writing game reviews for Too Much Gaming (www.2muchgaming.com) and fan fiction (https://www.fanfiction.net/u/550553/sandwichsupernova), listening obsessively to Rush, and doing just about whatever it is that nerds do.

Joe's favorite video games are *Final Fantasy VIII, StarFox 64, The Legend of Zelda* series, *Child of Eden, Bayonetta,* the *Metal Gear Solid* series, and most especially the *Smash Bros.* series.

He can be contacted at josvchoi@gmail.com.

<u>Notes</u>

www.ingramcontent.com/pod-product-compliance
Lightning Source LLC
Chambersburg PA
CBHW021117260626
47169CB00005B/1317